The
Divines

The Divines

Eden Sandoval

Wayward Storm Press

Chicago

THE DIVINES. Copyright © 2025 by Eden Sandoval. All rights reserved.

Library of Congress Cataloging-in-Publication Data is available upon request.

ISBN-13: 979-8-9993584-1-7 (Paperback)
ISBN-13: 979-8-9993584-0-0 (eBook)

For baby Marjorie. May all your dreams come true, and may you always be free.

1

DIVINE ACADEMY

"War does not exist at the Academy."

The president's voice echoed around the tall, magnificently domed room, filling every crevice with her sure authority. I shifted in my seat, agitatedly crossing one leg over the other in front of me. Even now, my muscles were slightly sore from the training session several hours earlier—my last in Dagmar before I'd left to come here. I released a frustrated breath. As a soldier, I knew better than most that the war existed everywhere. There might not be fighting on school grounds, but the war's consequences could be felt by every Divine at every level in every place.

"At the Academy, neutrality is our greatest strength."

I slid down in the pew as I crossed my arms over my chest and regarded her dispassionately. This speech had already gone on for too long, but it didn't look like she was anywhere near done. I sighed, letting my head fall back so I could take in the tall, arched ceiling above the room full of new students. Sunlight was spilling through the stained-glass windows, projecting bright smears of jewel-toned color across the stones. I'd never seen such an ornate building before. Most back home were utilitarian and in states of constant disrepair—a cost of being on the front lines of the war.

"The Divine world was not always filled with conflict as it is today," the president continued. "The gods, in their wisdom, created Divines and graciously left the human realm in our care."

I rolled my eyes. That was an extremely simplistic, sanitized retelling of our history. The gods hadn't left peacefully—a collection of newer gods had forcefully imprisoned themselves along with the older gods in a separate realm, attempting to protect humans from the sweeping violence that'd ensued on every inch of the planet when the gods had used humans to fight their battles with one another for them. That small group of gods had created Divines, leaving us, without true instruction or structure, to be the guardians of the planet—the Normal realm—in their absence.

"For many years, Divines of all factions lived in peace. Light Guardians, Dark Guardians, Blessed, and Demons provided balance for one another, and collectively used their powers to watch over the Normal realm and safeguard its humans from any further meddling of the gods. There was complete harmony."

I clenched my jaw, annoyance spiking through me. She was deluding herself—peace between the factions had been extremely short-lived, and the darker factions had soon veered away from the lighter ones in world view and action. The Dark Guardians and Demons had wanted to control the Normal world with might and fear, while the Light Guardians and Blessed preferred to let the Normals govern themselves and watch over them secretly from afar. That difference of opinion had quickly led to war and eventually led the Dark Guardians and Demons to create their own realm on a separate plane, isolated from ours, only connected via one heavily guarded portal and illegal rips in reality between the human world and their kingdom. It was from those illegal rips that they'd ruthlessly attacked Divine and Normal settlements alike for several centuries, trying to wipe us out so they could take complete control of the Normal world. It was because of them that I'd been forced to be a soldier my entire life.

"It is that original harmony that we embody on our campus," the president continued, her voice brimming with enthusiasm. "Here, Divines of all factions study and live together without conflict. Everyone is equal. Everyone is protected. Education, not violence, is our way of life. There are no border towns here—no rips in the plane between the Dark Guardian and Normal realms to guard. No need for soldiers. Here, everyone can be happy and free."

My stomach clenched. As much as I wanted to roll my eyes at the sentiment, it was the reason I'd ultimately chosen to come here. Not many soldiers did—especially not border town soldiers. I was the only one from Dagmar who'd enrolled in years. The last before me had been Matt. But I'd needed out. I'd been fighting and killing almost every day since I was old enough to hold a weapon. I'd experienced death more than I'd experienced life. And it'd begun tearing at me in a deeper way, killing any glimmer of hope that even briefly flared to life inside me. So I'd enrolled the second I'd turned eighteen. Just as Matt had done before me.

"The Academy is a place of hope, joy, and scholarship. Your faction is irrelevant here. Your level of power is irrelevant here. What matters is your dedication to your classes and fellow students."

Someone scoffed a few feet to my left. I lifted my head and glanced over to see who'd made the noise—who else was enjoying the president's speech as little as I was. I couldn't help the small smile that formed as I saw him. The young man was sitting in the exact same position as me, his tattooed arms crossed over his chest, his legs stretched out and crossed in front of him. He was dressed similarly too—black combat boots, ripped black jeans, and a black V-neck T-shirt that stretched over his broad chest and muscular arms. His hair was black, shorter on the sides, and a little shaggier on top, and he was pale—far paler than my own light brown, even in the dead of winter. And he was frowning darkly as he stared intently at the president.

As though he felt me looking, he turned his head slowly in my direction. Shock jolted through me as our eyes met. His were electric blue and stood out starkly against the dark of his hair. I'd never seen eyes like his before. It was almost like they were lit from within. I wondered what kind of Divine he was—whether his eyes were a result of his power somehow.

I hid my reaction as I stared back, and raised an eyebrow at him, as if to say, "What?" His gaze slid quickly over me, and I watched as he processed my outfit—my black heeled combat boots, the black ripped skinny jeans, the black long-sleeved shirt with the shoulders cut out that I'd pushed up to my elbows, revealing lightly tattooed forearms—and the way I was sitting. The corners of his eyes crinkled slightly before he turned away.

A polite smattering of clapping drew my attention back to the front of the room. The president was done speaking. *Finally*. It'd felt like an hour.

"Okay, now to getting you all settled in!" She clapped her hands together in front of her, a wide smile stretching her face. "As you know, your cellphones won't work here as we're not on the same plane as the Normals. We gave each of you an assigned phone when you arrived that will work only on this campus. We have already sent your dorm and room assignments to each of your devices and delivered your belongings to your rooms. We have also sent you a map of the campus, though you may still participate in the campus tour in a half hour should you desire to."

She beamed as she surveyed the students filling the chapel.

"Dinner will be served in the dining hall in a couple hours, and I encourage each of you to branch out and make new friends. Please remember, however, that we do not allow you to ask one another about your powers or Divine faction. If you wish to disclose these things, that is, of course, fine. However, our goal here is to bridge differences, not reinforce them. You will have professors assigned to you who know your classification so that they may train you to use your specific abilities, but that is the extent to which your faction will be known. Your classes will begin tomorrow, starting with training exercises in the morning. On behalf of the staff and administration, welcome again to the Academy! We're all looking forward to having a new group of students here this year. You are dismissed."

I pushed quickly to my feet and jumped over the back of the pew into the mostly empty one behind me so I could get out of the chapel faster. I wasn't used to being around so many people. Only in battle, and this was nothing like that. I had no prior experience to inform me how to act. So I simply ignored everyone and kept my expression a practiced blank. It'd served me well enough back home, and it'd serve me well enough here.

I pushed through the throng already at the doors and made my way outside. The sun shone brightly in the afternoon sky, illuminating the campus with golden light. It really was beautiful here. The buildings were elaborate creations of stone and wrought iron. The dorms looked like huge stone manors, while the main building with the dining hall and all the classrooms was essentially a moderately-sized castle. Sizable trees were strewn throughout the grounds, and bordered campus in a thick forest. Open expanses of lush grass softened the space between buildings. Flowers artfully surrounded each structure and filled several gardens built around quietly bubbling fountains. Precisely trimmed shrubs decorated and separated spaces. And spread throughout were wrought-iron tables, benches, and lounge chairs, designed to allow students and staff to enjoy the outdoors.

A neutral group of Divines had created the school and the small realm in which it sat several centuries ago, connecting it to the Normal world through a series of portals. They'd wanted it to be a refuge for young Divines from the war. And looking around, it was hard to claim it was anything but. I filled my lungs with fresh air, then exhaled slowly. The air wasn't as oppressive here. There was no foul, gritty stench that permeated everything. No smell of blood, fire, and death.

I made my way to a distant wrought-iron picnic table, then climbed up to sit on the tabletop, resting my feet on the attached bench. I pulled out and lit a cigarette. It was a bad habit I'd picked up over the last year when things in Dagmar had become truly unbearable. Something about it offered a kind of solace that I hadn't been able to find elsewhere. And I wasn't too worried about its negative effects—I was a quick healer. I'd be fine.

I continued to pull at the cigarette as I watched the new students spread across the grounds, exploring, meeting people, finding their dorms. I'd find mine eventually. Right now, I just wanted to let the sun soak into my skin. It was rarely this bright and clear in Dagmar. I'd hypothesized as a young child that all the death attracted and held the gloomy weather above the town. Matt had laughed that hypothesis away.

"It's just what the weather is like in this part of the country," he'd said, before ruffling my hair.

"Hey."

The deep voice behind me made me start. I whipped around and saw the young man from my pew walking toward me. He was tall and had a strong, lean build. His movements were smooth and calculated. Almost catlike. I took another drag of my cigarette and silently watched him approach.

He smiled and pushed onto the table next to me.

I narrowed my eyes at him. "I'm not giving you a cigarette." I kept my tone carefully bored. "I don't know how easy they are to get around here, so I'm not giving any away." I took a slow drag and released the smoke through my nose.

He reached into his pocket, then pulled out his own pack. "No need." My eyebrows rose as I watched him light one, then lean back on one arm. "They do sell them in the lounge, though. At least, that's what my sister told me."

I watched him closely, keeping my expression a practiced blank. Why was he here? What did he want? No one ever talked to me unless they needed something.

"I'm Gabriel, by the way." He shot me a smile as his gaze traversed my face again.

I frowned.

His smile broadened. "That's usually when the other person would say their name."

I blinked at him, then heat prickled my cheeks. "I'm Terah," I said, looking away. Something about his eyes was too intense. It felt like they could pierce through my exterior and see all the way to my bones.

"Terah," he repeated slowly, like he was thinking it over. "That means . . . wanderer, doesn't it?"

My eyebrows rose, and I glanced at him again. Not many people knew my name meant anything. I'd only found out because my mother had spoken about it derisively when I was younger, like she hadn't named me herself. Perhaps she hadn't.

He shrugged at my expression. "My parents are academics in their down-time. They're fascinated with religious history. I read a lot of the history and religion books we had around the house whenever I was bored, and I was bored a lot growing up. I also have a good memory." He sent me a crooked grin.

I smiled a little. "It does mean wanderer, which is funny since I've lived in one town my entire life. This is my first time leaving it."

He nodded and took a long drag of his cigarette. "Well, you've got plenty of time left to prove your name right, if that's what you want."

My smile faded. Only if I lived that long. People from Dagmar weren't known for their long lives. Too many battles for that. Too much violence.

"Anyway, *your* name is all good and holy," I said, changing the subject.

His shoulders shook in a small laugh. "Yeah, my mother takes her Light Guardian status and her mission very seriously, so she went ultra holy with it. Same with my sister's name. Rebekah." He shrugged. "Mine's not my first choice, but I'm stuck with it."

I nodded and blew out some smoke. I liked his name. It sounded strong, purposeful, meaningful. Whereas mine felt . . . neutral. A little weird. It made me wonder about my father—who he was, where he was, whether he was alive. I wondered if he'd named me. Given her station, my mother should've been more like Gabriel's, going the holy route. Many Divines, especially Light Guardians, did. And they evoked the new gods the most, even if few Divines truly believed in them.

"So, what were you scoffing at during the president's speech?" I asked.

Gabriel let out a long sigh before taking another drag of his cigarette.

"That bad?"

"I dunno." He pushed his hair back with one hand. "It's just the way she was talking about this place. Like it's achieved some sort of miracle of peace, neutrality, and understanding. Bothered me."

I shifted so I could face him more directly. "What do you mean? I didn't buy her whole thing about the war not existing here, but this place *is*

6

kind of an anomaly. With every kind of Divine living here without violence."

His brow furrowed slightly, as though he was trying to think of the right way to explain it. "Well, look at the administration for instance. While they have every type of Divine on the professor roster, the people who actually run the school are mainly Light Guardians. The school gets safety and strategy briefings from the Light Guardians. Most students here are either Blessed or Light Guardians. Dark Guardians and Demons are pretty few and far between, and fewer of them attend each year. Seems a little less than neutral to me."

I took a last drag of my cigarette, then put it out on the table. I hadn't really looked that closely into how the school was run—I'd mainly just wanted to get the hell out of Dagmar. But if he was right about the leadership, he'd have a point.

"I guess I hadn't really thought about it like that."

"And it's more than that." He flicked his cigarette into the grass and leaned back on one arm again. "Even though I think it's hypocritical to claim to be neutral while essentially being run by the Light Guardians, I wouldn't mind that much if the Light Guardians as a group actually fought for and supported who they claim to. But they don't. Their army fights for privileged Divines and Normals, and they fight at the largest plane rips, but that's it. They leave everyone else to die. Which makes this school and their association with Light Guardians even less neutral. We're supposed to look up to the Light Guardians as though they're all that's good, peaceful, and moral, but how can we? They're not. They only look after themselves and the people they deem worthy enough."

My jaw had tightened while listening to his rant, and tension stiffened my shoulders. I'd spent my entire life around Light Guardians. I'd fought with them to protect the Normals. I'd seen them die horrific deaths—sacrifice themselves every day for others. How could he think they didn't care?

"I've lost you, haven't I?" His smile was bittersweet.

I bit the inside of my cheek, unsure of how to respond.

"It's not like I'm a Dark Guardian sympathizer. I've just seen too much growing up to hold the Light Guardians on a pedestal the way that others do."

Curiosity loosened the tension in my chest. "What did you see?"

He watched me for a long moment, gauging my expression. Finally, he sighed and looked away.

"I grew up in Elareth."

Elareth. The name sounded familiar. I wracked my brain, trying to remember what I'd heard about it.

"It's a border town," he said, answering my unspoken question, "but not one like Dagmar or Glenhaven. We aren't solely a Divine town. We live side by side with Normals, and most of the Divines are Blessed and less powerful Light Guardians."

My eyes widened slightly as I remembered. Matt had told me about Elareth when I was younger—about how the Divines lived in the same community with Normals while trying to keep their powers, and the Demon attacks, hidden from them. It was uncommon. Most Divine and Normal towns were separate. Easier to keep our powers a secret from them that way. I couldn't imagine how the Divines in Elareth did it. It didn't seem possible.

"And we're just one of many border towns like ours," he continued. "There are a lot that sprang into existence over the years when the Dark Guardians figured out ways to rip open more unsanctioned passages between their plane and ours. So many that we couldn't just move whole cities and towns of Normals. We had to pull together as many local Divines as we could and try to keep the Normals safe where they were at. No warrior faction soldiers ever came to help us."

I frowned. I'd never heard about this before. I'd never heard there were so many places that Normals lived with us on the front lines. How had the warrior faction not set up adequate defenses there? How had they not found a way to move the Normals to safety?

"The Light Guardian leadership decided to start ranking these newly formed border towns based on their importance so they could prioritize resources." Disgust had crept into his voice. "Like how big the plane rip was, how many attacks were happening at each location, who the Normals and Divines were that lived in or near each city or town. They pooled their leadership and protection efforts into certain places, and left others completely without help. They depended on people like me and my family—people who just happened to live or be born near these towns—to pick up the slack and fight out of the goodness of our hearts, regardless of our resources or training."

He shook his head angrily.

"Needless to say, it's not sufficient. I've seen too many people die." He closed his eyes briefly. "Far too many. Normals and Divines alike. And the Light Guardian leadership has never sent us help or backup, no matter how many times we've begged. They've never provided us with any

8

support or formal training. We're not even officially in or run by the warrior faction. There's no reason we should be the ones placed in that position. We shouldn't have to be soldiers. But we don't have a choice. We would all die of we didn't fight. And the Normals would die if we left."

I stared at him, speechless, as anger bubbled hotly in my chest. But it wasn't directed at him this time. I was angry at the Light Guardians. It was one thing to expertly train people all their lives to fight in border towns, or to expect such a sacrifice from people who'd dedicated themselves to the warrior faction. But it was another to ask untrained civilians to do what I'd done my entire life—to face unimaginable danger, to kill—all without proper training or guidance. Without centralized leadership or support. Without a choice. I wondered if my mother knew about this. I wondered if she'd care.

"Our town, and many like ours, are full of Normals who've never been and never will be wealthy or well-known. They're regular people. Some are kind, and some aren't. Some are hardworking, and some aren't. But they're human, just like in every other town and city we try to protect. The Divines there are not as powerful overall, but they're still Divines. Yet none of us are considered 'important' by the Light Guardian leadership. They, and we, weren't deemed essential enough to help or save. They abandoned us to figure it out and try surviving on our own."

He looked at me then, his eyes flitting over my face.

"It's hard to feel like our side is better than the Dark Guardians when we pick and choose who deserves to live and die just like they do," he murmured. "Obviously not to the same extent or on the same scale, but I hope you can see why I feel like our leadership is a bit hypocritical." He pushed off his hand and scooted to the edge of the table. "It's hard to put the Light Guardian side on a pedestal when their methods leave so many innocent people unprotected and alone."

I bit the inside of my cheek and looked down at my knees. I felt . . . guilty. It wasn't like I'd made any of the decisions that'd left people so unprotected, but I felt deeply tied to the Light Guardian side. They were the ones I'd been around my entire life. They were the ones whose battles I'd fought. Whose orders I'd followed. I'd contributed to a system that was screwing over many of our own people. And my mother had probably been a part of those decisions. My stomach sank. I hoped Gabriel never found out who she was, or where I was from. He wouldn't be so eager to talk to me then.

"I get where you're coming from," I finally said, scooting to the edge of the table too. "I didn't know any of that."

He smiled a little. "Not many people do. Just those of us who live it." He turned to me again. "So, I haven't lost you after all?" His smile broadened.

I couldn't help myself. I laughed—something I hadn't done genuinely in a long time. "No, you haven't lost me."

Gabriel slid off the table, then turned to face me. "Does that mean we can be friends?"

I blinked at him, confused. And suspicious. "Why would you want to be my friend?" No one ever had. They were either too scared of me because of my transformation or were put off by my rougher attitude and style. Matt had been my only consistent friend.

Gabriel threw back his head and laughed. It was a warm, full-throated sound. "Seriously?"

My cheeks burned, but I nodded anyway.

He grinned and crossed his arms over his chest. "Let's just say I don't see too many people walking around and giving as few fucks about every-thing as me." Amusement danced in his eyes. "Seems like we'd get along."

I narrowed my eyes at him. It was the vibe I generally put out—that I didn't care about anyone or anything—but he didn't know me well enough to know just how true that'd become. I didn't want anyone close. I didn't want to care about anyone. Not again.

"Plus, we dress the same, so it seems expected." He grinned, ignoring my scowl.

I pocketed my lighter and pushed to my feet. Even with heeled boots, I was significantly shorter than him. It felt like a disadvantage in moments like this. I tilted my chin so I could meet his gaze. I didn't see any artifice there. No nefarious plan. But I couldn't trust that. He was a soldier—as experienced at hiding his true emotions as I was. I should turn him down. Send him on his way to find another friend who'd actually give a damn about him. That couldn't be me.

But don't you want at least one person to talk to while you're here? Don't you want one person who won't stare or glare at you?

My stomach tightened.

"Fine. We can try to be friends." I'd just have to be careful. Not get too close. Not incorporate him into my life too much. Keep myself closed off so I'd be fine when he eventually left—either by death or by choice.

Gabriel's grin morphed into an amused smirk as he watched me. "Don't sound so excited."

2

FIGHT CLUB

THE TRAINING COACHES HANDED OUT SWEATPANTS AND T-SHIRTS TO the first years as we walked into the large gym the next morning. After sending us to the locker rooms to change, they had us line up around the perimeter of the gym. There were enough first years to circle the room three times. Apparently, we were the largest incoming class that the Academy had seen in decades. The escalating war might've had something to do with that—everyone wanted an escape into what felt like a peaceful world. And more parents wanted their children out of the line of danger. My stomach tightened. My mother had never wanted that for me. She'd actively done the opposite, depositing me on the front lines before I was even a week old.

I leaned back against the gym wall, watching the trainers and a group of what looked like upper-level students conversing in the center of the room as we waited for more students to arrive. Next to them stood several racks of wooden training weapons, and beneath them lay thick mats that cushioned most of the floor.

"Hey."

I glanced to my left and saw Gabriel pushing through the crowd to get to me, a small smile on his face. He looked genuinely pleased to see me. I bit the inside of my cheek and kept my expression as neutral as possible. I'd agreed to this. I'd agreed to be friends.

"Where did you go last night?" he asked when he was finally at my side. "I looked for you at dinner but didn't see you."

I shrugged and turned back to watch the trainers. "The dining hall was crowded, so I just grabbed some food and took it back to my room."

"Makes sense. Wish I'd thought of that. It was awkward as hell trying to figure out where to sit. It seems like a lot of people already know each other and have grouped together."

I nodded and crossed my arms over my chest. "That doesn't surprise me. A lot of people probably grew up in the same towns together."

"True. Too bad I was the only one from my town the right age to attend the Academy this year."

"Same," I murmured, watching as the upper-level students spread out across the room. "I'm the first one in four years to decide to come here."

Not many people from border towns chose to attend. Most thought their roles in the war were too important to give up for four years of school, so they went straight into the warrior faction when they came of age, if they were powerful enough. Most of the students here had come from towns that'd never seen conflict. They'd never been in battle or experienced the worst of the war. They'd never had to fight or kill or watch someone they loved die. Most didn't truly understand what it was like to live and fight in a border town.

Gabriel nodded, watching me curiously. I knew he wondered where I came from, but he didn't ask. And I certainly wasn't going to offer that information unprompted.

"So, what do you think 'training exercises' means?" He leaned against the wall next to me.

"Dunno. Ma— my friend told me that they do daily combat training with us here. It's probably an assessment of some kind to see what our different fighting levels are. That's what I'd do first, anyway. Wouldn't make a lot of sense for them to train us all together with such different skill levels."

Gabriel nodded. "Makes sense. Especially because there are a few students from border towns here. Wouldn't want them to accidentally eviscerate the newbies." He grinned, his eyes dancing with mischief.

I smiled. He was pretty expressive—funny, even—for a border town soldier. "*You're* from a border town. Would you eviscerate a newbie?"

"Well, not on *purpose*." He smirked. "But in the face of my skills, who knows what would happen." He winked at me.

I snorted and nudged him with my shoulder, trying to suppress my smile.

"Okay, listen up," one of the trainers shouted, drawing our attention. The gym fell silent. "One of our goals here at the Academy is to help each of you become the best fighter that you can over the next four years. We're not necessarily training you to be military-ready, unless that's something you want. Our main objective is to make sure that all of you can defend yourselves should the occasion ever arise."

He looked around the room, his expression surprisingly serious.

"It's not a secret that it's dangerous to be a Divine. Between our war and the perils of the Normal world, there are always threats nearby. To that end, we'll work to prepare you for whatever you might encounter. Today we'll be assessing your current fighting skills so we can divide you into the training group that will best match your needs. There's no need to be concerned if you've never trained before. We have five training levels, spanning from beginner through advanced, so you'll fit comfortably somewhere."

Whispers filled the room, as people discussed with their neighbors what group they thought they'd be sorted into. I glanced at Gabriel—he'd crossed his arms over his chest and looked supremely unconcerned. He was probably a great fighter, being from a border town and all. A part of me hoped we'd end up in the same training group. At least that way I'd have someone to talk to. But another part of me knew that spending more time with him was against my best interests. It'd only make him more a part of my life, and I couldn't afford that. Not again.

"This is how we're going to do it," the trainer continued. "We'll call groups of you forward to have one-on-one fights with upper-level students. Physical combat only—please don't use your power. You will start with someone from the beginner training group. If you defeat them, you'll fight a student in the training group above them. You will do this until you lose. You'll then be assigned to the training group level that you lost to. If you lose to no one, you'll be assigned to the advanced group."

He looked around the room, assessing.

"There are a lot of you, so this will take some time. Watch all the fights. This is your first day of training, so take it as a learning experience. When you're called forward, proceed to the center and begin stretching. We'll then assign you to an upper-level student, and you may begin fighting. The trainers will be walking around and assessing while the fights are happening."

He turned and nodded at the upper-level students. A small group of them started pulling new students from the crowded wall and sending them to the center of the room. They all looked nervous—a couple looked like they might be sick.

"Do you think it'll be interesting or boring?" Gabriel asked quietly as we watched them stretch.

I frowned, my gaze sliding carefully over each of them. "Based on how nervous they look, I'd say boring. No experienced fighter will have those kinds of nerves for a simple exercise like this."

Gabriel nodded slowly as he watched them contemplatively. "You're not nervous," he finally murmured. "Does that mean you're an experienced fighter?"

My eyes narrowed as I glanced at his profile. He was fishing for information about me again. He glanced back and smiled as he saw my expression. Only then did I see the amusement in his eyes. He was . . . teasing me. He didn't expect me to seriously respond.

I blinked, surprised, then quickly hid my reaction. Instead, I pulled on a neutral mask. "Guess you'll just have to wait and see." I shot him a cool smile. Controlled. Unrevealing.

Gabriel's shoulders shook in a silent laugh.

The whistle blew, drawing our attention, and the fights started. Three ended within seconds as the upper-level students pinned down the new ones, but two managed to defeat their upper-level opponents.

"We'll need two beginner-intermediate upper-levels over here please," the lead trainer called.

He blew the whistle once they were in place, and the students ran at each other. One new student was defeated in under thirty seconds, and the other held out for around three minutes, before also being defeated.

"Alright," the trainer called after blowing the whistle again, "report to the trainer with the clipboard over there, and she'll take your names and record your training groups."

As they did that, the upper-level students pulled more first years from the wall, and the process began again. We watched as student after student was pulled forward, fought, and was sorted into different training groups. So far, most people landed in the beginner through intermediate levels, with only a couple students making it to the intermediate-advanced group.

By the time the upper-level students got to our side of the room, over half of the new students had already fought and been sorted. At least an hour had passed, and I was beginning to wish I'd eaten more than the banana I'd stolen from the dining hall last night. I wouldn't have said no to some coffee either. I'd have to see if I could steal some of that for future mornings.

Gabriel was pulled from the wall in the next group. He gave me a salute before leisurely making his way to the middle of the room. I crossed my arms over my chest and watched as he stretched. I wondered how good he was. He looked strong and seemed like he trained a lot given his border town situation, but looks could be deceiving. You could be strong and still not be a good fighter.

The whistle blew, and I smiled as Gabriel easily overcame his first opponent. It took under five seconds. They quickly sent a beginner-intermediate student, and he defeated them almost as quickly. The intermediate student held out for under a minute. The fight got a little more interesting as he faced the intermediate-advanced student. This fight lasted several minutes, and I finally got to see Gabriel's technique and style. He had a graceful, fluid way of moving, and each motion looked incredibly purposeful. He was also good at being unpredictable—subverting the expectations of his opponent and catching them off guard with his strikes. I was impressed. It said a lot about the quality and dedication of the teachers he'd had, that he'd learned to fight this well without any formal warrior faction training.

Once Gabriel had defeated his intermediate-advanced opponent, the first advanced upper-level student was brought forward. The lead trainer directed them to the weapon rack, where they were allowed to choose several wooden training weapons. Gabriel chose a short-sword and dagger, while his opponent chose a broadsword. The crowd was buzzing with excitement. No other student had made it this far. Everyone wanted Gabriel's last match to be good.

The whistle blew and the two of them circled each other. They were cautious at first, lunging and thrusting their weapons, more to feel each other out than to truly attack. Gabriel's opponent was broader and more densely muscular than him, but Gabriel was smart. He knew how to use leverage to overcome his opponent's strength, when and how to engage him, and how to mislead him into moving or blocking in the wrong direction. This gave him an edge, though it wasn't enough to fully win. While not as smart or creative a fighter as Gabriel, his opponent had clearly been trained very well. I tried to filter out the crowd's gasps and cheers, and watched, assessing, as their swords clashed again

16

and again. They had different strengths, but overall, they were evenly matched.

As the minutes passed, Gabriel became bolder and introduced more kicks and body-to-body strikes, making the fight more physical. Pushing his opponent to tire out. Striking his opponent's body with his wooden weapons. If this was real battle, Gabriel would've certainly been drawing more blood. But after ten minutes of fairly even fighting, the lead trainer blew the whistle, ending the round.

Gabriel shook his opponent's hand, then the hand of the lead trainer, who'd made his way over to them, smiling. The trainer spoke to him briefly, then pointed him toward the trainer with the clipboard. There was no doubt that he'd be assigned to the advanced training group.

"You next," an upper-level student said, pointing at me and a few others around me.

I pushed off the wall and walked calmly toward the center of the room with several other nervous looking students. I smiled a little as I passed Gabriel.

"Good luck," he murmured.

I gave him the identical salute that he'd given me earlier. He grinned.

We quickly stretched, then moved into position across from our opponents. I eyed mine appraisingly. He was small and didn't look very strong. This would be a quick fight.

The whistle blew, and I ran at my opponent, quickly tackling him and pinning him to the ground in only a couple seconds. He struggled but couldn't even slightly move me off him. Our whistle blew again, and I helped him to his feet, then waited for the beginner-intermediate student to walk forward. The whistle blew, and I defeated her just as quickly. My fight with the intermediate student only lasted a minute before he yielded. The one with the intermediate-advanced student only lasted two. Finally, the same advanced student who'd fought Gabriel walked forward, as the lead trainer rolled over the weapon rack.

I grabbed a wooden sword, and my opponent grabbed two long daggers. He sized me up as we moved into position. I knew what he saw: a short but sturdy young woman with lean muscles. He, on the other hand, was a boulder of a person, medium-tall in height and incredibly muscular. I saw the confidence in his gaze. He believed he could crush me in a couple seconds. He'd be wrong. I'd trained with people older and larger than me my entire life. I knew how to compensate. Beyond that, Demons, in their transformed state, were incredibly large and powerful. Some were larger than houses—sometimes significantly larger. His size wouldn't be the factor he thought it would.

The whistle blew and he ran at me. He swung both daggers, aiming for my stomach, but I dodged them easily and swung around him, whipping my sword at his back. The tip scraped across his T-shirt, hard enough to leave a welt, but not hard enough to rip the fabric. He spun, his expression darkening with frustration. I smiled coolly, then nodded in invitation for him to come at me again. I was nowhere near done with him. If that was all it took to frustrate him, he was in for a very bad time.

He growled and swung at me again. This time, I swung up my sword and blocked his downward strikes. His eyes widened in surprise as my arms held up against his onslaught. I was a lot stronger than I looked. He pressed down on me through my sword, trying to force my knees to buckle, but I locked my position and held firm. Matt had made me practice this a lot when I was younger, and since he'd been older and larger than me, he'd been the one on the other side. And he hadn't rested until I could consistently get out of this position in at least a dozen different ways.

I leaned back and kicked my opponent roughly in the stomach, winding him and shoving him back, disconnecting our weapons. Then I surged forward and whipped my sword at his stomach. This time the sword tip ripped his shirt and opened a shallow cut in the skin beneath. Not enough to fully bleed, but enough to turn his face red with embarrassed anger. He was clearly not used to being beaten.

He came at me with his wooden daggers, and I surged forward aggressively to meet him. We locked into battle, striking, blocking, turning, kicking, moving increasingly faster until our movements were almost a blur. This was where the quality of our training would show through the most. The fight was too fast to stop and think about each individual move before it happened. Our actions and reactions were all muscle memory and experience now, and the most experienced fighter would win.

I assessed him dispassionately as we continued fighting. He was decent, but I knew I could beat him without too much additional effort. I'd been fighting people more skilled than him since I was a young teenager. Matt had made sure of that. While the fight was quick, this student wasn't outmaneuvering me, and I knew by now that he couldn't. It was time for me to end the fight.

I feinted a strike from above, drawing his focus and attention there, then kicked him roughly in the stomach as his arms swung up to block me. He stumbled backward, unbalanced, and I swung my sword, striking both his hands on the knuckles. He swore, his grip loosening on his daggers, but before he could react, I whipped my sword back around and struck him there again. This time, both daggers flew from his hands. Before he could grab for them, I barreled into him low, propelling him backward onto the mat.

He landed a wicked punch to my ribs as we rolled, struggling for dominance, but I got him back with a sharp elbow to the face. He swore as his nose spurted blood, and I jerked out of his grip and shoved him over, so he was face down on the mat. Then I leapt onto his back and brought my sword across his throat, my other hand grabbing his hair and pulling his head back so he couldn't move. I had him.

"Yield," I ordered firmly. He struggled beneath me, but I pulled my sword tighter across his neck, restricting his breath. "If this was a real sword, you'd already be dead," I growled, my voice dark. I yanked his head back even further. "Yield."

He struggled for a moment, then held up his hands. "I . . . yield," he croaked.

I released him and stood as the whistle blew again.

The coach came over and shook my hand. "Nicely done." He looked both impressed and wary.

Then he turned, dark green power glowing around his fingers, and quickly placed them over my opponent's nose. In a few seconds, the bleeding stopped, and the injury was healed. He turned back to me and held out his hand.

"I can take your weapon."

I watched him carefully for a long moment, then held out the sword. He glanced at my wrist as his fingers closed around the wooden blade.

"Ah, Matt did say that a young woman from Dagmar would be coming through. I assume that's you?" He smiled, a little warmer this time.

My heart leapt at hearing Matt's name. It'd been so long since I'd seen him. "Yes. That's me."

"Very good. We'll be happy to have you in our advanced training group. You'll start tomorrow at 9:00 a.m. in gym room 201. Please see the trainer with the clipboard so she can record that."

I nodded tightly at him and walked over to her. It was only then that I realized how quiet the room had gone. It was eerie, like all the sound had been turned off. I glanced at the crowd and saw they were all watching me. Some with surprise, some with confusion, some with jealousy, and others with fear. I looked away as I reached the trainer with the clipboard, trying to let it roll off my shoulders. It wasn't like people fearing me was a new thing.

"Name?"

"Terah Alexander."

"Advanced?" Her eyebrow rose shrewdly at me.

"Yes."

"Very good. You may rejoin your classmates now."

I nodded, then turned sharply and began walking back to where Gabriel stood. Whispers filled the room now like an ominous hiss.

"That was vicious. Who is she?"

"I dunno."

"She must be from a border town."

"That would make sense."

"My bets are on Dagmar."

"Must be. They're the best trained and most powerful."

"That's pretty cool."

"More like scary. Did you see what she did to him?"

"There was so much blood."

"She was ruthless."

My jaw tightened as I passed.

"Nice job," Gabriel whispered as I reached his side. We watched the next group of students stretching in the center of the room. I clenched my teeth and didn't look at him. "Seriously. You're the best fighter I've ever seen."

I didn't respond. I wasn't sure what reaction he was trying to elicit from me, but I wasn't in the mood to talk. I could still feel the gazes of all the new students on me, and it was starting to make my skin crawl. I bit the inside of my cheek. Hard enough to hurt. What I wouldn't give for a cigarette right now.

"Border town?" His tone was serious—the most serious I'd heard it thus far.

I glanced up at him, trying to read his expression.

He smiled a little. "Thought so." Then he glanced down at my wrist. "May I?"

I frowned, not understanding what he was asking for. He reached slowly for my hand—slow enough for me to pull away if I wanted to—then his fingers closed around mine and he turned my arm, so the underside was facing up. He examined the tattoo on my wrist and smiled a little sadly.

"Dagmar." He nodded slowly. "That makes sense."

I glanced down at it as he released me. I had the tattoo that most people from Dagmar eventually got. It was of a large pair of wings on either side of a glowing sword. And engraved on the sword's blade was an elaborate letter D for Dagmar. It was a symbol of pride—something we were known for throughout the Divine world. You got it if you survived long enough to see your teen years. It meant you were powerful and skilled. Or extremely lucky. Matt had one just like it on his inner bicep.

I hadn't thought about how much I'd want to hide where I was from until I got to the Academy. A large percentage of the people here seemed to idolize and romanticize Dagmar as a place of power and heroics, while a smaller percentage didn't like us, or were just plain scared of us because we were soldiers. Gabriel made up the unique percentage who didn't like us because we were a Light Guardian stronghold that received all the best training, resources, and leadership the warrior faction had—everything he'd been denied his whole life.

"I was hoping you wouldn't find out," I said quietly, but matter-of-factly. "But yeah. That's where I'm from. Sorry to disappoint you."

I took a slow breath and didn't look at him. I didn't want to see the disgust in his eyes. I didn't want to see him backing away from me. I wished I didn't regret the loss of his friendship so soon. It wasn't like he was a part of my life yet. It'd only been a day. Letting go of him should be easy. All I had to do was put him behind me and move on. At least Matt would be around . . . at some point.

"I'm not disappointed," he murmured as the whistle blew for the next group. "I can't blame you for where you grew up any more than you can blame me for where I grew up. But it makes more sense now—why you reacted badly to what I said yesterday."

I glanced at him and saw a bittersweet smile pulling up the corner of his mouth.

"You grew up only around Light Guardians. Some of the most powerful in the world. Of course you wouldn't know how it is in other border towns. You wouldn't see the Light Guardian side's deficiencies in the same way from there."

I watched him for a long moment. He was good at keeping his expression neutral when he wanted to—a skill many of us soldiers shared—but he didn't seem to be judging me or talking down to me. I sighed and looked forward again, watching the new students struggle with the upper-level ones on the mat.

"All I've ever seen are Light Guardians giving their lives to protect the Normals," I said quietly. "I've seen them die over and over again. And many of them die very young. I've nearly died more times than I can count, all for protecting others. After living that, it was hard to hear you say that Light Guardians don't care. That they aren't doing enough." I released a slow breath. "But I believe you about the Light Guardian leadership. It isn't right. You shouldn't be forced to fight without training, resources, or official help."

Gabriel was silent for so long that I glanced up at him. My heart jumped as I saw that he was smiling at me. A real smile. I swallowed, a foreign warmth permeating my chest and easing some of the tension in my body. I hadn't realized how rigid my muscles had become.

"Glad you agree," he murmured.

I smiled. "Does that mean we can still be friends?" I asked lightly, parroting his words from yesterday.

Gabriel's shoulders shook with silent laughter. "Yep. Besides, I want you to teach me some of those sick fighting moves."

I rolled my eyes. "You're an amazing fighter. There isn't much I could teach you."

He smiled at me slowly, the color of his eyes seeming to deepen. "I very much doubt that."

My pulse spiked. "Want me to teach you how to sneak out of here so we can go smoke? I'm getting tired of being stared at."

Gabriel looked around then, and his eyes widened as he saw how many students were still gawking at me. "Oh, shit. I didn't notice. Yeah, let's get the hell out of here."

I smiled and grabbed his hand without thinking, pulling him through the crowd toward the door. We weaved through the mass of staring students until we managed to get behind a more densely packed group of them. Then, as the next whistle blew, we ducked through the doorway unseen and sprinted down the empty hallway. We laughed as we reached the stairs and jogged down them. Then we ran to the main door and pushed outside.

The sun was shining brightly, reflecting off the long blades of grass, making them look as though they were glowing. I inhaled the fresh, sweet-smelling air deep into my lungs. So different from home. So much nicer.

Gabriel led us to a wrought-iron table that was far enough from the building that the teachers wouldn't see we'd left early when they emerged.

"Gods, we were in there forever." I sat on the edge of the table and lit a cigarette. "I'm fucking starving."

Gabriel lit his own and leaned back on one hand. "Same. Too bad we don't have our regular clothes. I had a granola bar in my pocket."

"Oh shit, I totally forgot." I looked down at our training clothes and laughed. "People will definitely know we snuck out early now."

Gabriel smiled and blew out some smoke. "Probably. At least we had the foresight to bring our cigarettes."

My smile turned mischievous. "I almost didn't, but the draw of potentially leaving early was too strong."

Gabriel grinned and nudged me with his shoulder. "Troublemaker. Same though, honestly." He took a long drag of his cigarette, then slowly blew out the smoke. I watched it curl through the air in front of him before dissipating with the breeze.

We were silent for a few minutes, but it was a comfortable silence. We smoked and listened to the leaves rustling in the trees as the warm breeze whispered past us. Cheerful birdsong filled the air, accompanied by the gentle bubbling of the closest fountain. I wasn't sure I'd ever felt this relaxed before. Especially around another person. Inexplicably, it felt like Gabriel and I were old friends—comfortable, without pretense, in each other's presence. It wasn't something I'd felt since Matt had lived with me in Dagmar, and it wasn't something I should feel now. Not when my goal was to keep everyone a safe distance from me. I frowned and put out my cigarette on the side of the table. Perhaps I was letting down my guard too much with him.

"So," I said, deciding to break the silence, "how did you learn to fight so well without warrior faction trainers?"

Gabriel glanced at me, thoughtful. "Well, my dad taught me all the basics. He trained while he was a student here and then honed his skills by fighting so often in Elareth. And then when I was ten, a former warrior faction soldier—a Blessed—came to live in town and took pity on us. He was older and retired from military duties, but he saw how much we were struggling, so he dedicated his time to helping the kids improve. I think he was the main person who made me the fighter I am. Well, him and all the Demons I fought over the years."

He grimaced and put out his cigarette.

"What about you? When did you start living in Dagmar?"

I sighed and looked across the grounds at the trees bordering the far side of campus. "My mother brought me there and basically gave me to the training house not too long after I was born." I scowled. "By the time I could walk, they had me training to fight and handle weapons. I fought in my first big battle at age six."

Gabriel looked taken aback. "That's—"

"Really young, I know. But battles were huge and bad—they needed as many fighters as possible."

"Yeah, but still. Children that young? That's wild."

I nodded absently, the beautiful grounds vanishing as memories of dark, bloody battles swam into focus instead. Skin-crawling Demon roars rang in my ears as the smell of blood flooded my senses. My stomach clenched, and I pressed my eyes closed, trying to push the images away.

"We aren't known for our long lifespans in Dagmar," I finally said, opening my eyes to the bright grounds again. "The warrior faction does what it needs to do to keep the Demons from infiltrating the Normal world and killing all the Normals—even sacrificing some of its own children."

Gabriel's jaw clenched grimly as he watched me, but he didn't say anything.

"Anyway, I basically trained and fought almost every day. Killed and watched people suffer and die more days than I didn't. It was hellish. That's why I hate when people romanticize it. It's not great. There's nothing wonderful or heroic about it. It's brutal and deadly and sucks the life out of the people living there. That's why I came here. To get away from all that, just for a little bit."

Gabriel was silent for a long moment, his brow furrowed. "It doesn't seem like you had much more choice in the matter than I did," he finally said.

I smiled bitterly. "I guess not. But I did it. We all did. It was all any of us knew. And we knew what the cost would be if we didn't—countless Normals would die along with all the Divines on our side of the war. I guess it was our duty." I shrugged. "But at least we were well trained. At least we had leadership and support. I can't imagine living like that without it."

Gabriel smiled a little. "It sucked. But it sounds like it sucked for you too."

My smile turned genuine as I watched him. "It did."

Our first class after lunch was History of the Divines. Our teacher, Professor Jeriah, was an incredibly old and wizened man who droned on and on about the old gods and the new, and why our powers were bestowed on us. It wasn't anything I hadn't heard before. Ten minutes into his lecture on why it was an honor to have destinies touched by the gods, I was spacing out pretty hard, my chin resting on my crossed arms on the table. I really hoped this class would get more interesting, because as it was, I was barely holding off sleep.

Part way through class, Gabriel pushed a piece of paper in front of me. I glanced at him and raised an eyebrow, but he just jerked his chin at the paper. I sighed and straightened up, grabbing and unfolding it.

I heard from my sister that there's a student-teacher lounge on campus that has beer. Want to check it out tonight?

I smiled and grabbed his pen.

Sure, sounds fun. I'm gonna need a lot of beer to recover from how boring this class is.

I pushed the note back to him. He read it and smirked.

I'll buy the first round.

I gave him a thumbs up, and he pulled the paper back to him and tucked it into his pocket.

Our next class was much more interesting. It was meant to teach us other ways of using our powers beyond our transformations. By necessity, I'd learned to do quite a few things untransformed in Dagmar, especially healing, creating shields, conjuring light and fire, and some matter-shifting. But I was eager to learn more.

Every Divine was both fueled and limited by their own level and character of divine power. We could channel it into our transformations or out of our bodies in other ways, but it took practice and extreme concentration to learn to control it and make it take the forms we wanted it to. So much so than many Divines didn't bother mastering the use of their power beyond their transformations. Once you drained your power, whether through your transformation

25

or through other uses, there was no way to regenerate it quickly—you just had to wait for it to replenish itself, which could take hours or even days. If you weren't careful, you could spend not only your reserves of power, but also your very life force. And no one could come back from that. They'd simply die.

"Okay class," our teacher began, "welcome to Divine Power 101. I'm Professor Inez, and I'll be your instructor this semester. We'll be starting out with several basic uses of our powers that tend to be of assistance in many different situations. In the first part if the semester, we'll focus on conjuring light and fire, creating shields, and minor healing. In the second part of the semester, we'll move on to larger uses of power such as more major healing, moving objects, and matter-shifting."

I tucked my leg under me on the chair and listened intently. This was an area I could use improvement in. Especially if I didn't want to transform in battle—and I didn't—supplementing in some non-transformation power usage could give me an edge. It could help me survive longer while reducing my need to transform.

"We'll start today with conjuring light," Professor Inez continued. "I want each of you to partner up with the person sitting next to you so you can have peer feedback, and so you don't tire yourselves out too quickly." She smiled wryly. "Many people overdo it on their first day, so please try to reign yourselves in. We don't need a fire burning down *another* classroom."

Several students laughed nervously.

"Here's what I want you to do. I want you to hold your hand in front of you like this," she raised her hand, palm up as though she was grasping a ball, "and I want you to close your eyes and look inward. Look for the well of your divine power inside of you. I want you to concentrate on taking a *small* strand of the power and sending it down that arm. While you do this, think about forming a ball of light in your palm. Concentrate hard on this. *Will* your power to take the form that you want it to. Any questions?"

No one raised their hand.

"Good. Pair up and decide who's going first. I'll walk amongst you and offer feedback. Please begin."

I turned toward Gabriel.

"Partners?" he asked before I could even open my mouth.

A small smile pulled at my lips. He wasn't hiding how eager he was to be friends. But an immediate dread dampened that initial warmth, making my smile fade. No one ever wanted to be my friend, especially not openly.

The only person who'd ever been this enthusiastic was Caleb. And that had ended badly.

"Sure," I finally said, looking quickly away from him. Doubt filled me. What if he just wanted something from me? What if he was trying to manipulate me into letting down my guard? My jaw clenched. Well, I wouldn't, no matter how enthusiastic he was. I'd learned that lesson, and I wasn't planning on making that mistake again. "You can go first. Just don't burn down the room."

Gabriel smirked and held out his hand. Without even closing his eyes, a bright ball of white light appeared in his palm. "I've had a decent amount of practice." His eyes sparkled mischievously.

My jaw unclenched and I couldn't stifle a small smile. His mood was strangely infectious. I held out my hand and made a bright light appear just as fast. Gabriel grinned.

"Good job you two," Professor Inez said as she passed. "You can move on to conjuring flames if you feel comfortable doing so."

We nodded, and both of us closed our hands, causing the lights to vanish.

I turned my chair to face Gabriel. "You can go first."

He held out his hand and stared intently at his palm. In another moment, electric blue flames erupted from it. My eyes widened—the color matched his eyes perfectly.

"I was right," I murmured before I could stop myself.

"About?" He looked at me with those piercing eyes.

I bit the inside of my cheek. I could feel them beginning to prickle with heat. I wished I'd kept my mouth shut.

"I just thought your eye color was probably spill-over from your power. Looks like I was right." I nodded at the flames in his hand.

He smiled, warm amusement creeping into his expression as he noticed my blush. "Let's see yours, then." He closed his hand on the flames, then crossed his arms, regarding me silently.

Shit. I'd forgotten that, if the flames showed the color of his power, it'd show mine too.

Divine powers came in a variety of colors based on a person's faction. Dark Guardians had a gradient of black powers, Demons had varying shades of red, Blessed had a variety of colors loosely corresponding to the natural element reflected in their transformations, usually blues, browns, reds, oranges, and grays, and Light Guardians had bright white powers.

My powers definitely weren't bright white. They didn't correspond with the color of any Divine faction.

I swallowed, trying to push past my nerves. I should've known I wouldn't be able to hide my difference forever. But it was unavoidable now.

I lifted my hand and drew power from inside me, commanding it to become fire. Deep purple flames burst into my palm and flickered brightly.

Gabriel's eyebrows rose. "That's surprising," he murmured, almost to himself.

I quickly closed my hand around the flames, making them vanish before anyone else could see them. I didn't look at him. I'd been forced to reveal more than I'd wanted to, and I'd just have to live with the consequences. If he chose to abandon me for it, it was out of my hands.

"Doesn't match your eyes, though," he added lightly.

My gaze jerked to his. He was . . . smiling at me. He'd seen my power and hadn't recoiled in fear and confusion. That was . . . surprising. The knot in my stomach loosened slightly. Maybe he just assumed I was a Blessed? That would explain it. I'd just have to hope he'd never find out the truth.

Professor Inez approached us before I could think of a response. "It looks like you two have a decent amount of practice with this. Have you done much healing?"

"I have," I said. "During and after battle."

"I've done a little," Gabriel said, running a hand through his hair, "but it's not my strength."

"Okay, well I'll have you two work on that for a little while. Start small. Start with what you've done before. Please don't overly injure yourselves, and try to keep the mess to a minimum. I'll check on you in a few minutes, and you can call for me if you need help before then." We nodded, and she walked away.

I glanced at Gabriel. "What kinds of healing have you done before?"

He shrugged and his knee started bouncing up and down. Almost like he was nervous. "Mostly just emergency stuff when people were hurt in battle. I've healed some gashes, moderate burns, and smaller stab wounds, but not as completely as I wanted to. I haven't done anything more serious than that."

"Okay, well the concept for healing larger things is basically the same, but you pour more power into it, and you have to visualize more detailed internal workings. But we can start small."

I leaned back and pulled a knife from my waistband. I'd learned in Dagmar to never be without weapons. Gabriel smiled, amused, then leaned back and pulled a knife from his waistband as well.

"We've gotta stop matching like this," he teased.

I rolled my eyes, a smile pulling at my lips. "Want to go first?"

Gabriel swallowed, his smile fading. He really was nervous. "Sure."

I met his gaze and pulled the knife lightly down my arm, slicing into it just a little. Blood pooled and started to drip. Panic flashed across his face for a moment, but he pressed his eyes closed and took a deep, slow breath. When he opened them, the nervousness had turned to determination.

He took my arm in his hands and closed his eyes. I could feel the power vibrating through him before I even saw the electric blue strands of power snaking down his arms toward his hands. Then he pushed the power into my skin. It felt warm and tingly. It soothed the stinging of the cut and slowly, very slowly, the cut began to heal.

Gabriel finally opened his eyes and smiled when he saw that my skin was smooth and closed.

"Not bad. You just need a little practice, but you've got the gist of it."

He nodded and released my arm. "It's not as hard when there's not battle raging around me. My turn." He took his knife and made a similar cut down his arm.

"There are two main ways of healing," I said, moving closer so I could reach him. "You can either heal one wound at a time by concentrating your power over each spot, or you can heal more generally if someone has a bunch of injuries."

Instead of taking his arm, I ran a finger slowly down his cut. Deep purple poured from the tip, leaving healed skin behind it. Gabriel's eyes widened.

"If you pour power into someone who has too many injuries to heal one at a time, then you direct the power to treat multiple regions at once. This takes a lot of concentration and practice, as you have to picture the internal workings of more than one place at once. That's why people prefer to more precisely focus their power over individual injuries when they can. The good thing about topical healing, which is what I just did, is that it requires a lot less of your power. You concentrate on the wound itself, using just enough to heal it instead of pouring a ton of excess power into the person you're trying to heal."

Gabriel nodded as he looked down at his healed arm. "Which kind of healing did I just do?"

I wiped the remnants of his blood onto my pants. "You kind of did a combination of both. You poured power into the general vicinity of the wound, but not directly on it, so you used more power than you needed to, but you essentially still healed it topically."

Gabriel frowned but nodded. "Can I try again?"

I smiled. "Are you always this eager to make your friends bleed?"

Gabriel smiled, but it didn't reach his eyes. Instead, he looked grim. Almost haunted.

"Not generally, but I want to get better at this. I don't want to lose anyone else because I don't know what I'm doing."

My smile faded. He'd lost someone. Someone he cared about. I bit the inside of my cheek. I wasn't good at comforting people. In Dagmar, we'd always been expected to suck it up and move on. If we mourned every loss, we wouldn't have time for anything else. But in this moment, I almost wished I was. It was a strange feeling—wanting to lighten someone else's burden. It probably wasn't something I should feel. But . . . I couldn't say nothing. My stomach clenched. I couldn't just ignore his pain.

"Then let's practice," I finally said, matter-of-factly, "so you'll be prepared in the future." I didn't meet his eyes. I didn't want him to think I cared too much—about him, about anything. Instead, I picked up my knife and drew it down my arm again, focusing on the cut instead of him.

Gabriel's hand briefly hesitated over my arm before he placed his finger at the top of the cut. He took a deep breath, then moved his finger slowly down, pouring power into it as I'd done for him. He wasn't as quick as I knew he could be with practice, but it was certainly more efficient than when he'd poured way too much power into my arm. Finally, his finger reached the bottom of the cut, leaving behind healed skin.

"Good. That was definitely an improvement."

He nodded and wiped my blood onto his pants. "It felt better. Much less draining. I'll have to work on that."

Professor Inez brought over some damp towels so we could clean up. "Good work, you two. I'll have you work on healing for the next few weeks, and we'll go from there. You seem like a good tutor," she added, smiling at me.

I shrugged, a little uncomfortable. "I just had to heal people a lot growing up, so it comes naturally to me now."

She nodded. "Well, we're lucky to have you in our class. It'll help the other students to see how you approach healing."

She patted my shoulder, then turned and walked back to the front of the class.

"Alright everyone, I think this has been a good introduction for today. I'll be assigning you some readings about the theory behind your use of power for non-transformation purposes. Those readings will go into more detail about how to best complete some of these more basic tasks and will give you some practice tips. It'll be especially important in helping you master skills quickly and ensuring you can keep up in class. We have a lot to get through this semester, so please make sure you stay on top of your workload. I'll send a list of your assignments to your phones shortly, and you should've all received your books by now. Any questions?"

The class shook their heads.

"Great. It was nice meeting you all, and I'll see you on Wednesday. You're dismissed."

I made my way across the moonlit campus with the small map that Gabriel had drawn for me on a napkin at dinner. The building that housed the lounge was on the opposite side of the grounds, past all the dorm buildings, past the giant main classroom building, and past the ornate chapel that'd housed orientation. It was sitting just before the start of the staff residence buildings that sat on the edge of campus near the thick border of trees.

I pushed open the door when I reached it and walked purposefully inside. The entire building was essentially a large, dimly lit stone room with several small fireplaces around the walls. Seating areas of plush-looking armchairs and small tables were arranged around the fireplaces, high-backed booths lined the back wall, and round and rectangular tables of various sizes filled the remaining open spaces in the room. Most of the light came from large wrought-iron candelabras that hung from the high ceiling, filled with giant flickering candles.

The bar was situated in the center of the room, partially dividing one side from the other. It was made of highly polished dark wood that was elaborately carved with images of all the Divine factions. Behind the bar was an extensive line of taps—far more extensive than the bar in Dagmar—as well as a large collection of bottles holding every kind of liquor I'd ever heard of. And on the back corner of the counter sat a high-tech stereo system that was blaring music.

I glanced around the room, trying to locate Gabriel. It was already packed with both new and returning students, and it wasn't escaping my notice how many people were currently staring at me. I gritted my teeth. News of my earlier fight against the upper-level student had spread. *Great.* Just what I needed.

I finally spotted Gabriel at a small table in the back corner of the room. He already had two beers in front of him. Some of the tension left me as a smile pulled at my lips, and I pushed through the crowd to get to him.

"Is that beer for me, or did you have a particularly hard day?"

Gabriel looked up and grinned. "It's for you. Hope you don't mind, but it sounded really good, so I got one for each of us. I did promise to buy the first round."

"True." I pulled out the chair and sat across from him. "Thanks." I slid the beer toward me then took a long sip. It was frothy and malty with a small amount of bitterness, and a sweeter finish. A better beer than we'd ever had access to in Dagmar. "Mmm. It really is good. It's been a while since I've had a beer." I took another sip and sighed, relaxing back into my chair.

"I'm guessing there weren't that many parties in Dagmar." Gabriel set down his glass.

"No, not really any. We did have one bar in town that I went to sometimes, but it wasn't the greatest. Mainly went there for company when I wanted it."

Gabriel nodded. "Yeah, we only had one in Elareth as well. Though it was run and heavily frequented by Divines. We went there more than I'd like to admit. Especially after hard battles." He took a long sip of beer and looked around the room. "It wasn't as nice as this."

"I'm glad your sister told you about this place. It'll be nice to have somewhere to unwind that doesn't have to do with battles or loneliness." I took a large sip of beer, not meeting his eyes, and kicked myself for the loneliness comment. *Damnit.* I needed to get better at keeping my thoughts and feelings to myself. I'd just gotten out of practice at socializing. I hadn't wanted to, beyond a short fling here or there. Not since Matt. Not since . . . Caleb.

I could feel Gabriel's gaze on my profile. "Not much company in Dagmar?"

I shrugged as heat rose in my cheeks. "There was some. But my main friend left to come to the Academy when I was fourteen. We grew up together. Trained together. He was the one person who was consistently there for me."

Gabriel nodded and swirled his beer around his glass absently as he studied my expression. "Were you pissed when he left?"

My stomach clenched. I was beginning to think Gabriel might be more observant than I'd initially given him credit for. I'd have to be careful about that.

I took a slow sip of beer, watching him carefully. "It sucked, but I got through it."

Gabriel nodded slowly, and some of his jet-black hair fell into his eyes, hiding the piercing electric blue. He pushed it back over his head and leaned back in his chair, watching me in return. I swallowed, my fingertips digging into my glass. Something about him was . . . mesmerizing. But I couldn't nail down what.

Gabriel sighed and pushed his glass a little away from him. "My sister left to attend the Academy when I was fifteen, then dropped out and joined the warrior faction. She was the only friend I really had. I had a best friend when I was younger, but he died when I was eleven. Demon attack." He shrugged, but that haunted look returned briefly to his eyes.

My stomach clenched. "I'm sorry."

He shrugged again, but I could see the lingering pain. "It was a long time ago," he said quietly. "Anyway, my sister leaving kind of wrecked me. She was the person who knew me best and accepted me most. After she left, I shut down for a while. I didn't have many people to talk to. I avoided the Normals because I couldn't be honest with them about who I was, and I avoided the Divines because they looked down on me for the appearance of my transformation. I felt isolated from everyone."

Surprise lit my insides. People in Dagmar had avoided me because of my transformation too, but I'd never heard of that happening to anyone else. "Why didn't they like the appearance of your transformation?"

Gabriel watched me for a long moment, like he was trying to determine how much to tell me. "It's . . . untraditional looking," he finally said. "I've done research on it, and it's not unheard of, but it's uncommon. People didn't understand it, so they feared and avoided me when they saw it. It's why I stopped transforming as much and relied more on my fighting skills in battle."

My eyes widened. That'd been what I'd done as well. It was rare— every Divine usually transformed in battle. Curiosity burned through me. What did he look like? What kind of Divine was he?

"People are weird about mine as well," I finally said, leaning back in my chair and crossing my arms over my chest. "It's unexplainable, so they think it must be darker—evil—somehow. It's why most people apart from Matt—my friend—avoided me." I shrugged, as though it hadn't caused me lifelong sadness. I'd been rejected since I was a small child for something I had no control over.

Gabriel's eyes widened, and I saw curiosity spark to life there. He wanted to know about my transformation too. But neither of us could ask more questions—the Academy didn't allow it. If we wanted to know, we'd have to freely divulge that information, and I wasn't sure either of us wanted to. It was . . . kind of nice having a friend. I didn't want to drive him away so soon.

Gabriel eventually sighed and leaned forward so his elbows were propped on the table. "It's not easy being avoided for things we can't control. It's what made my sister leaving even more devastating for me. It's hard enough to build connections in border towns. People die so often that real friendships are few and far between. But with this added rejection over my transformation, it felt almost impossible. I eventually moved past it and made a few friendly acquaintances over the past couple years, but it took time. And I still had to hide my transformation from them."

I nodded and rolled my glass slowly between my hands. I wasn't sure how much to tell him. But he'd confided in me. Maybe . . . I could survive confiding a little in return.

"Matt was more than my best friend," I finally murmured. "He was my family. His mom took care of me when I was first placed in the training house as an infant, but she died when I was two. Matt took care of me after that. He basically raised me. We were almost inseparable. But living in Dagmar was hell for all of us, even Matt. That's why he left to come here. I was too young to fully understand his reasoning—at the time, it felt like a betrayal. Like he'd abandoned me. But I understand it better now." I smiled sadly. "I mean, I left Dagmar to come here too. I needed the escape just like he did."

"But it was still hard."

"Yeah. It sucked. He's been hired as a trainer here, so I may punch him when I see him again." I smiled.

Gabriel's eyebrows rose. "Have you not seen him since he left?"

My smile faded. "No. He wrote a lot, but he was never able to come back."

Gabriel grimaced. "Yeah, you should punch him. Just a little."

34

3
REUNION

I DECIDED TO HEAD TO THE TRAINING ROOM EARLY THE NEXT morning in case Matt was around. I hadn't seen him on campus yet, but I knew he'd been hired as an assistant trainer for at least one of the groups right after he'd graduated last semester. I kind of hoped he'd be assigned to mine. At least that way I'd see him regularly.

I slowly pushed open the door to our assigned training room. I was the first student to arrive, but not the only person here. My heart did a flip as I saw him. He was on the other side of the room organizing the wooden training weapons, his back to me. He was fairly tall, with broad shoulders, a muscular build, and golden-brown hair. I smiled. It'd been four years, but he was still so familiar. I watched him in silence for a long moment. His movements were measured and purposeful, as they'd always been. He exuded both power and careful control.

Finally, I decided to alert him to my presence. I cleared my throat and watched as he twitched in surprise then swung around. Even startled, he was still incredibly handsome. His face was just a little more angular than it'd been when I'd last seen him. He was fully an adult now—a reality that made my stomach feel a little weird. Almost fluttery.

"T-Terah?" His eyes widened.

"Forget about me already?" I smirked and took a step toward him.

"Of course not." His gaze roved over me, as though he was in disbelief. "You . . . you're grown up."

I laughed. "Well, it *has* been four years." I took another step forward.

Matt's shoulders drooped a little. "Yeah." He looked down, but not before I saw guilt flash across his face. "It's been too long. My fault, I know."

I walked closer to him slowly, almost afraid he wasn't real. That he might disappear again if I got too close.

"Did you miss me?"

He jerked his head up to look at me again. His gaze swept over my face, and a look of wonder grew there.

"Of course I missed you. Every day."

I smiled as I stopped in front of him. His eyes warmed in response.

"Did you miss me?" he asked.

I rolled my eyes. "More than I'm willing to admit." I smiled, trying to disguise the massive swell of emotion churning through me.

But he knew me too well. He stepped forward and swept me up in a tight hug. I yelped as he lifted me off the ground, his arms wrapped firmly around my waist. My arms circled his neck, and I buried my face in his shoulder. He still smelled the same. Woodsy and warm. It was such a comforting scent. So familiar. My grip on him tightened. He was here. Really here.

"I'm sorry," Matt murmured, pressing his cheek to my hair. "I shouldn't have left you there. I should've come back. I should've taken you away."

I shook my head. "They wouldn't have let me leave until I was eighteen. Not without my mother's permission, and we know she'd never have given it."

His arms tightened around me. I could feel his heart racing through his chest.

"I should've found a way. I'm so sorry."

"It's okay," I murmured into his shirt. There was no point being sad about the past. There was nothing we could do to change any of it now. Besides, it wasn't like he'd had a choice—I knew he would've returned to me if he could've.

"I missed you," he finally murmured. "So much." He pressed his lips to the top of my head, then slowly lowered me back to the ground. Then he took my shoulders in his hands and held me back from him so he could look me over again. "I still can't believe how grown up you are." He smiled and shook his head. "The last I remembered, you were a scrawny little girl."

36

I scowled at him. "I was fourteen! Hardly little."

His smile turned into a grin. "Compared to me you were."

"And now?" I smiled up at him.

I was surprised to see his cheeks redden slightly. He opened his mouth to respond, but before he could, footsteps behind me interrupted us. I stepped back, out of Matt's grip, and turned to see Gabriel walking over. He was watching us with interest, but his expression was carefully neutral.

"Hey," he said as he reached my side, his voice a little deeper from his proximity to sleep.

I smiled. "Hey. This is Matt, my friend from Dagmar." I gestured at him. "Matt, this is my friend Gabriel. He's from Elareth."

Matt looked Gabriel over warily but held out his hand for a handshake anyway. "Elareth. Another damn border town. I hope it wasn't too hellish."

Gabriel smiled slightly as he shook Matt's hand. "It was pretty bleak, though not as bleak as Dagmar sounds."

Matt nodded faintly and pushed his hands into his front pockets. He looked back and forth between us for a moment. Gabriel crossed his arms over his chest and returned Matt's stare with an assessing one of his own.

"Did you meet here?" Matt finally asked. "Or did you know each other before coming to the Academy?"

"We met here," I said quickly. "Gabriel is one of the few people who doesn't suck."

From the corner of my eye, I saw Gabriel's small smile.

"Likewise." His voice was warmer now.

Matt nodded slowly. "Well, I'm glad you're making friends." He turned toward me, angling his body away from Gabriel. "And I'm glad we're finally in the same place again." His hazel eyes softened as they met mine.

"Me too." My cheeks flushed.

"We should probably go change," Gabriel said, glancing at his watch. "We're supposed to start in five minutes."

I nodded and turned to follow him to the locker rooms, but I stopped about ten feet out from Matt and turned back again. Gabriel paused as I walked back to Matt.

"I promised myself I'd do this because you left me for so long." Then I punched him in the shoulder. Not hard enough to really hurt him, but hard enough to make a point.

Matt winced. "Damn it, Terah, that hurt." He rubbed his shoulder.

I smiled slowly as I backed away. "That's the point. Now we're even."

To my surprise, his cheeks reddened again as he watched me. *Interesting.* I turned to rejoin Gabriel and saw he was silently laughing.

"Nice," he murmured when I reached his side.

I grinned. "I won't lie—that felt good. Might need to revenge punch him again at some point."

Gabriel and I were assigned to each other as training partners since we were the only new students to join the advanced training group. Luke, the lead trainer, and Matt were responsible for raising the group's fighting skills to the level that the warrior faction demanded. Many of us were already there, but as Luke and Matt kept pointing out, the better we got, the higher ranking we could be if we chose to go in that direction with our careers, the better we'd be able to save people, and the more likely we'd be to survive.

The first day was hard. We trained for three hours, starting with intensive hand-to-hand combat, then moving to staff and swords. Gabriel was incredibly good, but Matt and Luke weren't satisfied with good. They wanted perfection. So they came around and corrected us often, nitpicking our form, fluidity, speed, and the power we put behind our movements. They made us repeat forms and movements again and again until we hit them correctly each time. And every time someone won a fight, they made the loser identify the winner's flaws and tells, then would make us go again.

I won all our fights, but I was surprised and pleased to find that Gabriel was a good sport about it.

"That was awesome," he said after I beat him again. "You're going to make me a much better fighter." He took my hand, and I pulled him to his feet.

Matt cut through the other fighting pairs and stopped at my side. "Not bad, but not perfect, either. Just because you know you can beat someone doesn't mean you should let yourself get sloppy." He skewered me with a look, and I scowled back, crossing my arms over my chest. I'd forgotten how much of a hardass he could be during training. "Did you spot any of her weaknesses?" He turned toward Gabriel, his expression mild.

Gabriel looked at him for a long moment before running a hand through his hair. "Not really. I guess she let through a few of my strikes, which would've caused her injury if the weapons were real."

Matt nodded and turned back to me. "Exactly. Untransformed, any of those strikes could've taken you out of the fight. You shouldn't be letting in any."

My scowl turned into a glare. I knew it was his job and everything, and he wasn't technically wrong, but that didn't mean I had to like it.

"And you," he added, turning back to Gabriel, "need to work on your speed and endurance. Terah's getting the better of you because she's quicker than you, she's creative about overcoming size discrepancies, and she's built up a lot of endurance. Work on speeding up your reactions, movements, and counterattacks. Work on keeping the same energy level throughout the fight even if you're tired. Okay?"

He looked between the two of us. We nodded glumly.

"Take those things into account and go again."

I sighed as he turned to leave, but he paused and stepped closer to me for a moment. To my surprise, he reached out and tucked a piece of my hair that'd come loose from my ponytail behind my ear. It was a familiar gesture. Close. And it made my pulse jump. It'd been a long time since I'd let anyone casually touch me. I swallowed and met his gaze, the expression there a little different than I remembered.

"Thanks," I whispered.

He smiled warmly, then squeezed my shoulder before walking away. I watched him go, adrenaline and uncertainty churning in my stomach.

After classes, Gabriel and I grabbed a quick dinner before gathering our homework and taking it to a quieter back corner of the lounge. We figured having beer while working was a much more bearable way of doing our homework, instead of locking ourselves in the library. I'd probably lose it if we did that. Sitting in classrooms all day was confining enough. We'd only had an hour of school per day in Dagmar, so the transition to a full afternoon's worth of classes plus homework was a rough one.

"Fuck, I'm sore," Gabriel groaned as he slid back into the booth across from me, carrying two beers. He slid one toward me, a smile pulling at his lips. "You really kicked my ass today."

I smiled. "We'll just call it even since you're the first person in a long time who's made my arms and shoulders sore."

"I did?" His smile turned downright cheerful.

I glared at him.

He laughed. "What? You kicked my ass all day. The least you can give me is a small amount of gloating."

I shrugged and took a long sip of beer. "Guess I'll just have to make sure you're even sorer tomorrow." I shot him a smug smile.

Gabriel groaned. "Gods, I believe you. Fine, no more gloating for me."

I smiled and took another sip of beer.

"Do they still hurt?" Gabriel asked, watching me closely as he held his glass between his hands. His eyes were fascinatingly vibrant, even in the dim lounge lighting. Almost as though they might glow in the dark.

"Hm?" I blinked, distracted.

The side of Gabriel's mouth pulled up. "Your arms and shoulders. Are they still sore?"

"Oh." I thought about it as I took a long sip of beer. I had quick-healing abilities, so my muscles had stopped being sore a few hours ago. But I didn't want to disclose that to him. Doing so would reveal more about my power than I wanted to. "They're not too bad."

He nodded slowly and took a sip of beer. "Well, if they're bothering you, I can always try to work out the soreness and knots for you."

My brows drew together as I considered him. "How? With healing?"

"Not really. It doesn't involve divine power. Have you ever heard of a massage?"

I shook my head.

"Well, my mom used to do it for my sister and me after hard days of training, when we were too sore to sleep. It doesn't get rid of all the pain, but it helps loosen things up. I can show you, but you'll have to come sit over here for a few minutes." He jerked his head at the space in the booth next to him.

I frowned. He wanted me to sit close to him and trust him to do something to me that I'd never heard of. A part of me wanted to, but another, larger part wanted me to stay away. I'd already let him closer than was wise. I'd already broken my own rules just by letting him be my friend. Trusting him more would only lead to negative consequences. Guaranteed heartache. And I was done being the naïve child who'd let that happen.

Gabriel's smile turned bemused as he studied my expression. "You're funny. You're acting like I've asked you to jump off a building with me, not sit next to me."

I bit back my response. I was tempted to tell him that it was just as bad.

Gabriel sighed and leaned back against the plush booth cushion, his bemused smile turning more knowing than I wanted it to. "It's alright. You don't have to."

I frowned, my hands tightening around my beer glass. I didn't want him to think I was afraid of him. I wasn't. That wasn't the problem. I just . . . didn't want to trust him. Or let him too close. I bit the inside of my cheek, weighing my options. Finally, I sighed and released my beer glass.

"Fine. Scoot over." I'd just have to keep the emotional barrier between us even while we were physically close.

Gabriel's eyebrows rose in surprise as I stood and moved to his side of the booth. But he slid over, making room for me.

"You'll need to sit with your back facing me," he said, moving his beer out of the way.

I did as he said and sat facing the crowded room. He turned to face my back and scooted a little closer. I could feel the warmth emanating from his chest. A small shiver ran down my spine, though not in a bad way. Maybe it was because I couldn't see him, but awareness sparked through me, like an electric current, centered where we were closest together.

Suddenly, I felt his large hands on my shoulders. I inhaled sharply, then tensed, preparing to throw him off me if I needed to. Gabriel immediately lifted his hands away.

"Do you want me to stop?"

My heart hammered in my chest, and I took a slow breath. He was giving me a choice. He wasn't attacking me. He wasn't forcing me to be close with him.

"No," I finally murmured. "It's fine."

"Okay." I felt his slow exhale on the back of my head. Then his hands came up to rest on my shoulders again.

When it was clear that I wasn't going to tense up, he moved, running his hands over my shoulders and upper back, gently pressing and evaluating.

"You definitely have a few knots here," he murmured, more to himself than to me.

Then he started pressing the pads of his thumbs firmly into my shoulder and back muscles. He pushed his fingers in different lines and circles, creating pressure between his thumbs and forefingers, and encour-

41

aging my muscles to stretch and relax. My head fell forward, and a small sigh escaped my lips. This felt . . . heavenly. Indescribably good.

"Nice?" he asked as he continued massaging my stiff muscles. I could hear the smile in his voice.

All I could do was nod faintly, my head still bent forward. As the minutes passed, all the tension I held in my shoulders melted away, and the warmth of his hands soaked into me, oddly relaxing from someone I'd only known a few days. His hands eventually slid from my shoulders to my upper arms, massaging the muscles there.

I groaned, my eyes sliding shut. I couldn't help it. I hadn't realized how tight my muscles had become. I'd never done anything to loosen or relax them. I felt the soft vibration of his laugh through the small amount of space between my back and his front. It sent warm tingles up my spine, and goosebumps erupted across my skin. But I couldn't conjure the wariness I knew I should feel at my reaction to him. All I could think about was the press of his fingers and the sensations they elicited—so good it was almost torturous.

Gabriel finally trailed his hands up to my shoulders again, then gave them a light squeeze before releasing me.

"There. Hopefully that helps you feel less sore."

I blinked, dazed. The loss of his touch felt wrong somehow. Which was absurd. I could only attribute it to not wanting the relaxing sensations to end.

"Thanks," I finally breathed. I glanced over my shoulder at him, managing a small smile. "It was nice."

His gaze met mine—close. Its intensity burned brighter and hotter at this distance. Inexplicably fascinating. Hard to look away from.

"No problem." His deep voice rumbled through me, and I swallowed.

I jerked my gaze from his and quickly stood, moving across to my side of the booth so I was a safe distance away again.

I took a long sip of beer, then pulled one of my books in front of me. "We should probably finish up our homework."

Gabriel nodded slowly, still watching me closely. As though he was trying to see past my exterior to what I was really feeling. But I had my expression on lockdown. I was used to pretending nothing fazed me.

We finally finished our homework a couple hours later, and it was good that we did, because the lounge had grown steadily louder and rowdier as more and more students had poured in and more beers were drunk. Even I was starting to feel a bit buzzed after the steady stream of beers, which was quite a feat given my quick-healing abilities.

"I'll get us one last round as a reward for finishing," Gabriel said, pulling himself from the booth.

I smiled. He was nice. Generous. He made it hard to remember why I shouldn't like him too much. "Thanks."

He shot me a warm smile, then made his way through the crowd to the growing line at the bar.

He'd only been gone a couple minutes before someone else slid into the booth next to me.

"Hey," Matt said, a bright smile on his face. "I noticed you were over here, and I wanted to say hi."

I smiled back, my insides feeling warmer and more liquid than usual. Yep, definitely buzzed. "Hey."

Matt glanced behind him before turning his body to face me on the seat. I wondered vaguely if he'd waited for Gabriel to leave before he'd come over.

"Don't tell me," Matt laughed, looking at the table in front of me, "you came here to study? That's bold."

I laughed and shrugged. "It's better than being in the library. I'd never get it done that way."

Matt's smile was warm. "I guess you *were* always fidgety. You were far happier training than you were sitting in class or reading."

I shrugged. That'd certainly been true, though I'd evolved in the years since he'd left. I'd been alone a lot more, so I'd had to. That was when I'd started reading all the books he'd left behind, and all the ones I could find lying around the training houses. It was part of the reason I'd decided to come here—to learn more. Broaden my mind as I'd been broadening it on my own in Dagmar. I'd found that reading could be an escape too—my mind could experience some degree of freedom even when my body couldn't. But I didn't correct him. We'd have plenty of time to catch up and rediscover who the other was. It wasn't important that he learn that about me now.

"I come here a fair amount to unwind," he continued, "though I've never tried studying here."

He looked a little distracted as his gaze swept over my face again, slowly this time, as though he was cataloguing every feature. Like earlier, there was something there that was different. Some quality that'd changed.

"I still can't believe how different you are," he murmured. He reached forward and traced his finger down the line of my jaw to my chin. I was too surprised to consider stopping him. "Different," he murmured, barely more than a whisper, "but familiar still."

I swallowed as nerves rushed through me. I wasn't sure what to say. I wasn't sure what to do. Matt had never been like this with me before. The intensity in his eyes made my stomach feel warm and fluttery, like there were a hundred moths taking flight there. It was . . . strange. A foreign, not entirely pleasant feeling.

"Four years is a long time," I finally murmured.

"It is."

He released my chin and reached for a lock of my hair instead. It was longer than he'd ever seen it—past my shoulders, down to my mid back. I'd worn it shorter when I was younger to keep it out of the way during battle. But I'd let it grow over the last couple years. I'd needed a change.

"It's not a bad difference," he clarified, twisting my hair around his finger, his eyes never leaving mine. "It's just weird to see you suddenly as an adult. I feel like I missed that happening." He sighed, letting my hair fall back to my shoulder, and rested his arm on the table.

"You did," I murmured. He'd missed most of my teenage years. I didn't blame him—I knew he'd had too many duties at the Academy to let him return—but it was still true. Regardless of his wishes, he'd been gone for years of my life. And beyond physical changes, I'd changed. Internally. Him and Caleb leaving had solidified that.

"I wish I hadn't," he whispered.

"Me too."

Matt swallowed, faint color flushing his cheeks again. It made my own prickle with heat. Finally, Matt released a long sigh and ran a hand through his hair, looking away from me for the first time.

"I regret leaving. I'll probably regret it for the rest of my life. It was . . . selfish of me."

I smiled a little and shrugged. "It's done now. You can't go back and change it. All regret does is waste energy. Besides, I turned out okay." I said it lightly, but we both knew it was a lie. No one who'd lived through the hell that was Dagmar was okay. But I'd survived, and that was nothing to brush aside. Matt of all people knew that.

Matt opened his mouth to speak, but Gabriel slid back into the booth across from me before he could, a beer in each hand.

"Hey, Matt." He didn't look surprised. He must've noticed Matt in the lounge before now. He slid one of the beers to me, then studied us curiously, his expression carefully neutral. I immediately picked up my beer and took a large gulp.

"Hey, Gabriel." Matt's voice was considerably less warm now. He turned back to me. "I should probably go—I just wanted to come over and say hi." He reached forward and took my hand with his. "See you tomorrow for training."

His fingers lingered against mine for a long moment as he held my gaze, then he released me and pushed to his feet, slowly stretching to his full height.

"Don't expect me to be easy on you both tomorrow morning just because you've been drinking." He smiled smugly at us. "I intend to work you into the ground."

Gabriel and I both groaned, and Matt smirked before walking off.

"You'll thank me someday," he called over his shoulder.

"I doubt it," Gabriel grumbled.

We ended up staying in the lounge for several more hours. Something about my conversation with Matt had me wanting more beer, and Gabriel also seemed eager to stay.

"I can't believe you haven't seen any movies," he said in disbelief, four beers later. Gabriel had revealed he was an avid movie watcher, and he'd become more and more shocked as he found out the extent of my lack of movie knowledge.

I smiled at his blatant shock. "I've seen parts of some on the training house TV in the background, but it was the only TV we had, and we were either too busy to watch the entire thing, or people kept fighting over what to put on and would change the channel."

"Well, I can't let you keep going through the world without seeing at least some of them," he grumbled. He drained the rest of his beer and set down his glass. "I brought most of my movies with me. We can have movie nights and get you caught up." He'd been leaning forward eagerly, but he suddenly looked self-conscious, as though he'd just realized he was being too enthusiastic. He sat back in his seat again. "I mean, if you want to," he added casually, crossing his arms over his chest, as though it wasn't a big deal. But I could see it was.

I smiled and bit the inside of my cheek to keep from laughing. He was

45

usually so good at hiding his emotions when he wanted to. Seeing him slip up, especially for something like this, was almost endearing.

I picked up my glass and drained the beer before setting it back on the table. "Okay. I can be persuaded to watch some movies."

Gabriel smiled, warm enough and sincere enough to make my insides feel like they were being gently heated by the sun. Perhaps the beer was getting to me too.

"We should probably head back now," I added, glancing at the clock behind the bar. It was well past midnight, and only a few stragglers remained in the lounge apart from us.

Gabriel sighed. "You're probably right."

We stood and gathered our books, then made our way out into the fresh, warm night air.

"I'll walk you back to your dorm," he murmured as we started down the long path back to the north side of campus. The moon was bright enough to light our way comfortably.

I lit a cigarette, then watched as the smoke rose like a twisting vine into the night sky. It was still dotted with stars—some intricacy of how the Divines who'd made this plane had attached it to the Normal plane. We shared the same sun, moon, stars, and seasons, but the rest of the plane was like a side pocket in the regular one, almost undetectable to Normals, and could only be accessed through special openings created when the plane was formed—portals.

"It's out of the way for you," I murmured after releasing another breath of smoke. "You really don't have to."

Gabriel smiled down at me as he lit his own cigarette. "It's not that far out of the way. Besides, I want to. If you're okay with it."

I couldn't help the smile that curled up the side of my mouth. But disquiet immediately followed. It shouldn't feel this good to have someone want to spend time with me. That's what'd gotten me in trouble before—letting it mean too much to me. Causing me to lower my guard. This was why closeness was dangerous. I needed to push the feelings away and return to the hardened soldier I'd become in Dagmar. It was the only way to protect myself. It was the only way to keep myself whole when people inevitably left me.

I tried to school my expression into something more neutral. "Okay." I wouldn't deny myself the company, but I wouldn't encourage it either.

We walked the rest of the way in silence, smoking and enjoying the quiet of the night. I didn't feel pressured to speak around Gabriel if I had nothing to say. He seemed equally as content simply existing alongside me as directly interacting with me. It was different. Nice. It lifted from my shoulders some of the pressure I usually felt when interacting with others. Like I had to perform a version of myself for them. While I'd never allow myself to fully remove my carefully controlled mask around him—around anyone—I felt able to pull back some of its layers and be closer to who I really was. It demanded less energy of me. Perhaps that was why it felt more natural than it should to accept him into my life, even in a limited sense.

We slowed as we reached the front of my dorm. It was the second to last one on the north end of campus, whereas Gabriel's was the closest to the main classroom building and the furthest south of all the dorms. He'd added quite a few extra minutes to his walk by seeing me back to mine.

Gabriel turned and smiled at me. "See you tomorrow. Fingers crossed that we're not too hung over."

I laughed in spite of myself. I knew I wouldn't be—I healed quickly, and my power wasn't depleted. But he didn't know that.

"For real. If we are, Matt will probably go out of his way to torture us."

Gabriel's smile turned sardonic. "I wouldn't put it past him. Though he'd probably torture me more than you." I saw a flash of speculation in his gaze before his hair fell in front of his eyes, blocking the vibrant blue.

I wasn't sure what made me do it—maybe it was all the beer, maybe it was his expression, maybe it was how he hadn't been able to hide his enthusiasm about sharing movies with me—but I stepped closer, reached up, and pushed his hair gently from his forehead. Unleashing his eyes again. They widened, surprised, as they met mine.

"Goodnight," I murmured, quickly losing myself in their vibrant depths.

I stepped slowly away from him, trying to extricate myself from the inexplicable pull they had over me. Finally, I managed to turn and reach for the door, but not before I saw how the surprise had mellowed into something warm and soft. I swallowed and pushed quickly into the building.

4

TRANSFORMATION TRAINING

I FOUND GABRIEL AT DAWN, SITTING ON A WROUGHT-IRON TABLE halfway between my dorm and his. I knew he was waiting for me—it was an out-of-the-way place for him to be otherwise. I smiled and took a deep breath of the fresh morning air as I made my way to the table. The sun was just beginning to rise over the trees surrounding campus, sending warm light in glowing rays across the grass.

As I got closer, I saw that Gabriel was eating something. He looked tired but relaxed. At peace. Objectively handsome. My stomach clenched. I hated to admit it, but it was true. Today he was wearing black combat boots, black jeans that hugged his muscular thighs, and a black V-neck T-shirt that bared many of his tattoos. I hadn't gotten a good look at all of them yet, but I'd spotted some constellations, a pair of Guardian wings, something that looked like waves that turned into wind, a detailed rendering of an elaborate church window filled with vibrant stained glass, and a name—Cainan—that looked almost like a memorial. Since he was from a border town, it probably was.

Gabriel smiled when he saw me approaching. "Hey. I figured if I got up early enough, I'd actually catch you before you got to the training room."

I smiled and climbed up to sit on the table next to him. I wondered if he'd waited for me yesterday too. "You'd be right. How's your head feeling?" He'd gotten far more intoxicated than me last night, though I couldn't gloat. Only my quick healing had saved me.

Gabriel shoved the rest of his food into his mouth, then rolled his eyes as he tilted his hand from side to side in front of him.

"So-so?"

He nodded and swallowed his food. "Not the worst hangover I've ever had, but let's just say I would've preferred to sleep in instead of going to training today. You?"

I couldn't help the smug smile that stole across my face. "I'm fine. I don't get hangovers."

Gabriel groaned and pulled out his cigarettes. "That's totally unfair," he grumbled as he lit one.

I laughed and shrugged. "Sorry."

Gabriel raised a sardonic eyebrow at me. "No, you're not."

I grinned and nudged him with my shoulder. He was right—I wasn't.

Gabriel grabbed a small parcel next to him, then held it out to me as he blew out a stream of smoke. "I grabbed you a muffin. Didn't see you take any food back with you last night, so I wasn't sure if you'd get a chance to eat before training."

Warmth and surprise filled me in equal measures. People didn't usually think of my needs like that. I was used to being the only one who looked out for me. "Oh. Thanks." I pulled on a neutral expression as I took it from him—I didn't want him to know how much his small act of kindness affected me. Instead, I bit into the muffin. It was warm and sweet, and a blueberry burst in my mouth. "Mmm." My eyes slid closed. It was good. So good. Better than any food in Dagmar. "I was prepared to wait until lunch to eat, but this is much better."

I opened my eyes and caught him watching me, the corner of his mouth quirked. "Glad I guessed right," he murmured before taking another pull at his cigarette.

I had a quick cigarette as we walked the rest of the way to the main classroom building. Other students were starting to pile out of their dorms in various states of dress and tiredness and were making their way to the main building for their respective group trainings.

Matt, Luke, and some of our classmates were already there and changed by the time we reached our training room. Matt smiled when he saw me, but it turned into a frown as he looked Gabriel over. I was starting to get the feeling that he didn't like Gabriel much. I rolled my eyes as I

49

pushed open the door to the locker rooms. Whatever Matt's problem was with him, he'd have to figure it out on his own. I wasn't going to just not be Gabriel's friend because Matt didn't like him.

Matt and Luke had us start training with hand-to-hand combat drills, before moving into full one-on-one fights with our training partners. Gabriel was a little slower today than he'd been yesterday, and after our first full fight, he laid on the mat and groaned as I pinned him down.

"Do you think they'll notice if I just stay down here and sleep?" He ran his hand down his face.

I frowned and loosened my grip on him. "Is your hangover that bad?"

Gabriel smiled wryly as I sat up, straddling him. "I'm honestly surprised I haven't thrown up all over the mat yet. Though if you throw me a few more times, I'm sure it'll happen."

"Come on you two," Matt yelled from the sidelines. "Get off your asses and go again." There was an edge to his voice that grated at me.

I shot him a glare over my shoulder but pushed off Gabriel and offered him my hand. He groaned as I pulled him to his feet, looking paler than before. Maybe he really was close to being sick. I bit the inside of my cheek. If his hangover was still this bad, it meant he didn't have any quick-healing abilities.

"Want me to help you?" I asked quietly as we lined up on our mat again. "With your hangover?"

Gabriel frowned. "How?"

I shrugged "I told you I'm good at healing. Do you want my help or not?"

He glanced at Matt, who was watching us with a frown. "Sure. If it can keep me from throwing up everywhere."

I dismissed Matt's frown with an eyeroll. "Don't worry about him. It should only take a few seconds."

I stepped closer to him and placed my hands on his chest before closing my eyes and locating the well of deep purple power that lived in me. I grabbed a moderate strand of it and pulled it down my arms to my hands. *Heal*, I commanded it, visualizing what I wanted it to accomplish. *Heal*. Then I pushed it out of me and into Gabriel. I heard his sharp intake of breath as my power rushed through him, burning away any remnants of alcohol and fatigue, rehydrating him, and rebalancing his system.

A few moments later, I released him and stepped back. "How do you feel?"

Gabriel flexed his arms in front of him, surprised. "Completely better. That's . . . incredible. Thanks."

I suppressed my smile and shrugged. "Not a big deal. Ready to go again?"

Gabriel nodded, but as he turned, I saw Matt stalking over.

"Please tell me you didn't just expend a bunch of your power to get rid of his hangover." His voice was brimming with misplaced anger. "And yes, I noticed he was slower and hungover." He shot a glare at Gabriel.

I crossed my arms over my chest and narrowed my eyes icily at him. He of all people knew that challenging me wasn't a good way to start a conversation with me.

"I was under the impression that you were our trainer, not the keeper of my power." I met his angry gaze with my stubborn one.

Matt glowered at me. "It was a blatant waste of your power, Terah. What if he hurts you in training? You won't be able to heal as fast. What if it's weakened you and thrown off your fighting?"

I scowled. I didn't appreciate Matt revealing my capabilities. I'd carefully avoided talking about my quick healing in front of anyone. While some Blessed had the ability, it was mostly associated with Guardians, Light and Dark. I glanced at Gabriel and saw that he'd crossed his arms as well and was giving Matt a hard but inquisitive stare.

I returned my gaze to Matt. He was much angrier about this than he should be. Maybe he still thought of me as the child I was when he'd left me. But I'd been looking after myself for years without him—I didn't need him stepping in now, throwing arbitrary worries and limitations at me.

"I know my limits and abilities." My voice was hard. Firm. "At this point, I sure as hell know them better than you do. Or did you forget you've been absent from my life for four years? So why don't you leave and let us get on with our training."

Hurt flickered across Matt's face before his expression hardened. "Fine. But add ten minutes to your training to make up for this waste of time." He stomped off.

"Asshole," I muttered, turning back to Gabriel.

He shrugged, not meeting my eyes. "He clearly cares about you. He just doesn't want you to get hurt."

"Well, he's got a hell of a way of showing it," I grumbled. But I glanced at Matt again. He was talking to Luke, but his eyes were still on me. Something in them seemed to flicker—intensify—as they held mine. I jerked my gaze away and refocused on Gabriel.

"Ready?" I took my starting position opposite him.

He smiled a little. "Much readier than I was before."

Matt approached me as I sat on the training room benches, waiting for Gabriel to emerge from the locker rooms. I clenched my jaw as he neared, preparing for another fight. But Matt just smiled.

"Lower your sword, warrior," he teased as he sat down next to me. "I'm not here to yell at you."

I glowered at him but relaxed against the wall again. "Maybe boss me around less, then."

Matt sighed and leaned back against the wall too. "I'm your trainer, Terah. I'm supposed to boss you around."

"Training wasn't what you were doing, and you know it. You just don't like Gabriel."

Matt stiffened slightly next to me. "It has nothing to do with how I feel about Gabriel. I'm just trying to look out for you," he added more gently. "Like I always have."

I frowned but didn't say anything.

"Anyway, I just wanted to talk to you about our one-on-one transformation training later. You saw they assigned you to me, right?"

I nodded blandly. They'd sent everyone their transformation training schedule, room, and assigned staff after dinner last night.

"I asked to be assigned to you," he added, watching me closely. "I thought it'd make you more comfortable."

I sighed and crossed my arms over my chest. "It does. At least other people won't have to see my transformation."

Matt frowned. "You shouldn't have to hide who you are, Terah. You're amazing, and so is your transformation. People just need more time to understand that."

"People in Dagmar had plenty of time to understand, and they still shunned me."

Matt sighed. "I know. But they were fools. Ignorant and elitist. You deserved better."

I bit the inside of my cheek and looked away from him. Yes, I'd deserved better. But no one had ever treated me better. He had no idea how lonely and isolated I'd been, especially after he and Caleb had left.

"There's more diversity here than in Dagmar," he continued. "More people with many kinds of transformations. You should give people a chance to see you and get to know you. I'm sure most of them will be far more understanding than the people in Dagmar were."

I frowned. Highly doubtful. "What did you want to talk about?"

Matt watched me for a long moment, likely trying to determine whether he should let me change the subject. He sighed, acquiescing for the moment. "I just wanted to talk to you about what I was planning for our sessions. Am I right in assuming you still have issues with burn-out?"

I nodded glumly. Of course I did. I didn't transform enough to practice building up and controlling my power in my transformed state.

"Okay. That's definitely something we need to address, then. We only have an hour at a time, so I think we should do some combat training in your transformed state as well as some work on using your transformation-specific abilities."

I nodded without enthusiasm. I knew I had to do it—it was a required class for first years—but I wasn't going to be happy about it.

"Hey," he murmured, reaching over and grasping my shoulder. My gaze jerked to his. The hazel was warm and familiar. "You'll be fine. And we'll get you caught up and in control in no time."

I nodded slowly, ensnared in his gaze. Maybe if I looked long enough, I'd be able to figure out what in it felt so different. What quality there had changed.

I finally pulled my gaze from his and leaned my head back against the wall, letting out a long breath. In the end, it wouldn't matter if I was in control of my transformation or not. It wasn't like I transformed enough to necessitate that kind of proficiency. I'd worked long and hard so I could get through most battles without transforming at all, and that's how I'd continue to fight once I returned to Dagmar.

Matt sighed, releasing my shoulder, then pushed to his feet. He likely realized he wouldn't get much more out of me about this. "I'll see you at 4:00. Make sure you eat a hearty lunch."

I spaced out through most of our History of the Divines class. Unfortunately, it hadn't gotten much more interesting since the first day. Gabriel sat next to me, looking bored and annoyed, but I knew he was listening anyway. And thank the gods for that, because I couldn't bring myself to, and *someone* had to get us through our homework. I knew I shouldn't depend on him for anything, but I couldn't for the life of me make myself focus through this class. The professor's voice was too monotone as he droned on and on about the dates and locations of different civilizations and their Divines. So I made an exception out of necessity.

Gabriel shook me out of my stupor at the end of the hour, then we packed up and headed to Divine Power 101.

"Alright class," Professor Inez said from the front of the room, "we'll be moving on from creating light and fire to some modest healing today. If you have experience healing, please move to the left side of the room. You and your partners can start off at whatever level you're currently at. Those without experience, please move to the right side of the room, and I will walk you through each step of the exercise. Gather your things and move now. Once you're settled, the left side of the room—those with prior healing experience—may begin."

I turned my chair toward Gabriel as students pushed to their feet and started relocating. We were already on the left side, so we didn't have to move. "Since I healed you earlier, maybe you could work on healing for a bit?"

Gabriel smiled, his gaze assessing as it swept over my face. "Worried you might burn out before transformation training?"

I narrowed my eyes at him, wishing he wasn't quite so observant. "No, I just want you to get better at healing. In case I ever get a hangover."

Gabriel rolled his eyes, but his shoulders shook with laughter. "Mmm, well Matt did spill that you're a quick healer, so I know you won't be getting a hangover anytime soon." He grinned at my glare. "But I guess I do owe you one."

I sighed and pulled a slim dagger from my belt. "Good. Don't let me bleed for too long." Then I drew the sharp edge down my arm, shallowly parting my skin.

Gabriel shot me a part frustrated, part amused look, but quickly focused on my arm as blood began seeping from it. He placed his finger at the top of the cut, took a deep breath, then drew his finger slowly down, electric blue power flowing from it. Veins and skin pulled back together, and in under a minute, I was completely healed.

I inspected my arm as he drew his hand back. "Nice. You're already improving. Want to try something more difficult?"

Gabriel winced, but quickly pulled forward a practiced neutral expression. "And what if I can't heal it?" His tone was casual, but I could see real worry in his eyes. Until his hair fell forward and hid them from me.

"Then I'll heal on my own or the professor can step in." I smiled, bemused. "Don't worry. You can do this." I'd been paying attention to his power output, and he seemed to have quite a lot of it. Which wasn't a surprise. A person usually needed to have an excess of power for it to spill over into their physical appearance like his did. And it meant that he'd eventually be able to heal much larger injuries without burning out. He just needed practice.

Gabriel took a deep breath and let it out slowly. "Okay. I'll give it a try."

"Good. What's the hardest thing you've successfully healed?"

Gabriel frowned, thinking. "One of the soldiers in Elareth was stabbed by a Demon claw through his upper chest near the shoulder. It went all the way through. I wasn't trained to heal, but we were in the middle of the battle, and we needed all our fighters, so I did my best. Managed to get it closed enough for him to keep fighting, but that was about it. It wasn't a very complete healing. I'd want to get more training in me before trying that again."

I nodded slowly. "Okay, so something smaller and less complex to heal, but also more complex than what we've been doing. Probably some kind of smaller puncture wound would be best."

Gabriel opened his mouth, alarm flooding his expression. "Wait. What are you going to—"

But I'd already lifted my dagger, and before he could finish, I plunged it into my forearm, carefully avoiding bone. He wasn't ready to mend bone yet. I winced at the pain, but I'd been stabbed probably thousands of times throughout my life. It was a pain I was used to.

Gabriel's mouth fell open and he stared at me in horror. "W-what the hell! Why would you do that?"

I pulled the dagger from my arm and dropped it on the table. "It's the right size and type of wound that you needed to practice on. You can do it. Just concentrate and visualize exactly what you want to fix while you heal."

Gabriel met my gaze, his frantic shock merging with anger and uncertainty. Perhaps even some fear. Fear that he couldn't heal it.

"You can do it," I repeated calmly.

Gabriel's chest rose and fell quickly, but whatever he saw in my gaze seemed to firm his resolve.

"Fine. Okay." He scooted his chair closer. "I can do this," he murmured to himself.

He blew out a breath, then placed his hand gently over the wound and closed his eyes. I felt power humming through him before I even saw blue power glowing around his hand. His grip tightened on my arm, and I winced as he poured power quickly into me. It wasn't the gentlest healing ever—I could feel the individual muscle fibers starting to pull back together—but he was doing it. His fingers shook, but his power never faltered. It soaked into me, soothing the pain as he pulled me back together, healed the veins, and finally skin. In a little over a minute, the wound was completely gone.

Gabriel released my arm, breathing hard.

I smiled smugly at him. "Told you, you could do it."

He glared at me. "That was completely irrational!" he exclaimed suddenly. "Don't do that again. You can't just . . . stab yourself."

My smile grew. I couldn't help it. I'd never seen him so frazzled before.

"What?" he asked angrily. "Why are you smiling?"

"Worried about me?" I tried not to laugh.

Gabriel glared, but I could see his anger receding. He sat back in his chair. "You can't just do that to yourself. Especially without giving me warning." He glanced at the table where my arm had been resting and winced. "Look at how much blood you lost."

"I'm fine. Whatever you didn't replenish when you healed me, my quick healing will get to soon. Besides, I'm used to it—how else do you think we practiced healing in Dagmar? In battle, obviously, but also by doing this." I nodded at my dagger sitting next to the small pool of my blood.

He frowned, unappeased.

"You should be proud of yourself," I added, waving my hand over the blood on the table. Deep purple flowed from my fingers, and the blood slowly vanished. "You successfully completed a more difficult healing, and without wasting a bunch of power. You're learning fast."

Gabriel leaned forward, staring at the table where my blood had been. "How did you do that?"

I shrugged. "Just turned the blood into the same material as the table. Less messy than cleaning it up with a rag. Which reminds me . . ."

I stood and went to the small sink built into the side of the classroom with a pile of small towels next to it. I quickly rinsed the blood off my arm, then grabbed a towel and dampened it. I brought it back to Gabriel and held it out to him.

"For your hand." It was still covered in my blood.

"Oh." He looked down at his red fingers, as though he'd forgotten. "Thanks."

We spent the remainder of class focusing on smaller uses of our powers—mostly summoning small objects to us, and some light matter-shifting. I didn't want to expend too much of my power before transformation training, and Gabriel had expended enough through the healing. He still seemed grumpy with me at the end of class, so I packed up my stuff and prepared to leave without him. But he caught up with me just as I reached the hall.

"Hey," he said, lightly touching my elbow to slow me, "good luck with transformation training. I'll meet you after near the dining hall for dinner."

I nodded and turned to leave.

"Terah . . ."

I paused and glanced back at him.

"Don't let Matt push you around too much." He smiled a little, but his expression was oddly serious.

This surprised me enough to bring a smile to my lips. "I never do."

Gabriel nodded, his expression difficult to read. There was something interesting there, buried in the depths, but I didn't have the time right now to worry about or determine what it was.

I checked the time on my phone—class had gotten out a little late—then turned to go. I didn't want Matt to lecture me about tardiness.

"Oh. Good luck with your transformation training too," I called as I retreated.

I glanced at Gabriel over my shoulder. Just in time to catch him smile.

"I hope you had a good lunch," Matt said as he paced the empty room in front of me.

We'd been assigned a room specifically made for Guardians who were learning to experiment with and control their powers. It had a very high ceiling, and all surfaces were lined with dense, nearly impenetrable metal. That way we wouldn't accidentally take down the whole building if something got out of control. Instead, we'd just kill ourselves and anyone else in the room.

"I did, though you cost me five bucks."

Matt raised his eyebrows curiously.

"Gabriel bet me that I couldn't finish all my food. He was right," I grumbled.

Matt's jaw tightened slightly, but he shrugged. "At least you actually listened to me for once. You'll want all your strength for this."

I rolled my eyes. Serious Matt was no fun.

"You should transform now, and I'll do the same."

"Okay," I mumbled. I really didn't want to.

Instead, I watched as Matt closed his eyes. In the next moment, his entire body lit up with bright white light. Enormous glowing wings burst from his back, as glowing silvery armor formed and covered his body. A large sword materialized at his side, and his skin, hair, and eyes glowed with warm light. It was hard not to feel awestruck seeing his transformation. He was unfathomably bright. Extremely powerful. I hadn't seen him transform in years, and I'd forgotten just how imposing it was. He looked like the truest form of an angel. As a Divine, and a Light Guardian at that, I supposed he was.

I smiled and moved closer to him. "I forgot how beautiful your transformation is." I reached out and laid a hand against his armored chest. I could feel his power vibrating around and through him.

He smiled at me, a beautiful smile that glowed with pure light, and reached out to gently touch my cheek. "Thanks." His voice was slightly fuller and deeper in his transformed state. "Now it's your turn."

My smile faded and my stomach clenched. I took a step away from him. "But my transformation isn't beautiful. It's just dark."

Matt shook his head, moving closer again. He reached forward and took my hand. "Your transformation *is* beautiful. And there's beauty in darkness as well as light."

I frowned at him. "I don't believe you, but I know I don't have a choice." And I wouldn't be able to stall for much longer.

I took a deep breath, then walked across the room and stood facing Matt. Then I closed my eyes and looked inward for the well of deep purple power. I felt rusty at this—I hadn't transformed for close to six months, and I'd only done so then so I wouldn't die in battle. Steeling myself, I grabbed the well of power and flung it outward in all directions, so it filled every inch of my skin. Warmth rushed through me, and with a flash of light, I transformed. Deep purple light radiated from my skin, glowing wings burst from my back, and deep purple armor formed around my body. A matching sword materialized at my side, shifting purple fire and lightning running up and down the sheath, and I felt my hair lifting and floating as though it was suspended in water.

I opened my eyes, which I knew were glowing intensely with purple, and looked at Matt. He looked awestruck and slightly taken aback. His body tensed, and he backed up a step. Away from me.

My stomach clenched. It'd been years since he'd seen me transform, and he'd clearly forgotten how strikingly different it was from his own. He was made of pure white angelic light, and I was made of stormy purple fire and lightning. A Guardian in form, but neither light nor dark. No one knew what I was. No one had ever seen a transformation like mine before.

My wings unfurled and lifted me into the air as I drew my sword. Lightning ran up and down the blade as purple flames rose from it. Matt's reaction had hurt. Even the one person who'd known and loved me throughout my life couldn't get used to my difference. He'd moved further from me. He'd reacted in fear. And his reaction made me feel more alone than I'd felt in a long time. *Damn him.* Anger burned through me, mixing with the hurt.

"So, what? You're scared of me now?" My transformed voice came out fuller and more powerful. At least it hid some of the emotion I was feeling.

Matt stepped forward slowly, but didn't speak right away. His silence sliced through me.

"I guess your whole speech about there being beauty in darkness was bullshit, wasn't it?" I taunted. "You can barely look at me."

Matt unfurled his wings and shook his head. Then he pushed into the air. "It wasn't bullshit. I meant it. I still do. I just . . . forgot what your transformation was like. I forgot how much power you put out. I just needed a minute to adjust. And . . . I'm realizing we'll have to be especially careful as we practice. We don't want to destroy anything or hurt anyone."

The hurt cut deeper as the anger burned more brightly in me, like a flash of lightning—hot and powerful. I gripped my sword tighter, and it blazed brighter in response. Why would he assume my transformation would cause any more damage or destruction than his? He could burn and destroy things with brilliant white fire just as I could with fire and lightning. They just looked different. The distinction was purely in his perception of the quality of his power—light, good—versus the quality of mine—darker, bad. And it was prejudice.

"You shouldn't have needed time to adjust," I murmured angrily, glancing at the ground twenty feet below us. "And I'm *not* more dangerous than you are." I didn't even know if he could hear me. I didn't know if I wanted him to. He'd hurt me—managed to get around the walls I'd so carefully created around myself for my own protection—and I couldn't forgive him immediately for that. Nor had he even asked to be forgiven. My mood darkened further.

Matt pulled his sword from its sheath and faced me, his expression grim. "Okay. We'll start with an in-air battle, then work up to multi-surface fighting. Then, for the second half of class, we'll focus on materializing different weapons in your transformed state. I want you to stay transformed for the entire hour," he added, sternly.

I ground my teeth together and nodded. Even in battle, I'd only stayed transformed for ten to fifteen minutes tops. And just doing that drained me. This was going to be hell. But I'd think about hell later. Right now, I had a lot of anger to burn through, and it was all directed at Matt.

"Good. Begin."

I shot toward Matt, letting my anger fuel me. My transformation burned brighter as our swords clashed with violent force, and Matt's eyes widened in surprise. *Yes, I've gotten much stronger in our time apart.* Matt might be able to beat me untransformed, but my transformation burned with fierce power, heightened my strength and reflexes, and removed many of my inhibitions. And now I had a point to prove. I'd not let him beat me.

Matt disconnected our swords and swung around me, but I spun quickly in the air and kicked him roughly in the chest before striking again, forcing him to defend himself. But Matt responded to aggression with aggression, and soon, we were fighting at lightning speed, spinning and tumbling through the air. It came naturally to us—we'd trained together almost our entire lives. We knew the rhythm and speed of the other. And we knew each other's weaknesses better than anyone.

Our swords clashed again and again—thrust, block, kick, spin, strike, dive, roll, over and over. We flew through the air, dark and light, locked in ferocious battle. Time stopped having meaning. All my focus was on his every movement, strike, expression, tell. It was how I saw the opening—the smallest pause as he tried to catch his breath. And it was all I needed.

I poured power into my wings and launched into him, propelling him into the wall with enough force to knock the breath from his lungs. Then I pinned him there, my sword tip against the side of his throat. Where his artery was.

"I yield," he gasped.

I released him, then flew to the ground, landing gracefully on one knee, and sheathed my sword in one swift movement. Matt landed in front of me, his expression unreadable.

"That was good," he finally panted. His voice was carefully neutral, but I sensed something beneath it. Fear? Anger? I wasn't sure. "But I can see that you're burning through a lot of power. You'll wear yourself out too soon if you keep doing that."

I stood and faced him. "I don't know how not to. My transformation seems to demand this much power from me. I'm not sure I can pull it back. I've never successfully been able to."

Matt sheathed his sword and crossed his arms over his chest, considering me. "Maybe it's not about rationing power, then. Maybe it's about building up your stamina, so you can withstand such a drain. The more you get used to it, the longer you'll be able to withstand it."

I shrugged. I didn't really know. I'd never been able to figure out why I burned out so much quicker than the Light Guardians I knew.

"We can try, but nothing's worked in the past."

"Well, that's why we have these trainings. To figure it out."

I crossed my arms over my chest, giving him a hard stare. There was a tension coming from him that I didn't like. It made me want to leave him and his judgment. I tried to hold onto the anger and push down the hurt. His rejection shouldn't matter to me anymore—not while I'd survived without him for so long. I shouldn't let it hurt me. I needed to remain as impenetrable as ever. It was the only way to keep myself safe.

"Ready to go again?"

"Fine," I bit out harshly.

Matt's eyebrows rose, but he didn't address it. "Okay. Back in the air."

I took off and turned to face him as he pulled level with me, drawing my sword quickly from its sheath. Adrenaline pumped through me as he drew his sword. He'd been absent for four long years, then he'd been an ass about my transformation after urging me to trust him with it. Yeah, I'd need to beat him again.

Matt lunged at me first this time, but I easily dodged, spinning around him. I sliced across his back with my sword, forcefully enough for him to feel it, but lightly enough that it wouldn't damage his armor. He swung around and came at me again. We locked swords, and he tried to force me back and down toward the ground. But I sent more power to my wings and threw him up and away from me instead.

Matt kicked off the wall above me and dove, his wings folding in then expanding, slowing him right as he reached me, and our swords clashed again. White and purple flames swirled together as he shoved me back, trying to overpower me and propel me into the wall. But I folded my wings and dropped quickly below him before rapidly rising behind him and striking him from behind. Matt spun and lunged at me, but I surged forward and met him aggressively. Our swords clashed, sending sparks and fire swirling through the air around us.

The fight became more physical than the last. To get leverage over me, Matt began incorporating more hand-to-hand combat into the fight, forcing me to duck and block more, or be kicked or punched. But it didn't faze me—I was used to fighting like this, and I was used to taking hits. In response, I used the walls to my advantage, kicking off them to fly at him with more power and speed. To disrupt his rhythm and land more strikes, kicks, and punches. I wasn't as large as him, but I knew how to compensate well.

Matt spun and landed a hard kick to my rib cage, shoving me backward and winding me. Then he tried to pin me against the wall. But I flooded my wings with power and shoved off the wall, then propelled him rapidly forward, our swords locked together. He pulled back, trying to disconnect and regain control, but I was moving forward too quickly and with too much power for him to disengage. I took advantage of his distraction and struck the back of his sword hand with my sword's pommel. Matt cursed, his grip loosening, and I twisted my sword around his, wrenching it from his hand, and causing it to drop to the ground. Before he could even react, I poured more power into my wings and propelled him quickly into the wall, my sword across his throat.

"I . . . yield," he rasped.

Satisfaction flooded me with warmth, though it didn't remove the sting of hurt that lingered there. I released Matt after a long moment, then quickly landed and sheathed my sword.

Matt returned to the ground and retrieved his sword before sheathing it, his shoulders stiff. "Nice job," he panted, an edge to his voice. "You definitely didn't hold back like you do in regular training."

He was baiting me, so I didn't respond. I just crossed my arms and waited for his next instructions. He walked to the other side of the room and grabbed his water bottle, then took a long swig. Now that I was on the ground, I felt my adrenaline ebbing, and a wave of exhaustion washed over me. I swayed on my feet.

I glanced at the clock as Matt returned to me, and surprise tunneled through me. Over half an hour had already passed. No wonder I was exhausted. This was the longest I'd stayed transformed in years. It was probably only sheer adrenaline that'd kept me strong for this long. I gritted my teeth. I didn't want Matt to see my weakness. After his reaction to me, he was the last person I wanted to show vulnerability to.

Matt's gaze traveled carefully over me as he stepped closer again. "How are you feeling?"

"Fine," I lied, my tone clipped.

Matt studied me for a moment longer before sighing. "Let's call it a day on fighting. We can spend the rest of our time working on materializing different weapons."

I nodded brusquely and stood with my feet shoulder-width apart. It was easier to lock my knees in that position, and there was less of a chance that I'd visibly sway.

"Like all Guardians, your sword is your standard weapon," Matt said, pacing in front of me, "but you should also be able to materialize other weapons that are specific to your transformation. They tend to be different from person to person, and are suited to each person's strengths, skills, and power level."

He stopped pacing and faced me again.

"For instance, besides my sword, it's also easy for me to conjure long knives and daggers. I can make other things appear, but they tend to cost a lot more power, whereas my standard weapons don't take much out of me."

I nodded sullenly. I'd grown up around Light Guardians—I knew all this just as well as he did.

"Have you noticed what other weapons you can conjure relatively easily?" It wasn't something we'd determined before he'd left for the Academy. I'd refused to transform enough to find out. But the battles had gotten worse, and I'd been forced to transform more in the past couple years.

"I can materialize two long knives, some shorter daggers, and a bow and arrows."

Matt's eyebrows rose in interest. "That's a good range. Why don't we start with those today, and we can work from there next time."

I sighed, my stomach clenching. "Fine."

My knees shook—tiredness was hitting me hard now. All I really wanted to do was transform back into my normal self and sleep. Instead, I closed my eyes and concentrated on the twin long knives that I favored. I felt them slowly materializing on my back, secured in crisscrossing scabbards. I reached behind me and pulled them from their sheaths, showing Matt.

"Good. Nice materialization, and those look like good all-purpose weapons."

I nodded and dematerialized them.

"Daggers next."

I closed my eyes and concentrated on my thigh-holster daggers. They materialized, but much slower this time. I could practically feel the power draining out of me as they became more and more solid. I was beginning to burn out. If Matt didn't let me transform back soon, I'd fall out of my transformation.

I opened my eyes and pulled the shorter daggers from where they rested on each armored thigh.

"Nice. Good for throwing, and for close combat. It looked like it took more effort to make those appear, though."

"You think?" I snapped. "You've had me stay transformed for close to forty-five minutes. Of course I'm getting tired."

Matt pursed his lips slightly. "Tiredness is to be expected when you've had so little practice in your transformed state, but Guardians should be able to stay transformed for a while, sometimes hours if they're powerful enough, without burning out as long as they're not expending too much power. We know you have a lot of power, so that's not the problem. We need to make you stronger and raise your endurance so you can withstand that like other Guardians. Try to keep your power working at the same levels, even if you're tired. It'll take practice, but that's why I'm pointing out where you need to improve."

I rolled my eyes before closing them. I knew he was just doing his job, but that didn't make me less annoyed with him. I hated feeling weak, and little made me feel weaker than rapidly burning out because of my trans-formation. I pulled forward the last of my energy and pictured my bow and arrows, then poured as much power as I could manage into the image, trying to make them appear faster than the daggers. My hands shook with the effort, but I felt my bow and arrows appearing more quickly on my back.

I opened my eyes and presented them to Matt. I couldn't hide how much my arms were shaking now. I tried to keep my knees locked, but they were starting to give out. I felt like passing out, and I could see how dim the glow of my power had become. I'd reached the limits of my transformation, and I was only minutes from falling roughly back into my human form.

"Good," Matt said quickly, his eyes on my shaking hands. "I think we've had enough training for today. You can transform back and head to dinner."

I made the bow and arrows vanish, then concentrated on pulling the dregs of remaining power back inside of me, reforming it into the discreet well in my chest. There wasn't much power left to collect. I staggered back slightly as I returned to my human form, then grabbed the wall to keep from falling over. My legs felt like soft rubber, and I wasn't sure how much longer they'd be able to hold me.

Matt transformed back much more smoothly and didn't even seem winded. His power had barely diminished at all. *Asshole.* He walked toward me, concern growing in his eyes.

"Are you okay?" His tone was gentler now than it'd been thus far. Perhaps because he'd taken off his trainer hat for the day. Or perhaps because I was no longer transformed.

"I'm fine," I said sharply. "Just worn out."

Matt reached for me, presumably to steady me or offer support, but I jerked away from him. Hurt flashed across his face.

"I'm fine," I repeated, pushing off the wall. It took all my strength, but I stood up straight and steady in front of him, meeting his concerned gaze with my angry one.

"What's wrong?" he murmured, taking a step closer. "You're mad. Why?"

I looked at him in disbelief. He was sharp and judgmental one moment, and soft and caring in the next. It was infuriating and confusing. It was . . . hurting me. And I didn't let anyone do that. Not anymore.

"I thought you were different," I said sharply, moving back so I could lean against the wall again. My knees shook. "I thought you meant it when you said you didn't have a problem with my transformation. When you said you saw good in it. But you're not different. You reacted just like everyone else when you saw me transform again."

Matt opened his mouth to speak, but I cut him off.

"You're afraid of me. And beyond that, you're being unfair. You're claiming my power is more dangerous than yours purely based on how it looks. Because it looks different and darker. It's bullshit. You turned out to be just like everyone else in Dagmar."

Matt winced. *Good.* I'd meant to hurt him. Because, despite my best efforts, he'd found a way around my protective walls and had sliced me open. Because he'd raised me. He was my family. The only one who'd cared for me. And I loved him. My fists clenched shut and tears stung my eyes. *Damnit.* This was why love was always a mistake. It only had the power to hurt. Even with him.

"Terah," Matt murmured, stepping closer, his expression pained.

"Don't," I said sharply, holding up my hand to stop him from advancing further. "Don't deny it. I know what I saw."

I stared up into the hazel depths and saw him pale as he noticed the tears brimming in mine, threatening to spill over. I hated that he could see how upset I was. If I wasn't so drained, I wouldn't be letting it affect me so much. I'd be better able to control myself.

"You let me down." My voice shook. "And I can't forgive you quickly for that."

Matt's shoulders fell. He looked upset. But he took another step toward me, closing the gap between us.

"Terah," he murmured again, reaching for my waist, "I'm sorry."

The tears escaped and spilled down my cheeks. I wiped them away angrily with shaking fingers.

Matt's hands closed around me, warm and familiar. "I'm sorry," he whispered again, pulling me close. Then he wrapped his arms around me and held me to his chest. I didn't have the strength or heart to shove him away, but I kept my back rigid. I refused to lean into him. If I did, I knew I'd just collapse into tears, let him hold me, and forgive him too easily.

"You're right," he murmured, his lips moving against my hair. "I should've been better. Reacted better. It won't happen again."

Anger surged through me, and I shoved away from his chest, backing away on wobbly legs.

"It doesn't matter if you don't do it again," I said bitterly. "You already did it. You can't erase that. I'll always remember it."

Matt looked stricken, and he sank onto the bench near the wall. "I'm sorry. I wish I could change what I did." His shock morphed into dejection. But I didn't want his apologies. I wanted him to be the person I'd thought he was.

"Save it," I murmured. I grabbed my bag and walked from the room as firmly as I could. I was drained down to my bones, but I refused to show him any more weakness. Not right now.

I made my way down the steps to the dining hall, holding the railing in a death-grip, and ignored the students around me. The world was starting

66

to spin and wobble. Gods, I needed to sit down. And maybe sleep for a year.

My legs were shaking violently by the time I made it to the ground floor. It took all my strength to keep from just sinking to the ground. I looked around, trying to spot Gabriel, and saw him leaning against the wall near the dining hall doors, waiting for me. I walked slowly toward him, bracing myself against the wall, trying to look as normal as possible. I didn't know how I was going to carry food and walk without dropping everything everywhere. Maybe I'd just skip dinner.

Gabriel smiled when he spotted me, but it soon faded as worry took over. He shoved off the wall and pushed through the crowd to reach my side.

"What happened?" He carefully looked me over. "Are you okay? You look really pale."

He glanced at my hand on the wall, then he met my eyes. I wondered if my eyelashes were still wet. His worry turned grim, and his jaw clenched.

"What did he do to you?"

"Nothing." I looked away from his piercing eyes. "I'm just a little worn out. I stayed transformed for much longer than I usually do."

I pushed off the wall and headed for the front door as steadily as I could. I wanted to get outside and sit down. Maybe have a cigarette. Try to regain my strength and control before attempting to get food. Gabriel walked with me, still watching me intently. I clenched my hands into fists at my sides so he wouldn't see them shaking. When we reached the door, I pushed against it as hard as I could, but my arms shook, and I couldn't put much force into the movement. Gabriel came up behind me and pushed on the door as well. It opened, and I stumbled through it.

I sighed, relieved, as the cooler air of the early evening hit my face and filled my lungs. It was refreshing, like drinking cold water after training in the heat. I started forward across the grass, heading for an empty table in the distance. Thankfully, not too many students were outside. Most had already headed to the dining hall for food. *Good.* I didn't want anyone to see me like this.

The world suddenly tilted sideways, and my knees gave out beneath me. Gabriel swore and lunged forward, managing to grab me around the waist before I hit the ground. He hauled me up against him with a grunt of effort and steadied me.

"I'm gonna call bullshit on you being okay." His expression was stormy and intense as it met mine.

I opened my mouth to reply—to deny it—but the world jerked again, tumbling over itself. My stomach lurched, and I gripped his arm tightly, trying to anchor myself to something solid as my legs shook violently beneath me. Gabriel's expression turned grim. He reached down and grabbed the bag I'd dropped, then placed it over his shoulder. Then he bent and swung me up in his arms.

"What are you doing?" I yelped.

"I'm carrying you to a table," he said, calmly striding forward.

"I'm fine. I can walk on my own."

Gabriel gave me a sardonic look. "I'd say you established you couldn't walk when you nearly fell on your face."

My cheeks burned—I wasn't sure what to say. He wasn't wrong. I sighed, giving up for the moment, and let him carry me to the empty wrought-iron table. His chest was steady and firm beneath my cheek, and his scent was warm and almost spicy, like amber mixed with pine. This was . . . surprisingly nice. Comforting in a way it shouldn't be.

I'm just tired. I wouldn't be noticing any of this if I wasn't so drained.

Gabriel set me down on the wrought-iron bench and placed both of our bags on the table in front of me. Then he sat down next to me and faced me.

"Explain please." His tone was matter of fact, but his eyes were worried. "What happened? Why are you this drained?"

I sighed and pulled out my cigarettes and lighter with shaking hands. Gabriel quickly took them from me and pulled out a cigarette. He lit it, pulling smoke into his mouth, then handed it to me, exhaling slowly. He probably though I'd burn myself if I'd tried doing it on my own. With my hands shaking as hard as they were, I probably would've.

"Thanks," I murmured, placing the cigarette in my mouth and inhaling deeply. Gabriel waited, his gaze never leaving my face. "Honestly, nothing in particular happened," I finally said. "I don't transform very often, so I haven't built up my endurance to withstand it for very long. Matt made me stay transformed for the whole session. Usually, I only stay transformed for fifteen minutes tops." I made a face and took another drag of my cigarette.

Gabriel nodded slowly, his brows furrowing.

"I . . . because my transformation is different, I burn through my power a lot faster than most other people. I can't sustain it for as long. Not without completely burning out."

"Does Matt know that?" There was an angry edge to Gabriel's voice.

"Yeah. That's why he wanted me to stay transformed the whole time. He wants me to build up my endurance." I rolled my eyes.

Gabriel's expression darkened, but he didn't say anything.

"We fought each other in our transformed states for over half the time, then worked on other transformation-specific abilities. By the time we were done, I'd pretty much burned out."

"And he just left you to fend for yourself when you're clearly not okay?" He lit his own cigarette, his expression grim. "What an asshole."

My mouth pulled up at the corner. Gabriel was angry on my behalf. That was . . . new for me. Even when people had treated me poorly in Dagmar, Matt had always shrugged it off, accepting it as reality instead of meaningfully pushing back against it. He'd done the same whenever my mother had scorned or ridiculed me. He'd commiserated, but moved on quickly, never becoming angry for me. Never trying to change anything for me. Never giving me the space to truly feel my feelings about any of it. Perhaps he'd been scared to. Perhaps he didn't know how to do that himself.

"I didn't give him a chance to help me," I finally said, my hand shaking as I lifted my cigarette to my lips. Gabriel's eyes followed my hand's progress. "I was angry at him for . . . well, it doesn't matter. I just left him there and came down to meet you."

Gabriel watched my expression closely as he blew out a stream of smoke into the darkening evening air. "What did he do to make you mad?"

My cheeks tingled with heat. "It's nothing. It was . . . foolish. Not that important."

Gabriel's eyebrows rose. "I highly doubt that. You don't tend to get mad over nothing."

My smile turned bittersweet. "He reacted poorly to my transformation." I looked down, the smile fading. "He's seen it before, but not for a while. When he first saw me transform tonight, he backed away from me. He looked . . . I don't know. Scared maybe? Repelled? And he said we'd need to be careful to contain my power, so I don't destroy things and hurt people. He thinks I'm dangerous, just like everyone else does. Just because my power and transformation look darker than theirs."

I looked out over the grounds, trying to force the tears stinging my eyes to disappear. I bit the inside of my cheek. Hard. I never cried. Before today, I hadn't in a long time. Not since Caleb. It'd been years. I desperately hoped Gabriel wouldn't notice. I didn't want him to think I was weak. Pathetically emotional.

"I thought he was different. I thought, because of our history, he'd accept me as I am. But I was wrong." I shrugged as though it wasn't a big deal.

"Terah . . ." It was a tone I hadn't heard from him before. Gentle. Quiet. No hint of teasing or suave confidence. Almost like he felt my hurt inside his own chest. And it was more than I could currently handle.

The tears escaped and fell down my cheeks. I heard his intake of breath and glanced at him. A flash of surprise and pain crossed his face, but he shuttered his expression quickly, wrestling a neutral one into place instead. But he didn't back away in horror or disgust as I'd feared. At least, not yet. Instead, he lifted his hand and trailed the backs of his fingers slowly down my cheeks, gently wiping away the tears. My lips parted in surprise, but I didn't stop him.

"That's not foolish." His voice was a little deeper than usual. "He shouldn't have reacted that way. He's an ass."

I shook my head, biting the inside of my cheek again, trying to keep more tears at bay. "No. The problem is me." I tried to sound matter of fact. Unfazed. "My transformation is just . . . too different. Too dark. I think I might be asking too much of people to just accept it. It's not reasonable to want that. Even from him. Maybe fear is the reasonable reaction to me."

Gabriel tossed his cigarette angrily, shaking his head. "No. The problem isn't you, and it's not asking for too much to be accepted for who you are. No matter what your transformation is like, it's not your fault. You aren't any lesser for it, and you shouldn't have to accept bad treatment because of it. We were all created the way we were for a reason. You were *meant* to be exactly who you are. We're all Divines. It shouldn't matter what transformations look like." He ran his hand agitatedly through his hair. "It's just elitism. And prejudice."

He looked back at me, but I wasn't sure what to say. My tears had stopped at least. Gods, I couldn't imagine what he thought of me now. To get upset over something so trivial—this wasn't who I usually was. It wasn't who I wanted people to see.

Gabriel sighed, his anger ebbing. "I told you that I don't transform very often either," he said quietly. "It's because people also react poorly to my transformation. But as much as I still avoid that conflict by fighting without it whenever I can, I've come to understand over the years that it's their shortcomings and not mine that make them react the way they do. My transformation is valid regardless of what it looks like. Regardless of whether it's familiar to people. It's *others* who choose to react to that difference with hatred and fear. It's not my fault, and it certainly isn't yours." His intense gaze met mine. "You trusted Matt to see that part of you, and *he let you* down. Not the other way around."

I nodded slowly and extinguished my cigarette on the side of the table. "I want to believe that. But it's hard to believe that everyone else is wrong, not us."

Gabriel smiled a little. "It took me a long time to get there and stop blaming myself. Still struggle with it sometimes—the rejection isn't easy to deal with. But I hope you can get there someday too. It's not fair to ask us to accept worse treatment because of something we have no control over. We were born like this. Nothing can change that."

I nodded again, and the world tilted unsteadily around me. I swayed and placed my forehead in my hand. *Ugh.* I shouldn't have moved so much.

Gabriel watched me closely for a moment before pushing to his feet. "I'm gonna grab you some food. We need to try getting your energy back up so you can regenerate your power. Then I can help you back to your room."

I shook my head and made to stand up. I'd already shown him too much vulnerability—I didn't want him to think I couldn't take care of myself. But Gabriel moved forward quickly and placed his hands on my shoulders, stopping my attempt to rise.

"Terah," he said, slightly exasperated, "I can see you barely have any strength or energy left. You won't make it halfway to the building before you collapse again. Please just let me help you."

My breath stalled as the vibrant blue of his eyes met mine. Close. Very close. Gabriel smiled and took a step back, releasing me.

"Besides, if I carry you through the dining hall, people might get the wrong idea about us." He smirked, his eyes glittering mischievously.

I rolled my eyes but sat back down without further complaint. "Fine," I grumbled.

"Good," Gabriel said smugly. He knew he'd won this fight. I resisted the urge to flip him off—barely—but he read my expression and grinned. "Be back soon," he called over his shoulder as he walked away. "Don't run off."

I shook my head, part amused, part frustrated. As if I could.

A smile pulled at my lips as I watched his long, purposeful strides carry him quickly back to the main building. He . . . hadn't left me to fend for myself when he saw I was struggling. He hadn't met my involuntary display of emotion with disdain or indifference. He'd cared enough to stay with me, not only to make sure I was okay, but to talk me through things. No one had done that for me before.

"Thank you," I called after him. "For . . . everything."

Gabriel turned and flashed a devastating smile before reaching for the door and disappearing through it. Warmth grew in my chest. I didn't know what to do with him sometimes, but against my will, I was starting to really like him. Against my will, I was beginning to feel truly glad that Gabriel was around.

5
AWAKENING

"Not bad," Matt said grudgingly to Gabriel as he walked over after our most recent hand-to-hand combat fight.

It'd been six weeks since the start of the semester, and Gabriel's combat skills had improved significantly. Instead of losing every match, he was pushing me to work harder and harder to win, and he'd started winning some—quite a feat, given that I'd had warrior faction training, and he hadn't.

"But you need to learn how to get out of that hold in a more technical way. You won't always be able to use your size as your way out." Matt gestured for me to come over to him, a smug smile pulling at his lips. "We'll show you how."

He pulled me into him, so my back was pressed to his front, and wrapped his arm tightly around my waist. Then he held a wooden practice knife in front of my throat, his fingers splaying over my rib cage.

Gabriel crossed his arms over his chest, his expression relatively neutral. But I'd learned enough of his nuances so far this semester that I could tell he was annoyed.

"Asshole. You just wanted an excuse to touch her."

I started. The words had been in Gabriel's voice, but his mouth hadn't moved. At all. I stared at him, speechless. I couldn't have imagined it, could I? His voice had sounded so clear. I glanced over my shoulder at Matt, but his expression hadn't changed. He hadn't heard it.

73

Matt met my gaze and smiled. "Now watch Terah to see how she gets out of this hold."

I shook myself to clear my head—I'd have to think about this later. I faced forward again, weaved my leg backward through his, then pulled them forward, breaking the stability of his stance and forcing his legs to bend. I simultaneously grabbed and twisted Matt's wrist so the knife was pointed away from me. Then, lightning fast, I grabbed Matt's upper arm and bent forward, throwing him over me and down onto the mat. Before he could react, I kicked the knife out of his hand, grabbed it midair, then leapt onto him, pinning him beneath me with my thighs, and pressing the blade across his throat.

Matt smiled up at me, his chest heaving. "Nice." He rested his hands on my legs as he caught his breath. His gaze held mine. It was warm. Too warm. My stomach clenched and nerves rushed through me. I wasn't sure I liked the feeling.

I pushed off him quickly but offered him my hand. He took it, and I pulled him to his feet.

"Think you've got it?" He smirked at Gabriel.

Gabriel nodded shortly, his shoulders tensing.

"Fuck off."

Once again, I heard Gabriel's voice, but his mouth hadn't moved. And Matt hadn't heard him.

"Good." Matt looked pleased with himself. "Go again."

I frowned as he walked away. It was like . . . I was hearing Gabriel's thoughts. But that wasn't possible. That wasn't a power that Divines had. Nor was it something I'd ever been able to do before.

"What is it?" Gabriel asked as I faced him again, preparing for our next fight.

I blinked and refocused on him. His brow was furrowed as he watched me. "Oh. Uh, nothing. Ready to go again?"

Gabriel watched me closely for a long moment, then nodded. "Yeah. Let's go."

"Were you mad when Matt made me show you how to get out of that hold?"

We'd finished training and were making our way across the grass to a table for a smoke break. The sun was bright today, reflecting off the light beige stones that made up the buildings, and warming the air that'd finally started to cool. It'd be autumn soon.

Gabriel glanced at me, his gaze quickly sweeping over my expression. He cleared his throat and pulled out his cigarettes, looking away. "Not mad. More frustrated. But not at you."

I nodded slowly and lit my cigarette. "Why were you frustrated?"

Gabriel lit his and took a long draw from it. Then he released the smoke through his nose. "He was being manipulative. He should've worked with me directly to teach me what he wanted to teach me. But he chose to use you as a prop."

I watched him closely as I released a breath of smoke. He was so good at neutralizing his expression when he wanted to. But I still detected an edge to it. A hint that he felt more strongly than he was letting on. Could he have really thought the words that I'd heard in his voice? It was so hard to tell. But I didn't want to ask him. That'd not only be embarrassing, but also over revealing. And what if he hadn't thought those things? Would it just be proof that I was losing my mind?

I nodded and looked away from him. "Matt's always done things his own way, even if it's not the way I would've done them." Usually, his way corresponded closely with whatever my mother or the warrior faction had ordered. And once decided, he was hard to sway.

Gabriel released a stream of smoke and ran his hand agitatedly through his hair. "I get that. And I get that his position as trainer allows him to decide. But that doesn't mean it's okay for him to use you to fulfill whatever . . . goal . . . he might have. Especially when he could've done his job better another way."

I frowned, watching as students milled about, some with food, others simply enjoying the nice weather before afternoon classes began.

"What do you think his goal was?"

Gabriel's mouth set grimly, and he looked away from me. "To be close to you." He said it quietly. Almost like he didn't want me to hear it.

My heart lurched, but I kept my expression neutral. There'd been an edge to Matt during training that I hadn't been able to decode. I'd attributed it to his general dislike of Gabriel. But was Gabriel right about why? It didn't make a ton of sense. Matt could be close to me whenever he wanted. He knew where to find me. Why would he need that during training?

"In the future, I can tell him to work on the moves directly with you, if that makes you more comfortable."

Gabriel glanced at me, his gaze moving carefully over my expression. Almost like he thought he was missing something. Or that I was. He sighed and looked away a moment later, then flicked some ash from the end of his cigarette.

"It's not about my comfort. It's about yours."

I frowned as I put out my cigarette on the edge of the table. *Had* it made me uncomfortable? Matt had always been physically close with me. He'd raised me, trained me, cared for me. I barely thought twice about his proximity because it felt so normal from him. It was everyone else that I was usually careful about keeping away from me.

But I'd seen heat in his eyes as I'd pinned him down—an expression I wasn't used to seeing from him, especially not directed at me. My cheeks prickled with heat. There'd been a different quality to his gaze since we'd reunited, but I'd attributed it to this new, older version of him. Could it be that he . . .

I shook my head and stood quickly, pushing the thought from my mind. It was probably nothing. And it didn't matter either way. I'd never let myself be compromised like that again, no matter who was in question.

"Ready to go in?"

Gabriel sighed and pushed to his feet. "Yeah."

"My friend is having a party this coming Friday," Matt said as he paced across the armored metal surface in front of me. Since that first transformation training, he'd been careful not to react to my transformation. It was the reason I'd forgiven him. He was trying, at least. "She's hosting it in one of the dorms."

My eyebrows rose. I hadn't heard of many parties happening on campus. Most people just went to the lounge to decompress. "That's cool."

Matt gestured at me, and I released the fire at him that I'd been holding. He created a white shield around himself to diffuse it.

"Good. That was a much more controlled shot."

I nodded and shook out my arms. Staying transformed still took a lot of power from me, and I could feel myself quickly draining.

"Is there a reason for the party?"

Matt smiled. "Well, this is her last year, and she decided she wants to make it as fun as possible. She has money to spare, so she thought a big party would be a good way of doing that."

I nodded and watched him closely. I hadn't met any of his friends yet. I wondered if he had any romantic attachments to any of them. I wondered if he'd let himself open up to other people enough to allow for that. It'd always just been the two of us, for the both of us.

"Try again, but with lightning this time."

I nodded and put my hand out in front of me. I closed my eyes, pulled power to my hand, and concentrated on what I wanted to happen.

"Anyway," Matt said, waiting for me to shoot, "I was wondering if you wanted to come. The party's pretty open, so I can invite whoever I want."

I shot a beam of lightning at him, the same size as the shot of fire I'd sent before. Matt's shield flared up again and absorbed the shot.

"Perfect. Nice job. You're improving with that very quickly." He smiled at me, warm. Very warm.

I swallowed and looked away. "Um, a party could be fun. Though I don't know any upper-level students besides the people in our training group."

Matt shrugged. "I'll be there. And we haven't really had time together outside of training. It would be nice."

I bit the inside of my cheek, thinking. "Can Gabriel come too?" I'd be more comfortable going if I knew there'd be someone else there that I knew. I didn't want to have to follow Matt around like a lost child. Or be left in the corner alone.

Matt's smile faded a bit as his body tensed. "I guess that's fine. If it would make you more comfortable."

"It would," I said quickly. I knew they didn't like each other much, but I trusted Gabriel to have my back in that kind of situation. "If he even wants to go," I added to defuse the tension that Matt was suddenly radiating. "I don't know how he feels about parties."

Matt shrugged. He didn't like talking about Gabriel.

"Try a shot with both fire and lightning this time. But try to keep it smaller."

My fingers trembled with exhaustion. Making these shots small took more energy than just unleashing a ton of power all at once. It took precision and control. Extreme focus. And Matt had been making me practice measured shots for most of the training session today.

"And what if I accidentally hurt you?" I was starting to reach my limit. And my concentration wasn't at its strongest anymore.

Matt smiled, the tension melting from his body. "I won't let you. It'll be fine. Trust me."

I took a deep breath and released it slowly. "Okay."

I raised my hand in front of me and closed my eyes, then pulled the last of my power from the well in my chest and sent it down my arm to my hand. Then I pictured what I wanted, and how big I wanted it to be. My hand shook in front of me, and I clenched my jaw, trying to reign in my concentration and the last of my energy so I wouldn't lose my grip on the power.

Suddenly, my mind snapped away from the present, and an image flared to life around me, forcefully filling my consciousness as though it was really happening. Matt stood close to me in a dimly lit room. He was staring down at me, his expression filled with so much raw emotion it shocked me. I'd never seen him like that before. He took my face in his hands and leaned toward me, his eyes closing. Shock rang through me. He was . . . going to kiss me.

I gasped and jerked back into myself, the training room reappearing abruptly around me as power burst from my hand. My concentration had been broken, and I'd inadvertently released the shot of fire and lightning without limiting it. It burned powerfully and out of control as it barreled across the room. Toward Matt.

"Matt! Move!" It was too strong for his shield to absorb.

Matt cursed and threw himself out of the way, and my power hit the wall instead with such force that the room shook around us. But the walls were made to repel damage, not absorb power, and in the next moment, my power rebounded back at me. I threw my hands up, trying to materialize a shield around me, but my power was too diminished to make a strong one. The shot of my power obliterated the shield the second it touched it, and slammed into my shoulder and chest, throwing me forcefully backward into the far wall. It burned through my armor and shirt like they were nothing and ate away at my skin and muscles. My body was absorbing the power of the shot, but it was burning me alive.

I collapsed onto the ground, falling out of my transformation. I was in too much pain to move or even scream. The room blurred around me, and I felt my consciousness slipping rapidly away. Everything was losing its shape. But Gabriel's face slowly formed in front of my eyes, swimming hazily, in and out of focus. I clung to it even as I faded. I didn't care why it was there. I instinctively felt that, if I didn't hold onto it, I'd be lost. I put all my concentration, all that I had left, into clinging to it.

"Gabriel," I thought, as a clearer image formed of him walking down the stairs to the dining hall. He stopped in his tracks.

"Terah?" He looked around him, his brow furrowing.

"*Help me. Please.*"

Worry flooded his expression. "Where are you? What's happened?" He spun around on the stairs.

"*Transformation training room,*" I forced out, even as the image of him began to fade. "*I . . . fucked up.*"

Gabriel sprinted back up the stairs. "Hold on. I'm coming."

But my mind couldn't hold onto the connection anymore. My consciousness faded, and darkness grew around me.

"Gods, Terah," Matt's shaky voice echoed around me. I faintly felt him turning me over. "What did you do to yourself?"

The training room door burst open. "What happened?" *Gabriel*. He sounded angry. I heard him approach, but I couldn't see anything anymore.

"I'm s-sorry," I whispered. "S-sorry."

"Damnit. *Do* something, Matt! Fix this!" Gabriel sounded frantic.

"Come on, Terah," Matt murmured, placing his hands over me. Pain shot through me, dragging me deeper into the dark. My heartbeat slowed. My breath stilled. "Stay with me."

Power slammed into me. White hot. Overwhelming. Familiar. It was a power that'd pulled me back together hundreds of times throughout my life. It filled my body, rapidly reforming damaged bone, tissue, muscle, and vein. My lungs filled with air again, and my heartbeat steadied and strengthened as the darkness slowly receded.

The hands on me began to shake. "Shit. I'm running out of power. There's just too much damage."

"Use your remaining power on the more difficult internal healing," Gabriel said quickly, "and I'll heal everything on the outside. I just don't have enough training to heal her insides."

"I can try," Matt gritted out, his hands shaking harder now. The power flowing into me was waning, and I knew he'd burn out soon. But he pushed hard, grabbing every bit of available power he had and shoving it out of his arms into me. Pulling me together as much as he possibly could. Finally, his hands fell away. "That's all I can do," he gasped.

I heard movement and felt another set of hands gently covering my upper chest and shoulder. Then I felt a burst of new power enter me. Electric blue. Soothing like water. Warm like a summer night, but cool enough to ease the burning pain that still lingered. The power blanketed my injured skin, then pulled me slowly together like gentle fingers. Blood regenerated, muscles regrew and fused, and skin reformed.

When I finally opened my eyes, Gabriel and Matt were sitting over me, panting, looking down at me with concern. Blue faded from Gabriel's hands as a breath of relief whooshed out of him.

"You're okay," he panted sinking to the ground next to me. He took my hand in his. "Don't ever scare me like that again," he huffed as Matt collapsed on my other side.

"I won't," I murmured, squeezing his hand. I knew it wasn't something I could actually promise—we were at war—but I'd stopped caring about reality for the moment. I reached out and took Matt's hand with my free one. "Thank you. Both of you."

Matt turned his head and smiled at me as he squeezed my fingers. "Don't make a habit of forcing us to save you."

I narrowed my eyes at him, and he grinned.

"I'm kidding," he murmured, squeezing my hand again. "I'm glad you're okay."

Gabriel sat up, then turned and offered me his hand. I took it, and he pulled me slowly into a sitting position. I grabbed the top of my charred shirt and bra to keep them from falling off me.

"Here," Matt said, sitting up and unzipping his sweatshirt, then handing it to me.

I quickly pulled it on and zipped it before pulling off the remains of my burned clothes, then Gabriel helped me to my feet. I swayed a little— even healed, I was still exhausted from burning through all my power— and Gabriel quickly slid his arm around me, steadying me against his side.

"So, what happened? What were you practicing that almost killed Terah?" I felt the tension returning to his body as he looked at Matt.

Matt's jaw clenched, but he pulled his gaze from Gabriel and looked at me. "It shouldn't have happened. We were just practicing routine transformation power usage, but something went wrong."

I bit the inside of my cheek. I wasn't sure how to respond. How could I just tell them that unexplainable things were starting to happen to me?

Matt's eyes narrowed as he watched me closely. "What aren't you telling me?"

I tensed, and Gabriel's hand tightened on my waist in response.

Matt sighed and ran his hand down his face, but his expression softened. "Terah . . . whatever it is, you can tell me. I won't be angry with you. What happened?"

I bit the inside of my cheek. Should I trust them with this? What if they didn't believe me? I glanced up at Gabriel. His worried gaze met mine, and he nodded slowly, silently encouraging me.

I let out a deep breath and looked away from both of them. My fists clenched. I wasn't sure I had much of a choice. "When I was preparing to send the shot, my consciousness was pulled away from here. I was dropped into a scene with other people happening around me like it was real. It wasn't a memory—nothing that happened in it has happened before. I experienced it like I was there. When the scene faded, I snapped back to this room, but my concentration was broken, and I released the shot on accident, without measuring the amount of power in it. That's what made it out of control."

I glanced at Gabriel and caught him frowning, but with thought, not judgment.

"It was too large for Matt to block, so he jumped out of the way, and it hit the wall and rebounded back at me. I didn't have enough power left to shield myself, or enough time to move, so it hit me instead."

I glanced at Matt and saw that he'd paled, and his eyes were wide with shock. Whatever he'd thought had happened, it clearly wasn't this.

"Has . . . this ever happened before?" he managed to ask. He was trying to school his expression into a more neutral one but was largely failing.

My stomach clenched. *Damnit.* Maybe they both thought I was losing my mind. "No. But . . . it's not the only different thing that's started happening to me."

"What . . . do you mean?"

I glanced at Gabriel again. He didn't appear shocked like Matt. More curious than anything else.

"You spoke to me," he murmured, meeting my gaze. "In my head. That's how I knew something was wrong, and where to find you."

"*What?*" Matt ran both hands through his hair. "Is that true?"

I swallowed. "Yeah. When my consciousness was fading, I suddenly saw Gabriel walking down the stairs to the dining hall. It wasn't like the other image—it wasn't like I was there—it was more like I was watching him on a screen. And I knew somehow that what I was seeing was happening now. So I called out to him. I told him I needed help."

Matt retreated a few steps as he looked back and forth between the two of us. "And . . . you heard her speak to you? In your head?"

"Yes."

"It's the first time I've tried talking to someone like that. But . . . it's not the first time I've heard other people's thoughts."

Matt closed his eyes and rested his forehead in his palm for a long moment. "How is that even possible? How is any of this possible? This isn't something Divines can do."

I felt Gabriel tense. "Just because we haven't seen it before doesn't mean it's impossible. And it doesn't mean that it's bad."

Matt scoffed and shook his head dismissively. "I don't even know what to do with this information. But we clearly have to do something. You could've died! You could've killed someone else! Without knowing what's going on with you or how to control these new abilities, you're putting yourself and those around you in danger."

My eyes widened even as hurt sliced through me. He thought they were new abilities? I supposed it was possible. I'd refrained from transforming as much as I could throughout my life to avoid further ostracization, and in doing so, I'd distanced myself from my power and abilities. But at the Academy, I was forced to transform and use my power multiple times a week. It was forcing a connection between my power and my mind that'd never existed before. Perhaps that included connecting me to abilities I'd inadvertently blocked myself from utilizing. But Matt thought they were dangerous. *I* was dangerous. I clenched my jaw. He always assumed the worst from me when it came to my power.

Gabriel's arm tightened around me. "That's bullshit," he said sharply, glaring at Matt. "Terah almost died because *you* insist on pushing her to the brink of burnout. Of course she couldn't adequately shield herself. It's your training that's putting her in danger, not her abilities."

Matt's entire body tensed, and his fists clenched at his sides. "You don't know what the hell you're talking about. I'm pushing her because it's the only way to make sure her endurance grows. I'm trying to make sure she survives!"

"How are you making sure she survives if you're routinely draining her? That's not a good way to ensure she's in control of her abilities. Every Divine has powers that could injure themselves or others. But we don't suppress or control them from the outside. We teach them carefully how to experiment with their own abilities. How do you think we deal with training Blessed? None of them have powers that perfectly resemble each other. They surprise us with their abilities all the time. We safely train them through careful experimentation, moving slowly, and letting them gradually grow into their abilities. *You're* pushing her too far too fast. That's what's dangerous. Not her."

Matt and Gabriel stared each other down angrily. They'd probably yell at each other all night if I let them, but my exhaustion was growing, and my legs were feeling less and less stable by the minute. Even before I was injured, I'd almost burned out. Now, I felt dead on my feet, and close to passing out.

I cleared my throat, cutting through the tension radiating between them. "I don't think we're going to solve this right now. And I need to go rest. We can talk about it more tomorrow." I glanced up at Gabriel and he nodded, the anger receding.

"I'll take you back to your room."

I nodded gratefully, then looked at Matt. His jaw was clenched as he looked back and forth between the two of us. But he nodded, tightly.

"Go rest. I'll need to think about this and figure out what to do about our training sessions. I'm not convinced it's a good idea to keep training you to use your abilities, especially these new ones. I'm not sure it's safe."

Tension radiated down my body as glared back at him. But hurt was pinging around in my chest, bruising me. Anger and pain swirled together into an indistinguishable mix.

"I wish you didn't let your fear of my power take over your reasoning. You may not show it anymore, but I can still see it there."

Hurt flared in his eyes. I had no idea why. *He* was the one rejecting me for things I couldn't control about myself.

"I'm just trying to protect you. Even if that means protecting you from yourself."

"That's bullshit," I ground out. "It's not like not training me makes the abilities go away. Gabriel is right. I should be trained and trained well, not restricted and isolated. It would be safer for everyone if all my abilities were well-developed and under control. And that takes practice."

Matt's jaw clenched, his mouth tight. He shook his head. I could see he didn't agree with me. He thought his way was best. Safest. The only right way. My stomach clenched. He thought he knew better than me, even about myself. He always had.

"Why are you doing this?"

Matt's eyes widened as the connection between our minds snapped into place. I hadn't even tried. But something about my roiling emotions seemed to have triggered it.

"Because I care about you, Terah," he finally responded once the shock

faded. "*So much. You're my family, and drastic measures will keep you safe. Even if you hate me for them in the moment.*"

I ground my teeth together. "*If you cared so deeply about me, you'd believe in me enough to help me, not hold me back and control me. And you'd care about what I want and how I want to handle my own power.*"

Matt's expression turned stubborn again. I could tell from the thoughts swirling around in his head that he wasn't about to change his mind. No matter what I said.

Frustrated and exhausted, I looked up at Gabriel. "Let's go." There was nothing more I could accomplish with Matt tonight.

His gaze quickly searched mine, but he nodded. He slung my bag over his shoulder, then we turned and headed for the door, Gabriel continuing to brace me against his side.

"*Terah, wait,*" Matt called in my mind. I could feel his desperation. He didn't want me to be upset with him. But more than that, he didn't want me running to Gabriel instead of him when I was upset. "*Please.*"

My fist clenched at my side as my mood darkened. Instead of responding, I forcefully shut Matt out of my mind. I didn't want to hear him anymore tonight.

"Nice room." Gabriel whistled as he spun around, taking in the large space. "It's enormous."

My dorm room was at the back corner of the building, meaning it had an unusually large footprint, and an abundance of windows. My canopied bed was sizable and sat on the wall opposite the door, resting on an enormous plush rug that covered most of the room's stone floor. To the left of the door sat a small fireplace with a flatscreen TV mounted above it and a small seating area of several plush armchairs and a couple small tables gathered around it. On the far left wall sat a wooden desk with a minifridge and small microwave beside it. And on the far wall to the right of the door were two doorways, one leading to a generous walk-in closet, and the other leading to a moderately sized bathroom. I knew I'd lucked out—most rooms didn't have a bathroom, and students had to use the shared ones on each floor.

I smiled as I sank onto the foot of my bed. "Thanks. It's the largest room I've ever slept in. And it's the first time in my life that I haven't shared a room."

I'd shared with Matt until he'd left, and then I'd shared with other kids. The children's training houses in Dagmar had always been overfilled. With how quickly the war was escalating, they'd had a never-ending need for child soldiers. Like me.

"I'm glad you got it, then. You deserve a nice space. Oh man, you even have a fireplace and a bathroom! Okay, I might be a *little* jealous about that." He smiled as he walked over and sank onto the foot of the bed next to me. "I have to use the shared bathroom with everyone else on my floor. It's a nightmare trying to get ready in the mornings."

"You could always come here and use mine if you need to." I'd said it without thinking, and my cheeks immediately prickled with heat. Why the hell had I offered that? That wasn't keeping him at a distance. My fingers tightened around my comforter. My head was just in a weird place after all I'd experienced today. That was all.

Gabriel glanced at me, surprise widening his eyes as he scanned my expression.

"I mean, if it's an emergency or something," I added quickly, trying to downplay it. I bit the inside of my cheek, trying to school my expression into something bland and neutral.

Gabriel smiled a little but looked away. He was silent for a long moment. "I should probably go grab us some food."

My cheeks burned. He'd changed the subject. That was worse, somehow, than accepting my too-eager, misguided offer.

"Okay."

"Want anything in particular?"

I shrugged, trying to push down the embarrassment. It was good that he'd ignored my offer. He was keeping the space between us that I should've kept. He was doing what I should've done. I should be grateful. "Not really. At this point, anything edible will do."

Gabriel nodded and pushed to his feet. "Sounds good. I'll be back soon."

"Wait." I pushed shakily from the bed as he headed for the door. "I might be asleep by the time you get back, so . . ."

I pulled open the door and went to the high-tech hand scanner that served as the room's lock. It was another of the dorm's idiosyncrasies. They were outside of each student's room and were programmed to only unlock with that student's handprint. The scanner also allowed us to secure our rooms with retractable armored walls and shutters in case the school was ever under attack. Rumor had it that all this security was installed to appease the worries of prominent Light Guardian parents who didn't want their sheltered children to be murdered by "darker" Divine factions who might also attend the school.

I pressed the "add entrant" button and placed my hand on the scanner to authorize it. Then I grabbed Gabriel's hand and placed it on the scanner. The scanner beeped, and a green light appeared. I hit save, then turned and smiled up at him.

"There. Now you can get in when you get back."

To my surprise, Gabriel's cheeks heated with faint color as his gaze held mine. But he swallowed and quickly turned away, pulling his gaze from mine.

"Thanks." He started back down the hall toward the front door. "Be back in a little bit." I watched him go until he disappeared into the darkening night.

I shook off the weird anxiety churning in my stomach and returned to my room. My eyes were growing heavy, so I changed into my pajamas—a soft tank top with a built-in bra, and loose flannel pajama pants—before sinking into my bed and pulling the covers over me. I was so tired. So so tired. I just needed a little sleep. Then things wouldn't feel so strange and confusing.

I stood outside in the darkness, the cold air whipping around me. A horrible sound tore through the night air, and I spun around, fear flooding me as I saw an enormous Demon—the largest I'd ever seen—barreling toward me. The world around me dissolved.

I sat at a table in the dining hall with Gabriel, watching in disbelief as a young man I'd never seen before sauntered through the dissipating crowd of students who'd been trying to bother us, and approached me, his gaze curious. Something about him drew my attention. He seemed strangely familiar somehow, even though I knew I'd never seen him before. But his eyes were cold and hard, and sent a shiver of trepidation through me. A person only had eyes like that if they'd been through hell and hadn't emerged fully whole on the other side. I wondered what his hell had been. The image dissolved.

We ran from our cars toward the town overrun with Demons. The attacks were getting worse and worse lately. I glanced at Gabriel before looking at the seventy trainees running behind us. They'd signed up for this. I knew that. We were all here for the same reason—to protect our people. But my stomach still sank. There weren't truly enough of us to defeat all these Demons. We'd pay a heavy price if we survived at all. Gabriel reached over and squeezed my hand, his expression firm. Determined.

"We stay together," he murmured.

I clenched my jaw and nodded. The image dissolved.

I hovered over a battlefield, resignation and determination filling me. I knew we were probably going to die here. This was the final front. If we didn't succeed now, nothing would be left of the world as we knew it. Death and destruction would reign. And now we truly didn't have a choice. We lifted our joined hands as power shuddered around us. There was no going back now. I glanced at the ground before releasing the power. I just needed to see him. One last time . . .

"Terah?"

I jerked awake, gasping. My forehead was covered in a sheen of cold sweat, and my pulse was racing. Gabriel was sitting on the edge of the mattress, his hand on my shoulder, peering down at me with concern. What the hell had happened? I looked around, disoriented. I was in my dorm room, still lying in bed. I must've fallen asleep. But . . . that hadn't felt like a dream. Far from it.

"Are you okay? You were tossing and turning in your sleep."

I sat up and wiped away the perspiration with the back of my hand. "I think . . . I had another vision. At least, it felt the same as it did in the training room—too real to be a dream."

Gabriel's eyebrows rose. "Really? What did you see?"

I shook my head, trying to remember. It'd been all over the place. Jumbled, as though large parts of the scenes were missing. Context, people, everything felt incomplete. But it'd still felt too real. Like I was really there. I'd been able to smell the blood. Feel the sting of ash in my eyes and lungs.

"It's hard to describe. It jumped around to several different times and places. All things that haven't happened yet. But a lot of it was about the war. There were so many Demons. A town burning. A huge battle that felt like some kind of final front." I rubbed my hand over my eyes, almost like I could wipe away the remnants of what I'd seen. "It felt like . . . we were losing the war."

My eyes met his and held—I needed a tether. Something to keep me grounded as a whirlwind of inexplicable things happened around me. I didn't want to tell him how much what I'd seen had impacted me. How much it all scared me. Why was I even having these flashes or visions in the first place? How much should I trust them? What if I was imagining them? Or worse, what if they were true? What if the future really was that bleak?

Gabriel's expression was difficult to read. He hesitated for a moment, seeming to struggle with his words. Finally, he reached forward and took my hand. "Maybe it's not a definite future," he murmured, his thumb tracing a slow path back and forth across the back of my hand. "Maybe you're just seeing possibilities—trajectories if things don't change. It could be that your visions are warnings and not just predictions."

I swallowed and pulled my gaze from his, looking instead at our joined hands. His engulfed mine, and I could feel the faint evidence of calluses on his palm, formed from a lifetime of wielding weapons without quick-healing abilities. Something about the contact was comforting, like his calm was engulfing all of me, not just my hand.

"You think they're real?" My voice was barely more than a whisper. "You don't think I'm losing my mind?"

I heard Gabriel's intake of air. It surprised me. He was usually so good at measuring his reaction to things. His fingers tightened around mine.

"You're not losing your mind, Terah. I promise. You know yourself, you know what you saw, and you know it's felt different from anything you've ever experienced. Trust that knowledge. It's not a coincidence that this is happening at the same time that you're starting to gain other new abilities. I heard you speak to me in my head. I know what you're experiencing is real."

I nodded slowly, trying to hide how much his words meant to me behind an indifferent mask. Trying to hide how overwhelmed and exhausted I was after everything that'd happened today. But I knew I was largely failing.

"Do you think these abilities are showing up now because I'm being forced to transform more?"

Gabriel nodded slowly, looking thoughtful. "That's a good hypothesis. I've certainly been feeling a greater connection with my power and abilities because of transformation training, so connecting for the first time with abilities that we've suppressed feels plausible."

I nodded, releasing a slow breath. "If you're right about them being warnings, I'm not sure what I could do to prevent those things from happening. It didn't show me that. There was barely even context for what I did see."

Gabriel ran his free hand through his hair, pushing it back from his forehead. "Let's keep an eye on it. You're only just starting to see things and develop this ability. Maybe, as you better understand it, the visions will pull themselves together more, or you'll learn how to make them more complete.

"*If* Matt agrees to train me with them," I said bitterly.

Gabriel's expression darkened and his jaw clenched. "He'd better. And if he doesn't, we'll figure out a way to work on them without him. Your power is your own—it's not his to control."

I nodded, biting the inside of my cheek. Trying to push down the lingering hurt from Matt's continued rejection of my power.

Gabriel sighed, releasing me, and pushed to his feet. He retrieved a tray of food from my desk and brought it to the bed, a bittersweet smile pulling at his lips.

"You should eat. You've had a pretty shitty day."

I couldn't help smiling. "I really have."

Gabriel's smile broadened into something warmer as he sat on the edge of the bed to share the food with me. He'd grabbed a variety of dinner options including pasta, roasted chicken, salad, roasted vegetables, bread, and a couple desserts. He'd even grabbed an iced coffee for me—something I'd developed an intense appreciation for since coming to the Academy. It wasn't something I'd had in Dagmar.

I ate as much as I could and began to feel a little better. Definitely less shaky. I leaned back against the headboard, resting my hand over my stomach. "That was good. So much better than the food in Dagmar. Thanks for bringing it all the way here."

Gabriel shrugged, wiping his mouth with a napkin. "Not a big deal." He pushed to his feet and returned the tray to my desk. "I'll take this back to the dining hall later."

I nodded and pushed from the bed, stretching before retrieving my cigarettes from my side table. Then I headed to one of my open windows. I raised the screen, then lit a cigarette and held it outside.

"Wanna join me?" I turned to look at Gabriel. "I don't feel up to going outside just to smoke."

Gabriel's eyes slid over my outfit, and I suddenly remembered that I was in pajamas—a low cut tank top and flannel pants sitting low on my hips. My cheeks prickled with heat as I began to feel self-conscious. But Gabriel looked away quickly and pulled his own cigarettes from his pocket.

"Sure." His voice was carefully light. "I could probably use one. Didn't expect to have to save your life today—it's been stressful." The corner of his mouth pulled up, as humor danced in his eyes. He was teasing me.

I rolled my eyes but smiled and made room for him at the window.

"Matt invited me to a party this Friday," I said as Gabriel lit his cigarette. "Want to go?"

Gabriel leaned against the windowsill and released a long breath of smoke. "I thought you were mad at him."

I exhaled my own breath of smoke. "I am. But . . . he's still my family. Even when he's being an ass. It seemed important to him."

Gabriel nodded, resigned, as he took a long drag of his cigarette. "But you're not going to just give in to his ideas about your power, right?" A hint of frustration had entered his voice. "Just because you care about him doesn't mean he should get to control you."

I tensed, slightly offended. "Of course I won't. I care about him, but that doesn't mean I'm going to let him decide what's best for me. Only I get to do that. And I did it for a long time without him."

The tension dissipated from Gabriel's shoulders. "Good." He shot me a small smile.

"Does that mean you'll come with me?"

Gabriel chuckled. "I doubt Matt wants me there."

I shrugged. "I don't really care what he wants. If he wants me to go, then I'll do so on my own terms."

"And you want me there."

". . . Yes."

Gabriel's smile was genuine this time.

"Plus," I added, nudging his shoulder with mine, "there'll be free beer."

Gabriel laughed and tossed his cigarette. "You had me at free beer."

6

COMPLICATIONS

I STOOD IN MY CLOSET, STARING AT MY CLOTHES, AND WONDERED what people wore to parties. Fuck if I knew—I'd never been to one. Whenever I'd gone to the bar in Dagmar, I'd always worn my usual clothes. Guys I'd wanted to hook up with had never cared about what I was wearing, and I hadn't cared about their clothes either. Loneliness and physical want had been the driving factors of those encounters on both sides, not fashion. But this felt different. This was a real party. I wanted to at least try.

I finally settled on a pair of heavily but artfully torn black skinny jeans that I knew hugged my curves nicely, a flowy dark purple tank top that bared a lot of my back, held together by two crisscrossing straps between my shoulder blades, and a pair of black knee-high, lace-up heeled boots. I liked them, as they allowed me to stash decently sized knives inside but were flashier than my usual heeled combat boots. To finish the outfit, I secured a small silver necklace with a pendant of a tiny flying bird around my neck. Matt had given it to me before he'd left for the Academy. He'd said it reminded him of me. It was the only present I'd ever received.

I quickly dressed, then went into the bathroom to deal with my hair and makeup. My hair was naturally straight, so I'd decided to try making it wavy just to add a different element to my look. I pulled out and plugged in my barely used curling iron from under the sink and got to work. It took about half an hour to get through all my hair, but I managed to achieve gentle waves and only burned myself once. I lifted my hair to examine my neck, but the cylindrical burn had vanished—it looked like my quick healing had already gotten to it. *Good.*

Next, I pulled out my bag of makeup. I didn't own much, but I often liked to wear sharp eyeliner to match my sharp personality. Waterproof, of course—I didn't want to die in battle because makeup had gotten in my eye. That'd be embarrassing. I decided to swipe on a little of my darker eyeshadow, blending it until it looked smoky, my usual eyeliner, mascara, and a little tinted lip balm that stained my lips a shade of deep berry. I glanced in the mirror when I finished and shrugged. I looked decent. Different. Hopefully good enough for a school party.

I pocketed my phone and cigarettes, then headed out to meet Gabriel. The moon was bright and full this evening, and the night air smelled earthy and almost sweet. How would I ever return to Dagmar after four years of living in such a beautiful place? The hell I'd left would feel even worse, now that I knew how different a place could be. No wonder Matt had immediately taken the trainer job here.

I found Gabriel sitting on a wrought-iron table outside his dorm, enjoying a cigarette. The moonlight reflected off his dark hair, almost as bright as the moon itself, and his eyes looked even more ethereal and glowy in this setting.

He grinned and stood when he saw me, his gaze sweeping over me. "You clean up nice."

I smiled. "Thanks. So do you."

And it was true. Gabriel was wearing black slim-fitting jeans with an untucked, dark gray button-down with epaulettes on the shoulders, and the sleeves rolled up to his elbows, baring many of his tattoos. He was freshly shaved and had styled his hair in an intentionally messy way, highlighting the angular cut of his jaw and revealing the vibrance of his electric blue eyes. Something in my stomach tightened. He was . . . striking to look at.

"Ready for your first party?" he asked as we meandered from his dorm to the dorm west of his, where the party was located.

"I guess. I just hope it's not too awkward. I don't know anyone there. I don't even know what we're supposed to do."

Gabriel shrugged. "Mostly just hang out and drink. Sometimes dance or play games, usually around drinking. And if it's awkward, we'll just leave. You never promised Matt you'd stay the whole time."

"True." It did make me feel a bit better. It wasn't like I'd be trapped there. "Are *you* ready for your first Academy party?" I nudged him with my shoulder. "Ready for flocks of young women to throw themselves at you?"

Gabriel rolled his eyes.

"Don't be scared," I teased. "I'll have your back. I can fight them off or bring you more—whatever you're going for."

Gabriel made an exasperated sound, but I could see the humor in his eyes as he leveled a glare in my direction. I laughed, feeling lighter and less anxious than I had all evening.

As soon as we passed Gabriel's dorm, we could hear the pounding music and loud voices from the party. It'd only started a half hour ago, but there was already a large crowd of students congregating on the grass in front of the dorm. It looked like the party was as much outside as it was inside. And it looked like half the school was there.

Several wolf whistles followed us as we made our way through the crowd to the front door. I rolled my eyes as a few of the perpetrators made suggestive eye contact with me. They were already quite drunk—it seemed like they'd started drinking before the party had even begun. I ignored them and let the unwanted attention roll off me. I could literally kick all their asses if I needed to, so I wouldn't waste energy worrying about them.

Gabriel touched my shoulder as I reached the door, and I paused and glanced up at him. "You said you'd have my back during the party, so it's only fair that I have yours too."

He was smiling in that cavalier way he often did, but I could see the seriousness in his eyes. I blinked, surprised. Had those obnoxious guys bothered him?

I smiled. "Thanks. Though I could kick their asses on my own."

Gabriel's smile turned warmer. "True. But you won't need to do that alone unless you want to."

Warmth grew in my stomach as his eyes held mine. He . . . meant it. My cheeks heated, and I spun forward and pushed through the front door, not meeting his gaze again.

"Thanks," I murmured.

We walked into the dorm's large common area. It was packed with tons of people, most of whom I'd never seen before. People were laughing, dancing to the pounding music, playing drinking games, and talking loudly. I rose onto the balls of my feet to see around the room, but even in heels, my eyes still only reached people's shoulders. I scowled, irritated. It was times like this that I wished I was taller.

"Can you see where the drinks are? All I can see are people's shoulders."

Gabriel glanced down at me and smirked. "I guess you *are* a shorty. I don't usually notice—your personality tends to make up for your height."

I punched him lightly in the arm.

His grin widened. "A *violent* shorty."

I glared at him, and he laughed. Then he spun to look around the room. He was at least a half head taller than most people here. *Jerk.*

"I see the fridge. This way." He grabbed my hand and led me through the crowd. His height and breadth carved a clean path through the partiers.

"Beer?" He pulled open the fridge. "Or do you want a mixed drink? Looks like they bought out pretty much all the stuff the lounge carries."

"Beer for now. But I'll probably try a mixed drink later."

Gabriel pulled two beers from the fridge and popped the caps off by leveraging them against the edge of the counter and hitting the tops with his hand. He handed me one, then clinked his bottle against mine before taking a sip. I leaned forward against the counter and looked around the room, but I didn't see Matt anywhere. I at least wanted him to know I'd bothered showing up. Even if things were still tense between us.

I took a swig of beer. "Do you see Matt?"

Gabriel looked around the room dispassionately and shrugged. "No." He took a swig of his beer. "But I'm sure he'll find you eventually."

"Since he clearly has a thing for you."

I kept my expression carefully blank. I didn't want him to know I'd heard his thought. I frowned as I took another swig of my beer. Was he right? Matt had never seen me that way before, even when I'd had misguided feelings for him as a child. But lately . . .

"Hey," a deep, casual voice broke through my thoughts. "I haven't seen you around before. Are you a first year? Wanna dance?"

I turned, straightening up, and saw a guy with shaggy blondish hair sidling up to me. He leaned on the counter next to me and looked me over unsubtly. He was clearly already drunk. Gabriel tensed beside me, but when I glanced at his face, he was examining the guy next to me with the same cool, dispassionate expression he'd worn as he'd looked around the room for Matt.

"I'm good. Thanks for the offer though."

The guy's gaze shifted to Gabriel for a moment, but returned to mine quickly, seemingly dismissing him.

"Too bad. I would've enjoyed dancing with you. And I can *guarantee* you would've enjoyed dancing with me." His gaze raked up and down me again.

I smiled at him sweetly as I swirled my beer around in the bottle. "Tragically, I guess we'll never know. Feel free to leave." Gabriel stifled a laugh.

The guy's smile vanished, and he looked back and forth between the two of us. "Fine." His expression morphed into something dark and bitter. "It's your fucking loss." He spun around and stomped away from us.

I rolled my eyes and took another swig of beer. "Do guys really think pulling shit like that will work? It's gross."

Gabriel leaned his hip against the counter and smiled. "Drunk, desperate guys do. But they don't tend to be the smartest. Or the best people."

I nodded and drained the rest of my beer. He grabbed the bottle along with his empty one and tossed them into the trash can.

"Want another drink?"

I smiled. "Sure. Can I have a mixed drink this time?"

"Yep." He opened the fridge. "Anything in particular?"

I shrugged. "Surprise me." I turned my back into the counter and leaned against it so I could watch him.

Gabriel pulled out several bottles of liquor, several mixers, and other odd ingredients, then started pouring things into a metal shaker. He seemed to be doing it by eye, as though this was something he was familiar with.

"Perks of spending too much time at the bar in Elareth," he said as he caught me watching. He added ice to the shaker, closed it, then vigorously shook the mixture. Then he poured it into two cups and slid one to me. "If this whole Divine thing doesn't work out, I guess I can always become a bartender." He grinned.

I touched my cup to his, then took a sip. The light beige concoction was sweet and tasted like fruit and ginger. The burn from the alcohol was carefully masked, which was quite a feat given how much liquor I'd seen him add to it.

I took a longer sip, savoring it this time. "Mmm, it's good."

Gabriel smiled and took another sip. "Glad you like it. Be careful though. It's got a lot of alcohol in it."

"So, you're telling me to drink it slow."

Gabriel's smile turned into a grin. "Yeah. Unless you're trying to get fucked up."

I laughed, then took another sip. "Not really."

We leaned against the counter with our drinks and watched the growing chaos of the party unfold in front of us. It was weirdly fascinating. Everything happening was so foreign to me—not even the bar in Dagmar had been like this. There was a level of freedom and wild abandon to the party that I'd never seen Divines display before. I took a long sip of my drink as I watched the growing group of people dancing. Perhaps it was because most of them had never been soldiers. They'd never lived under the warrior faction. They'd never seen everyone around them die. They'd never had to kill. The war hadn't changed them like it'd changed us. And because of that, they felt a freedom that many of us had never known. A foreign ache throbbed in my chest.

"Want to dance with me after we finish our drinks?" I asked Gabriel, suddenly. I wasn't sure what made me do it. Maybe it was the atmosphere, or the warmth washing over me from the drink. Maybe it was seeing how much fun the dancers were having. Maybe it was the need to drown out the melancholy that'd begun creeping into my mind as we'd stood and watched the crowd.

Gabriel looked at me, surprised and a little taken aback.

"As friends, I mean," I added quickly, not wanting him to think I was trying to push our friendship into something else.

Gabriel regarded me, his brow slightly furrowing, seemingly conflicted. My stomach twisted, and I quickly regretted asking. It'd clearly made him uncomfortable. It was obviously something he didn't want to do, at least with me.

"Never mind," I said quickly, looking away. "We don't have to." My cheeks burned, but I hid them behind my cup as I raised it and took a long swallow.

I saw Gabriel shifting in my periphery, his mouth opening to respond.

"Terah?"

I spun and saw Matt approaching us. He looked handsome and relaxed in a tight V-neck T-shirt and dark blue jeans.

I smiled, grateful for the interruption. I was pretty sure Gabriel was about to turn me down.

Matt grinned and set his beer on the counter. "You came. I wasn't sure you were going to."

"I wasn't sure I was going to either, but the call of free beer overcame my reservations."

Matt chuckled, his eyes going soft and warm as he regarded me. It was an expression that'd usually having me backing away from him, unsure and confused. But not right now. Right now, I needed the distraction.

"I'm glad you came," he said quietly. "I've missed spending time with you."

"Me too. Even if I'm still mad at you."

To my surprise, Matt laughed and stepped closer. He reached forward and curled a wavy lock of my hair around his finger. "Guess I'll have to work hard for your forgiveness then." His gaze heated as it met mine.

Gabriel stepped forward so he was standing next to me instead of behind me. "Hey, Matt." He inclined his head slightly in greeting.

"Hey, Gabriel," Matt said, dropping his hand back to his side. His expression was carefully polite, but his shoulders had gone stiff. "Glad you could make it."

"*Liar*," I thought, biting the inside of my cheek to keep from smiling. Matt looked down at me and a smile pulled at his lips. He'd . . . heard me. *Damn*.

"Mind if I steal you away for a little bit?" Matt asked. "I want to introduce you to my friends."

"Sure." I picked up my drink again. The cup was almost empty. "I'm not really doing anything else."

I felt Gabriel tense next to me, but he didn't say anything. I glanced at him, but his expression didn't give anything away. He was too skilled at hiding what he was thinking.

"You'll be okay?" I asked him, barely meeting his gaze.

"Always am." He smiled, but it didn't reach his eyes.

Something about it made me want to stay. I wanted him to tell me what he was thinking. What was wrong. Why he wouldn't dance with me. Not knowing his thoughts was starting to undo me.

But Matt grabbed my hand and pulled me through the crowd, away from Gabriel. I glanced back at him one last time before disappearing into the mass of people. His vibrant gaze met mine, unreadable, but intense. My heart contracted, as though someone's hand had closed around me there. But in the next moment, I could no longer see him.

Matt steered me around the crowd of dancers to the other side of the common area, where a group of his friends had congregated near the wall.

"Hey, everyone," Matt said, pulling me to his side. He still held my hand tightly. "This is Terah—my friend from Dagmar that I've told you about."

The group turned, and as one, their eyes landed on me. They smiled as they looked me over.

"Another Dagmar kid," one of his friends said. "All of you look so tough." She laughed, but not unkindly, as she stepped forward and reached her hand out to me. "I'm Eva. I'm a fourth year here, and this is my party."

I shook her hand and returned her smile, trying to make it seem natural. I was used to avoiding people, not making new connections.

"We've heard so much about you! It's nice to finally meet you!"

"Thanks. It's nice to meet you too." I wondered what Matt had said about me. I wondered how much he'd shared.

One by one, each of his friends stepped forward and introduced themselves. Jesse, another fourth-year student, Omer, an assistant trainer for the intermediate training group, Leah, an assistant school medic, Simon, an assistant trainer for the intermediate-advanced training group, and Zamir, a graduate who'd stuck around the Academy to do research at their library on the complexities of relationships between Divine factions for a future book. They all seemed so smart and accomplished.

My stomach tightened around a small pang of jealousy. Matt had a lot of friends. But he deserved to. We'd always been isolated in Dagmar. He deserved to have a group of people who cared about him. I just hadn't been as lucky. Everyone had always avoided me because of my transformation. And I'd never seen the appeal of having more than one friend. Until now.

"So," Omer said, casually, "Matt says you're the best fighter in Dagmar. It's hard to imagine someone could actually beat him in a fight, but if it's true, I'd love to see it." He grinned.

I smiled. "I'm not sure that's a fair assessment of my skills. We're all trained to be good fighters in Dagmar."

Matt rolled his eyes and draped his arm casually around my shoulders, taking a sip of his beer. "Yeah, right. You've beaten me multiple times in the past month alone, especially transformed. And you were always at the top of the training class growing up." I had been. With him.

My cheeks heated as all of Matt's friends looked at me, impressed.

"Luck?" I grinned and sipped my drink.

"Not a chance," Simon said, crossing his arms over his chest. "I've gotten my ass kicked by Matt enough times to know how good he is. You must be beyond warrior faction levels to get the best of him."

I was, but I shrugged and smiled a little mischievously.

"Ah, a modest Dagmarian." Omer laughed. "That's pretty refreshing."

"Yeah," Zamir chimed in, smirking. "When Matt first got here, he walked around like he was untouchable. Took the trainer several weeks of trying to kick his ass to convince Matt that he had anything left to learn about fighting."

"Good old Luke," Simon laughed.

I laughed in disbelief and turned to look at Matt. It was hard to imagine a brash eighteen-year-old Matt walking around like he knew everything. It certainly hadn't been what he was like in Dagmar.

Matt scowled. "I was not that bad," he grumbled. But he clearly enjoyed the banter with his friends.

"Were too," Omer grinned. "We're all just glad you got over it eventually, or you would've been insufferable."

"Um, he kicked my ass in training every day for four years," Simon interjected. "I'm pretty sure that still counts as insufferable." His expression was warm as he looked at Matt, a familiar smile pulling at his lips.

Matt grinned sheepishly. "Sorry. You were a good training partner, though. Besides, we border town kids had to stick together."

I glanced at Simon, curiously.

"Glenhaven," he said, answering my unasked question. That made sense. Glenhaven was the second largest border town in the country. Dagmar was the first.

Matt slid his arm from my shoulders and took my hand again. "I'm feeling a bit attacked here." He shot a teasing glare at his friends. "Want to go dance?"

I blinked at him in surprise, then looked at his friends. Some of them were grinning suspiciously at us. Simon studied me, shrewdly. *Great.* They thought there was something between us too. Which was false. But after Gabriel's rejection, I wanted *someone* to want to dance with me.

"Sure." I smiled at his friends as Matt pulled me toward the dance floor. "It was nice meeting you all," I called over my shoulder.

They laughed and waved.

"They liked you," Matt said as we made our way through the crowd.

"Really? They seem far more interesting and worldly than me. It's hard to compete with that."

"You were great." He beamed at me, a touch of pride in his eyes. "And there's no reason for you to feel like you have to compete with them. You're remarkable yourself, you know."

I laughed. Remarkable? No. Fucked up and a decent fighter? Sure.

I threw back the rest of my drink as we wove through the crowd, then tossed the cup into a trashcan as we passed. Matt tossed his empty beer bottle. The dance floor was extremely crowded now, but Matt managed to carve out a space for us at the back wall of the common room near one of the halls that led to the dorm rooms.

Matt pulled me toward him and placed my arms around his neck before sliding his hands around my waist. He drew me closer so there was barely any space between us and began swaying and bobbing to the upbeat music. I mimicked his movements the best that I could and found that I caught on pretty quickly. It was just like memorizing moves for fighting, but softer.

I smiled up at Matt as I got the hang of things. "This is fun," I shouted over the music. "I've never danced with anyone before."

Matt's smile was somewhat self-satisfied. "I'd never danced until I came to the Academy," he said, leaning forward so he could speak into my ear. "But my friends like parties, so I learned pretty quickly."

I could believe it. With his handsomeness, plus the fact that he'd never hidden that he was from Dagmar, he'd probably never had an absence of partners. It suddenly occurred to me that I didn't know whether Matt had ever dated anyone during his time here. He'd never mentioned it in his letters, but I couldn't imagine he'd gone so long without falling for someone.

Matt's eyes carefully traversed my expression, his face close to mine. There was enough heat and intensity growing in his own that my cheeks began to burn.

He pulled me closer, pressing me into his chest. "But I've never enjoyed dancing as much as I'm enjoying it now."

I swallowed, nervously. I didn't know how to handle Matt when he was like this. It was a version of him that I wasn't familiar with. His hands splayed over my back, one hand finding the skin bared by my shirt. Gentle warmth and a rush of nerves tumbled through me as his fingers caressed my skin. I was breathless. A bit unnerved. Unbidden, my vision from Wednesday popped into my head—Matt leaning forward to kiss me.

I broke away from him suddenly, something akin to panic pounding through me. I'd vowed to never let anyone that close to me again. And he'd been pushing against the boundary line of what we'd always had, and new, frightening territory, since I'd come back into his life.

"Can I grab another beer?" I tried to smile—tried to disguise my sudden emotional shift. I just needed a little space. I needed room to think and breathe. And it was hard to think and breathe when he held me close.

Matt watched me closely for long moment, then nodded. "Of course. I'll come with you. I need another beer anyway."

It took a while to push through the crowd of rowdy dancers, but we finally made it back to the kitchen area of the common room. Matt pulled open the fridge and grabbed two beers, then looked around for a bottle opener. I grabbed the beers from him, rolling my eyes, and popped the caps off on the edge of the counter.

Matt's eyebrows rose. "Nice trick." He grabbed one of the beers and took a long swig.

I shrugged. "Just saw Gabriel do that earlier." I took a sip of beer and looked around the room, trying to spot Gabriel. I felt bad—I'd been gone for a while, and he'd only come because I'd asked him to.

"He's over there." Matt pointed at the wall by the front door, a knowing look in his eyes. The warmth from earlier was gone.

I glanced in the direction he'd pointed, and my stomach automatically clenched, then dropped. Gabriel was standing there with a young woman. A beautiful one, with long, curly blond hair and a tall, slim build. She looked angelic and feminine—pretty much the opposite of me in every way. She was talking and laughing, leaning forward and touching his arm a lot. Gabriel was swigging his beer and responding, a small, familiar smirk playing on his lips. He was . . . being charming.

As I watched them, I swallowed a larger gulp of beer than I'd intended, and ended up coughing, my eyes watering. I'd offered to back him up tonight, but I hadn't thought about what'd happen if he actually took an interest in someone. And I hadn't thought about what'd become of our friendship if he started dating someone. I doubted he'd have much time left for me then. And he wouldn't choose me over her.

I spun away. This was just another reason why I shouldn't have let him in so quickly. I hadn't properly weighed the consequences. I hadn't truly considered what it'd do to me if he left too.

I reigned in my feelings and carefully smoothed over my expression. Then I looked back at Matt, pulling a cheerful smile onto my face. "Just making sure he wasn't sulking for being abandoned," I said lightly. "But he can clearly take care of himself."

Matt studied me for a long moment, trying to decipher how I was really feeling. But I didn't want him to know that. I didn't want anyone to know that. So I took a step closer to him and slid my hand into his, smiling slowly up at him. I needed to distract him. I needed to distract myself. I wanted the knot in my stomach to go away. And Matt was the perfect person to divert me.

"Want to dance more?" I tilted my chin up, bringing our faces closer together. I tried to create the warmth in my eyes that I'd seen earlier in his. "I liked dancing with you."

Matt's cheeks flushed, and he seemed at a loss for words. I tried not to feel too guilty about manipulating him. I *did* enjoy dancing with him. And the nerves I'd felt before as he'd held me were completely gone now. I didn't feel like I needed space between us anymore. In fact, the less space there was between us, the less I'd probably be thinking about Gabriel and what he was doing.

"Sure," Matt finally said, a tentative smile forming. "I'd love to." His gaze slid back over to Gabriel, but I refused to look again. I already had the image of him and the young woman seared into my brain. And I didn't want Matt to think I only wanted to dance with him because of Gabriel.

I stepped even closer, causing his eyes to snap back to mine. The front of my shirt just barely brushed the front of his.

"Will you lead the way?" I tried to get lost in his eyes as I had briefly while dancing, but it didn't feel the same. Not to me, anyway. But Matt's gaze heated again, and his other hand slid to my waist.

"Of course." But he didn't move. He seemed entranced. His eyes traveled over my face and down to my lips. He swallowed, and I felt warmth slowly flowing through me again. My stomach was still in knots, but not quite as tight as before. *Good.* Maybe I needed to keep doing this.

Matt released my hand and cupped my cheek, his thumb running gently over my skin there. Then, tentatively, he ran his thumb slowly across my bottom lip. My mouth opened on a small gasp. Gentle tingles were beginning to fill me. Matt's gaze seemed to darken with . . . desire. I swallowed nervously, but didn't back away from him.

"Terah," he murmured, taking my face between his hands. His expression was filled with so much raw emotion it shocked me. I'd never seen him like this before. Yet it felt familiar somehow. His face moved slowly closer to mine, and shock rang through me. He was . . . going to kiss me. Then it hit me. *My vision.* This was what I'd seen. And it was coming true. Panic rushed through me, but it was tempered by the warmth I felt as I held his gaze. There was so much there. So much that I was scared to understand. But Matt cared about me. And he'd promised he wouldn't leave me again. Unlike Gabriel.

Matt's eyes slid closed as his face neared mine. He hesitated for a brief second, then pulled my face forward and pressed his lips to mine. A wave of shock rushed through me followed by a wave of gentle warmth. Matt's lips were soft and warm, and his familiar scent surrounded me. It comforted me. I let my eyes close.

Matt's lips moved across mine in gentle caresses and pulls. I relaxed into him. This felt . . . nice. Comfortable. I allowed myself to kiss him back. Matt groaned softly at my response and pulled me tightly against him, his kiss deepening. I could taste the hunger in it. The slow burn of desire. And I realized, surprised, that Matt had wanted to do this for weeks.

His hands tangled in my hair as the kiss became fiercer. His tongue slid along the seam of my lips before pushing into my mouth. And he desperately plundered, sliding his tongue against mine. I could barely move. Or breathe. Or think. I was *kissing Matt*. Something I'd dreamed about in my youth but had never thought would actually happen. Long enough ago that I'd stopped wishing for it. *Did* I still want this?

Suddenly, an image of Gabriel flashed into my mind. He was still leaning against the wall by the door, but his focus wasn't on the young woman in front of him anymore. I watched his muscles tensing, his grip on his beer becoming vice-like. He was watching us.

I gasped and pulled my mouth from Matt's, staggering backward a few steps. My chest heaved, and my mind slowly cleared as I stared up at him. *Gods.* What had I done? What had I let us do? I hadn't thought it through. And this could ruin everything. Our friendship. Our closeness. The emotional fortress that kept me safe. Panic filled me and I backed away from Matt in horror. I'd foolishly repeated my past mistakes. I'd let him in. Too much. Just because I'd needed a distraction.

Matt was breathing hard from our kiss, but his expression filled with confusion and hurt as he watched me put more space between us. *Shit.* My stomach sank. I was already ruining things.

"I . . . I'm sorry." I continued backing away, my knees starting to tremble. "I didn't . . . I didn't think . . ." but I couldn't finish my sentence. I was flooded with a thousand feelings, each one overwhelming to me.

And then I did the most cowardly thing I'd ever done—I turned on my heel and ran from the room. Ran from him.

I pushed through the crowd outside and kept running. I wished I could turn back time. I wished I could undo what I'd done. I'd used Matt, and then hurt him. I'd kissed him without thinking about the consequences. And Gabriel had seen it all.

I ran past Gabriel's dorm and across the soft grass of the open grounds, the light of the moon guiding me. I needed to get as far from the party as possible. Only then would I have the space I needed to think. I ran until my chest felt tight and I was gasping for air. Finally, I collapsed onto a wrought-iron bench near the edge of the trees that bordered campus. Then I curled over into myself, resting my elbows on my knees. I felt cold. Hollow. Irresponsible. I hadn't fucked up this bad in quite a while.

I sighed and turned on the bench to face the trees. This far from the party, the night air was still and quiet, only the gentlest of breezes swayed the leaves. I took a deep breath, filling my lungs with the cool air, then let it out slowly, trying to re-regulate. I repeated this process until my pulse slowed. Then I pulled out my cigarettes and lit one, inhaling deeply.

How would I face either of them now? Had I just pushed away everyone I cared about through one foolish decision? I let out a humorless laugh, shaking my head. Matt had told me that I was remarkable, but I knew the truth—all I was remarkable at was sabotaging what I had. Destroying what I cared about. Driving people away. I was remarkable at ending up alone. Perhaps I shouldn't have come to the Academy. Maybe the strict structure and dismal atmosphere in Dagmar were all I could flourish in. All I deserved. At least it kept everything predictable. It enforced my solitude and kept me strong. I'd softened at the Academy. I'd let my guard down too much. I'd begun letting people in. And the results were telling.

"Hey."

I jumped and spun around on the bench, my pulse racing. I hadn't heard anyone approaching—another sign that I was losing important abilities at the Academy. Gabriel stood there, his hands shoved into his front pockets. His face was hidden in shadow.

My stomach clenched and I turned back around without saying anything. I wasn't ready to face his judgment. I wasn't ready to explain myself. Or to lose him.

Gabriel walked around the bench and sat next to me. He pulled out his cigarettes and lit one quietly. Then we sat there together in silence for a while, watching the shadows lengthen and listening to the soft whisper of the leaves.

"Are you okay?" he finally asked.

My stomach sank. No. I wasn't okay. But I didn't respond.

"You looked pretty shaken when you left," he murmured. "If I hadn't needed to find you, I probably would've punched Matt in the face."

This surprised me into looking at him. "Why?"

Gabriel's expression was unusually serious as his eyes held mine. "Because he pushed you too far too fast. Like he always does."

I mulled this over in my mind. Had he? Or had I been the one that'd pushed him? In my desperation to get the image of Gabriel and that angelic-looking young woman out of my mind, I'd made advances on Matt that weren't fully honest.

"But I kissed him back." Shame rushed through me, tying my stomach into knots.

Gabriel shrugged. "That hardly matters. He's been angling to do that for weeks. He just jumped at the first viable opportunity. And you weren't ready. You care about him, but that doesn't mean you were prepared to move forward like that."

I stared into the trees and thought this over.

"Am I wrong?"

No. He wasn't wrong. I hadn't been ready. But I felt like it'd mostly been my fault. I'd pushed myself to be close to him, and he'd just responded.

"No," I said quietly. "You're not wrong."

Gabriel nodded. Part of me was grateful for his insight, but the other part of me felt like it was a weakness. He could read me better than I wanted him to. Better than I read myself sometimes. It felt like something I should be able to control or stop. I should be able to hide myself from others better than this.

"Do you think I ruined everything with him?" I finally asked.

Gabriel studied me closely for a minute. Then he sighed and looked away. "No. But he probably won't stop trying to be with you. It'll come down to you deciding whether you want to be with him like that or not."

I nodded and flicked my cigarette away. "I don't really know what I want." It felt horrible to admit out loud, but I needed to let out the truth that was pinging around my head. "I care about him. A lot. I even had a crush on him when I was younger." I smiled ruefully and shook my head. "But I got over it and moved on when I was still a child, and he never saw me like that. Until now. I'm not the same person I was then. I . . . can't tell if I care about him like that or not."

Gabriel tossed his cigarette, then crossed his arms over his chest, stretching his legs out in front of him. "I think," he began slowly, his voice quiet, "that being from border towns messes people up in deeper ways than are obvious. We deal with so much death, destruction, and violence all the time that we learn to push down our own feelings and emotions. We have to, to survive."

I nodded, crossing my legs in front of me. I knew this all too well.

"But I think it makes it hard for us to open up to other people," he continued. "And it makes it harder for us to be in touch with how we really feel. I mean, how could we possibly know how we feel when we spend our whole lives trying *not* to feel?"

He was right about closing off to survive. I'd done that for most of my life. Hell, I was still doing that now, though not completely successfully. A shiver ran through me that had nothing to do with the temperature. How could I make it through the world—life—if I couldn't even trust or discern my own feelings? How would I ever know what was real? But on the other hand, why would I want to feel if feeling would only lead to heartbreak and pain? It only ever had.

"Maybe it's better not to feel at all then." My voice went cold and hollow. "Maybe people like us aren't meant to. We were made to fight and save lives, not have lives of our own. Feeling . . . caring about people . . . it never ends well for me. Maybe I should stop trying to connect at all."

Gabriel uncrossed his arms and turned to face me, sorrow bleeding through his neutral expression. "But don't you think you deserve to feel? To care for others and be cared about in return? Isn't that worth the potential pain?"

I looked away from him, my fingers curling into my palms. It hadn't been worth it. Not for me. Caring for people and having them leave or die had hollowed me out. Made me less complete. It'd caused too much pain, and the pain continued to live in me long past the point of being cared for. It tormented me. How could that be worth it?

"I don't know," I finally said. "Experience tells me no. That I don't deserve it. That it isn't worth it. But . . . I guess a part of me still wants it anyway. It's so self-defeating. I wish I could destroy that part of me."

"I don't," Gabriel murmured. "It's what keeps you grounded. Human. If you lose the ability to feel, who do you become?"

I'd become Caleb. A shiver ran through me at the thought. I'd leave hurt and destruction behind me like he had. I'd hurt others. But . . . maybe it would save *me* from being hurt? That'd been his rationale. But thinking about it that way felt selfish. I let out a defeated breath. Nothing seemed like the right path. Nothing seemed painless.

I closed my eyes and leaned to the side so my head was resting on Gabriel's shoulder. I was overwhelmed. Lonely. Feeling too vulnerable in this moment to push away my need for comfort and closeness with another person. It was a failing. But maybe that was me. Maybe all I was good at was failing.

Gabriel shifted and wrapped his arm around my shoulders, pulling me into his side. He didn't mind, then. The knots in my stomach loosened slightly. His warmth enveloped me, chasing away the chill that'd begun to settle into my skin from the night air.

"I'm a fucking mess, aren't I?" I whispered.

He rested his head against the top of mine. "Aren't we all?"

I smiled a little. Perhaps we were. Maybe there was some comfort to be had in that.

A loud crash from within the trees broke through the quiet of the night, and we bolted upright.

"What the hell was that?" I pushed to my feet and spun, looking all around us. But nothing looked out of place.

"I'm not sure." Gabriel pushed to his feet and squinted into the darkness between the trees. "There shouldn't be anything on this plane big enough to make that kind of sound. Apart from students or staff."

"Maybe a tree fell?"

Another crashing sound broke through the air, followed by loud shuffling and the unmistakable sounds of snapping branches. Whatever it was, it was moving closer.

I backed away from the tree line. "What do we do?"

Gabriel grabbed my hand and pulled me over to a small set of bushes to our right. Then we crouched behind them and peered through the branches.

"We need to know what it is first," he whispered. "It could be nothing, but I'd rather see it before it sees us." I nodded, glad that I'd hidden knives in my boots. Just in case.

The rustling and sounds of breaking branches grew louder as whatever it was drew closer to the edge of the trees. I tensed, waiting, adrenaline pumping through me. Whatever it was, it sounded big. Finally, a large, hulking shape burst through the tree line, and the exact thing I'd desperately wished not to see appeared before my eyes.

A Demon.

It was transformed and looked to be on the smaller side—about twice Gabriel's height and much, much broader. Demons took many shapes and forms, but all were created to be powerful and to strike fear, literally, into the hearts of their opponents. This Demon certainly lived up to that purpose. Its body was muscular, beast-like, and deliberately misshapen. No trace of the human remained. Instead, enormous knife-like claws and huge, jagged teeth ominously reflected the light of the moon. Both looked caked in blood. My stomach clenched and dark anger spiraled through me. I wondered whose blood. Like all Demons, its skin was thick, rough, and a dark steely gray. This particular Demon looked like it oozed skin-burning acid from its pores. I'd seen several like this before in Dagmar.

The Demon lumbered purposefully toward the closest dorm buildings. Without further thought, my training took over. I pulled both knives from my boots and made to stand so I could intercept it. But Gabriel grabbed my arm and pulled me back down next to him.

"Wait," he whispered. "We can't just attack it."

I stared at him like he'd lost his mind. We had to. We had to stop it before it hurt someone. Neither of us had been gone from our border towns long enough to forget *that*.

"You're forgetting where we are," he whispered quickly, placing both hands on my shoulders. "Demons are also students at the Academy, and it's not like they're not allowed to transform."

Oh. I *had* forgotten about that.

"We have to make sure it's not a student or some other person authorized to be here." He stood slowly, keeping a hand on my shoulder. "Wait here."

I tensed, tightly clutching my knives, as I watched him jog to catch up with the Demon.

"Hey," Gabriel called, smiling casually as he slowed in front of it. "I don't believe we've met before." He turned to face it, but it didn't stop moving, so he jogged backward to keep his eyes on it.

I snuck out from behind the bushes and followed them at a respectable distance. I wanted to be close. Just in case.

"My name is Gabriel. What's yours?"

The Demon let out a terrible, snarling roar that made my skin crawl. "My name is immaterial, filth." The Demon's voice was horrible—like the deepest baritone combined with the sound of enormous boulders being crushed. "Just know that I am the one who will deeply enjoy killing you."

It swiped its large, deadly claws at Gabriel, but he ducked easily out of the way.

"I'm gonna guess you're not staff or a student, then." Gabriel smiled coolly. I crept up behind the Demon, ready.

The Demon laughed—a horrific sound that made my ears burn with pain and forced the air from my lungs. Demon powers were no joke. There was a reason the Dark Guardians had strived so hard to get the Demons on their side of the war. They were not only huge and deadly in form, but they also possessed the ability to cause extreme physical and psychological fear to manifest in their opponents on command. This combination of abilities made them difficult to fight. You had to be strong in more ways than one to succeed.

"No self-respecting Demon would ever be found at a filthy Light Guardian institution," the Demon roared. "They would deserve to die. Just as you do. Just as everyone here soon will."

It laughed—a grating sound that made my hair stand on end—then swiped at Gabriel again, sending acidic goo flying as its sharp claws sought to tear into him. Again, Gabriel was a step ahead and ducked.

"Cool." Gabriel straightened. "Thanks for clearing that up for us."

Lightning fast, he grabbed two daggers from his waistband and threw one into the Demon's chest. The Demon screeched with anger more than pain and ran at Gabriel. He threw himself out of the way just in time. I ran at the Demon from behind and sliced fiercely across its back with one long knife, then stabbed into the back of its thigh with the other. We needed to slow it down so it couldn't get anywhere near the dorms. Most of the students here didn't have enough training to defend themselves against a Demon.

The Demon spun on me and hit me forcefully across the stomach with the back of its hand, throwing me off my feet. My skin stung as its gooey acid ate through my shirt. But I ignored the pain. My quick healing would get to it soon. I rolled to my feet and ran at it again, hacking powerfully into its arm with my remaining knife. Black blood spurted from the Demon's wound, and I ducked the stream. I knew from experience that it'd burn as much as the acid-goo.

Gabriel threw his second dagger at the back of the Demon's other leg, trying to incapacitate it enough that we could kill it. I pulled my knife free, then hacked at its arm again, slicing it completely off. One less set of claws to kill us with. As it screamed with rage and pain, I jumped and grabbed Gabriel's dagger from its chest. Taking a cue from me, Gabriel grabbed my other knife and his second dagger from the Demon's leg. At least we were evenly armed now. But we'd have to act quickly. Demons had specialized quick-healing powers that differed from Guardians. This Demon would be able to regrow its arm and completely heal its wounds in an incredibly short amount of time.

Unfortunately, this Demon was no novice. It quickly bent and picked up its severed arm from the ground, then threw it at Gabriel, claws first. Gabriel ducked, the claws just missing him, but the blood and acid didn't. He hissed with pain as both substances liberally splattered his skin and began to burn him.

I swore and launched myself at the Demon, repeatedly stabbing and ducking, slicing and moving so it couldn't catch up with me. I ignored the blood and acid that splattered generously over my skin. The pain hardly registered—I was too focused on my goal. The Demon roared, swiping at me, trying to grab me off the ground with its remaining hand, but I threw myself through its legs before it could. I struck out with my knife as I rolled under it, cutting deeply into its leg. Then I rolled away before it could stomp on me and crush me.

Gabriel ran at it again as I shoved to my feet, then launched himself off its partially extended leg, propelling himself higher, and slashed viciously across its throat. Blood spurted, and the Demon gurgled, its vocal cords destroyed. Its head wobbled, but it was still attached. With a ragged gurgle, the Demon grabbed Gabriel out of the air with its remaining hand, and its claws sliced deep into his side as they tightened around him. Gabriel grunted in pain and stabbed through the Demon's hand, trying to force it to drop him.

With a growl, I threw myself onto the Demon, sinking my blades into its back up to the hilts, then braced my feet against its back and used my blades as anchors. Then I pulled myself up its body, climbing until I reached its shoulders. With a grunt of effort, I propelled my long knife as hard as I could into the top of its spine. The Demon twitched uncontrollably, releasing Gabriel, and dropping him roughly to the ground. I yanked my knife free, and in one swift movement, I swung the blade at its neck. Metal parted skin, tissue, and bone, and with a squelch, its head toppled from its body. It was the only way to kill a Demon.

The Demon's body swayed, and it tilted forward.

"No," I gritted out. If it fell forward, it'd crush an already-injured Gabriel.

I grabbed the Demon's shoulders and threw all my weight backward.

I'd rather the Demon fell on me. It might crush me slightly, but I'd survive. Probably. I wasn't sure whether Gabriel would, and that wasn't a chance I was willing to take. The headless body swayed, then tilted backward. The blood from its severed neck poured down my arms and chest in droves, burning my skin and clothes. I tossed my weapons into the grass as far from me as I could—I didn't want to accidentally stab myself if the body fell on me. It'd happened once when I was younger, and I'd learned my lesson. Then I threw myself off the Demon before it hit the ground and rolled away from it. It thudded into the grass with enough force to shake the earth around us.

Breathing hard, I shoved quickly to my feet and ran to Gabriel. He'd pushed himself into a sitting position and had his hand clamped over his side, trying to stop the bleeding.

"Shit," I murmured as I dropped down beside him. Blood oozed energetically from between his fingers. Worry knotted my stomach—the punctures must be deep.

But Gabriel ignored his own injuries and urgently looked me over instead. His eyes widened in horror. "You . . . you're covered in blood. Are you hurt?"

A small smile pulled at my lips and warmth reentered my chest. "I'm fine. None of it is mine."

Gabriel released a relieved breath and nodded.

"Take off your shirts. I need to heal you."

Gabriel winced but pulled the blood-soaked fabric over his head. I grimaced as I saw his skin. He was covered in angry red welts from the blood and acid burns, and he had four deep puncture wounds in his side from the Demon's claws that were heavily bleeding. I quickly wiped my hands on my pants, then reached forward and pressed them to the puncture wounds. Purple power gathered around my fingers, and I began healing him—fixing organs, pulling together and reknitting muscles, veins, and skin. Fortunately, the punctures were neat, making them a little easier to close. And fortunately, I had a lot of experience healing.

When I'd finished with the puncture wounds, I ran my hands slowly over his firm stomach, chest, and arms, purple flowing gently from my fingers, healing all the welts and burns from the acid and blood. I glanced at his face briefly and saw him watching me intently, his eyes warm.

I swallowed hard and sat back, power fading from my fingers. My pulse pounded in my ears. "There. That should do it."

"What about you?" Gabriel leaned forward, his brows pulling together as his gaze swept over me again. "You're covered in blood and acid too."

I shrugged and pulled my shirt over my head. "It'll heal." I used what was left of the fabric to mop the excess blood and acid from my skin. Gabriel hissed in sympathy as he saw my skin covered in large patches of red welts.

"They'll be gone in a couple minutes." I stood and pulled Gabriel to his feet.

He looked back toward the trees at the edge of campus. "How the hell did it even get onto this plane? The school is supposed to be a neutral area. Plus, there are protections on the boundaries. The portals are shielded."

"I don't know." I pulled my phone from my pants. It was thankfully unscathed. "But we need to let the school know." I opened my phone and hit Matt's contact information. The phone rang a few times before he picked up.

"Terah." His voice was tight with concern and regret. "Are you okay?"

"Matt, there was a Demon attack."

"What? What do you mean? How is that even possible?"

"I don't know. A Demon got through the barrier around the Academy's plane somehow, and it tried to kill us and reach the dorms. Gabriel and I stopped it, but you should come here quick. We need to report it to the school."

Matt let out a stream of curses. "Okay. Where are you?"

"We're in the field between the dorms and the trees on the east side of campus."

"Okay. I'm on my way." He hung up.

I sighed and pushed my phone back into my pocket. Then I went and gathered the weapons I'd thrown, wiping them on the grass to clean off some of the blood and slime. Gabriel did the same, then we exchanged our weapons back as we walked over to the Demon's body.

"Hey," Gabriel murmured, lightly touching my shoulder. "The welts are gone."

I looked down at my skin and smiled. "Quick healing."

"Thanks for healing me, by the way." I met his gaze and saw that it was warm again.

I shrugged. "Not a problem. Thanks for fighting with me." I nudged him with my shoulder. "You're good in a fight."

Gabriel grinned down at me. "I thought you'd know that by now since we train together every day."

"True, but you never know how people will react when things actually get bad. You could be good in training and bad in battle."

Pounding footsteps interrupted us, and we turned to see Matt running across the field. His eyes zeroed in on our shirtless torsos before sliding to the Demon lying headless on the ground beside us. I shifted, suddenly self-conscious. I was only wearing a partially burned bra. I crossed my arms quickly over my chest.

"Shit," Matt murmured as he circled the Demon. He ran his hands through his hair. "I don't understand how this could've happened."

He pulled out his phone and quickly dialed a number.

"Yes, this is Matthew Darian," he said as the call connected. "There's been an outside Demon attack on several students on campus. We're not sure how this happened, but we need the president down here quickly." He fell silent as the person on the other line spoke. Matt's eyes slid over us again and lingered on my bare torso. My cheeks heated, and I suddenly wished I had a spare shirt.

"No," he replied. "It doesn't look like there are injuries. No need for a medic. Sounds good. Please tell her that we're on the east field. Thanks again." He hung up and pocketed his phone, then pulled his shirt over his head and handed it to me.

"Thanks," I murmured, my gaze meeting his. It was searching and intent, and I knew it didn't have anything to do with the Demon attack. He was wondering where we stood. Why I'd run from him. I swallowed and broke eye contact with him, focusing instead on pulling on his shirt.

"This shouldn't have happened," Matt said, finally glancing at Gabriel. He returned Matt's gaze, his own icy and slightly narrowed. "But I'm glad you two were the ones who crossed paths with it. I'm afraid to think what would've happened if students with less training had gotten in its way."

My stomach tightened at the thought. They would've died. Countless students could've died.

We heard voices approaching and turned to see a group of people hurrying across the lawn toward us. The Academy's president was at the front, her eyes wide as she stared at the Demon's corpse. I took a small step closer to Gabriel as I watched them approach. Nerves fizzled through me. What if they blamed us? What if we hadn't done the right thing? I didn't want to be kicked out. I didn't want to be sent back to Dagmar. Not yet.

Gabriel stepped closer, and his fingers found mine. He squeezed them gently, then held onto them. I glanced up at him, and he met my gaze, his sure and warm. I could see the wordless reassurance there. He was telling me that things would be alright. He was telling me that, for once, I wasn't in this alone.

The president sent a team of trainers, including Matt, to do a sweep of the grounds and the perimeter of the plane to make sure the school was secure. Then she took statements from Gabriel and me about the attack, what the Demon had said, and how we'd determined it was an outsider.

"I'm glad you two were able to deal with the situation before anyone got hurt," she said when we'd finished answering her questions, "but as our students, you are under the Academy's protection. You never should have been placed in that position, and for that, I am sorry."

Gabriel and I nodded blandly. It didn't matter what should've happened—it was done, and we'd dealt with it like we always would've. We were soldiers, and being students here wouldn't change that, no matter how much she might wish it could.

"We will be looking into this incident and may need to speak with you both further. I must ask, however, that, until we know more about the situation, you keep these events private. We don't want students to feel unsafe, or for some students to turn on other students. We must protect *all* Divines that attend, no matter their faction."

Gabriel and I both agreed, then we were allowed to leave.

"Well, no part of tonight went as planned," I murmured as we walked back toward the dorms.

Gabriel smiled sardonically. "That's the understatement of the year." The moonlight gleamed off his bare skin, making him look almost luminescent. I tried not to look too much.

"Not all of it was bad, though," I said, watching our shadows move with us as we walked. "I went to my first party. I danced for the first time." It'd been fun. Until it wasn't.

"I didn't know that was your first dance," Gabriel said quietly. I glanced at him. He looked subdued. Almost upset.

I shrugged and adjusted Matt's shirt to keep it from sliding off my shoulder. "Sorry I was a bad party-mate. I shouldn't have just left you there. And when you finally found someone you were interested in, I ruined it, didn't I? Making you leave to come find me."

Gabriel glanced at me, studying me carefully. "You didn't make me leave. I chose to go find you. I was worried about you. Also, I wasn't interested in her romantically."

I raised an eyebrow in disbelief. He'd seemed into her. Too into her. He'd let her touch him and be near him.

"She remembered me from our training group sorting day. I was just killing some time and making small talk." He shrugged. "Just waiting for you to come back."

"It's okay." I looked away from him and up at the stars instead. "You don't have to explain yourself or anything."

"I know." His expression was unusually serious. "But I wanted to," he added quietly.

I nodded, and we walked in silence for a while. I still had my doubts about his interest in her. Who'd let someone hang all over them like that if they weren't interested in them? But what I'd done with Matt flashed into my mind. I'd kissed him from a place of surprised jealousy, confusion, and desperation, not because I'd determined I was genuinely interested in him like that. Maybe things were more complicated than they appeared. But either way, I shouldn't care. His romantic life shouldn't be a concern of mine. All I cared about was that we could remain friends— that his future girlfriend wouldn't make him choose between her and me.

"Anyway," I finally said, "I'm just sorry that things didn't go as planned. If there's ever another party, I promise I'll be a better party-mate."

The corner of Gabriel's mouth pulled up. "You were great when it mattered most." I frowned, confused. "We fought well together," he clarified, running a hand through his hair, smoothing it down before messing it up again. "And you healed me. You expended your power on me, and you didn't have to. That's more than I can usually ask for from a party-mate or a fighting partner."

I smiled. "We make a good team." But my smile faded as I thought about the Demon. "I'm just glad we got it before it got to the dorms. What if we hadn't been out there?"

"It would've been bad," Gabriel murmured, somber again.

"Oh, um, I think my visions might not just be warnings," I said a long moment later. "One of them came true."

Gabriel turned to look at me, his eyes widening. "Really? Was it about the Demon?"

I bit the inside of my cheek, willing them not to burn. "Not exactly. I had a vision that Matt would kiss me. I didn't know it was going to happen at the party, but it all lined up and happened exactly as it did in my vision."

Gabriel stopped walking as we reached the side of his dorm. His expression was carefully unreadable. "Was that the vision you had during your transformation training?"

I nodded and looked away from him. It felt like a ridiculous reason to have almost died. But a small detail about that day kept plaguing the edge of my thoughts. I'd been with Matt. My vision had been of Matt. But my mind had shown me Gabriel as my consciousness was fading. I'd called for Gabriel to help me. He hadn't even been in the room. I hadn't even known him for that long. Why hadn't my mind reached for Matt—the person I'd known my whole life, who I knew cared deeply for me—who was only a few feet away? It was nonsensical. Every time I thought about it, I was left with more questions than answers.

"Did you tell Matt about the vision at any point before it happened?"

I shook my head. "It seemed . . . I don't know. Too personal, I guess. And I had no idea whether or not it would come true. I didn't want to make things awkward for nothing."

Gabriel blew out a slow breath and nodded. "Well, we'll have to keep an eye on your visions, then. I don't think it's a coincidence that you had visions about a larger conflict with the Demons and Dark Guardians right before a Demon attack on the school."

"I was thinking that too. I just hope there's some way we can prevent the worst of my visions from coming true. Things seemed . . . bad. Really bad." I shivered a little, as I remembered them.

"I hope so too," he said quietly.

After a moment of silence, I looked up at him. "Are you heading to bed?" I wasn't up for going back to the party, but I wasn't sure I wanted to be alone just yet. Too many things had happened tonight, and my mind was racing with a million thoughts. I wanted a distraction—company—for a little longer.

Gabriel glanced down at me, quickly assessing my expression. "I was thinking of running in and grabbing a shirt and maybe a movie to bring back to your dorm, if you don't mind hanging out for a little longer. I have too much adrenaline to go to sleep right away."

"And I don't want to leave you yet."

His thought was a light whisper that drifted through my mind. And I could see it wasn't one he'd meant for me to hear. My cheeks heated.

"Sounds good," I said lightly. "I don't think I could sleep right away either."

Gabriel smiled and started for the front door. "Be back in a minute."

"Maybe pick a lighter movie?" I called after him.

He shot me a smile over his shoulder. "That's probably a good idea."

7
THE HIGH LIGHT GUARDIAN

I AWOKE THE NEXT MORNING TO POUNDING ON MY DOOR. AT FIRST, I thought it was a part of my dream. It'd been a weird melding of my visions with the Demon attack the night before. The result was a horrifying whirlwind of activity, violence, and gore. The pounding had fit right in. But I eventually jerked awake and realized that part of my dream had been real.

I grumbled and pushed out of bed, wiping sleep from my eyes.

"Alright, I'm coming."

I still felt exhausted. There was no way I'd gotten a full night's sleep yet. I glanced at the clock on my bedside table and confirmed that it was only 9:00 a.m. *Ugh.*

I pulled open the door and came face to face with Matt.

"Oh. Hi. What are you doing here?" I yawned in the middle of my question, but he got the gist of it.

Matt was frowning. "Why haven't you been answering my calls?"

My eyes narrowed as annoyance spiked through me. "Um, because I've been asleep?"

Matt glanced over my head into my room, almost like he was checking if I was in here alone. My eyes narrowed further. But he ignored my annoyance and instead ran his gaze over my outfit, lingering on my sleep tank top which was sitting fairly low on my chest as I'd tossed and turned in my sleep. My cheeks grew warm at his perusal. So did his.

He pulled his gaze from my clothes and met mine again. "Mind if I come in?"

I stepped back and let him through. "Did it have to be this early? I wanted to sleep until at least noon."

"Unfortunately, this can't wait." He sank into one of the chairs in front of my fireplace as I closed the door.

I plopped down in the chair opposite him and waited for him to explain.

"The Academy president is convening a taskforce to investigate the circumstances surrounding the Demon attack last night. She's asked that you and Gabriel attend so you can answer any questions they might have about the attack."

I frowned and pulled my feet up onto the chair in front of me. I'd prefer to sleep.

"Did you already wake up Gabriel? Or am I the only one who's lucky enough to get an early morning door pounding?"

Matt rolled his eyes. "I called him, and he actually picked up his phone."

"Whatever," I grumbled. "I was sleeping. Sleeping outweighs phone calls."

"And," Matt continued, holding my gaze intently, "I thought we could use some time alone to talk over what happened last night."

My jaw clenched and I looked at the rug. I knew he didn't mean the Demon attack. He meant our kiss. But I wasn't sure I was ready to talk about it with him.

"Okay. What do you want to talk about?"

Matt sighed, exasperated. "Terah, we kissed and then you ran away from me."

"Yeah," I said slowly. "I'm sorry about that." I rested my chin on my knees. "I guess I didn't think it through very much. And then I panicked."

Matt nodded slowly. "I can understand that. Our relationship has never gone into this territory before. It's a lot of change to process. But . . . how do you feel about it now?"

I bit the inside of my cheek. I wanted more sleep before having this conversation. I wanted coffee. A cigarette. More time to think. Or maybe just . . . to never have this conversation.

"I'm not sure," I finally answered, honestly. "I've cared about you my whole life. You're my family. One of my best friends. But I'm not sure about us being together romantically."

Matt's hands clenched in his lap, but he didn't speak. He waited.

I pulled my gaze from him and looked at the rug instead. "You knew me so well when we were younger, but you aren't as familiar with who I've become. How hard I've worked to keep people out. I've distanced myself from my emotions so much that I can't even tell how I feel most of the time. And . . . I don't want to lose you as a friend by being wrong about how I feel. I don't want our relationship to be ruined."

Matt ran his hand through his hair and took a deep breath, then let it out slowly. "You're right. I don't know you as well as I used to. Another reason not to forgive myself for leaving you." He smiled sadly. "You may not know how you feel," he stretched forward and took my hands in his, "but I can tell you're attracted to me. You kissed me back, Terah."

My cheeks grew hot. I knew I had. I trusted Matt. Felt comfortable with him. And his kiss had been nice. But . . . shouldn't it be more than nice? More than comfortable? If it was right, wouldn't I have stayed? Or would I have always panicked and run, no matter how right it was? I just didn't know.

"I guess the problem is, I don't know where my love for you as family ends and where other feelings begin," I finally murmured. "I don't know how strong the attraction itself is, and I don't know if what I feel is enough to actually be with you romantically." I felt horrible saying it, but it was the truth. I loved him, but I wasn't sure I wanted to date him. I just didn't know.

Matt's shoulders went rigid, and he released my hands. His expression had turned into something sad and distant. He couldn't meet my eyes now.

"I'm sorry, Matt. I'm not trying to hurt you. All of this is because I don't want to end up hurting you even more down the line." And I didn't want to hurt myself in the process either. Letting anyone that close was dangerous.

Matt sighed and leaned forward, resting his elbows on his knees. "Don't apologize for how you feel. You're just being honest." He considered me for a long moment. "I . . . care about you deeply. Which I believe you already know. You're beautiful and strong, badass and determined. You make me laugh, and you understand me better than anyone else. But . . . I can understand why you might not be as sure. If you're willing to, we can take things slow. Give you time to figure out how you feel."

I nodded, relief trickling through me. "I think I need that. Time. Time to learn to decipher my emotions after a lifetime of pushing them down."

Matt sighed and pushed slowly to his feet. "Dagmar wasn't kind to any of us." He glanced out the closest window, a far-away look in his eyes. "We all need time away from it to figure out who we are and what we want."

He walked over to my chair and reached out a hand to take mine. Then he pulled me to my feet.

"Can I at least try convincing you?" he murmured as he slid his hand up my arm, over my shoulder, and up my neck. He cupped my cheek in his palm and stared into my eyes, his thumb trailing gently over my skin. "Once in a while? Can I try showing you how good we'd be together?"

My breath caught in my throat. I wasn't sure that was a good idea. And I wasn't sure that counted as taking things slow. It might do more harm than good. For both of us.

Matt leaned forward and rubbed his nose gently along mine, his lips so close. "Please," he murmured, his voice unsteady. "Just this once?"

Conflict brewed in my stomach as uncertainty swept through me. But my heart hurt for him. I could see how much he wanted this. I could see how much my uncertainty was hurting him.

"Just once," I whispered, reluctantly.

Matt immediately drew me against him, and his mouth descended on mine. The kiss was passionate, but slow, like he was trying to reign himself in. His lips captured mine in deep, unhurried pulls, one melting into the next. His warmth enveloped me, chasing away the slight chill of the morning air, and his scent invaded my senses—familiar, comforting. I could feel his heart racing through my chest. I could feel the shudder of his breath between kisses. I could feel his care. His desire. But I couldn't stop the uncertain thoughts. I couldn't empty my mind. Maybe I wasn't trying hard enough.

I let myself kiss him back. My arms encircled him and held him close in return. And I let him in deeper. Maybe that was the only way to tell how I really felt. Maybe it was how I'd get my answer. I let his kiss sweep through me, his tongue slide against mine. My pulse quickened as Matt's fingers explored the curve of my back, the indent of my waist. And I tried to clear my mind without closing it. I didn't want to suppress my feelings, I wanted to discern them. That required a certain amount of openness. A certain amount of vulnerability. Just this once.

I relaxed my grip on my mind, easing some of the control I'd relied so heavily on in the last few years. But instead of gaining clarity, an image formed rapidly behind my closed eyelids. *Gabriel*. He was sitting on a bench outside my dorm building, smoking as he waited for me. *Damnit*. This wasn't what I'd been trying to do. Gabriel stilled, his eyebrows furrowing as he glanced around. He felt me there. *Shit.* I shouldn't have opened my mind at all. Especially right now. I didn't want him to see—

I gasped as Matt pulled me closer, crushing my chest to his, as he deepened the kiss. He groaned against my lips, his hands sliding up to my waist under my tank top. His skin burned hot against mine. Gabriel tensed, his consciousness filling my own. He could see what I was seeing. He could feel what I was feeling. And I couldn't for the life of me shut him out.

"Terah," his voice whispered through my head. There was so much emotion in that word. He didn't want to be seeing this. He didn't want it to be happening. But he didn't want to leave and let it continue, either.

"Gabriel. I'm . . . sorry. You shouldn't be seeing this. I can't . . . close my mind."

"Is this what you want?" he asked quietly. *"Is this who you want?"* The second question slipped out before he could suppress it. I felt his stomach clench.

Gods. I didn't know. I had no idea what I wanted. I'd tried opening my mind to find out, and I'd failed. I'd immediately connected with Gabriel instead. Something inside me was broken. I couldn't do this right. I couldn't just feel. I couldn't keep myself away from people like I knew I should, but I also couldn't let them in. I couldn't simply accept what Matt was begging to give me. Instead, I was stunted and uncertain. Tormented and trapped. And Gabriel could see it all.

I pulled my mouth from Matt's, staggering back, and the connection with Gabriel severed. I backed up, panting, and collapsed onto the edge of my bed. Matt was breathing hard, flushed, his eyes full of pent-up desire.

"I don't think . . . that was taking it . . . slow." I placed my hands on my knees and tried to catch my breath.

Matt grimaced, running his hands through his hair. "I'm sorry. I . . . lost control." He swore and turned away from me. But I knew some of the responsibility was my own. Once again, I'd let him in. I'd responded.

"I should get dressed," I said quietly, pushing to my feet. "I'm sure people are waiting for us." Gabriel was.

I dressed quickly in my closet, making sure to arm myself—just in case —then emerged and headed for the door. Matt followed me silently down the hall. It didn't look like anyone else was awake yet. Most students had partied hard last night and were likely still passed out. Lucky them.

I pushed through the front door, stepping into the morning sunshine. The sky was clear and bright, and the air was crisp and cool—much cooler than last night. Gabriel was standing near the front door, leaning against the side of the building, his arms crossed over his chest. I swallowed as our eyes met, and my cheeks burned. He'd seen too much. Heard too much. Things I'd never wanted anyone else to know about me. But his gaze wasn't accusatory, as I was afraid it might be. Instead, it was assessing.

"Hey," he murmured, pushing off the wall. He completely ignored Matt. "Are you okay?"

Matt stiffened next to me.

"Yeah." I looked down, my fingers curling into my palms. It was a lie. On all fronts. When I glanced back at him, I could tell he understood. He might not be able to hear my thoughts anymore, but he knew how I felt.

He took a step closer to me. "I figured it would take you a few minutes to get ready after Matt called me, so I swung by the dining hall and grabbed you some food."

He pulled a small object wrapped in a napkin from his jacket pocket and held it out to me.

"It's a blueberry muffin." Warmth grew in his eyes as a small smile pulled at his lips. He'd noticed they were my favorite.

Something in my chest lightened as a genuine smile lifted my lips. My first of the day. I stepped closer and took the muffin from him, my breath catching as my fingers slid over his.

"Thanks," I whispered, lost in the vibrance of his eyes. They pulled at me somehow, drawing me in like a magnet.

"We should get going," Matt said sharply, cutting through the pleasant haze. "They'll be waiting for us." He started down the path, his shoulders stiff, and Gabriel and I trailed behind him.

I opened the napkin as we walked and took a small bite of the muffin. My eyes slid closed for a moment. It was still warm. And good. So good.

"I wish they could've convened their super-secret meeting later," I murmured to Gabriel once I'd swallowed. "I wanted to still be sleeping right now."

Gabriel smiled. "Same. I feel like we earned a sleep-in. We *did* defeat a Demon without warning last night."

"Right? No thoughts for our comfort," I teased. "Super rude."

Gabriel laughed, shaking his head. And whatever lingering tension was between us dissolved. I smiled and took another bite of the muffin, my spirits lifting.

Matt took us to a smaller structure just beyond the main classroom building that held all the administrative offices. The inside was covered in rich, dark woods, tufted leather furniture, and plush ornate rugs. Simple wrought-iron chandeliers hung from the ceiling every ten or so feet, creating little spotlights of warm light. The space exuded elegance and tradition.

We followed Matt down a long hallway to the highly polished door at the end. He knocked, then pushed it open, revealing a large meeting room. There were already quite a few people there—the president, members of the Academy's administration, and several members of the warrior and political factions. I frowned. They were all representatives from the Light Guardian side of the war. I'd expected to see at least some representatives from the other factions as well. I glanced at Gabriel. His shoulders had stiffened, and his eyes had narrowed. He'd definitely noticed.

The president came forward and briefly greeted us before showing us to several seats on the far end of the enormous meeting table. Matt took the seat on my right and Gabriel the one on my left.

"We're just waiting for a couple more people to arrive before we get started," the president announced to the room, before rejoining a conversation with a warrior faction representative.

"I feel super out of place here," I grumbled to Gabriel. "What could we possibly tell them that we didn't last night?"

Gabriel shrugged. "It's possible that they want us here to answer questions from people who weren't there last night. And it gives the Academy's account of the attack more legitimacy if it comes from student witnesses and not just the president."

"So we're here because of politics." I leaned back in my chair and crossed my arms over my chest, scowling.

"Likely," he murmured, looking around the room dispassionately. "And it helps that at least one of us isn't a Light Guardian. Makes everything seem more neutral."

My eyebrows rose as I glanced at him. I'd guessed he was a Blessed based on the color of his power, but he'd never explicitly excluded himself from a faction before.

His smile was bittersweet, and he shrugged. "You were probably going to find out during this meeting anyway." I frowned and looked back at the table. I wondered if that meant he'd find out about me as well. I hoped not.

The door to the meeting room opened again, and two more figures walked in. My stomach dropped, and I gripped the edge of the table so tightly that the blood left my fingers.

"What the hell is *she* doing here?" I hissed at Matt. "Did you know she was coming?"

Matt met my gaze with his steady one. Yes. He'd known.

Rage boiled through me. Enough to make my fingers shake. Enough to obliterate all rational thought from my head.

"If I'd told you, you wouldn't have come," he said quietly.

I glared at him. Hard. Of course I wouldn't have come! I would've been right to stay away!

"And that would've been *my* fucking decision to make!" I whispered harshly. "Seriously, Matt, what the hell?" I turned away from him, angling my body so I couldn't see him anymore. I was furious. Livid. He knew better than anyone how much it'd hurt me to see her. Just how much she'd hurt me in the past.

Gabriel glanced at me, curiosity and concern blending on his face, but I didn't meet his gaze. Instead, mine strayed back to the woman who'd just entered. Beautiful. Cold. The president had immediately approached her, and they were speaking in low voices. But her eyes strayed around the room and finally met mine. Tension tightened my muscles all the way down my body. I didn't want to see her. I hated her. All she'd ever done was judge me and use me. I hadn't spoken to her in four years. I hadn't seen her in two. I clenched my jaw and glared at her. I would've been fine not seeing her again for the rest of my life.

The president moved to her seat. "Alright, everyone. We're all here, so let's call this meeting to order."

Everyone took their seats, and the room fell silent.

"Most of you are already acquainted with each other," she continued, scooting her chair closer to the table, "however, we have two students and an Academy trainer present who witnessed the attack and its aftermath."

She gestured at us, and all eyes trained on us. I fixed my gaze on the opposite wall, refusing to acknowledge them. I didn't want to be here. I was a soldier, not a political pawn. The Light Guardian side had only ever wanted me for my battle skills, not my mind. That was our only value to them. I didn't want to be paraded out now for people to pretend to listen to me, all for the false appearance of neutrality.

"The main question we need to address," she continued, "is how the unsanctioned Divine, in this case a Demon, got through our security and onto the Academy's plane. Additionally, we need to ensure that such a thing does not occur again. We need to guarantee the safety of our students. We sent professors last night to examine the integrity of the plane border, and we asked the warrior faction members here today to do the same."

She turned to the warrior faction representatives.

"Would you like to brief the room on your findings?"

"We did a perimeter check this morning," said a tough but stately woman several decades my senior. "We also followed the trail of broken trees from the main campus to the plane barrier. We found no obvious breach points anywhere."

I frowned as people around the table looked startled. No breach points. Had that meant they'd gotten on the plane through the various portals the students used to come to campus? Those were heavily guarded and also sealed from inside the Academy's plane by a series of shields fed by divine power.

"The portals didn't appear to be disturbed," she continued grimly, "so we're investigating how the plane barrier might have been opened and closed again. If plane tears were used, they weren't like the ones in our border towns. Once opened, those tend to stay open."

"The two most likely options," the warrior faction representative next to her added, sitting forward in his chair, "are that the Demon was working with someone on campus who arranged for their access, or that somehow they have infiltrated or bypassed the technology used to seal the Academy's plane."

"After hearing the warrior faction's analysis," the president said, "we have asked them to investigate which of these has occurred, determine who opened the plane, and determine where it was opened from. All those with access to this technology, or who know how to gain access to it, will be questioned."

"There is another way this could have happened," an authoritative voice said from the other end of the table. I tensed, refusing to look at her. "While it is unthinkable to consider, for our safety, we must."

"For those who don't know," the president cut in quickly, "this is Serafina Alexander, the High Light Guardian. She directs and oversees the warrior and political factions of the Light Guardian side of the war."

Tension radiated down my body. Why had she had to say her last name? I glanced quickly at Gabriel to see if he'd noticed. His brow was furrowed, and he was giving Serafina a hard glare. My stomach tightened. He'd come face to face with the person who'd dictated how his life had gone. What his border town had gone through. How little support they'd

126

received. And if he put two and two together, he'd probably never forgive me.

Matt reached out under the table and rested his hand on my leg to comfort me. I jerked away from him and glared. This was his fault—me being here with her. He could've prevented this, but he'd chosen to lie to me instead.

"We must consider," Serafina continued, calm and authoritative, "that the Dark Guardians have amassed enough power to breach the plane and transport people at will." Shock traveled in a wave around the table. A couple people even gasped.

"That's impossible," one of the Academy's administrators said, firmly shaking her head. "They could never have enough power to do that. Besides, why would they choose to target the Academy? It's neutral ground!"

"That theory does seem rather alarmist," a second administrator said, though he looked apologetically at Serafina as he said it. "There's only been one attack, and nothing I've heard about it connects back to the war or to the Dark Guardians. Besides, if they had the power to do this, why would they only send one Demon? It wasn't a very successful attack."

The first Academy administrator nodded in agreement. "And the Demon was defeated by first year students," she added, glancing at us. "Not a very deadly attack."

"These are not regular first years," the president cut in. "One is from Dagmar, and the other from Elareth. Both are highly skilled in combat and in our advanced training group. I'm sure their trainer Mr. Darian can vouch for their abilities."

Matt inclined his head in agreement. The group around the table looked us over again, surprise and curiosity blending on their faces. Even the warrior faction representatives were looking at us with respect. I clenched my jaw and scowled back. I didn't want their respect—I wanted to leave. I glanced at the head of the table and saw Serafina eyeing Gabriel coolly. She must not have known he was from a border town, and she clearly didn't think highly of Elareth. To his credit, Gabriel was staring straight back at her, his jaw set. He didn't cower or address her with reverence. A little warmth reentered my chest. Not many people stood up to her—I liked him more because of it.

"I have no doubt," the president continued, "that, if any of our other students had come upon this Demon, or if the Demon had reached the dorms as it was attempting to, there would have been many fatalities. We owe these students a great debt of gratitude."

"It is possible," Serafina said, finally pulling her gaze from Gabriel, "that this was a scouting mission. This may have been an attempt to test their control at entering and exiting the Academy's plane, and to test the school's security." She looked around, haughty and regal. "If this is the case, we must expect further attacks by the Dark Guardian side. The Academy must be ready for this eventuality. It is far better to over-prepare than to leave our children's safety to chance."

I tried not to snort. She cared about winning, not about the individual lives that could be lost. Not about the lives of young students. Not even mine. She'd always thrown me into danger, not kept me away from it.

The president sat forward. "The High Light Guardian has suggested the perimeter of the plane barrier be protected by a small group of warrior faction soldiers. However, this poses several potential political issues. We are on neutral territory, yet the warrior faction represents one side of the ongoing war. Our use of their protections could be seen as the Academy taking a side, which is not our intention. We'd like to preserve the important function that is a neutral space for all Divines to congregate." She turned to the political faction representatives. "What are your thoughts on this?"

I listened irritably as the political faction representatives droned on and on about neutrality, about how other Divines could technically join the warrior faction—not just Light Guardians and Blessed—and how the benefits of some form of protection outweighed the costs. Most at the table seemed to agree. But I felt instinctively that they were simply rationalizing the answer they most wanted. Anyone with clear eyes could see the Light Guardian side was eager to bring the Academy under its wing. They wanted to gain more ground in their battle against the Dark Guardian side, and they weren't above using the school and students to do so.

"We will now vote on this issue to determine the best course of action," the president said as the political faction leaders fell silent.

"Do we get to vote as well?" Gabriel asked, crossing his arms over his chest and leaning back in his chair. He eyed the president, his gaze firm and steady.

She blinked at him and was silent for a long moment. "I . . . suppose you are the only representatives of our student body present. Therefore, I believe that would be appropriate."

Serafina pursed her lips, her eyes narrowing. She hated not being in control, and she hated that we'd be able to vote with the rest of them.

The president stood. "All in favor of the warrior faction guarding the perimeter of the Academy's campus, please raise your hands." Everyone around the table lifted their hands into the air. Everyone except for Gabriel and I. Eyebrows rose all around us as people noticed. They'd assumed that, as students, we'd definitely agree with their plans to defend the Academy's plane. But I didn't. Not like this. Not without all factions of Divines represented at the table.

"All opposed?" the president asked slowly.

Gabriel and I raised our hands. Serafina glared at us. Matt shifted uncomfortably in his seat. The president nodded at us, acknowledging our vote, and we lowered our hands.

"Any abstentions?" No one raised their hand. "The motion has passed, and we will be welcoming the protection of the warrior faction on campus."

People around the table nodded in approval. Serafina looked pleased, bordering on smug.

"For the record, however, I would like to hear why our student representatives voted against this option." The president turned to us.

Gabriel and I glanced at each other. I felt drained. He looked determined.

"You can tell them," I murmured silently. It got easier to connect with his mind each time I did it.

Gabriel nodded, then turned to face the president. "I voted no because it's far from neutral, and it's not the best or only option." He was calm and firm. Commanding of attention without the haughtiness I was used to seeing in leaders, especially Serafina. "I find it troubling that there are no representatives from the Dark Guardian and Demon factions present as we weigh our options. The main leadership present are representatives from the Light Guardian side. That's not neutral, as the Academy professes to be.

"Many of our students are not Light Guardians and do not agree with the Light Guardian agenda, nor have they taken particular sides in the war. Perhaps some have even taken the opposite side. Only welcoming the protection of the Light Guardian side and *their* warrior faction is abandoning neutrality." He calmly met the accusatory gazes around the table. "I believe it would be more prudent to amass well-trained individuals from among *all* factions who are interested in protecting our younger generations, as well as protecting the neutrality that the Academy stands for. This would allow *all* Divines that attend the Academy to feel represented and protected without bias."

I smiled as he sat back in his chair. He—a student, a soldier from Elareth, not a Light Guardian—had spoken the most eloquent and rational words thus far. Warm pride expanded like a bubble in my chest.

The president nodded thoughtfully as she regarded him. Most of the warrior and political faction reps were now eyeing him suspiciously or with open dislike.

"And you?" the president asked, turning to me.

"I agree with Gabriel. That's also why I voted no." Matt tensed beside me. From my periphery, I saw him shaking his head. He was disappointed in me. He disagreed with me. Well, tough. I was beyond disappointed in him.

"We will consider your viewpoint moving forward," the president said. "Ultimately, they are valid concerns. For now, however, we will proceed with the most expedient protection we can gather." She turned to address the group. "We will reconvene when the investigation has made more headway. I will be in close contact with the High Light Guardian, who will keep me abreast of any new developments with the warrior faction's investigation."

Serafina stood and regarded the president regally. "Thank you for your trust in us. It is born from experience that, unfortunately, these students do not yet have." She shot us a glare. "We shall have warrior faction soldiers guarding the perimeter of the Academy's plane by early this afternoon. We will send enough guards so that they may take shifts—we don't want the barrier to be unguarded at any point, day or night. The president has kindly extended the use of campus facilities so our representatives can be housed and fed. With our soldiers in place, we have faith that we can protect all people on this plane."

Gabriel and I scowled as those around the table smiled and nodded. They were all clearly very proud of themselves.

The president stood. "If no one has anything to add, I will call this meeting to a close. Thank you all for attending during this troubling time. We have greatly valued all your help and wisdom."

The group around the table clapped, then stood, gathering their belongings. I quickly stood, my fingers curling into fists. I wanted to get out of here. As quickly as possible.

"A moment, you three," Serafina called from the head of the table, gesturing at Gabriel, Matt, and me. My stomach clenched and sank. I didn't want to be anywhere near her. And she *usually* didn't want to be anywhere near me.

Serafina's sharp gaze bored into mine as we walked over to her. What could she possibly want? Gabriel stood beside me, his arms crossed over his chest, and Matt came to stand on my other side, though he'd put a small amount of distance between us. We waited there, awkwardly, as the room emptied. Then Serafina stepped toward me.

"Matthew has informed me that you have been developing new abilities. Potentially *useful* abilities." She hadn't bothered with a greeting. There was no attempted affection or familiarity. My insides went cold and hollow.

I clenched my fists and turned to glare at Matt, anger radiating off me. How fucking *dare* he report to her about me, especially without asking me first. He knew all she'd ever done was use me and my abilities for her own gain. He knew how much I wanted her out of my life. Matt was in a *world* of trouble.

He studied my expression, clearly a little worried about my reaction, but held his head high. He clearly believed he'd done the right thing. *Asshole.*

"My abilities have nothing to do with you," I said sharply, turning back to look at her. "They, like me, are no concern of yours."

Gabriel looked back and forth between us, his brows pinching together. It was clear that Serafina and I knew each other, but he hadn't realized how. Yet.

Serafina smiled at me, slow and dangerous. "On the contrary, my daughter. Your power and abilities have *everything* to do with me. Half of them came from me, after all."

Gabriel turned to me, his mouth opening in surprise. I could almost see his brain working—putting together what he knew about me and what he knew about her. That my mother was the reason for his suffering. That I'd known that and kept it from him. His eyes hardened slightly, and he turned away from me, his jaw clenched. Pain speared me in the chest, like an invisible blade had plunged into me there. He wouldn't forgive me for this. I knew that. Our friendship was . . . over.

"I'm not a child anymore," I said firmly, trying to hold onto what little remained of my composure. "Nor am I an official member of the warrior faction. You can't give me orders, and you can't dictate how I use my power."

Serafina smiled again. "We'll see."

A shiver ran through me. Serafina usually got her way. She was the most powerful Divine on the Light Guardian side and held the most powerful position. But I was stubborn and determined too. And I'd long grown tired of her manipulations. I'd fight her on this, even if I fought her alone.

"I have instructed Matthew to train you to use these new abilities and to foster better control." She beamed at Matt. "He has generously agreed." Matt nodded silently beside me.

I glowered at him. Of course he had. Because *she'd* asked him to. Not because I had. The stabbing pain in my chest intensified.

"He has informed me that you have *visions*," she continued, her eyes glittering greedily, "and that you can see and even speak into other people's minds. Imagine how useful those skills will be to our side. You may finally turn the tide of this war. I've never been prouder."

I stared at her, my fingers shaking. I felt as though a sword had been plunged into my gut. She'd never been proud of me. She'd never told me that she was proud. There'd always been sharp critique and open disdain. She'd always been sure that I could be much more skilled if I only tried harder. No, she wasn't proud of me. She'd simply saved the words like weapons, to use at the precise moment she needed the most from me. That moment was now. And it hurt. But it also sparked a protective anger in me. She might be crushing me on the inside, but she'd *never* have absolute control over me. Only I could decide what to do with my power. I'd never cede that to her.

"No." My voice was clear and steady—far steadier than I really felt. "You're not proud of me. You're proud that this weapon you made is finally showing it's worth something. Your mistake was having your weapon be a person. I have free will and my own conscience. Only I can decide what to do and who to help. And I am *not* willing to help *you*." I sucked in a deep breath, trying to steady my fingers. "You abandoned me. You forced me to grow up in a living hell. You treated me with cold disdain. You neglected and ignored me, and never once gave me affection. You barely visited, and when you did, it was only to fulfill your orders, not to see or speak to me. You pitted Matt and me against each other every time you visited us in Dagmar and turned him into your spy and pawn here."

I shot him a glare.

"I am who I am today because of my own strength. Not because of you. I'll make my own decisions. I'll train how I want to train. And I'll use my power how I see fit. I'll not become your weapon. I'm not your means to an end. I *will not* help you."

Serafina stared at me in stunned silence, her eyes wide and filling with rage. Her hands clenched at her sides, her whole body going rigid. Gabriel glanced at me, his eyes skimming over my face, his expression unreadable. My stomach clenched. I couldn't take it. I couldn't stand being here with people I cared about who didn't truly care about me in return. It was worse than being alone.

"You . . . you're being completely childish and selfish," Serafina squawked. "The whole world can burn as long as you get your way, is that it? Matthew, make her understand! You've always had sway over her."

I trained my gaze on Matt coolly. His cheeks warmed under my icy stare. He could see, now, that things were incredibly damaged between us. And he was torn. He didn't want to make things worse.

"He doesn't anymore," I said quietly, my insides like ice. Matt's eyes flickered with hurt, but I turned away. "I'm done speaking about this. Goodbye, mother."

I walked past her with long, sure strides, and pushed through the meeting room door. I walked quickly down the hall and made it outside before breaking into a run. All the panic, emptiness, and sadness I'd recently felt bubbled up in me, spilling over. Making me run faster. I wanted to escape. I was tired of being a Divine. Being a means to an end. Being used but not cared for. I wanted to simply . . . be.

I ran until I made it to the opposite end of campus, past all the buildings, over the large expanse of grass. I glanced behind me, but I didn't see anyone around. Of course. No one would follow me this time. Matt had betrayed me. Gabriel was disgusted by me. Serafina didn't care about me. No, I was truly alone now.

A cry of anger and agony pushed out of my throat, uncontrollable, and I burst into my transformation as I ran. Deep purple wings erupted from my back, and I pushed into the air before all my armor had formed around my body. I flew over the large expanse of trees bordering campus, until I was about two-thirds of the way to the barrier, then slowed. I didn't want to run into warrior faction soldiers. Instead, I glided down to the top of a large tree and transformed back, then carefully climbed through the branches until I found a thick one to settle on that was hidden from the ground by dense leaves.

I turned off my phone, then pressed my back against the thick trunk,

133

tilting my head to gaze through the leaves above me to the clear, bright sky. I took deep breaths, trying to slow my pulse. The air was cool and crisp—soothing. But nothing could erase the explosion of emotions rampaging through my insides. I pressed my eyes closed. I couldn't push them down anymore. They'd been building in me my whole life, and it finally felt like I couldn't suppress or hide them anymore. I'd hit the maximum threshold for what I could hold in, and I needed to let some of it go or I'd explode. I knew it was a weakness—feeling this much, being this close to breaking—but I couldn't bring myself to care about that right now. There was no room left in me for that shame. So, for the first time in my life, I let myself do something I'd always been terrified of doing. I let myself truly feel.

I shuddered, curling forward as I released my control on myself and my mind. And sadness hit me as hard as a Demon strike. Tears welled in my eyes and spilled down my cheeks in torrents. There was so much to mourn. So much had torn me apart over the years, and I'd pushed it all down to survive. To keep moving forward like the disciplined soldier that I was. But I'd never succeeded in killing that softer part within me.

A sob spilled from my mouth as I mourned the maternal love and affection that I'd never received. I let myself feel and sit with the deep absence and emptiness I felt without it. I mourned the lack of a father, and the love and care he might've provided that my mother never could. I mourned the death of Matt's mother, the closest person I'd had to a caring parent. And I mourned the fact that I couldn't remember what she looked like.

My body shook as I mourned my lack of a real childhood, and all the horrendous, violent experiences I'd had from a young age in Dagmar. The terror and helplessness that'd dug into my soul because of it. I mourned my experiences with Caleb. Everything I'd given him. How betrayed I'd felt. How broken and alone he'd left me. I mourned the loss of my connection with Matt. He'd been my family, my caretaker, my closest friend. The one who'd raised me, who'd known me best. But that person felt gone, replaced by someone who didn't listen to me or respect my wishes.

And I mourned the loss of Gabriel. He'd become my best friend and closest companion. The person who listened to me and supported me, who liked me as I was. Another sob spilled past my lips as another deluge of tears fell. I already missed the loss of his warmth, his understanding, his humor, care, smile.

Pain throbbed in my chest like a festering wound. The world around me blurred through the torrent. I supposed crying was a part of feeling—a part I'd closed off for far too long. I hated the pain and the heartbreak—I'd tried to avoid them my entire life—and I didn't care for the tears, but . . . at least I actually knew how I felt in this moment. Sad. Heartbroken. Alone. But aware. Awake. Still here.

I ceded control to my sobs. I let them shake my body as I clung to the tree for comfort, and I let close to two decades of pain pour out of me. It was exhausting—almost as draining as burning out—but also . . . freeing. It felt like an invisible weight I'd been carrying around my neck my whole life had suddenly been lifted. I could suddenly see how tired I was of shoving things down and just surviving. I'd been in survival mode since I was a young child, and it'd separated my mind from my emotions and my body. It'd split me apart and kept me from myself. And I was tired of it. For the first time in my life, I wanted to live.

The tears slowed, and I leaned back against the tree trunk, wiping my cheeks on my sleeve. How would I move forward? Should I leave the Academy so I could be free of the people I'd lost? Should I just run away and travel the world? I sighed, my eyes sliding shut. I knew I'd never be able to outrun the war. Divines were everywhere. The fighting was everywhere. Now it was at the Academy, too. My dream of being free from it had been unrealistic and naïve. But I was tired of fighting the war on other people's terms. If I was going to fight, it needed to be my choice. My way. For my own reasons, not just because someone ordered me to. And I'd need time to figure out what all those reasons were.

I released a deep breath and finally let my exhaustion overtake me. I relaxed fully into the tree trunk, emptying my mind of thought and worry, and let sleep overtake me.

"*Terah*," Gabriel's voice whispered through my mind. *No*. I tried to push it away. It was too painful to think about him. Too painful to see him or hear him, knowing he'd never willingly be my friend again. Not after I'd lied to him. Not now that he knew. Even on the edge of sleep my mind was cruel, forcing me to look at an image of his sad face. "*Please come back.*"

My heart twisted painfully. It couldn't be real. The real Gabriel had hardened and turned away from me. The real Gabriel didn't want anything to do with me. I pushed his voice and image firmly from my mind and fell into a deeper sleep.

The trees were burning. Black fire set the vegetation ablaze. Dark clouds swirled overhead, and thunder rumbled through the air. A young man was standing in front of me—the same one I'd seen in my last set of visions— regarding me, his expression resigned and cold.

"You've made the wrong choice." His words were firm, but his gaze flitted over the people around me. Uncertainty wavered in their depths. "If you don't choose differently, you'll die. All of you."

Anger speared through me. "They won't stop now! No matter what he promised you. Open your eyes! You know it's true!"

The young man's eyes flickered for a moment, before he turned to look behind him. His fists clenched and unclenched. The image faded.

I shivered in my sleep and wrapped my arms around my middle. Another image formed.

"Why haven't you told him?" the young man from before asked, smiling slightly. He was sitting on the couch next to me in a room full of morning sunshine.

I sighed. "You know him. He'll just worry. And I doubt he'd want me to fight if he knew. You know as well as I do that we need all the soldiers we can get right now. We can't afford to be a fighter down."

He nodded, his expression turning solemn. "You can't keep it a secret forever." His eyes betrayed some of his worry. "And it's hurting him. Not knowing what's going on with you. Not knowing what to do or how to help."

I sighed, long and slow. I was getting a headache, and my nausea was growing. "I know," I murmured, placing a hand against my forehead. "I'll tell him. I promise. I just . . . need to think about the right way to do it."

The man studied me closely, then nodded. "Just don't draw it out too much," he finally said. "The worry is undoing him."

My heart clenched and my stomach dropped. I knew he was worried. I knew I was hurting him, and it was tearing me apart. I'd only wanted to spare him from even greater worry. Shame swept through me, twisting my stomach into knots of guilt and anxiety. He had a right to know, even if I was scared. Even if I was afraid of what it might do to us. My desire to protect him by keeping him from the truth, wasn't truly protecting him.

"I'll tell him today," I said quietly, looking down at my lap, my throat tight. "But I want to be the one to do it. Promise you won't tell him before I do?"

His eyes searched mine, then he sighed and looked away. "I promise. But do it soon."

The image dissolved, and another took its place. This one felt familiar, like I'd been here before. I was standing outside in the darkness, alone. A million emotions swirled through my chest, and I felt dizzy. I pulled air into my lungs, trying to calm myself, but it barely helped. I'd had too much to drink, and this current state was my own fault. I wished my quick healing would kick in. I was tired of feeling this out of it. This out of control.

I walked through the grass, away from the loud noises of the crowd. I needed some time to think. Some time to resign myself to what'd become clear this evening. Pain ripped through my chest at the thought, and I suddenly wished I'd brought a beer outside with me. I swore and lit my cigarette as I walked, making my way past the building and through the grass toward the trees on the west end of campus. I'd still be able to see the building, but at least I'd put some distance between myself and its occupants. The chilly wind whipped around me, making goosebumps form over my skin. I shivered, wishing I'd thought to grab my jacket.

A rustling in the trees behind me broke the quiet of the night. Suddenly, a horrible sound tore through the night air, and I spun around, fear flooding me as I saw an enormous Demon—the largest I'd ever seen—barreling toward me.

I gasped and jerked awake. I was still sitting in the tree, the sun still shining above me, though in a different position in the sky. I must've been asleep for a few hours at least. I rubbed my eyes, feeling slightly disoriented. I'd had visions again. Confusing ones, filled with unfamiliar people and with conflict that I couldn't decipher but could feel. I'd felt the fear and desperation as though I was there, but I had no idea what I was scared of, or what was happening around me.

I took a few deep breaths, trying to calm my racing heart. Then I dug into my pocket for my cigarettes and lighter. I needed the calm and clarity they seemed to bring. I inhaled, then leaned back against the trunk of the tree, releasing a slow stream of smoke into the leaves above me. I couldn't stay up here forever. I'd have to face Gabriel and Matt eventually. But fear of further pain from those encounters kept me in the tree. It was cowardice—I should face their anger and disappointment head on. I should stand behind my choices and face the consequences of my decisions. But the past few days had been overwhelming.

Seeing my mother unexpectedly had been overwhelming. I just needed more time.

I finished my cigarette and sat in the tree for a while longer. It was calm up here. Chilly, but peaceful and refreshing. I listened to the sound of the leaves rustling gently in the trees and relished the feel of the breeze blowing softly through my hair. I listened to the calming birdsong that filled the open spaces around me. There was something about sitting out here surrounded by nature that felt perspective-altering somehow. The world wasn't just made up of the war and my problems. There was beauty in it. Peace. I needed to remember that, especially when my personal world got too chaotic. It didn't necessarily lessen my own problems, but it reminded me that there were still places where my mind could be calm. There were still quiet places in the world untouched by human violence and war. Places worth fighting for.

After a while, I got too cold to stay in the tree, so I climbed down, not bothering to transform again. The physical exertion and concentration required were distracting and felt nice anyway. I took my time walking back to the main grass of campus, then finally exited the trees and made my way back to my dorm. There were a few students milling about, but most people seemed to be staying indoors. At least this meant I'd run into fewer people.

By the time I made it to the front of my dorm building, my hands were pale and cold, and my cheeks felt a little raw from the chilly breeze. I shivered and pulled open the door, then made my way quickly past the students in the common area. They had the television on in the background, but most were playing card games and chatting. They gave me an odd look as I passed, but no one said anything to me. I *had* cried for the better part of an hour before passing out in a tree. So . . . yeah. I probably didn't look my best. I shrugged. Nothing I could do about that now.

I stopped short halfway down the hall to my room and squinted at the end of the hall. Someone was slumped on the floor in the shadows in front of my door. I frowned, and walked slowly toward them, hoping my mother hadn't sent someone to apprehend me when I returned to my room. But the breath whooshed out of me as I got close enough to see them. My heart squeezed as though a vice had closed around it.

Gabriel. He was slumped against my door, asleep, phone in hand, his head resting against the doorframe. His hair fell over his face, and I fought the urge to reach out and push the soft looking strands back over his forehead. I bit my lip. How long had he been waiting here? *Why* was he waiting here? He knew he could unlock my door and wait on the much comfier chairs. But he'd chosen not to enter. He'd chosen the cold, hard floor.

I let out an unsteady breath and walked to his side before sliding down the door so I could sit beside him. My shoulder and hip pressed to his, and I tried not to enjoy how warm he was. If we were still friends, I would've placed my icy hands on his neck just to scare him. And get warm. But we weren't still friends. My heart sank.

"Hey," I murmured, nudging his shoulder with mine. I knew he'd probably come here to yell at me for my deception and to end our friendship, but I also knew I deserved to be yelled at. I'd kept a lot from him. There was no point postponing the inevitable any longer, especially when it seemed like he'd waited for me to return for such a long time.

Gabriel stirred, lifting his head from the doorframe, and rubbed his eyes groggily. Then he turned his head in my direction. His eyes widened as he saw me, then softened as he took in my features.

"Terah," he murmured, his voice a little gravely, "you came back."

I bit the inside of my cheek and nodded, bracing myself for his anger to hit me. For the shouting to start. Gabriel lifted his hand and trailed his fingers down my cheek, sorrow filling his expression. My breath caught.

"You've been crying."

My gaze jerked to his, surprised. Why did he care whether I'd been crying or not? Why wasn't he yelling at me?

"It's . . . been a hard day."

Gabriel nodded and wrapped his arm around my shoulders, then pulled me gently into his chest. The gesture was a surprise—filled with a care I hadn't expected. So, naturally, I started crying again. I hid my face against his chest, trying to keep him from noticing, but my tears soaked through his shirt. His fingers rubbed gentle circles into my upper arm, and he rested his head against the top of mine.

"Why aren't you yelling at me?" I finally asked, my face still buried in his shirt.

"Why would I yell at you?" He sounded genuinely surprised.

I lifted my head from his chest and looked at him in confusion. "Because I didn't tell you who my mother was. I kept the information from you even though I knew she was the person who made your life hell. And . . . because I refused to help her and Matt with my power." I wiped my tears on my sleeve, trying to push down the new tears threatening to fall. "It's . . . okay. If you don't want to be friends with me anymore. If you can't forgive me for keeping it from you. And for having her as a mother. I understand."

Gabriel watched me closely for a long moment before reaching forward and catching a tear I hadn't been able to stop against the back of his finger. His expression remained gentle. Not mad. Not even closed off. It was confusing. Not what I'd expected, especially from him.

"I don't hold who your mother is against you," he finally said, leaning back against the door. "That's not something you can control. And she seems to be just as horrible and inconsiderate to you as she is to everyone else." He shook his head disparagingly. "I'm not mad at you for not wanting to help her and Matt, either. They never bothered to think of you as a person, and they didn't respect you. What you told her . . . it was right. You're your own person, and only you get to decide how and if you want to be involved."

I frowned. "But . . . you seemed mad when you found out that we were related. I saw your expression. You . . . closed off from me."

Gabriel sighed and stretched out his legs in front of him on the floor. It seemed like he was trying to find the right words. "I wasn't mad that she was your mother," he finally murmured, not looking at me now. "I was upset because I knew why you hadn't told me before then." A bittersweet smile lifted one side of his mouth. "You didn't trust me enough. You decided our friendship wasn't strong enough to handle the truth. That's what upset me."

I stared at his profile, speechless. This was far different from what I'd expected. I'd never thought Gabriel cared enough about me to be bothered by the absence of a deeper trust or complete honesty. I'd thought he'd mainly befriended me so he wouldn't have to go everywhere alone, not because he particularly cared about me as a person.

Gabriel finally looked at me, and his keen gaze quickly took in my surprise. Understanding lit his eyes, but also sadness. "Do you really think no one cares about you?" The electric blue bored into me, as intense as a light shining directly into my eyes. But I couldn't look away. "Do you not see how you could be genuinely valued by other people? By . . . me?" he added quietly.

I bit the inside of my cheek, trying to push down the threatening tears. No. I couldn't see that. With me, everyone always seemed to have an agenda. Or at the very least, they never cared enough about me to think twice about leaving me behind and moving on with their lives whenever being with me was no longer beneficial. It made it hard to put my trust in others.

I pulled my gaze from his and looked down at the rips in my jeans instead. "I'm sorry I didn't tell you. I thought I'd lose you as a friend. And . . . I didn't want that. Not . . . yet." *Not ever.* I shifted uncomfortably at the admission.

Gabriel smiled, that unfamiliar soft warmth emanating from him again. He reached forward and took my hand. "Holy shit, your hands are like ice." He grabbed both and pressed them between his, rubbing them and trying to get blood flowing back into them. "Where were you?"

I bit the inside of my cheek. "I was, um, in a tree. In the middle of the forest that borders campus."

Gabriel stared at me. "You were . . . in a tree? For the whole time you were gone?"

I nodded. "I, uh, flew to the top of a tree so I could have time to think. And then I fell asleep for a while."

"In a tree . . ." Gabriel raised an eyebrow exasperatedly. He'd completely ignored the fact that I'd disclosed I could fly. "And what if you'd fallen out of the tree while you were sleeping?" His voice had an edge to it, but his hands remained gentle on mine.

I shrugged. "I'm a quick healer?"

Gabriel shook his head, his eyes pressing shut. "You're gonna be the fucking death of me," he murmured under his breath.

I blinked at him, confused, but he just shook his head and smiled wryly. "I'm glad you didn't fall out of the tree. Maybe don't sleep in one next time. Also," he added, a little gruffly, "maybe don't disappear off the face of the earth for hours and turn off your phone. I've been really worried. For all I knew, your mother's cronies could've kidnapped you."

He released my hands and pushed to his feet. "Oof." He stretched his arms over his head and twisted his body, first one way, then the other. "I'm gonna be sore tomorrow." Then he held out his hand and pulled me to my feet. "We should get you under some blankets or maybe get your fireplace going. To fix your ice hands. If you want me to come in, that is," he added, looking a little uncertain.

I placed my hand on the scanner, then pushed open the door. "Of course I want you to come in," I grumbled, grabbing his hand and pulling him behind me. I could almost feel him smile.

I sat in one of the armchairs as Gabriel stripped the top blanket from my bed. He draped it around me before sitting in the chair across from me.

"I wanted to come after you," he finally murmured, staring at the empty fireplace. "Right when you left. But your mother kept me there. She tried to convince me to help change your mind."

I winced. Of course she had. She could never take no for an answer, no matter how firmly it was said.

"I basically told her to fuck off. She . . . doesn't like me." He smiled.

I smiled too, warmth filling my chest. I loved his refusal to defer to her.

"Then she and Matt started arguing. She wanted him to force you to help them, but he said that wouldn't be possible or ethical. She was pretty mad about that. But he did say he'd try his hardest to convince you." Gabriel rolled his eyes.

"Good luck with that," I murmured resentfully. "I'm not going to let him near me for quite a while. Not after everything he's done." My jaw clenched as tension returned to my shoulders. "I can't believe he was reporting on me to the one person he knows I hate most in the world. He knows how much she's hurt me, how little she's cared, and how cruel she's been over the years. How can he claim to care about me while doing that?"

Gabriel let out a long, slow breath. "He does care. But he's also an asshole. He doesn't listen to you the way he should, and he doesn't respect your decisions. Him caring doesn't make up for that."

I nodded slowly. I was starting to realize that myself.

"I don't think I want him to train me anymore," I said quietly, staring at the patterns on the rug. "Not for my transformation and power at least. I don't trust him with it. And I can't trust him not to report on me to her."

Gabriel nodded and ran his hand through his hair, pushing it back over his head. "I can help you with it whenever you need or want me to. And we can use the Academy's library as a resource whenever we need to."

"Thanks. That sounds good. And I can still use my assigned training room to practice, just without him."

I sighed, my stomach clenching. Pushing Matt away like this hurt, even though it was the safest way forward. Anger ignited in my chest. *He'd* put us in this position. His choices were forcing me into mine.

"By the way," I finally murmured, staring into the empty fireplace grate, "I'm a Guardian." I didn't want any more lies or large secrets between us. I didn't want to give him any more reasons to leave in the future.

In my periphery, I saw Gabriel look up, surprised. He clearly hadn't expected me to be this forthcoming.

"Not a regular Guardian, though. I don't seem to be either Light or Dark. I'm something in the middle. That's why my power is purple."

When I finally looked at him, I saw him nodding, thoughtfully. "That's interesting. I've never heard of a Neutral Guardian before."

"Me neither." I grimaced. "Even Divines with one Light and one Dark Guardian parent turn out either one or the other, not something in between. That's why everyone is so weird and suspicious about my transformation. I don't look like anything they've ever seen. I share similar abilities, but mine tend to look a little different or burn a little hotter. Everything is just a little . . . off. Different. Darker. Plus, these weird extra abilities." I shrugged. "That's why I don't like to transform in front of other people unless I have to. Everyone always freaks out and avoids me."

Gabriel nodded slowly. To my surprise, I didn't see any disgust or wariness there. Just curiosity and commiseration.

"I understand where you're coming from." He sat back in his chair and crossed his arms over his chest. "I really do. I feel similarly a lot of the time about mine. But honestly, your transformation sounds really cool." The corner of his mouth pulled up. "I'd like to see it someday, if you ever want to share."

I bit the inside of my cheek. I'd love for him to react differently to it than everyone else. I just wasn't sure that, when he actually saw it, he'd be able to respond with anything other than fear.

"Since you finally told me about yours, I might as well tell you about mine." A smirk played across his lips, but the smile reached his eyes. He looked . . . almost cheerful. As though he'd been waiting for this conversation for a while. "I'm a Blessed."

I smiled. "I did guess that, but I wasn't sure."

"I know. The color of my power pretty much gave me away." He smiled and shook his head. "My mother is a Light Guardian, but my father is a Blessed, so my sister got the Guardian power, and I ended up with the Blessed." He shrugged. "But even for a Blessed, my transformation is unusual. When I change, I keep my shape, but my skin and all my features alter. I look . . . almost like a shadow. I become stronger, lighter, and I can jump far higher. I'm also a bit studier, so it's harder to injure me. But most significantly, I can make parts of myself, or my entire body, dematerialize. You can still see me, but if you try to touch me, you'll go straight through."

My mouth dropped open. I'd never heard of Blessed powers manifesting in that way. It sounded . . . really cool.

"I'm sure you can see how much that can help during battle. I can make my hand solid enough to hold a weapon, but the rest of me can be dematerialized and essentially untouchable. I can fight with minimal to no injury."

"That's amazing," I whispered, my eyes wide. "I've never heard of abilities like that."

Gabriel smiled, clearly pleased I wasn't shrinking away from him. "That's why people think it's weird. To them, my transformation seems dark—not as tied to natural elements as most other Blessed. Though, if I had to pick, I'd say mine connects to air and wind more than anything else. But I look different, so people inherently distrust my power and me. That's why I don't transform much in front of other people."

I sighed and nodded sympathetically. This we had in common. And it was bullshit.

"Your transformation sounds incredible, though." I pulled the blanket more tightly around me. "People really are ignorant about transformations, aren't they?"

Gabriel's shoulders shook in a silent laugh. "Seems like it. People will always fear what they don't understand."

"Well, I'd like to see your transformation someday too. If you ever want to share it."

Gabriel's smile lit up his face and seemed to turn his eyes a slightly deeper shade of blue. My heart skipped a beat.

"Just imagine the terror we'd create if we showed up somewhere both transformed." I laughed, trying to ignore the odd sensation.

Gabriel chuckled. "If we ever want to clear a room . . ."

"Next time the lounge is super crowded, we'll know what to do." I grinned, feeling lighter than I had in a while. Having someone understand and validate my feelings instead of pushing past them, helped more than I'd expected it to. And this was the first time that I'd been able to laugh or joke about the exclusion that'd defined my life. It'd always felt too heavy and painful to do so before. It felt like growth, somehow.

"Well," Gabriel said ruffling his hair absently, "since we've finished disclosing our deep, dark secrets, want popcorn and a movie?"

I smiled and nodded. "That sounds perfect."

A loud knock on my door pierced through the calm of the movie credit music. Gabriel and I glanced at each other uncertainly, and I pushed slowly from the bed. We both hoped it wasn't my mother.

I pulled open the door, just enough to see out of it. Matt was standing there, his eyes wide with worry. My jaw clenched and my insides went cold. I had zero desire to see or talk to him. I slammed the door in his face.

"Terah, wait!" I heard his fist slam against the door as he swore.

I turned and gave Gabriel an exasperated look. I couldn't believe Matt was trying to talk to me so soon after betraying my trust. Gabriel's eyebrows rose, but he kept his expression carefully blank.

"Please," Matt called through the door. "I just want to talk to you for a second. I promise it won't take long."

A frustrated growl rose from my throat as I pulled open the door again. "I don't want to talk to you. I'm really fucking mad at you. You've consistently ignored my thoughts and wants ever since I came to the Academy, and you've let me down in a variety of ways since then. You're not being a good friend, Matt. Let alone a good anything else."

Matt's face had furrowed with sadness, and I could see the guilt nagging at him. It was a sad enough sight that it made me want to reach out and comfort him. But I clenched my fists at my sides instead. I couldn't give in this time. If I did, he'd never take my boundaries seriously. And he needed to if we were still going to be friends.

"I'm sorry," he murmured. "I know I've failed you. I do." He ran his hands desperately through his hair. "But I don't want to lose you. Please, give me another chance to make this right. Please."

I frowned, shaking my head slowly. "I don't think I can do that right away. Not this time. I need time to process everything enough to move forward. And I need time to forgive you, because I can't right now."

Matt opened his mouth to say something, but nothing came out. He looked both stunned and dejected.

"I'm also not going to train one-on-one with you anymore. Not for a while, at least. I'll work on my transformation myself and with other help."

This propelled Matt past his speechlessness. "That's not safe," he gritted out through clenched teeth. "I can't let you do that."

"You don't have a choice," I said sharply. "It's my decision, and I *will* do it, without your help. It doesn't feel safe to train with you anymore. Can't you see that? I won't let you and my mother use me. I won't let you report on me again."

Matt opened his mouth to argue, but I cut him off.

"It's not negotiable, Matt. I've decided. Do you have anything else to say to me, or can I get back to my night?"

Matt's gaze sharpened with anger, but I could see the sadness underneath. He pressed his eyes closed and took a deep, slow breath. "I just wanted to apologize." He opened his eyes and met my gaze again, his imploring. "I wanted to let you know that I care about you. Deeply. More than I care about anyone else. And I don't want you to forget that, even though I've messed up."

My stomach clenched. "How you feel about me doesn't excuse your actions. In fact, your actions tend to contradict your claim that you feel so deeply for me. You've used me. Ignored my wishes and boundaries. Betrayed my trust."

I shook my head sadly. This wasn't how I wanted things to be between us. I missed the days when he'd been my source of comfort and stability. But he was quickly removing himself from that position in my life.

"You have no idea how much I wish I could lean on you while all of this is happening," I added quietly. "But I can't right now. I have to respect my needs and choices, even if no one else will. And doing that means I need some distance from you for a while. If you care, you'll give me that space. And if you care, you'll change how you treat me."

Matt bit his lip, and I thought I saw a sheen of tears growing in his eyes. But he looked down quickly. Finally, he nodded.

"Okay." He sounded miserable. "I'll give you some space. And I'll try to regain your trust. I'll be better, Terah. I promise."

He reached for me, his fingers trembling. But he couldn't agree to give me space while trying to pull me closer. He already wasn't adhering to what I'd asked from him. I stepped away, the vault around my heart closing tightly.

"Goodnight Matt." I closed the door on his devastated face, trying to ignore the sinking in my chest.

8

MEMORIES

OCTOBER PASSED AND ICY WINDS SWIRLED AROUND CAMPUS, blowing the leaves from the trees and seeping through the buildings. The stone walls and floors of our dorms became colder, the sky cloudier, and snow seemed imminent. I was extremely glad my room had a fireplace. While the buildings on campus had been upgraded and renovated over the years, nothing could take away the chill that leaked through the old stone construction. Hallways and classrooms were drafty, and most of the common areas relied on fireplaces for warmth. I'd made sure to keep my room stocked with enough firewood to keep my fireplace going all night, and Gabriel and I spent most of our free time huddled around it.

By the last week of October, things had gotten frigid, and Gabriel and I walked toward the main classroom building huddled in heavy jackets and smoking with chilled fingers. We were more tired than usual this week. Our teachers had started piling on homework in anticipation of exams in a few weeks, and our Divine Power 101 class had begun practicing larger and more complex uses of our powers, demanding much more energy from us. The combination had left most first years extremely drained and grumpy.

"Would it kill them to let us sleep in every once in a while?" Gabriel grumbled. He took a drag of his cigarette, then exhaled, the smoke mixing with the steam that was now visible every time we breathed.

I released smoke through my nose. "Probably. Matt and Luke are hardasses about our training, so they'd definitely never let us have a day off."

Gabriel scowled and inhaled deeply from his cigarette as we rounded the corner of the curving path that led to the front of the main classroom building. I was surprised to see the president standing outside the front door, gesturing to the buildings around her as she spoke to what appeared to be a student. A *new* student who clearly didn't know what every building was. A ripple of unease traveled through me as I looked at the newcomer's back. They looked . . . strangely familiar. Caramel-colored hair that reached the top of their shoulders, an athletic, medium-heighted build, and a posture that exuded detached coolness. My steps slowed as fear slid through me.

Oh gods, please let it not be him.

It couldn't be. It wouldn't make sense for him to be here. He'd never wanted to attend the Academy. His plan had always been to join the warrior faction as soon as he came of age. But he turned slightly, and I saw his face. Caleb. It *was* him. Older and broader than before, but definitely him. *Shit.*

I jerked to a stop, then spun around and started walking in the opposite direction. Nope, not today. I wasn't ready for this right now. I was only just getting a handle on myself in a new environment. I was just starting to figure out who I could be if I opened up a little more to the people and situations around me. I didn't need him coming here and messing everything up. And I didn't want to revert to blocking off my emotions again just to survive his presence.

I pulled out my phone as I continued walking in the opposite direction, my heart pounding wildly. Then I pulled up my texts from Matt for the first time in several weeks and started typing.

"Caleb seems to have transferred in," I wrote. "I believe he's being shown to our training group by the president. I can't deal with that today. Sorry, but I'm gonna be skipping. Gabriel might too." I hit send, then pocketed my phone again.

Gabriel caught up with me, clearly confused. He glanced over his shoulder at Caleb and the president again before looking at me. "What's wrong?" He lengthened his stride, trying to keep up with my hurried footsteps for the first time ever. I was practically jogging across the frosty ground.

"I know that new student." I tossed my cigarette and pulled my jacket more closely around me. "I have zero desire to interact with him today or really ever again, so I'm not going to training today. I'm ninety-eight percent sure the president was showing him to our training group."

Gabriel frowned but kept pace with me. "Who is he? What did he do? Is he from Dagmar?"

I shook my head. "He's not from Dagmar. He lived there, though, for about a year. Then he left to live gods know where."

I felt a buzz from my phone and pulled it out again.

"Okay," Matt wrote. "I'll look into it, and we can talk later. Sorry you had to see him again."

I shoved my phone back in my pocket and grabbed another cigarette, lighting it quickly and inhaling deeply from it. Gabriel watched me, worry furrowing his brow.

"I let Matt know that I'm not going today, and I said you weren't sure if you'd go. You can if you want. You don't have to skip just because I'm skipping."

"I'm not going if you're not. Besides, who would I train with? I don't want to train with Matt, and I'm certainly not training with this new guy. Not when he's got you this wound-up." He watched me closely, clearly trying to discern what I was feeling.

I faced forward and grimaced, walking a little faster. I hated that I was, in fact, wound-up at all. It'd been over three years since I'd seen Caleb. I was no longer a young and vulnerable teenager. And I'd gotten over him and what he'd done. Mostly. But seeing him had been a shock, and I'd reacted more than I thought I would. I'd never thought I'd see him again. That was what he'd wanted, after all. I never thought he'd come to the Academy. I never thought I'd *have* to deal with him in person again.

I finished my second cigarette as we reached my dorm, and I pushed open the front door, sighing in relief as the warmer air inside reached out to envelop me. It was too damn cold. I grabbed an apple that was sitting in a bowl in the common area, then headed for my room, Gabriel following silently behind me. When we got inside, I pulled off my jacket and bag, and started building a fire. If we were going to barricade ourselves in my room for the morning, we might as well be warm.

I finally sank into one of the armchairs and bit into the apple. Gabriel sat across from me, sinking back into the chair and studying me silently. He wasn't demanding an explanation—he wasn't demanding anything. Instead, he simply waited, more patient than I'd ever be, for me to say whatever I wanted to say. I sighed, sinking back in my chair.

"That guy's name is Caleb. He moved to Dagmar right around the time Matt left to come to the Academy."

I paused to take another bite of the apple. Gabriel nodded slowly, waiting for more.

"As much as I hate to admit it, I was pretty devastated when Matt left. I didn't have any other friends, and most people steered clear of me because of my transformation. But Caleb didn't. I mean, he wasn't a fan of my transformation or anything, but he didn't avoid me because of it."

I stared into the lively flames, remembering that time. A time I'd actively worked to not think about over the years.

"Caleb was . . . funny. Confident. Charming. A really good fighter. Better than me. And he chose to train with me and teach me how to fight better. He pushed me to improve. But he also spent time with me outside of training, which no one besides Matt had ever done. We quickly became friends. Caleb was a year older than me and was much more assertive and confident. He made it clear that he wanted to be more than friends, and I was so swept up in his presence and his enthusiasm for me, and so lonely from Matt's absence and Dagmar's shittiness, that I let myself fall for him pretty quickly."

I grimaced and took another bite of apple, chewing slowly. Gabriel's eyebrows rose slightly, but he didn't say anything. He just waited.

"He was my first boyfriend." I scowled. "My first a lot of things. We were together for close to a year. And I gave him . . . everything. All my thoughts, all my hopes and dreams, all my damage and despair, all my affection and love. And he gave me those things in return. It was the least lonely I'd ever felt. But obviously, things didn't work out so well."

I shrugged. Gabriel crossed his arms loosely over his chest and watched me as I fidgeted in my chair.

"It was almost a year after he moved to Dagmar that he planned this romantic day for us." I lowered my hand with the apple to my lap, memories filling me again. "It was just after my birthday, and we were given a rare day off to do whatever we wanted. He made a makeshift tent in the forest that bordered town, and brought food, champagne, and blankets there so we could spend the day together. We talked, drank champagne, made out, and, um . . . did more. It was the first time I'd ever trusted anyone with myself like that."

My cheeks heated. I hated sharing this part, but it mattered for him to fully understand my devastation.

"Afterward, he just held me and told me over and over that he loved me." I stared into the flames, refusing to meet Gabriel's gaze. I couldn't. Not right now. "He said he'd never loved anyone romantically before, but that he hadn't been able to help falling in love with me." I rolled my eyes. "Of course, I was completely infatuated and told him I loved him too. And I meant it. He'd opened me up and cared for me in ways I hadn't thought were possible. In ways no one else had ever cared for me. So of course I loved him."

I shook my head and let out a slow sigh.

"Then the sirens started blaring through town. Dagmar was under attack on the day that a lot of the adult soldiers were gone getting supplies, visiting family, and taking time off. We had so few of those days that it usually wasn't a problem. But because of that, there was only a small group of soldiers in place to protect the plane rip. Caleb got dressed quickly and begged me to stay in the tent and not fight. He said he didn't want to have to worry about me while he fought. He said he couldn't bear the thought of me getting hurt. I'd never seen him look so worried and desperate, so I agreed to stay behind, even though I didn't want to. And then he ran off to fight."

I glanced at Gabriel. There was an expression there that I couldn't quite identify. But he didn't seem to be judging me.

"I stayed there for maybe five minutes before ignoring his request. After all, I was a trained soldier, and I knew it was my job to fight. With so few soldiers in town, they needed me. I couldn't just never fight again because it worried him. So I got dressed and ran toward town.

"When I got there," my voice wavered slightly at the memory, so I stopped and took a slow breath. "The destruction was overwhelming. Half of Dagmar was destroyed. Many unsuspecting Guardians had been killed. And the Demon that was attacking was huge. There were so few left in town to fight it, and so few of those who were there were still alive. I transformed immediately and joined the fight next to Caleb and a handful of other Guardians. Caleb was pretty unhappy to see me there, but it was clear that they needed all of us, so he didn't fight me on it.

"A couple Guardians died while we fought. They were young— around my age at the time. No more than fifteen or sixteen. But brave. Determined. Unfortunately, that didn't save them. They were . . . torn apart by the Demon. There was blood everywhere." My chest felt more and more hollow as I remembered the scenes from that day. "And we had to ignore their brutal deaths and keep fighting. We had to stop the Demon from destroying the rest of town and getting to the surrounding Normal towns.

"We fought harder than we ever had. We sliced at it, burned it, stabbed it, tried to incapacitate it however we could. But it used the destroyed buildings as weapons against us. It picked up pieces of wood, glass, and metal, and tried to kill us with them. Caleb got a pretty bad gash across his chest, and another Guardian was impaled with a jagged metal pipe. But we finally started getting the upper hand. We took turns distracting it while each of us tried to behead it. When it was finally my turn, I gathered all the power I had left and pushed it into my sword, then flew behind it to attack. But it knew what we were doing, and it spun around and ran me partially through with a sharp wooden beam."

I touched my stomach lightly, wincing at the memory. Remembering the pain. Gabriel shifted in his chair. I glanced at him and saw tension tightening his limbs. He looked upset.

I smiled a little. "Obviously, I survived." There was no point in him stressing about it now. It'd happened years ago. "Anyway, I used the last bit of my strength to strike the Demon across the neck with my charged sword. And fortunately, the strike plus my power was enough to behead it. But at that point, I'd been transformed for too long and used all my power. I fell out of my transformation, all the way to the ground, with the wooden beam still mostly through me. I had nothing left to heal myself, so I started dying.

"Caleb landed and ran over to me. He grabbed me and yelled and cried, but I passed out before I understood what he was saying. But obviously his fear had come true. To him, I'd ignored his request to stay behind at the cost of my life. As though I'd had any other choice," I grumbled. Long-buried annoyance sparked to life in my chest, and I clenched my jaw.

"I woke up the next day in the medical building and was told that a bunch of Guardians had returned and pooled their powers to heal me. It was the only reason I'd survived. But I was still incredibly weak. Caleb came to see me right after I regained consciousness, but he looked . . . different. His face looked gaunt and pale, and his eyes were cold and almost empty looking. It was . . . frightening to see him like that. He told me in this dead, flat voice that he knew it was my job to fight, and he knew he couldn't stop me from fighting in the future, but that he couldn't live with that. He said this was why he'd never allowed himself to love before.

He said falling in love with me had been a giant mistake." I bit the inside of my cheek, willing the memory not to sting.

"He said seeing me almost die had ripped him apart, and that he wasn't willing to go through that again. Not for anyone. Not even for me. He said caring for me hurt him too much. That it made him weak and distracted him from what was important. It was a burden he didn't want or need, and it'd hold him back. So, to fix all this, to protect himself, he said he was leaving. Immediately. He was going to a different town, as far away as possible, to leave me and his feelings for me behind. He said he wouldn't write. He wouldn't visit. If he was lucky, he'd forget about me quickly. He'd never have to feel that way again. Then he gave me this cold, closed off look, and turned and left me there, barely conscious on a medical bed. He grabbed the bag he'd already packed, and just walked out of Dagmar. He never came back. That was the last time I saw him."

I glanced at Gabriel again and saw a mixture of shock and anger on his face.

"Caleb left me . . . broken," I continued quietly, glancing away. "All I could think about was that I'd been abandoned again—by Matt, my mother, him. He'd left me alone to deal with the physical pain from the injury, and the emotional pain from losing every person I'd ever cared about. For months, I returned to the tent in the woods and cried and cried, clinging to my memory of him. Trying to remember that he'd been real and had, at one point, cared about me. That I hadn't just imagined him. He was the one who'd taught me to love, but he was also the one who'd taught me that love hurts. That loving and trusting people could destroy me, and that it wasn't worth it.

"I closed off after that day and tried to kill that part of myself. I became more self-sufficient, but I also became colder and shoved down all my emotions. I never cried after that. Not until recently. And I never let anyone in like that again. He's the main reason why I've never let any relationships or hook-ups since then be serious. I'm only now trying to figure out whether that was the right reaction to what happened. I'm only now trying to connect with myself again. *Feel* again, just a little."

Gabriel shook his head slowly, anger winning out over the stunned horror. "He was a fucking coward." His voice was quiet, but there was a dangerous edge to it. "He ripped you apart to avoid being ripped apart himself. He left you while you were injured and punished you for doing what you were trained to do. What you *had* to do. You probably saved his life and the lives of the other Guardians that day, and he left you for it.

That's not love." His fists clenched on either side of his legs. "He's . . . the worst kind of person. Selfish and cruel."

My smile was bittersweet as I met and held his gaze. He was . . . angry on my behalf. "It took me a while to get there, but I agree with you." I tossed the remainder of the apple into the fire and watched it sizzle and blacken. "Despite my reaction to him this morning, I've mostly gotten over it. It's been over three years, and I've grown a lot as a person. I definitely don't have feelings for him anymore, but I guess I never thought I'd see him again, especially without warning. It caught me off guard and was a bit too much for morning-me to handle." My smile broadened slightly.

Gabriel nodded and finally unclenched his fists. "I understand." He seemed to be wrestling with a plethora of emotions, but he also seemed to be trying to reign himself in and not dump all his thoughts and feelings onto me at once. "And . . . Matt knows?"

I nodded. "I wrote to him after Caleb left and told him everything. I was too torn apart to keep it to myself. And I'd desperately hoped Matt would come back and visit me if I told him how much I was hurting. But he was too busy with school to come back."

"Yet another time he's failed you," Gabriel murmured, his voice dark with anger.

I shrugged noncommittally, but it was hard not to agree with him, at least a little. "I just wish Caleb wasn't here," I finally murmured, staring into the dancing tendrils of flame. "I don't like the reminder that I'm so easy to leave. That my love is inconsequential compared to other people's needs and agendas." I sighed. "I'm three for three on the people I've loved leaving me behind. It's hard not to feel like that's what'll always happen."

Gabriel leaned forward and took one of my hands in his. My gaze jerked to his, surprised. His eyes looked stormy, but warm. Intense and intriguing. I couldn't look away. Or breathe.

"Just because they failed you, doesn't mean everyone will. The people who are worth it are the people who will stay."

My cheeks heated as he held my gaze.

"I don't know if people like that exist," I whispered. "I don't know if anyone will ever think I'm worth that." I swallowed, the admission stinging.

"I *know* people like that exist," he murmured, rubbing the back of my hand with his thumb. "And you *are* worth that."

"You're worth everything."

My cheeks burned as the breath caught in my throat. The thought was silent—he clearly hadn't meant for me to hear it. But his gaze remained steady on mine. For once, he wasn't hiding himself or his feelings. My stomach clenched on a feeling that was akin to agony. Why did he have to say such perfect things?

"Anyway," he murmured, slowly releasing my hand and sitting back in his chair, as though he wanted to give me some space, "thanks for telling me all of that. It can't be easy to talk about."

"It's not, but it was nice to get outside validation that I wasn't the one in the wrong. That leaving me like that wasn't normal or okay."

Gabriel shook his head, crossing his arms over his chest. "It was neither. He's an ass, and I'm honestly surprised you didn't just walk up to him and punch him in the face. Hell, *I* want to punch him in the face."

I smiled. "Well, if he gets in my way during training, I absolutely will."

Gabriel smiled. "Good."

I returned to training the next day, Gabriel at my side. I'd dressed to kill—metaphorically speaking—in all black, curve-hugging clothes with my heeled combat boots and my sharpest eyeliner. I wanted Caleb to see that he hadn't broken me. I wanted to disarm him. After all, *he* was the one who'd run away, not me.

Gabriel slung his arm across my shoulders as we pushed through the door to the training room. I glanced up at him, surprised, but his gaze was aimed forward, looking at the people already congregating in the room. His stance was . . . protective. He didn't want me to face this situation alone. I smiled a little, my chest seeming to warm from the inside at this visible sign of his care. Some of the tension eased from my shoulders, and the anxiety bubbling in my stomach seemed to calm to a low simmer.

We started across the room, and my eyes immediately zeroed in on Caleb. He'd already changed and was stretching. He turned as he noticed our movement and froze in his tracks as his eyes landed on me. His mouth fell open as shock washed over him, and he visibly paled. I raised my chin and unflinchingly met his gaze, my own as bored and cold as I could make it.

Caleb's mouth snapped shut as his eyes slowly roamed over me before landing on my face. Then his gaze flicked to Gabriel and narrowed slightly. He straightened slowly, and a cold, distant mask settled over his face. His shoulders and jaw stiffened, and he turned purposefully away from me.

I released a small breath as we walked the rest of the way across the room to the locker rooms, Gabriel's arm still around my shoulders. Gabriel paused as we reached the doors and glanced behind me. He smirked.

"He's not doing a good job of ignoring you," he murmured in my ear.

"Good," I grumbled. "I want him to suffer at least a little for what he did."

Gabriel chuckled, his eyes meeting mine. "Same." He glanced quickly behind me again, before a slow smirk spread across his face. "To make him jealous," he murmured, leaning toward me. Then he brushed his lips across my cheek, close, so close, to the corner of my mouth. My breath stalled in my lungs, and my heart leapt before hammering wildly in my chest. Which was . . . odd.

"At least he won't think you're pining over him now," Gabriel murmured, pulling away from me slightly. But as he looked down at me, I saw uncertainty overshadowing his usual confidence. I wondered what he was uncertain about.

I pulled myself together and tried to will my cheeks not to burn. "I hope you're right." Our gazes held for a long moment, as though neither of us could look away. I wasn't sure what made me do it—Caleb's presence, or Gabriel's uncharacteristic uncertainty—but I reached up and ran my forefinger gently across his chin, right below his bottom lip. *I'm just playing along. That's all this is.*

Gabriel's gaze heated for a moment, before he stepped away from me, a carefully neutral expression descending over his face again. "See you in a couple minutes." He flashed me a quick grin, then disappeared into the locker room. I took a deep breath and pushed open the door to mine.

When I emerged, Gabriel was waiting for me, and we walked back to our usual spots on the mat. Matt had finally appeared, and he glanced at me nervously as I approached. I could tell he was worried about how Caleb's closeness would affect me. I smiled a little at Matt, trying to reassure him. I wouldn't give Caleb the power to impact me like that anymore. Matt smiled back, clearly happy that, despite the stress of the current situation, I wasn't keeping as much distance from him anymore. Caleb reappearing had kind of forced my hand on that.

Luke assigned us some drills, then some hand-to-hand combat fights with our partners. Gabriel and I trained hard, ignoring Caleb on the other side of the room who was training with Matt for the day. Matt had purposefully situated them as far away from us as possible, for which I was grateful.

In the last half hour of training, Luke decided to have us pair up with people we didn't usually train with for one-on-one battles in front of the rest of the class. I immediately asked one of the guys training next to us if I could be his partner, and Gabriel asked the other guy. At least I could ensure that I wasn't paired with Caleb, though I was sure Matt would've tried to intervene if that'd happened.

Gabriel's pair went first, and I was happy to see he held his own much more easily against them than he had at the beginning of the semester. He'd gotten stronger, quicker, and had gained a lot of endurance over the past few months. I smiled, pride welling in my chest as I watched them. As his training partner, I'd experienced his improvements firsthand, but I was happy that the rest of the group was getting to see it as well. Gabriel's quick learning had forced me to push myself hard to keep beating him. I'd gotten stronger and faster as a result of training with him.

Gabriel eventually won his fight, and I clapped enthusiastically with the rest of the room. I glanced in Caleb's direction and saw him eyeing Gabriel warily. I knew Caleb well enough to know that he felt threatened by him. Luke called David and me forward next.

"Good job," I whispered to Gabriel as he passed. Gabriel smiled and squeezed my hand.

David and I lined up on the mat across from each other. I took a deep breath and cleared my mind. It didn't matter that Caleb was here. I was a soldier. I'd faced countless Demons and countless horrifying situations, and I'd do what needed to be done regardless of who was watching or how I felt. Fiery determination rushed through me, and all doubt left me. I smiled at David—a deadly smile—and saw a flicker of nervousness in his eyes. The psychological battle was no less important than the physical one, and I had the upper hand.

Luke blew the whistle, and we circled each other. David lunged at me, and I easily dodged him, then tripped him with my foot as he passed. He recovered fairly quickly and lunged at me, grabbing me around the waist, and throwing me to the mat. I immediately kicked up into his stomach, sending him reeling backward. I jumped to my feet and landed a forceful kick to the side of his ribs. He managed to grab my arm, but I spun into his chest and heaved him over my shoulder, propelling him into the mat.

"Oy," Luke called from the sidelines. David and I glanced at him.

Luke threw each of us a practice sword. "To make things more interesting." He smiled, good-humoredly.

David pushed to his feet, and we transitioned into a fierce sword battle. Our wooden swords clashed with speed and power. David was good. Very good. He'd been training in this group for two years. But I could tell he got slower as he got more tired. So I tried to use that to my advantage. I pushed him into elaborate sword and footwork passages, forced him to use up a lot of his strength as I pressed toward him with my sword, and winded him as I added hand-to-hand combat elements to our fight. Finally, after what felt like at least ten minutes of fighting, I saw an opening. The barest of pauses from David. But it was enough. I swung my sword around his and yanked up, disarming him before he could register what was happening. Then I lunged at him low, grabbing him around his hips and propelling him off his feet. As his back hit the mat, I jammed my sword point against his chest, right over his heart.

Luke blew the whistle, and I dropped my sword and pushed to my feet. I smiled at David and extended my hand, then pulled him to his feet.

"Nice job," Luke said, collecting our practice swords. "Both of you. And I'm pleased with your progress, Terah. You and Gabriel seem to be pushing each other to improve quickly." I nodded at him in thanks, then returned to Gabriel's side. I avoided Caleb's gaze, but glanced at Matt. He looked proud.

"That was amazing," Gabriel murmured as the next pair got ready for their fight. "You should be proud of that."

I smiled. I was. Caleb had always been an amazing fighter, but a small part of me hoped I'd surpassed him. I wasn't sure, though. As a fighter, Caleb was ruthless and to the point. I'd be surprised if that'd changed.

We watched several more groups go before Caleb stepped forward with the guy that Gabriel and I had fought in our training group trials. I winced. I'd beaten this guy without too much effort. Caleb would slaughter him.

"They're going to be sending him home in a coffin," I whispered to Gabriel. "Caleb was far better than him even when I knew him in Dagmar. And he was never good at pulling his punches."

Gabriel's brow furrowed. "I'm sure either Luke or Matt will stop it if it gets out of hand." But he glanced at Caleb's cold, deadly expression, and I knew he wasn't sure.

Luke blew the whistle, and Caleb's opponent immediately threw a punch at his face. But Caleb caught his fist before it could make contact, then twisted his opponent's arm until his opponent let out a yell of pain. I grabbed Gabriel's arm, tense. Caleb was already using unnecessary force for a training exercise, especially so early in the fight.

Caleb punched his opponent in the stomach twice—hard—then released him. To his credit, his opponent recovered much quicker than I would've expected from Caleb's use of force. He turned on Caleb, a growl of frustrated anger rumbling out of him. But Caleb's expression remained cold. Dispassionate. Almost lifeless. It sent a shiver of apprehension through me. Caleb let his opponent run at him again, then dodged at the last minute, and twisted around, weaving his leg through his opponent's, unbalancing him. Then he grabbed him around the hips and propelled him to the ground. Caleb leapt after him and slammed his knee forcefully against his opponent's sternum. Before his opponent could react, Caleb wrapped his hands around his throat and started choking him. In earnest.

My grip on Gabriel's arm tightened.

"I yield," his opponent gasped, barely able to form the words. But Caleb didn't let go. His hands seemed to tighten further. Luke blew his whistle, and Matt shouted at Caleb to end the match, but Caleb ignored them. He had a wild look in his eyes. Dark and murderous. It wasn't a look I'd seen there before.

"He's going to kill him," I murmured. Gabriel looked down at me, his eyes wide with astonished fear.

Luke blew the whistle and began moving forward. But something overtook me. My blood pounded in my ears as I watched Caleb. I released Gabriel and took a few steps forward. Then I was running. I could see his opponent's face turning a deep purple, and his legs were thrashing. If someone didn't do something, he'd die. So I decided to do something.

I slammed into Caleb's side with as much force as I could muster, managing to knock him off the other student and to the floor. Matt ran forward and dragged the other student out of the way as I landed on top of Caleb and restrained him. Caleb's face went white with shock, but the cold, murderous look soon returned.

"You," he whispered furiously.

"Me," I replied, my voice steady. Then I smiled slowly at him. "What are you gonna do about it?"

Caleb's eyes narrowed with fury, and he shoved me away from him then kicked me hard in the stomach, throwing me backward off him and onto the mat. I was right: he still didn't pull his punches. Or kicks. I'd have a wicked bruise. But I rolled quickly to my feet, as he did, ignoring the pain. I knew better than to attack him head on, so I feinted hard to the right, misleading his block, then attacked him lightning fast from the left. I managed to land two solid punches, one to his rib cage, and one to his stomach, forcing the air from his lungs. Then I grabbed him and threw all my weight at him, propelling him back down to the mat. As soon as he hit the ground, I straddled him and surrounded his neck with my hands as he'd done to his opponent. I wouldn't kill him, but I *would* force him to surrender.

"Yield," I commanded firmly.

"Like. Hell." Caleb gasped. He twisted his body under mine with all his strength and toppled me off him. Then he straddled me and began choking me. But that was a mistake. I, unlike his original opponent, knew numerous ways to get out of a hold like this. And I, unlike his original opponent, could keep a calm head about me, even while being strangled.

Since Caleb's hands were busy on my neck, I brought my hand up and smashed his nose up and back. I was pleased when I heard it crack. I'd broken his nose. Blood spurted out, coating the front of my shirt as Caleb swore, blinking in pain. His grip on me loosened, just a little. But it was enough. I punched his arm hard in the elbow, causing it to bend, then rolled with as much force as I could manage, dumping him off me. Then I pinned him down and exerted pressure on his broken nose. Caleb grunted in pain. I closed one hand around his neck as I continued pushing on his broken nose.

"Yield!" I yelled, panting. My hands were covered in his blood. Matt and Luke both started forward but stopped when I glared at them.

"*Let me finish this.*"

Matt nodded, holding Luke back with a hand on his arm.

Caleb scrambled, punching my arms and sides, trying to roll over. But I ignored the blows and exerted more pressure on his nose and neck. The pain had to be mind-melting by now.

"Yield!" I yelled again.

Caleb let out a roar of pain and fury, but there was no way for him to escape. I'd beaten him.

"Fine!" he finally yelled. "I yield!"

Matt and Luke rushed forward as I climbed off Caleb. I looked down at his bloody face and gave him a cold, hard look.

"I would've expected better from you after all these years," I murmured. "But I guess leaving didn't do you as much good as it did me." I smirked at him, then walked away, not looking at him again.

Luke grabbed Caleb and dragged him to his office. Fighting with the intent to seriously injure or kill one's opponent was not allowed at the Academy. I'd be surprised if he wasn't expelled for that. Matt knelt next to Caleb's original opponent and healed the strangulation bruises from around his neck.

"Don't worry," he murmured. "Luke will make sure the administration knows what he did. He'll face repercussions."

Gabriel beamed at me as I walked back over to him. "That was fucking badass!" He pulled me into a hug, ignoring the blood on my shirt. "You broke his nose! And you beat him! This is . . . a great day."

I couldn't help grinning back. It *had* felt great to best Caleb at what he took the most pride in. And he'd been totally out of line. I had no idea where he'd been living these past few years, but it certainly hadn't been a good influence on him.

Matt dismissed the class a little early, then walked over to Gabriel and me. He shook his head and blew out a frustrated breath.

"That was wild." He rubbed his hand through his cropped hair. "I can't believe he went berserk on another student like that. Thanks for stepping in, by the way," he added, meeting my gaze. "You shouldn't have had to, of course. Luke or I should've gotten to him sooner, but I think we were both in shock."

I shrugged. "It's fine. It was nice to be able to beat him. Granted, using some of his own dirty methods. But I figured, since he tried to kill another student, you and Luke wouldn't get too mad about a broken nose. Especially since he's a quick healer."

"Not mad at all. Seems like it was the only way to snap him out of his murder trance." Matt reached forward and touched the bruises on my neck, his eyes filling with anger.

"Not as bad as this one." I raised the front of my shirt to show them the deep, boot-shaped bruise that'd formed there. Matt and Gabriel both winced.

"Let me heal it for you," Matt murmured, reaching for me.

I dropped my shirt and shook my head. "No need. The bruises will be gone in a few minutes. I'm more concerned about getting that asshole's blood off me." I gestured at my shirt and held up my hands.

Matt nodded slowly, lowering his arms. But he didn't look happy about it.

"Did you get any information about why he's here?" I asked, changing the subject.

Matt sighed. "It seems like Serafina put out a call to a handful of border towns, asking them to send people—good fighters that are close in age to Academy students. She wants to make sure that, if there's another attack, there are enough people here that are used to fighting Demons, to defend the school and students."

I gaped at him as Gabriel swore under his breath.

"But . . . she's treating the Academy like a border town! She can't do that. The Academy is neutral territory."

Matt grimaced. "Believe me, the administration is extremely unhappy about it, but Serafina pulled rank and cited the well-being of the students as her reason. It's becoming clearer that she's using the attack to create another front in the war."

I raised my eyebrows at Matt. I was surprised to hear him talk about my mother like this. Usually, he was loyal to her to a fault.

Matt rubbed his neck, self-consciously. "I've been thinking a lot about what you said—what you both said—at the meeting for the past few weeks. And with all that's happened, it's hard not to see that you both have a point, especially about the Light Guardian side overstepping." He sighed and rubbed his eyes. "I've vowed to look more critically at how things are dealt with moving forward, and to change things if I can. I believe in the Academy's neutrality, and I want to preserve it if I can."

I was genuinely surprised. Was it possible that Matt was actually growing as a person? That he'd started taking my words to heart? Maybe his days of blind loyalty to the High Light Guardian and all she represented were coming to an end. I hoped it was true—it was much more likely that we could remain friends if it was.

"Anyway," Matt continued, "I found out that Caleb was the first to agree. He packed up from Glenhaven and came here, technically as a student, but he and the administration both know he's really here as a soldier. Though we'll see about that after today . . ." Matt trailed off, looking in the direction of Luke's office.

"Glenhaven," I muttered darkly. "Of course he'd choose to move from the most hellish border town to the second-most hellish border town." My fists clenched. "And no wonder he's turned into such a monster. Dagmar has a reputation for its skill and power, but Glenhaven has a reputation for its sheer brutality."

Matt nodded. "Not everyone from there is unhinged, but I learned from my friend Simon that many people fall down that hole of viciousness and cruelty. They're encouraged to from a young age, and few escape it.

All border towns cause their own specific damage, and Glenhaven's is that it makes its fighters lose themselves." Matt sighed. "If he isn't expelled, we'll have to keep a close eye on him. He may be good in a fight against Demons, but we don't want to sacrifice the safety of other students just for his help in the unlikely event of another attack."

There was a long moment of silence as we all shifted uncomfortably. No one knew why or how the Demon had come to the Academy. And without knowing the motive, we had no idea whether it would happen again.

Matt finally turned to look at me, a smile pulling at his lips as he looked me over. "You should probably go shower. I'll text you later if I hear any more news about Caleb."

I nodded and turned to walk to the locker rooms, Gabriel at my side.

9
ONSLAUGHT

Unfortunately, Caleb wasn't expelled. My mother pulled rank, and after having a strong word with Caleb, forced the school to keep him enrolled. He was, she asserted, too important for the protection of the school, though she did restrict him to training only with Matt, for now. Caleb was one of the Light Guardians' best fighters who wasn't officially in the warrior faction yet, and she apparently didn't want to waste all the warrior faction's resources by pulling them from various fronts to guard the school.

When Matt told me this, I suddenly knew why Caleb had agreed to come to the Academy in the first place: my mother had probably promised him a higher-ranking position in the warrior faction in the near future if he agreed to do this. Caleb was, and always had been, obsessed with being the best warrior. The best *recognized* warrior. Which meant that he wanted to eventually be the highest-ranking officer in the warrior faction. I bet he even wanted to supplant my mother. I was glad, for the first time, that I'd never revealed her identity to him. I'd shared everything about her and how she'd hurt me, but I'd never talked about who she was or what position she held. Something had always held me back from it. If I had, I was sure Caleb would've tried to use that to his advantage. *If I had, he might've stayed.* But I quickly pushed that thought away. *If* he'd stayed—and that was a big if— he would've only done so to use me. He would've stayed for the wrong reasons, and I would've let myself be manipulated. Because I'd loved him.

Eager to rekindle our friendship, Matt kept his word about distancing himself from my transformation work, especially because, in return, I'd agreed to hang out with him sometimes, either at dinner or in the lounge. Neither he nor Gabriel was pleased about spending more time with the other, but they put up with each other anyway so I wouldn't be forced to awkwardly decide who to hang out with in a given day.

Matt hadn't tried to kiss me again, though I could still see the desire to lingering in the depths of his eyes. He also didn't try convincing me to help my mother, nor did he ask for any information he could relay to her. I felt, for the first time since the last Demon attack, he wasn't going to my mother with information about me. Consequently, my trust in him grew again, as he'd promised it would.

Every Monday, Wednesday, and Friday, while Gabriel went to his one-on-one transformation training, I used the room I'd been initially assigned. There, armed with a rubber training dummy, I transformed and worked on developing and controlling skills by myself, and if I ever had questions about how Guardians generally used their power, Gabriel and I would spend time in the library after hours, looking things up. Even by myself, I knew I was improving. I'd taken great care to perfect my fire and lightning throws—the ones that'd almost burned me alive—and I'd also learned to use the metal walls of the room to have my power bounce back at me so I could practice different styles and strengths of shields. This was how I'd discovered I could use incoming power to bolster my shield instead of diffusing against it. It took a lot of concentration, and quite a bit of endurance, but I'd begun perfecting it. Of course, I'd only been able to practice it with my own power, so I had no idea if it'd work with anyone else's, but I hoped it would. I'd never heard of anyone else successfully catching their or another's power. Usually, it'd blow them apart like mine had when it'd hit me earlier in the semester. It was yet another skill I hadn't seen from other Divines.

By mid-November, Gabriel and I spent many of our evenings holed up in the student lounge, studying for our upcoming exams. While it was loud and far from the ideal studying spot, it also had roaring fireplaces and warming beers to help us survive the now frigid temperatures on campus.

On a particularly cold, clear night, Gabriel and I decided to take a meandering, leisurely path from the lounge back to our dorms while smoking our cigarettes, preferring to walk a wide arc through the frozen lawn than stick to the slippery paths. We wanted time in the fresh air after nearly four hours of studying, which had left our brains feeling like mush. We were willing to brave the cold if it could help clear our heads.

As we walked, we traded stories of what it'd been like to grow up in our respective border towns.

"It was hard to keep the battles quiet from the Normals," Gabriel said, after releasing a breath of smoke. "The only reason we could at all was because the plane rip wasn't directly in town. It was outside of it, along the outskirts of a forest. Divines built all of our homes and businesses on that side of town to try shielding the Normals from it—it ensured that we'd always see the attack before they did and gave us a chance to defeat the Demons before they made it too far into town."

I shook my head slowly in disbelief, releasing smoke through my nose. "That's wild. How did they explain all the damage to just your side of town?"

Gabriel smiled. "Most of the Normals either figured out that something more was happening and stayed out of it, or they decided the town was just particularly susceptible to natural disasters."

I raised my eyebrows incredulously. It was amazing what people could convince themselves of just to keep the more uncomfortable truths at arm's length.

"Either way, they tended to stay out of it. The hardest things were actually school and dating." Gabriel let out a huff of laughter before taking another drag of his cigarette. I watched, fascinated, as smoke curled through his lips, mixing with the steam of his breath as he exhaled. "We were expected to go to the school in town, which was incidentally the only school, and was also attended by all the Normals."

"Weird." I pulled my gaze from his mouth and looked up at the stars instead, as I brought my cigarette to my lips. With the cold had come a crisp clearness to the sky, revealing far more stars than we'd been able to see earlier in the semester. They twinkled warmly at us, almost like they could see us in return. "That's asking a lot of you to keep so much of yourselves hidden all the time."

Gabriel sighed. "Yeah, we had varying degrees of success with it. We'd have to leave school sometimes to protect the town from attacks, which was hard to explain away. Plus, most of us didn't have quick-healing abilities and there weren't always enough people around who could heal us right away, so we'd return to school all beaten up and with a variety of injuries. I think most students thought we were in a fight club or something." A wry smile pulled at his lips.

"How did you not get thrown out of school for that? Especially if Normals were the main people running it."

"Well, it helped that there were a few Divines who worked there too. They made excuses for us or would explain it away as impromptu field trips or something. And, like I said, a lot of adults in the town figured out that there was something going on that was bigger than the students. They mostly just let us get away with stuff."

I nodded, exhaling smoke, and thought this over. It seemed like an extremely stressful thing to worry about on top of already worrying about Demon attacks and not dying. Grades, other students, hiding who you were—I grimaced. I didn't envy that experience.

"That sounds shitty and complicated," I finally said. "And wild to have to worry about when you're just trying to survive and protect people."

Gabriel nodded, exhaling smoke. "Most of us resented it—always pretending, always being questioned about what we were involved in, getting dirty looks for having injuries, like we had any choice in the matter, getting dumped because we couldn't tell Normals about the Divine aspect of ourselves." He smiled a little ruefully.

My stomach clenched and my chest seemed to tighten. I wondered for the first time if Gabriel had ever had his heart broken. "So . . . you dated Normals?" I tried to keep my voice light. Neutral. I *wanted* to hear about his life and experiences. No matter what they involved.

"Yeah." He rubbed his free hand through his hair and looked out over the dark, frozen grounds. "There weren't really alternatives. There weren't that many Divines in town, especially around the same ages. Most of us ended up dating Normals, being friends with Normals, or keeping more to ourselves. I did a little of each. Figured out it was easier to isolate myself than pretend to be someone I wasn't, but every once in a while, I'd get drawn back in. It's hard to convince yourself that being alone is better when you're really lonely." He smiled wryly.

My heart clenched at his admission. I knew all too well what it felt like to be isolated and alone, and I'd never wish it on anyone. Especially not him. I nodded as I put out my cigarette under the toe of my boot.

"So, I'd occasionally date a Normal from school, until I remembered why I'd decided to stop doing that, or they'd dump me—whichever came first. Usually, they'd dump me because we Divines seemed like unreliable troublemakers. We'd run off at odd hours day and night to fight Demons, but the Normals weren't allowed to know that. All they could see was that we left them or would cancel plans with them and then not be truthful about why."

He took a drag of his cigarette, then exhaled the smoke at the stars.

"Plus, they really did think we were all in some sort of illegal fighting group. Every girlfriend I had told me that, if I cared about them, I'd abandon whatever violent club or gang I was in." He chuckled, shaking his head. "I always assured them that I wasn't in one, but they never believed me."

I smiled a little, but something about it pulled at me. "Did it hurt you?" I finally asked. "When they broke up with you for things you couldn't control? It sounds shitty, and like a quick path to heartbreak."

Gabriel took a last pull of his cigarette before putting it out in the frozen grass. His expression turned thoughtful as he exhaled the smoke. "Hm . . . well, I definitely got upset about it sometimes, but I think most of that came from the unfairness of the situation. They were wrong about me, but I could never tell them that, and I could never tell them the truth. I just had to nod and go along with it. I had to shoulder whatever blame or accusations they put on me without explaining myself, all to protect my actual identity. But I don't think I ever had my heart broken." He sounded almost surprised, like he'd never thought about it before. "I think because I could never really be myself around whoever I was in a relationship with, I never felt really close with them or anything. Even if I really liked them, I never fell in love."

I glanced up at him then, trying to read his expression. He was smiling a little, but it was a resigned smile. My stomach tightened and I swallowed. I had the strange urge to be closer to him. To comfort him. But I didn't know how to do that, or what that would look like. So I simply looped my arm through his as we walked near the trees bordering the west side of campus.

"Do you regret that?" I asked quietly. "Not having fallen in love?"

Gabriel looked down at me then, his gaze traveling slowly over my face. His expression was softer than I was used to seeing it, but I couldn't nail down what he was feeling. My lungs constricted, like they could no longer hold air.

"I don't think so," he finally said, releasing me from his vibrant gaze. "It wouldn't have gone well there anyway. It wasn't the right time or place. But I'd say I at least learned enough about infatuation to tell the difference between it and love. Which is a positive, I guess."

He shrugged and smiled down at me. His eyes seemed to glimmer in the darkness, and I found myself getting lost in them again. His smile grew, and he pulled me closer to his side, placing his hand on my arm still linked through his. My cheeks prickled with warmth even in the freezing night air.

I pulled my gaze from his and looked up at the stars again. "Well, I hope you find the right time and place to experience that someday, if that's what you want. You . . . deserve it."

Gabriel's smile was warm and genuine. "Thanks. So do you," he added, not looking at me. Which was good, because my cheeks chose that moment to burn scarlet.

We meandered by the trees for a bit longer before the shivering started taking over.

"Want to head back?" Gabriel asked, no doubt feeling my shivers against his arm.

"Yeah. It's freezing out here."

Gabriel's shoulders shook on a laugh. "Yep. It's almost like it's winter or something." He grinned as I shot him a glare, and he rubbed his hand up and down my arm, trying to impart some warmth.

We picked up our pace as the breeze made the trees sway harder. Cold wind whipped around us, and I reached up and flipped my hood over my head to provide a barrier. But the rustling of the trees got louder and louder, even as the wind subsided. Confused, I stopped in my tracks, my arm falling from Gabriel's. I stared at the trees incredulously, a sliver of fear slicing through me.

"Um . . ." I looked at him in alarm, then back at the trees.

Gabriel's brow furrowed as he turned to stare at them as well. "It can't be."

But I wasn't sure what else it could be. I pulled off my gloves and stuffed them in my pockets, willing my frigid fingers to warm up, then grabbed my knives from my boots.

"I'd rather be prepared. Just in case."

Gabriel hesitated for a moment, then nodded, and pulled his daggers from his boots. "What about the perimeter guards?" he murmured as we backed away from the tree line.

"I'm not sure. Maybe it managed to get past them. Or killed them." I shivered, and not just from the cold. If it'd killed all those warrior faction soldiers, what was it capable of doing to us? I didn't want to think about it too much.

The crashing grew louder, and Gabriel and I tensed, each taking our fighting stances. I wished we hadn't been out in the cold for so long. I felt stiff. Not ready to fight.

The Demon finally burst through the trees with a roar, confirming our fears. It was twice the size of the first Demon we'd battled together, and its roar caused our eardrums to burn in protest. The sound filled my head and chest, overwhelming me. I felt a trickle of blood running down my neck from my ears, but I couldn't raise my arms to cover them while holding my weapons at the ready. With another earsplitting scream, the Demon charged at us. There was no need to check whether this Demon was an innocent student. Its intent was clear. It wanted to kill us.

I pushed through the physical terror the Demon's screams created, and ran at it, Gabriel on my heels. This Demon's form was wildly different from the first one we'd battled. Instead of two legs and arms, this Demon seemed to glide over the ground on a slug-like base, and had at least ten long, wildly flailing arms that slightly resembled octopus tentacles but without the suction cups. These would be tricky to avoid—we'd have to take off as many arms as possible. This Demon also only had one large eye that burned red. But at least it didn't have acid skin. So that was something.

I raised my knives as the Demon got close, and ran between its flailing arms, slicing down hard on one near its base, and hacking at it repeatedly until it severed. The Demon let out a terrible, bone-chilling roar and grabbed me roughly with another arm, lifting me off the ground. Upside down, I sank my knife deep into the arm that held me. The Demon shrieked and transferred me to a different arm, and I quickly stabbed into it too.

Gabriel ran toward me, dodging the flailing arms, then swung his daggers at the base of the arm holding me, severing it. I fell along with the severed arm at least ten feet to the ground but managed to quickly extricate myself and push to my feet, only slightly winded.

"You okay?" Gabriel called as he hacked at another limb.

"Yeah. Thanks for that."

I ran around the back of the Demon while Gabriel dealt with its front, and most of its attention. I frowned as I looked it over. Beheading it would be a challenge since it didn't have a delineated head. Just an eye and a slightly slimmer top. We'd just have to estimate—if it still started healing and regenerating, we'd know we got it wrong.

I ran at the Demon's back and leapt into the air, then drove my knives

170

as deep and as high as I could into the Demon's back, then used my body weight to pull the blades all the way to the ground, slicing open a good portion of its back. The Demon's blood, black and acidic, poured from the large wound. I dodged as much of it as I could, but a decent amount spilled onto my hands, burning me.

The Demon spun with a terrible, gurgling roar, and hit me hard across the chest with one of its many arms. The force of the hit threw me close to twenty feet and knocked the breath from my lungs. I landed hard, my head slamming into the ground, and stars burst like small shimmering sequins in front of my vision as I gasped for breath. Gabriel ran at the Demon and slashed fiercely at its limbs, trying to take more out so they couldn't keep injuring us, and buying me time to recover.

I pushed to my feet as quickly as I could, trying to catch my breath, then ran at the Demon again. I'd almost reached it when it managed to grab Gabriel's arm and ferociously whipped it behind his back. A crack split the air, and I winced, knowing Gabriel's arm had broken. Gabriel swore and dropped his dagger but drove his other dagger deep into the Demon's torso. The Demon screeched and went to grab Gabriel again, but I ran between it and him just before it reached him and hacked off its limb.

"Thanks," Gabriel panted, grimacing in pain.

"Can you kneel for a second?" I dodged another arm and hacked it off in the middle. "I need to use your knee as leverage."

Gabriel knelt quickly, and I ran at him, stepped onto his knee like a stair, then launched myself off it as high as I could onto the Demon. I dug my knives into its flesh, then quickly used the base of its flailing limbs to climb higher. The Demon thrashed at me with its tentacles, and whipped its body back and forth, trying to dislodge me, but I clung tightly to it and propelled myself upward. In another few seconds, I leapt off its highest limb and drove one of my long knives into its eye. Thick black goo oozed from it and spilled down my arm as I stabbed into it again, twisting my knife, ruining its vision. If it couldn't see us, we'd have a much better chance of ending it before it could heal. Then I pulled my knife from its eye and slashed across its neck as hard as I could.

"Terah, look out!"

I turned my head but saw too late. The Demon grabbed me with one of its three remaining limbs, this one as thick as a tree trunk. It wrapped around my middle like a snake and squeezed tightly. I struggled, gasping for air, but its arm just continued to tighten. I cried out as one of my ribs broke. Then another. Growling, I stabbed into its arm furiously with my knives, trying to get it to release me. But the Demon ignored its injuries and slammed me against the ground, once, twice, three times. I blinked rapidly, dazed from the impact. I could feel blood streaming from my mouth and nose. *Shit.*

"No!" Gabriel shouted, fighting the Demon's other two arms so he could get to me. He finally broke through and jumped, hacking at the arm that was still holding me.

I stabbed into its arm again, even as the Demon tightened its hold on me. Another crack rent the air as the Demon broke another one of my ribs. This wasn't working. If I didn't get out of its hold soon, it'd kill me.

My power. I can use it without transforming.

Of course. I closed my eyes, pushing the pain to the edges of my consciousness, and reached for the well of deep purple inside of me. *Fire*, I thought as I pulled it forward. *Fire.* I opened my eyes and shot a powerful beam of flames from my hand at the Demon's arm. It immediately released me and screamed as a good two feet of its limb burned off.

I fell to the ground and groaned as my broken ribs were jostled. I'd be lucky if none of my organs were punctured. But I pushed through the pain. We needed to finish this. Taking a cue from me, Gabriel shot bright blue flames at the Demon's neck, trying to sever it. I pushed to my feet, gritting my teeth against the blinding pain from my ribs, then ran to take out the remaining two limbs so it couldn't attack Gabriel while he tried to behead it. I hacked through one arm with my knife while simultaneously sending a powerful shot of purple fire at the other. Finally, both limbs fell twitching to the ground.

I jogged over to Gabriel, gasping against the pain.

"Almost done," he gritted out. He looked even paler than usual.

I raised my hand in front of me and pulled more power from the well in my chest. *Fire. Powerful fire.* Purple flames practically erupted from my palm, and shot in a large beam at the Demon, fully engulfing it in a swirling tornado of fire. The Demon screamed and flailed, but it couldn't escape the flames. It burned alive and was quickly reduced to ash and goo. There would be no need to behead it now. There was nothing of it left.

My hand shook as the fire subsided from it, and I sank to my knees. I'd expended too much power, not just on the fire, but on all the healing my body was trying to do. I dropped my knives and collapsed on my back, groaning. My ribs felt like they were on fire—like someone was holding a torch against them. I was too scared to look at them. I felt like one might be poking through my skin.

"Terah," Gabriel gasped as he collapsed next to me. "Are you alright?"

"I'm fine." I tried to speak without moving my torso. "Just a couple scratches."

"Bullshit," Gabriel said fiercely.

"Your injuries are more important anyway. You don't have quick healing to get to them like I do." I turned to look at him, and he winced as he saw my blood-covered face. I was sure it looked more gruesome than it was.

I reached out and lightly touched Gabriel's broken arm, wincing as I saw it hanging at the incorrect angle. It must be hurting him like hell. I pressed my eyes closed and took stock of what I had left. I had just enough power to heal it, but only if I did it now. Otherwise, I'd quickly drain it as my body healed itself. I knew he wouldn't like it, since I was injured too, but I had every intention of healing him.

"Can you reach into my pocket and grab my phone with your good arm? We need to call Matt and warn the administration. I just need a few minutes before I can move again."

Gabriel nodded and slid his hand into my pocket. "Are you sure you'll be okay?" His brow was furrowed as his gaze swept over me again. "You look really beat up."

He dropped my phone into his lap, then reached out to gently touch my face.

"You'd tell me, right?" His deep voice was unsteady, his eyes pleading. "If you were really hurt?" Shock tunneled through me. I'd never seen him like this before.

I winced in pain but reached up and placed my hand over his. "Yes. If I was really hurt, like life-threateningly hurt, I'd tell you." I squeezed his hand and managed a small smile. "Now call Matt. The sooner this is sorted out, the sooner we can get inside." Though, to be honest, I could no longer feel the cold. Not through the pain.

Gabriel nodded and quickly found Matt's contact information. I vaguely heard him speaking to Matt and describing what'd happened, but my focus was on other things. My power was diminishing more and more each second as my body pulled itself back together, but that meant less power to heal Gabriel's arm with. I had to do it now.

"Yeah, she's injured," I heard him say, "though she claims it's not too bad." He looked at me and scowled. "I'm not sure I believe her, though."

I stuck my tongue out at him. He smiled a little and turned away again. I winced, pulling my tongue back in—I'd gotten a mouthful of my own blood. I spat into the grass, then reached out to touch Gabriel's arm. I quickly pulled my remaining power down my arm and pushed it out through my hand. *Heal*, I told it firmly, envisioning exactly what I wanted it to do. My hand closed more tightly around him as it pulsed with power. *Heal*, I commanded again, sending more—all I had left. I could see, almost as though my power was a camera inside his arm, how his bones were reconnecting and sealing, how his veins were being repaired, how his muscles were returned to their correct configuration and all bruising and pulling injuries disappeared. My arm dropped back onto the frozen grass as soon as I knew his arm was fully healed.

"Damn it, Terah!" Gabriel growled. "Why did you do that?"

I didn't respond. I just closed my eyes, giving over momentarily to the exhaustion, a small smile pulling at my lips. I'd done it because I knew I wasn't seriously injured. Just a few broken bones—nothing that wouldn't heal in a few hours, maybe overnight with how depleted my power was. And I knew he couldn't heal himself. I'd gladly be in pain for a few extra hours if it meant that he wouldn't have to suffer.

"No, she just healed me when I wasn't paying attention," Gabriel said angrily into the phone. "Just get your ass over here, Matt!" Gabriel hung up and slid my phone into his pocket before moving closer to me. He reached out and cupped my cheeks between both shaking hands.

"Terah?" he murmured, a slight quake in his voice.

I opened my eyes and smiled at him to reassure him. I'd never seen him this worried before. It cut at me—made me want to ease it in whatever way I could.

"I didn't lie, you know. I'm not actually seriously injured. Just a few broken ribs and a busted lip and nose. Nothing that won't heal in a few hours. I'm mostly just tired from throwing all that fire at it."

Gabriel blew out a sigh of relief and sat back a little. "You still shouldn't have used your power to heal me," he said grumpily. "You need it to heal yourself."

I smiled and reached out to take his hand—an instinct I didn't bother to question right now. "I wanted to." I shrugged a shoulder. "I didn't want you to be in pain. Plus, you can't heal yourself."

Gabriel frowned at me, but his cheeks colored slightly. He squeezed my hand, then laced his fingers through mine. "Thanks." His voice was quiet. "But I don't want you to be in pain either."

"I won't be," I mumbled, looking away from him. "Not for long."

"I'll make sure of it." Determination had entered his voice. "I'm going to make Matt heal you."

I grimaced and tried to sit up, but pain ripped through my middle, and I gasped, giving up. "No really, that's not necessary. I'll be fine soon."

"Bullshit," Gabriel murmured again. Then he bent and quickly pressed a kiss to my forehead.

I blinked up at him, flabbergasted. Had he really just—

"I don't want you hurting for a second longer than you have to." His voice was gruff, but his expression was warm. It was my turn to blush. "I don't feel confident healing your ribs yet, but I can heal your nose and mouth."

I nodded reluctantly. I'd healed him, it was only fair to let him heal me in return. Gabriel kept his fingers entwined with mine and raised his other hand to gently touch my nose. He closed his eyes, and I felt warmth seeping into my skin as electric blue gathered around his fingers. I felt his power gently guiding the bone and cartilage back into the right places, healing the veins that'd been punctured and the skin that'd been opened and bruised.

Then he lowered his hand to rest lightly over my mouth. His power glided gently over my lips and into my mouth, filling the space with warmth. The bleeding stopped as he healed the veins and cut skin, reduced the swelling, then let his power overflow from my mouth to cover my lips, healing the cut skin there. His power was warm and soft—it felt like the very essence of him. And right now, his essence was filling and caressing my mouth. My eyes slid shut and my heart pounded in my ears. *You're just tired. Pull yourself together.*

He finally sat back, his power dissipating as his fingers slid over my lips before returning to his side. A small smile lifted the corners of his mouth.

"Thanks." My voice was a little unsteady.

I slid my hand from his and pushed onto my elbows. I winced, but with my face healed, I knew the small amount of power I had left would focus on healing the bones soon. Footsteps pounded through the grass, and I turned my head to see Matt approaching us.

"Terah," he panted as he got close, "are you alright?"

I sighed. "I'm fine. Just a couple broken ribs. And Gabriel already healed my nose and mouth. It looks worse than it is."

Matt nodded, though he didn't look entirely convinced, then turned and examined the Demon's remains. Apparently, he believed me enough to not assess my injuries.

"I don't understand how it wasn't stopped by the warrior faction soldiers," he murmured, walking around the large, charred spot with lingering remains of ash, goo, and Demon blood. He ran a hand agitatedly through his hair. "I've already informed the president. She's calling the High Light Guardian about it before coming here. But she gave you both permission to return to your dorms or go to the medical wing if you need to. She'll speak to you both tomorrow if she has any questions."

"Okay." I tried to sit up—I really wanted to get back to my dorm so I could lie down—but I felt one of my broken ribs poke into my skin, and I gasped. I knew I could walk, but someone might need to lift me to my feet first.

Gabriel gave me stern look, then placed his hand on my shoulder, pushing me gently back into the grass. "Matt, get your ass over here and heal her."

Matt shot Gabriel an annoyed glare, but walked over to us anyway, and knelt at my side. "You said broken ribs?" His expression softened as I nodded, and he reached forward and carefully unzipped my jacket. "Sorry, this will be cold, but I need to see what kind of damage I'm working with."

I sighed, frustrated. I knew what healing entailed. He didn't need to explain it to me like I was a child. Matt pushed my jacket open, then lifted my shirt so he could see my entire rib cage. Both he and Gabriel hissed in sympathy. I glanced down and saw that my entire torso was covered in deep blue-black bruises, and I could clearly see where several of my ribs were poking against my skin. Well, at least they hadn't broken through.

"It'll heal in a couple hours," I murmured. "I've had worse."

Gabriel rolled his eyes and shook his head. I could tell he was about to argue with me.

Matt sighed. "I know you've had worse." He met and held my gaze. "I've been there when you've had worse. And I know you can heal on your own. But I'm still going to heal you now, whether it's necessary or not." His expression was firm. Decided. And it sparked my annoyance.

I scowled but let him rest his hands against my torso. I knew I should be grateful that they were so intent on taking away the pain. But . . . I didn't like needing to be helped. Nor was it necessary for my survival. I didn't need to be saved, and I didn't like giving people an excuse to fuss over me.

Instead of arguing with them, I closed my eyes and focused on how nice the cold air felt against my bruised skin. It was almost soothing.

Matt's power burned into my torso, and I felt my insides being pulled back together. I gritted my teeth as the bones moved, then fused. The muscles were mended next, the veins were repaired, and the bruising was eliminated. Finally, my scraped skin was mended, and I was fully healed.

Matt lifted his hands from my torso and opened his eyes. "There." He smiled and slid my shirt back down before zipping my jacket again. "That wasn't so bad, was it?" There was a cocky edge to his voice that grated at my frayed nerves.

I sat up and scowled at him. "It wasn't bad, but it also wasn't necessary. I'm not weak."

Matt raised his eyebrows. "Never said you were. But you don't have to be in pain for the rest of the night just to prove that."

My scowl deepened, and I pushed to my feet. I knew he was right, but I also didn't like feeling vulnerable or frail. Especially when I knew I was neither. And especially when Matt already felt that, in many areas of my life, I didn't know what was best for myself.

"You're welcome, by the way." Annoyance filled Matt's voice as he stood.

Gabriel pushed to his feet and rolled his eyes. He knew as well as I did that Matt was just baiting me now.

"Did you give Gabriel this much shit for healing you?" Matt crossed his arms over his chest, his eyes flashing with annoyance.

"I told him, as I told you, that it wasn't necessary," I said sharply. "But thank you. Thank you for agreeing to heal me after Gabriel yelled at you to do it. How generous of you."

Matt's expression grew even angrier. "I would've healed you anyway." He stepped closer. "It's not like I want you to be in pain either." He paused and looked at me intently. "Is that why you're mad? Because I didn't heal you first?"

I pinched the bridge of my nose between my fingers and took a deep, slow breath, trying to recenter myself as a wave of deep exhaustion swept over me. I wasn't even sure why we were fighting. Or why I felt so angry. I just wanted to leave.

"No," I finally said, my voice calmer. "That's not why I'm mad. I'm just tired, and I don't like being fussed over. I didn't mean for this to blow up into a fight. It doesn't matter anymore—it's done. I just want to go back to my room." I took a step toward Gabriel, and he walked over to me.

Matt looked at us for a long moment, a tinge of sadness entering his eyes, but nodded. "Okay." He sighed and ran a hand through his hair. "Get some rest. I'll talk to you tomorrow."

I nodded and turned to walk back toward the dorms, Gabriel at my side.

"I grabbed your knives and stashed them in my boots," Gabriel murmured as we stepped back onto the icy path that led to my dorm.

"Thanks," I sighed. Now that I was healed, I could more fully feel the cold and the fatigue.

"Also, I'm sorry," he added quietly. "I didn't mean to fuss over you. The last thing I wanted was for you to feel weak or incapable. I know you're strong and you could've healed on your own. I just didn't want you to hurt longer than you had to."

I reached over and slid my arm through his, leaning on him a little for support. "I know. That's why I didn't yell at you." I stared down at the path as we walked and frowned. "I don't know why Matt's healing made me mad. It just felt different. Like he *was* trying to save me, and like he wanted me to know that he'd saved me. Like I should owe him even though it wasn't necessary." I shook my head slowly. "I know I overreacted. But . . . he's been getting under my skin a lot lately. I think I'm having a harder time trusting his motives, and apparently that's coming out at weird times for me."

Gabriel nodded, watching me closely as I sighed.

"I just wish things were easier between us," I murmured, almost to myself. "Like they used to be."

Gabriel's arm tightened around mine. "Give it some time. You're trying to find a new normal as an adult with someone who only knew you in childhood. And he's certainly not making things easier for you both. But things are bound to even out eventually."

I rested my head briefly against his shoulder. "Thanks." We slowed in front of my dorm building. "I hope so."

Gabriel pulled open the front door and glanced inside. "No one in the common area," he said, looking back at me, "so we don't have to come up with a weird lie about why you're covered in blood." He smirked slightly and took my hand, pulling me inside behind him.

I smiled. "I hadn't even thought of that. What would we have said? That I got drunk and fell over?"

"Sounds plausible." Gabriel grinned at me. "We'll keep that excuse for next time."

I laughed and followed him down the hall to my room. Gabriel reached the door first and unlocked it with his hand, then pushed it open and turned on the light before immediately starting to build a fire.

"You're freezing," he said, noticing my surprise, "if you haven't noticed."

"Oh." I looked down at my chalk-white hands, seemingly devoid of blood. "I guess I am." Gabriel chuckled and pulled out his lighter, then flicked it on and brought its flame to the kindling.

I closed the door and meandered to the bathroom. I needed to wash my face at the very least. I flipped on the light and grimaced as I saw my reflection. The whole lower half of my face was covered in blood, as well as my neck, ears, and the upper part of my jacket. Some blood had also matted in my hair from being upside down, and there was Demon goo on my sleeve.

"I'll be out in five minutes," I called to Gabriel before shutting the bathroom door.

I turned on the shower and quickly undressed, then stepped carefully into the hot water. I sighed as the steam surrounded me and the hot water drenched my skin, washing away the blood. Then I quickly soaped my skin and washed my hair, making sure to work through all the bloody mats. Finally, I rinsed off, turned off the shower, and wrung the water from my hair. The hot water hadn't taken away my exhaustion, but it'd made me feel more regulated. I dried off, then wrapped myself tightly in a towel before carefully picking up my soiled clothes. I grimaced, trying to keep the grossest parts from touching my clean skin. I'd have to do laundry in the morning.

I opened the bathroom door and padded out into my room. "Shower's free if you need it."

Gabriel looked up from an armchair near the fire and his gaze slid over my damp skin and towel-covered body. It didn't look like he could form a cohesive response. My cheeks burned.

"I'm gonna change," I mumbled, walking toward my closet.

I flicked on the light and closed the door. Then I dumped my dirty clothes in the laundry basket before gathering some warm pajamas. I quickly donned them—the air in my room was still very chilly—then toweled my hair as dry as I could.

When I emerged from the closet, Gabriel seemed to be taking a shower, so I went and sat by the fire. I absently finger-combed my hair in front of it, using the heat to help dry it, and thought about the battle. About the Demon squeezing me and snapping my ribs like they were twigs. The pain had been so sharp and intense. I hadn't been injured like that in months. I'd almost forgotten what it felt like to be hurt in battle. I shivered. That was one thing I should never forget. Not if I wanted to survive.

I sank back in my chair, closed my eyes, and released a slow breath. I remembered Matt's warm fingers on my skin as he'd healed me. The sadness in his eyes as he'd watched me step closer to Gabriel. My heart squeezed and guilt slid through me. I'd been too harsh with him. He'd been trying to help me, and I'd bitten off his head. There was just something about him that'd been bothering me lately. But I wasn't sure the feeling was rational or fair. Matt cared about me. He always had. Of course he didn't want me to suffer. Of course he would've always healed me, as he'd done countless times in the past, as I'd done for him countless times in the past. So why did it suddenly feel too vulnerable? Too intimate? And why had I felt the need to push him away?

I sighed and emptied my mind, then reached out, holding an image of Matt in my thoughts. I didn't know if it'd work, if I'd be able to intentionally connect with him, but I wanted to try. I wanted to apologize. And I wanted there to be less conflict between us all the time. I loved him, after all. He was my family. And the constant tension between us lately hurt. More than anything, I missed how things used to be between us. The ease we'd felt when we were younger.

"*Matt,*" I whispered in my mind. "*Are you there? Can you hear me?*"

My heart pounded with anticipation and nerves as I waited. I had no idea if I could even connect with someone so physically far from me. After a long moment of silence, I sank further into the armchair, relaxing my body as much as I could. And I opened my mind even more, making myself far more vulnerable than I generally liked to be. I let myself feel how much I wanted to talk to him. How much I wanted this to work.

"*Matt,*" I whispered again. "*Can you hear me?*"

Warmth filled my mind, and an image formed—Matt lying on his bed in just his boxers, a book in his hand.

"*Terah,*" his voice whispered through my mind. He set his book down. "*I hear you. Are you okay?*"

"*Mhmm. I just . . . wanted to talk.*"

I felt Matt smile. "*That'd be nice,*" he murmured, "*as long as you don't yell at me again. It's been a while since we've talked alone.*"

It had been. I'd been mad at him for weeks about his behavior toward me and his involvement with my mother. And all other times he was around, so were other people. Namely Gabriel.

"*I'm sorry about all that,*" Matt murmured, hearing my thoughts. "*About everything with your mother. And your transformation. But I promise, I won't betray your trust like that again. I thought I was doing the right thing, but you made me realize I was wrong.*"

"*I know you won't,*" I said quietly. "*I believe you.*"

I sighed as I watched him lay there, and imagined I was with him. That I could lay next to him and press my cheek to his chest as I had when we were younger. That he'd wrap me in his comforting embrace—the only one I'd known in childhood. He was familiar. Important to me. And I missed his easy affection.

Matt groaned softly, feeling my imaginings almost like I was really there. He wanted to pull me closer and kiss me without consequence. Kiss me until I agreed to be with him the way he wanted me to be. My cheeks burned in response to his thoughts.

"*I . . . I just wanted to apologize for yelling at you earlier,*" I said, trying to redirect his thoughts. "*I think I was afraid you were acting for the wrong reasons again. That you didn't think I was capable of handling things myself.*"

"*I know. Believe it or not, I know you pretty well.*" He smiled. "*I figured it was a trust issue, especially because I've failed you on that front multiple times recently.*"

"*I'm sorry,*" I whispered, tears gathering in the corners of my eyes. "*You were right. I didn't yell at Gabriel for healing me. Just you. I know you care about me. I should've trusted you more.*"

"*It's okay, I deserved it. I broke your trust and haven't fully won it back. I know it'll take time.*" His smile turned bittersweet as he rested his hands on his stomach.

I was quiet for a moment, my gaze sweeping slowly over him. I rarely looked at Matt as just himself. I'd always thought of him as my older caretaker, or trainer, or friend. But not just as himself. He was . . . young. Only twenty-two. But he carried so much on his shoulders—he always had. More than anyone his age should. And it isolated him, then and now. I'd just never noticed how much, because to me, he'd been everything. Always there. A constant companion. I'd never been truly alone while he was around, and I'd thought that'd applied to him as well. But I hadn't considered how much his age would impact his experience of things. He was older—to him, the togetherness hadn't been one of two equal people, like it'd been in my mind. It'd been him taking care of me. Being responsible for both of us, not just himself. My stomach clenched and my heart throbbed. Something about that realization . . . hurt.

He sighed and his stomach muscles clenched, drawing my attention. My gaze traveled down his bare torso like a soft caress. Deep shadows settled into the valleys of muscle on his chest and stomach, and the light from his lamp gently illuminated the peaks. Enraptured by this play of dark and light, I imagined reaching out and trailing my fingers softly over his skin, following the path of shadows.

Matt's breathing accelerated. *"Terah,"* he groaned, his voice gravelly and full of pent-up desire. I knew he'd experienced my perusal almost as touch.

I let out a shuddering sigh, overwhelmed, as Matt thought about pulling me close. Pressing my torso to his. Kissing me passionately. My cheeks flushed and my heartbeat sped up.

"I miss you," I murmured, trying to change the subject. Trying to refocus things on us in a different way. And it was true. I did miss him. I missed the way things used to be with us. I missed when I'd trusted him unconditionally. Missed when he was the one who'd known me best and cared for me most.

"I miss you too. And I still care for you the most."

But my mind flashed to Gabriel.

Matt's jaw clenched. *"He hasn't known you for as long as I have, and he doesn't know you like I do. He can't possibly care for you as much as I care for you."*

"But he knows who I am now better than you do. And he cares about me as I am. I know he does."

I could feel Matt biting back a response. He didn't want to argue with me. He didn't want to talk about Gabriel, or even think about him. He didn't want to think about how much time Gabriel got to spend with me. Time that Matt couldn't have.

"You should come here," Matt murmured, pushing away his thoughts about Gabriel. *"Come to my room. I'll hold you like you wanted. We can talk and spend time together like we used to. Just the two of us."*

My cheeks heated again. I did want to spend time with him. I missed him. But I also wanted—

I heard the bathroom door open, and my heart leapt. I wasn't alone anymore.

"I wish I could," I murmured, *"but—"*

182

"*But you're not alone anymore.*" His voice was bitter and resigned. "*I didn't know Gabriel was still there.*"

"*He was in the shower,*" I clarified quickly. "*Sometimes it's easier for him to use the one here than the shared one in his dorm.*"

I could feel Matt's bitter laughter. "*I'm sure that's what he told you.*" But behind the bitterness I felt real hurt. Matt was hurting because of me. My stomach clenched as pain throbbed through my chest. I didn't want to cause him pain.

"*I'm sorry, Matt,*" I whispered, as I heard Gabriel walking across the room toward me. "*You know I love and care about you, too.*"

Matt swallowed and pressed his eyes closed. I could feel the pain burning in his chest. "*I know. I just wish I was the only one you felt that way about.*" Then he shut his mind to me, and our connection was severed.

I opened my eyes and saw Gabriel sitting across from me, his hair wet and endearingly disheveled, watching me with a carefully neutral expression. I took a slow breath in and let it out. I thought talking to Matt would ease my stress and guilt. But I felt overwhelmed again. Confused and sad. I met Gabriel's eyes and saw understanding there. Resignation. He knew I'd been talking to Matt.

"Everything okay?"

I pulled my legs onto the chair in front of me and rested my chin on my knees. Some of my wet hair fell forward, landing in front of my face.

"I don't know. I can't seem to talk to Matt without hurting him, or without him hurting me. I'm tired of it. I miss how things used to be between us, but I also can't give up who I am, what I believe in, or who I care about just to make him happy. And I guess that hurts us both." I shrugged, trying to seem less upset about it than I really felt.

Gabriel nodded slowly, still observing me closely. As I melted into the vibrant churning depths of his gaze, I wondered if Gabriel really cared about me as much as I wanted him to. As much as I'd told Matt that he did. As much as I cared about him. I'd always care about Matt, but what I felt for Gabriel was different. I trusted him more, even in such a short time. He knew me best as I was now. He forgave me when I wasn't my best or most honest self. Supported me even when he knew the worst about me. Never barreled past or shoved down my emotions—he encouraged me to feel and talk about them. We fought together, laughed together, took care of each other, healed each other, learned together, listened to each other. We were always there for each other. Without me fully noticing, Gabriel had wheedled his way into my life and my heart. He'd become my best friend, filling an emptiness in me that Matt couldn't. He let me be me—exactly as I was now—without judgment. Just as I let him be him.

I suddenly realized I hadn't broken eye contact with Gabriel for at least a minute. I started a little and blinked, my cheeks beginning to burn. Amusement entered his eyes, but also something warmer. He leaned forward and gathered the wet strands of my hair that were still in my face. Then he swept them slowly toward my ear, his fingers gliding gently over my cheek, leaving a trail of warm tingles behind. His gaze met mine—steady, close—as he tucked the strands behind my ear. My breath stalled in my lungs. I couldn't take in any new air. I couldn't move or think. Then Gabriel leaned casually back in his chair, the corner of his mouth lifting in a small smile.

I blinked, coming back into myself as though my consciousness was suddenly reconnected with my body. He was teasing me, that was all. Getting under my skin in the way that only close friends could. It made me want to do the same to him. Tease him. Take him off guard, just a little.

So I smiled at him slowly, warmly, as my eyes held his. Then I gathered my damp hair to one side, exposing the bare skin of my neck and shoulder on the other. I looked down, as though I was uncertain, then looked back into his eyes, biting my lip. His smile faded as his gaze slid over the curve of my shoulder and neck, finally returning to my face to land on the lip I was biting. His cheeks grew warmer as his eyes seemed to darken to a deeper blue. And just like that, I knew I had the same effect on him that he had on me. But just as suddenly, I knew I didn't want to tease him. What I felt for him wasn't fake, so messing with him like this felt wrong. I didn't want to treat him the way I'd treated all other guys since Caleb, even Matt. I just wanted us to be close. To be friends. Real friends.

I pushed quickly to my feet, my cheeks burning at my own behavior. Then, avoiding his gaze, I turned and walked to the bathroom. I stood in front of the mirror and took several deep, calming breaths as I looked at my reflection. A pink-cheeked, bright-eyed version of myself looked back. I looked . . . riled up. Which made no sense. There was no reason to be. Perhaps it was simply embarrassment.

I shook my head and grabbed my brush. I'd need a minute or two for the color to recede from my cheeks. So I took my time brushing my hair. It'd grown a bit over the last few months, and consequently tangled much more easily. Now, it almost reached my waist. I'd considered cutting it short again, like I'd worn it when I was younger—easier to keep out of the way when fighting—but all this cold weather had encouraged me to keep it long.

I heard footsteps and looked up, still running my brush through my hair. Gabriel leaned casually against the bathroom door frame, watching me, though more cautiously this time. Like he was afraid he had upset me. Like he didn't want to chase me away. But he had no reason to worry. I was pretty good at upsetting myself without any help from anyone else, and if I was worried about someone's behavior right now, it was my own.

I gave him a small smile before turning back to the mirror and starting to braid my hair over my shoulder. "What do you want to do now?" I kept my voice as light and cheerful as I could, hoping it'd reassure him. I wanted him to stay.

Gabriel's gaze swept over the reflection of my face in the mirror, then he smiled a little and shrugged. "Stay with you for a while longer." He crossed his arms over his chest, his damp hair falling in front of his eyes. "I'm not too picky about what we do."

Warmth filled my chest, and I found myself blushing again. *Damnit.* What the hell was wrong with me? We were just friends. And I wasn't an inexperienced fifteen-year-old anymore. I wished I'd stop reacting like one.

"We could re-watch that movie from last weekend," I suggested, looking around for a hair tie to secure my braid. Looking anywhere but at his face. "You left it in my room, and it was pretty light and fun."

"Sounds good." He shook his hair out of his eyes, and the electric blue was unleashed on me again. My mouth went dry. I licked my lips, nervously.

"Want me to make popcorn?"

"Sure." I jerked my gaze from his and finally located a hair tie. I secured it quickly to the end of my braid.

Gabriel's eyes lingered on me for a long moment before he nodded and pushed off the wall, heading back into the main room. I let out a slow breath and tried to pull myself together.

"I just wish I was the only one you felt that way about." Matt's words floated through my head again. I hadn't given them much thought at the time, but against my will, they began taking on new meaning now. I looked toward the door Gabriel had just disappeared through. Was it possible? Was I really that out of touch with my own feelings that I just hadn't noticed?

No. That could ruin everything. You could scare him away and end up alone again.

Popcorn started popping in the other room, and the scent of warm butter wafted lightly over. I shook myself. No. I was overthinking it. Overblowing it. I was just tired. My reaction to him didn't mean I felt more than I thought I did. I needed to relax. To stop reading so much into things. Just focus on the friendship. I didn't need further complication in my life.

I gave myself another fortifying shake and walked back into the main room. Gabriel smiled at me from where he sat on the bed. He'd abandoned his black sweater, leaving just his white undershirt on. He was holding a bag of popcorn and had already queued up the movie.

I returned his smile and plopped down next to him, then grabbed a handful of popcorn. *Just friends.* The benefits of closeness without the drama and uncertainty of more. It was far better this way.

10

BURIED FEELINGS

THE SOUND OF MY ALARM PULLED ME FROM A DEEP DREAM. I WAS warm. So warm. A temperature I hadn't been able to achieve in my room since late summer. It was perfect. So comfortable. I didn't want to leave the bed—certainly not in favor of the chilly air I knew awaited me outside the blankets.

I groaned and lifted my arm, my eyes still closed, trying to reach my side table and my phone. But I couldn't. Not without shifting to the other side of the bed. And I was too comfortable to move. I dropped my arm back onto the bed and burrowed closer to my warm pillow. It felt firmer than usual, but no less comfortable. I sighed. Maybe my alarm would turn itself off after a couple minutes? I could do with a little more sleep anyway.

A deeper groan reverberated beneath my cheek. My eyes flew open as my heart lurched, then started racing. *What?* I looked down and color immediately flew to my cheeks. Gabriel. All I could do was stare down at him, flabbergasted. But he wasn't awake enough to have noticed yet. Instead, his arm tightened around my waist, pulling me more firmly against him as he reached blindly for my side table and phone. He grabbed it and pressed the side button, silencing the alarm. Then he opened his eyes groggily and looked up at me.

He looked confused for a second, then color flooded his cheeks as well. He realized, right as I did, that we must've fallen asleep during the movie last night. We'd fallen asleep and somehow ended up holding each other. I'd been using his chest as a pillow, my arm draped around his waist, and my leg resting between both of his as he held me tightly to his side. No wonder I'd been so warm.

"Um . . . this is unexpected." My voice was a little raspy from sleep. I wasn't sure what else to say.

Gabriel ran his hand down his face. He looked like he was trying to make his brain catch up with what was happening. "I guess we fell asleep during the movie." His voice was a little deeper than usual. "Sorry about that."

His hand slid from my waist back to the bed. I felt instantly colder.

"It's okay," I said lightly. "I don't mind. Just a bit surprised. But I can't complain—it was much warmer with you here. I usually wake up cold."

Gabriel blushed again and looked away, almost like he was uncomfortable. My stomach sank as I watched him. It didn't have to be a big deal—it'd been an accident, after all. I'd hoped he'd just laugh it off. I guess he couldn't.

I carefully pushed off him, disentangling our legs, then climbed out of bed. I immediately shivered—the chill in the room was no joke—and glanced out the window to see a liberal amount of snow covering the grounds. No wonder. I turned, refusing to look back at Gabriel in my bed, and padded quickly to the bathroom. He clearly needed some space to regather himself, so I busied myself with getting ready for the day.

I emerged once I'd brushed my teeth and hair, washed my face, and put on eyeliner. Gabriel was out of bed and in the middle of straightening the covers. That was nice of him. I left him to it, and went into my closet, closing the door behind me, so I could dress. I quickly pulled off my pajamas and pulled on some black skinny jeans, a bra, and a black V-neck sweater that had horizontal slashes across the arms from shoulder to wrist, allowing a little skin to peek through. Warm, but not too warm for the few rooms that had fireplaces. Then I grabbed a pair of thick socks and my flat black leather boots that laced up to just below my knees. I was pretty sure they'd handle the snow reasonably well. Enough to keep my feet dry, at least. Finally, I grabbed a clean, black, wool jacket that had a hood. It was slightly warmer than the one I'd worn yesterday, and, importantly, wasn't currently covered in blood.

I pushed open the closet door and my stomach sank. Gabriel was gone. I bit the inside of my cheek and walked out into the main room, peering into the bathroom just to make sure. Yep. He'd left.

I sighed and sank onto the foot of my bed, feeling deflated. Seemed like I'd finally scared him off, at least temporarily. *Damnit.* I clenched my hands in frustration. Should I have pretended to be more uncomfortable about waking up in his arms? I grimaced. That would've been pointless. It *wasn't* a big deal. I shook my head slowly. There was nothing I could do. I couldn't control his reactions—I'd just have to let Gabriel feel however he currently felt, and hopefully we'd be back to our normal friendship soon. I'd just have to wait in uncomfortable solitude until then.

I bent over and pulled on my socks and boots, carefully pulling and tying the laces so no snow would get through, but leaving enough room around my calves that I could slide in some short daggers before I left. Then I sighed heavily and leaned my forearms on my thighs, a sinking feeling taking hold of my stomach. As much as I wanted to not care, Gabriel's absence filled the room. The silence rang louder because of it. I glanced at my desk chair and saw that he'd grabbed his sweater, but not his jacket. He'd left in such a hurry that he'd forgotten it. I shook my head, dropping it forward, my hair falling around my face like a curtain. It felt like there was a ten-pound weight in my chest pulling me down. The day had barely begun, and I already wished it was over.

There was a small commotion outside my door before I heard a beep and saw the handle turn. Gabriel pushed open the door while trying to balance several things in his arms. I gaped at him, totally unprepared for his reappearance. He grinned and shoved the door shut with his foot.

"Snagged some coffee from your dorm's common area," he nodded at the mugs he was balancing in one hand, "then stole some bagels and cream cheese from the fridge." He gestured to the paper-towel-wrapped objects he was holding between his upper arm and his ribs. Then he walked over to my desk and set everything down. "No one was out there, so they'll never know who took them. Lucky for us." He smirked and turned to face me, his hands free now.

I stared at him in confusion. I felt like I had whiplash. So . . . he hadn't run away? I . . . hadn't scared him off? He'd just gone to find us food and coffee like a thoughtful person, and not the coward I'd tried to make him in my mind. Yet again, I'd underestimated him. I'd assumed he was that easy to push away.

Gabriel's smirk grew a little wider as he watched me, and he crossed his arms over his chest, leaning back against my desk. "Thought I'd run away?"

My cheeks burned as I straightened up. "Maybe. You didn't have the best reaction when we woke up."

Gabriel's smirk turned into a softer smile, and he turned back to the desk and grabbed a mug and bagel. He brought them over to me and held them out. I took them tentatively, careful not to brush his hands with mine.

"Sorry about that," he said, as he walked back to the desk to grab his mug and bagel. He returned and sat next to me on the edge of the bed. "I'm not really a morning person. I was more disoriented and surprised than anything else. I'm not upset about it or anything."

I frowned slightly, not sure I fully believed him, and took a sip of coffee. The warm liquid slid down my throat, warming my insides, and I sighed, my eyes sliding closed for a moment. The coffee had just the right amount of sweetness. It was perfect. I opened my eyes and glanced at Gabriel. He was watching me closely. Assessing my reaction.

His eyes narrowed. "If you don't believe me, I'll just be forced to spend a bunch of nights in here to prove it doesn't bother me." He smirked before taking a sip of coffee, his eyes dancing mischievously. "But then I'd have to demand closet space in here so I can have changes of clothes. Otherwise, people will assume we're together, since I'd keep emerging from your room in the clothes from the day before." He waggled his eyebrows at me, his eyes full of amusement.

I laughed and swallowed a mouthful of bagel. "Pfft. You always wear black. No one's going to notice the difference between this black sweater and the next."

Gabriel's shoulders shook with laughter, and he took a bite of his bagel. "You never know." He shot me a sly smile. "Don't want to ruin my flawless reputation with scandalous gossip."

I snorted at that. He was ridiculous. But my heart felt lighter than it had all morning.

I was surprised to find that no one had noticed the Demon attack the night before, especially as it'd been closer to the dorms than the first attack. There were no anxious whispers between students on our way to training. No general aura of anxiety or tension from those we passed as we entered the main classroom building and walked up to our training room. Everyone was simply focused on exams and how tired they were.

I looked around the room, assessing as we stretched for training. The students in our group were the most likely to feel an obligation to step in and protect students and the school in the event of an attack. They were some of the few who were trained well enough to do so without dying. But none of them seemed stressed beyond the norm. There was no grim edge to any of their expressions. No extra tension held in their bodies.

The only person who seemed to be behaving differently was Caleb. I'd caught him watching Gabriel and me multiple times since we'd arrived, when he usually did his best to pretend like we didn't exist. His gaze on us was appraising. He'd even stationed himself closer to us, when he usually chose to train on the opposite side of the room.

"I wonder if he knows about the attack," I murmured to Gabriel as we started our drills.

"I bet he does," Gabriel murmured, glancing at him briefly as he blocked my strike. "Your mother might be feeding him information, since he's technically a part of their defense team."

I scowled. "I don't see why he needs to be closer to us, just because he knows we fought a Demon last night."

Gabriel shrugged a shoulder, blocking another of my strikes. "Maybe he thinks if he sticks closer, he'll be around if there's another attack."

"Or my mother ordered him to stay close to us." My mood darkened. "Maybe she thinks we have information that she doesn't."

Gabriel nodded slowly. "She might. Especially since she knows about your mind reading ability. Maybe she thinks you've overheard something in your head that's allowing you to predict where and when the attacks are happening. And she wants him to get information on that for her."

"But I haven't. There's nothing to overhear."

"Yeah. That's why it's annoying."

I sighed, blocking his strike. "Even if I did, I'd never willingly give him information. Especially not to help her. They're the two people I like least in the world."

Gabriel smiled, blocking my strike. "Maybe if you say that a little louder, he'll go back to ignoring us."

I smiled, grudgingly. "Don't tempt me. I'm pretty sure the president would be extremely mad at us if we revealed to the room that the Academy was under direct attack, just to make my ex leave us alone."

Gabriel's shoulders shook with laughter. "Can't fault me for trying."

I laughed and glanced over at Caleb again. My gaze immediately met his icy one—he was watching us again. But instead of jerking his gaze forward as he usually did, it dipped to my smile and lingered there for a long moment. Matt landed a strike against his ribs, and Caleb winced and jerked his head forward again. My smile faded, a frown taking its place.

Strange.

After lunch, Gabriel and I were called into the president's office to give her our statements about the most recent attack. She didn't give us a lot of new information, but she did divulge that the closest warrior faction perimeter guards were stunned with enough power to knock them out before the Demon had crossed all the way through. This was a troubling development, and it confirmed that the Demons weren't working alone. It'd take a lot of people to have enough power to open an unsanctioned rift in the Academy's plane while also knocking out powerful warrior faction soldiers.

"As with before," the president said, "please keep these occurrences quiet for now. We're expanding our security and our investigation, but we don't want to cause any panic, especially with exams coming up."

Gabriel and I glanced at each other, then nodded reluctantly. But I was starting to feel like the student body should be told. The attacks clearly weren't a one-time occurrence. Whatever the Demons were trying to do, it seemed like they'd keep trying until they achieved it. At least if the students knew, they could be on their guard.

"And I must thank you two again for your brave service," she said as she pushed to her feet. Gabriel and I stood as well. "It was a horrible coincidence that both of you were there for yet another attack, but I'm glad you were able to hold your own."

Gabriel's brow furrowed, and he glanced at me. I felt an uncomfortable stir as well. It *was* weird that we'd been there both times. At different times of night, in different parts of campus.

"We're some of the few smokers here," Gabriel said slowly, "so we're outside more often than most other students. Maybe that raises the likelihood that we'll see the attacks before anyone else does." But he didn't look convinced by his own words.

The president nodded. "That could very well be the reason. I'd encourage you both to stay near the dorms when you do that from now on. Even though we're increasing our security measures, it would be best for you to stay away from the perimeter of the grounds until we're certain the situation is under control. Which reminds me, I will send each of you the phone number for the warrior faction commander on the grounds. If you see another infiltration attempt, call the commander first. We don't want our students having to risk their lives to defend the school."

Gabriel and I nodded.

"Thank you both again. You're free to go."

A hush fell over campus as exams neared, and everyone threw themselves into studying with a fervor we hadn't bothered with up until this point. Gabriel and I had finally abandoned the lounge in favor of the library, so we could get as much studying done in the quiet as possible. This drove me stir crazy, but through our diligent work, I was slowly starting to feel like I might not fail every class.

Amid the general panic over exams, the school started preparing for the traditional end of term holiday party that it threw for the students and staff each year. The campus buildings were decorated with garlands entwined with rich, embroidered ribbons, sprigs of mistletoe were hung from doorways, and wreaths with pinecones, cinnamon sticks, and winter berries were hung from each building's door. Additionally, several large pine trees were brought into the dining hall where the holiday party would take place. They glowed with tiny white lights and were draped with gold ribbons.

If I hadn't been so wrapped up in schoolwork, I would've taken more time to enjoy it all. We'd never decorated for the seasons in Dagmar, and we rarely took time to celebrate anything. Celebration wasn't deemed necessary, as we were soldiers on a battle front, and all things that weren't necessary weren't thought of as important. At most, we'd have a slightly nicer meal or two a couple times a year if someone remembered. So I enjoyed the Academy's dedication to making things nice for the people who lived here. It might not be necessary, but it added a warmth to the grounds.

Exams started the following Monday. Gabriel and I would have several a day through Wednesday, starting with History of the Divines, and ending with Ethics. I tried to apply the lifelong training I had in dealing with overwhelming battle situations to dealing with overwhelming academic situations. It wasn't something I'd ever experienced before, and all I could really do was keep my head down and press forward. Push for another hour of studying. Push to finish the exams in the time given to us. Push to keep my nervousness from affecting my performance. Push through my exhaustion to keep going.

By the end of our last exam on Wednesday, I was thoroughly and completely exhausted. Gabriel and I had a quick cigarette together before each heading back to our separate dorms, bleary-eyed, to collapse into long-overdue sleep. I barely even remembered making my way from the exam room to my dorm, and I fell onto my bed, fully clothed, and immediately passed out.

I slept all through the night and well into the next day. I barely cared that I'd missed training, though I secretly hoped Gabriel had slept through it too so he wouldn't have to train with Matt or Caleb, which I knew he'd hate. This was our last week of classes for the semester, and therefore our last week of training for over a month, so I *should* be taking advantage of it, but not today. I couldn't make myself care today. I was too exhausted.

I rolled out of bed and made my way to the shower. I knew the hot water would soothe my aching muscles and exhausted body. I slowly washed my hair and thought about winter break. After much internal agonizing, I'd decided I didn't want to return to Dagmar for the break. My heart sank just thinking about returning to the blood, grime, and distrustful looks. The constant fear and injury. The grim bareness of life there. The loneliness. I'd worked so hard these past few months to start undoing some of the damage Dagmar had inflicted on me, and I instinctively felt that it'd cause me more damage if I returned now. I'd therefore submitted a request to stay on campus over the holidays. It's what Matt had done when he'd been a student here—he'd agreed to some kind of job on campus that'd kept him busy between semesters. I hadn't mentioned my plans to Gabriel or Matt, mainly because I didn't want them changing their plans because of me. I was prepared to accept a month or two of loneliness in exchange for not having to return to a place that destroyed my soul.

I sighed and turned off the water, then wrung out my hair and stepped onto the bathmat. The air was chilly, so I quickly dried off and wrapped the towel tightly around me before walking out of the bathroom. But I stopped in my tracks just past the door, my cheeks immediately burning.

"Hey." Gabriel looked up from the chair he was leisurely lounging in.

I gaped at him and secured my towel more tightly around myself. As it was, this particular towel only covered me down to my upper thighs.

"Sorry," he murmured, looking sheepish, "I should've just waited outside. But I knocked and called you and didn't hear anything, so I got worried. I should've just realized you were probably either sleeping or showering. And once I was in here . . ." he gestured at the crackling fireplace. He'd gotten warm and comfortable and hadn't wanted to wait where it was colder. I couldn't fault him for it—I would've done the same thing.

A smile pulled at my lips as I watched his gaze heating as it slid slowly over my skin, almost like a caress. It made me feel tingly inside. Braver. So I walked over to the chair opposite him and sat down, my towel just barely covering me. Now it was his turn to blush.

"Aren't you cold?" He tried to keep his gaze on mine.

I shrugged and leaned back in the chair, crossing one leg over the other. "Not really. I just took a hot shower, so I still feel warm from that."

Gabriel swallowed and nodded. My smile broadened. It wasn't often that I could catch him off guard. I enjoyed making *him* blush for a change.

"I brought you some food." His voice was a little hoarse. He cleared his throat and gestured to my desk where he'd set the tray. "You slept through breakfast and training, so I thought you might be hungry."

My smile turned genuine. "I am. Starving, actually." I pushed to my feet and raised on my toes, trying to see the tray over Gabriel's tall form.

"Uh, maybe you should put on clothes first?" His voice sounded slightly strangled.

My smile turned mischievous as I lowered my heels to the ground. "Does my towel make you nervous?"

Gabriel's gaze heated as it traveled warmly over me again. A heated shiver ran through me in response.

"Not nervous," he murmured, his voice a little deeper. "But it's definitely distracting."

I laughed, trying to ignore the sudden fluttering in my stomach. "Fair enough. I'll be right back."

By the time I'd emerged, dressed, Gabriel had pulled over one of the side tables to rest between our chairs and placed the tray of food on it.

"Oh, one more thing." He pushed to his feet and walked to my desk, then returned with an iced coffee in his hand. "For you." He held it out to me.

I smiled, wrapping my fingers around the cup. "You really are the best." I sat across from him and took a long sip of the coffee. I sighed, happy. It was my favorite.

Gabriel grinned and shrugged. "It's just food. It's not like it's difficult or anything."

I rolled my eyes. "But it's nice of you, and you never have to. Therefore, you're the best. Stop arguing with me."

Gabriel's shoulders shook with silent laughter. But he didn't argue.

When night fell, Gabriel and I grabbed a quick dinner from the dining hall before heading to the lounge to celebrate the end of the semester. The lounge was crowded, specifically with first years since we'd all finished our exams the same day, but Gabriel managed to spot an empty table in the back corner of the room.

I rolled my eyes as we passed Caleb, who was loudly entertaining a group of followers, all of them clearly deep into their beers. Somehow, even with his new frosty demeanor and murderous tendencies, he'd gained a group of admirers who hung on his every word. It was mind-boggling to me. But being from the second largest border town in the country, and being handsome on top of that, had given him a lot of social credit at the Academy. And he ate it up. He wanted to be the best *recognized* warrior, after all. Caleb's eyes followed me as we passed, but I refused to look at him. I wasn't sure if he watched because of his hatred of me, because it still unsettled him to see me around, or because my mother had asked him to. But whatever the reason, it put me on edge.

Gabriel bought the first round of beers, and we sat in the low-lit room talking about what classes we wanted to take next semester. There were some mandatory ones, but I'd also heard we'd be able to pick a few elective courses, specially designed to help us in whatever Divine careers we wanted after graduation. I'd always assumed I'd be a soldier for the rest of my life, but coming to the Academy seemed to offer people paths to futures I'd never considered before. My original plan had been to run away to school for four years before having to return to Dagmar, but I wasn't so sure that that had to be my path anymore. At the very least, I was tired of having my life choices dictated by others. Maybe my time at the Academy would allow me the opportunity to forge my own path.

I decided to buy our second round of drinks, so I pushed back from the table and made my way to the bar. Gabriel had asked me to pick a beer for him, so I scoured the tap list and tried to find a nice dark one. I'd found those to be the best and most warming on cold nights like this. I greeted the bartender and placed our order, then leaned against the rich, wooden bar and waited. There were several students in line in front of me, so it'd take a few minutes.

Another student sidled up to the bar and leaned against it, right next to me. I glanced up and tension immediately stiffened my body.

"Hey," Caleb said, his voice light. He was looking at me intently.

I glared at him. "What the hell do you want?" I'd gone out of my way to never have to interact with him again, and here he was, bothering me for no apparent reason. Perhaps all the beer had gone to his head.

"Still sharp as a dagger, I see." He smiled slowly at me. It was a smile that used to make my knees go weak, and Caleb knew that. Now, though, all it did was put me on edge and make me angry. Caleb wouldn't willingly talk to me now. Not unless he needed something. My stomach tightened.

"Just wanted to know if you're going to the holiday party with anyone," he said lightly.

I stared at him like he'd grown an extra head. "Why would you give a shit about that?"

Amusement suffused his features, though his eyes remained cold—how they'd looked the day he'd left me behind. "Maybe because I want you to go with me?"

Warning bells pealed through me. I knew where I stood in Caleb's mind, and it wasn't as a dance partner or a date. He'd made that *very* clear.

"Bullshit. You'd never willingly do anything with me again." But a thought struck me, and I turned to look at him in triumph. "Unless someone ordered you to . . ."

Caleb's eyes narrowed slightly, and I had my answer. Cold rage swept through me, and I felt myself hardening toward him even more. He'd willingly put himself through the torture of being near me, if it meant gain for him, of course. What an absolute asshole.

Caleb pulled his smile back on. "Don't be ridiculous. Maybe I just want to get to know you again. Maybe I want to apologize." His gaze was imploring. Eager. But the stony hardness remained. And I knew instinctively that he hadn't changed. He wasn't sorry. He only cared about himself and his ambition.

"Don't pull that bullshit with me." My voice was like ice. "We both know you're only asking me because someone ordered you to get closer to me. The High Light Guardian, perhaps?"

His jaw tightened, and I knew I was right. But Caleb was a charmer—he had been since the day I'd met him—and a relatively good actor when he wanted to be. He placed his hand against his middle and winced convincingly. As though my words had hurt him.

"That's a pretty harsh accusation," he said, somberly. "Especially to someone you used to love. What if I want to go back to that time again? What if I still . . . want you?" His gaze swept warmly over me. But I knew he didn't—he didn't want to go back in time, and he didn't want me. He'd left me behind, and he'd still be distancing himself from me if someone hadn't forced him to interact with me. It was the only reason he was even talking to me.

My blood boiled from head to toe, the rage enough to make my fingers shake. He'd crossed a line by bringing up the past—by bringing up my old feelings for him when *he'd* been the one who'd torn me apart and abandoned me. I wasn't sure I could stop myself from punching him. Repeatedly. Until he could never smile again. I didn't still have feelings for him. He had no power over me like that anymore. But he clearly believed he did, and he wanted to use that power to get what he wanted. He was despicable.

"If I had the choice," I said, my voice dark and quiet, filled with barely contained rage, "I'd never willingly spend another second with you." Fury practically radiated from me, and Caleb took a small step back, trepidation stealing into his expression. "You're a horrible, manipulative person, and no one, not even my *mother* could compel me to do anything with you other than punch you in the face and send you to hell."

At that moment, the bartender returned with my beers and placed them in front of me. *Thank the gods.* I needed to walk away before I attacked him. Caleb looked confused for a moment, likely not realizing why I'd brought my mother into this. *Good.* I'd let him ruminate on that one until he figured out that his most respected mentor, the key to his ambitious dreams, was also my family. Even if I hated her. I knew he wouldn't like it. He didn't like any reminder of me.

Before he could respond, Caleb's eyes shifted to a spot over my shoulder, his gaze turning hard again. Gabriel stepped up next to me and slid an arm around my waist, pulling me gently but firmly into his side. I felt the anger and protectiveness radiating off him. And it thawed my heart, just a little. I leaned into him. I didn't need him to fight this battle for me, but it was nice to know he had my back—that I didn't have to do this alone.

"Why the hell are you bothering Terah?" His voice was quiet, but deadly.

"I didn't know you were her keeper," Caleb sneered as he glanced at Gabriel's hold on me.

I stiffened, but Gabriel ignored the bait. "It's pretty clear that Terah wants nothing to do with you. Fuck off."

"I don't know," Caleb smirked, his gaze slowly and purposefully sliding over me, from my head to my toes, "she used to want *everything* to do with me. And I bet she still does."

This dig hit the mark, and Gabriel tensed, the muscles down his body going rigid. But I just laughed. Audibly. Genuinely. I couldn't help myself. Caleb's smirk faded as his gaze shifted to me, uncertainly. This wasn't the reaction he'd foreseen. But his suggestion that I might still want him after everything he'd done to me was frankly hilarious. And completely wrong.

"Oh, hun," I finally gasped, wiping tears of mirth from my eyes, "you may have been the first guy I dated, but I've had *so much better* than you for years. I hope you don't think I've mooned over you and eagerly awaited your return."

I laughed again and grabbed my beer, then took a large sip. Caleb stiffened, anger tightening his features, along with a barely perceptible hint of hurt. But I no longer cared about his feelings.

"The answer is no," I said firmly. "I don't want to go to any party with you, I certainly don't *want* you, and I'd frankly rather shovel shit for the rest of my life than spend another minute with you."

I handed Gabriel his beer and turned on my heel, away from Caleb.

"You'd better find someone else if you want a date to the party," I said over my shoulder as I started walking away. "Oh, and give my regards to my mother," I called. I laughed again at his dumbfounded expression, then took Gabriel's hand, winding my fingers through his, as we walked back to our table.

We sat back down, and I let out a long sigh. "He's such a conceited asshole." I took a long sip of my beer. It was dark, thick, and strong— exactly what I needed right now. Gabriel took a large gulp of his as well and nodded at it approvingly.

"What was that even about?" He glared darkly over my shoulder in Caleb's direction.

I sighed. "I'm ninety-nine percent sure my mother ordered him to get closer to me, and he decided inviting me to the holiday party would be a good way of doing that."

I shook my head in disgust.

"He may hate me, but if there's one thing that'll make him spend time with me again, it's the prospect of securing a better position for himself with the Light Guardians. He's always been mercenary and ambitious."

Gabriel shook his head angrily and took another sip of beer. "I can't believe he thought he could just walk back into your life like that after everything he did. Like you would ever let him."

"He has a rather high opinion of himself. I think he genuinely thought I'd still have feelings for him that he could manipulate to get what he wanted. Too bad for him, I grew the fuck up and moved on. I used to think the world of him. Thank the gods he disillusioned me of that. Now all I see him as is pathetic and hilariously transparent."

"I'm glad for that." Gabriel leaned back in his chair, his expression oddly serious. "Especially since he's such a manipulative creep. I hope he and your mother will now see they can't control you so easily." He sent another glare over my head at where I presumed Caleb was now sitting.

I shrugged. "Who knows. But I hope he'll at least leave me alone from now on. If he doesn't, I may not be able to refrain from punching him next time. Came pretty close to it this time. Still want to, actually."

Gabriel smiled and took another sip of beer. "When we're done with this round, want to get out of here? I'd love to not have to stare at that asshole's face anymore."

I smiled at him, my chest lightening as though it was filling with air. His fierce dislike of Caleb because of what he'd done to me had me feeling warmer and happier. Gabriel was an incredibly loyal friend.

"Sure."

My smile turned mischievous as I picked up my glass and chugged the thick liquid that still filled about two-thirds of it. Gabriel gaped at me, then started grinning as I kept going. I set the glass on the table a couple seconds later, now empty.

"What?" I asked innocently. "Why prolong your suffering?"

Gabriel threw his head back and laughed, loud and unreserved. I stared at him in wonder. I'd rarely seen him so open. I . . . liked it.

"True." He grinned at me, warmth in his gaze. "Gimme a sec . . ."

He picked up his own glass and downed the rest of the contents in a few large swallows. Then he grinned and pushed to his feet. We donned our jackets and walked back through the lounge toward the door, ignoring Caleb's glare. Finally, we pushed through the front doors out into the chilly night air.

I took a deep breath, gathering the coolness into my lungs. It'd grown quite hot in the lounge with the thick crowd and all the fireplaces going.

We pulled out our cigarettes and lit them, then blew tendrils of smoke into the frigid night as we meandered away from the lounge toward the paved path that would take us back to the dorms.

"I can't believe we've finished a whole semester already," I murmured as we walked. "It feels like everything went by so quickly."

Gabriel took a drag of his cigarette. "True." He released the smoke through his nose. "But it's nice to have it under our belts. And don't worry, you're still stuck with me for another three and a half years." He shot me a playful smirk.

I smiled. I liked the thought of that. "I'm glad you made me be your friend." I meant for it to be a teasing statement, but it came out oddly earnest.

Gabriel glanced down at me, the smirk fading from his lips. But a warmth grew there instead. "Me too. Though I wouldn't say I *made* you." He nudged my shoulder with his, a softer smile pulling at his lips.

"Well, you didn't leave when I made it more difficult," I amended. "So . . . thanks for that."

Gabriel grinned and surprised me by wrapping his free arm around my shoulders and pulling me into his side. "You didn't make it difficult. You were just being yourself. And I happen to like you."

He said it lightly, but that didn't stop the deep blush from forming on my cheeks. I laughed, taken a little off guard. But not in a bad way.

"Thanks. I happen to like you too."

Gabriel's grin broadened. He opened his mouth to respond, but a horrible sound cut across the grounds and stopped us in our tracks. I jerked around, my stomach dropping in dread, and my cigarette fell from my chilled fingers, sputtering out on the cold, frost-covered ground. And then I saw it. A huge Demon was emerging from the tree line across the grounds. It was still far from us, as we were near the buildings, but I could tell even from here that it was huge. *Shit.*

Gabriel pulled out his phone, fumbling with it. "We should call the commander. The president gave us their number."

I nodded absently and started jogging toward the Demon. We'd call, but I wasn't willing to leave the grounds unprotected until then. Gabriel jogged after me, holding the phone to his ear. "Fuck." He shoved the phone back into his pocket. "No answer."

I reached out as we ran and grabbed Gabriel's arm. I was mostly free from the effects of the beer we'd been drinking because of my quick healing, but I wanted to make sure that he had a clear head for this fight. It looked like it'd be a bad one. Purple power poured from my fingers into his arm and quickly burned the alcohol from his system.

"Thanks," he panted.

I sized up the Demon as we ran toward it. It was at least forty feet tall, gunmetal gray with burning red eyes, and in the form of a spider, but with far more legs. Each leg ended in a long, sharp, metal point, almost like a sword. And it was fast. At this rate, it'd make it most of the way to the buildings before we'd make it even halfway to the trees. *Damnit*. We needed to keep it as far from the buildings—and students—as possible. Which meant only one thing. I grimaced as the reality set in.

"I have to transform," I said as we sprinted toward it. "It's too large and too fast. We can't let it get closer."

Gabriel's mouth set grimly, but he nodded. "I'll transform too and follow as fast as I can."

I reached out briefly and grabbed his hand, squeezing it. "Good luck."

Then I released him and pushed my power outward as fast as I could, transforming in a huge flash of purple light. My hair lifted to float around me, my eyes burned with purple fire, and purple armor encased my body. I pushed off the ground, not willing to look at Gabriel's reaction to my trans-formation, and flew rapidly toward the Demon, pulling my glowing sword quickly from its sheath. The Demon let out a roar that vibrated roughly through the air, hitting and tearing at my psyche like a serrated knife, and turned toward me. Even forty feet off the ground, I was still only at its eye level.

"How did you get past the guards?" I shouted, my voice deeper and more amplified in my transformed state.

The Demon laughed—a rough, lurching sound like boulders tumbling over each other. All the hair on my body stood on end in response to it.

"The guards are dead," it hissed in a voice that made my eardrums feel like bursting. It was like the loudest, shrillest bell combined with a thou-sand fingernails screeching over a chalkboard. Cold fear shuddered through me. Could it be true? Could it have really killed all the guards? I clenched my fist and pushed the fear aside. I couldn't worry about that right now. I needed to focus on the battle. I needed to *win* the battle.

The Demon reared up on its back legs and slashed at me fiercely with its front ones, the long shards of sharp metal whipping toward me with powerful speed. I shot up, avoiding them, and threw a bolt of lightning at the metal points. The Demon screamed as the metal conducted the light-ning to the rest of its body, sending forks shooting through its flesh, electrocuting it. The Demon roared and shot venom at me from its pincers. I quickly materialized a purple shield around me and blocked the stream. It sizzled over the surface and dripped to the ground, burning the grass below. I quickly dematerialized the shield and sent a burst of fire and lightning out of my hand at the Demon's pincers, trying to eliminate them. But the Demon dodged, and the shot hit its back instead. It hissed in pain, but the fire and lightning hadn't done much damage. I cursed under my breath. I'd need to do something larger to materially injure it.

A shadowy figure brandishing knives ran past and launched into the air, carried high almost like a leaf in a gust of wind. Far higher than a normal person should've been able to jump. I couldn't make out any features—the figure almost blended into the night air. They landed on the Demon's back and stabbed into it. Hard. The Demon screeched and threw the figure from its body to the ground. But the figure fell more slowly than any normal person would and seemed unaffected by the fall. I gasped as the Demon stabbed its leg through the figure, but it passed through as it'd pass through smoke—without making contact or causing any damage. My heart pounded in my ears. *Gabriel.* He'd transformed and finally caught up.

Reinvigorated, I charged my sword with lightning and flew at the Demon, then struck one of its front legs. I aimed near the top, where it looked to meld from metal into skin. The lightning burned through its flesh as I made contact and burned the leg down to the bone. It didn't sever it though. *Damnit.* This Demon was incredibly large, strong, and difficult to injure. The Demon thrashed, hitting me across the front of my armor with its bloody leg, sending me tumbling through the air away from it. But I caught myself midair and flew back with a burst of speed, pouring power into my wings. I charged my sword again and targeted the same leg in the same place. This time, my sword hit, and its power discharged with a boom. The bone shattered, and the leg fell to the ground with a heavy thump. One leg down, eleven or so to go.

I swung around the back of the Demon as Gabriel jumped onto its front. Then I shot a stream of fire at it, burning the sharp hairs from its back. Once I'd cleared a patch of skin, I lunged and plunged my sword there with all my strength. But the Demon had thick skin, thicker than rubber, and my sword barely punctured the surface. Meanwhile, Gabriel was attempting to take out the Demon's eyes with one hand while slicing at the back of its neck with the other. He crouched on its head, as though he weighed nothing, and stabbed ferociously. The Demon roared and went up on its hind legs, sweeping its front legs over its head, trying to dislodge him. But Gabriel hung on, and its legs just went through him.

I took advantage of the Demon's new position and flew at it from a distance with as much speed as I could, holding my sword with both hands and charging it with even more lightning. I was determined to break through its skin and actually cause some damage. With a yell, I plunged my sword into the small gash I'd already created, and this time, the sword sank in, deep and true. Lightning shot out from the stab, burning forked paths through its body.

The Demon roared and jerked away from me, returning all its legs to the ground. And before I could move, it shot thick strands of glowing, acidic webbing at me. The webbing burned my armor and stuck to me, wrapping around me like a thick rope, tethering my wings to my back and sides. I plummeted almost forty feet, and only managed to create a shield around myself at the last moment to keep myself from slamming into the ground. Winded, I dropped my shield and fell into the grass. I struggled against the webbing, trying to release my arms and wings. But it held me in a firm, sticky cage that also glued me to the ground. *Shit.*

The Demon screamed in triumph and brought one of its legs quickly down on me. I gasped as its sharp point punched through my armor and drove clean through my shoulder just beneath my collarbone, embedding into the ground beneath me. I cried out as the Demon jerked its thick, metallic leg violently out of me. Blood poured from the puncture wound in a thick stream as I tried to roll away from another strike, but I couldn't overcome the webbing.

Gabriel leapt from the Demon's back and drove both of his knives deep into the Demon's face, hanging from it and materializing more so he could drag his knives down with the weight of his body. The Demon screamed and turned its attention from me to him. Thinking fast, I gathered power inside me and pushed it out of my body in the form of a giant fireball. The fire burned through the webbing as it shot away from me, freeing me again. I pushed quickly to my feet, ignoring the blood dripping liberally from my shoulder, and launched into the air again. I also ignored how my arms had started shaking. I knew my transformation, injury, and heavy use of my power was draining me, but I needed to hold on and push forward. Of all the Demons we'd fought at the Academy, this was the deadliest, the hardest to destroy, and we *couldn't* let it reach the students.

I took a deep breath, trying to pull calm rationality around myself. I needed to think about this battle more strategically. Taking out all its legs would take too long and wouldn't actually kill the Demon. I needed to take a more direct approach. I needed to find a way to behead it, and fast.

I sheathed my sword and materialized my bow and arrow, then flew high above the Demon as I notched an arrow and charged it with as much lightning as it would hold. I drew back the string, ignoring the screaming pain from my injury, and aimed at the Demon's oozing neck. Then I let the arrow fly. It plunged into the Demon with a loud crack of thunder, and exploded, sending bolts of lightning shooting outward into the Demon's flesh, tearing through skin, muscle, and bone. The Demon teetered and fell to the ground with an earth-shaking crash, twitching and writhing. But its head wasn't severed. Before it recovered, I took another arrow and charged it, then let it fly at the same spot. Thunder cracked around us as it buried itself in the Demon's neck and exploded, sending thick lightning bolts through its body. The Demon's scream was cut off as most of its neck was blown apart.

I quickly dematerialized my bow and arrows and pulled my sword from its sheath again. Then I gathered the rest of my power and shot at the Demon from above, charging my sword with everything I had left. With a cry, I brought my sword down on the Demon's neck with both arms. Fire and lightning shot from my sword into the Demon's neck, severing most of the remaining muscle and skin. There was so little left. We were almost there. Gabriel jumped high into the air from the ground, and with a cry of effort, fully materialized and brought his knives down into the deep neck wound, severing it the rest of the way. The Demon's head rolled away from its body, and its legs twitched violently, curling up onto its back.

It was dead.

I jumped to the ground and let out a shuddering sigh of relief. We'd done it. It was finished.

Gabriel sheathed his knives and walked toward me. I stood there, still in my Guardian form, purple power still swirling through me, though much weaker now. My transformation was dimming, and I'd soon fall out of it. But I couldn't think about that now. My heart pounded as Gabriel approached me, and all thoughts of the battle and my injury vanished. He was finally seeing me. Seeing my transformation—a part of me that I could never change or get rid of. A part of me that was integral to who I was. And I was terrified he'd run from me.

Gabriel stopped directly in front of me, and I could finally fully see his transformation. He was the shape of the Gabriel I knew, but the rest of him looked totally different. His skin was no longer skin, his hair, features, and clothes no longer visually defined by different colors, patterns, and textures. He was as dark as the night, hovering between opaque and transparent. Like a shadow. But he wasn't all dark. He had small specs of light covering him from head to toe, almost like stars. He looked like a clear night sky come to life. He was . . . beautiful.

I smiled and reached a glowing hand forward. My fingers slid through his chest as though he was made of nothing more than air. There wasn't any resistance or even temperature difference as I passed through. It was like his chest wasn't there at all.

Gabriel took a step closer and reached out, his hand turning more opaque, more solid, and lightly touched my hair that was floating around me like it was suspended in water. His gaze roamed over me, taking in every detail of my transformation. My smile faded, and I tensed, waiting for and dreading the moment when he'd move away from me in fear and disgust.

But it never came.

Instead, Gabriel reached up and cupped my face between both his hands. My gaze jumped to his, startled, and I realized he was smiling at me.

"But . . . you're so beautiful," he murmured, his voice warm and genuine as he stroked his now-solid fingers down my cheeks. "How could anyone run from you?"

My heart jolted as though I'd been hit by one of my own lightning bolts, and tears prickled the corners of my eyes. No one had ever thought my transformation was beautiful. Only dangerous and different. Dark and untrustworthy.

I reached up and placed my shaking hands over his, still cradling my face. "You're beautiful too," I murmured, unable to control the waver in my voice as a wild tumble of emotions swept through me. And I meant it. His form was ethereal—mesmerizing. "Like constellations in a night sky." I released his hands and reached forward to touch his cheek, which grew solid beneath my fingers. He still felt like him—warm, soft, a hint of stubble—even though he looked different. "How could anyone be afraid of you?"

His chest rose and fell more quickly. I could feel the intensity of his gaze on mine even without seeing its color. My breath caught in my throat and my pulse pounded through me in response. We stood there for a breathless moment, neither of us moving or speaking.

"I—" Gabriel tried, but he stopped, like he couldn't form whatever he wanted to say. Instead, he pulled me against him, and his mouth covered mine.

Fire blazed through me the moment our lips touched—a fire that had nothing to do with my power. I inhaled sharply and clung to him, kissing him back feverishly. As though my life depended on it. As though I'd die if we stopped. His lips were warm and strong and sure. Every pull and caress had jolts of lightning running through me, and heat pounding through my veins. He kissed me as though he was starving for me, delving deep, hardly coming up for air, filling all my senses as he held me close.

I wound my arms around his neck, ignoring the sharp sear of pain from my injured shoulder, raised on my toes, and deepened the kiss. His tongue slid into my mouth, and I moaned as his essence filled me there. His groan rumbled through his chest as I met his tongue eagerly with mine, and one of his hands slid down my back, and molded around my hip, feeling how I curved there. I let my mind open to him as he held me close, delving into my mouth again and again, and everything intensified. I could feel what he was feeling. I could hear the blood pounding through his veins. It was overwhelming. Intoxicating. Amazing.

I took his bottom lip between my teeth and scraped over him lightly as I released him. Gabriel's groan was deeper this time, and he lifted me off the ground before crushing me to him. Then he delved back into my mouth, taking the kiss impossibly deep. My fingers shook as I tilted my head back, welcoming him in. Meeting him enthusiastically. Holding him to me. And we moved together, learning the taste and feel of each other. Stroking and exploring. Taking and giving. I'd never experienced a kiss this intense. I'd never experienced the intensity of desire that was swamping me, overwhelming all my senses. I felt dizzy with it. But I desperately wanted to keep feeling it. I never wanted us to stop. My body crackled with awareness everywhere we were pressed together. Everywhere he was touching me. I wanted more of this. More of him.

Suddenly, Gabriel set me back on the ground and staggered away from me. I stumbled forward, still reeling from the kiss. But Gabriel backed further away. I touched my shaking fingers to my lips, dazed. They felt swollen and tingly from the kiss. But . . . why had he stopped?

Gabriel transformed back into his usual self, a look of horror spreading across his face. Pain and confusion stabbed through my chest as I watched him—it wasn't the expression he should've had after a kiss like that.

"I . . . I'm so sorry," he said shakily, taking another step away from me. I frowned, lowering my hand from my lips back to my side. His gaze shifted to my lips, and guilt flooded his expression. "I shouldn't have done that," he panted. "It was . . . a mistake. I know we're just friends." He ran his hands through his hair. "I just . . . got caught up, I guess. With adrenaline."

The pain stabbing into my chest intensified, and I stumbled backward a step, feeling weaker by the second. My power was drained, I was injured, and I'd stayed transformed for too long. But I couldn't for the life of me focus enough to transform back now. My nerves and emotions were in a jumble. I shook my head a little as I stared at him, trying to understand what he was saying. What he was feeling. He thought our kiss was a mistake? He'd only kissed me because of adrenaline? Tears stung my eyes, and I bit the inside of my cheek, cursing silently, wishing they'd disappear.

"Please," he murmured, desperation lacing his words, "please forgive me. I wasn't thinking. I shouldn't have done that." He took another step back, his fists clenching as he hung his head and shook it sadly.

My mind was reeling. I couldn't figure out what to say. How to feel. To me, the kiss had been enlightening and staggering. It'd been perfect. The best kiss of my life. And it'd forced me to see where Gabriel really stood in my heart—no mean feat, as I'd been shoving away my emotions my whole life. But to him, it'd been a mistake. Nothing more than an adrenaline-filled whim. And that reality tore painfully through me. Tears spilled down my cheeks, and Gabriel's face convulsed with pain as he saw them.

"I'm sorry," he said again, his voice shaking now. "I never meant to do that. It was a fucking horrible mistake. I . . . I'll never do it again."

More tears spilled down my cheeks now, and my whole body shook. Every word he uttered felt like a dagger to the heart.

"I . . . I don't want to lose you," he said, a frantic edge to his voice. His hands shook as he plowed them agitatedly through his hair. "You . . . you're my best friend. I want you to feel safe with me. I want you to be able to trust me, and I don't want you to feel pushed by me. I want you to feel clear on where we stand."

Oh, I was clear on that, alright. He'd made it very clear that he cared about me, but just as friends. He'd kissed me because he'd been over-whelmed with adrenaline and gratefulness that I hadn't backed away from his transformation. That I'd accepted him when no one before me had. But he didn't want more. For him, more had been a mistake. He regretted going there. And he'd discovered this at the same moment I'd discovered that more was exactly what I wanted with him. That my feelings for him were far deeper than I'd allowed myself to believe. But I desperately wanted to be wrong about where he stood. I wanted some hint that maybe, just maybe, a small part of him might want more, too. So I opened my mind to him, trying to see his thoughts, but I felt him firmly close it off, slamming the door between us. He didn't want me to see. He didn't want to hurt me more and drive me away.

"I can't . . ." Gabriel stammered. He stopped and ran a hand down his face, cursing under his breath. "I'm sorry I hurt you," he finally murmured.

He sounded . . . devastated. And he looked terrified. My heart felt like a Demon's claws were slashing through it, tearing it to ribbons. Tears spilled down my cheeks. What kind of monster was I to make someone react like this with just a kiss? How could I drive people away, alienate them, and disgust them so quickly? My knees shook as I watched Gabriel back further away from me. I was losing him. I'd pushed him too far— responded too enthusiastically to something he hadn't wanted. I'd shown too much of how I really felt and scared him away.

Gabriel swore again and turned on his heel. He walked quickly away from me, leaving me shaking and bleeding in the cold. I watched numbly as he disappeared into the darkness, tears rushing down my cheeks in a continuous river. He'd . . . left me. He'd just turned and left me behind. Like Caleb. Like Matt. I'd trusted him. Trusted him not to just leave when things got tough. Trusted him to be the person who wouldn't turn his back on me. To be the person who'd care enough to stay. But he'd gone. Just like the others. And he'd come to the same conclusion as Caleb—that more with me was a mistake. So he'd left me with an injury, a beheaded Demon, and . . . a broken heart.

My vision blurred, and my knees collapsed beneath me. I fell out of my transformation as I hit the ground. Blood dripped freely from my shoulder as I stared at the spinning sky above me. I'd been too caught up with Gabriel to notice how much I'd burned out. How injured I was. That I wasn't healing. I'd used up too much power to heal on my own.

Pain ripped through my chest again. I'd fallen for Gabriel without even realizing it. How had that happened? And worse, he wanted nothing to do with me. Not like that. And he'd left me. Walked away from me. Rejected me. Yet again, I'd made a horrible choice in opening up my heart. A choice that might very well destroy me. Why could I never learn?

11

LOSSES & GAINS

I ached with exhaustion and pain, and darkness clouded the edges of my vision. But I wasn't sure I even wanted to keep myself from bleeding out. I hurt too much. Internally. And what was really left for me? I was alone. More alone than I'd been in a while. I had no path. No real family. No friends who wouldn't leave me. No one who'd fight for me or stay for me. No one who truly loved me. All I had was my ability to fight. My identity as a soldier. And that wasn't a life at all.

My eyes slid closed, and I let the darkness hovering around the edges of my vision overtake me—fill me slowly with cold emptiness. I hated my life. Why not just let it end? But something inside me rebelled against the inaction. I was a fighter, and I'd fought too long and hard to stay alive to just give up now. Even if I longed for the peace that giving up would offer. Even if surviving meant feeling the pain of being alone. Of having been left again.

I forced my eyes open. I needed to make it someplace where I could be healed. I groaned, pain searing through me, as I forced my shaking arms to push me into a sitting position. Then I shoved to my feet, stumbling as the world spun around me. I shakily stepped over the pool of my own blood and staggered toward the staff residences. I had no idea where the medics were located, but I knew Matt could heal me. If I could find him in time.

Stabbing pain shot through my shoulder with every step I took, and blood dripped down my jacket onto the frozen ground, but I forced myself to keep going. I tried to remember which building Matt lived in, but I'd never been to his room before. I closed my eyes and tried opening my mind to him, but I had almost no power left. I staggered to the nearest staff residence building and leaned against the cold stone exterior. Then I closed my eyes and reached out again, pouring all my strength and concentration into it, until I felt the tiniest connection snap into place.

"Matt," I called out weakly, "*your building and room number. Quickly. Please.*"

The feeble connection wavered, but I forced it to hold, my legs shaking as I drained further. Matt's confusion and worry filled my mind, but he answered quickly.

"*Building four. Room eighteen.*"

The connection broke as I staggered away from the wall again. My vision swam, and the ground seemed to sway beneath me. *Shit.* I was only at building one. I braced a hand against the wall and made my way toward building two. Then I staggered over to building two and braced myself against it as I headed for building three. Finally, I reached building four. I fell against the front door, leaving a trail of blood on the surface, and managed to turn the nob. The door creaked open, and I staggered inside, pushing it closed behind me.

The staff residence building was essentially set up just like the student dorms. There was a common area, and then halls leading to different rooms, and stairs leading to different floors. I stumbled across the empty common area and looked down the closest hall. It held rooms one through five. The staff's rooms were clearly larger than the students' rooms, so there were fewer down each hall. I counted the halls quickly and realized room eighteen would be on the second floor. *Damnit.*

My legs shook violently as I made my way to the stairs. They were too weak to carry me up the flight, so I crawled up instead, using my uninjured arm to propel me. Finally, I reached the landing and pulled myself up using the banister. Blood dripped freely from my shoulder onto the floor, and I grimaced as the world spun violently again. I wouldn't be able to remain conscious for much longer. Clutching the wall, I made my way down the first hallway. If I'd counted right, Matt's room should be down here. I reached the end of the hall and saw Matt's room number. *Finally.* Relief swept through me as I fell against the door, smearing blood across the polished wood.

I knocked, and Matt immediately opened the door, expecting me. I fell through and landed on the rug with a groan.

"Terah!" Matt shoved the door closed and knelt next to me. Then he carefully rolled me over. "What happened? You're covered in blood!"

Darkness swam before my eyes as his worried face flickered in and out of focus. I couldn't talk anymore. But tears slid down my cheeks. Not from the pain of the wound, but from being left again by the person I cared about most.

Matt swore and quickly unzipped my jacket. He pulled a dagger from his belt and sliced the jacket off me in several quick, efficient motions. Then he did the same with my sweater. The tank top went next. He needed to see the injury before he could heal it, and he didn't have time to waste undressing me. Matt swore again as he saw the large puncture wound that went straight through me. He dropped his dagger onto the rug and placed both hands over the wound. White light surrounded his fingers and burned into me. I cried out in pain as Matt's power began pulling me back together, healing and fusing everything that was torn. Trying to replenish the blood I'd lost.

"Hold on, Terah," Matt murmured as he poured more of his power into me, healing me as quickly and thoroughly as he could, "it'll be done soon."

I nodded, my eyes closed, and reached a shaking hand up to grab a handful of his shirt. I needed to feel grounded somehow. I needed to feel like he was tangibly here with me. I clutched his shirt like it was the one thing keeping me tethered to the earth. Matt finally sat back with a sigh and rubbed his blood-covered hands down his pants.

"It's done," he panted. He'd expended a lot of power.

I nodded, but barely registered the change. I supposed my shoulder didn't hurt as much, and Matt had replenished enough blood for me to survive, but I felt incredibly weak. And the pain in my chest wasn't the kind that could be healed with divine power.

Gabriel's face, his look of horror, swam before my eyes, and more tears streamed down my cheeks. He'd backed away from me. Run from me. I clutched Matt's shirt more tightly. I needed him. His familiarity. His comfort and care. I looked up into his eyes through my watery ones and saw the deep worry there. He didn't like seeing me hurt. And he especially didn't like seeing me visibly vulnerable. Because it meant things were particularly bad. But he also looked a little uncertain, like he wasn't sure what to do with me now. Like he wasn't sure what his role should be. But his uncertainty melted away as his gaze swept over my tear-streaked face, replaced by firm resolve. He stood quickly, forcing my hand to drop from his shirt, then bent and scooped me into his arms. Then he carried me across his large living area and down a small hallway that had two doors. He nudged one open with his foot and brought me into the bathroom.

Matt set me down on the edge of the tub, then leaned around me so he could turn on the hot water. He rinsed his hands, secured the plug in the drain, and let the tub fill. I stared numbly at the bathmat as the uncontrollable stream of tears continued. Matt unlaced my boots and pulled them off along with my socks, then stood me up and gently removed my blood-stained pants, setting my phone from the pocket on the counter. Then he lifted me in his arms again and placed me carefully into the tub with my bra and underwear still on. Blood immediately seeped from my skin into the water, creating swirling tendrils of red. Matt opened the cabinet under the sink and grabbed a washcloth, then dipped it in the water and gently started wiping the dried blood from my skin.

"Terah," he murmured as he continued his ministrations, "what happened?"

I swallowed and looked up at him, fresh tears spilling from my eyes. I hurt too much to talk about it. But Matt's expression was so warm and caring, and I had no defenses against that right now. So I told him. Everything. The Demon attack, transforming, defeating the Demon, Gabriel and I seeing each other's transformations, the kiss, and Gabriel regretting it and leaving me there. All the while, Matt continued to wipe my skin with the washcloth, periodically adding soap. But I could tell from the set of his jaw that he was angry. Furious, in fact. But not with me—with Gabriel. My stomach clenched. That wasn't what I wanted either.

"I can't believe he just left you there injured like this," Matt murmured darkly. "He's worse than Caleb."

I bit my lip, trying to stifle the sob that was attempting to escape my mouth. But I was only partially successful. Caleb's abandonment had left me devastated, but it was nothing to how I felt now. I felt hollowed out. Gutted. Broken. Gabriel meant so much more to me than Caleb ever had.

Matt set the washcloth on the side of the tub and bent to place a kiss against my forehead. "Give me a second. I need to report the attack to the administration."

I nodded numbly as Matt pulled out his phone and called the president. I closed my eyes and relaxed into the warm water as Matt described the attack and relayed what the Demon had said. He also told her about my injuries and assured her that he was monitoring me and ensuring I was okay. After several moments of silence, in which the president spoke hurriedly on the other end, Matt told her that he understood, then ended the call.

"She's going to have all the off-duty warrior faction guards woken to assess the damage and determine how the Demon got through." He ran the washcloth gently over my face, wiping the tears and dirt away. "And they'll also be shoring up the defenses around the Academy. I'm hoping the Demon was lying about killing the warrior faction soldiers, but we need to know for sure. Either way, this is a bad sign. I'm not sure what the Academy will end up doing, or what the High Light Guardian will do, but it unfortunately seems like the Academy is no longer a neutral zone. The war is being brought here against our will."

I shivered, despite the hot water. I hated that war seemed to be such an inescapable inevitability. Matt sighed heavily and reached into the water, then pulled out the plug. He waited for the dirt and blood-filled water to drain, then replaced the plug so the tub could fill again with clean water. He added a generous squeeze of liquid soap this time, and it foamed up, filling the tub with comforting-smelling bubbles.

I sighed and sank deeper into the water, willing it to soak away all my pain and fear. Matt sat next to the tub and gently stroked my hair. I knew he was trying to reassure me—comfort me. But I felt very alone. The person I'd given my heart to, albeit unknowingly, had left me like it was nothing. It seemed like I was never good at placing my care and trust in the right people—in people who wouldn't hurt me. It was why I should've stuck to my old ways of survival. I never should've let him in like that in the first place. I never should've taken down the walls around my heart.

My phone buzzed violently on the vanity's stone counter, and I jumped in surprise. Matt and I exchanged a confused glance before Matt reached over and grabbed it. His expression went grim as he saw the identity of the caller.

"It's Gabriel." His voice was dark with anger. "Do you want me to pick up?"

My stomach fluttered, half with hope, half with dread. Why was he calling me now? He'd run away. Why would he contact me again so quickly? Unless . . . he needed something from me. My heart sank. That tended to be why people came back.

"No," I finally said, sinking further into the water. "I don't think I have it in me to deal with him right now."

Matt nodded and hit the button on the side of my phone, silencing it. He regarded me quietly for a while, observing my devastation. "I didn't know you felt so strongly about him," he finally said. There was no anger in his voice. No accusation. Just sadness.

"I didn't know either." I closed my eyes against the pain. "Not until it was too late. I'm pretty horrible at decoding my own emotions."

Matt released a slow breath, his hand gliding softly over the top of my head again. "I'm sorry. I'm sorry he hurt. And . . . I'm sorry he doesn't feel what you want him to feel."

I opened my eyes and glanced up at him. I knew it'd cost him a lot to say that, especially since he didn't want me to care about Gabriel like that. He'd made clear that he wanted to be the one I fell for.

I reached out and took his hand with my soapy one, squeezing his fingers. "Thank you."

His expression filled with warmth as he watched me, and he reached out and slid his fingers down my damp cheek. "You can stay here." His voice turned slightly gravelly. "For as long as you want. I don't want you to feel alone."

My eyes stung with tears again, and I nodded. "Thank you. I'd like to stay for a while." The thought of returning to my room and sitting there alone with my own emotions was too much to handle right now.

After my bath, I donned a pair of Matt's boxers and a T-shirt, then walked out to the living room and plopped down on the couch. Matt brought me a cup of hot tea, then sat next to me.

"He's been calling a lot," he murmured, handing me my phone. "Just so you know."

I pressed my eyes shut and let my head fall back against the top of the couch. I couldn't imagine what Gabriel wanted to say to me that badly. Especially now.

"Maybe I should answer it for you next time. That way you don't have to deal with him, and hopefully it will keep him from calling again."

I nodded, even as my chest tightened with tension, and handed my phone back to him. Then I curled up against the arm of the couch, bringing my knees up in front of me. I took a tentative sip of the tea and tried not to pull a face. I'd never had it before—it wasn't as good as coffee. But the warmth was comforting, so I focused on that as I took another sip. More than anything, I just wanted Gabriel to be here. I wanted to hear his voice and laugh. See his smirk. Experience the warmth of his presence. I already missed him. But how could I forgive him for abandoning me, especially when he knew how much that, in particular, would hurt me?

My phone started buzzing again, and Matt sighed and accepted the call. "What do you want?" he said gruffly.

My heart squeezed painfully as I heard Gabriel's voice on the other end. He was speaking quickly. He sounded upset.

"Yes, well, she's fine, no thanks to you. I've healed her and she's here with me. You should stop calling."

There was silence for a moment before Gabriel spoke again. He spoke less quickly now, but he still sounded upset.

"I don't think that's a good idea." Matt's voice was darker now. Angry. "She's exhausted and she doesn't want to deal with you right now."

Gabriel sounded angry as he spoke again.

"Fine," Matt snapped. "I'll ask her." He muted the call and turned to me. "Gabriel wants to come by to speak with you. He says he made a mistake and wants to explain." He rolled his eyes, clearly not buying it.

I clutched the tea close to my chest, worrying my bottom lip with my teeth, thinking. I *wanted* to see Gabriel. But I didn't want to hurt more.

Matt watched me carefully. "You don't have to say yes. He doesn't need to speak with you tonight. He's done enough damage for one day."

I closed my eyes for a moment and thought of Gabriel.

"*Terah, please,*" his voice whispered through my head. He sounded tired. Sad. My heart contracted.

"He can come here, but just for a few minutes. I don't have the energy for more than that."

Matt looked displeased, but he relayed the information to Gabriel, adding directions to his room. Then he hung up. I put the mug of questionable content on the wooden side table, then leaned my head on Matt's shoulder and closed my eyes. Matt wrapped his arm around my shoulders and pulled me closer. And I tried to draw strength from him. Enough strength that I could speak to Gabriel with dry eyes and some form of dignity. It'd be hard. And I was so tired.

Several minutes passed before there was a knock on the door. Matt sighed heavily and pushed to his feet. He pulled open the door and stepped to the side, letting Gabriel in. I looked up tentatively and winced when I saw him. He was still in the same clothes he'd worn during the battle, and the front of his jacket was covered in my blood. His face looked drawn, tired, upset, almost gaunt. I'd never seen him like that before.

"I'll give you two a few minutes," Matt said, an edge to his voice. He walked over to me and pulled me against him briefly, then leaned over and pressed a kiss to my forehead. "I'll be in my room down the hall if you need me." I nodded and smiled a little in thanks. Then he left, and Gabriel and I were alone.

Gabriel took a deep breath, then walked over and sat on the opposite end of the couch. He regarded the rug for a few moments in silence, then finally looked up at me. I could see the pain reflected in the electric blue of his eyes. My heart did a sad flip in my chest.

"I fucked up, Terah," he murmured, his voice a little hoarse. "I'm . . . I'm so sorry."

I chewed on my lip as I watched him. I wasn't sure what of the many things he'd done to hurt me he was apologizing for.

"I never should've left you there." He shook his head in disgust. "I know how much that hurts you. I just wasn't thinking." He looked at me imploringly. "I was so afraid that I'd pushed you away and lost you. I just couldn't take it, and I didn't know what to do, so I panicked and left."

He ran his hands through his hair. They looked even paler than usual.

"I realized the second I reached my dorm that I'd fucked up and done the last thing I should've done. The worst thing imaginable. So I turned around and went back to where I'd left you." He took a shaky breath. "But you were gone. All I saw was a pool of blood on the ground. And that was the first time I noticed my jacket was covered in blood too. I . . . I don't know how I didn't realize you were that injured before."

His fingers trembled as he let his hands fall to his sides again.

"I panicked. I ran back to your dorm and pounded on your door, but I didn't hear anything. I was afraid you might've passed out, so I let myself in, but it was clear you hadn't been back there. So I ran to the medical wing, but you weren't there either. I was so scared that someone had taken you, or that you were lying injured somewhere. That's why I started calling you. I just . . . wanted to make sure you were okay. I knew I'd already failed you twice this evening, and I wasn't willing to let it happen again."

I picked up my cup of tea to give my hands something to do. I felt conflicted. He'd left me, but he'd also quickly tried to come back. But that didn't erase the fact that he'd left in the first place. And that he'd broken my heart. But I supposed he didn't explicitly know that.

"I'm not Caleb," Gabriel murmured, his voice wavering slightly. "And I'm not Matt. Or your mother. I would never willingly leave you behind. And the fact that I left at all tonight instead of talking things out with you was a massive mistake. I'll never just leave like that again—not unless you ask me to go."

I pressed my lips together, unsure of what to say. Unsure of how I felt.

"What about the kiss?" I finally asked, my voice shaking a little. I needed to know why he'd pulled away. Why he'd looked horrified. Why he'd promise to never do it again.

Gabriel ducked his head, looking miserable. "I'm sorry about that too," he said quietly. "I promised myself that I'd never treat you like Matt did. I promised never to push you too far or take advantage of you. And I broke that promise. I broke your trust in me and acted without thinking. It was . . . inexcusable." He shook his head sadly. "All I can do is beg for your forgiveness and promise I won't do anything like that again."

His eyes met mine, shinier than usual, as though he was holding back tears. The breath rushed out of me, as though I'd been punched in the stomach.

"I care about you, Terah. You mean . . . so much to me. I don't want to lose your friendship. Not for anything."

My heart sputtered to life, but it also hurt. It wasn't the declaration I wanted from him, but it still meant something. He did care. Just not in the way I cared about him. Not in the way I wanted him to care about me. Could it be enough? I wasn't sure. But I also knew I didn't want to lose him either. Maybe I could suffer through the pain and still just be his friend. Maybe, after time passed, my feelings would pass too, and I could be content with just friendship. It'd be better than not being with him at all. Better than not having him in my life. It'd have to be enough. But something still gnawed at me.

"After you kissed me, you looked . . . disgusted. Horrified. Are you really that repulsed by me?" Tears sprang to my eyes again. I tried to blink them away—tried to keep him from seeing. His expression after he'd kissed me had hurt. It'd made me feel like a monster. Like I was horrible and revolting.

Gabriel turned to look at me, shock spreading across his face. "No. Terah, I'm not repulsed by you at all. I . . . thought that was clear. I was just horrified by my own actions. I was horrified I could break those boundaries I cared so much about without even a second thought." He shook his head again. "The problem was with me, not with you. My expression had nothing to do with you, I promise."

I bit my lip again. I still didn't fully understand. But perhaps his lack of romantic feelings for me didn't have to stem from a shortcoming of mine. Maybe. He'd never seemed to mind my proximity before. Surely, if he was truly repulsed by me, he would've reacted similarly at some other point. But I wasn't sure. I wasn't sure about anything at the moment.

"So . . . what do you want to happen from here?" I asked quietly.

Gabriel studied me for a long moment, as though he was trying to discern my true feelings. "I guess . . . I want us to be friends again," he finally said, leaning back into the couch. "I want you to trust me and feel safe with me. I want us to share things and spend time together. And I want to make up for all the mistakes I made tonight." He smiled at me—a beautiful, bittersweet smile. "But most of all, I just want you to be happy. Whatever it takes."

Being with him made me happy. It always had. But now I'd be with him knowing exactly how he felt about me, and that it wasn't what I wanted him to feel. But perhaps that was better. Perhaps it would make things easier, now that the lines around our friendship were more clearly drawn.

"I want that too," I finally said. And it wasn't entirely untrue. I wanted his friendship and presence in my life. I'd just have to be satisfied with that. I'd need to romantically move on.

Gabriel reached out slowly, giving me time to pull away or stop him, and gently took my fingers. The devastating warmth of him surrounded me there, seeping into me. I blinked back tears. I wanted more. So much more. But I'd have to get used to this. I'd have to push through it and move on. If I didn't, I'd lose him completely. So I took a deep breath and offered him a small smile in return.

Gabriel's smile broadened, and warmth reentered his eyes. He squeezed my fingers. "Thank you. For forgiving me and all my fuck-ups."

He slowly released my hand, then pushed to his feet. He sighed, stretching his arms above his head. He looked sore. Beyond exhausted.

"I'll let you get some rest," he murmured, lowering his arms and meeting my gaze again. He took a step backward toward the door, his eyes shifting briefly to the hall Matt had disappeared down, before returning to mine. "This is horrible timing, I know, but I never found the right time to ask. I was wondering if you wanted to go to the holiday party with me. As friends, of course," he added quickly.

His clarification cut through me like a knife. He was reminding me, yet again, where we stood. But I wanted to go with him. To be honest, I wanted to do everything with him. Going as friends would have to be enough.

"I was going to ask you earlier," he murmured, sliding his hands into his jacket pockets, "but the Demon attack kind of prevented it."

"Sure," I said quickly, trying to pull a smile onto my face. Trying to look like I was okay. That I was happy to remain just friends. "That sounds nice."

Gabriel smiled at me, warm and genuine, and nodded. "Thanks. And . . . I'm glad you're okay. I'll see you tomorrow." I smiled a little and nodded. Then he pulled open the door, gave me one last smile, then left.

I sat there in silence for a few moments. I should've felt happier than I currently did. He'd come back. He'd apologized. He'd told me how much he cared about me and that he'd never willingly abandon me. But all I could feel was the absence—the absence of the feelings I wanted from him.

I pushed to my feet, sighing heavily, and walked down the hall to Matt's room. The door was closed, so I knocked lightly.

"Come in."

I pushed open the door and walked inside. Matt had changed out of his clothes and was now just in some boxer briefs and a T-shirt. He was sprawled over his bed with a book in his hand. But he put it down as I came in, his worried eyes sweeping over my face.

"How did it go? Are you okay?"

I sighed heavily and shrugged. "We worked things out." I walked toward the bed. "He explained why he did what he did and apologized. And we're friends again. But . . . just friends. I guess that'll have to be enough."

Matt's expression grew sad as he watched me climb into bed next to him. I sank back against the pillows with a sigh, and he reached over and pulled me close. I buried my face in his chest, trying to accept his offer of comfort.

"It'll be okay," he murmured. "Not right away, but eventually it'll be okay."

I nodded, rubbing my nose into him. He was so warm. So familiar. I needed those things right now.

"I can go sleep on the couch," Matt murmured, his voice a little deeper as his hand rubbed comforting circles over my back. "You can take the bed."

I shook my head and grabbed a fistful of his shirt. "I want to stay with you. If . . . if that's okay." I wouldn't assume anymore. I wouldn't believe people felt a certain way unless they told me. Maybe that would save me from future heartache.

"Of course it's okay." His lips moved against my hair. "I'd always prefer to be with you."

My heart tugged sadly. Matt leaned over and pulled the covers over us, then settled his arms around me again. He pressed his lips to my forehead and the top of my head, his hand rubbing over my back, soothing me.

"Matt?"

"Mm?" He rubbed his nose gently against my hair.

"Do you still . . . feel romantically toward me?" My cheeks heated. It was an embarrassing question to ask.

Matt pulled back from me a little, so he could look down at my face.

"I . . . do," he said slowly, looking nervous. Like he was afraid I'd pull away from him.

I nodded slowly, silent for a long moment. "Can you . . . would you mind . . . kissing me?"

Matt's eyes widened. He looked stunned. Confused.

"But . . . you're in love with someone else." Sadness blanketed his features again. My heart squeezed. He wasn't wrong.

"But I love you too," I murmured, trying to reign in my other emotions. "Maybe not completely in the same way, but it's still there. And . . . I shouldn't dwell on what I can't have."

Matt's eyebrows lowered a little, uncertain. I could tell by the way his eyes were drawn to my lips that he wanted to kiss me, but I could also tell that he wasn't sure it was a good idea. It probably wasn't. But I desperately craved the affection. I desperately wanted to feel like I could move on. Like I could feel something with someone else. Like someone, at least, wanted me.

"I don't know if that would help either of us," he finally said, though he looked reluctant to say it.

I sighed, the heavy weight of disappointment filling me. But I nodded. He was probably right. I was being reckless. I laid my head back on his chest and blinked away the stinging tears. Matt held me close. I could hear his heart pounding beneath my cheek.

"Fuck it," he said a few moments later.

Much to my surprise, he rolled me onto my back, leaned over, and pressed his lips to mine. Warmth filled me. Slowly. A little at a time. Like I was thawing lightly in the sun. It was nothing like the fire that'd raged through me when Gabriel had kissed me, but it also wasn't nothing. It gave me a little hope.

I clung to Matt, wrapping my arms around his back as he kissed me tenderly and slowly. His lips moved over mine, warm and soft, his breath mingling with my own. And I sighed, relaxing and sinking into the soft mattress. This was, as it'd always been with Matt, oddly comforting. Familiar. Matt's tongue slid gently over my bottom lip before sliding into my mouth. Our tongues softly caressed, and Matt let out a deep groan. He pressed himself into me, his hard chest unyielding against my soft one. He slid his hand gently over my waist and stroked the bare skin there where my shirt had ridden up.

He finally broke the kiss and rested his forehead against mine, breathing hard. "Terah," he groaned quietly. I could hear the longing in his voice. And the restraint.

I reached up and pulled his face back to mine. This time we kissed with more urgency. His lips pulled insistently at mine, and his tongue delved deep. I gasped and threaded my fingers through his hair, pulling him closer. Our legs intertwined, his body completely covered mine, his scent and essence filled me. And I let him in. I desperately wanted his kiss to put me back together. I desperately needed this to be enough.

Matt pulled his mouth from mine and trailed his lips over my jaw and down my throat. I sighed, arching into him, giving him more access.

"Gods, Terah," he groaned before latching his mouth over my skin there, sucking insistently, his tongue swirling over me. I grabbed handfuls of the back of his shirt as pleasure sparked to life. *Yes.* This was what I wanted to feel. What I *needed* to feel. With someone other than Gabriel.

Matt returned his lips to mine, and we kissed desperately, clinging to each other. But I knew we were desperate for different things. Gabriel's face swam behind my closed eyelids as Matt's hands slid further up my sides under my shirt, moving warmly over my skin. I knew what he wanted. I could feel it in the speed of his pulse, his gasps of breath, the contraction of his stomach against mine, the hardening length of him.

And suddenly I knew. I knew I'd never be able to erase Gabriel from my mind and heart this way. It only made me think about him more. Want him more. Wish he was the one kissing me and pressing me insistently into the mattress instead of Matt. And it devastated me. But above all, it wasn't fair to Matt.

I pulled my mouth away from his and rested my forehead against his shoulder, gasping for breath. Matt gathered me in his arms and rolled off me, pulling me gently into his side.

"We should . . . probably stop," he panted.

I nodded against his chest, my hand splaying over his ribs. Tears stung my eyes. I loved him. I really did. But not like this.

Matt reached over and switched off the small lamp on his bedside table. Now the only light in the room came from the moonlight streaming through the windows.

"Thank you," I finally murmured, once my breathing had become more even. "For helping me tonight. For everything."

Matt smiled and pressed a soft kiss to my forehead. "I'll always be here for you. No matter what."

I nodded and settled against him more, his warmth surrounding me like a protective cocoon. I tried emptying my mind and heart of all the pain. I needed rest. I'd think about everything in the morning. My eyelids grew heavy as the seconds passed, and before long, I was asleep.

***

They were coming. Everything had led to this moment. All the attacks. All that violence. It all came down to this. His choice, and mine. But it hadn't really been a choice. I could never turn my back on everything and everyone I loved. And now I'd probably die. We all would. I ran, trying to reach Gabriel and Matt in time, but an explosion rent the air and the alarms began blaring. We were out of time. They were here.

The image dissolved, and I found myself in the cold and the dark. I was lying on the ground, gasping, struggling to breathe. Smoke from the vanquished Demon still billowed around me. I'd won, but I'd also lost. I could feel that with every fiber of my being. Snow fell quietly from the sky, not knowing it would land amongst such violence and carnage. I tried to breathe, but I couldn't draw in much air. My lungs were filling with liquid. I coughed a little, and blood dripped from my mouth. This was it. It was finally happening. But I didn't want to leave here alone. I didn't want the dark sky to be the last thing I saw. I closed my eyes, fighting to stay conscious. Fighting to concentrate through the agony that was my body.

"*Gabriel.*"

***

I jerked awake and bolted upright in bed, my chest heaving. The pain had felt so real. So all-consuming. I shivered and looked around. Nothing looked familiar. Nothing was in the right place. Panic jolted through me.

Then memories came flooding back. *Right.* I was in Matt's room. I'd forgotten.

Matt stirred next to me and brought his hand up to my shoulder. "Terah?" His voice was soft and gravelly. "Are you okay? What's wrong?"

I took a deep breath in and let it out slowly, trying to calm my racing pulse. "I'm okay. Just bad dreams."

Matt rubbed his eyes, then pushed into a sitting position. His tired, hazel gaze bored into mine, searching my expression. Then he moved his hand from my shoulder to me face, cupping my cheek and running his thumb over my skin.

"Bad dreams, or bad visions?"

I kept my expression neutral as I thought. Did I trust Matt enough to tell him what I'd seen? He'd promised not to report on me anymore, but I wasn't sure he'd be able to keep that promise. Not when my visions might hint at more attacks on the Academy. It wasn't that I wanted the Academy to be unprepared, I just wasn't sure how my visions worked yet. Whether they were certain or not. Where or when they'd take place. Each time I had a vision, a little more seemed to be revealed. But until I knew more, I didn't think the information would be very helpful. It would just cause panic.

I sighed. "Bad visions."

Matt nodded and laid back down, then pulled me down next to him. He wrapped his arms around me and held me to his chest.

"I'm sorry," he murmured. "Having visions sounds terrifying. I'm sorry you have to suffer through them."

I nodded, closing my eyes. Willing my heartbeat to return to its normal speed after all I'd seen and the immense pain I'd felt.

"Do you want to tell me about it?" I could hear the curiosity in his voice. But I could tell he was trying not to push me.

"Will you promise not to tell anyone about them? I know you'll want to, but you need to respect my decisions. I need to be the one who tells people, and I need to be the one who decides when and how to do that."

Matt's muscles tightened beneath my cheek. I glanced at his face and saw his conflict. His instincts and loyalties were warring against one another. He finally let out a long sigh.

"I promise. I can't pretend it'll be easy, but I promise to keep your secret."

My own tension eased slightly. "Thank you."

And then I told him about the visions, and even connected them to visions I'd had before. I wanted him to understand the scope, but I also wanted him to see that my visions revealed a little more each time. I wanted him to understand why I wanted to wait a bit longer before telling anyone about them.

Matt was silent for a while, and I sensed his regret that he'd promised not to tell anyone. "That makes it seem like there will be another attack on the Academy," he finally said, sounding resigned.

"Potentially. Though we could've probably guessed that anyway, since there have already been multiple attacks."

"True, but these sound much worse. And . . . it sounds like you'll get really injured."

I hadn't revealed to him the extent of my injuries in the last vision. I didn't want him to panic and break his promise because of that.

"But I've gotten really injured my whole life, Matt. It's not like that's a new thing for me. And if I continue fighting in this war, injuries are inevitable. It's a risk all soldiers take, and we all have to face the consequences of that. Besides, nothing in my visions showed me not recovering."

Matt made an unhappy sound at the back of his throat, but his arms tightened around me. He hated the thought of me being injured, and he wanted to prevent it, but he'd also promised not to tell anyone. I'd hold him to that promise. And in the meantime, I'd try to learn more about each vision so I could maybe prevent them or alter the circumstances somehow. Nothing was fully written in stone. I had to believe I had some power to change things, otherwise, it'd just be a cruel method of torture—showing me what would happen with no chance of stopping it. In my experience, Divines were given powers for a reason.

"You promise you'll tell the administration?" Matt asked quietly.

I nodded against his chest. "As soon as I have enough information to be helpful."

I felt Matt nod. I knew ceding control in this would be hard for him. But it was also a test. A test that he could step back and trust my judgment. That he could believe in me when it mattered most. Matt didn't say anything more, so I settled against his chest again and closed my eyes. His warmth seeped through me, and sleep overtook me again.

Matt woke me up around noon the next day as he came into the room and collapsed on the bed next to me. He'd insisted I skip training, given how much blood I'd lost the night before. He sighed heavily and placed his hand on top of my head, gently stroking my hair.

I yawned and turned over so I could look at him. "Tough day of training?"

"Brutal." He grimaced. "Had to split my time between training with Caleb and training with Gabriel, and both seem pretty eager to beat me up. Had to work extra hard to be on top of my game."

I couldn't help the smile that pulled at my lips. "I feel like I should apologize for that, or something."

Matt smiled wryly at me. "You do seem to have a strong effect on people. But I can't complain." He smirked. "Not when you're here in my bed."

My cheeks burned, and I looked away, suddenly uncomfortable.

"Sorry." Matt's smile faded. "That was meant to be a joke. In poor taste, I know . . ."

"It's okay. You're not wrong."

He cleared his throat. "So, am I right in guessing you don't have a dress for the holiday party?"

"Yeah. I never needed one in Dagmar, and I don't know how I'd get one delivered here. So I guess I'll just make do."

"Well," he said slowly, pulling at his lower lip, "I was thinking that maybe we could go on a small adventure. As a professor, I'm allowed to leave the grounds." He smirked. "What do you think? Want to get out of here for the afternoon and go find you a dress back on the Normal plane?"

I sat up, my pulse racing. "Seriously? You're allowed to take me off campus?" I'd never traveled outside of Dagmar, and I was itching to see more of the world—more of what I was supposed to be giving my life to protect.

Matt's smile was crooked, but genuine. "Yeah. I got the president's permission and everything."

I grinned, a bubble of excitement expanding in my chest, making it feel lighter than it had in a while. "That honestly sounds amazing."

Matt grinned, looking pleased. "I was hoping you'd think so. I brought some clothes from your room for you. Used the Academy override code to get in—hope you don't mind. But I didn't think you'd want to walk all the way back there in my clothes."

I laughed. "Yeah, that might've looked weird. I don't mind."

"Good. I left them on the dresser over there." He nodded across the room. "I'll make you lunch while you get ready." He pushed off the bed and headed for the kitchen, closing the door behind him.

I pushed slowly out of bed and winced. Even though Matt had healed me, my body was carrying the after-effects of all the strain it'd gone through. I was pretty sore. And, as I'd almost completely drained my power yesterday, it hadn't fully replenished yet, so there was little to alleviate the soreness. I walked over to the dresser and grabbed the clothes he'd picked out for me. Along with a new bra, underwear, and socks, I saw a navy tank top, a matching navy sweater, and a pair of dark blue skinny jeans. They were my nicest pair. I hadn't bothered wearing them much this semester as they weren't quite my style. I wondered if Matt had chosen them because they were one of the few pairs that weren't intentionally ripped. I rolled my eyes. The rips were my favorite parts. That's what made them my style. And underneath all this lay the necklace he'd bought for me four years ago. I smiled. Matt had never mentioned noticing that I wore it, but he clearly had, and he clearly liked it.

I dressed quickly, pulled on my boots, stashed my knives down the sides, and freshened up in the bathroom. Then I walked to the living room. Matt had finished preparing lunch in the tiny kitchenette, and brought the plates and cups to the small, round table near the window.

"Just made us some sandwiches." He sat down opposite me. "I figured we can get other food when we're on the Normal plane."

I nodded and bit into the sandwich. "Where are we going?"

Matt swallowed his food. "It's a large town not too far from one of the plane exits. It's a mixed Divine and Normal town, but it's not a border town. They have a good selection of stores and some great food. I think you'll like it."

I nodded, taking another bite of my sandwich. I'd probably like any town that wasn't Dagmar. "Sounds nice. I still can't believe you're allowed to take me off-plane."

Matt smiled and shrugged. "Like I said, staff members are allowed to leave pretty much whenever. Plus, the president knows you and I grew up together, and I'm pretty sure that she's eager to keep you happy, especially after all these Demon attacks. She doesn't want you blaming the school for your injuries."

I laughed, surprised. I'd never thought about blaming that on anyone other than the Demon that'd injured me, and the Dark Guardians who usually sent them.

"And how will we get from the plane exit to the town?" I took another bite of the sandwich.

"Well, the specific plane exit we'll be using is guarded on the other side by a small facility that also keeps cars around for staff who need to run errands. We'll take one of those."

My eyebrows rose. We didn't have cars in Dagmar. "When did you learn to drive?"

Matt grinned. "When I went to school here. One of my friends was from the town we're going to, and I stayed with him a lot over breaks. He taught me. And the Academy issues all the paperwork that the Normals usually require, so if we're pulled over by their police, we should be good."

I nodded slowly, trying to mask my expression as shock trickled through me. Matt had told me he'd stayed at the Academy over breaks. That he'd been too busy doing work for them to return to Dagmar. Too busy to visit me.

"You mean . . . between jobs that the Academy had for you?"

Matt swallowed his bite of food and set down his sandwich. His eyes carefully met mine. "Of course. It was an easy trip, since the town is so close to campus."

I narrowed my eyes as I watched him. He didn't look like he was lying, but it was hard to tell. My stomach tightened, my appetite vanishing. I wondered for the first time how true it really was. It'd be a big lie, even for him. An inexcusable one. But if he *had* lied, I doubted he'd so flippantly reveal that now. Maybe he'd simply misspoke.

"We can leave as soon as you finish eating." Matt picked up his glass and drained it of water. He'd already finished eating his sandwich.

I nodded, pushing my plate away from me. I couldn't eat any more right now. "I'm ready. I just need to grab my stuff."

I pushed from the table, wanting a little space from him for the moment. I didn't like the doubt that'd infested me. All I really wanted to do was banish it. Matt had made a lot of mistakes, but one thing he'd never done was leave me behind to die for no reason. He'd raised me. Loved me when no one else had. Wrote to me constantly. Missed me. He wouldn't have left me alone in Dagmar unless there was absolutely no other choice.

I grabbed my phone from the side table next to the couch and saw there was a text waiting for me. I smiled, releasing a slow breath, something akin to relief tunneling through me. *Gabriel.* I hadn't realized how worried I'd been that he'd changed his mind about being friends. That he'd had time to dwell on how much I'd responded to his kiss—too much—and no longer wanted anything to do with me.

"Missed you at training," the text read. "Hope you're feeling better. Text me when you're up and I can bring you some food and coffee."

I sank onto the arm of the couch. He still wanted to spend time with me. He still wanted to be friends. While he'd said that yesterday, I wasn't used to people coming back the way he had. And it was hard to banish all the doubts that'd resurfaced when he'd left. I read the message again and smiled.

"Thanks, I'm feeling a lot better. Just a little sore and drained. Matt's taking me off-plane so I can buy an outfit for the holiday party. We're going to a Normal-Divine town near one of the plane exits. I've never been to a town other than Dagmar, so I'm excited. My phone won't work off-plane, though, so I'll text you when I get back."

I sent the message, pocketed my phone, then looked around for my destroyed jacket. I found it folded on a chair by the hall, so I quickly rummaged through the pockets and retrieved my cigarettes and lighter. The cigarettes were a little smooshed but were salvageable. And they were thankfully free of blood.

Matt grabbed a bundle of fabric on the corner of the couch and walked it over to me. "I also grabbed this, since I kind of destroyed your jacket from yesterday."

I took it from him and saw that it was my coat that'd barely survived my last battle with a Demon. But I'd washed and mended it since then, so it was currently my most functional warm outerwear.

"Well, I value my life over my clothing, so I don't mind losing it. Besides, I can fix it if I really want to." I pulled on the coat and zipped it up. "Thanks for grabbing this."

"I stuck some gloves in one of the pockets. They might be a bit big, since they're my spares, but it's better than freezing off your fingers. I'm not sure how much we'll be outside, so I wanted to be prepared just in case."

I smiled, some of the tension I'd felt toward him easing slightly. "Thanks."

Matt donned his jacket, then we exited the staff residence building and walked toward the plane barrier on the east side of campus. The sun was bright today, but the air was freezing, and our breath rose in little puffs in front of us as we walked.

I shivered and pulled out a cigarette. Matt frowned at me as I lit it, but didn't say anything. I knew he didn't like that I smoked, but we all did what we had to, to survive, and this was my way, for now. He'd left—he didn't get a say in what I'd had to do to endure that loss. I inhaled a soothing stream of smoke, then blew it gently into the air above me.

My phone buzzed as we reached the trees, and I pulled it from my pocket with my free hand. Gabriel had responded.

"Woah, I didn't know anyone was allowed to leave campus. Sounds like fun. Enjoy the town and be careful. I'll miss you."

My cheeks warmed. Gabriel wasn't usually this straight forward and transparent about his feelings. Matt glanced at me and then at my phone. Again, he didn't say anything, but his shoulders took on a new stiffness, and I knew he guessed Gabriel and I were talking.

"I'll miss you too," I wrote back quickly. "Wish you could come. I'll see you later."

I pocketed my phone, put out my cigarette, then pulled on the gloves Matt had given me. Just a few minutes in the cold had made them stiff and frigid. The gloves were a little big, but warm, so I didn't mind.

Matt and I finally reached the plane barrier and were greeted by several warrior faction soldiers posted there. They straightened up and nodded at him as we got close.

"I believe the president called ahead about our departure," Matt said to the closest guard.

"Yes, she did. Just give us a moment, and we'll have the portal opened for you."

Matt nodded. "Thanks."

We stood to the side as the guard called the administration office to have the barrier opened around the portal we needed. A few minutes later, a hole formed in the barrier, revealing a swirling gray circle—the portal—just large enough for us to pass through one at a time.

"It'll only be open for twenty seconds," the warrior faction soldier said, "so please hurry through."

Matt grabbed my hand and pulled me toward it. "I'll go first." He glanced at me. "Make sure you follow as quickly as you can."

I nodded, and he released me. Then he walked into the swirling, opaque gray, and vanished. I took a deep breath and followed. Walking through the portal felt weird—like walking through jelly. But I quickly emerged from the other side and found myself standing on browning grass, gray clouds swirling angrily above me. The portal closed behind us.

I followed Matt to a small building about thirty feet to our right. It was non-descript, but I could tell it was where the Academy personnel were stationed. The building was very old, and like all the buildings at the Academy, was made of stone with wrought-iron accents.

Matt scanned his Academy ID at the front door, and it clicked open, allowing us to walk into a small reception area. Matt walked up to the desk and handed over his ID, then mentioned the president's call-ahead, and asked to borrow a car. The receptionist nodded and had Matt fill out a form while she went to find the car keys. A few minutes later, she led us back outside to a parking lot behind the building. Just like at the Academy, it was funny to see something so modern attached to a building so old. The receptionist led us to a small, sleek-looking car and gave Matt the keys.

"When should we expect you back?" she asked, as Matt unlocked the car and opened the driver's-side door.

He glanced at me before responding. "Probably around ten or eleven?"

The receptionist nodded and handed Matt a small, old-looking flip phone. "Keep this on in case we or the Academy need to contact you."

Matt nodded and thanked the receptionist, then motioned for me to get in the car. I pulled open the door and slid onto the black leather seat. The car smelled new, and the interior was covered in dark, highly polished wood. I fastened my seatbelt as Matt pulled out of the parking lot. The car's engine hummed pleasantly as he drove. It sounded like, if he wanted to, Matt could push the car to go pretty fast. He grinned at me and reached over to turn on the radio. He already looked more relaxed.

"It's nice to get away from the Academy sometimes." He directed the car down a small, deserted road. "It's kind of freeing."

I smiled and watched the landscape speed by us. "I always wanted to travel more, see more places, but never got the chance while living in Dagmar."

Matt nodded sympathetically. "I never got to travel until I came to the Academy, as you know. Then I got to see several different cities and towns because of my friends. I even got to fly in an airplane for the first time. It was kind of wild, but also awesome."

My stomach clenched and I frowned, glancing at him. When had he had time to do all that? And if he had, why hadn't he had time to visit me?

He glanced over at me and saw my frown. His smile turned patient, and he reached over and squeezed my hand. "Not every job the Academy had for me was on campus, Terah."

I let out a breath I'd been holding and nodded. That made sense. He'd just never told me about his off-campus adventures in his letters.

"Have you ever thought about leaving the Academy?" I tried keeping my voice light. "Leaving the Divine world and the war behind and starting a new life somewhere else?"

Matt frowned, returning his hand to the steering wheel. "I won't lie—I've thought about it. But . . . my place is with the Light Guardian side of the war, and my loyalty belongs to them. I've been given gifts that can protect people, and I can't turn my back on that. I think the guilt of doing that would be worse than my lack of freedom is now."

My stomach sank. I knew he was right. It was mostly how I felt as well, but I really wanted *someone* to consider it. I wanted someone to validate my own longing to leave it all behind. But Matt was right. How could I live with myself if I knew people were dying and that I might've been able to prevent it? But that reality stung, because I knew what it really meant: because of who and what we were, we'd never be free. We'd never truly have a choice about our lives.

I sank back into the leather seat, feeling deflated and hollow. It was a waste of energy to wish for a different life—to long for something I couldn't have. All I could do was enjoy moments like this—small moments of freedom and adventure.

Matt glanced over at me, his gaze sweeping over my face. "I know it's not fair, but I truly believe we can find happiness anyway. We just have to grab meaningful opportunities and moments. Try to live as fully as we can whenever we can. It's hard, but I think it's possible."

I nodded, turning my head to look out the side window. I couldn't summon the same optimism, but it made me feel a little better that someone in the same position as me *could* feel optimistic about the future. I hoped Matt was right—that even within all the violence, we could all find some kind of happiness and fulfillment.

Thirty minutes later, we reached the edge of the town. I sat up eagerly and peered out the window as we drove down the main street. There were so many buildings. Countless stores and restaurants with bright signs and gleaming windows. Unbroken sidewalks ran in front of the buildings, bordered with small, manicured trees, bushes, and seasonal flower arrangements. Strands of twinkling lights and strings of garland twined up the poles of the streetlights. Everything looked so clean. So bright. So cheerful. There were no signs of destruction. No perpetual repair. No scorched earth, dead plant life, piles of rubble. Was this what all non-border towns were like?

Matt turned into the parking lot of a large shopping center in the middle of town and found a parking space near the entrance. Then we made our way inside and Matt found a directory of all the stores. The mall was huge—there had to be at least fifty stores—and was bursting with people. I tried my best not to gawk, not to seem too out of place, but I'd never seen anything like it. Everything was colorful and vibrant. There were stores full of things I'd never seen before. And the voices of hundreds of people all melded together creating a loud hum that rolled and shifted as people moved around us.

Matt picked out a handful of stores that might meet our needs, then took my hand and guided me through the crowd. We went through the first few stores on our list, but neither of us found clothing we liked, so we decided to go to one of the larger department stores that had a little bit of everything.

I perused the dress section there, which was thankfully much larger than the dress sections at any of the smaller stores we'd been to. Matt ran off to look at suits while I browsed. Apparently, he'd gotten a little taller and broader since the last time he'd purchased one.

I picked through the dresses, wrinkling my nose at many of them. Most were too flashy, too sparkly, or too ruffly for my tastes. I wanted something that straddled the boundary between edgy and feminine, revealing and covered. I finally found what I was looking for when I reached the last rack. Buried in the middle was a short, long-sleeved dress that had a plunging deep-V neckline, and a collection of rhinestones that decorated the shoulders. Other than that, the dress was plain black. It looked elegant and sexy, with just the right amount of edginess. Plus, it was my favorite color.

I smiled, found one that looked like the right size, and pulled it off the rack. I'd need to try it on though. I glanced around, but Matt wasn't in sight, so I shrugged and walked into the dressing room anyway. He was smart. He'd figure it out.

I quickly pulled off my clothes and boots and pulled the dress over my head, shimmying it down my hips. It was made of dense but stretchy mate- rial, which made it form-fitting, but not restricting or uncomfortable. The hem showed off quite a bit of leg, landing around my mid-thigh area, and the deep V in front went down to my waist, baring quite a bit of my chest and torso. It was too low and wide for a traditional bra, so I'd need to buy an alternative while we were here. It'd be a daring dress to wear, but it also felt just right.

I smiled at my reflection, then opened the dressing room door. Matt was leaning leisurely against the door frame leading from the dressing room back into the main part of the store, and he had the components of a suit draped over his arm.

"What do you think?"

Matt looked up and his eyes went a little wider in surprise. I did a slow turn for him, so he could see the dress from all angles, and had to suppress my laugh as I saw his cheeks turning pink.

"I know I don't have the right bra for it yet, but I think it suits me. Thoughts?"

Matt opened his mouth, but no sound came out for a long moment. Then he snapped his mouth shut and shook his head, a smile forming. "Clearly, I like it." He straightened and walked closer. "It looks good on you. Perhaps a little too good," he murmured, his gaze heating as it traveled slowly down my body.

I smiled, trying to push down my discomfort. He wasn't the one I wanted noticing me like that.

"Are you going to the party with anyone?" Matt reached forward and caught my fingers with his. He pulled me closer, so I was standing less than a foot from him.

I tensed, knowing my answer would upset him. "Gabriel asked me to go with him . . . as friends. I told him I would."

As predicted, Matt's shoulders stiffened, his expression hardening. "Is that wise? After everything that's happened?"

"He only asked me yesterday," I murmured. "When he came over to your place to talk to me. He didn't seem to think it'd be a problem. We did work things out . . ."

Matt shook his head in disbelief. "How did he possibly manage to stick that question into the conversation you had?"

"Why do you ask?" I skirted around the question. "Were *you* going to ask me? It's a bit late, you know. The dance is tomorrow."

Matt ducked his head and nodded. "I know. I waited too long. I was just debating with myself about whether I should ask you at all. I didn't want to pressure you or anything. Especially after the mistakes I've made this semester. But I guess I waited too long." He smiled sadly.

Secretly, I was relieved he hadn't asked me before today. I wasn't sure I would've felt comfortable saying yes. Not before what'd happened between Gabriel and I. Even now, I was still glad I was going with Gabriel, even if it was only as friends.

"It barely matters who I go with." I stepped back and pulled my hand from his. "Especially since I'm just going with Gabriel as friends. You and I can hang out and dance too." I spun one last time and gave him a mischievous smile.

Grudgingly, Matt smiled back and nodded.

"Just give me a sec to change."

I pulled on my regular clothes and slid into my boots. Matt had made me leave my knives in the car—he'd said we'd set off the security systems in all the stores if we kept them on us. I'd grudgingly agreed, but keenly felt their absence, like I was missing a vital piece of clothing.

"Okay, where to next?" I asked as I emerged from the dressing room holding the dress.

"You mentioned needing a different bra?"

"Oh yeah. Also, some shoes and maybe some jewelry and makeup."

We wandered around the large, multi-level department store and found the shoe section. I picked out a pair of tall, black velvet heels with a stripe of rhinestones and sharp spikes down the back in the same color as the rhinestones on my dress. Matt also picked out some black leather dress shoes to go with his suit. In the undergarments section, I found a stick-on bra with individual adhesive cups that'd be completely invisible under the dress. I also grabbed a pair of thigh-high nude tights. In the jewelry section, I found some long, sparkly, silver earrings that almost reached my shoulders, and a simple, thin necklace of silver chain that had a single spike hanging from the center. Finally, I grabbed a tube of dark red lipstick on our way to the check-out line. It was a cross between blood red and a deep maroon—it'd be the perfect small pop of color.

Once we made our purchases, we exited the mall and hurriedly stored our bags in the trunk before hopping in the car to get out of the cold. Matt drove us further down the main road as the sun began to set, pointing out restaurants and stores that he'd frequented when he'd stayed in town between his jobs at the Academy. It occurred to me for the first time that I'd never asked what those jobs had entailed. He'd never volunteered the information. I'd always just assumed it was important and was required for him to be able to keep attending the school. I didn't know if they'd given him a scholarship like they'd done for me, or if he'd had to work to pay his way through. I'd always assumed the latter. I bit the inside of my cheek as I watched the colorful lights from all the stores go by. Now probably wasn't the time to ask him about it. But I eventually should. I deserved to know what was more important than returning to me—the child he'd left in a war zone.

We finally reached the other side of town and Matt pulled into the parking lot of his favorite restaurant.

"I used to eat here all the time with Javier and his family," he said enthusiastically. He parked the car smoothly and turned off the engine. "Usually at least once a week. I think you'll really like it."

We got out of the car, and I followed Matt to the front doors of the brightly lit building with a colorful neon sign out front. We pushed inside and were hit with a wall of sound. There were people everywhere, talking, laughing, eating. It was a bit overwhelming. But the atmosphere was also cozy. Happy. It wasn't the loudness of chaos, violence, or battle, but of community, friends, and family.

A couple minutes later, Matt and I were shown to a table at the back of the restaurant. I looked through the menu once we'd settled in, but Matt had so many favorites that he wanted to share that I ended up letting him order for the both of us. I couldn't help smiling as the food was finally delivered to our table.

"Woah, this is a lot. It looks amazing though."

Matt grinned. "It tastes even better." He started dishing the food onto plates for us. "We have a few different kinds of tacos here," he pointed, "and fajitas, sopes, a couple tamales, rice, beans, and fresh guacamole. Oh, and horchata," he added, gesturing at our cups. "I almost cried when I ate here for the first time." He smiled and passed me my plate. "It's so much better than border town and cafeteria food. I never knew food could taste this good."

I smiled and picked up a taco filled to bursting with spicy smelling meat. I took a bite, and my eyes promptly slid closed. Flavor burst through my mouth—rich meat, warm spices, tangy lime, the bite of onion, the cooling of cilantro—combining to create a flavor that was totally new to me. I groaned. I couldn't help it. It was the most flavorful thing I'd ever eaten.

Matt laughed, and I opened my eyes to see him grinning at me. "It's amazing, right?"

I nodded and took another bite, sighing as the flavor filled my mouth again. It was heavenly. I understood why Matt had been happy to eat here so often.

"Sometimes, when I have a lighter day, I go off-plane and come here just to remember what good food tastes like." Matt took a large bite out of one of his tacos and sighed. He closed his eyes and nodded as he chewed. "It never gets old."

We ate until we couldn't fit anything more in our stomachs, then donned our jackets and made our way back through the bustling room. It was dark when we finally exited the restaurant, and soft flurries were drifting down from the sky, melting before they accumulated on the ground. I pulled the cold air into my lungs on a deep breath. It felt refreshing after the warmth of the restaurant and the rich food.

We climbed into the car, then Matt pulled out of the lot and headed back in the direction we'd come. I gazed out the window as we drove down the main street that'd take us out of the town, and I tried to memorize everything I saw. The many lights, the glimmering storefronts and restaurants, the people laughing and smiling, the lack of war. It was so vibrant here. So different. I wanted to remember this. Maybe someday I'd be able to come back.

"Thanks for this, Matt," I murmured as we exited town and sped down the dark country road, the car engine humming cheerfully.

Matt smiled and reached over, taking my hand with his. "I wanted to give you something special," he murmured. "Something no one else could give you. I'm really glad you liked it."

I glanced at his face and saw his cheeks burning. I bit the inside of my cheek and looked back out the window, discomfort turning my stomach. It felt too soon to be accepting romantic gifts and words from him. And I knew that's how he'd intended this gift to be taken. But . . . Matt had given me freedom and new experiences. I should feel grateful, not awkward that he felt more for me than I did for him. I needed to focus on the gratefulness, and how wonderful the experience was, not on how much I wished I'd experienced this with Gabriel instead.

I sighed and sank back in the passenger seat, watching as the road stretched ominously before us, vanishing into the dark of the countryside. It'd be hard to go back to a life of no freedom or travel after seeing such a different world. But I didn't regret it. I'd rather know what amazing things the world held, even if it was just a glimpse. Maybe it'd help me feel more passionate about protecting it.

"I wanted to talk to you," Matt said, breaking the silence as we sped past barren fields. "About us. Our relationship."

I tensed slightly and glanced over at him. He was frowning, but he didn't look angry or sad for a change.

"Okay . . ." I wasn't sure what we were going to talk about. He knew where I stood right now. He knew I wanted Gabriel and not him. Not like that.

"I just want you to know that I . . . well, I want to date you." He sounded slightly embarrassed. "I know that's not what you're ready for yet. I realize that, I really do."

I nodded and looked out the window again. The tightness in my chest was returning little by little.

"But I didn't want to leave you with any doubts about my feelings for you. I want to be more than friends. And . . . I want to know how you feel about that."

I pressed my lips together and glanced at him again. How *did* I feel about that? Well, I supposed it felt nice to be wanted, even if it wasn't by the person I wanted. And it *did* offer me some kind of reassurance about the future. I cared deeply about Matt, and I was attracted to him to a certain extent. It was . . . easy with him. Comfortable. I could see us being happy. Mostly. But I knew deep down that I'd never be ecstatically happy. There wouldn't be unbridled passion. And I hadn't known I wanted that until I'd kissed Gabriel. I hadn't known what it *could* be like. But Matt was here, offering himself, and Gabriel wasn't. He'd made it pretty clear that he didn't see me or want me that way. But could he? Should I so quickly give up on what I'd glimpsed between us just for stability and more assured care? I wasn't sure. But Matt was waiting for some kind of answer.

I took a deep breath and let it out slowly. "You're right that I'm not ready yet," I said quietly. "I only just discovered how I feel about Gabriel, and it seems like a bad idea to jump straight from that into something else."

Matt nodded slowly, gripping the steering wheel tightly. He was nervous.

"But I obviously care about you. And I like spending time with you. I always have. So . . . maybe, with enough time, I might be open to dating. But . . . not right now."

I weaved my fingers through each other in my lap, nervously. I didn't want to hurt him, but I knew I'd hurt him more if I lied and jumped into something with him that I wasn't ready for. It wouldn't be fair to either of us. I needed enough time to put my feelings for Gabriel behind me before I could move on. I'd discovered at least that much last night when I'd tried to use Matt's kiss to wipe Gabriel from my mind. It'd truly backfired, for me at least.

"I understand," Matt said quietly. "And I don't need a promise or anything. Just a possibility that you might be interested in a relationship with me."

He smiled over at me briefly, his eyes sad again. I knew, now, that this was another reason why Matt resented Gabriel so much. I'd thought it was just an ego thing between the two of them, but I'd been wrong. Matt hadn't liked Gabriel because he'd seen me let him in, in a way I'd rarely let anyone in. And Matt had guessed what that could mean. To Matt, if Gabriel hadn't been around, I probably would've said yes to him much earlier. I wouldn't have had any feelings for anyone else to compare against my feelings for him. I wouldn't have known better. But he couldn't turn back time and erase Gabriel's influence on me. It was much too late for that.

I knew we were too far for me to communicate with him, but I closed my eyes and thought about Gabriel anyway as we sped deeper into the dark countryside in silence. I thought about his mischievous smile, his piercing blue eyes, the way he always looked at me closely—closer than anyone else—to figure out what I was really feeling, the way his hand felt in mine, his laugh, the way his hair fell forward in front of his eyes. In just one semester, all these things had become dear to me. *He'd* become dear to me.

I smiled a little, giving space to those feelings in my mind. There, they didn't have to be bad or wrong. They weren't rejected. They didn't make me weak. They just were. And they were proof that, after everything I'd been through, I was still capable of love, even though I'd tried so hard to lock away that part of myself. Love was tearing a hole in my chest right now, but it was simultaneously filling me with warmth and light. What I'd thought could only lead to heartbreak and pain was also teaching me about beauty, care, and capacity. About gentleness amidst the violent fray. And someday, someone would love me back. I'd just have to wait—become a stronger version of myself, while still being open enough to care. That'd been what I'd failed to see before—that you could be strong and vulnerable at the same time. That the two could, and perhaps *should* coexist. I could be strong enough to survive the violence and pain, and open enough to see the beauty and care. Only through openness could I ever hope to find a semblance of balance. And only balance could help my soul survive.

Thirty minutes later, Matt parked the car in the lot behind the outpost near the portal. We exited the car and grabbed our bags.

"Just give me a sec to run in and get the portal opened," he called over his shoulder, already walking toward the building.

I nodded and walked slowly to the place we'd materialized from earlier. I shivered as chilly wind whipped across the open field of dead grass and pulled my jacket more tightly around myself. It was a little eerie out here in the dark countryside with only the sounds of the howling wind for company. I hoped Matt would hurry.

Matt exited the building a few minutes later and walked toward me with a different receptionist from the one we'd dealt with earlier. The receptionist was on the phone, presumably one that allowed him to be in contact with the Academy even from here.

"The barrier should be opened soon," Matt reassured me, noticing my shivers. "The warrior faction guards have already called in the request to the administration, so we're just waiting for them at this point."

"M'kay." I shoved my hands into my jacket pockets, my bag dangling from my wrist.

The receptionist ended the call and walked over to us as a portal appeared—a wall of barely visible shifting gray.

"You have twenty seconds."

Matt and I nodded and hurried forward. Then we stepped through, one at a time. I trudged through the jelly-like atmosphere and emerged back on the Academy grounds right behind Matt. The portal closed with a small pop behind us.

We were greeted on the other side by at least three times the number of warrior faction soldiers we'd seen here earlier. A vast company, more like an army than a security presence, spanned the border to each side of us, as far as I could see. I looked around, startled. This was a much more militarized border situation. I quickly glanced at Matt to see his reaction to this. His expression was fairly neutral, but I noticed him glancing around as well. I stepped closer to him and grabbed his sleeve, worry hammering through me, outpacing my pulse.

"Do you think something happened while we were gone?" I whispered.

Matt shrugged as the soldiers closest to us nodded at him. He nodded back. "Not that I heard." He shouldered his bags and pulled out his gloves. "But you never know." His tone was mild. Too mild.

Fear overwhelmed the confusion and pulsed thickly through me. If something had happened and I wasn't here . . .

I pulled out my phone and opened my texts to Gabriel. "Are you okay?" I wrote as I followed Matt through the dark trees back toward the campus buildings. "We just got back and there are triple the amount of soldiers at the plane barrier than were here when we left. Did something happen? Was there another attack?"

I sent the text, then slid my phone back into my pocket and jogged to catch up with Matt. After everything that'd emerged from these trees at night thus far, I didn't want to be caught in here alone.

Matt and I finally exited the line of trees and started making our way across the grass. But I tensed as I noticed a figure walking toward us. Even with only the light of the moon, I could tell it was the president. My stomach tightened. Something must've happened. Why else would she be out here at this time of night?

Matt inclined his head as she approached us, but I couldn't move. I was cold with fear. Gabriel hadn't texted me back yet. What if something had happened to him?

"Hello, you two." The president smiled cheerfully as she stopped in front of us. My fear turned to confusion. Why would she be smiling if something bad had happened? "I hope you enjoyed your day off campus." She looked from Matt to me.

I cleared my throat. "Yes," I managed to say, trying to mask my confusion. "Very much so. Thanks for allowing it."

"Oh, not a problem." She waved her hand dismissively. "Especially after all you've done to help us."

I managed a small smile. She must mean after fighting and defeating Demons on the grounds.

"And I must thank you for the newest insight you've given us." She gestured toward the tree line. "I was just on my way to check in with the new warrior faction soldiers. You saw them on your way back in I presume."

I nodded mutely, highly confused. I felt like I was missing something. Matt tensed at my side.

"Thanks to the information from your visions, we've had the opportunity to bring in more warrior faction guards, so we're prepared in case of further, larger attacks." Her expression grew serious. "This is invaluable information, and I really can't thank you enough for disclosing these insights to us."

It was my turn to tense. I *hadn't* told the school about my visions. Not at all. Not yet. The only people I'd ever revealed my visions to were Gabriel and Matt, and I knew Gabriel would never willingly offer to help the administration or the warrior faction unless it was an emergency. And if that was the situation, he'd still tell me first. Which meant . . .

My stomach dropped as I turned and looked at Matt, my eyes hardening.

"Tell me you didn't," I thought at Matt, the connection between our minds snapping into place as a result of my anger. *"Tell me you didn't break your promise to me the same fucking day that you made it."* Matt glanced at me, sadness in his eyes, before looking away. He didn't bother to respond, which was, in itself, an answer.

I turned back to the president and plastered a fake smile onto my face. "Of course. Always happy to help protect my fellow students."

She beamed at me and reached forward, placing her hand on my shoulder. "We greatly value your skills and your loyalty." She seemed oblivious to the thick tension gathering between Matt and me. "I hope, upon your graduation, you'll consider joining the warrior faction like Matthew. They need all the bright and skilled young people they can get, especially in these increasingly dark times." She patted my shoulder and bade us farewell, continuing toward the trees. But I was frozen with dread. What was she talking about? Matt wasn't in the warrior faction.

I turned slowly to face him, cold tension making my muscles rigid. He'd betrayed me. Lied to me. Again. After everything we'd been through and all his promises to change. He'd promised to trust me in exchange for my trust in him. To let me decide when it was right to tell the administration. But he'd just gone and told them anyway, seemingly with no hesitation. He'd betrayed my trust when I'd needed it from him the most. And then he'd lied about it. The deep affection I'd felt for him, especially after our adventure today, now felt hollow and fleeting.

"What. The. Actual. Fuck." It was all I could get out. I was shaking now. With rage. And a deep hurt I couldn't put into words. Did he truly think so little of me that he couldn't trust me to tell people when I felt I had enough information? Did he truly still see me as a child?

Matt sighed, resigned. "I didn't have a choice, Terah. I battled with myself all night and all morning, but I couldn't keep it a secret from them. Not without betraying my orders."

"Your orders?" I asked with harsh disbelief. "You don't have any. You're an assistant professor." He hadn't had to tell them. He'd wanted to. More than he'd wanted to trust me.

Matt shook his head sadly. "That's not true anymore."

I ground my teeth together. "What do you mean?"

Matt ran a hand through his hair and looked up briefly at the sky, as though looking for something to save him. "After the first attack, and after the meeting with your mother, I got an offer to join the warrior faction with a decently high-ranking position. The position would allow me to stay at the Academy and continue teaching but would also give me the responsibility of helping oversee the protection efforts at the Academy. I . . . accepted the offer. I was inducted in shortly after."

Matt refused to meet my gaze. My fists shook. I wanted to punch him more than anything. To hurt him even a fraction of how much he was hurting me.

"And why the hell wouldn't you tell me that?" I shouted, losing all semblance of calm and control. "Why wouldn't you warn me that anything I might tell you would have to be reported?"

Matt finally looked at me. His jaw was set, his expression stubborn, but I could see the sadness in the depths, intensifying. "Because I knew you might know things that would help protect the school, and that you might not tell me if you knew about my new position."

The breath whooshed out of me as shock and hurt hit me like a rampaging Demon. So . . . he'd used me. Intentionally. Unabashedly. He'd used me against my will for my abilities and for information. Had he . . . ever really cared about me? Because this wasn't how a person treated someone they cared about. My fists clenched as a deep, hollow ache gripped my chest.

"Then why did you even bother promising not to report on me?" My voice shook. "Why intentionally lie to me?"

"It wasn't intentional. I thought I could get around my orders. I thought I could keep your visions a secret until you were ready to tell them. But they were too specific. They were clearly about the Academy. I struggled with myself for hours and hours, but I didn't have a choice. I had to tell them."

"You're full of shit, Matt." My voice had gone hollow and cold. It felt like a void was opening inside of me. A great chasm, sucking everything in, making me collapse in on myself. "I trusted you, and you kept things from me. You made the *choice* to lie to me. You joined the warrior faction, knowing what that would mean. And you made the *choice* to ask me about my visions and mislead me about your ability to keep them secret."

Matt looked miserable, but he also looked, as he'd so often looked throughout my life, as though he was certain he'd made the right decision. The only decision. But he hadn't. He'd just made the easiest one. He'd pushed me to trust him again, while never completely putting his trust in me. He'd pushed me to trust him all the while knowingly misleading me. I suddenly knew, with a deep and painful certainty, that I could never fully put my trust in him again. He was the friend I'd known the longest and had loved the most for so much of my life, but he couldn't be that for me anymore. And that broke my heart. It was a different heartbreak than what I felt about Gabriel, but it was no less potent.

"I can't do this with you anymore," I finally said, much calmer than I actually felt. Because inside, I was falling apart. "I don't trust you, and it's become clear that you certainly don't trust me or my judgment. You don't listen to me, you don't respect me or my decisions, you keep lying to me, and you keep betraying my trust. I can't . . . keep letting you in like I have before. I can't be your friend like I was before. And I certainly can't date you. What we had . . . it's broken now. And believe me, that's not what I've ever wanted to happen. I loved you the most for so long. You were my family, Matt. But you're hurting me. You *keep* hurting me. *You've* pushed us here, and now you have to face the consequences of your actions."

Matt opened his mouth to speak, fear and alarm widening his eyes, but I cut him off.

"Goodbye, Matt. I hope you learn to trust someone someday, and that you can earn their trust in return. But that can't be me anymore."

I turned from his pain-filled face and walked away, blinking back the tears stinging my eyes. It was over. After a lifetime of friendship and companionship, it was all over, irrevocably broken from too many secrets and too many betrayals.

"Terah!" he called from behind me, his voice filled with anguish. But I ignored him and walked faster. This hurt. So much. But I needed to hold firm to me beliefs and boundaries. And that meant walking away from him, even if each step felt like a knife to the chest.

My phone buzzed as I roughly wiped an escaped tear from my cheek. I quickly pulled it from my pocket and glanced at the message. It was from Gabriel, of course.

"I'm okay. Just been hanging out in my room. Nothing's happened that I've heard of, but the increased warrior faction presence is definitely weird. Are you heading back to your room? Can I come by? We can talk about it then."

I shoved my phone back into my pocket and changed course. I didn't want to wait for Gabriel to come find me. I wanted to see him now. I needed his company. And I needed to not be in a place that Matt would find me if he wanted to try changing my mind. Because I was afraid he'd succeed. And for both our sakes, I knew I couldn't let him.

I knocked on Gabriel's door a few minutes later, trying to brush the last evidence of my tears from my face. I heard footsteps behind the door, before it was pulled open. And then I was staring up into Gabriel's unfairly handsome face. It felt like it was the first time I'd seen him in a year—I'd missed him much more than I should've after only being away from him for a day.

Gabriel was in a simple pair of dark jeans and a dark gray sweater that hugged his chest and arms. He'd pushed up the sleeves, revealing his tattooed and leanly muscular forearms. My mouth went dry, which seemed unfair, since I was trying to get over him.

"Terah." He smiled broadly at me—a rare, completely genuine smile that lit up his eyes. "I missed you."

He reached forward and folded his fingers around mine, then pulled me slowly into his room, leaving me space and time to pull away if I wanted to. But I didn't want to. Instead of stopping, I moved forward until my forehead was pressed to his chest. The past couple days had been over-whelming. I . . . needed him.

I heard Gabriel's breath of surprise, then felt his long arms wrap around me, holding me gently to him. He nudged his door closed with his foot, then leaned over and rested his chin on top of my head. I closed my eyes and inhaled his scent deep into my lungs, as I wrapped my free arm around his waist. This was where I wanted to be. With him. Like this. I'd stay here forever, if he'd let me.

Finally, Gabriel pulled back and looked down into my face, his gaze carefully assessing. "Are you okay?"

I wondered wryly what'd tipped him off—the remnants of tears in my eyelashes, the deep sadness in my eyes, or my uncharacteristic affection.

I watched him as he did another sweep of my face.

"You look . . . sad."

I smiled a little and walked over to sit on the edge of his bed. "It's Matt," I murmured, looking down at the rug. "He lied to me again. Betrayed my trust. Used me."

Gabriel frowned as he walked over and sat next to me. "Want to tell me about it?"

I sighed and placed my bag of clothes on the floor before unzipping my jacket. "Yeah. If you don't mind."

"I never mind."

I smiled a little and nudged him with my shoulder, like nothing had changed between us. But everything had changed. It was hard, even now, to forget about kissing him. And I couldn't unlearn my feelings for him. It made moments like this both comfort and hurt me—a constant throbbing ache in my chest.

"Thanks," I murmured.

Then I told him. First about my visions, then about Matt's promises. I explained why and how he'd broken them, and his new role in the warrior faction. When I finally finished, I looked up at Gabriel's face, unsure of how he'd respond. Perhaps he'd think that telling the administration was the right thing to do, as Matt had.

But Gabriel's face was scrunched in incredulous disgust. "What an asshole. I can't believe he joined the fucking warrior faction after everything he saw your mother say and do. After she ordered him to force you to help them! And I can't believe he lied to you about all of it. You're supposed to be his closest friend."

"I always thought I was," I said quietly, "but he never put his trust in me. Not completely. Not like I put my trust in him. He's always thought of himself as the one in charge. The one with all the responsibility who had to take care of everything, even me. And he did, for a lot of my life, but not anymore. I guess he never learned how to give up that power and control, even now that I'm an adult. He just tramples over me and my autonomy to do whatever he thinks is right, regardless of how I feel and what I want."

I shook my head, the cruelty of the situation still burning at me.

"Gods, he even told me he wanted to date me." I laughed derisively. "On our way back from the town. He said he wanted a romantic relationship with me, all the while knowing he was intentionally lying to me about so many other things. How did he possibly think that would go down? Did he truly think I'd never notice or wouldn't be mad?"

I made a sound of frustration and threw my hands up in the air in front of me.

"Asshole," I finally murmured, lowering my hands and balling them into fists on my lap. "At least I told him no, even before I knew what he'd done."

"You said no?" Gabriel sounded genuinely surprised. I glanced at him, my gaze traveling carefully over his expression. I saw a lot of curiosity there, and something lighter that I couldn't put a name to. "I wasn't sure you were still uncertain." He pulled his gaze from mine and looked down at the rug. "I thought maybe you'd decided you wanted to be with him."

I blinked at him, startled. Why would he think that? Especially after last night? Had he somehow not interpreted my reciprocation as genuine interest in him?

"No," I finally said, fighting to keep my voice mild. I had too many thoughts and questions running through my head at once. "It never felt right with him. I always felt uncertain about it, and I recently realized that I don't feel the same way about him as he does about me. I love him, but as family, as a friend, not as a romantic partner. That's why I told him it wouldn't be a good idea—not anytime soon, at least. But that was before I knew what he'd done and how much he'd lied to me. Now, it wouldn't be a good idea *ever*."

Gabriel nodded slowly, a far-off look in his eyes. He looked like he was thinking hard about something. But he didn't reveal whatever it was. Instead, he reached over and folded one of his large hands around my balled-up fist, gently rubbing my skin with his thumb.

"I'm sorry," he murmured. "I'm sorry he did that, and I'm sorry you had to find out like that. But most of all, I'm sorry he betrayed your trust and damaged your friendship. I know how much it's meant to you throughout your life. You deserve respect and good treatment from those you care about, and I'm sorry he let you down."

My eyes stung with tears, and I leaned my head over to rest against his shoulder. "Thanks. It's a different kind of heartbreak than I've experienced before, but it sucks just as much."

Gabriel shifted his arm and wrapped it around my shoulders. We sat there in comfortable silence for a while, him offering comfort, and me soaking it in. I hoped I'd never lose him, too. That, I felt, would truly break me. Matt's loss had me feeling like a plate that'd been dropped on the floor, the impact causing fissures to shoot across the surface, threatening to fracture it into many parts, but just holding onto its form. Losing Gabriel would be like dropping that ruptured plate again. I'd finally burst apart at the seams, and the wholeness of my being would be irreparably damaged. The pieces of me would survive, but I wouldn't be who I'd been before. And I was beginning to like who I was now. I didn't want to lose myself to more loss. If only it was controllable.

"Want to watch a movie or something?" Gabriel finally asked, releasing me slowly and smiling warmly at me. "Movies tend to help me escape from my problems for a little bit."

I returned his smile, warmth growing in my chest, easing some of the throbbing ache there. "That sounds nice, if you're not too tired."

Gabriel's mouth hitched up on one side as he considered me. "Never too tired to spend time with you." He nudged me gently with his shoulder.

My cheeks heated a little, and I looked away quickly. He was making it hard to put my romantic feelings for him to the side. It would help if he'd stop being so damn charming.

"Thanks," I said, as matter-of-factly as I could, trying to disguise my blush.

Gabriel's smile broadened a little as he watched me, then he pushed off the bed and started setting up the movie. I scooted back so I could sit against his headboard, then watched him move around his room. As the movie was loading, he brought over a long-sleeved shirt of his as well as some boxer briefs and placed them on the bed next to me.

"You can stay, if you want. You've had a pretty shitty day—I don't want you to feel alone. No pressure, though."

I smiled and pulled his clothes into my lap, accepting them. Of course I wanted to stay. "Thanks."

Gabriel's expression went soft as he watched me, but he turned away quickly, before I could nail down what he was feeling.

I held his clothes against my chest and sank against his headboard again as I watched him cross the room to start the movie. Even if he didn't care about me the way I cared about him, even if he could always see through me, whether I wanted him to or not, being with him made me feel at peace. Despite all the complications, whenever I was with Gabriel, I felt like I was home.

12

SACRIFICES

The evening of the holiday party arrived with a flurry of activity. We'd all had to eat early, as the dining hall would be closed well before its usual time so the school staff could prepare the room for the party. Even as we ate, we watched workers drag in pieces of a stage that they pushed into the back corner of the room, while others strung up lights across the vast ceiling. I had no doubt that, by the time they were done, the room would look magical and no longer resemble a cafeteria.

After a quick but hearty dinner, Gabriel and I returned to our separate rooms to prepare for the party. I took a long, hot shower, then painstakingly got to work on a smoky eye makeup look that I'd been working on perfecting since the last party. Over that, I applied my usual black liquid eyeliner and made sure the wings were dramatic and perfectly sharp. Next, I dug out my new lipstick from the bag of clothes and applied it, careful to make sure it was symmetrical. Fortunately, it was the kind that dried into a matte after application, so I wouldn't have to worry about it smudging throughout the course of the night.

Finally, I blow-dried my hair and got to work on curling it from the halfway point down. I'd decided on a curled, pinned style that would bare my neck on one side, sending the cascade of curls over my other shoulder. It seemed glamorous, and was, most importantly, fairly easy to achieve.

When I was satisfied with my hair, I padded back into my room and pulled out my dress, undergarments, and shoes. After getting the cups of my silicone stick-on bra symmetrically aligned, and pulling on my thigh-high nude stockings, I pulled the dress over my head and made sure it was situated properly. Finally, I donned my necklace and earrings, then stepped into my spiky velvet heels.

I walked back into the bathroom to examine myself and smiled happily. I'd somehow managed to pull everything together. I looked . . . well, different from the person I was used to seeing in the mirror. But in a good way. I looked a little older, and much more pulled together than usual. And I couldn't help smiling at the way the dress made me feel. I'd never felt particularly pretty or sophisticated before, but this dress made me feel both. But damn, it was daring. I hadn't exposed this much of my chest and torso, well, ever. If any dress could help a guy fall for me, it was this one. I just hoped it worked on the right guy.

I packed my cigarettes, lighter, and lipstick in my jacket, then pulled out my phone to check the time. 9:00pm. Which was perfect. The party would just be starting now, and it'd give Gabriel and I the opportunity to arrive fashionably late.

I sent Gabriel a quick text letting him know I was ready, then settled into one of my armchairs to wait for him. I felt a little nervous. Maybe because I was hoping tonight could be just magical enough that Gabriel would start feeling a little more for me than he currently did. It wasn't that I wanted to force him to like me or anything, I just wanted to know, to *fully* know, whether he'd considered us as a possibility. If I knew for sure, then I'd be more able to move on. But the confusing signals between us had me clinging to hope in a way that'd be detrimental to any other relationship I'd try to have if this wasn't sorted out. Whatever tonight brought, I hoped certainty, one way or the other, would be part of it.

Gabriel knocked on my door about fifteen minutes later, and I hurried to open it. My pulse kicked up as my gaze slid over him. He was standing there in a black, perfectly tailored suit that hugged his muscles without being too tight. He'd told me earlier that it was left over from going to his high school prom. Instead of wearing a traditional button-down, he wore a dark gray and black striped V-neck T-shirt that hugged his chest and torso. He was also wearing black high-tops instead of dress shoes, and his hair was arranged in a messy, but stylish, way. It was all perfect, and perfectly Gabriel.

I smiled and stepped to the side so he could enter, but he didn't move. He was staring at me, seemingly at a loss for words.

"You . . . you look . . ."

I smiled up at him innocently as he tried to pull himself together. He ran a hand nervously through his hair.

"Well shit," he finally said, rubbing the back of his head. "You look gorgeous."

I laughed and grabbed his hand, pulling him into my room. "Thanks." I closed the door behind him. "So do you." I sent him a playful smile over my shoulder, and I saw his eyes warming as he watched me. My heart skipped a beat.

"Are you ready to go?" Gabriel finally looked away and fidgeted with his jacket, which he'd draped over his arm. He seemed nervous too, and it was oddly endearing.

"Just about." I walked over to the armchair and grabbed my jacket. "Just need to put this on first."

I pulled on my jacket and pocketed the phone, and Gabriel took the opportunity to pull on his as well, then we exited my room. When we got outside, I saw that it'd started snowing. Large flakes peacefully floated down from the sky, leaving a light dusting of white over the grounds and buildings. Gabriel offered me his arm for stability, since I was in heels, and I happily took it, curling my fingers over his forearm.

I laughed as the snow fell harder and landed in my lashes and on my nose. It'd gotten fairly cold in Dagmar in the winter, but it'd rarely snowed. Maybe, just this once, I could let myself enjoy it. Hardly anyone was around, and I trusted Gabriel enough to not think lesser of me for it. I started trying to catch snowflakes in my mouth as we walked, and I laughed as they inevitably hit me in the eye or the cheek. When I finally caught one in my mouth, I was so surprised that I inhaled it as I gasped and ended up coughing.

Gabriel laughed and wrapped his arm around my waist, pulling me into his side. "You're too damn adorable for your own good."

My heart warmed, and I glanced up at him. "I think you mean fearsome and badass." I shot him a fake glare.

He chuckled. "That too."

When we reached the main building, we walked through the main doors and went across the entryway to the dining hall door. Once we pushed inside, we saw that the room was already packed with students, teachers, and staff, all dressed in their finest, and a DJ was supplying pumping club music while the live band set up the stage that'd been placed where the food counters usually were. Strings of lights and fresh garlands were gracefully draped from the ceiling, providing a gentle light, and ornately decorated pine trees lined each wall, filling the space with their fresh scent. The room looked totally different—If I'd never been in here before, I'd never have guessed it was usually a cafeteria.

"I think there's a coat rack over there." Gabriel pointed over the heads of the crowd to the side of the room.

"I'll have to take your word for it," I grumbled. "I can't pretend to see over anyone, even in these heels." Gabriel smirked at me, then took my hand and led me through the crowd. As usual, his height and breadth carved a path for us much easier than I ever would've been able to.

We hung up our coats on the heavy-duty rack, then decided to find the bar. Gabriel led us across the room to the opposite wall where, apparently, he saw a large bar set up. People gaped at us as we passed. Possibly because they'd never seen us out of our torn up, mostly black wardrobes. Also, because we tended to exude a tough, unapproachable front around others, born from our time in border towns, that our finery was possibly clashing with.

Much to my discomfort, a decent number of guys stared openly at my dress and the particularly low-cut front. I rolled my eyes and occasionally glared at them when their reactions crossed into the so-obvious-it-was-rude category, but I supposed it meant the dress was doing a good job of making me look nice. Perhaps even desirable. But theirs wasn't the attention I wanted.

"Forget it, man," one guy said to his gawking friend as we passed. "I *told* you they were together."

I glanced at Gabriel to see his reaction to this. Gabriel rolled his eyes, but he also wrapped his arm around my waist and pulled me into his side. I was surprised at this reaction to the accusation that we were dating, especially because of his negative reaction to kissing me a couple days ago. But I wasn't going to be the one who inserted more space between us. I liked being this close to him. Besides, I'd noticed quite a few young women eyeing him with interest as well, and the fewer of them who tried to approach him tonight, the better. How would I ever ascertain if there was something between us if they kept pulling him away to dance?

We finally reached the bar at the other end of the room, and saw that, apart from the normal beer, liquor, and wine, there was also a menu of themed holiday drinks that we could order from. And everything was free. My eyebrows rose and I whistled as I looked down the themed drinks list. When the Academy threw a party, it really went all out.

We ordered our drinks, then stood to the side as they were being prepared. There was already a line forming behind us at the bar, and we didn't want to be in the way. Once we had our drinks, we found a small, round, standing table to the side of the bar to settle at. It was one of the few tables still open, and it'd give us a place to lean and set our drinks. I took a sip of my spiced citrus cocktail and sighed happily. "Those bartenders really know what they're doing. This is seriously good."

Gabriel set down his drink. "Can I try it?"

I nodded, and we swapped glasses. Gabriel had ordered a mulled cider cocktail, which was sweet and tart, and just as good as the one I'd ordered.

"Mm." I set his glass back on the table and slid it toward him. "That's really good. I may have to order every drink on that list."

Gabriel grinned as he slid my glass back to me. "Does that mean you expect me to carry you home when you inevitably pass out?"

I rolled my eyes, suppressing my smile. "I'd never pass out. Quick-healing abilities, remember?"

"Ah, yes. Your unfair advantage in the war against hangovers."

I smiled and took another sip of my cocktail. "I'm glad for it tonight, though. These drinks are *strong*."

"Yep." Gabriel took another sip of his drink and smiled. "You may have to carry *me* home later."

I laughed as an image of this popped into my head. Small-statured me trying to carry an enormously tall Gabriel. I doubted I'd be very success-ful. It'd be easier to just drag him.

We talked for a while and leisurely sipped our drinks as the room became more and more crowded. We'd lucked out in picking a table so close to the bar. Whenever there was a lull in the line, either Gabriel or I would hop in and quickly procure more drinks before the next wave of students flooded the table. By the time the live band had finished setting up, I'd had over half the holiday drinks on the list, and I was starting to feel the effects of all the alcohol, even with my quick healing. I felt warmer and more relaxed. Braver. Which was why, when the live band started playing an upbeat tune, I threw back the rest of my drink and slid my arm through Gabriel's.

"Want to dance with me?" I smiled up into his face. I just hoped he wouldn't turn me down as I suspected he almost had at the last party. "You *did* ask me to come here with you. Seems like dancing would be a part of that."

Gabriel blinked down at me for a moment, his cheeks flushing a little as his gaze swept slowly over my face, landing for a prolonged moment on my lips. "It is." Gabriel pulled himself together, and a smirk pulled at his lips. "Calling that in already?"

I frowned. "What do you mean? Are you saying you're only going to dance with me *once*?" I took a step away from him, indignant.

Gabriel laughed and pulled me back into his side, his hand curling around my waist. "No, that's not what I'm saying. I just wanted to see how you'd react when I implied it."

I gave him a frustrated glare and flipped him off. He laughed again and threw back the rest of his drink.

"Sorry." His eyes danced with amusement. He took my hand and pulled me toward the dance floor. "No more teasing. For now." He winked at me. I smiled, in spite of myself.

The live band's first song ended as we took our places in the small amount of open space we'd found amidst the students already dancing. But they started up again almost immediately with another upbeat tune. I smiled and grabbed Gabriel's hands, then started swaying and bouncing to the beat of the music. I didn't have the most experience dancing, but with Gabriel, it hardly seemed to matter. His enthusiasm was infectious, and I was having too much fun to second-guess my movements or feel nervous or awkward. Gabriel seemed to have experience dancing. His motions were smooth, confident, and always on beat. It was, unfortunately, extremely attractive. *Damn.* As though I needed that.

Every few songs, we'd break away from the dance floor to get more drinks from the bar. I was pretty serious about trying all the holiday cocktails. When would I have another opportunity to try such high-quality and inventive drinks, especially for free? Well, probably not until the next Academy holiday party. But even I had to admit, as I became slightly unsteady on my heels, that maybe I was drinking a little too fast for my quick healing to keep me fully lucid. But I wasn't too worried. Gabriel was always there to steady me by wrapping his arm around my waist, which I liked very much. Plus, the more we drank, the closer Gabriel seemed to hold me while we danced. Perhaps I should've been more worried about whether sober-Gabriel would approve of how close drunk-Gabriel was holding me, but there was a burning in his eyes that always stopped me when I thought about inserting some kind of space between us. And that burning looked a lot like desire. I couldn't make myself move away—not when that was a part of what I wanted him to feel.

Several hours into the party, we grabbed another round of drinks—our eighth? Tenth? I'd lost count—and headed back toward the dance floor, now overflowing with jumping and gyrating couples. I skimmed the crowd, looking for any open space we could squeeze into, and my gaze collided with a familiar hazel one. I froze in my tracks. He was leaning against a wall about twenty feet from us, looking impeccable in his suit, button-down, and tie. He looked . . . sad. Lonely. Handsome. *Matt.*

His gaze roamed over me before flicking briefly to Gabriel. When it met mine again, despair had taken hold. And it wrecked me. Before I even knew what I was doing, I reached out to him with my mind. I just needed to know he was okay. I wasn't sure why I bothered. Even if he wasn't, I wouldn't change my mind about our friendship after all he'd done, but as hard as I tried, I couldn't turn off the lifetime of care I'd had for him.

"Terah," he murmured as our minds connected. *"Please. Please forgive me."*

His eyes filled with tears, and it hit me like a dagger to the chest. *Shit.* If I didn't disconnect with him now, I'd be in danger of taking back everything I'd said yesterday. And those were words that I'd meant. It was a boundary that I needed to keep, no matter how much it hurt him and me. My eyes stung with tears as I shook my head slowly at him. I couldn't just forgive him. There wasn't a reason to. He hadn't changed. I took a deep breath and severed the connection between us, turning away from him.

"What is it?" Gabriel's smile faded as he saw my expression.

"It's Matt. He's here." I raised my glass and threw back my very strong drink in three gulps. Then I spun and headed directly for the bar. I needed another drink. I needed to wipe Matt's anguish from my mind.

Gabriel followed me, but spun as he walked, trying to see where Matt was. "Aw, hell," he finally said, running a hand through his hair as he spotted him. "He looks miserable."

I got back in line and crossed my arms impatiently over my chest. I wished it was moving faster.

"I know. It's not fair. It's not like this is what I wanted. But he forced my hand. He has no right to look so dejected."

Gabriel sighed and wrapped his arm around my shoulders, pulling me gently into his side. Then he leaned over and pressed a kiss to the top of my head. My cheeks warmed, and a little of the tension I was carrying eased. I pressed my eyes closed and leaned into him. The room felt like it was spinning a little.

"What if I get you a beer this time?" he murmured into my ear as his thumb rubbed soothing circles against my shoulder. "It's a little less strong. I don't want you falling off those heels and breaking your neck."

I smiled at this. Trust Gabriel, even when he was drunk, to always have an eye on my well-being.

"I guess that's fine. If you promise to dance with me more."

Gabriel glanced at Matt again before turning and sliding me, so my back pressed to his front. He wrapped his arms around me and pressed me to him. "Of course I'll dance with you," he murmured against my hair. It was hard to think straight when he did this. It was hard not to turn in his arms and kiss him again, but that would only scare him away, so I refrained.

When we finally got to the front of the line, Gabriel ordered me a beer, then took a large swig of it himself before handing it over to me. I narrowed my eyes at him, but he just smirked. He knew I didn't need to drink the whole thing by myself. But still. I took the bottle from his fingers, held his gaze defiantly as I put it to my lips, and quickly drank ninety percent of the remaining liquid.

Gabriel's smirk turned into a grin, then he laughed. "Alright, alright. I'm overruled. I really *will* have to carry you home later."

He set down his partially finished cocktail on the bar and pulled me back toward the dance floor. With both hands free now, he wrapped his arms around me and pulled me firmly against him, pressing my torso to his. Then he swayed with me to the beat of the pounding music. His hands slid down to my hips and guided them to move against his. I sighed —the contact was intoxicating—and wrapped my free arm around his neck, anchoring myself to him.

While our dancing earlier in the evening had been exuberant and happy, our dancing now was slower and closer. Our hips moved in unhurried circles, pressed firmly together. Agonizing and incredible all at once. It was quickly making me breathless. I slid my hand up his neck and into his hair as I drowned in the intensity of his electric blue gaze, bright even in the darkness of the room. He dipped me back, then pulled me slowly up against him again, his lips grazing my ear and neck. Warm shivers flooded my body. I threw back the rest of my beer and slid the empty bottle onto a passing waiter's tray to free my hands. Then I wrapped my arms around Gabriel's neck and pressed closer.

Gabriel dropped his forehead against mine, his breaths shorter now. "Gods, Terah. You're so beautiful."

My cheeks burned crimson, and my pulse beat heavily through me.

This was what I wanted. To be with Gabriel like this. To be pressed against him. To have him holding me to him as though in desperation.

The song ended and the next began, but we hardly noticed. It didn't seem like anything in the world could break through our heated trance. I gently rubbed the tip of my nose against the skin that his V-neck exposed, then slid my lips over the exposed part of his collarbone. I felt the air whoosh from his lungs, and his hands slid down my back and over the curve of my backside, squeezing gently and pulling my hips more firmly against his. A quiet moan escaped my lips. What I wouldn't give for Gabriel to fully let me in. For him to realize that what he felt for me was the same as what I felt for him. Because if he didn't, I might just lose my mind. As it was, I was practically trembling from this contact.

He slid his hands from my backside to my thighs, his lips trailing down my neck. Then he ran his fingers over my tights, nudging my dress up my thighs little by little so he could touch more of me. And it was making me blind with need.

"*Gabriel.*" His name shuddered out of me. I wasn't sure how much more of this I could take before I'd need to pull him into an empty room so I could quench the fire burning uncontrollably through me.

But instead of continuing his exploration, instead of giving into that fire with me, he froze. I pulled back a little and glanced up at him, confused. A look of dawning horror was spreading over his face.

Oh no.

Gabriel pulled suddenly away from me, putting at least two feet between us. I stumbled from being released so quickly, and adjusted my dress, pulling it back down my thighs. Gabriel was breathing hard, staring at me like he'd only just realized I was there. He ran shaking fingers nervously through his hair.

"I did it again, didn't I?" He spun around and cursed, his face in his hands.

I stood there, stunned, not sure what to say. My blood was still pounding hotly through me, and my mind was a little fuzzy from all the alcohol. What was happening? He'd done what again? It wasn't like he'd kissed me or anything.

"Shit. I'm sorry, Terah."

He turned back to face me, his eyes frantically searching my expression. Like he thought I'd be mad. It didn't make any sense. Why would I be mad at him? I thought I'd made it pretty clear when he'd kissed me that

I was more than interested. Which was what confused me the most—I could've sworn he was interested too. So . . . why was he acting this way?

"I shouldn't have . . . gods, I'm so sorry." He shook his head. "I shouldn't have done any of that. I got . . . carried away. It was inexcusable. I . . . I know we're just friends."

Hurt was filling me now, deep and tormenting. The room around me blurred as tears filled my eyes. *Damn.* I tried to blink them away. But I felt transported back to the moments just after he'd kissed me. When he'd looked horrified. When he'd said it'd all been a mistake. When he'd promised to never do it again. And then the full weight of his rejection landed on me. He had desire, but not for me. Sure, I was there, and the alcohol had brought it out, but when he'd remembered it was me, he'd backed away. I wasn't who he wanted. I was just his friend. Nothing more.

"Gods, I can't believe I did this again." He scrubbed his hand down his face. "I'm such an asshole. I'm sorry for crossing those boundaries. It was . . . a mistake. I . . . I hope you can forgive me."

Hurt cracked through me, tearing at my heart. Ah yes. A *mistake*. I was wondering when those words would appear again. Being with me like this always seemed to be. For him. For Caleb. It was a mistake that Gabriel only made when he was drunk with adrenaline or alcohol. But in his right mind, he'd never choose me like this. And that reality, asserted again so clearly, tore through me, more painful than a Demon's claws ripping through my flesh.

I'd hoped he could see me as more. I'd wanted him to realize how good we could be together as more than friends. But I could see now that that was an impossible dream. I wasn't who he wanted.

A tear spilled down my cheek as I looked at him. I couldn't form words. I could only stare at his anguished face. His fists clenched at his sides as he saw my tear. But he didn't move toward me. He didn't try to offer any comfort. Which, I supposed, gave me my answer—the certainty I'd been looking for at the start of the night. But it wasn't the answer I'd longed for.

A young woman sidled up to Gabriel as we stood there, staring at each other. I quickly wiped the tear from my cheek. I didn't want anyone else to know what was happening. I didn't want anyone else to see how vulnerable I'd become since letting Gabriel into my heart. I needed to be as impermeable as I'd always been. Or at least make others think I still was.

"Hey," she said loudly over the music, stepping between Gabriel and me, very close to his chest. "Are you dancing with anyone?"

She glanced at me over her shoulder, sizing me up, then turned back to him, dismissing me. "Or are you already taken?" She offered him a seductive smile. I couldn't really begrudge her for it—she seemed extremely drunk, and he was extremely handsome. "It's just . . . I'm a *really* good dancer. I bet *I* wouldn't disappoint you."

I bit the inside of my cheek. Hard. Until I tasted blood. Just because I understood didn't mean I didn't want to haul off and punch her. But I knew how much of a disappointment I was to Gabriel. Always around, but never who he longed for. Never who he needed. But this young woman was pretty and seemed . . . enthusiastic. And she wasn't me.

"He's all yours," I said, pulling as much give-no-fucks confidence into me as I possibly could in the moment. After being rejected and all. "I certainly wouldn't want to get in the way of him having *real* fun."

The young woman smirked at me and wrapped both arms around Gabriel. But he just stood there, staring at me, seemingly confused. Like he didn't quite understand what was happening. But he raised his hand and settled it against her waist. Perhaps it'd been a reflex, or perhaps he really did find her more desirable. But suddenly, I couldn't take it any longer. I couldn't be here and see him with someone else. I couldn't watch him as he responded to someone else. I needed to get out of here.

I turned on my heel and walked away, pushing through the crowd, heedless of whether I was being rude. I somehow made it to the coat rack and fumbled through my jacket, grabbing my cigarettes and lighter. Then I pushed back through the crowd and made it out of the dining hall into the main building entry way, then out the front doors into the cold, fresh air.

Snow continued to swirl from the dark sky, but I ignored the weather and walked unsteadily across the wide expanse of snowy grass. A million emotions swirled through me, centering in my chest like a heavy weight, and I felt dizzy. I pulled more air into my lungs, trying to calm myself, but it barely helped. I'd had too much to drink, and this current state was my own fault. I'd known, though I'd wished otherwise, that Gabriel didn't feel the same way about me. But I'd let him behave as though he did, just because he was drunk. And because I'd wanted it so badly. And it'd pushed him from me again. But now I truly knew how he felt about me. I knew he'd never return my love.

My dizziness increased as I stumbled forward, tears streaming from my eyes, and I wished my quick healing would kick in. I was tired of feeling this out of it. This out of control. I walked through the snowy grass toward the trees on the west end of campus, wobbling slightly on my heels,

259

moving away from the loud noises of the crowd inside the dining hall. I needed some time to think. Some time to resign myself to what'd become clear this evening. Pain ripped through my chest at the thought, and I suddenly wished I'd brought a beer outside with me. Fuck being sober. If there was ever a night where I really needed the pain of reality to disappear, it was this one.

I swore and lit my cigarette as I walked. Even at the tree line, I'd still be able to see the building, but at least I'd be putting some distance between myself and its occupants. I'd give myself the time and space to think and pull myself together. I couldn't act like this was the end of the world. Gabriel had been pretty clear with me after we'd kissed that he didn't want to be with me romantically. It was my own foolishness that'd allowed me to hope. And this was where that'd gotten me.

The chilly wind whipped around me, making goosebumps erupt over my skin, as I headed toward a wrought-iron bench near the edge of the trees. I shivered, wrapping my free arm around myself, and wished I'd thought to grab my jacket. But no—I'd only thought about grabbing my cigarettes. I really wasn't thinking tonight.

I reached the bench on unsteady legs and brushed off the snow that covered it. Then I sank onto the freezing metal and inhaled deeply from my cigarette. What a fucking mess. I shook my head in hopeless frustration as I sat there, listening to the faint thumping of music escaping the dining hall into the night air. I tried not to think about Gabriel in there, dancing and laughing with someone else. Desiring someone else. Forgetting me and moving on with someone he was actually attracted to. I balled my fist and pressed it hard against the cold metal beneath me. I knew I should feel relieved. This was essentially the permission I'd been looking for to move on. But I couldn't summon any feelings of relief in this moment. Only devastation.

I needed to go back to my room after this cigarette. That would be the smartest course of action. I shouldn't hang around the party and watch Gabriel and his new dance partner from the sidelines. I shouldn't find Matt and forgive him just so I could dance with him and feel something. I shouldn't go back in and find a random guy, any guy, to pull against me on the off chance that it might make Gabriel jealous. I knew all these options would only lead to my own destruction, and that I'd regret them afterward. No, it was time for me to accept defeat, as hard as that was for me. Someday I'd be able to move on, but tonight was not that night. Tonight, I needed to let myself feel the loss. And I needed to remove myself so I wouldn't create more messes for sober-me to clean up later.

I nodded, decided, and took a last long drag of my cigarette before dropping it in the snow. It sputtered out, and I sent a small stream of power at it, matter-shifting it into snow. Then I pushed to my feet and waited for the swirling world to settle around me again. I'd just go back inside and grab my jacket. Then I'd leave.

I turned and took a few wobbly steps back in the direction of the main building. But before I'd made it very far, a rustling in the trees behind me broke the quite of the night. I froze, dread flooding me. *No. Not now. Anytime but now. Please. Please let it be the wind.* Just the wind. Yes, that's all it was. Just the wind. I'd keep walking. I'd go back inside. Everything would be alright. There was nothing out here but my own overactive imagination. Besides, the boundaries had been fortified recently. It'd be impossible for anything to get through. Yes, it must be nothing.

I took another step forward. And then another. Suddenly, a horrible sound tore through the night air, and I spun around, fear flooding me as I saw an enormous Demon—the largest I'd ever seen—breaking through the outer edge of the trees and barreling toward me.

Shit. SHIT. What was I going to do? What *could* I do? I had no weapons. No phone. No battle-ready clothing. No help. I looked quickly at the main building, wondering if I could sprint there and raise the alarm. But it was too far away, and I was too drunk to make the trip in time. I turned back and watched with sheer panic as the Demon lumbered toward me. It was easily three times the height of the tallest buildings in Dagmar and was as broad as two long training houses pressed together. I hadn't seen a Demon this size in my entire life. I didn't even know they *could* be this size. And it was barreling toward me while I was alone, drunk, and in a fucking dress. *Great.*

But my training kicked in as it always did, even in my less than lucid state. I took a deep breath and closed my eyes, finding the well of deep purple power in my chest. Then I grabbed it and threw it outward, transforming in a flash of light. I didn't have a choice. Not only was I faced with a nightmarishly large Demon, but I was also without armor or weapons. My transformed state was the only thing that could protect me now. I pulled my sword from its sheath, kicked off my heels into the snowy grass, and launched into the air. I sure as hell wasn't going to let this Demon trample all over the things and people I cared about. I couldn't let it reach the main building. I couldn't let it hurt a single student in there. And if I had to sacrifice myself to protect them all, so be it.

I charged my sword with lightning and flew at the Demon with enormous speed—the most I could shove out of my wings. I hit it across the chest with a bright flash of purple fire, and pierced its skin, causing a gush of black acidic blood to spill down its front. But the Demon laughed. It *laughed*. Like I'd given it a mere paper cut. Then it grabbed me out of the air with one of its many arms and threw me into the trees. I slammed hard against a tree trunk, my head cracking against the bark. I felt a trickle of blood making its way down the back of my head, but I shook myself quickly and launched off the tree. I wasn't about to let a Demon get the best of me. Not even an enormously large one.

I surrounded myself with a shield of purple power and charged my sword with lightning as I pushed toward it again. At the last moment, I dropped my shield, and with a cry, swung my sword up, severing the Demon's top arm cleanly from its body. The enormous hand and arm crashed to the earth with a massive amount of force. But I didn't have time to feel satisfaction. One of the Demon's other arms whipped around and grabbed me out of the air and threw me brutally into the frozen ground. The wind was knocked from my lungs, and the world spun violently around me. My whole body ached, and I felt like I was going to vomit. Maybe if I did, I'd feel better. I should've known better than to drink so much. It was making me slower. Sloppier. Less creative.

I pulled myself together and pushed to my feet before the Demon could stomp on me. Then I threw myself back into the air and sheathed my sword, summoning my bow and arrows as quickly as I could as I flew high above the Demon. I needed to create significant damage while out of its reach, to prevent further injury. It's what I should've started with, and probably would've if I'd been sober. I grabbed my bow and an arrow from my back and infused the arrow with as much lightning as it'd hold. Then I notched it and pulled the bowstring back to my cheek, aiming carefully at the Demon's neck, before releasing it.

The arrow exploded with a crack of thunder as it imbedded in the Demon's skin, and forks of lightning shot through its body from the impact point. It screamed, stumbling forward a few steps. Unfortunately, the arrow didn't seem to have done any major damage. It'd hurt, but the Demon was largely in the same condition it'd been in before. *Shit*. I threw my bow onto my back and summoned all the power I could to my hands. With a cry, I released a deluge of fire and lightning at the Demon, creating a giant, purple tornado around it. I'd never practiced something this large in training before, but this Demon called for the most extreme measures I had. Like it or not, my power was the only thing between it and all the students happily enjoying themselves at the holiday party. It was all that was keeping the Demon from destroying my new home.

I growled with effort as I continued to swirl the tornado of fire and lightning around it. I could feel my power ebbing as I expanded the tornado, trying to push the Demon back toward the trees. It staggered back a few steps, screaming in pain as the fire and lightning ate away at its skin. It was causing real damage. But I couldn't sustain an attack of this magnitude for long. So I sent out one last wave of power at it before unsheathing my sword and diving at the Demon while it was still blinded by purple fire.

I struck the Demon across the neck with all the strength I could muster, my arms shaking with the effort. The blade sliced deep into the Demon's damaged skin, sending a giant wave of black blood down its body and over my arms. I ignored the stinging of the acid as the blood seeped through the cracks in my armor and burned through the sleeves of my dress. I pulled back, panting, and flew around for another pass at it. Its neck was far too thick to sever with only a couple hits. Until I managed it, injuring it would only make the Demon more desperate and angry. So I needed to hurry.

I made it halfway across its neck, slicing deeply, almost deep enough to hit bone, before the Demon spun and grabbed me with two of its arms. Then it pulled me, one arm in one direction, one leg in another. I cried out as the Demon stretched me, attempting to rip me in half. I desperately struggled to release myself, twisting this way and that, but all I managed to do was dislocate my shoulder. The Demon laughed, a horrible sound as deep as thunder yet as shrill as the scream of a kettle. It thought it had me. It thought it was about to kill me. *Not today, asshole.* Not while my friends were in danger.

I sent out a large burst of flames from every part of my body, engulfing the Demon's hands, and twisted violently with all my strength. My leg let out a loud crack as it broke, still in the Demon's grasp, but the fire had startled it enough to loosen its grip. I used my other leg to kick free of it, trying to ignore how much my own fire had burned me. At least the alcohol had one good effect—it made it harder to feel my injuries.

I flew away from it, trying to regather myself and look at the Demon with fresh eyes. I saw that deep, angry burns covered its skin where the tornado of my power had enclosed it, and huge patches of skin had been stripped away. This gave me hope. It meant my power had an impact on it. Maybe, if I could summon something bigger . . .

The Demon ran at me, its bellow burning my ears and making my bones quake, before I could form a plan. I flew backward as quickly as I could, trying to pull myself out of the way as it swiped at me with an enormous, clawed hand, at least the size of the car Matt and I had just been in. I raised my sword to counter whatever part of the blow I couldn't get out of reach for, and the side of my blade sank deep into the Demon's hand between its claws, cleaving it almost in two. But it just laughed as blood flowed freely from it. It was playing with me. Having fun with me. It seemed certain it could kill me easily, if it really tried.

I clenched my jaw, my mood darkening as rage bloomed from my chest. I might be drunk and alone, but I was still a formidable opponent. This Demon would pay for messing with me. I shot rapidly up over its head, then tucked my wings and dropped until I was level with its neck. Then I expended my wings, rapidly slowing, and swung my sword into the gash that was already healing. This time, I connected with bone, and a crack rent the air. The Demon's head fell forward as its neck broke, but the remaining muscle and tissue kept it from fully swinging forward off its shoulders. I was close, so close, to beheading it. If I could just—

The Demon screamed and spun, its arms extending from its body. I poured power into my wings, flying backward as quickly as I could, trying to avoid the sharp claws, but the Demon had moved too quickly. One of its giant hands raked across my body, and the claws pierced roughly through my armor and sliced deep into the skin underneath. I cried out as burning pain seared through me, making my body tremble, and blood started pouring quickly from the wounds. *Shit.* My heart sank. My odds now weren't good, but I couldn't give up. Not with so much at stake. I was only one life. There were hundreds only a hundred yards behind me. And they needed me. They needed me to stop this Demon before it crushed them without warning.

I pulled a massive amount of power down my arm and opened my hand, releasing a giant inferno of purple fire at the Demon's injured neck. The smell of charred flesh filled the air, and the Demon opened its mouth on a silent scream. The fire burned through several layers of skin and muscle on one side, diminishing its remaining tissue. If I could just hit it again before its specialized quick healing could reform the bone, muscle, and tissue, I'd have a shot at beheading it. But the Demon knew that as well, and wasn't interested in letting me end it. It spun and threw its remaining hands protectively around its neck, shielding itself from further attack.

Growling with frustration, I dodged another one of its arms and flew around to its front. Then I plunged my sword as deeply as I could into its chest. I sent huge bolts of lightning through the sword as it was still embedded, and the lightning tore deep into its body, causing it to stagger backward, pulling my sword away with it. I threw more lightning at it as I flew back from it, trying to stay away from its arms. I was running low on power. I couldn't afford any more injuries now.

But in a move I never saw coming, the Demon grasped one of its enormous hands with another and tore it from its own body. I hung in the air, flabbergasted, as I watched black acidic blood spurt from the injury. What was it doing? Why was it hurting *itself*? But quicker than lightning, the Demon threw its severed hand claws-first at me. I gasped, trying to fly out of the way, but I couldn't move quickly enough. Several claws embedded deep in my chest, and before I knew what was happening, I was falling out of the sky under the weight of the enormous hand.

I hit the ground on my back with a loud thud, and stars burst in front of my eyes. My wings had protected me from the impact, but only marginally. I feebly grasped at the claws that were buried deep in my skin and tried to pull them out of me. But its hand was so large that it pinned my entire body to the ground. Only my remaining armor had stopped it from being an immediately deadly blow. But the claws had gone almost clean through me. It was bad. *Really* bad.

With enormous effort, I managed to yank the claws out of me and roll out from under the hand. But the Demon barreled forward and raised its giant leg to stomp on me. It was clearly done having fun—it wanted to end me. I rolled again, faster, trying to get out of the way. But the Demon's foot still landed on my arm. I screamed in pain as I felt my bones flattening under its weight as though they were made of nothing more than paper. I'd never felt pain like this. Ever. I couldn't think through it. I couldn't even cry. It was all-consuming. But I'd die if I couldn't push through it. And then it would attack the main building.

I blinked through the blinding pain and shot a bolt of lightning up at it, this time with my dislocated arm—the only one still with whole bones. But it barely grazed the Demon's shoulder. I couldn't move it well enough to aim right. The Demon's rolling laugh haunted me as it ground its foot down, crushing my already crushed arm beyond recognition. My stomach heaved as the pain overtook me. I tried to push down the nausea and the horror at what the Demon was doing to my body. And I tried to push down the brain-melting levels of pain that flooded every inch of my form. I refused to give up. I had to keep going. I had to push through, no matter what.

Even through the blinding pain, I managed to blast the Demon's leg with fire, forcing it off my destroyed arm. Then I rolled over and slammed my dislocated shoulder into the ground, relocating it enough so I could move it a little more. It was all I had left now. I used my wings to raise me off the ground so I could stand on my one good leg, then I pulled the last remaining dregs of my power into my partially functional arm. Every last ounce of power that wasn't attached to the life force keeping me alive. With a yell of effort, I raised my arm and sent the power up at the Demon, into my sword that was still embedded in its chest. My sword flared brighter and brighter as I filled it, until it was blinding. Then the power exploded outward from the sword, tearing through the Demon's body, sending chunks of its torso and chest flying through the air. The Demon's ruined ribcage was exposed as my sword was blown backward off the Demon and landed in the grass.

The Demon's remaining arms scrambled over its destroyed torso, as though it was trying to hold itself together. I hopped backward a few steps as acidic blood rained from its body, and I materialized my twin long knives on my back. I couldn't infuse it with much, as my power was basically gone now, but I did what I could. Then I aimed and threw the knife as hard as I could. It pierced the Demon's heart and exploded. Its heart was gone. The Demon fell to its knees. But I knew it wasn't enough to kill it. It could, and would, regrow its heart unless I beheaded it. I needed to retrieve my sword and hit its neck one last time. It should be enough.

I pushed into the air as the Demon scrambled across the blood-soaked grass toward me. Even kneeling, it was easily sixty feet tall. I shot toward my sword, but the Demon swiped a giant hand forward and hit me from the side, throwing me out of the air and onto the ground. I felt several of my ribs crack from the impact of the hit. I blinked rapidly, trying to bring the world back into focus even as blood poured from me. I couldn't give up. Not now. I was so close.

The Demon scrambled forward and grabbed my glowing sword from the ground, gurgling in pain as the purple fire and lightning that ran up and down the blade burned into its hand. Before I could so much as move, the Demon brought the sword down over me with a forceful thrust . . . and impaled me through my stomach to the ground.

I blinked up at the sky, dazed. I tried to move, but my sword kept my body pinned to the ground like a bug pinned to a display. The Demon's horrible face split into a wide grin, even as blood continued to spill from it.

And that's when I knew.

I knew, without a doubt, I would die. I knew I couldn't win this fight. Not really. But more importantly, I knew that every student, teacher, and staff member at the Academy would die if I didn't do something. Even with its injures, the Demon could heal. It could crush the entire main building and everyone inside it to dust with barely any effort, and without any warning to the building's occupants. Whereas my wounds seemed beyond repair now. But by the gods, I'd try to take this Demon down with me. It was the most I could do now. The best I could do. It'd be my last act on this earth. My last sacrifice. My last battle.

I closed my eyes and gathered my life force from within me—the one power we were never supposed to expend, and the one power that would definitely kill us if used. I'd burn out, totally and completely. Without my life force, no amount of healing would bring me back. But what did that matter now? I was impaled with my own sword. My body was crushed and torn and broken. No part of me was whole. I wasn't going to survive this. Why shouldn't I use the only power I had left? There was truly nothing left for me to lose.

My body began to hum as I pulled my most sacred power from my center. My strongest power. The power that bound itself to my soul and kept me on this earth. The power that fueled the divine. The sky above me gathered in deeper, darker clouds, swirling violently like a tornado above us as thunder rumbled ominously. I was thankful for the live band and thumping music at the party, keeping everyone from hearing this and spilling outside to see what was happening. Thank the gods for small favors. No one needed to see this. No one needed to see me die.

My body glowed brighter and brighter as I freed more and more of my life force, until I was blinding. It hurt. This power hurt. Pure divine power was far too powerful for a mortal to interact with and control in this way. It was buried deep inside us and attached to our souls for a reason. Using it like this would destroy me. But I'd stopped caring about that. All I could see were the faces of all the students at the Academy. Gabriel's face. Matt's face. I couldn't let any of them die. And this was all I had left. My last chance to defeat the Demon. My last chance to make my life worth something.

The Demon staggered backward, confused, trying to shield its eyes from the glow. I couldn't let it retreat more. I needed to end it. Now. I grabbed all my life force and pushed it to the surface of my skin, not giving it time to be wasted on healing me. I needed it all for the Demon. Then, with all the strength I had left in every inch of my battered body, I pushed the power out of me and at the Demon with a loud scream of effort—a scream so loud it made my own eardrums burn with pain.

And then my body was ablaze. I wasn't on fire—I *was* fire. And lightning. The purest essences of each. I ceased to be human in that moment and became power. Pure power. Pure divine. Wave after wave of ferocious fire and huge bolts of lightning launched from my skin at the Demon as I screamed, burning it and electrocuting it alive. Burning through it like it was made of paper. Huge lightning bolts struck the Demon from the sky, piercing its head and shoulders as thunder roared around us. The fire and lightning shot from me so fast that it swirled together, becoming an enormous tornado over our heads, engulfing the Demon, pulling trees from the ground, and lifting the Demon into the air. I wasn't sure if it was my impalement or my power that kept me on the ground.

The Demon rose higher and higher into the air as my life force stripped away its skin and muscle and burned it down to bone. But that wasn't enough. I wouldn't stop, *couldn't* stop, until the Demon was completely gone. With another scream, I shoved the last of my life force out of my body at the Demon. The Demon's bones disintegrated in one last loud explosion of power that sent a shockwave from it, powerful enough to snap several large trees in half.

And it was done. The Demon was gone.

The sky calmed, the thunder and lightning receded, and the last whisps of my divine power began ebbing from my skin, blowing away with the wind. I felt the life fading from my body as my power left me. My sword disintegrated from my torso, and I fell out of my transformation. Blood spilled rapidly out of me and darkness clouded the edges of my vision. I was alone in the cold and the dark. But I'd done it. I'd defeated the Demon. I'd saved the people here.

I laid on the snowy ground, gasping, struggling to breathe. Smoke from the vanquished Demon still billowed around me. I'd won, but I'd also lost. I could feel that with every fiber of my being. Snow fell quietly from the sky, not knowing it would land amongst such violence and carnage. I tried to breathe, but I couldn't draw in much air. My lungs were filling with liquid. I coughed a little, and blood dripped from my mouth. This was it. It was finally happening. I was going to die. But I didn't want to leave here alone. I didn't want the dark sky to be the last thing I saw. I closed my eyes, fighting to stay conscious. Fighting to concentrate through the agony that was my body.

"*Gabriel.*"

I reached out with my mind even as my mind shut down. Even as the last traces of my power were fading from my skin. But I needed to see him. One last time. I clung with all my strength to life and what little traces of the divine remained. There was nothing left for me now. No future to worry about. No drama of uncertain feelings to make me miserable. I had this one chance to tell him how I felt about him. To let him know how much I cared, even if I'd soon be gone.

"*Gabriel,*" I called out again in my mind. "*Please. Come find me. I need to see you. One last time . . .*"

Gabriel's startled consciousness suddenly filled my own. He was sitting on the floor in the entrance hall, swigging a beer sadly even as the deafening music pumped through the door to the dining hall. He was devastated. And lonely. I wondered why. Had the young woman he'd been dancing with left him?

"*Terah? Is that you?*"

"*Come find me, Gabriel. Please. I need to see you. Before I go.*"

Gabriel staggered to his feet as our minds connected more firmly, and he dropped his beer on the ground in a sudden wave of startled fear. The glass shattered around him, but he ignored it.

"*You're hurt!*" He could feel my presence now. He'd felt my injuries. He had a sense of what'd happened to me.

I winced as his fear flooded through me, overwhelming in its scale. The darkness around the edges of my vision was growing larger. More impenetrable. I was quickly losing consciousness.

"*Hurry,*" I murmured. "*I won't . . . last long. Outside. Near . . . the trees.*"

Gabriel ran as though the hounds of hell were at his heels. I'd never seen him so frantic before. But I couldn't maintain the connection any longer. My mind snapped away from his as I coughed, more blood spilling from my mouth.

I wasn't sure how long I laid there waiting for him, clinging to life so I could say one last goodbye. But I eventually heard pounding footsteps through the ground as he ran toward me from the main building. When his face finally loomed over mine, I couldn't help smiling a little, even through the blinding pain that was my entire body.

"Gabriel," I gasped.

He looked down at me in horror, surveying the damage. Seeing clearly what I knew in my heart—that I was dying. And there was nothing that could be done to fix me now.

He collapsed onto the ground next to me. "Terah." His voice shook as he reached out and touched my cheek. Then tears were spilling from his eyes. "No."

"I'm sorry," I gasped, trying to drag air into my lungs. "So sorry."

Gabriel shook his head and cupped my face between his hands. "No," he said more firmly, as his tears continued to fall. "We'll fix this. We'll heal you. I already called Matt. He and the medics are on their way."

I smiled up at him. At his tortured face. Even in his terror, he was the most beautiful person I'd ever met. Inside and out.

"It's . . . too late for that," I said weakly. "I used . . . my life force. Can't . . . fix that. But I . . . I did it. I protected the Academy. I . . . protected you. One last time."

Gabriel leaned over, dropping his head onto my shoulder as sobs wracked his body. "No," he murmured, shaking his head in denial. "No no no." He clutched my shoulders desperately. "Please." His voice cracked. "Please don't leave me."

I wished I could reach up and hold him. Comfort him. Tell him it'd be alright. He'd be alright. I wouldn't change what I'd done, not even now. I'd done what I always knew I'd have to do someday—give up my life to protect others. And I wasn't even mad about it anymore. In the moment, I hadn't hesitated. It was right. This sacrifice. I knew it was.

"Gabriel," I whispered, the darkness closing in as my pulse slowed. "Look at me. Please."

Gabriel lifted his tear-soaked face and looked down at me in anguish.

"I needed to tell you . . . before I go . . ." I gasped, trying to draw in more air. But I couldn't. The darkness was pulling me under. I had to say it. Now. Before I was gone. "I . . . I love you, Gabriel. I . . . love you."

I couldn't see him anymore. I couldn't see anything anymore. The world was dropping away beneath me. Darkness curled around me like a hug from an old friend, finally coming to claim me after all these years. This wasn't so bad after all. I just hoped I'd see Gabriel again one day. In whatever came next. If anything did. But above all, I hoped he'd be happy.

"Terah," I heard Gabriel's shaking voice say from miles above me. "I—"

But the darkness swallowed me.

13

FALLEN

(GABRIEL'S PERSPECTIVE)

"Terah." My voice shook with anguish. "I love you too."

But her eyes slid shut and her labored breathing ceased.

"No!"

Tears spilled from my eyes so fast I could barely see. This couldn't be happening. This couldn't be how it ended. Pain tore through me like no pain I'd ever felt before. I doubled over, gasping at the intensity of it. I pressed my shaking hand to my stomach, barely able to breathe.

I . . . was losing her. But . . . I loved her. With my entire being. My feelings for her had grown and evolved over the past few months into something so deep I could barely put it into words. And she'd . . . she'd said she loved me too. She'd answered every hope I had and tore down everything I'd foolishly assumed. That had to *mean* something, right? Our love had to mean something. This couldn't be the end. It *couldn't*.

I looked down at Terah, shock paralyzing me. Her face was covered in blood, but her expression was peaceful. Almost like she was sleeping. I reached out a shaking hand and slid my fingers gently down her cheek, wishing I'd done this a million more times when I'd had the chance. Wishing I'd known how she felt about me—that she hadn't minded that I'd crossed the boundaries of friendship into the romantic too many times. Gods, if I'd only known, we could've been together so much sooner, and she never would've come out here alone. She never would've had to sacrifice her life.

My entire body quaked as I cupped her face between my hands. I was stunned. Dazed. I couldn't force my mind to accept what I was seeing. Beneath my fingers, Terah's skin was still warm. I wanted her to just open her eyes. I wanted her to smile up at me in the playful way she did and ask me teasingly whether I really thought a Demon could get the best of her. I stared at her intently, hoping, needing to see some indication that she was still there. That she hadn't left me. But the seconds ticked by and there was no change. No smile. Nothing. And her skin grew colder beneath my fingers.

Pain ripped through me again as reality hit me, permeating the dazed fog. And then anger like nothing I'd ever felt before surged through me. No. *NO*. I couldn't just let her go. I couldn't accept what was happening. I couldn't move on. I wouldn't. I had to do something, anything, to fix this. To bring her back to me. I let out an anguished cry into the night sky above me, and fiercely pulled all my power toward my hands. I didn't care if it killed me—I had to heal her.

Blue light glowed around me brightly as I leaned over Terah's still form. "Please come back to me," I murmured, before grabbing her shoulders. Then I shoved out every ounce of power I could pull from inside myself through my hands and into her.

Terah's skin glowed blue from the amount of power she was receiving all at once, but I didn't stop. *Heal*, I ordered my power as I fed wave after wave into her. *Heal*. Tears streamed down my face as my power showed me how much was broken, punctured, and crushed inside of her. More than all my power could ever heal. A sob broke free from my lips, but I kept going. Kept pushing my power into her. I wouldn't stop. I wouldn't give up on her.

Footsteps pounded across the frozen snow, but I didn't glance up. I didn't want to break my concentration. But I could tell from a familiar sound of anguish, that Matt was one of the people who'd arrived. Finally. Maybe with more people, as many as we could possibly find, we could save her. Maybe we could bring her back.

The last of my power drained from me, and I slumped back on the grass, gasping. But I reached out and pressed my fingers to her neck, feeling for a pulse. Nothing. I pushed back onto my knees and started giving Terah CPR. Maybe it would keep enough of her vitals going so we could revive her.

"Matt." I looked up at him desperately. "We're losing her. Help me. Please."

Matt had tears running down his face as well. He looked frozen, like he'd been dropped into hell and couldn't believe what he was seeing. I knew exactly how he felt. This *was* hell. The president stood next to him, horror in her eyes, her hands clasped over her mouth.

"I'll call more teachers to come help while the medics are on the way," she murmured shakily as Matt collapsed onto the ground next to Terah, his hands already glowing with white light.

Matt grabbed her shoulders and poured his power quickly into her. Blinding white light grew and grew around them as Matt drained every ounce of power he had into the woman we both loved. Terah's skin glowed white as her body absorbed it all.

Please. Please let it be enough.

Matt collapsed on the ground, gasping, when all his power was spent. I reached out and felt for a pulse again. There was the smallest movement— the faintest pulse—but it was already fading. *No.* I swore and compressed her badly injured chest again, trying to pump any blood she still had left through her body, then wiped the blood off her mouth with my sleeve before tilting her head back and blowing air into her lungs. Thank the gods for my Normal education. They'd made us learn common Normal healing as a part of our physical education requirements. I looked at Terah's chest as I blew another breath into her, but her chest remained still. Her lungs weren't filling with the air.

"Shit." I straightened up and continued the chest compressions. "Something's keeping her from taking air. We need healers *now*."

The president stepped forward and knelt with Matt next to Terah. She was incredibly pale, and her hands were visibly shaking. I didn't blame her. Not only was this horrific, but a death on Academy grounds from a Demon attack could mean the end of the Academy.

"The healers are ready and almost here, and I've sent word for more help. We'll need it all if . . . if we are to revive her." Her voice shook.

"Can you help her too?" My voice was hoarse with desperation. "We need all the power we can possibly get."

The president nodded, a little hesitant, but leaned forward, her hands starting to glow with white light. "I will do my best."

The medics arrived with a stretcher and a handful of professors as the president was giving her power to Terah. Several of the medics gasped when they saw her, and some of the professors swore.

Matt looked at the crowd that had gathered and shook his head, his hands balling into fists. "This won't be enough. It's not enough power to save her."

He pulled his phone from his pocket, his hand shaking badly, then quickly pressed a contact's number. "Simon, there's been an attack. Grab as many of our friends as you can find and run to the tree line behind the main building. Terah's hurt and we need your help."

He hung up and shoved his phone into his pocket, then grabbed a second phone from his other pocket—one I hadn't seen before—and called another number.

"Yes, it's Matt. There was another attack and Terah's dying. We need you here. We need your power if she's going to survive. Please." And then he hung up. I didn't know for sure who he'd called, but I guessed it was her mother. I hoped she'd come. We needed her power. But I wouldn't rely on her to show up or do the right thing. She'd made it clear during our last meeting just how much she valued her daughter. And it wasn't very much.

After the president had expended her power, the medics surrounded Terah and trailed their power over her, doing a quick analysis of her injuries.

"She's almost gone," one medic said. "Barely still there. I'm not sure if we'll be able to revive her."

"She's been impaled and has multiple other deep puncture wounds," another said. "Most of her organs are damaged. Extreme blood loss."

"Her arm is crushed and the other is dislocated and fractured," another murmured.

"Her lungs are filled with liquid. We need to clear that first if we don't want her to get brain damage from lack of oxygen."

"We need to close up the wounds too, if we don't want her to completely bleed out, and we need to get her heart beating again."

My ears rang as I listened to them list her injuries, and I suddenly wished with a startling fierceness that I could somehow trade places with her. That I could suffer and die instead of her. She never deserved this. She deserved . . . everything. The world. Her happiness. But the world seemed intent on consistently throwing its worst at her.

The medics ushered professors forward and instructed them on where to focus their powers. The professors, all grim and in shock, obliged without comment or hesitation. Terah's lungs were cleared out first, and I was given permission to resume breathing for her. I did so, even while the healings were taking place. But I knew it was a temporary fix. Unless we could heal her insides and eliminate internal bleeding, her lungs would just fill again.

"Even if we get her closed up, she doesn't have enough blood left to survive," one of the medics murmured to another. "And it's too much to regenerate. We'll need to do a transfusion."

The other medic nodded. "I agree, but we may not have enough in storage for that."

My stomach clenched painfully, panic and anger tumbling over each other there. How could the Academy have a medical wing that wasn't prepared for graver injuries? Was their fucking hubris so large that they thought serious injury could never happen on campus?

"We need to get her back to the medical wing *now*," the lead medic said firmly. "All those who haven't expended their powers, please follow us there."

The remaining professors nodded as the medics lifted Terah onto the stretcher. I groaned in agony as I saw how much blood was pooled on the ground where she'd been lying. Hot tears spilled down my face again as I pushed to my feet and followed the medics, but I didn't give a shit. I didn't care about what anyone thought of me now. I didn't care if I was letting my vulnerability show. Because I couldn't for the life of me hide it. Not now. All I cared about was Terah. Nothing else mattered anymore.

Matt's friends ran over as the medics carried the stretcher with Terah to a side door in the main building.

"Holy shit," one of his friends exclaimed as he saw her.

"Simon! Thank the gods you're here." Matt grabbed his friend's arm and pulled him along with us. "Follow us to the medical wing," he said over his shoulder to the rest of his friends. "She'll need all the power she can get. She's . . . barely alive." Pain bled through his voice. Matt's friends exchanged looks of horror and followed us.

Impatience gnawed at my stomach as I watched blood continue to seep out of Terah. This was taking too long. Every second we weren't healing her, we risked losing her. I grabbed the end of her stretcher, relieving the medics of some of the weight, and started walking more quickly. The medics looked at one another, but no one told me to stop. Which was good. I wouldn't have stopped even if they'd told me to. And I'd gladly fight every person here to make sure Terah got the care she deserved. And quickly.

We practically jogged down the halls of the main building with the stretcher until we reached the medical wing.

"The largest room," the president ordered from behind us. The medics nodded and ran toward it.

Once in the room, Matt and I held the stretcher, and the medics transferred Terah onto the hospital bed. My gut clenched tightly as I saw how much blood she'd left behind on the stretcher. The medics threw a sheet over Terah's torn, bloody clothes, and called the remainder of the professors forward while they hooked her up to an oxygen machine and a heart monitor. The heart monitor let out a continuous, terrifying beep. Because Terah's heart wasn't beating. My jaw and fists clenched as terror shuddered through me. We weren't moving fast enough. We were losing her.

Another medic ran back into the room with emergency wound-sealing tape. "We can't focus on the outside injuries right now," he panted. "We'll just have to seal them, so she doesn't lose more blood, and focus on the internal healing."

He got to work as the other medics instructed the professors and Matt's friends on where to focus their power and healing. The medics wanted to heal her punctured organs, clear out all the stomach acid, internal fluids, and blood from where they didn't belong, and seal all the blood vessels and veins they could so a transfusion could take place. One by one, person after person stepped forward and poured their power into Terah. I grasped her hand tightly in mine as I watched. I felt the strong need to tether her here somehow. I wanted her to know she wasn't alone. I needed her to know I'd never leave her, no matter what.

After every person in the room had expended themselves, the medics ran their powers over Terah again, doing another full-body analysis.

"We need to try restarting her heart manually," one medic said, his voice tight with worry. "If we don't, she'll die in a matter of minutes."

A spasm shuddered through me, leaving rigid tension in its wake, and I gripped Terah's hand tighter. I couldn't believe after so much power was poured into her, so little had been achieved. But I couldn't give up. I flat out refused to believe we could still lose her. There was no way in hell that I'd let that happen.

The medics rolled out and charged a defibrillator, while another brought over a screen.

"Everyone needs to step back to the other side of the curtain. Including you," he added, his gaze meeting mine. I released Terah's hand to make room for the medics but crossed my arms over my chest and stared him down fiercely, anger churning through me. I wasn't going to leave her side.

"Don't waste your time or energy trying to move me," I said darkly. "I'm not going anywhere."

Trepidation crept into the medic's expression as I towered over him, but he finally shook his head and stepped around me, dropping the issue. The curtain was pulled around us, and the medics cut Terah's dress off her chest and shoulders. Then the defibrillator was charged, and they sent a powerful jolt through Terah's body. I whipped my head around to look at the heart monitor, my pulse accelerating until I almost couldn't breathe. Nothing. It was still flatlining. I swore and ran my hands through my hair. The medics charged the defibrillator again and sent another jolt through her chest. Still nothing. Tears pooled in my eyes again as my clenched fists shook at my sides. *Come on. Please work. Please.*

They sent jolt after jolt through Terah's body, and I felt each one in my own chest, tearing at me. Ripping my heart to shreds. The medic wielding the machine finally set it down, panting, and shook her head. My legs shook and nausea hit me like a truck. *No.* This couldn't be it. We couldn't just give up.

"Try it again," I said harshly to her. "We can't give up on her."

The medics looked at each other before the lead medic turned to address me.

"We need more power to restart her heart. More than just a defibrillator. We need a powerful healer. But we don't have enough power left between us to fix it."

Desperate anger seethed through me. "Then why the hell didn't you focus on healing her heart first?" I shouted, losing all semblance of self-control.

"Because," she responded, remarkably calmly given the circumstances, "she would've died much sooner if we hadn't fixed those other things first."

My entire body shook as I stood there, livid. I wanted to force them to try again. They couldn't give up. I couldn't let them. But their expressions were set—decided. Fine. If they wouldn't keep trying, I would. I'd never give up on her. I took a step forward and reached for the defibrillator paddles myself.

"Where is my daughter?"

I froze as I heard the voice, imperious even when laced with fear, my eyes widening. I spun around to see the High Light Guardian walking quickly around the screen. She made brief eye contact with me before looking down at Terah. Her expression was fairly neutral as she looked at her daughter's blood-soaked body, but I could tell she was distressed by the way the creases around her eyes deepened, and the cunning, dangerous light within them dimmed.

In a quick motion, Serafina tore off the blood-soaked sheet so she could see the damage more clearly. And her eyes pressed shut at the sight.

"They can't restart her heart," I said, my voice hoarse. "They need more power to heal it. Can you do it?"

Serafina glanced at me, haughtiness radiating from her, but her derisive expression softened slightly as she studied me more closely. I could feel the remnants of my tears still damp on my cheeks. My anguish must be visible.

"I can absolutely do it," she said crisply, "though I am not sure how wise that would be. As the High Light Guardian, I need to retain a significant amount of my power in case something more serious happens and I am called to defend our people in some larger way. I cannot simply expend myself outside my duties as leader. It could be disastrous for the Divine world, and my allegiance, above all others, even my family," her eyes flicked back over Terah's lifeless form, "is to the Divine world."

Rage tore through me so strongly I could barely see clearly. I took a step toward Serafina, practically vibrating with it. "I don't give a shit about your other assignments or responsibilities. She's your fucking daughter! And she *is* a part of the Divine world. She's a part of who you're supposed to be protecting! She gave her life to defend the school and all the people here while your warrior faction soldiers were nowhere to be found. The least you can do is help her. If you have a heart at all, if you ever loved her, even a little, then you *will* heal her!"

Serafina retreated a step, her eyes widening as my rage engulfed her. I doubted anyone had ever spoken to her like that. But instead of unleashing her own imperious rage at me, she looked back at Terah, her mouth twisting as she considered her.

"I suppose . . . I do owe her something," she said, almost to herself. "She is mine, after all. And she is . . . important . . ."

She stepped closer to Terah, her hands beginning to glow white. I swallowed hard and took Terah's hand again. I hated her mother. Deeply. I could never forgive her for how she made Terah suffer. How she used her. How she didn't love her. But if she saved Terah's life, I'd push those feelings aside for the moment.

As Serafina pressed her hands over Terah's chest, the sparkling white light around her fingers became immediately blinding. I squinted as everyone else slammed their eyes shut. Serafina's divine power was staggering. I'd known she had to be powerful to hold the High Light Guardian position, but I'd never witnessed power so strong. It flowed into Terah's body, and she absorbed wave after wave until she glowed as brightly as Serafina. They looked . . . like angels. Purely Divine. But Terah was the only angel here—Serafina was far from it.

I held my breath as the healing continued, and glanced at the heart monitor every couple seconds. If anyone could make Terah's heart start again, if anyone had that much power, it was Serafina. But I also knew that, if Serafina failed, there'd truly be no hope left. And I'd lose her. My grip tightened around her hand, and I prayed to any and all good that might exist in the universe, that this would work, and that Terah would be saved.

Breathless moments passed as the medics, the president, and I all watched the healing. But finally, as the glowing white light shimmered and faded, I heard the only sound besides Terah's voice that could bring me complete joy. A beep. From the heart monitor. I spun around and looked at it just to be sure. Another beep came from it. And another. Little squiggles began connecting across the screen, showing a steady heartbeat. The breath whooshed out of me as I turned back to look at Terah. She was *alive*. Truly alive.

The medics rushed forward and placed a new sheet over Terah's body, trying to preserve her privacy. Serafina stepped back and brushed her hands together lightly.

"I have healed and stabilized her heart and other internal organs, but I will do no more." Her voice was firm, and her expression was cool again. "It should be enough to keep her alive as long as her other wounds are seen to quickly." She turned to the president. "I expect regular updates on her condition. Additionally, we should retire to examine the security situation around the borders of campus. Matthew, you will join us."

I looked up as the curtain was wheeled away and saw Matt's pained expression. He clearly didn't want to leave Terah here. But he had orders now that he was a part of the warrior faction. My jaw tightened. I would've told Serafina to fuck off, regardless of her orders, but I knew Matt wouldn't. Not even for Terah. With one last agonized glance at her, Matt followed Serafina and the president from the room. I shook my head in disgust.

As soon as they left, Matt's friends and the professors filed out as well. There was nothing left that they could do, as they'd all expended their power trying to keep Terah alive. I made grateful eye contact with a few of them. They'd come to her aid without really knowing her, and I'd never forget it.

Once the room cleared, a medic stepped forward and quickly took a small blood sample from Terah's arm, then got to work analyzing it with a machine. Another medic brought out the equipment for a transfusion.

"I'll give her my blood," I said quietly, as they inserted a needle attached to a thin tube into her arm. They'd said earlier that they didn't have enough for her—I'd make sure they did.

"I thought you might," the medic said, not even bothering to glance at me. "Do you know your blood type?"

"I'm a universal donor." We'd had a decent amount of blood drives at my high school. Not to mention other Divines who'd needed transfusions after battles in the past.

The medic nodded and brought over a chair for me. "I'm assuming your blood alcohol content is about as high as hers? It's not ideal, but I suppose we'll have to overlook it, given the situation."

I stiffened and gave her a hard look. It wasn't like any of us had planned for this to happen. If I'd known what was coming, I obviously wouldn't have had any alcohol, and neither would Terah. It'd just been extremely bad luck that the attack had come the night of the holiday party. I frowned as the medics hooked Terah up to a saline drip. *Had* it been bad luck? Or had it specifically been planned for a time when everyone would be at their most vulnerable? My mood darkened.

The medics came over and swabbed my arm before inserting a needle attached to a thin tube. Blood flowed from my arm into a collection bag, which in turn, distributed my blood into Terah's veins. I reached over and took Terah's cold fingers again, rubbing them gently. Her fingers always seemed to be cold. Though now, the coldness had more to do with her health than anything else. But I'd still give her my warmth. I'd give her anything to make her suffering stop.

The transfusion took a decent amount of time, but I had nowhere else I was willing to be anyway, so I sat back in my chair and stroked Terah's fingers as my blood continued to flow into her. And I whispered to her in my mind, telling her how much I loved her. That I'd be here by her side until she woke up again, and for as long as she'd have me after that. Desperately hoping she'd hear me somehow.

As the transfusion continued, the medics focused their remaining power on healing the damage in Terah's crushed arm. Before the transfusion, they'd placed a tourniquet above the injury while also creating a blockade of power between her arm and the rest of her body to make sure no blood flow interacted with it while it was still crushed—they didn't want any bone fragments to get in her bloodstream. But they were having a rough time. Apparently, apart from breaking every bone almost to dust, the Demon had also caused bone, muscle, and skin to all meld together. Separating it out and putting it all back together was proving to be extremely difficult. But, inspired by all the help received and effort that'd already been put into saving Terah, they seemed determined to keep working on it until they figured it out. My respect for them grew as I watched them troubleshoot as a team and painstakingly, little by little, heal the internal workings of her arm. Over an hour later, they finally removed the tourniquet, her arm beat up, but whole once again.

"Does she have quick-healing abilities?" one of the medics asked while they worked on stitching closed all her external wounds. They had no power left to heal any of them.

"She does," I said quietly, watching them work. "When she has enough power reserves. But before she lost consciousness, she told me she used all her power on the Demon, even her life force. So I wouldn't expect her power or her quick healing to return anytime soon."

The medics all paused and looked up at me, startled.

"That's . . . not possible," he said, once he'd gotten his reaction under control. "She must not have used it all. Otherwise, we wouldn't have been able to revive her, regardless of how much power we had."

I frowned. I'd heard that before as well, but I trusted Terah to know her own power levels. She'd said she'd used all her life force, and I believed her. But there wasn't a point in arguing the fact with this medic. Terah was responding to the healing, and that's all that mattered right now.

"Anyway," the medic continued, "It'll be a while before she builds up her power again, so for now, we'll have to settle for the more rudimentary Normal healing methods."

I nodded shortly—I'd figured as much. And it was another reason I wasn't willing to leave her. All the power that I regenerated, whenever I regenerated any, belonged to her. I'd drain myself as many times as needed to speed up her recovery.

When the medics were done stitching her up, the male medics left and the female medics brought buckets of water, sponges, and towels to clean Terah, as well as a clean mattress pad and sheets for the bed.

"You should really close your eyes for this part," the lead medic said to me kindly. She was the oldest person here. Older even than my parents.

The only elders I'd ever met were Normals—Divines didn't usually live to reach old age. Because of the war. "I doubt she'd want any onlookers while she's fully uncovered."

I nodded again. I didn't want Terah to be exposed unless she chose to be. So I closed my eyes as they got to work. Finally, a medic came over and removed the needle from my arm and placed a bandage over the small puncture.

"Just a few more minutes and you can open your eyes again," the lead medic said.

I nodded silently and waited, listening to them shift Terah around as they cleaned her and remade the bed.

"Alright, you're free to look."

I opened my eyes and saw the medics had cleaned all the blood and dirt from Terah's skin. They'd also put her in a hospital gown, changed the bed linens, and covered her with a blanket. I swallowed hard as tears stung my eyes again. Like this, Terah really did look like she was just sleeping. Like her eyes might open at any moment, and she'd smile up at me. My stomach clenched, and I reached forward and ran my fingertips slowly down her cheek. Her skin was warm again under mine. A tear broke free and spilled down my cheek.

"The last thing we can really do for her tonight is fix her dislocated shoulder," the lead medic said. "We'll have to work on healing her other injuries more completely when our powers regenerate more. We'll likely be able to start doing that tomorrow afternoon or evening."

I nodded, quickly wiping the tear away, and stood so they could access her shoulder. They quickly crowded around her, some lifting her arm, while others stabilized her shoulder. Then, with a pop, they snapped her joint back into place. I winced and looked at Terah's face but saw no expression of discomfort.

"Is she in pain?" My voice came out gravellier and more lifeless than I'd intended. My ability to mask my despair was gone.

"I doubt she can feel anything right now," the lead medic said, sympathetically. "But we'll also be giving her some pain medication before we leave."

"Thank you." I sat at Terah's side again and took her hand.

The medics worked on cleaning up the room and their equipment, then gave Terah pain medication, and left the room. Only the lead medic stayed. I glanced at her once I noticed she was watching me.

"Am I right in assuming you won't leave her?" She smiled a little.

My shoulders stiffened, and I gave her a flinty look. "I'm not leaving. Not until she's better."

The medic nodded and was silent for a long moment. "Well, it's not really a policy of ours to let other students—well, anyone who isn't family—stay with the ill while they're in our wards."

I opened my mouth angrily to protest, but she held up a hand to silence me.

"*However*," she said slowly, "I believe, with a student in such bad condition, we might be able to make an exception. We don't have many medics who can monitor her overnight, so if you're willing to stay, I may allow it for those purposes."

I looked away from her and back at Terah's peaceful face. "I'll do anything I need to, to stay."

"I believe you would," she said quietly. "It's nice to see such devoted friendship, especially since her family seems . . ." She shifted uncomfortably. "Well, I'm just glad she's got such a strong advocate in you."

"Thank you," I finally murmured. "For saving her. And for letting me stay."

The medic smiled and placed a hand on my shoulder. "Don't forget to take care of yourself too, dear." She squeezed my shoulder and released me. "I'll bring in a cot and some blankets for you. Just give me a moment."

She left the room and returned a few minutes later with a cot, pillow, and small pile of blankets, which she set near the large bay window to the right of Terah's bed. Through it, I could see snow was still quietly falling from the sky. It felt strange that something so normal and peaceful could be happening while I felt like my own world was falling apart. It seemed like everything else should stop as well. But the world kept going, and the snow was a painful reminder of that.

The lead medic walked back over and showed me where all the light switches were and pointed out the attached bathroom. Then she rested a hand briefly on my shoulder and departed for the night.

Finally alone, I released a slow, shaky breath. This had easily been the worst night of my life. And the worst night of Terah's. I leaned over until my forehead rested on her forearm. And I stayed there, feeling her warmth, listening to the comforting sound of her heartbeat through the monitor. I'd come so close to losing her. A part of me was still afraid that I would. Exhaustion and a fresh wave of anguish swept through me.

"How is she?"

I straightened up and saw Matt, looking exhausted and haggard, walking slowly in, his eyes glued to Terah.

I scrubbed a hand over my eyes. "She's mostly stabilized. They healed her arm and gave her a transfusion, but they weren't able to heal a lot of her injuries. She's still just . . . hanging on."

Matt nodded as he stopped at her side and slid his hand into hers. "Gods, Terah," he murmured, his voice shaking. "What did you do to yourself?"

Anger spiked through me. "She sacrificed herself to save everyone at the Academy, including you." I didn't try to conceal the hard edge to my voice. I hated how he always seemed to put the blame on her, as though she'd done something wrong or made the wrong decisions. But she'd made the bravest decision. The hardest one. And she usually did. I couldn't understand why he never saw that.

"I wish I didn't have to leave," Matt said quietly, ignoring my last statement. "I wish I could've stayed with her. That I could continue staying with her."

"But duty calls?" I couldn't keep the sarcasm out of my voice or the sneer off my face. Yeah, I knew he had orders, but I didn't give a shit. I would've told my superiors to go to hell. Nothing would've made me leave her, especially when she was like this.

"Yes." Matt glared at me. "I'm a ranking member of the warrior faction now. I can't just drop the protection of the school because I want to stay here."

I rolled my eyes and shook my head in disgust. I knew nothing we said to each other would convince the other of the rightness of our positions.

Matt glanced over at the cot and blankets near the window, then looked back at me. "You're staying, aren't you?" His voice was quiet. Serious.

"No shit." I crossed my arms over my chest and surveyed him coolly. "I won't leave her."

Matt studied me closely for a long moment. "She was wrong, wasn't she?" His gaze was intent on mine. "When she assumed you didn't love her back."

My stomach clenched tightly as pain ripped through my chest. "Is that what she told you?" I tried to keep my voice steady. "That I don't love her?"

Matt's lips pursed as his body went rigid with tension. He clearly didn't want to tell me much.

"She interpreted you . . . leaving her that night you kissed her . . . as a rejection of her. She thought you were saying you didn't care for her as more than friends." He looked at the floor, his jaw tightening.

I dropped my forehead into my hand, tears threatening again. But I clenched my jaw and shoved them down. I'd worked so hard not to hurt her. Not to push her too far or be yet another guy who forced his own wants onto her without thinking about what she wanted. Not to be like Matt or Caleb. But I'd hurt her anyway. She'd thought I was rejecting her. I sank against the back of my chair, defeat flooding me.

"Yes," I said, my voice hollow. "She was wrong."

Matt looked at my sharply. "So, you *do* love her?"

All I could do was nod. I hated myself right now. I hated that I hadn't told her how I felt. I hated that I'd hurt her. And I hated that she'd run to him when she'd thought I'd rejected her.

"You should tell her if—when—she wakes up." Matt's voice was almost too quiet for me to hear. I jerked my head up and looked closely at his expression. He looked conflicted. In pain.

"I tried. Before she . . ." But I couldn't finish. I looked at her face again and swallowed. Silence blanketed the room for a long moment, only filled by the beeping of her heart monitor. "Why do you want me to tell her?" I finally asked. "I know how you feel about her. You can't want us to be together."

Matt's shoulders slumped. "Yeah, well, I've done a lot of what I want and very little of what she's wanted. And . . ." he took a deep, steadying breath, "I just want her to be happy. Besides," he straightened his shoulders a bit, "it's not like I'm going anywhere. I know how I feel about her won't change. She may decide, someday, that she'd prefer to be with me."

My jaw tightened instantly. Only he could want her happiness in the most asshole-ish way possible. He couldn't simply think about her wants and needs—it always had to include his own interests somehow.

"Don't count on it," I murmured gruffly. "If she chooses to be with me, I don't plan on fucking up our relationship. Ever."

Matt smiled a little, though it didn't reach his eyes. "I'd expect nothing different. But just remember, it's not ultimately up to you. She decides."

I nodded curtly. In this one thing, we agreed—it was her choice. But his message was clear. In this one moment, we'd come together for her to see that she recovered. But after that, we'd be enemies again, each unwilling to give her up. Well, that was fine with me. I didn't intend to

286

repeat my mistakes or leave anything between us unsaid. I didn't intend to ever lose her again.

"Since I can't stay with her," Matt said, breaking the tense silence, "I'd like to help you stay." My eyes widened. "Someone who cares about her should be here, at least," Matt added quietly as he noticed my surprise. "Am I right in assuming you haven't thought about changes of clothes or food or anything?"

I shook my head stiffly. I hadn't, but I was prepared to go without, if it meant I could stay with her.

"Right," Matt continued, businesslike, "then I can pack a bag for you. Bring you some clothes and toiletries. And I can also bring you food from the dining hall as often as I can manage between my warrior faction duties."

"Thank you," I ground out. It would be helpful. I just wished the help wasn't coming from him.

"I'll bring those by in the morning."

I nodded as Matt's attention shifted back to Terah. He stepped closer to her and leaned over, pressing his lips to her forehead. Then he murmured in her ear—too quiet for me to hear—before kissing her cheek and running a hand over her hair. I stiffened in my chair—he certainly felt physically entitled to her—but I didn't say anything. If he kept going though, I would. And it might be with my fist, not my mouth.

Matt straightened up, his eyes overly bright, as though he was struggling with tears. "Let me know if anything . . . if her condition changes."

I pushed down my anger for the moment. "I will."

Matt nodded, his eyes narrowing on mine, then he turned and left the room.

I let out a slow breath before pushing to my feet. I dragged the cot away from the bay window and brought it over next to Terah's bed. Even though the window was only about ten feet away, it still felt too far from her. With a heavy sigh, I kicked off my shoes, shrugged out of my suit jacket, pulled off my belt, and stripped out of my dress pants. It'd been such a fucking long night. Full of some pretty great highs and the absolute lowest of lows.

I closed my eyes briefly and remembered Terah's smiling face as we'd laughed and danced earlier. She'd seemed so happy. So enthusiastic and full of life and energy. I remembered her soft sigh as I'd pulled her close to me as we'd danced. How her arms had encircled my neck as she'd pressed into me. It had made my heart pound wildly. But I still hadn't seen it. How could I not have? How had I missed all the signs that she'd had feelings for me as well? Perhaps because I'd been so damn wrapped up in myself and my own reactions to her that I'd refused to see what was right in front of my eyes. And I hadn't just talked to her about it, as I should've. In short, I'd been a fool.

I shook my head, disgusted with myself. I wished I could turn back time and change what I'd done and how I'd reacted. Change how the attack had taken place and how much Terah had been hurt. Sighing, I walked over to the light switches and flipped them off before returning to the cot. Then I sank onto it and pulled the blankets over me. The cot was a good foot shorter than me, but I was too exhausted to care about that minor discomfort now. I reached up and squeezed Terah's hand as I finally let myself relax and close my eyes. And with her soft skin against mine, I finally fell asleep.

"Hey," Matt said as he walked into the room the next day, his eyes immediately seeking out Terah. He was carrying a bag of my belongings along with a tray of food that he set down on the small table near the door. "How's she doing?"

I shrugged a little, trying to hide my deep worry. "She's stable," I murmured. "They've mended her broken ribs and fractured arm, set her broken leg, and are working on healing her puncture wounds. It's slow going, though." I scrubbed a hand over my face. "They can only heal a little at a time as their power regenerates."

Matt nodded and looked at me appraisingly. I was pretty sure he was trying to figure out how I was doing. It didn't take a genius to notice I wasn't doing great. I was trying not to show it, but there was no hiding the toll Terah's injury was taking on me. It was hollowing me out and tearing me apart. I couldn't even escape the torture of it as I slept. I'd had vivid nightmares about finding her broken and bleeding in the snow. Nightmares about trying to tell her I loved her, only to find myself further and further away from her as I tried to speak. It also didn't help that I hadn't had a cigarette in a while. But I wasn't going to leave her side. Not for anything—especially not for something as unimportant as that. But the headaches and restlessness I was getting from the withdrawal were fucking terrible and made it harder to deal with everything.

Matt finally looked away from me and pulled up a chair to the other side of Terah's bed. He took her hand, and I saw a faint glow of white light around his fingers. He was doing what I'd done this morning—giving her some of his power to speed up her recovery. I could only hope it helped in some small way.

"I have some updates from the plane barrier," he finally said, once his power faded from his fingers. But he kept Terah's hand in his. I watched him from across the bed and waited.

Matt sighed and glanced at me.

"From our investigation so far, it doesn't seem like the barrier was breached around the perimeter of the grounds like the other attacks. None of the guards were killed or even alerted to the infiltration. Not until Terah brought down a huge storm from the sky to defeat it. The fight was over, and we were already in the medical wing before they made it from the perimeter to where the fight had taken place. This seems to point to one thing: the Demon must've come onto the grounds in its human form to avoid detection, and likely from a breach in the plane above instead of around the grounds. A breach that's since been closed. It seems likely that the Demon hid in the trees and only transformed when it saw Terah nearby."

I tensed. It'd long since bothered me that Terah was always around when the Demons attacked, and it bothered me even more now. Before, when it'd been the both of us, it'd been easier to convince myself that it was a coincidence. But it seemed like the Demon had . . . *waited* for her this time. The thought was terrifying.

"Do you think they're targeting her on purpose?" I tried to keep my expression and voice calm, even as terror gripped my stomach in a vice. I wanted to scoop Terah up and take her far away from here to keep her out of their reach.

Matt shifted uncomfortably in his seat. "I'm not sure. It's possible that the Demon just waited until the first available student was near it. But . . . it's unclear why it would do that instead of just attacking the building where all the students and staff were." He shook his head, his brows furrowing. "I've tried thinking about it in a rational, detached way, but even then, it seems like too much of a coincidence that she's been there for every attack."

I nodded. We were on the same page about that. "Why would they target her? What could they want with her?"

"I don't know. They could be trying to get to the High Light Guardian through her. Or take revenge on Serafina by killing her. But beyond that,

I'm not sure. She doesn't have any other connection with the war or the Dark Guardian realm other than being a border town soldier. Nothing that would make her stand out from plenty of other students here."

I sank back in my chair and crossed my arms over my chest, frowning. "Do you think they might be trying to take her out because of her unique power?"

Matt's gaze jerked to mine, his eyes widening. "How would they even know about that?"

"I dunno. But the Light Guardians know. The Academy administration knows. Maybe there's a spy."

Matt swore under his breath and looked away. "That's possible, I guess. I'll have to look into that. But it would be pretty disastrous if that were true."

Of course it would be. But the situation was already disastrous. It didn't seem like too much of a stretch to assume that someone was working for the Dark Guardians from inside the Academy.

Matt sighed and rubbed his eyes before grasping Terah's hand in his again. "Additionally, I think Terah's visions are starting to come true."

I raised my eyebrows mildly at him and waited silently for an explanation. I already knew that at least one had come true—Matt kissing her—but I doubted Matt knew that.

"The night that you and she . . . fought . . . she had several visions in her sleep. She described them to me, and one of them sounded like the attack that happened yesterday, though there wasn't any indication in her visions about when that was going to happen. Obviously, if there was, I never would've let her out of my sight."

I nodded slowly, thinking. It didn't exactly surprise me, but it was unsettling. And it meant that worse things were coming. If all her visions came true, it would mean horrible things for the Divine world.

"Yeah, well, it's not the first time that one's come true."

Matt's startled gaze met mine again, but I didn't elaborate.

"Well . . . those visions she shared with me along with this most recent attack mean that the Academy's not safe anymore. It means that more Demon attacks are likely coming, and the Academy's not built to handle that. We're a school, not a war zone. We can't keep having attacks on students."

"Maybe the Academy shouldn't remain open." I sent him a hard stare. "If it can't retain its neutrality, and if it can't keep its students safe, why keep it open? One way to stop more attacks on the school is to not have students here anymore."

"I know," Matt murmured, looking at Terah again. "I've brought that up with the president. But no one can order the school to close. As much as the Light Guardian side has respect here, the Academy is still technically neutral. It isn't beholden to any orders, and the president isn't willing to close the school after centuries of being open." He shook his head, and I could see his frustration.

"Then I hope the president is ready to have a lot of blood on her hands if the Academy is attacked again," I said darkly. "Not that she doesn't already," I added, looking at Terah again. I reached forward and closed my hand around hers.

Matt nodded and sighed. "I tried to make her see that, but she's too concerned about the history and tradition of the school to consider closing it for any reason. I did encourage her to send out information to all new and returning students about the attacks this semester and the lack of guaranteed safety here moving forward. It'll at least let students make informed decisions about whether to return next semester. She does seem open to that, at least."

I nodded, my fingers tightening around Terah's hand. A part of me wanted to leave and not return next semester—to take Terah far away from here before the Demons accomplished whatever they were trying to accomplish. They couldn't attack her if they couldn't find her. But as much as Terah struggled with the roles we were expected to fill as soldiers —the roles we hadn't had much of a choice in—I also knew she was incredibly brave and loyal. I'd seen how many times she'd put her life in jeopardy to protect people who couldn't protect themselves. Even with her reservations and bitterness about the life she'd been forced into, I doubted she'd choose to leave the Academy, even now. And if she didn't leave, I wouldn't either.

"Well," Matt said, after an extended silence, "I should probably go. Just wanted to give you an update." He stood then bent and cradled her face between his hands. He pressed his lips to Terah's forehead, before murmuring quietly in her ear. Then he straightened up and looked at me again.

"Keep her safe." His gaze was intense. Serious. He meant it.

I nodded curtly at him. I'd always try to keep her safe.

Matt nodded at me, then turned and walked from the room.

The days passed slowly and blurred together, only differentiated by the increased agony I felt each day Terah didn't wake. Every morning, I woke up, ate something if Matt was able to bring food, poured whatever power I'd regenerated overnight into Terah, exercised in the room's open space so I wouldn't lose strength or endurance between now and when training restarted next semester, and read to her. Then I watched closely and held Terah's hand as the medics continued to heal her various wounds. Once the medics left for the day, I told her stories about growing up in Elareth, and the trouble my sister and I had gotten into. Then I ate dinner, poured any power I'd regenerated during the day into her, and quietly told her how much I cared about her, while desperately trying to stave off the despair I felt whenever I saw how injured she still was. Then I turned out the light and slept, before waking up the next morning and repeating it all over again. And this was how it continued, day after miserable day.

Each day I awoke with a renewed hope that today would be the day that Terah would regain consciousness. That I'd see her smile, hear her voice, and see the bright vibrancy in her eyes again. And each day those hopes were crushed. She remained unconscious, too injured and busy healing for her body to sustain consciousness. I knew it was probably for the best, but it was torture. Not being able to heal her. Not being able to interact with her. Not truly knowing whether she'd return to me. But I knew my despair was nothing to what she was going through, so I pushed through and was there for her in every way I could be.

A little over a week after the attack, the last person I ever expected to see here walked through the door to Terah's room. *Caleb*. I slowly closed the book I'd been reading to Terah, and lowered it to the side of the bed, regarding him coolly. The last time he'd been in the vicinity when she was injured, he'd left her and the town behind in his desperation to not be affected by his feelings and worry for her. I'd assumed he'd react similarly now, if he reacted at all. But here he was, walking uncomfortably but firmly into her room.

"Caleb." I didn't bother keeping the hardness out of my voice. He deserved my anger. He'd had Terah's love and trust and had been foolish enough to throw it all away to save himself from discomfort, hurting her in the process. He was the worst kind of scum—an asshole of the first degree. "What the hell do you want?"

I crossed my arms over my chest and gave him a hard stare, my gaze flicking over his face. He looked upset. Not mad, though. More . . . worried.

"Gabriel." Caleb nodded a little at me, his own voice hard. He liked me about as much as I liked him. "I only just heard about the attack." He took a hesitant step closer to Terah's bed. "The president . . . she told everyone at today's end-of-year assembly about the Demon attacks and how Terah stopped this last one on her own. She said she protected the school but almost died . . ."

He took another hesitant step toward her bed, uncertainty, reluctance, and pain simultaneously filling his expression as he looked at her.

"I just wanted to see how she was before I leave for Glenhaven in an hour."

My body tensed as anger burned through me. "Since when do you care about her condition? I thought for sure you'd just run away and leave her behind. Isn't that what you did last time?"

Caleb shot a glare in my direction. "Guess she didn't hold anything back," he muttered darkly.

I scowled. "Why would she? You got her to trust you, treated her like shit, then abandoned her when she needed you most. She hates you for it. But she's also grown enough past it that she doesn't feel the need to keep it a secret. Believe me," I added, my voice darkening, "she's better off without you and your whole, 'feeling-things-makes-me-weaker' bullshit."

Caleb's glare intensified as his jaw clenched. A vein protruded from his neck and pulsed as anger clouded his eyes. But he pressed them closed, squeezed the bridge of his nose between his fingers, and took several deep breaths. When he finally opened his eyes again, he looked more under control.

"I'm . . . trying to be better," he finally said, quietly. "I can't pretend that I don't regret what I did to her sometimes. I mean, I wouldn't change what I did. Feeling like that—how I felt when we were together—isn't something I can afford in my life. It distracts me. Makes me weaker. But . . ." he looked down at Terah's peaceful face as he took another step closer to her, "I never wanted her hurt. Not then, and not now."

I shook my head, my jaw clenching. I fundamentally didn't understand him. How could he not see that shutting himself off from emotion was what actually make him weaker, not love. As soldiers caught up in a multi-generational war, there was so little good in our lives. Why rob ourselves of one of the few forms of happiness available to us? But I remembered, earlier in our friendship, Terah had felt similarly to Caleb about love. She'd only seen its potential to hurt. She hadn't been able to see its capacity to heal and create joy. But she'd been working so hard on overcoming the hurt that Caleb, Matt, her mother, and Dagmar had inflicted on her. Unlike Caleb, she was starting to open herself up again and reevaluate her stance on connection with others. And I wasn't interested in letting Caleb hurt her more.

"Well, you've done absolutely nothing to help her, then or now, so what do you want?"

Caleb sighed and pushed his longer hair over his head and away from his face. "I just wanted to give her something this time," he said quietly. "To make up for how I left her injured last time."

"And what do you plan to give her?"

Caleb smiled a little, though his eyes remained cold and hollow. Like they always were. "The only thing I have to give. My power."

I hid my surprise behind a stony expression. I genuinely never thought he'd even do that much. But I wasn't about to turn down something that would help Terah heal faster. I finally nodded curtly at him.

Caleb walked the rest of the way to her bed and stood there, looking down at her, his expression difficult to read. "How bad was it?" His gaze remained on Terah's face.

"Her injuries, or the battle?"

"Both."

I scrubbed a hand over my face. I didn't like thinking about it. I'd had enough nightmares of Terah lying in a pool of her own blood, dying. I didn't like bringing it into my waking thoughts as well.

I finally sighed. "Really bad. I was the one who found her. Most of her bones were broken or crushed, she had head wounds, gashes, deep puncture wounds, and she was impaled through her stomach." Caleb's eyes widened as he paled, and his fists clenched at his sides. "Her heart stopped beating, she bled almost all the way out, and she couldn't breathe. She'd also burned completely out. It took more than a dozen people draining themselves to keep her barely alive, and the High Light Guardian's intervention to get her heart and organs healed enough to function. As for the battle, no one knows how large the Demon was, since she'd disintegrated it by the time any of us got there, but from the markings on the ground and the damage to the trees, it looks like it was massive. The largest Demon I've ever encountered."

Caleb's clenched hands shook, but he just nodded curtly, his expression a cold mask.

"Okay," he finally said, his expression shuttered. I shouldn't have been surprised—if the guy had been able to leave Terah when she'd almost died before, he could probably do it again. Or at least not be as affected by it as he should've been.

He stepped to the side of the bed and reached forward, placing his hands on Terah's shoulders. He took a deep, shaky breath, then closed his eyes, white beginning to glow around his fingers. I watched quietly as wave after wave of power pulsed down his arms and into her, causing her to glow. My stomach clenched, an aching wave of hope cresting over me. She hadn't received this much power since the night of the attack. Maybe it would be enough to at least allow her consciousness to return. *Please. Please be enough.*

When the dregs of power finally ebbed from Caleb's fingers, I sat forward and took Terah's hand in mine, hoping to see something, anything, that would indicate his power had a substantial effect. Caleb watched her closely as well. But after a long moment of nothing, I pressed my eyes closed and took a deep breath, trying to shove down my disappointment. Trying not to give into despair. Instead, I laced my fingers through Terah's and held her hand between both of mine.

"Well," Caleb finally said, "at least I did something this time."

He turned and walked to the door but paused in the doorway.

"You know, you're doing more for her than I ever could." He was still facing away from me, his voice so quiet I could barely hear him. "I couldn't stay then, and I can't stay now. Not for anyone. Not even . . . for her."

I frowned as I watched him. Why was he telling me this? Why was he sharing with me at all?

"Maybe I always knew," he continued, his head falling back so he could stare at the ceiling. "Maybe I knew she deserved better—that I could never give her what she needed."

I lifted my eyebrows, surprised. It . . . sounded like a part of him still cared deeply for her, despite all the energy he'd put into shutting her out and antagonizing her. I didn't know what to do with that information. But I supposed even someone as fucked up as Caleb couldn't completely succeed in making himself an emotionless robot soldier. Not yet, anyway.

"I guess it doesn't matter now," Caleb sighed, straightening his shoulders. "I should go."

With one last glance over his shoulder at Terah, he walked quickly from the room and out of the medical wing.

Another week passed without Terah regaining consciousness, and I was quickly losing my sanity. While her body was healing, no one really knew that was going on in her mind. No one knew for certain that she'd wake up. And the uncertainty was killing me.

The worry ate at me more and more every day, and every day I fell apart a little more. But I tried to keep a gruff mask of neutrality on at all times. I tried to keep people from seeing how much of a mess I really was. But inside I was dying—flooded with too many worries and emotions that had no place to go except to stew in my feverish brain. I was terrified that I'd still lose her. I was terrified that after saving her body, her mind might never return. And losing her would kill me. I knew I'd never recover from that.

Each night, after everyone left, I'd finally let myself fall apart. Every night I held Terah's hand and let silent tears soak the shoulder of her hospital gown as the agony of her absence ripped me apart. I hated it, but I couldn't help it. After holding everything in all day, I had to release the stress and tension, or I'd explode. I wasn't proud that I couldn't seem to keep it together, but where she was concerned, I couldn't seem to measure my emotions. The firm control I'd cultivated my entire life to survive seemed to give way in the face of my feelings for her, and the devastation I felt at seeing her suffering. During the day, I wore the mask of calm consistency. I bottled everything up and saved it for when we were alone. When no one could see my shoulders shaking or my uncontrollable tears. Then I'd fall into a restless sleep and awake, only to don that neutral mask again. Like I was my old self. But I wasn't.

The only reprieve in this never-ending torture came in my dreams, and even then, only occasionally. Sometimes, instead of the fucking horrific nightmares about finding Terah dying, I'd hear her voice speaking softly in my mind. Sometimes I heard her say my name, and I'd reach out with all my might, trying to connect with her. Trying to tell her I was here with her. Trying to lead her back to me. But she always faded away, never materializing more firmly, and I'd feel freshly torn apart.

I realized it was probably my own mind, desperate for any trace of her, inventing these faint encounters. Taunting me. But even so, I clung to her voice, even if it wasn't real. Her faint presence banished the nightmares and lulled me, temporarily, into a less painful state. It was the closest I came to feeling like we were together again.

But even in all my distress, I refused to give up on her. I refused to fully believe she was gone. Because she fucking deserved someone who'd fight for her and believe in her, and I was going to be that person for her, even if it tore me apart. I'd never stop fighting for her, and I told her this every day. I murmured it to her as I poured my regenerated power into her morning and night. I told her as my uncontrollable tears soaked her shoulder. I told her when her voice drifted faintly into my dreams.

"Terah, I'm here. I love you. I'll never stop fighting for you. Come back to me."

And maybe, just maybe, if I never stopped telling her that, if I never gave up, she'd come back.

14

A GUARDIAN AND A BLESSED

I don't know how long I was gone. A while, at least. For the longest time, I knew only darkness. It was death, I was certain. I knew I'd died. I was prepared for it. I'd let it take me. Yet I was surprised that I was still . . . here. Still an entity somehow. I'd always assumed death was the end. That I'd just stop—cease to exist. Flicker and fade from the universe. But somehow, I was still here. Wherever *here* was.

The darkness wavered back and forth, consuming me and filling me, then retreating to the edges of my mind, before consuming me again. It felt like waves—cascading in and over me, then retreating, only to send more waves behind it. And that's how it stayed for the longest time.

I thought maybe this was it. This was what death was—a gentle but monotonous dance of darkness and light. Forever suspended in nothingness, while somehow still existing. It wasn't so bad. Nothing hurt. Nothing was expected of me. I just . . . was. But I was alone. I'd hoped that, in death, I'd either cease to exist entirely, or I'd go someplace where I could be with others. But it seemed that luck truly wasn't on my side. I was as alone in death as I'd often felt in life. It didn't seem fair, but it was clearly far beyond my control. So I just let the tides of light and dark sweep me along like a leaf on a stream. I let myself drift and my mind empty.

Sometimes I forgot who I was and what my life had been like. I wasn't too worried about this. I seemed to know, instinctively, that parts of my mind were gone, but I doubted any of it really mattered in death. But sometimes glimpses of it came back. Faces, voices, scenes, feelings. Sometimes they'd wash over me, filling me with emotions that I'd forgotten existed. But all too briefly. Just enough for me to feel a wave of longing or sadness or joy or fear. But then it was all gone again, and I just continued to float along, remembering nothing.

Sometimes I heard him. Just at the edges of my consciousness. Sometimes I felt him calling for me or murmuring to me. Sometimes I tried to call back. I knew it wouldn't do anything—we were worlds apart. But a small part of me hoped that, if I could hear him, some part of him might be able to hear me. Maybe I could comfort him the way his voice comforted me, even now. But it was all probably an illusion—memories left over from my life that popped briefly into existence before fading away. I wondered if my memories would eventually fade forever, and I'd be left here, an empty husk of former existence, floating in nothingness for eternity. That thought made me sad, but I'd soon forget what sad was, and I'd return to just being.

Whenever I heard him, though, warmth spread through me, and a sharp longing followed. His murmurs tethered me to my memories and to some notion of myself. Who I was. Who I still wanted to be. It was hard to forget everything when his voice drifted through the darkness and enveloped me. I wanted to be closer—to his voice and to him. I wished he was here with me. But that was selfish. He had the rest of his life ahead of him, and mine was over. I'd willingly given it for something larger than myself, and I couldn't regret that. So I just survived on the faint, deep sound, letting it feed my soul and comfort me, wherever I was now.

Sometimes I forgot my name. It barely seemed to matter here. There was no one to call by it. There was no one to tell it to. But he never forgot it. He said it sometimes, reminding me about a part of myself. And the other words he said, when I could make them out, reminded me about other parts of myself—the beautiful, the painful, the intense. And when he reminded me of these overwhelming emotions, I remembered his name, too. *Gabriel.* The one I'd loved. The one I'd love until the nothingness finally took all of who I was. The one who, even in death, didn't leave me. Perhaps I wasn't alone after all. Perhaps I'd gotten what I'd always wanted —someone who'd stay. Someone who'd never give up on me. But it hurt that I couldn't be the same for him. It hurt that I couldn't give him everything I wanted to in return. So I gave him his name. And my voice. And my love. It was all I had left, and I knew I wouldn't have this much for long.

"Terah, I'm here. I love you. I'll never stop fighting for you. Come back to me."

If I had a body, I'd cry for him. If I had a heart, it'd squeeze as his words washed over me. If I had a mouth, I'd tell him to find happiness without me. I'd tell him the truth—that I could never come back. That I didn't even know where I was.

But I couldn't do any of that. And he never left. Neither did his words. His voice returned often to my darkness, fighting it back, bringing a small sliver of light with it. I clung to the light and the pieces of him that he sent me. I tried desperately to hold onto myself by holding onto him. Sometimes I tried to follow the light to his voice, but I never seemed to make it very far. And before long, his voice would fade away, leaving me sad and lonely. But at least I wasn't feeling nothingness. I wasn't ready for the nothingness yet.

Perhaps I was only delaying the inevitable. Perhaps I was unfairly clinging to pieces of life—things I had no right to cling to in death. Perhaps I was keeping him from moving on. Keeping myself from moving on. But each time his voice swept over me, I couldn't remember why I should push it away. Instead, I threw my existence at it and fiercely clung to it. Each time, I clung harder and harder, like I thought it could transport me out of this nothingness. Like I thought it could really bring me back to him. But I knew it couldn't. Nothing could, now.

But his persistence brought light with it. And the light declared war on the dark nothingness that surrounded and suspended me, pushing it back. He really wouldn't stop fighting for me, so I decided to fight too. For myself and for him. I wasn't sure what it could accomplish now, but how could I give up if he wasn't going to? I fought by trying to remember who I was. I fought by clinging to his voice. I fought by rejecting the darkness and trying to follow the light. I fought by reaching out to him with all that was left of me. I fought by trying to go back to him.

Little by little, the darkness receded. And little by little, he became clearer to me. Gabriel. The man who'd freed my heart and accepted my soul. The man who was fiercely passionate, tough, loyal, and also funny, understanding, and secretly soft. The one who genuinely gave no fucks but also deeply cared. The one who saw through me and into me, who accepted and believed in me. The one who stayed. The one I loved.

Gabriel. His smile beckoned me forward, leading me away from the edge of the abyss. His electric blue eyes burned a path through the shadows and lit my way.

"Come back to me."

Yes. I would. I was trying. I'd never stop trying. I'd never stop fighting for him.

"Terah."

"Gabriel."

"Come back to me."

"Yes. I'm trying."

"Please."

"I will."

I don't know how long I was gone. A while, at least. For the longest time, I knew only darkness. It was death, I was certain. I knew I'd died. I was prepared for it. I'd let it take me. But . . . I was wrong. It wasn't death. And I wasn't gone. Not really. Not forever. Gabriel hadn't given up on me, and it turned out that I hadn't either. I wasn't done yet. He'd asked me to come back—he'd believed that I could. So I believed it too.

I wasn't sure how I did it. One moment I was trapped in wavering darkness, fighting with all my strength to break through, and the next, I was bathed in light and warmth, the darkness receding—nothing more than a distant, shadowy memory. One moment I was simply a vague whisper of existence, and the next, I was falling into my body, feeling its matter closing around me, securing and reconnecting what'd become disconnected far too soon. And before long, I remembered myself. All of myself. Body, mind, and soul. Things came back to me in overwhelming waves—memories, feelings, sensations—but I just held on and soaked it all in. I'd take the overwhelming waves of life any day over the dark waves of nothingness. For the first time in my life, I'd prefer to feel, even if it was sad or hard, than to just exist, empty and alone.

When the overwhelming waves subsided, and I soaked in all of myself, letting it settle into the crevices of my being, I was finally able to open my eyes. At first, I blinked rapidly as the bright sunlight streaming through the bay window overwhelmed me. I'd only seen darkness for gods-knew how long. But they slowly adjusted, and I moved my head the smallest amount, taking in my surroundings. I was in a large room I'd never seen before, but it looked like it was part of the Academy. I assumed I was in the medical wing. I was lying in a large bed, and a machine next to me was making steady beeping sounds. A heart monitor—we'd had a few in Dagmar, only used for serious, longer-term injuries. The warrior faction had embraced certain aspects of Normal healing that it thought would give it an advantage over the Normal-rejecting Dark Guardian side.

I finally looked down at the edge of my bed, and the heart monitor started beeping much faster. He was asleep, his head resting against the edge of the mattress, a book lying next to him. *Gabriel.* It looked like he'd fallen asleep while reading. My heart squeezed, and I took a deep, shuddering breath. Some twinges of pain shot across my chest and torso, but I ignored them. I was injured, but I was also alive. *Alive.* I'd thought it was over. I'd thought I'd never see the world or Gabriel again. But here I was. Here *he* was. I'd been given another chance. I'd try my best not to waste it.

A smile lifted my lips as I looked down at him. Handsome—devastatingly so—but exhausted, and his hair looked like he'd run his hands through it often before passing out. My stomach clenched and my smile faded. He must've been worried. I had no idea how long I'd been out of it, but I suspected, based on the severity of my injuries, that it hadn't been a short time.

I moved my fingers a little, making sure I still could. No pain shot through my hand or arm, so I shifted, reaching over so I could slide my fingers through his hair, putting the dark strands back into some semblance of order. The heat from his scalp radiated outward, enveloping my chilled fingers in his warmth. Then I ran my fingers gently down his face, tracing the sharp angle of his jaw. I needed to feel that he was real. That I was real. That the thick veil of darkness no longer separated us. A shiver shuddered through me at the thought, and my fingers trembled.

Gabriel shifted and sighed. Then his hand came up to rub his eyes. I watched him, frozen, enraptured. My fingers fell back to the bed as he shifted his head and straightened up in his chair.

And then his intense blue gaze collided with mine.

"Gabriel." My voice was little more than a whisper—hoarse from disuse.

Gabriel gaped at me like he wasn't sure if I was real. He seemed almost frozen, like he was afraid to believe what he was seeing. Perhaps he was worried he was in a dream. I lifted my fingers again and covered his hand with mine, reassuring him. The second my skin touched his, his disbelief melted away. With a happy cry—something between a laugh and a sob—he pushed from his chair and leaned over me, hugging me as gently as he could. Too gently—like he thought I'd break. I pushed into a sitting position, ignoring the faint twinges of pain across my torso, and wrapped my arms around his back, pulling him onto the edge of the bed, then closer to me. It was the only sign he needed. He wrapped his arms around me and pulled me close.

Finally.

My eyes slid shut, and I buried my face against his neck, soaking in his warmth and breathing in his comforting scent. Tears welled behind my closed eyelids. I'd thought I'd never see him again. That I'd never be close with him like this ever again. Gabriel cradled the back of my head and murmured my name—a whisper of relief, pulled from deep within his chest—before gently rubbing his face against the top of my head. I smiled as I felt his lips press to me there. I'd missed this. I'd missed him.

"You came back. You came back to me."

I laughed a little, a tear spilling free. My fingers splayed over his back. "Of course I came back. You asked me to. You believed I could."

Gabriel pulled back so he could look at me. His eyes burned with an intense warmth, even as they searched mine. I smiled at him, not bothering to hide my feelings from him. There wasn't a reason to—I'd already told him how I felt. I'd made sure to, before I'd faded away. But he didn't seem to be running from me this time.

With a laugh—a sound of pure joy—Gabriel crushed me against him again. "Gods, Terah, I'm so glad you're okay. I'm so glad you're back."

I pressed my forehead to his shoulder. "Me too. And I'm glad you're here with me." *That you didn't leave me.*

Gabriel pulled back a little, his hands sliding up to my shoulders. His expression had grown serious. "I'll always be here," he said quietly. "I love you, you know."

I pulled back further and looked up at him in surprise. "W-what?" I wasn't sure I'd heard him right. I wasn't sure I could believe it. How could it be true, after all the times he'd pulled away from me in regret?

The corner of Gabriel's mouth hitched up in a bittersweet smile. "I said I love you. I told you the night you were injured, but . . . I think you lost consciousness as I was saying it. But I do. I have for a while. I was just too foolish to tell you, and even more foolish to not realize you had feelings for me too."

I stared at him, stunned. "But . . . you said it was a mistake. Every time we got close, you regretted it. You regretted when we were together as more than friends."

Gabriel shook his head slowly, the bittersweet smile faded as pain shot across his features. "I didn't mean it was a mistake because I didn't want you like that, I meant it was a mistake because we'd never talked about being more than friends, and I felt like I was forcing my feelings and wants onto you without giving you a chance to have a choice in it

303

all. And I felt horrible for that. I just didn't want to push you too far too fast, and I didn't want to lose you as a friend. I . . . didn't want to treat you the way Matt was treating you. But in the end, all I did was make you believe I didn't return your feelings." He dropped his head forward in defeat, shaking it slowly. "I should've communicated with you about everything instead of assuming where you were coming from. I'm so sorry."

My mouth opened in surprise as my heart squeezed. But I was afraid, so afraid, of misunderstanding. "So . . . so you *do* want to be more than friends?"

Gabriel's smile was warm as he reached forward and tucked some of my hair behind my ear. "Of course I want to be more than friends. I'm in love with you, Terah."

My pulse leapt, and Gabriel's smile widened as he glanced at the heart monitor, then back at me. *Damn.* It really wasn't ideal that he could hear how much he made my heart pound. But I could tell he liked it—he liked knowing he had an effect on me.

"And if you let me," he murmured, his face moving closer to mine, the smile fading as heated intensity took its place, "I can show you how I feel."

The heart monitor was beeping out of control now, but I shoved the sound to the edges of my consciousness as his face neared mine. Intense electric blue held my gaze, searing through me, stealing my breath. But he waited there—waited for my permission.

"Yes," I whispered. "Please."

Gabriel closed the rest of the distance between us, then his lips collided with mine. Soft. Warm. *Finally.* Relief shuddered through me, and then heat. The kiss started slow—a gentle unfolding, an awakening made of soft presses and pulls that sent my pulse reeling. I took hold of his face and pulled him closer, angling my head to deepen the kiss. He inhaled sharply, then groaned, pulling me against him.

His lips moved desperately over mine, no longer slow and gentle, the pulls long and insistent now. My fingers slid into his hair as he tilted my head back, deepening the kiss. His tongue slid over mine, slow and decadent, and I moaned, my fingers trembling against his scalp. Heat rushed through me, fiery tingles like sparks under my skin, a frenzy of need taking hold. I gasped against him as we kissed like that again and again, faster and more urgent now, not wanting to sacrifice a moment of this, even for breath. I arched against him, pressing my chest to his as I pulled his bottom lip between mine—a teasing bite, a soothing sweep of my tongue. This time his groan was deeper, vibrating through his chest, only muffled by my mouth.

I could feel the heat of his chest and stomach against mine through my thin hospital gown. The heat of his fingers, splayed over my back, keeping me close. The pounding of his heart against mine. It melted away all common sense and self-control. It didn't matter that I was injured. It didn't matter that we were in the middle of a staffed medical wing. All I wanted was to be as close to him as possible. To feel his skin against mine. To kiss him until every uncertainty and every painful memory was banished from my brain. Until I felt like myself again.

We only stopped kissing when the medic came into the room and cleared her throat loudly. Even then, it took us a few more moments before we could pull away from each other, our chests heaving.

"You're awake, I see." The medic looked me over before giving Gabriel a playfully disapproving glare. "And *you* haven't wasted any time. Have you even given her a chance to figure out if she's okay before pouncing on her?"

Gabriel slid back into his chair and leaned back, crossing his arms over his chest, smirking. He looked too pleased with what'd just taken place to be shamed by the medic.

I bit back a smile and turned toward the medic. "I feel alright. Just a little pain across my chest and torso."

Gabriel's smirk disappeared, and he leaned forward, worry flooding his expression and tensing his muscles. And I finally saw the deep exhaustion and tormented worry that must've filled his days for however long I'd been unconscious. My stomach clenched, and I reached over and covered his hand with mine, trying to comfort him. I didn't want him to worry anymore.

"That's to be expected," the medic said, stopping next to the bed. "We've healed most of the internal damage, but you still have the surface wounds from the impalement and multiple punctures. We stitched them up for now until we can fully heal them, or until your quick healing has a chance to get to them, but you can expect some pain from those."

I nodded absently and gently touched my stomach. Where the Demon had impaled me with my own sword. I winced at the memory, a shiver racing through me.

Gabriel turned from me to the medic, his gaze hard. "Is there anything you can do to help with the pain?" His voice was a little gruff. I could tell he hated that I might be hurting. My fingers tightened around his.

305

"We can give her a little more pain medication, but mostly it'll come down to her getting plenty of rest so the wounds can heal more quickly on their own."

Gabriel opened his mouth, his expression darkening, like he didn't think the medic's response was good enough.

"That's fine," I cut in before he could say anything. "It doesn't hurt too much."

Gabriel gave me an exasperated look as the medic smiled at me, but he simply squeezed my fingers and leaned back in his chair again. I couldn't help the smile that formed. He was a fierce advocate, but he also wasn't willing to steamroller me for the sake of his own worry, like Matt had always done. And I loved him more for it.

"I'm going to check your vitals to make sure everything is where it should be, and then I'll inform the president that you're awake. She may want to speak with you."

I nodded and let the medic get to work. She took my temperature, pulse, looked into my eyes with a light, examined my ears, mouth, and nose, listened to my heart and lungs, and then examined my arms and legs, bending and manipulating them. It didn't hurt, exactly, but I did feel a dull ache deep in my limbs, and some moderate throbbing as stitched-up wounds moved and twisted.

"We had to do quite a bit of healing on your arms and legs," she said, noting my discomfort. "A little soreness should be expected, especially without your quick healing. Additionally, it may take you some time to build up muscle strength again. I wouldn't expect you to be able to walk on your own right away."

My head jerked up and I stared at her, fear trickling through me. "How long will it take for me to be fit to train again?" I needed to be ready for future Demon attacks. I couldn't be weak or off my game. Not for long, if I wanted to protect the Academy and not die again.

The medic blinked at me, startled. "Don't you think you've had enough fighting for a while?"

My stare turned icy as I crossed my arms over my chest, trying not to wince as I touched some of my stitched-up wounds. "I'm from Dagmar." My voice was hard. "And there's a war. It's what I'm trained to do."

The medic pursed her lips but decided not to fight me on this. "Well, it'll probably take a few weeks of hard work, *after* you're fully healed, to regain your strength and mobility. You'll probably be ready to start training again at the beginning of next semester, but you should expect to be a bit behind."

I frowned and looked at Gabriel for his reaction. He looked conflicted, but he squeezed my fingers as my gaze met his.

"I'll help you," he murmured. "We'll make sure you're strong enough before next semester starts."

I nodded at him, some of the tension in my shoulders relaxing. "Thanks."

"Well," the medic said, changing the subject, "all your vitals look good, and your injuries are healing as expected. We'll definitely want to keep you here for the rest of the week, but we may be able to release you back to your dorm room after that. You're planning to stay on campus for the holiday, correct?"

I nodded.

"And you as well?" She glanced at Gabriel.

Gabriel nodded. "Filed my paperwork to stay before exams."

I glanced at him, surprised. We hadn't talked about our plans.

He shrugged, a small smile pulling at his lips. "I guessed you'd stay." I smiled, warmth filling my chest.

"Good," the medic cut in. "We'll want to continue monitoring you for a few weeks at least, and you'll need someone around to help you if you plan to stay in your dorm instead of here." Gabriel and I nodded.

She pulled the blanket back over me and walked to the door.

"I'll be sending in several medics to help you get cleaned up, and to change the linens on your bed. They'll be here in a few minutes," she added, giving Gabriel a meaningful look. As in, don't get too carried away making out, because we wouldn't be alone for long.

Gabriel rolled his eyes as the medic left. "It's like she thought I was going to jump you in your hospital bed," he grumbled.

"You're not?" I feigned shock. "Well shit. There go my evening plans."

Gabriel shot me an exasperated look, but the corner of his mouth twitched, like he was trying not to smile. "Don't give me any ideas," he grumbled. But he leaned forward and brushed his lips over mine.

I smiled and grabbed the front of his shirt, keeping him close, and kissed him properly until I could no longer breathe. "What if I like giving you ideas?" I finally panted as I broke away.

The blue of Gabriel's eyes seemed to darken as a low rumble emanated from his chest. In the next moment, I found myself crushed to him again, and his mouth came down over mine. I sighed and held him close as he delved deep with an urgency that matched mine. It felt like we'd been waiting years to be together like this. And now that the barriers between us were gone, all I wanted was to forget the rest of the world and indulge in this closeness with him.

We broke apart as the medics returned a few minutes later, trying to disguise our heated cheeks and shortness of breath. They unhooked me from the various machines and IVs next to my bed and helped me to my feet. Apparently, "help you get cleaned up" meant escorting me to the attached bathroom and helping me shower. This turned out to be a difficult task. The first medic had been right when she'd said I wouldn't be able to walk on my own for a while. Two medics had to haul me up and practically carry me to the bathroom, since my legs felt like they were made of soft rubber.

They closed the door behind us, then helped me out of my hospital gown. I grimaced as I caught sight of myself in the mirror. My torso and chest were covered in angry looking, stitched-up wounds, surrounded by deep purple bruises. There were also scabs and pink scars all over my skin where smaller injuries had begun slowly healing. They'd all disappear if my power regenerated more, but since I'd drained myself completely, even of my life force, I knew that'd take a really long time, if it happened at all.

Once the medics had the shower going, they sat me down under the stream of warm water and proceeded to wash my hair and skin thoroughly. I bit the inside of my cheek and tried not to wince as they washed around my wounds. I knew I'd feel better once I was clean, but it sucked. When they'd finished washing my upper body, the medics hauled me into a standing position and washed my lower body as I clung to a stabilizing bar that'd thankfully been installed on the shower wall. Even though they worked quickly, my legs still shook violently from holding my weight after so many injuries and so much time in the hospital bed.

After the shower, the medics toweled me off and put me in a large, fluffy robe that almost reached my ankles, then led me to the sink and produced a toothbrush and toothpaste, which I eagerly used. Finally, the medics flanked me on either side, their arms around my waist, and led me slowly back into the main room. Gabriel smiled and set down the book he'd been reading, then pushed to his feet. When we reached the side of the bed, he took me from the medics and carefully lifted me back onto the bed, which was newly adorned with clean sheets and blankets.

"We'll bring you a clean hospital gown in a few minutes," one of the medics said as they moved back toward the door.

I scowled. "Do I have to keep wearing a hospital gown? Can't I wear real clothes?"

The medics paused and looked at each other.

"We don't have any other clothes for you to wear," the other medic finally said.

"I have a clean shirt and some boxers you could wear, if the medics say it's okay," Gabriel said, reclining in his chair again.

I looked at them eagerly.

"Well . . . I guess that's fine as long as they're clean," the first medic said, resignedly.

"Yep." Gabriel pushed to his feet and went to retrieve his bag. "Haven't worn them yet."

The medics took the clothes from Gabriel and made him turn around so they could help me out of my robe and into his clothes. When I was finally dressed, the medics left, and I settled back against the pillows, sore and already a little tired.

"So, what's been happening while I've been out of it?"

Gabriel sighed and scrubbed his hand over his face. "You mean besides me losing my mind with worry?"

My stomach clenched and I looked down at the blanket covering my lap. "Sorry." I could only guess what he'd gone through because of me.

"No, don't apologize," he said quickly, leaning forward and taking my hand. "I didn't mean it in a blame kind of way. You're the bravest, strongest person I've ever met. And you made the hardest choice. The *right* choice. Don't ever apologize for that."

My cheeks heated and my mouth opened then closed then opened again. I didn't know what to say. Every person I'd ever been close with had made my injury's impact on them my fault. I'd been punished for it. Chastised for it. Left for it.

"Th-thanks. I just . . . don't want to make you worry about me."

The side of Gabriel's mouth pulled up in a bittersweet smile. "That's what it means to care about someone. Worrying about them. Wanting only good things for them. But also sharing the difficulties in life. Supporting each other and taking care of each other when things are hard and when bad things happen, as they inevitably will. Worry isn't bad—it's a sign of care. And I'll take on all the worry in the world if it means I get to have you in my life."

Tears stung my eyes, and I looked quickly down at the blanket again. How did I respond to such selfless care? How did I deserve it?

"*It's not selfless,*" his voice whispered through my mind, making me jump. My eyes widened and I jerked my head up to meet his gaze. This had to mean I'd regenerated enough power for some of my abilities to return! I'd been afraid my power would be gone forever after I'd drained all of it. "*This is how people are supposed to care for each other. Just because people in your life didn't care like this before, doesn't mean it isn't normal. And you* do *deserve it. You deserve unconditional care and love.*"

A smile broke across my face as relief and joy intermingled, making my chest feel like it was filling with air. I wanted to laugh. And cry. I wanted to hug him.

Gabriel's shoulders shook with silent laughter as he heard my thoughts, and he pushed to his feet and reclined on the edge of my bed. Then pulled me into his arms. I pressed my face against his shoulder and my fingers against his back, holding him close.

"How did you learn how to care for people like this?" I whispered. I needed to know. He was from a border town too—notorious for causing emotional damage and stifling feelings.

A laugh rumbled through his chest. "I don't know. My family, I guess. This was always what it was like with them. We were always there for each other, no matter what was happening. Celebrated the good and took care of each other through the bad. They kept me grounded. They did their best to keep Elareth from completely crushing me and my soul."

I smiled and pulled back a little so I could look into his face, close to mine. "So you learned to love through being loved. That's . . . nice."

Gabriel smiled then leaned forward and pressed his lips to my forehead. "I don't think I've thought about it like that before, but you're right."

"You're lucky to have them," I murmured, my gaze drawn to his lips as he pulled back again. "And they're lucky to have you."

I watched his mouth widen as he smiled, a roguish edge to it this time. I swallowed and pulled my gaze from his mouth, returning it to his eyes. But he'd already caught me looking. He moved toward me, not breaking eye contact until his lips were centimeters from mine. Then his eyes slid closed, and his lips brushed slowly over mine. Our exhales mingled as our pulses spiked, and I angled my head, my lips parting to let him in deeper. He surged forward eagerly, and our lips collided in a deep pull.

Heat shuddered through me, and I reached forward and closed my hands around the front of his shirt. I pulled him closer, held him to me, as my mouth desperately moved with his. How could something physical feel so life giving? Physical intimacy had always felt unbalanced or transactional in the past. But now . . . it felt like air. Soul-lightening. Sustaining. Needed for existence. I breathed him into me, dragging his essence deep into my lungs. Our chests heaved together, pressed closer as we sank into an oblivion of desire. And we lost ourselves there for a while, giving into our need. Everything felt so new, so heightened, with him—every touch, every slide of his tongue, every pull of his mouth, every shared breath. It was almost too much—too overwhelming—but anything less would feel like not enough.

Gabriel finally pulled back, and rested his forehead against mine, his chest heaving. "Gimme a sec. I need to remember we're in a medical wing full of people and not in one of our rooms."

I smiled, panting, and slowly released him. "Me too. It's hard to remember that when you kiss me."

Gabriel's laugh blew gently across my lips, making them tingle. "Likewise."

He pulled slowly back, and I saw his cheeks were flushed and his eyes were still dark with desire. My stomach clenched pleasantly, and I bit my lip. I wished we didn't have to stop.

Gabriel shook his head, a smile pulling at his lips. "Don't look at me like that, or I really *won't* be able to remember where we are."

I smiled and sat back against my pillows. "Okay, okay." I crossed my arms over my chest and watched, amused, as he slid off my bed and back into his chair, trying to institute a little space between us for restraint's sake. "Are you going to tell me what happened while I was out of it, now?"

Gabriel sighed and ran his hand through his hair, pushing the strands back over his head. "Yeah. Things were . . . bad. It took a ton of people draining their powers to keep you alive that night, and even then, we were only successful because your mother showed up and helped. After I yelled at her."

A grin spread across my face. "You yelled at her?"

He scowled. "Of course I did. She came all the way here then almost didn't help heal you. I wasn't about to let that happen."

I nodded slowly. Her actions didn't surprise me, but someone fighting her on them did. Matt had *never* pushed back at her over anything. But Gabriel had. He wasn't afraid of her. He didn't defer to her just because of her title. And it made me like him even more.

"What is it?" He frowned as his gaze slid carefully over my expression.

"I hope you aren't mad about that. My priority was keeping you alive, not keeping her happy."

I smiled. "Of course I'm not mad. Just thinking about how much I like you." Gabriel's eyes widened slightly, and his cheeks flushed again. I tried not to laugh. He clearly hadn't expected me to be so forthcoming. "I especially like that you don't fall in line and take shit from her."

He smiled, looking pleased. "A thing we have in common." I grinned. He was right.

Gabriel then told me Matt's theory about how the Demon had gotten onto campus, Matt's role in the Academy's fortifications, and how they agreed it was too coincidental that I'd been there at every attack. As inexplicable as it seemed, the Demons appeared to be targeting me. Then he told me about the president's end of term speech and Caleb's visit. This surprised me the most, but I also felt confused and a bit bitter. Nothing he did now would make up for all he'd done to me in the past. He was responsible for a good deal of damage that I'd carried with me for years. A moment of humanity from him wasn't enough to erase that. Still, it made me hope that someday, Caleb wouldn't be the cold, hardened person he was so desperately trying to be. But I also knew I didn't want to be a part of his transformation. He'd burned all bridges between us, and no small act of help would rebuild those. Nor did I think he truly wanted to.

"That reminds me," Gabriel said, pulling his phone from his pocket, "I promised I'd let Matt know if your condition changed at all. I guess I should tell him that you're awake."

"Yeah," I murmured noncommittally. "I guess so."

Gabriel paused, glancing at me. "Do you not want me to?"

I sighed. "No, you should. I just don't know how to feel about him right now. I know a lot has happened, and that he helped you stay, but he still lied to me and betrayed me. He's still willing to blindly fight for the Light Guardians no matter what they do and how many boundaries they cross. It's hard to let all that go just because he doesn't want me to die."

Gabriel released a long breath and nodded. "I can't say it'll be easy. Just from talking to him, I don't think he'll understand why you're still mad at him. You have every right to be," he added quickly, "but I don't think he's put much effort into understanding it. I don't even think he truly believes what he did when he lied to you was wrong."

I scowled and pulled my knees up in front of me. "For a pretty smart person, he can be pretty fucking ignorant."

Gabriel's mouth quirked on one side. "I should also mention he's probably not going to give up on the idea of you and him being together romantically." He crossed his arms over his chest, his gaze growing stormy. "He told me as much while you were unconscious, after he found out that I returned your feelings. He wants to wait for you to change your mind and pick him."

Anger flared to life like a small match in my chest. Matt never took my feelings or decisions seriously. And I was tired of it. In many ways, I was tired of him. But it hurt me to feel like that. Because he was my family and I loved him. But I couldn't keep doing this with him.

"I guess . . . that doesn't surprise me." I sighed. "But I was clear with him—after his most recent betrayal, I'm not even sure we can ever be friends, let alone anything more. And he knows how I feel about you. He knows I'm picking you over him."

Gabriel nodded slowly, his gaze intense on mine. "And . . . how *do* you feel about me?"

I frowned at him. He knew how I felt. I'd told him.

"You only said it once." His enigmatic expression broke slightly, and I saw the amusement underlying it. He was teasing me.

I narrowed my eyes at him. "Yeah, because I was unconscious for the rest of the time after that."

"Mmm." He was silent for a long moment. "That still wasn't you telling me." A grin broke across his face as he saw the exasperated look I was leveling at him. "I'm just saying, I've told you twice and you've only told me once."

This time I laughed. Gods, he could be ridiculous. And I loved him for it. "Okay. Fine. You win."

He crossed his arms over his chest and waited, smiling as he watched me blush.

"I . . . I love you, Gabriel."

My cheeks were burning crimson now. It was much harder to openly state my feelings when I wasn't on the verge of death.

"There. Are you happ—"

But he leaned forward, and his mouth covered mine before I could finish. I sighed as he took my face between his hands and tilted my head back. His kisses were long and lingering this time. Tender as opposed to urgent. Like he wanted me to feel what he felt for me through his lips. And I felt it. Gods, how I felt it. It was staggering—immense—this feeling between us.

He finally broke the kiss, panting. "I love you too, Terah." He was serious now. "With everything that I am."

I smiled, my throat tightening, and I reached forward and ran my fingers down his cheek. I could feel the beginnings of stubble there, a gentle scrape against my fingertips.

"With everything that I am, too," I whispered.

A couple hours later, the medics brought in a dinner tray for me, which I split with Gabriel. I wasn't feeling up to eating much yet, but the taste and feel of solid food was comforting and had me feeling more like myself again. A little stronger.

After dinner, Gabriel decided to shower, so I took the opportunity to borrow one of his books. I'd gotten through most of a chapter when I heard footsteps pounding down the hallway. I set the book on my lap, dread lurching through me. Had there been another attack? As eager as I'd seemed earlier to rejoin the fight, it was hard to push aside the memory of being torn apart by a Demon. I didn't want to relive that experience. Ever.

But the footsteps weren't because of another attack. I realized this with a simultaneous wave of relief and a twinge of discomfort as Matt burst into my room, panting.

"Terah," he gasped, his chest heaving, "you're awake! I got Gabriel's text. I was only just able to leave the perimeter of the Academy."

He walked quickly over to the side of my bed and peered down at me, worried. "How are you feeling?" He took my hand and squeezed it between his, his gaze roaming over my face, as though he thought he'd never see it like this again. Well, he almost hadn't. I'd come far closer to dying than I ever had before.

"I'm okay." I gave him a hesitant smile. Part of me was happy to see him after everything I'd been through, but I also felt a thick wall of tension between us. The last time we'd talked, I'd ended our friendship. "I'm a little sore, and the medics said it'd take me a while to regain enough strength to walk on my own again, but otherwise, I'm fine. Not dead at least." I shrugged.

Matt winced, then sank onto the edge of the bed, his fingers tightening around mine. "You came far too close, though." His eyes grew haunted. "I don't think I'll ever be able to get that image of you out of my head . . ." He stared at the sheets, seeing something I couldn't.

"Sorry." I shifted uncomfortably under the blankets. "Obviously it wasn't great for me either."

Matt raised his eyes to mine, the haunted look receding a little. "I'm so glad you're okay." He reached out with his free hand and trailed the back of his fingers over my cheek. It was a familiar gesture from him—one that'd been comforting in the past—but now it felt off. And I wasn't sure how much I should let him touch me. Our boundaries had been so out of whack these past few months that I wasn't sure where to draw the lines now.

"Thanks for everything you did to help." I shifted slightly away from him. "Gabriel said you helped him stay here. That was nice of you."

Matt's expression darkened at hearing Gabriel's name, but he just shrugged it off. "It wasn't a big deal." His voice was harder than before. "I couldn't stay with you as much as I wanted, so I wanted to make sure someone could."

I nodded and glanced at the bathroom door over Matt's shoulder, hoping Gabriel would be done soon. Even though it'd increase the tension, part of me wanted him here to help me navigate this weirdness with Matt.

Matt watched me closely, his jaw clenching. He'd seen me look away, and he knew why. Suddenly, he leaned toward me and took my face between his hands.

"I didn't do it for him." Intensity burned in his gaze, his face only inches from mine. "I did it for you, Terah. You have to know by now," he continued, a pained, almost desperate look in his eyes. "You have to know that I love you."

I stared back at him, my mouth opening slightly as I tried to think of the right thing to say. Yeah, I knew how he felt about me. But I also knew it wasn't enough. And I knew with complete certainty that I didn't return his feelings. I loved him as family, but nothing more. And that truth would hurt him.

"Please," Matt continued, pulling my face a little closer to his, "tell me that I'm not too late. Tell me that I still have a chance with you."

But he didn't. He *was* too late. And my heart squeezed painfully at the thought of hurting him. *Damnit.* But Matt knew me too well, and he saw the truth in my expression even though I hadn't said a word. His expression shuttered and his body tensed. But he didn't let go of me.

"He won't stay, you know," he said quietly as he took my shoulders in his hands. "Not forever. Not like I will. I've known you your whole life. He's only been around for a few months. He doesn't care about you like I do. He doesn't know you like I do." His grip on me tightened, his gaze turning imploring. He hadn't given up yet, and his stubborn expression told me he wouldn't anytime soon.

I shook my head, trying to push down the anger that'd begun bubbling in my chest at his words. He was trying to plant seeds of doubt, but I didn't have any. I knew how Gabriel felt about me, and I knew how I felt about him. Matt couldn't change that, no matter what he said.

"He may not have known me as long," I said carefully, trying to keep my temper under control, "but he knows me—who I am now—better than anyone. Even you. And he loves me for exactly who I am now. And . . . I love him too, Matt."

Matt flinched, and pain streaked across his face. "Please," he implored, his voice cracking a little, "give me another chance. I know you love me too. I can tell, Terah. I know I have an effect on you. If you'd just give me another chance, I know you'd be happy with me."

I started shaking my head in protest, but Matt cut me off.

"I can prove it." Determination flooded his expression. "I can prove I have an effect on you."

And he pushed me suddenly back against my pillows, his chest pressing into mine, and began kissing me fiercely. I was too stunned to react for a few moments. One second we'd been talking, and the next he was practically on top of me. Yes, he was warm, yes, he was familiar and comforting, and yes, a small part of me responded to his kiss, but he wasn't Gabriel. And Gabriel was who I loved and wanted.

"Matt," I gasped, pulling my face away from him. But his lips found mine again, and he continued desperately kissing me.

"Just let me in, Terah," he pleaded against my lips. His fingers tangled in my hair. "Please. Let me in."

It would've been easier to let him kiss me. It would've been easier to not break his heart. To just let him continue until he gave up or stopped on his own. But I couldn't. Not now that I knew my own feelings and knew Gabriel returned them. It'd made everything clearer for me. I knew what I wanted now, and I wasn't about to let that go anytime soon. So I pushed Matt off me as firmly as I could, until I'd forced him back into a sitting position on the edge of the bed.

"Matt, stop," I panted, trying to catch my breath after being crushed under his chest. "You can't just kiss me whenever you want. And kissing me isn't going to change my mind about us."

Matt's chest was heaving from the kiss, but he looked incredibly sad. Also frustrated and angry. But before he could respond, the bathroom door opened, and Gabriel emerged, his damp hair sticking up from being recently toweled dry, his T-shirt sticking enticingly to his damp stomach and chest. My pulse sped up at the sight of him.

Gabriel smiled a little at me, his eyes warm, but he also looked warily at Matt, and Matt's position on the bed. Then his gaze swept over my face again, appraising, before landing on my lips. I saw his jaw tighten, and he ran a hand tensely through his hair as he ambled, seemingly leisurely, to the other side of my bed. To my surprise, he reclined on the bed next to me and put his arm around my shoulders, stretching his long legs out next to mine. His expression remained bored as he studied Matt, but I could feel the tension rolling off his body as it pressed into my side.

"If you kiss her again without her permission," Gabriel said calmly, correctly guessing what'd taken place, "I'll punch you so hard your jaw will never be the same."

Matt glared at Gabriel with a hatred that surprised me. "Go to hell, Gabriel. I told you I wouldn't give up."

I interrupted before Gabriel could speak again. "I don't give a shit about whether or not you give up." I glared at Matt. "What I do give a shit about are my boundaries. If you do that again, Gabriel won't be the one you'll have to worry about. You know very well that I can beat you in a fight if I want to."

Matt turned his gaze on me. The hatred was gone, but the anger was still there. "You know you feel something for me, Terah." He shoved to his feet. "You can lie about it to Gabriel and me all you want. You can even lie to yourself. But I know it's there. And someday, you'll choose to be with me, not him. Someday, he'll leave you behind like he did before, and you'll realize I'm the only one who'll always be here for you."

Gabriel's anger broke through his neutral expression. "That's bullshit. I'd never leave her behind. Or have you forgotten which one of us left her here and which one of us stayed?"

Matt glared at Gabriel, then started yelling about duty, honor, and loyalty, which he said Gabriel wouldn't know anything about. I felt Gabriel steadily tensing, and I knew he wanted to physically throw Matt from the room. I reached over and entwined my fingers with his. Matt was upset and heartbroken, and he was lashing out at both of us. I didn't even really hold it against him. I knew how much heartbreak hurt. But I wanted Gabriel to know nothing Matt said would change how I felt. And that Matt wasn't right about my hidden feelings. So I reached out to him with my mind. The connection solidified almost immediately—the quickest I'd ever joined minds.

"I'm sorry about him. I think I just broke his heart."

I felt the tension ease in Gabriel's shoulders, and he leaned his head over so the side of it rested against the top of mine. *"I know. That's the only reason I haven't punched him already."*

I smiled. *"Same. Just so you know . . . he's not right about my hidden feelings. I don't love him like that. And . . . nothing he says can change my feelings for you."* My cheeks burned from stating my feelings so clearly, but it felt important, especially right now.

Gabriel's arm tightened around me, and he pulled his head back so he could look at me. My blush deepened as I saw how warm and intense his gaze was.

"Same," he murmured, a small smile tugging at the corner of his mouth.

Gods, I really wanted to kiss him again. Gabriel's smile grew into a smirk as he heard my thought, and his gaze went from warm to smoldering. I was pretty sure he was about to give me what I wanted.

Matt swore and kicked the chair next to my bed, breaking us out of our trance, and snapping the connection between our minds. His hands were fisted at his sides and shaking as he watched us. Seeing Gabriel and I together like this was undoing him. Guilt twinged in my chest. I wasn't trying to hurt him.

"I wish you'd never come here," Matt growled at Gabriel, his voice shaking with anger. And I knew he meant it. He'd always felt this way about Gabriel. From the moment he'd seen us together, he'd seen the potential for more to grow between us. My heart hurt for him. It really did. If he felt anything near what I'd felt when I'd thought Gabriel had rejected me, then he was suffering enough.

Before Gabriel or I could respond, Matt turned on his heel and stormed from the room. But instead of feeling relief, my gut clenched tightly with pain and regret. I pressed my eyes shut and dropped my head forward. Matt had been an angry and manipulative ass this evening, but I'd also seen the tears in his eyes before he'd turned away. I knew I'd hurt him. Deeply.

Gabriel's arm tightened around me. "I'm sorry." His lips grazed my temple. "I know you don't like it when he's in pain."

I lifted my head and looked at him. I was surprised to see his expression was gentle and understanding. Even with all his negative feelings about Matt, he wasn't celebrating my loss of him. Because he knew that loss hurt me. My heart warmed, radiating gentle heat through the rest of my chest, easing some of my tension.

"Thanks. I just hope he'll be okay." I sighed and reached up to push some of Gabriel's hair out of his eyes. "I just hope he can move on. Grow. Be happy. And maybe not yell at us as much."

Gabriel smiled, then pressed a kiss to my forehead. "He'll be alright eventually. It may take a bit, but he's a strong person. He'll find a way to move on."

I nodded, trying to push down the guilt.

"Are you okay?" He reached up and slid his thumb gently over my chin.

I melted in the blue intensity of his eyes. "I . . . I think I am." I was almost surprised. Because I was. I hated that I'd hurt Matt, but I wouldn't change my decision or my enforcement of boundaries.

A small smile tugged at his lips. "Do you still want to kiss me?"

I laughed. "Always."

Gabriel grinned and slid his hand up to cradle my cheek. His gaze trailed softly over my face, and he traced his thumb slowly over my chin again before lightly tracing my bottom lip. His gaze heated as he ran his thumb over my lip again, leaving a trail of tingles behind. I slid my hand up his chest as he slowly lowered his mouth to mine. I was already breathless.

He kissed me slowly this time, with a tenderness that had me trembling. My lips tingled as they slid against his, and blood pounded through my veins, making my entire body feel like it was pulsing. I slid my arms around his neck and pulled him closer as he lowered me back against my pillows. Then he deepened the kiss, his tongue sliding against mine in torturously slow caresses. My moan was echoed by his deep groan as he pressed into me, his weight sinking me deeper into the soft mattress. But where I'd felt suffocated by Matt, I only felt pleasant heat and pressure from Gabriel. And I wanted more.

He kissed his way down my neck to my collarbone as I sighed and arched into him, dragging my fingers down his back before sliding them under his shirt. His skin was hot and smooth against mine. He nipped at my collarbone, causing me to gasp as a heated shiver rushed through me, then returned to my mouth again. This time, his kiss was more urgent. His hand slid up my side under my shirt, eagerly feeling the curve of my waist, the gentle ridges of my ribs, as though he was carefully mapping me. My

319

skin tingled—the feel of his warm fingers against me was intoxicating. I wanted him to keep touching me—to not stop until he'd touched me everywhere. I groaned as his tongue slid slowly over mine, need now pounding through me like a giant drum. My breath shuddered out of me as I brought my knees up around his hips, then arched my hips into his. Gabriel groaned into my mouth.

"Gods, Terah," he panted against me. His fingers shook against my waist.

I smiled and gently nipped at his bottom lip with my teeth. "What?" I asked, innocently. "Can't handle my kisses?"

Gabriel groaned again, and his fingers slid higher under my shirt, until he gently grazed the underside of my breast with his knuckles. I gasped, then arched into him, encouraging him. I wanted him to do it again. I *needed* him to do it again. Gabriel grinned before taking my mouth with his. And as his tongue slid against mine, he cupped the lower swell of my breast and ran his thumb gently over its peak. I cried out into his mouth. I was trembling now. Need had turned from a pounding drum into rolling thunder. I raised my hips against his as he rocked his into mine. Pleasure spiked through me like lightning. Gabriel's groan rumbled through his chest into mine, tightening the skin there. Making me ache in the best way. Then he rocked against me again.

It was probably good that we heard the medics walking down the hall toward my room. If we hadn't, I wasn't sure what they would've walked in on. Actually, I was pretty sure. And even though we would've been enjoying ourselves, I doubted the medics would've appreciated it. But we managed to pull away from each other, albeit with difficulty, and Gabriel slid back into the chair next to my bed as I pulled the covers over me again. Then we quickly readjusted ourselves and our clothes before they walked in. The only telltale signs of our activities were our red cheeks and heaving chests. At least the medics were tactful enough not to say anything.

They rolled up my shirt to work on healing some of my stitched-up torso wounds, and I tried my best not to flinch as they poked and prodded at my tender flesh. Gabriel took my hand, and I saw him trying to control his own reaction as he saw how much bruising still covered my torso. But I caught the flash of anguish, and I squeezed his hand, giving him a small smile. I wished I could've told him that it looked worse than it was, but he knew as well as I did that the wounds were evidence of serious injuries that weren't healed yet. I *had* been impaled, among other things.

The medics removed the stitches on a couple of my wounds and focused their powers on healing those as deeply and completely as they could. As a testament to their skill, the healing didn't hurt as much as I knew it could. There were only twinges of pain here and there as they worked to more completely knit my muscles back together, eliminate bruising, and seal my skin. After about half an hour of work, the medics gave me a little more pain medication and firmly told me to rest soon. Then they left for the night, and Gabriel and I were alone again.

"Are you in pain?" he asked quietly, sitting forward in his chair.

"It's not too bad." I scooted down my pillows, then took his hand again. "Just sore. But nothing I can't handle."

Gabriel nodded slowly, worry still pinching his features. "And you'd tell me if it *was* more than you could handle?"

This wasn't the first time he'd asked some version of this question. I smiled and squeezed his fingers again. "Yes, I'd tell you. I promise."

Gabriel nodded again and looked across the room at his cot. The sun had set, and the moon was casting shadows through the room's bay window, engulfing his cot in strange patterns of darkness and light.

"I've been staying in here with you every night," he murmured, nodding at the cot, "but I can head back to my dorm room if . . . if you want me to."

I watched him closely, trying to discern whether he actually wanted to go or not. He'd been sleeping on a horrible, small bed for several weeks—anyone would miss their real bed after that. But his eyes told me that he wanted to stay. And to be honest, I wanted him to stay too. While I'd been putting on a brave face about basically dying and coming back to life again, I still felt the cold darkness hovering around the edges of my consciousness, like a nightmare I'd just woken up from that still hovered near. I didn't want to be left alone with that. Maybe a part of me thought it was all too good to be true, and the darkness would swallow me again and refuse to release me this time. But I felt instinctively that Gabriel wouldn't let it take me. He'd fight for me like he had when I'd been consumed by darkness before. He'd anchor me to the light and guide me home—a beacon in the darkness, illuminating the path back to him.

"I'd like you to stay," I finally said, "unless you want to go back to your room. I'd understand if you do."

Gabriel raised a quizzical eyebrow. "Do you seriously think I'd prefer my dorm room over you?" he asked dryly, leaning back and crossing his arms over his chest.

I rolled my eyes but couldn't keep the smile from pulling at my lips. "I mean, I was hoping I ranked slightly higher in your mind than your bed, but that cot looks pretty horrible."

The corner of Gabriel's mouth lifted, and he shrugged. "It's not so bad. At least it's close to you."

My cheeks burned as warmth filled me. How had I ever not realized how I felt about him? It seemed so obvious to me now. I'd been falling for him from the very beginning.

"Well, fortunately for you, you don't have to sleep on the cot anymore." I patted the bed next to me.

Gabriel's cheeks went a little pink, which was funny after what we'd been doing in the bed so far this evening.

"Are you sure you don't mind?" He ran his hand nervously through his hair, causing it to stand on end. "I don't want to take up too much of your space."

"*If you're not ready for that,*" his voice whispered through my mind—a thought he hadn't meant for me to hear.

I smiled. I liked that he didn't take things for granted with me, especially intimacy. He didn't assume anything, push, or feel entitled to anything physical when it came to me. He never saw his wants and needs as more important than mine. He never wanted me to feel pressured into giving more than I was ready to give.

"I don't mind. I . . . like it when you're close." I blushed again and looked up to see a smile tugging at his lips as he watched me. "As long as you're comfortable with it too." I didn't want him to feel pressured either. I didn't want to make him stay if he wasn't ready to.

His smile morphed into a grin. "I am."

I released a breath of relief and nodded. "Thanks. I just . . . I guess I feel safer with you here." I looked away from him and fidgeted with the edge of the blanket. "I don't think . . . you'll let it take me again."

Gabriel stilled, and I could see his look of confusion from my periphery.

"The darkness," I clarified softly, still not looking at him. But my fingers shook against the blanket. "That's . . . where I was . . . before I woke up."

Before I had time to react, Gabriel was on the bed next to me and was pulling me close, folding his arms protectively around me.

"Anything that wants to take you will have to go through me," he murmured, his voice edged with steel. He pressed his lips to the top of my head.

I smiled into his chest. His warmth was already surrounding me, banishing the chill that'd taken hold as I'd thought of that never-ending darkness. "Thanks."

I fell asleep a little while later in Gabriel's arms. And sure enough, the darkness didn't take me. I didn't think it ever could, as long as I was with him.

15
NEW STATUS QUO

THE PRESIDENT CAME BY THE MEDICAL WING A FEW DAYS AFTER I regained consciousness and gave me a personal briefing on the Demon attack situation, as well as a heart-felt thanks for all I'd done to protect the school. She also expressed hope that I'd seriously consider staying at the Academy next semester, even though my most recent experience here had been so horrifying. The whole thing was pretty uncomfortable—both being thanked and having to relive the most recent Demon attack with her —but I assured her that I planned on staying, and that I didn't hold the Academy responsible for what'd happened to me. Besides, I knew that without the Academy's healers and resources, I probably would've died after that attack anyway. Fully persuaded, and far more cheerful than she'd been upon entering my room, the president took her leave after thanking me again.

The president was the only person, besides Gabriel, who came to see me. Matt hadn't returned since that first day, and I didn't expect him to. He'd been so mad and hurt that I wasn't sure he'd ever talk to me again. Part of me was relieved, but a deeper part of me ached for losing him. The only other visitor I thought might come was my mother. I would've automatically dismissed the possibility, since she never did anything caring that was unrelated to her own gain, but after Gabriel had told me about her role in healing me, I thought she might want to see that I was alive and awake. But she didn't come, and I wasn't truly surprised. Sure, it hurt a bit

—I'd basically died and not even my mother cared enough to see that I'd improved—but I was also used to her ways by now. So I just added this to the list of things she'd done to disappoint me and moved on. That was all I could do anyway.

The medics finally approved my departure at the end of the week, on the condition that I came back for check-ups and continued healing several times a week until my power was fully regenerated. The day we were finally allowed to leave, Gabriel went ahead to my dorm room and grabbed clothes for me so I wouldn't have to hobble across the cold, snowy campus in his boxers and T-shirt. When he returned, I managed to pull on the clothes and winter gear myself, though slowly. I was regaining my strength a little more each day with Gabriel's help. He not only gave me some of his power each morning and night to help speed up my recovery, but he'd also been helping me practice walking, stretching, and lifting things each day. The only thing I needed help with was putting on my boots. Leaning over like that hurt the still-healing injuries on my torso. But Gabriel strapped them on me in no time, packed up all our things, slung his bag across his chest, then wrapped his arm around my waist to support me as we walked, finally, out of the medical wing.

We made our way through the cold, empty stone halls of the main building, then pushed through one of the side doors to get outside. The wind immediately whipped around us and slapped against our exposed cheeks like tiny, frigid hands, pushing against us and slowing us down. The snow was coming down thick, making visibility around us low. But what I could see of campus still looked magical. Like a snowy castle out of a fairy tale. I was careful, though, not to look in the direction I'd fought the Demon in. I didn't want to see the broken trees or evidence of the fight. I didn't want to see where I'd almost died. A shiver ran through me that had nothing to do with the cold.

Gabriel finally pushed open the front door of my dorm building and we made our way through the empty common area and down the hall to my room. The building was unusually quiet, as most of the inhabitants had left for winter break. I appreciated the emptiness though—it would've been much more unpleasant to have a ton of students staring at me upon my return, especially after the president had told the school what'd happened.

Gabriel unlocked the door to my room with the hand scanner, then pushed open the door and turned on the lights. It looked like he'd already started a fire in here when he'd come by earlier to grab clothes for me, so the air was warm and comfortable. He shoved my door shut with his foot before dropping his bag on the floor and stripping out of his jacket. I took mine off as well as I meandered over to the foot of my bed, then I collapsed backward onto it with a happy sigh. It was so much more comfortable than the one in the medical wing.

"I'm so glad I'm finally back."

Gabriel smiled as he watched me, then walked over and sat on the edge of the bed next to me. He folded his hand around mine and gently squeezed my fingers. "Me too. Welcome home."

I smiled.

Gabriel spent the rest of the day helping me settle back into my room and back into normalcy. He went to the dining hall and brought back an armful of food to make sure my room was fully stocked so I wouldn't have to drag myself across campus when I was hungry, and he'd swiped some bags of coffee beans from the kitchen so I could make coffee in my dorm's common room. He'd also brought back bundles of firewood so I could keep the fire going for the next few days at least. He seemed pretty focused on making sure I didn't overtax myself as I continued healing. But I didn't realize how set he was on that until that night when he told me he was planning on returning to his dorm room in the evenings to sleep.

"I just . . . have a hard time keeping myself in check, especially without the medics around to interrupt us." His cheeks burned, even as he tugged me closer to brush a warm kiss across my lips. "And you're still healing. I could hurt you without meaning to. It's selfish to stay and risk it, and sharing a bed with you *definitely* risks it. You need to focus on resting and healing. Not on your asshole boyfriend who can't keep his hands to himself." The corner of his mouth lifted in a small smile.

A smile tugged at my lips—I wanted to tease him about this—but a few of his words distracted me. "You're my boyfriend?" I crossed my arms over my chest and smiled mischievously at him. Sure, he'd said he wanted to be more than friends, and that he loved me, but we'd never talked about what to call it. I'd assumed he'd shy away from formal labels. Apparently not.

He straightened up and crossed his arms over his chest too, glowering at me. "I damn well better be."

I tried not to laugh at his frustrated expression. "I just didn't think labels were your style."

Gabriel rolled his eyes and ran his hands through his hair. "Anything that ties me to you is my style," he finally grumbled. I grinned, pleased.

He tugged me gently into his arms and kissed me slowly, lingering, taking my lips in long, unhurried draws, until my fingers began to tremble. It was his turn to grin.

———

Gabriel moved back to his dorm room with the promise that he'd return as soon as I healed enough that we wouldn't accidentally hurt me with our . . . enthusiasm. But he was still around during the day, and his presence made my recovery go by quickly. We fell into an easy rhythm together, as we always had. And while I missed his company and warmth during the night, his careful, slow-burning kisses during the day tided me over and kept me warm.

Each day, Gabriel worked with me to regain my strength and get back to the level of training and fitness I'd been at before the last attack. My torso wounds had finally healed enough that the medics had cleared me to start training again, if disapprovingly. But no amount of disapproval could make me forget the war was still raging around us, and more attacks were likely coming. I had to be in top shape if I wanted to survive, and if I wanted to protect the people and places that I loved. But, if I wasn't healed enough to lose control with Gabriel physically, then I also wasn't healed enough to be thrown to the ground or tackled in training. So he made us start small and focus on foot and arm work, drill movements, and strength training.

Gabriel still pushed me hard, like I wanted him to. Whenever my arms screamed with tiredness, he'd push me to hold out for a little longer. Push a little harder. I knew it was difficult for him—I could see his internal struggle around doing anything that could potentially hurt me or cause me discomfort—but he tried his best. We both knew the better trained I was, the more protected I'd actually be, even if I got a little sore on the road back to strength.

Day by day, I got a little stronger and healed a little more. I was beginning to feel more like my old, tougher self. I teased Gabriel and joked around with him more, spent more time out of bed and out of my room, felt my stamina in training growing, and my confidence and sense of self-worth expanding far past what it'd ever been.

The only thing that pulled me back down was the recurring nightmare. I'd basically died, and it was pretty unrealistic to hope my only injuries would be physical and not psychological. But the nightmares still took me off guard. I'd never had them like this before. Every once in a while, I'd close my eyes and find myself back on the ground on the snow—crushed, battered, bleeding, and alone. The Demon would loom in front of me, my sword in its hand, and I'd lie there, paralyzed, as I watched it plunge my sword through my stomach and into the ground beneath me. The pain would tear through me like it was really happening. The stunned panic would fill me again, and I'd realize yet again that I was going to die. That my life was ending, and I'd never grow old or have a partner or a family. That I'd die alone. Then, when the pain became unbearable, I'd jerk awake, covered in sweat and shaking.

The first time I'd had this dream, it'd felt so real that I'd called to Gabriel in my mind just as I'd done the night of the attack. I'd awoken to him bursting into my room in the early hours of the morning to make sure I was okay. Since then, I'd tried to keep the nightmares to myself—I didn't want him having to relive his pain and worry just because I was. He'd already committed so much of himself to my recovery. I didn't want to take more from him.

Christmas arrived with a fresh blanket of snow covering the grounds, and the sun shining brightly from a clear, blue sky. The air was crisp and cool, and smelled fresh, almost like the atmosphere itself was new. Like nothing bad had ever happened here.

Gabriel swung by mid-morning with breakfast. He grinned as I opened the door, and he saw my outfit. I'd decided to dress up a bit in honor of the holiday, even though I didn't usually celebrate any, and put on an emerald-green tank top, a dark blue jean miniskirt, thick black tights, a black leather bomber jacket, and my heeled combat boots. A smile pulled at my lips as I saw his outfit—a dark green V-neck sweater with the sleeves pushed up to his elbows, dark blue jeans, and his combat boots. We'd both had the same idea.

"We've got to stop matching like this," he teased, his eyes full of amusement as he repeated what he'd said to me in the early days of our friendship. I laughed, a familiar warmth blooming in my chest.

Gabriel nudged the door shut, then set the food items on one of the small tables near the fireplace. He threw his jacket over the back of a chair, then pulled me gently into his arms, his hands splaying over my waist.

"Mmm, you're beautiful," he murmured, pressing his lips to my forehead. "Merry Christmas."

I smiled and slid my arms around his neck. "Merry Christmas." I tilted my chin up in invitation, and he smiled, then kissed me soundly.

We ate breakfast and watched one of the Christmas movies Gabriel had brought from his room, then bundled ourselves in warm jackets and went for a long walk around campus. Neither of us smoked this time. Gabriel said he'd gone through withdrawal when he'd refused to leave my side in the medical wing, and he hadn't picked up the habit again since then. He didn't feel the need to anymore, and to be honest, neither did I. Whatever internal restlessness that'd been put at ease by the habit seemed to be mostly gone. I'd finally stopped shoving my emotions so completely to the side, and consequently, I didn't feel the need to compensate with the habit anymore.

We strolled hand-in-hand across the bright, empty grounds, enjoying taking steps into the untouched snow and seeing how far we'd sink in. We even made our way into the beautiful chapel that'd hosted our orientation. I hadn't been back since then, so we took advantage of the empty grounds to explore. We walked around the perimeter of the enormous stone room, gazing up at the arches that met in points high above us and marveling at the ornate stained-glass windows that depicted the history of the Divines. Our creation, forms, and mission were immortalized in vibrant panes of colored glass that stretched high above us, larger than life.

I stood, mesmerized, in front of a window that portrayed each form of Divine kneeling around a large book, each figure extending a hand to touch the cover—symbolic of our shared mission and purpose in the world. But I was most mesmerized by the artist's depiction of each Divine. No piece of glass was the same color. Instead of depicting the Light Guardian in all white and the Dark Guardian in all black, each Guardian was formed with hundreds of varying shades. The Dark Guardian was made of deep blues, grays, browns, blacks, maroons, and purples, while the Light Guardian was made of pale yellows, pinks, blues, whites, greens, and grays. A dynamic mixture of colors was also used to depict the gray-skinned, red-eyed Demon and the blue and green-tinged Blessed. It was like the artist had seen more nuance in each Divine faction than most Divines usually did. They hadn't represented things in the stereotypical way—white and black, good and bad—where factions were clear opposites. They'd chosen to represent us in a far more complicated, beautiful way.

"Hey, Terah," Gabriel called. "Come look at this."

I turned and saw him examining one of the large stones that made up the chapel floor. My curiosity spiked, and I walked over to him.

"What is it?"

"Look." He pointed at the corner of the stone. "There are markings on it."

I squinted and bent down so I could take a closer look.

"Huh." I frowned as I finally saw it. He was right—on the bottom corner of the stone was a small carving of a symbol I didn't recognize.

"And it's not the only one like that. There are a ton more."

Gabriel took my hand and pulled me toward another stone with a different marking on it. And then another. And another. Yet not every stone on the floor was marked. Some—probably most—of the stones in the room were just plain. But every so often there seemed to be a cluster of these marked stones, none of which shared symbols with any other. One had a spiral made of a collection of tightly packed dots, while another had what looked like stag horns. Yet another had a stylized eye, while another had bones crossing each other at their centers.

I bent and ran my finger over another symbol, tracing the pattern in the cold stone. "What do you think they are?"

"They're symbols of different gods," Gabriel murmured, squatting next to me to examine the symbol as well.

I frowned. "Then why are they only on some stones? There have to be enough gods to fill every stone in here many times over."

Gabriel shrugged and pushed to his feet, then held his hand out to help me up. We meandered down a path of the marked stones toward the center of the grand room, before they abruptly trailed off.

"That's why I thought it was weird," he murmured, turning to look at other trails of the symbols. There didn't seem to be any pattern or reason to them. "But maybe it's just for decoration or something. You know, to pay homage to our origins as Divines, kind of like the windows do."

"Probably. We could look it up in the library if you're interested."

Gabriel shrugged again and turned toward me, a smile pulling at his lips. "That's alright. I'm not too bothered by it." He slid his arms around my waist and pulled me against him. "Just thought it was interesting."

My pulse kicked up, and I stared into his vibrant eyes, melting in them. "It is interesting," I breathed, a little absently.

His smile widened into a grin as he saw how distracted I was by him, and he leaned forward slowly and brushed his lips over mine. I sighed as his scent filled my nostrils—warm, with a hint of spice—and I pressed closer, kissing him back. His arms tightened around me, and he deepened the kiss, the soft yet insistent pull of his lips against mine spiking my pulse and slowly setting me on fire.

But suddenly I was snapped out of my body and out of the present. The room and the cold faded, as did Gabriel and his warm kiss. I found myself in a dark stone passageway, lit only by the bright white light glowing in Matt and Caleb's hands ahead of me. We were traveling carefully down a steep, narrow set of stairs that seemed to go on forever, and eerily disappeared below us in the darkness. I swallowed down the fear and adrenaline that were pumping through me and tightened my hand around Gabriel's. The young man at the front of our small group turned to glance back at us with his cold, yet familiar-looking, eyes.

"Be on your guard." His voice was deep and quiet. "There are bound to be traps in here to keep out trespassers. There's a reason it's been hidden for so long. It isn't meant to be easy to find or take."

I nodded—that'd been my guess too—and took a deep, calming breath as we continued our descent. I had a bad feeling about this. A feeling that was growing with every step we took.

"Terah?" a worried voice echoed around me from far away. "Terah, can you hear me?"

Suddenly, I snapped out of the dark passageway and found myself back in the chapel. Gabriel was looking down at me with concern, his arms still folded tightly around me.

I blinked up at him, slightly dazed. It was so bright in here compared to where I'd just been. "Sorry." My voice was hoarse. I reached a shaking hand forward and pressed it to his chest, trying to steady myself. "I think . . . I just had another vision."

Gabriel nodded, his brows still furrowed. "That's what I figured, but I wasn't sure. One second you were there and the next you were completely unresponsive, so I got worried." He led us over to the closest pew, then sat and pulled me down next to him. "Are you okay? What did you see?"

I released a long sigh. "I'm okay. It wasn't terrifying or painful like many of my others have been. I just don't know what it meant."

I quickly told him what I'd seen.

Gabriel looked thoughtful. "And there was a person there you didn't know?"

"Well, I haven't actually met him before, but he's been in several of my visions. I don't know who he is, though. I've never seen him at the Academy or in Dagmar."

Gabriel nodded and ran his hand absently through his hair. "But you said Matt, Caleb, and I were there too?" I nodded. "Hm. That does make it sound like it happens at the Academy."

"Maybe. But it wasn't a part of the Academy I've ever seen. It was completely dark. And I don't know of any building on campus that would have stairs like that. They went on forever."

Gabriel sighed. "Me neither. I guess all we can do is keep an eye on it. And also keep an eye out for the person in your visions."

I nodded and reached over, sliding my hand into his. This was probably the least horrifying vision I'd had thus far, but it still made me tense and worried.

"Want to head to dinner?" Gabriel finally asked, squeezing my fingers. "I heard they have a pretty good feast for the holiday, even with so few of us on campus."

"Sure."

We stood, and Gabriel pulled me close for a last soft kiss before we headed out. We pushed through the chapel doors and saw that the snow had started up again, this time propelled by substantial gusts of wind, and the sky had darkened with clouds as the sun sank behind the trees. We quickly made our way the short distance from the chapel to the main building, the grounds lit by the little remaining daylight, our boots crunching in the snow as we went.

I sighed with relief as I pulled open the front door and the warmth from the building enveloped us. It was too damn cold outside. We made our way into the dining hall and saw that several of the tables usually scattered throughout the room had been pushed together into one long table. My mouth fell open. Almost its entire length was filled with food and decked out with sprigs of pine and winter berries, grand candelabras of softly glowing tapers, glimmering gold ribbons woven throughout, and some kind of paper decoration on each plate. They'd gone to great lengths to make things as homey and celebratory as they could for everyone stuck on campus. Most of the teachers who'd remained for the break were already here, along with some school administrators, staff, the president, and a few dozen students who'd chosen to remain for the holidays.

My mouth snapped shut and my body tensed as my gaze collided with Matt's. He was sitting at one end of the table with a few of his friends, but his gaze hardened as he looked between Gabriel and me. Gabriel didn't say anything, but his shoulders stiffened as he took my hand and led me to the opposite end of the table, as far from Matt as possible.

I tried not to look in Matt's direction as I sat down and stripped out of my jacket, but I could feel his gaze burning into me. It made me uncomfortable, but also sad. I knew him too well to not see his loneliness and sadness, even behind his anger. And I'd be lying to myself if I said I didn't miss him. But every time the president leaned over to speak with him, my resolve firmed again. He was a part of the warrior faction now. He was loyal to them over everything and everyone, and he'd shown that many times. I couldn't afford to keep him as close as he'd been. Nor would it be fair to him or to Gabriel to do so. Not while Matt still had feelings for me. So I turned resolutely in my seat and faced away from him, trying to forget he was there.

Gabriel finally grew less tense as we talked and teased each other. He explained that the paper decorations on our plates were actually holiday crackers, and that you were supposed to pull them with another person. He showed me how, then grinned as my mouth opened in surprise as the cracker exploded with a satisfying pop, dispensing a paper crown and various miniature toys. I donned my paper crown, even though Gabriel refused to wear his. But his shoulders shook with silent laughter each time he looked at me with it on. It probably looked ridiculous, but I decided not to care for once. I'd been through too much and had lost too much to care about small shit like that anymore. Why did it matter whether other people thought I was an impenetrable fortress? I was beginning to realize I could be a strong soldier without killing all joy within myself. And I was dedicated to putting that new attitude to practice.

"I regret to inform you that you're completely adorable," Gabriel said as he slid his arm around my shoulders and pulled me into him.

I couldn't help smiling. I'd punch anyone else for saying that, but from him, it didn't feel like an insult.

"Which reminds me." He pulled back a little and gave me a mischievous smile. "I have a gift for you. And a surprise. But I'll have to bring it by later."

My eyebrows rose. "You have a gift? Really?"

Gabriel smirked as some of his hair fell over his eyes. "What, you assumed presents weren't my style either?"

I shrugged. "Not really. Plus, I assumed people wouldn't have access to things from the outside world on the Academy's plane. Besides," I paused and took a sip of wine, "I don't need any presents. I already have you." I said it casually—it was only the truth—but Gabriel's cheeks heated, and he seemed to have lost the capacity to speak for a moment.

"It's probably not cool for me to make out with you in front of the rest of the school," he said, once he'd recovered, mischief in his eyes, "but if you keep saying things like that, I might not have a choice."

I laughed. "Is that a promise or a threat?" I slid my hand slowly up his stomach then his chest.

Gabriel's eyes slid closed for a moment, and he swallowed. "Both," he finally murmured, his voice a little deeper than usual.

Gabriel returned to his room after dinner to get whatever present he had for me, and I headed back to mine to get warm. I still couldn't believe he'd gone to the trouble. The only present I'd ever gotten was from Matt, and just the one time. But it was hard not to love that Gabriel had thought about it and cared enough to do something like that. It wasn't a thoughtfulness I was used to.

I pushed open the door to my room and flicked on the lights, then immediately started a fire in the grate. In just the few hours without it, the room had already grown frigid. I used my power, which had finally fully regenerated, instead of my lighter this time, so the wood glowed with warm purple light as it caught and held the writhing purple flames. Then I pushed to my feet and walked to the edge of my bed, pulling off my heavy winter gear. But I froze as I looked down and noticed a small box lying in the center of the comforter.

I frowned as I picked it up and sank onto the edge of the bed. I was a little afraid to open it, especially as the only other person I knew who had access to my room was Matt. But my curiosity got the better of me, and I pulled off the lid. I stared at the contents of the box as a wave of sadness rolled over me, dampening the warmth I'd felt this evening. Inside, lay a pair of small silver earrings in the shape of flying birds. Just like the necklace Matt had gotten me years ago. And there was a note written inside the lid of the box in Matt's tidy scroll. "Merry Christmas, Terah. I always have and always will love you. -Matt."

Tears flooded my eyes as my heart squeezed painfully. What was I going to do with him? How were we all going to get through this? I knew only time and change could heal what'd been broken between us, and only time would allow him to move on. But how much would all of us be hurt before that happened?

I brought the box to my desk and left it there with a sigh. It would upset Gabriel to see, but I didn't want to hide it from him. It'd hurt him more if I did. Then I plopped down on one of the armchairs, decidedly less cheerful than I'd been at dinner, and waited for Gabriel to return.

Gabriel arrived a few minutes later, his knock jerking me out of a downward spiral brought on by Matt and his gift. I pushed out of the armchair with a sigh and went to open the door. As soon it swung open, I was greeted with Gabriel's familiar smile.

"Hey," he murmured, stepping inside and nudging the door shut behind him. "Sorry, that took longer than I expected."

I shrugged and managed a small smile. "No big deal." I moved away from him and returned to my armchair.

Gabriel's smile faded as he watched me, his gaze trailing over my forced smile and stiff shoulders. "What's wrong?" He sat across from me in the other armchair, his brows pulling together. "What happened?"

I shrugged again. "It's nothing. I can't believe I'm even letting it get to me."

The worry in his gaze deepened. "As I've said before, you don't usually get mad over nothing. What happened?"

I sighed and leaned back in the armchair, crossing my arms over my chest. "On the desk," I finally said, motioning behind me.

Gabriel gave me one last appraising look before pushing to his feet and walking over to the desk. I heard him pick up the box that contained Matt's present, then open it. There was a long moment of silence, then he sighed, long and slow.

"Well, that sucks." He returned the box to the desk, then pulled off his jacket, and draped it over the back of the chair before sitting again. "He's persistent. I'll give him that."

His tone was light, but I could see the anger swirling in his eyes and the tension in his shoulders. But I also saw uncertainty there as his gaze slid appraisingly over my face again, trying to figure out what I was really feeling. My stomach clenched as I realized he couldn't tell whether Matt had succeeded in changing my mind toward him or not.

I shook my head sadly and pulled my feet onto the chair in front of me. "It'd be cool if we could fast forward to the part where he's moved on and we don't all have to suffer because of it." Bitterness filled my voice. "I hate hurting him. I hate being hurt by him. I hate seeing him hurt you. And it's never going to change my mind. I want *you*, Gabriel." I met his gaze firmly with my own. "I'll always want you."

Gabriel's eyes filled with warmth and the traces of uncertainty faded. The corner of his mouth hitched up—a small smile, but still beautiful. My heart tilted then clenched at the sight. He reached forward, holding his hand palm up for mine. I slid my fingers into his, and he gave a small tug, pulling me from my chair. I smiled as I landed in his lap, and his arms closed around me. He held me tightly to his chest and pressed his face against my hair.

"I hope you know," he murmured, his lips moving against the top of my head, "that you're everything to me." His tone was uncharacteristically serious.

Tears stung my eyes. My world simultaneously felt as though it was tilting on its axis and was the most stable it'd ever been. Everything with him was so new and intense—more intense than anything I'd experienced in the past. Yet I wasn't scared of it as I'd been for everyone before him. Finally, it felt right. Balanced. Additive. True. Our closeness wasn't forced, manipulated, or one-sided. And consequently, making myself this vulnerable with Gabriel felt safer than all the walls that I'd put around myself to keep me safe and everyone else out.

I turned on his lap, so I was facing him, and wrapped my arms around his neck. Our faces were close now, our torsos just brushing. And I watched as his eyes darkened as heat grew in them. "You're everything to me, too," I whispered, for once, entirely honest about my feelings.

A smile bloomed across Gabriel's face before he leaned forward. His lips parted mine, soft and warm, then took them in a long, slow pull. It vibrated through me and every nerve in my body, waking each one until they were humming with warmth and expectation. I pressed closer, my lips moving with his, eager and hungry. Quickening our pace until both of us were gasping. His kiss, as it always did, consumed me, but it also centered me. I could feel the certainty in it. It was like the stable foundations of a building—strong and even, so everything above it was sturdy, buildable, manageable. Our feelings for each other had a solidity to them that was nothing like the infatuations I'd had when I was younger. This was different and life-alteringly immense. For the first time, love felt . . . right. And it was a feeling I'd fight for and be vulnerable for.

Gabriel pulled back and rested his forehead against mine, his eyes still closed, breathing hard. "I should probably give you your present and your surprise before you distract me more." His voice was uneven.

I smiled and slid my hands down his chest. "Probably a good idea. Though I'm pretty sure you're the one who started it."

Gabriel shot me a roguish smile, before reaching behind him into his jacket and pulling out a small box. "Well, I guess we should start with the surprise. I left it in the hall so we could talk about it first."

I tilted my head at him, curious.

"It's my bag of stuff. I promised I'd return when you were healed, and you finally are, so I'm here, ready to stay with you if you want me to. But no pressure if you're not ready for that. Seriously—I want you to be one hundred percent sure. But that's why it took me so long in my room—I was packing up most of my stuff, just in case."

A brilliant smile spread across my face as warmth grew in my chest. "Of course I want you to stay." I ran my fingers up his neck and into his hair, then leaned forward and brushed my lips over his.

Gabriel smiled. "Thanks," he whispered, before brushing his lips over mine in return. "Okay." He pulled back a little. "Present time, before you distract me again." He grinned, then held up the small box. "It's not . . . big or anything, but it made me think of you. Had my sister help me get it, since I couldn't leave the Academy plane."

I took the box from him, warmth growing in my chest. To get this for me, he'd had to tell his family about me. And he'd been willing to. I lifted the lid and found a small, velvet drawstring pouch inside. I pulled open the pouch and carefully tipped the contents into my palm. It looked like jewelry, made of delicate silver chain. I spread it in my palm and saw that it was a necklace, with a small pendant at the end. My mouth opened in surprise as I turned over the pendant—it was a lightning bolt made of the same delicate silver as the chain, but the center was entirely filled with tiny, deep purple gemstones that twinkled up at me. He'd . . . found a representation of my power. A *beautiful* representation. And he'd thought of me.

"It's . . . lovely," I breathed, staring down at it. Gabriel was the only person who'd ever seen my transformation and hadn't been repelled by it. He was the only one who'd seen good in it. Tears prickled the corners of my eyes.

I looked up and caught Gabriel watching me closely, his brow creased with worry. He quickly smoothed his expression into a more neutral one. "So . . . you like it?"

"I love it." I smiled up at him, but I knew it wasn't sufficient. He deserved to know how I really felt. Only . . . I couldn't quite pull it all into words. So, instead, I connected our minds and, after a deep breath, opened my thoughts to him.

I watched as he sorted through my jumbled emotions. The deep hurt of lifelong rejection caused by my unique looking power. How that hurt continued cutting into me, keeping it a deep, open wound. How much his acceptance of my transformation and of me exactly as I was helped temper that hurt. How grateful I was for his acceptance. How amazed I was that he could even see beauty where others had only seen darkness and evil. My surprise that he'd thought to get me a gift when only one other person in my life had ever done that. How beautiful I thought the gift was. My continued wonder that he could so freely accept a part of me that no one else had. The burgeoning part of me that was beginning to accept and even like that part of myself as well. How his acceptance had fostered and encouraged my own. How he was making it impossible for me to not fall even harder for him . . .

Gabriel smiled, a gentle smile. He knew how I felt now. He could see the full context of my feelings. He cupped my cheeks in his hands, his gaze growing intense, and he opened his mind to me as well. But he did it more broadly. Beyond his immediate thoughts, I was flooded with the intensity of his emotions as his gaze burned into mine. It was the first time he'd let me see everything.

I saw how long and how deeply he'd cared about me. I saw the anguish he'd felt as he'd seen me with Matt, believing I'd never choose him over Matt. The gut-wrenching panic he'd felt when I'd been badly injured during transformation training and had called to him for the first time. His fear that I'd be injured or killed every time we fought a Demon. His terror that I wouldn't tell him if I was seriously hurt, and his fear that he wouldn't be able to heal me if I was. I saw how beautiful and powerful he thought I was, and how he thought my transformation was just as beautiful. How brave and strong he believed I was. How he'd felt when I'd accepted his transformation—when I'd seen beauty in it and him. When I hadn't run like all people before me had. How it made him feel when he saw me smile and laugh—warm, happy. How much he liked spending time with me and sharing things with me. How his insides felt like they were glowing when we were together. How much he wanted to touch me, hold me, kiss me, spend his life with me. How deeply my almost death and painful recovery had torn him apart. How he'd cried over me each night in the medical wing when he was finally alone. How he didn't want to live without me . . .

I didn't realize I was crying until the side of Gabriel's mouth quirked up and he chased my tears with his fingers, gently wiping them away. I hadn't known these past few months how much and how deeply Gabriel had felt . . . about everything. Perhaps because he was so adept at keeping his emotions hidden when he wanted to. I wondered if I'd had the same success at hiding my own emotions, or if he knew, *really* knew, how deeply and how quickly I'd fallen for him. How, despite my best efforts, I'd let him in and trusted him with record speed. I'd never let in anyone like I'd let him in—not even Caleb—even though it'd taken me a while to realize exactly what that meant.

Gabriel's smile broadened, his gaze warm. *"I won't know unless you show me."*

So, I decided to.

I carefully fastened on the necklace, then rose to my knees, wrapped my arms around his neck, and rested my forehead against his, closing my eyes. Then I let him in—fully in—to my mind. And I let him see it all. All the pain and loneliness that'd led me to intensely guard myself, my emotions, and my heart. All the times love, in its various forms, had torn me apart. All the times it'd ripped out and destroyed the gentler parts of me, leaving me raw and exposed. How I'd turned inward. Closed myself off to the world and to other people because of that, and because of the violence that'd always surrounded me—the countless people I'd seen die in front of me. How none of that had ultimately mattered when it'd come to him. He'd gotten around those deeply ingrained things in me like they were nothing, quickly bypassing every wall I'd erected to keep other people out.

I showed him how he'd challenged me and helped me grow. How he'd made me feel seen, heard, and appreciated. How his smile made my heart pound and my cheeks warm. How his vibrant eyes made me melt. How his close scrutiny of me so he could understand me and my emotions was entirely new to me and made me feel overwhelmed in a positive way. How he made my world a brighter place. How his first kiss had thundered through me and changed my life. How it'd forced me to reckon with my own emotions. I showed him the moment I'd realized I loved him. The moment he'd broken my heart when I'd thought he'd rejected me. The moment I knew Matt could never be a substitute for him. The moment I'd decided to die to protect him. How, even as I'd died, I hadn't regretted my decision. Because I loved him. More than anything. More than anyone.

Gabriel's sharp intake of breath broke my concentration, causing the connection between our minds to snap. I pulled back a little and opened my eyes to look into his. Moisture had collected along the bottom rim of his eyes.

"Terah," he whispered, his voice shaking. His arms tightened around my waist. He looked at a loss for words. But I knew how he felt. We both felt undone and remade. We'd shared so much with each other. We'd exposed our frayed edges, trusting the other not to use it against us. To understand. To see who we truly were and to stay anyway. Perhaps, that's what love truly was.

I tightened my hold around Gabriel, pressing closer. Tingles rushed through me as I continued to hold his gaze. It'd darkened and turned molten. And I knew he felt how I did. I knew he wanted what I did.

His mouth caught mine in a heated pull that scorched me down to my bones. It traveled through me like an electric shock, waking every nerve, making every hair stand on end, and every muscle clench then melt. This wasn't one of the careful, slow-burning kisses he'd been working hard to stick to these past few weeks. This kiss was like our first—filled with urgency, desperation, and fire.

He pulled me flush against him, and his hands slid over my back and up my sides as he continued to kiss me with abandon. I clung to him as his lips moved heatedly with mine, like he might die if he stopped. I felt the same. I arched into him, and Gabriel groaned. Then he released me and slid my leather jacket down my arms, kissing a burning trail from my jaw to the edge of my shoulder. I sighed and let it fall to the floor. Then I slid my hands under the hem of his sweater and shirt and trailed them up his firm stomach. He was perfect, and I wanted—needed—to feel all of him.

Gabriel pulled his sweater and shirt over his head, quickly discarding them on the floor, then pulled me against him again. The heat of his chest enveloped me as our mouths collided. His tongue slid against mine as he tilted my head back to deepen the kiss. We groaned in unison, and Gabriel's fingers found the hem of my tank top. He slid the fabric up as he explored my finally healed torso, the heated pads of his fingers sending warm shivers cascading through me. His thumbs traced slow circles over the front of my rib cage as his fingers lingered in the curve of my waist, stroking my skin, memorizing my shape, before he slid the tank top up until it bunched above my chest. I lifted my arms above my head, and Gabriel pulled it off and tossed it to the floor.

I eagerly pressed my torso to his and sighed as his bare skin pressed to mine. Our lips crashed together again, fiery and urgent, as we continued to explore each other. My hands roamed up his stomach and chest, feeling the dips and swells of his muscles, the rapid expansion and contraction of his chest. I explored his firm shoulder muscles, then slid my fingers down his arms, squeezing his triceps and biceps, my stomach tightening as I felt the flex of firm muscle there. Gabriel's hands molded around my hips, gripping me there and pulling them flush against his. Then his fingers slid slowly over the curve of my lower back before traveling up until they slid underneath the back band of my bra. He hesitated for a second.

"Do you want me to stop?" he asked, panting.

I knew he would if I asked him to. But I didn't want him to stop. Maybe ever. Gone were the days where restraint, fear, and numbness had guided my interactions with love and intimacy. This was different. *I* was different. I'd grown and become more whole. I finally knew how I felt and what I wanted. And I wanted Gabriel. I loved him, and he loved me. I wanted to give him everything. All of myself, inside and out. I wanted to let him in, in a way I'd never fully allowed myself to do with anyone before him, no matter how intimate things had gotten with them. And, even more staggering, I knew Gabriel wanted to do the same with me.

"Don't stop," I panted, pressing myself urgently against him. "Please."

He groaned and captured my mouth urgently with his again. He slid his hands up my thighs, pushing up the hem of my skirt until it bunched around my waist. Then his hands trailed up my body until he reached my bra. With a few quick movements of his fingers, it unclasped and fell away. He pulled me tightly against him again, his kiss filled with both tenderness and fire, as his hands splayed over the unimpeded skin of my back. And I sighed as I felt this new contact of my skin on his. Every part of me felt molten now. And alive. So alive.

I rocked my hips against his as his hand came up and cupped my breast. He captured my sigh with his mouth as his thumb trailed over its peak. Jolts of pleasure shot through me with each swipe of his finger. And when he pulled me back and replaced his fingers with his mouth, I couldn't stifle the half-sob, half-cry of pleasure. I rocked my hips against him more urgently now, sliding over the hardening length of him. He groaned against me, the vibrations shuddering through my skin, making it tighten. Then he took my hips in his hands and slid me against him again. We groaned in unison. Desire throbbed through me, making my fingers shake, drowning me in heated electricity until everything felt fuzzy except him. Like he was the only one in focus while the rest of the world blurred.

"Gabriel," I finally gasped, my head falling back as I pressed my eyes closed. He released me slowly from his mouth, sending one last jolt of pleasure through me, before straightening up and meeting my gaze. His eyes were as cloudy with desire as mine must be.

I slid my hands over his shoulders and up his neck until my fingers were buried in his hair. My brain was too scrambled for coherent speech. So, instead, I connected our minds and showed him what I wanted. Gabriel smiled, then nodded. It was what he wanted too.

He stood with me still in his arms, pressing me to him, and I wrapped my legs around his hips. He adjusted his hands, supporting me, as his lips trailed down my neck to my shoulder. Then he bit me there, not hard enough to hurt, but hard enough to make my whole body clench. I gasped, scorching heat pounding through me. Then I grabbed his face and pulled his mouth to mine again.

He groaned as my legs tightened around him and my tongue slid into his mouth. I could feel him starting to tremble against me as he clutched me tightly to him. I could feel him losing control in the best kind of way. And slowly, as he kissed me deeply, as we lost ourselves more and more in each other, he walked me to my bed.

16

CONSEQUENCES

THE NEW SEMESTER STARTED MID-JANUARY, BUT STUDENTS BEGAN arriving on campus a week or so before then so they could get settled in their dorms. Yet even as the start of classes loomed nearer and nearer, the difference on campus was palpable. Heavily armed warrior faction guards openly covered the grounds, not only surrounding the perimeter of the Academy's plane, but also periodically patrolling around the buildings. And a lot of students hadn't returned.

I knew the president had told everyone about the Demon attacks and that the campus was no longer fully safe, but I hadn't known how much of an impact that'd have on attendance until I saw how many had chosen not to return. At least a third of the student body hadn't come back. And it changed the entire vibe of the grounds. At least over winter break, the campus had been empty for a reason. But now, with all the teachers bustling around, and with so many fewer students, campus felt off, the atmosphere eerie and foreboding.

So, with a distinct lack of enthusiasm, we all returned to classes, many of the remaining students pretending that nothing significant had changed. The worst part for me, though, was facing the rest of the student body. By now, everyone knew what'd happened with the Demon attacks last semester, and who was involved. Everyone knew Gabriel and I had fended off several attacks. Everyone knew I'd almost died in the last one. And everyone knew I'd chosen to sacrifice myself for the protection of those at the school. If I'd thought they'd stared at me a ton before—when they just knew I was from Dagmar—that was *nothing* to how they stared at me now. It seemed like most had come down with the unfortunate urge to thank me for what I'd done. To ask questions and force me to relive it. And I damn well hated it.

I spent ninety percent of our first day of classes glaring at people, my shoulders and jaw tense, trying to get them to stop staring. Trying to discourage people from approaching. And Gabriel donned his fiercest scowl, trying to shield me from the worst of it. But no matter what we did, no matter how tough and mean we looked, we weren't successful at completely keeping people away.

Lunch on the first day of classes was the worst. Because of the freezing, damp weather, Gabriel and I had been forced to eat in the dining hall instead of outside like we'd preferred for most of last semester, before it'd gotten unbearably cold. And because of that, we now had to deal with the rest of the student body. But we tried our best to keep to ourselves. We'd ignored the open stares and loud whispers as we'd passed with our trays of food, and we'd picked a table in the back corner of the dining hall and made sure no one else felt like they could join us there. Then we deliberately faced away from the crowd so that, at the very least, we wouldn't have to see them gawking at us. But a few brave—or foolish—students didn't seem to get the message and decided to approach us anyway.

"Incoming," Gabriel murmured, nudging me lightly with his shoulder and nodding to a place just over my head.

I sighed, feeling deflated, and glanced behind me. "You've gotta be fucking kidding me," I groaned, turning back around, my shoulders immediately tensing. There had to be at least fifteen students *lining up* to speak to us. It was completely ridiculous. "Can't we just leave? I'm not hungry anymore anyway." My stomach had turned the moment I'd caught sight of all the eager-looking students, and I wanted to get as far away from them as possible. I didn't want to look into their expectant faces, and I didn't want to talk about—and relive—the last Demon attack. Just because I'd chosen to save everyone didn't mean I wanted to dwell on it. I just wanted to be left alone.

Gabriel nodded and took my hand, lacing his fingers through mine, and glaring at the people behind me. "Yeah. Let's get the hell out of here."

We were about to push to our feet when a deep voice cut through the noise of the crowd.

"Excuse me, everyone," it boomed in a confident, commanding tone,

"I've been sent to discuss private security details with these two. I must insist, for the sake of confidentiality, that you all disperse. You'll have to talk with them another time."

There was a moment of silence in which everyone looked confused, and no one moved, but the person soon rectified that by speaking again.

"Come on! Move it!" he barked, this time more like a military trainer. This finally got the crowd moving, and people scrambled back to their tables, whispering, and staring at the newcomer.

Gabriel and I exchanged confused glances, then looked around to see who the speaker was. We both knew that no one actually wanted to speak with us about security. If they had, they would've done so before the semester started, and not in a place as public as the dining hall. As I looked through the dispersing crowd, I saw one person still walking toward us. My stomach clenched and my breath stalled. He was strangely familiar, even though I knew I'd never seen him before. Not in real life, at least. But I *had* seen him. In my visions. It was him. He was here.

I forced my lungs to suck in a breath of air as I watched him approach. He was tall, though not as tall as Gabriel, strong, as though he trained a lot, and had light brown skin and dark brown hair. His face was handsome and angular, and his dark brown eyes were framed with thick dark lashes. But his eyes were cold and hard. A shiver of trepidation rushed through me. A person only had eyes like that if they'd been through hell and hadn't emerged fully whole on the other side. I wondered what his hell had been.

My heart pounded as my anxiety grew. The young man's expression was unreadable as his gaze met mine, though I thought I glimpsed some curiosity there. Gabriel stiffened next to me, his hand tightening around mine. It was enough to break me out of my anxiety-induced paralysis. Lightning fast, I connected my mind with Gabriel's. I needed to tell him before we talked to this man.

"Gabriel, it's him. The guy from my visions."

Gabriel's gaze snapped to mine, his eyes widening. But he squeezed my hand in acknowledgment.

"I don't know if he should be trusted or not," I added quickly as I turned back to watch the newcomer pull out the chair next to me and sit down. *"We should be careful."*

"Agreed."

I broke the mind-connection as I studied the young man next to me.

"Hey," he said, leaning his arms leisurely on the table in front of him as

345

he regarded us, "thought you might like some help getting rid of that mob." He jerked his head toward the rest of the students in the dining hall.

I kept my expression blank as I watched him. I didn't know what to make of his presence. It was hard not to feel like his appearance was a nightmare coming to life. After all, many of my visions were horrific and frightening, and almost every time I'd seen this man in them, a variety of stressful things were happening.

"I'm Damian," he continued, "and don't worry, I'm not actually here to talk to you about security. I'm a transfer student." He shrugged and gave us a cocky smile—one that didn't reach his eyes.

I squeezed Gabriel's hand, trying to dispel my anxiety as I studied Damian. His eyes narrowed slightly as he stared back. His gaze felt familiar—too familiar—and penetrating, almost like he could push past my expression and into my thoughts. But I didn't let anyone access my thoughts without my permission, so I instinctively pushed back, closing myself off and breaking eye contact with him.

Damian shifted, and I glanced back at him. He looked frustrated for a split second before the cold, neutral expression descended once more.

"So, uh, do you all not talk or something?" A faint smile pulled at his lips—one that would've been charming had his eyes not been so cold.

"Generally, not to people we don't know," I finally responded, my voice carefully bored. I leaned back in my chair and crossed my arms over my chest, regarding him coolly.

"That's not very open minded of you," Damian said, his tone mild and teasing. "I'm here from a different country, and I'm just trying to make some friends. I heard you all were in my training group, so I thought you'd be a good place to start." He shrugged.

This got my attention. "How do you know you're in our training group?" I tilted my head and watched him closely.

Damian shrugged again. "I went through the training test yesterday, and when they finally decided I'd be in the advanced group, I asked who else was in it so I could meet people." He sat back in his chair. "I've been asking around to see if anyone knows the faces to the names that I got, but so far, you two have been the only ones who've been identifiable. I see, now, why that is," he added, raising an eyebrow and glancing at the rest of the crowd of people still staring over at our table. "Must've been some attack to have the school in such a frenzy. Back home, people barely blink at Demon attacks anymore."

"They cared because the Academy is supposed to be neutral ground, free of whatever wars are being waged on the outside," Gabriel said, examining Damian shrewdly, his arms crossed over his chest. "Attacks aren't supposed to happen here at all."

Damian studied Gabriel in return. I wondered if Gabriel would feel the intrusive sharpness of his gaze like I had—like his brain was being searched.

Damian frowned, then broke eye contact with Gabriel and looked back at me. "That makes sense, I guess. I've heard of the Academy's supposed neutrality, though I've never known anyone who's gone here. I kind of thought it was a myth."

"No myth," I said shortly, "though it's definitely not as neutral as it used to be. Not with the Demon attacks, not to mention the Light Guardian side taking over security." I tried to keep as much of the bitterness out of my voice as possible, but I wasn't sure I was entirely successful.

Damian looked at me curiously for a moment, his cold eyes piercing into mine, then pulled a charming smile slowly onto his face. "So, I do know your names from the trainer, but care to introduce yourselves for real?"

I sighed heavily, but ultimately, this felt inevitable. I knew from my visions that we wouldn't get rid of him easily. "I'm Terah. I'm a first year, originally from Dagmar."

I glanced at Gabriel. His gaze was still hard and distrustful as he watched Damian, but he rolled his eyes and let out an impatient breath. "I'm Gabriel. First year, from Elareth."

Damian nodded slowly. "Huh, so you're both from border towns. Nice. Explains why you're in the advanced training group. I'm from a border town too, but in Europe. My family was originally from here, hence my accent, but we moved to Europe when I was a kid, and I've lived there ever since."

"What brings you here?" I didn't know much about border towns in other parts of the world, or Divine schools in other countries, but I knew the Academy was the only purportedly neutral one. All the other Divine schools I'd heard of were divided by Divine faction and political stance. They were the opposite of neutral. Had Damian come here to escape as well?

Damian considered us silently for a moment, like he was trying to determine how much to tell us. "We got word in town of a request from the High Light Guardian for more highly trained, Academy-age people to fortify the school's defenses." He sighed. "I wasn't planning on going to school or anything, but I'm eighteen and my father decided that the opportunity for potential advancement was too good to pass up. So here I am." He shrugged. "Not my first choice, but at least I get to escape that hell hole for a while."

His voice had hardened, and a deep grimness briefly entered his eyes. A grimness I was familiar with. It was a look that most people who grew up in war-ravaged border towns had—like they'd seen too much and were too tired far too young. And it was this, more than anything he'd said, that made me relax slightly toward him. It was the first real human reaction I'd seen from him.

"Anyway," he said, snapping out of his reverie and training his eyes on us again, "I just wanted to introduce myself. It might be nice to have a few people to talk to while I'm here." He gave us a crooked smile that almost looked bittersweet as he pushed to his feet. But it did nothing to warm the coldness in his eyes. It seemed untouchable—like nothing could ever breach the hard exterior to warm them. "See you in classes or training," he said as he turned away. "Whichever comes first."

I watched him as he walked away, nerves churning in my stomach. Damian grabbed his jacket from a nearby table, quickly donned it, then left the dining hall. A shiver of unease traveled through me.

"I don't know what to think," I murmured, turning back toward Gabriel. "He's hard to read."

"He seems . . . slippery," Gabriel finally said, leaning back in his chair and taking my hand again. "Like he's used to hiding layers of secrets. Like he never shows who he really is or what he's really thinking. It makes him almost impossible to read."

"Agreed." I chewed on my lip for a moment. "But I can't tell if that's just the effect of his border town on him, or if it's something else. Either way, we should keep an eye on him. Also, we should try to keep him from getting too much information from us until we know whether we can trust him or not."

Gabriel nodded. "I'm guessing you felt it too, then. Like he was trying to get into your brain."

I looked up at him, startled. "I did. Though I was hoping I was wrong about that."

Gabriel shook his head a little, his brow furrowing. "It felt like it does when you try to connect with my mind." My eyes widened. I'd never experienced the sensation before—I was always the one trying to connect, not the one being connected with. Gabriel looked around at the people still staring at us, then leaned closer, lowering his voice. "It's not an ability I've ever seen from a Divine other than you. We should be careful. If he somehow has that power too, and if he's not on our side, he has the potential to be dangerous to us."

I nodded, grimly. It was better to keep him at a distance until we knew more about him. We sat in silence for a few minutes, each in deep, troubled thought. But I finally snapped out of it as I saw a student at a nearby table push to her feet, looking determined as she turned toward us. My stomach clenched. With Damian gone, people felt like it was safe to approach us again.

"Can we get the hell out of here now?" A smile pulled at my lips as I glanced up at Gabriel, then jerked my head at the person heading our way.

Gabriel smiled and squeezed my hand. "Yep. Let's go."

***

We didn't see Damian again until training the next day. I already wasn't looking forward to it, due mainly to the fact that Matt would be there. Matt, who not only hated me for breaking his heart, but who also probably hated me for returning the present he'd gotten for me by leaving it outside his door. The combination of Matt, Caleb, *and* Damian made me not want to go at all.

As we pushed through the training room doors, I was pleasantly surprised to see that our entire training group had returned this semester. I wasn't sure if it was because they felt an obligation to protect the students from any future attacks, since they were well trained enough to do so, or if they'd just come back without worry, knowing they could defend themselves. But whatever the reason, I felt a little better knowing this many highly trained people remained at the Academy.

Gabriel and I walked across the room to the locker rooms, trying to ignore the looks from the rest of our training group—who had, at this point, all heard about the attacks—as well as Matt's pointed glare. I glanced around only once before we pushed through the locker room doors and briefly made eye-contact with Caleb. To my surprise, he nodded at me, his expression . . . complicated. The coldness was still in his eyes, but the hatred had faded and been replaced by a conflicted, regretful look. Next to Caleb stood Damian. They'd probably be training partners now. Damian was also watching us, his expression almost calculating. My stomach clenched a little with unease.

Once changed, Gabriel and I made our way to an open spot on the mats and waited for Luke to address the group.

"Alright, everyone," Luke finally called, cutting through the buzz of conversations. "First, I want to say welcome back. It's good to see all of you returned this semester. As I'm sure you've noticed by now, not everyone made that same decision. We've lost a lot of people on campus because we've lost their confidence in our ability to keep them safe. It's a fair reaction to the attacks that took place on the grounds last semester."

A couple people shot Gabriel and I curious side-glances. Luke cleared his throat, demanding all attention again.

"While it should never be a student's job to protect themselves or others while at the Academy," he continued, looking around at us, his expression grim, "you in this room are some of the only people on campus, apart from the new guards, who can actually do so. As some of your fellow trainees have already shown," he added, nodding at Gabriel and me. "Keep that in mind as you train this semester, and as you remain on campus. If something happens, it might not be your job to help, but I want you to think about doing so anyway. I want you to think about what the other students here, the ones who aren't well trained enough to fight, will do if you choose not to help."

Luke looked around the room again, meeting each of our eyes. I'd never seen him so serious. The expressions of those around me were equally as grim, and no one said a word of protest. I wondered again why they'd all chosen to return. Did they feel the same responsibility that I'd felt when I'd chosen to protect the school?

"I hope you keep this in mind as we work to improve our abilities this semester," Luke concluded. "Now, with that addressed, let's jump right back into it. I want you to stretch and then start with our hand-to-hand combat routines from last semester. Caleb, you can catch Damian up on what those are. Then we'll move to some sword work after that. Matt and I will come around and offer suggestions as we did last semester. You may begin."

Gabriel and I stretched before facing each other to start our drills. I took a deep, fortifying breath and tried to tell myself that it'd be fine. I could do this. I had no reason to feel nervous. Gabriel and I had been working incredibly hard since the attack to build back my strength and endurance, and we'd made great progress. But this would still be my first time training in front of anyone else since the attack. And I definitely felt behind.

A warm smile spread over Gabriel's face as he read my expression. "You've got this," he murmured from across the mat. He looked confident, and his eyes told me that he believed in me. Warmth entered my chest, banishing some of the anxiety that'd taken root there, and I nodded at him, grateful that he was here with me. Then we squared off and began our drills.

Gabriel eased me in, wanting me to see that I'd gotten much stronger than I thought I had. He was trying to boost my confidence—something I didn't usually need when it came to my fighting skills, but this past month had really changed that for me. I'd never had to come back from such a large injury. It'd never taken me this long to recover before.

Once I was sufficiently warmed up, Gabriel pushed me hard, as he'd been going during our one-on-one practices. He forced me to move quickly and to think fast and critically about how to get out of certain holds or situations. And he pushed me on my endurance. While I still got tired sooner than I had before, and while I wasn't quite as strong as I'd been before, I was quickly catching up to Gabriel. He still ultimately beat me each time, but the fights were getting longer and longer, and it was getting harder and harder for him to win.

Neither Matt nor Luke came over to critique our forms as we fought, but I caught Matt watching us a lot, sometimes with concern—he hadn't seen my recovery, so I supposed his concern made sense—and sometimes with anger and hurt. Which . . . there was nothing I could do about. So, I tried to ignore his stares and focus on my fighting.

Gabriel ended another round of hand-to-hand combat spectacularly, by throwing me over his shoulder and onto the mat, then pinning me with his entire body weight, which, as a super tall and muscular man, was substantial. The wind was knocked from my lungs in a whoosh, and all I could do was stare up at his grinning face, my cheeks flushed. Gabriel's grin softened as his gaze traveled over my face.

"That was the best round yet," he murmured, still over me, his body heat soaking into me as he pressed me into the mat. "You came incredibly close to beating me. A couple more days of this and you'll be back at the level you were before the attack."

"Thank the gods for that," I panted, a mischievous smile pulling at my lips. "It's about time for you to be on the bottom again."

Gabriel's cheeks warmed, and his eyes turned molten as he leaned over and brushed his lips over mine, softly at first, and much deeper the second time.

"Terah! Gabriel!" a voice boomed, making us jump. "Get off your asses and come over here!" Damnit. It was Matt.

Gabriel rolled off me and shoved to his feet, rolling his eyes. He reached down and helped me up, then we walked over to Matt on the sidelines. He looked livid. Yeah, we probably shouldn't have been kissing during training, but still. That warranted a small telling off, not boiling rage.

"You two training together isn't working anymore." Matt's voice was as hard as stone as he looked between the two of us.

"Gods, Matt," Gabriel groaned, running a hand agitatedly through his dark hair, "it was just a kiss. Let it go."

Matt's hands clenched into fists. "That's not what I'm talking about. You're not pushing Terah hard enough. You're being soft with her because of the attack and because you're together. And that's not acceptable. She needs to be pushed if she's going to get back up to speed and not die in the war."

I scowled at Matt. He was being completely unfair. And inaccurate. Gabriel was pushing me plenty hard.

"You're full of shit," Gabriel ground out, angrily. He crossed his arms over his chest and leveled a glare at Matt. "I'm pushing her incredibly hard. Of course I don't want her to get hurt, but I also want her to survive future battles. I want her to be well trained too. But you know that. That's not what this is really about. *You* just don't want Terah and me to be together, and you don't want to have to see us together. Cut the crap."

Matt's eyes flashed dangerously, though his cheeks reddened, proving that Gabriel had pegged his intentions correctly. "Maybe you've forgotten," he said, his voice a deadly calm, "but I'm your trainer, Gabriel. I have authority over you in this room. What I say goes. I don't give a shit what you think about it. And what I say, is that you and Terah won't be training together anymore."

They glared at each other, and I felt like it'd probably only end when one of them attacked the other.

"Matt, come on," I cut in, frustrated. "You're being unreasonable. You know I wouldn't let him go easy on me. You know how much my training means to me. Don't do this."

Matt's hard gaze turned on me, and I was blasted with the full force of his anger and hurt. And I knew he wouldn't change his mind. He couldn't handle seeing Gabriel and me together, and he'd use his professional authority to make sure he wouldn't have to. I shook my head sadly, anger bubbling through my veins. This wasn't going to end well. Not if it continued like this. So I reached out to him in my mind. I wanted to reason with him in a place where he felt less defensive.

"*Matt*," I murmured silently.

"*No!*" Matt shouted as he felt me trying to connect. The hurt he felt was too much. He couldn't let me see. He didn't want me to know how much I'd wrecked him.

My heart clenched painfully as Matt shoved me out of his mind and slammed the door between us.

"There's no one else to train with," I said, out loud this time, trying to shake off the haunting glimpse of Matt's sadness. "Come on, Matt, this doesn't make any sense."

But Matt had a gleam in his eyes that I didn't like. "Caleb! Damian! Come over here please." He didn't break eye contact with me.

Dread swiftly crashed over me, sending a chill down to my bones. *Oh no. Please no.* He wasn't so far gone that he'd do that to me, was he? I glanced at Gabriel. He was trying to keep his expression neutral, but I could see the dread in his eyes too, and the tight clench of his jaw.

Caleb and Damian walked over to us, Caleb looking confused and Damian looking . . . intrigued and mildly entertained? I gave him a hard, distrustful look before turning back to Matt.

"We're switching up training partners," Matt said shortly to Damian and Caleb.

Caleb glanced at me, tense concern in his eyes. He didn't want to train with me any more than I wanted to train with him. I waited, eyeing Matt warily. I'd prefer to train with Damian over Caleb any day, which was saying a lot, as I didn't trust Damian either.

Matt met my gaze again, his eyes glittering dangerously. They were colder than I'd ever seen them. "Terah, you'll be training with Caleb. Gabriel, you'll be training with Damian."

My stomach dropped and anger boiled through me. *Seriously?* I understood Matt was hurt, but this was going too far. Way too far. He knew my history with Caleb. And he used to care. Now, all he seemed to care about was hurting me and Gabriel as much as he felt we'd hurt him, just by falling in love with each other. And it was bullshit.

"No," Gabriel said, his voice deadly. He took an ominous step closer to Matt. "I'll train with Caleb. Don't be a jackass. Terah should train with Damian."

I glanced at Damian, who had an eyebrow raised in a slightly bemused manner as he watched this all go down. He clearly didn't give a shit about the outcome.

"No, she shouldn't." Matt's voice was like ice. "She'll train with Caleb because I said so. And you'll train with Damian. If you say another word against it, I'll kick you out of this group, Gabriel. Test me on that, and you'll be *very* sorry."

I reached out and grabbed Gabriel's arm. "It's okay," I murmured as he turned and looked at me. I hadn't seen him this upset in a while.

"It's *not*, though," he said, forcefully. "It's—"

"I know," I cut him off. We both knew it wasn't actually okay. But we didn't have a choice. Matt had the power here. "But I'll be okay." I tried to ignore the rest of the group's gazes.

"Trust me," I murmured in his mind. *"It'll be okay."*

Gabriel's eyes softened a little, and he nodded. *"I trust you."*

I offered him a small smile and slid my hand down his arm, wrapping my fingers around his.

"Everything okay over there?" Luke yelled from the other end of the room.

Matt turned to look at him. "It's all good. Just changing up some training partners."

Luke studied Matt for a moment, then nodded and turned back to the group he'd been working with.

"Let's go," Matt said, his voice hard as he turned back to us. "Break into your new training groups and get back to work."

Caleb heaved a deep sigh and turned to walk back to the area of the mat that he and Damian had occupied. Damian shrugged and walked over to where Gabriel and I had been training. I sighed and turned to go, but Gabriel tugged on my hand and pulled me into him, wrapping his arms tightly around me. Then he kissed me with abandon. Right in front of Matt. I could feel all the tension, worry, and anger he was holding in his body, like he was a tightly wound coil, but as we kissed, and as I wrapped my arms around his neck, pressing close, I felt his tension easing and his muscles relaxing. I knew he was upset and didn't know what to do. I also knew that he'd mainly kissed me to get back at Matt by forcing him to see us together anyway. But that didn't bother me. Matt was out of line, and I wasn't going to let him think he'd won that easily.

We finally broke away from each other, breathless, our cheeks warm and our chests heaving. Gabriel smiled as he glanced at my lips, which were now tingling with heat, then tucked some of my hair behind my ear.

"Sorry," he murmured, before pressing a kiss to my forehead, "I probably shouldn't have done that."

I pressed a kiss against his shoulder through his shirt and squeezed his hand. "I don't mind." I smiled as I backed away and headed toward Caleb. Gabriel's smile was warm as he watched me go.

I glanced at Matt as I turned around. He looked like he'd just been stabbed. My stomach clenched, and I looked quickly away. A part of me felt guilty for forcing him to watch us make out, but that feeling faded as I glanced at Caleb and remembered that Matt was knowingly forcing me to spend time with and trust my body to someone who'd hurt me so deeply and intimately.

I took a deep breath as I approached Caleb and squared off with him on the mat. I could do this. It would suck, but I could do it. I'd just try not to think about how good Caleb was at fighting and how I was behind him at this point because of my long recovery. I'd try not to think about how we used to train together when we were younger. And how he'd used training to get close to me, physically and emotionally. Now, though, Caleb's face was a mask of coldness. He clearly knew, as I did, that this wasn't going to be easy, so he'd brought up his defenses fast and hard. *Good.* It was better this way. I'd try to do the same.

Caleb and I started our hand-to-hand combat fights in stony silence. But less than a minute into our first, I was astonished to realize that he was . . . holding back. Caleb had *never* pulled his punches before. Not even when we'd been dating and were training partners. It was only because of this that I managed to beat him within a few minutes, which shouldn't have happened at my current state of fitness. I shoved off him after he yielded and regarded him with disgust.

"Seriously? Come on, Caleb. I know what you're doing. Cut it out."

Caleb raised an eyebrow coolly at me but didn't say anything.

"Stop holding back," I growled. "Yeah, I'll probably lose continuously for a few days, but that's the only way I'll get back up to speed. So cut the shit and actually fight me. I need to train in earnest if I want to survive future battles."

Caleb stared at me for a long moment, his expression unreadable. Finally, he gave me a short nod and squared off with me again.

The next fight wasn't pretty. While I managed to hold out for a few minutes, I was just a hair slower than I usually was, which was all Caleb needed to thoroughly defeat me. He eventually slammed me forcefully into the ground, then pinned me so I couldn't move. I winced, my head twinging from where it'd hit the mat. But at least he wasn't holding back anymore. As painful, mentally and physically, as this would be, it'd help me get better fast.

We fought hand-to-hand a few more times, each fight ending with a hard trip to the mat for me, before Luke blew his whistle and called for the wooden practice swords to be brought out. Matt rolled out the racks of practice weapons, and all of us moved forward to grab swords.

Caleb and I squared off again, and I tried to ignore how much more tired I felt at this point in the training process than I usually did. I tried to remember that I needed to be patient with myself—that I'd almost died and therefore it was okay for me to be behind and have less endurance, but it was still pretty discouraging. I'd been top of my training class for years, and falling behind like this was emotionally taxing in a way I hadn't been prepared for. And it scared me. I had no idea when the next attack might be. What if I wasn't ready?

I shoved those thoughts from my mind and re-centered myself as Caleb and I circled each other. Caleb made the first move and swung his sword at me lightning fast. I blocked him and went on the offensive, striking quickly and fluidly, pushing him back. Forcing him to keep blocking instead of launching an attack. Caleb looked mildly impressed, then mildly annoyed. He'd never been one to take being bested well. After several minutes, it became clear that he and I were at a stalemate when it came to our sword work, so Caleb introduced more hand-to-hand combat elements into the fight. At first, I handled this pretty well. After all, this was also Gabriel's preferred method of sword fighting, so I was used to dealing with it. But it was that hair of reduced speed that finally got me.

Caleb swung his sword in a high arc over his head, attacking from above and forcing me to raise both arms to block him. But before I could sidestep the other attack I knew was coming, Caleb's leg came up and he kicked me forcefully in the stomach, sending me reeling backward. I landed hard on the mat, and only just managed to keep ahold of my sword. I tried to shove quickly to my feet, but Caleb was already there, and kicked me back again.

Before I could counter his attack, Caleb raised his sword above me with both hands, point down, and something inside me went cold. I was paralyzed as I watched him, as though in slow motion, bring down his sword over my stomach. I couldn't raise my sword to block him like he thought I would. I couldn't hear anything other than the loud pounding of my heartbeat in my head. And suddenly it wasn't Caleb over me, but the enormous Demon. Grinning horribly at me as it brought my own sword down over my stomach and impaled me to the ground.

I felt the impact of Caleb's training sword like I'd felt the impact of the Demon's sword. To me, they'd become one and the same. My sword fell from my hand with a clatter onto the mat as I gasped. Pain shot through me, amplified by the flashback I was having. I felt the agony and terror of being impaled like it was happening again—like a drawn-out, waking nightmare. And with it came that horrible certainty that I'd die. Alone.

When the horrors of the Demon's grinning face and the pooling of my own blood finally faded from my vision, and the training room came back into focus, I rolled over on the mat and threw up.

I heard Caleb swear and other footsteps hurrying toward me. I rolled back over onto my back, wiping my mouth on my sleeve. Well, this was embarrassing.

I looked up as Gabriel knelt next to me, worry bright in his eyes. He reached forward and took my shoulders in his hands.

"Terah, are you okay? What happened?" He looked down the length of me, trying to see if I was hurt anywhere. I sighed. No, I wasn't hurt, beyond my ego.

"I'm okay." I pushed onto my elbows, wincing a little at the bruise forming on my stomach from Caleb's training sword. "Just had a flashback of the last attack when Caleb stabbed me in the stomach." I shook my head, frustrated. "I should be over this by now."

Gabriel's expression turned stormy as he looked at Caleb, who'd walked over while I was speaking. Caleb stepped back as he saw Gabriel's murderous expression, and he held up both hands in surrender.

"I'm sorry," he said quickly, "I forgot. I didn't mean to—" He sighed and turned to look at me instead. "Really, I'm sorry, Terah."

I was surprised to see sincerity in his eyes along with the usual coldness. Honestly, I was surprised he'd bothered apologizing at all—that he even felt like he needed to. It wasn't something he did very often, if ever. I'd expected him to simply shrug and accuse me of showing weakness. Instead, the coldness in his eyes receded just a little.

"I thought you'd block me. I didn't—" He sighed deeply and held the bridge of his nose between his fingers for a second before looking at me again, slightly more composed. "I didn't mean to make you relive it."

It was the most genuine thing he'd said to me in close to four years. I was a bit stunned. I pushed into a sitting position and rubbed my hand across my stomach absently.

"It's okay. I told you not to hold back. It's not your fault."

Gabriel rubbed circles into my back as I took a few deep, calming breaths, trying to banish the echoes of the Demon attack from my head.

"Are you sure you're okay?" Gabriel asked. He still looked concerned, but the murderous expression hadn't gone—it'd grown.

"I'm okay. I promise. Just mad that I reacted that way."

Gabriel nodded and leaned over to press a soft kiss against my forehead. Then he pushed to his feet, shoved past Caleb, and made his way to Matt, who'd been watching us with a look that was half hard, like he didn't care what was happening, and half full of pain. Gabriel didn't even stop when he reached Matt. He just raised his arm and plowed his fist into Matt's face. Hard.

My mouth fell open. So did everyone else's in the room. Everyone seemed frozen. Shocked. No one knew how to process what was happening. Clearly, though, Gabriel blamed Matt for what I'd just experienced. And that was on top of everything else Matt had done to us today. After all, if Matt hadn't made me train with Caleb, this wouldn't have happened. Gabriel would've known not to stab me in the stomach. He would've known to avoid things that might make me relive my impaling—something he knew I still had nightmares about.

Matt wasted no time in attacking Gabriel back, and soon both were throwing hard punches at the other, both managing to draw blood. I shoved to my feet, my pulse racing. I needed to put a stop to this *now*. Before Gabriel got thrown out of the Academy. But I'd only made it a few steps toward them when Luke got there and pulled them apart.

"Enough!" he bellowed. "Matt, go outside and walk it off!" He grabbed Matt by the shirt and shoved him toward the training room door. Matt's nose was dripping blood, but he just wiped it on his sleeve. "You may return when training is over, after which you and I will have a chat. Now go!"

Matt was shaking with anger, but he followed Luke's orders and stormed out of the room.

"Gabriel, go to my office," Luke said firmly, after Matt was gone. "I'll come speak with you shortly."

Gabriel brought his hand up to wipe some blood from his lip. He nodded at Luke before turning to glance at me, remorse practically pouring from his eyes. I quickly connected our minds.

"*Gabriel,*" I murmured, letting him know I was there.

"*I'm so sorry, Terah,*" he said quickly. "*I shouldn't have done that. It was . . . pretty fucking reckless. I just kind of lost it.*"

"*It's okay. Are you hurt?*"

Gabriel gave me a sad but beautiful smile. "*Naw. Just foolish. I'll see you at lunch.*"

I nodded and offered him a small smile before he turned and walked to Luke's office. I hoped he wouldn't get into too much trouble. But if they kicked him out for what he'd done—which would be supremely unwise after everything he'd done to protect the school—I knew I'd leave the Academy with him.

Luke walked over to Caleb and me and motioned for Damian to join us. Then he bent and waved his hand over my vomit, dark green power shimmering around his fingers, and matter shifted it into ash. He encased it with his power and sent it on a wave of green to the trash can near the locker room doors.

"Right," he said matter-of-factly, as he turned to the three of us. "I think I know what happened to lead to that fight, but I'll arrange for a meeting with you if anything is unclear after I speak with both Matt and Gabriel. Until then, I want the three of you to train with each other for the last half hour of today. We'll work out who will train with whom from here on out after I meet with those two." He nodded in the direction of his office.

Luke then turned to address the rest of the room, which was no longer filled with training. People were grouped together, talking about what they'd just seen, and shooting Caleb, Damian, and I curious looks. This was much more drama than our training room usually saw. Well, at least since Caleb had almost killed a fellow student last semester. And this time, the drama involved one of our instructors. People were ravenous for the details. I stared grimly back and crossed my arms over my chest.

"Everyone listen up," Luke called, his voice filling and quieting the room. "You will resume training. Now. You will train for another half an hour, at which point you may all see yourselves out to head to lunch. I will be out of the room for the rest of our session to deal with this mess. If there are any serious problems, you may come get me."

With that, he turned and strode toward his office. Everyone returned to their spaces on the mats, and before long, the sounds of fighting—controlled this time—filled the room again. I turned to Caleb and Damian. Caleb's cold mask was back, and Damian was regarding me with a mild, partially bored expression. But it didn't seem like he was going to ask about what'd just happened, so that was good.

"How do you want to do this?" Damian asked, looking from me to Caleb. "Do we want to fight each other all at once, or would you prefer taking turns? I'm used to both, so I have no preference."

I chewed my lip, considering. What'd just happened—specifically my reaction to Caleb stabbing me in the stomach—was really bothering me. And this might be my one chance to address it. It'd be exposing myself, making myself vulnerable with two people I didn't trust, but I was maybe willing to do that if it'd help me in the long run. Which was . . . new for me.

"I need to ask a favor of you," I said, turning to Caleb, hating that I had to speak to him at all, let alone ask anything of him.

His eyes briefly widened, before he pulled out a heavily guarded mask. "What is it?" His tone told me that he didn't really want to know.

"I need you to stab me in the stomach a bunch more times."

This time, Caleb's cold mask slipped even further, and he looked alarmed and confused. Even Damian looked surprised.

"What? Why? Are you trying to get Gabriel to murder me? Because if I do that, he definitely will."

I smiled a little at this. Gabriel could be pretty damn protective, but I knew he wouldn't be pissed at Caleb if this was something I wanted.

"It'll be fine. He won't because I'm *asking* you to do this. I *need* you to do this. I can't . . . that can't be how I react every time that happens to me. I can't just freeze up. I need to work past it. The only way I can think of doing that is by exposing myself to it a lot. I need to take the edge off the experience. I need to make sure it doesn't have power over me anymore."

Caleb raised an eyebrow at me, his eyes cold. He looked unconvinced.

"Please." I winced internally. I hated being in any way at his mercy. It was truly painful. But I knew he'd be willing to do this to me—hurt me, that is—whereas Gabriel probably wouldn't. And I didn't want to hurt Gabriel by forcing him to do something that would upset him. He'd already sacrificed enough of his own mental and physical health during my recovery. But I had no qualms about making Caleb uncomfortable. "Come on, Caleb. I need you to do this. You know hurting me won't affect you the way it'll affect Gabriel."

Damian raised an eyebrow and looked at Caleb appraisingly. His mouth twitched slightly, like he was privy to a secret that I wasn't.

Caleb stared at me coldly for a few more seconds. I could almost feel the conflict and tension radiating off his body. Finally, he swore and broke eye contact.

"Fine," he snapped. "Whatever. I'll do it. But only while Gabriel isn't here. Or Matt," he added, rolling his eyes.

I smiled at Caleb, probably for the first time in close to four years. "Thanks."

Caleb looked away from me quickly.

"And what about you?" I turned to Damian. "Want to join in?"

Damian shrugged. "Sure, why not." He gripped his sword and twirled it around in his hand a couple times, looking supremely unconcerned. "Two on one?"

"That's fine," I said, knowing they'd murder me. Figuratively, that is. But I supposed that was the point. I needed to snap out of this debilitating fear brought on by the Demon attack. I wouldn't be able to fight as well if it was hanging over me, clouding my judgment and dampening my abilities.

I turned and grabbed my sword from the mat, then faced the two of them. Adrenaline rushed through my body as I took a centering breath. I almost felt excited. The call of a challenge, especially a fighting challenge, was one of my favorite things. And this was bound to be one.

Caleb positioned himself in front of me, while Damian stepped behind me. Then they started circling me. I kept my sword at the ready and kept a watchful eye on each of them. Damian moved first, feinting right, then lunging at me from the left. I managed to block his blow and sent an additional kick at him, which he dodged, before I spun and blocked a simultaneous blow from Caleb. I disconnected my sword from Caleb's and quickly swept it behind me, correctly guessing at Damian's next strike. I blocked it just in time. I was already impressed. Damian was *fast*.

I dropped suddenly to the ground, sweeping my leg out at Caleb and my sword out at Damian. Damian blocked the surprise blow, but I managed to sweep Caleb's legs. He rolled to his feet quickly as I spun on my knees and blocked Damian's next strike. I hadn't been able to fully stand before he'd swung at me again. Damian pressed down, trying to use his body weight to force me to the ground. With a growl, I shoved to my feet, pushing his sword up and away from me. Then I spun out of range of Caleb's swinging sword.

We went on like this for several minutes, each trying to attack me, and me just managing to fend them off and get in a few smaller attacks of my own. I was pleased, though, that I was holding out this long at my current state of fitness. It felt good to push myself like this. A couple weeks ago, I wouldn't have been able to hold my own against even one of them, let alone two. Holding out this long was a good sign that I was quickly regaining my old strength and skill.

Eventually, though, they managed to work together enough to disarm me and for Damian to restrain me. Then, true to his word, Caleb shoved the tip of his practice sword at my stomach. My stomach heaved as nausea hit me, and I clamped my hand over my mouth. Cold shivers raced through my body and my knees went weak as Damian held me up, the Demon's horrible laugh echoing through my mind. But a fierce stubbornness took over, and I shook myself, forced the bile back down my throat, and forced my legs to hold me again.

Damian released me, and both men looked at me, a little uncertainly.

"Okay," I panted, wiping cold sweat from my forehead. I shook my head to clear it. "That wasn't quite as bad. Again."

Both looked at me, surprised. I might've even seen a shadow of respect in each of their gazes. Or maybe they just thought I'd lost my mind. Who knew.

Caleb and Damian circled me, and we began again. Each time we fought, they managed to disarm and restrain me, and one or both of them would shove their swords at my stomach. But it took longer and longer each time for them to manage that. I was getting better and better at fending them off, perhaps because I was becoming less scared of how it'd hurt when they eventually beat me. Yeah, it sucked, but it was manageable. I'd survive. I'd dealt with the same pain a thousand times before, and I was beginning to remember and believe I'd be able to deal with it a thousand times again. Each time they stabbed my stomach, my reaction was smaller. Finally, by the end of the half hour, I didn't have a reaction at all. Just a slight wince at the bruises that were forming on my torso. But even that didn't really bother me. The pain was so small compared to most other battle injuries. They'd heal in a couple minutes anyway.

I felt much closer to being back to my normal self than I had in my recovery thus far, and thanks to two people I didn't really trust or care for. *Who would've thought.* I thanked them, as each watched me like they couldn't quite figure me out, then hung my practice sword on the rack and headed to the locker rooms.

I showered quickly then grabbed my stuff and headed down to lunch. Gabriel was waiting for me at the bottom of the stone stairs near the dining hall doors. He'd changed back into his normal clothes and was leaning casually against the wall with his arms crossed over his chest. He had a laid-back smile waiting for me. Hopefully it meant that he hadn't been punished too harshly.

"Hey." He wrapped his arms around me and pulled me into him.

I smiled. "Hey yourself."

He had a small scab on his lip where Matt's fist had split it. My smile turned rueful, and I touched it with the tip of my finger, releasing a small stream of power. In a couple seconds, the scab and traces of swelling and bruising were gone.

"Thanks," Gabriel murmured, lifting my chin for a soft kiss. "Though I probably deserved to keep it. That was a pretty bad move on my part."

I laughed and took his hand, then led him into the dining hall. "I mean, it wasn't the most well thought out thing you've ever done," I teased, "but I can't blame you. Matt had me really wanting to punch him in the face today too."

Gabriel smiled, shaking his head a little self-deprecatingly. "Still, Luke almost killed me. Though he'd pretty much correctly guessed what'd happened to lead up to that fight. Seems like he's been more observant about our dynamics in training this past semester than I've given him credit for. He basically just shouted at me a bit about how irresponsible it was to start a fight, especially with a staff member, then told me not to do it again, or he'd seriously consider kicking me out of the training group. Then he asked me what I'd prefer to have happen in terms of training partners, and I said I'd prefer to be yours again. He said he'll be speaking with Matt about what happened, and he'll decide how he wants to move forward after that. So I guess we'll just have to see what he decides at training tomorrow. It could've been much worse, though. I get the feeling that I got off pretty damn easily."

I nodded. It sounded like it. But overall, I was relieved.

"That's good." I started piling food onto my plate. "I mean, I was prepared to leave the Academy with you if they kicked you out, but I'm glad it didn't come to that." I shot him a teasing smile. To my surprise, Gabriel's cheeks warmed, and he seemed momentarily at a loss for words.

"If you don't want me to make out with you in public," he finally murmured, his voice deep as he leaned down to brush his lips against my ear, "then you'll have to stop saying things like that in public." His free hand curled around my waist, pulling me against him.

I laughed, even as a warm shiver raced through me. To be fair, I'd never told him *not* to kiss me in public. Perhaps he was trying to prevent even more attention being drawn to us, which he knew I hated.

"Fine, I'll keep my romantic declarations inside until we're not in public." I rolled my eyes in pretend exasperation, but I turned and raised onto the balls of my feet, then pressed a lightning-fast kiss against his lips anyway, before moving down the line like nothing had happened. I caught Gabriel's smile as he followed me.

Training the next day was . . . awkward. Matt and Gabriel wouldn't look at each other, and the rest of the training group couldn't stop staring at them. Luke had forbidden Matt from talking to us in training unless it was an absolutely necessary, professional comment about our fighting forms. And Matt, as both an assistant professor *and* a ranking member of the warrior faction, was not taking this restriction on his authority well. He was practically fuming on the sidelines. But I had little sympathy for him. He'd abused his power, so the restrictions seemed appropriate.

Luke had also determined that both Matt and Gabriel had some valid points when it came to who we should train with and why. Luke had been at an impasse until, apparently, Damian had arrived early to the training room with the idea that the four of us could swap partners with each other each day. That way, Gabriel and I would still be training together sometimes, but not every day. This gave Matt a break from seeing us together while also keeping each of us on our toes by forcing us to deal with different fighting styles each day. It wasn't a horrible idea in theory, but the fact that I'd be forced to train with Caleb regularly made me supremely unhappy. Besides, I really liked training with Gabriel. I deeply resented having to give that up. But Luke grabbed Damian's idea and ran with it, officially implementing it immediately.

So, with a heavy sigh, I prepared to train with Damian, while Gabriel went to train with Caleb. We stretched in silence, though I noted Damian closely scrutinizing me. Occasionally, I felt gentle pushes at the edges of my mind, but I always pushed back, blocking out whatever it was. I had no idea whether he was responsible for it, but I instinctively resisted it. Damian's scrutiny of me made me feel like I was some weird puzzle he was trying to figure out. And that there were stakes in it for him. It was incredibly possible that the High Light Guardian had instructed him, as she'd done with Caleb, to try getting

364

close to us to determine whether we knew more about the attacks than we were letting on, or to see if I'd disclose more about my unique abilities to someone who wasn't her. It was also possible that she'd asked Damian to report on me since Matt was no longer near me enough to do so.

"So," Damian said, as we faced each other and began our drills, "I was talking to Caleb, and he said you were at every Demon attack last semester." He watched me appraisingly, his gaze steady and cold as he moved through the drills like they were as natural for him as breathing. I could tell he wasn't even thinking about them, he was just waiting for me to respond.

I raised an eyebrow at him and studied him coolly. "Why do you care about that?"

Damian eyed me almost contemptuously. "Seriously? I care because it's the only reason I came here—to help mount a defense for the school. Seems like I should know what's going on so I can figure out how to do that."

I narrowed my eyes at him. "Seems like the president should've briefed you. Or the warrior faction. That's not my job. And I don't appreciate you talking to Caleb about me," I added, as we spun around each other, continuing our drills. "We have a bad history, and I don't like him anywhere near me or my life."

"Noted," Damian said blandly, though he seemed neither surprised nor affected by this information. "And the president did brief me, but barely. She just said there were a variety of Demon attacks last semester that grew in intensity each attack, and that students had been forced to defend the school. That's basically it."

I shrugged. "Sounds accurate to me."

Damian rolled his eyes and shook his head. Yes, I was being difficult on purpose. But I had my reasons. I wasn't going to give him information until I knew whether or not I could trust him. Especially information that he couldn't get easily otherwise.

"So, I guess you're not going to tell me anything." It was more a statement than a question.

I smiled at him coolly. "See, you're getting to know me already."

To my surprise, Damian almost smiled. Apparently, it was a surprise to him too, as a second later, his cool mask was firmly back in place, all signs of humor gone.

"I'm guessing you have no idea why they've suddenly started attacking the school?" he pushed, as we continued circling each other, striking, blocking, repeating.

"No fucking idea. Just seems like everyone in this war, no matter what side they're on, is looking for a new front. Like we aren't all killing each other enough as it is," I added bitterly.

Damian stared at me, pausing for a moment mid-drill. He looked . . . genuinely surprised. But he caught himself quickly and began moving again, the cold mask descending once more.

"I thought all people at the Academy were Light Guardian enthusiasts." He eyed me curiously. "But it doesn't seem like you fall into that camp."

I shrugged and blocked his strike with my arm. "No side is above criticism at this point. And I have my own moral compass. I don't need it dictated to me by any one group of Divines."

"Yet you fight for the Light Guardians," he said shrewdly, raising an eyebrow at me.

I thought about this for a moment. That'd certainly been true in the past—that was basically my whole life in Dagmar—but I wasn't so sure it was true anymore. I wasn't willing to be used by the Light Guardians as I'd let myself be before. I wasn't willing to blindly follow orders anymore. And Gabriel had opened my eyes to the many flaws and failings of the Light Guardian side that I'd never known about or considered before. Because of that, I'd never be willing to join the warrior faction, as I'd initially planned. I'd never trust them enough to submit myself permanently and unconditionally to their orders.

"I used to," I finally said. "Now I'm committed to fighting for those who can't fight for themselves and using my abilities according to my own moral compass. Sometimes that aligns with the Light Guardians, sometimes it doesn't. I choose when and how I want to help. They don't get to decide that for me."

Damian considered me silently as we continued our drills. He seemed lost in thought, though I couldn't tell where his mind was going.

"Are you saying you're not on any side in particular, then?" he finally asked, his expression carefully bland. "You're not implicitly loyal to any side?"

I narrowed my eyes at him. I couldn't tell what emotion was behind those words, or what his motivation was. But it felt like he had one. And for the first time, I thought about trying to get into *his* mind. I wanted to see where he was coming from. Why he was pushing this.

Gingerly, I opened my mind outward only, not leaving a path open in the other direction, and tried to prod quietly into his thoughts. Damian's eyes narrowed almost imperceptibly, but otherwise his expression remained the same. But I couldn't get in. All I could feel was a smooth wall around his thoughts. Like cold, polished stone—impenetrable like a fortress. It was startling. No other person's mind had ever looked like that. No one else had been so efficiently guarded. I carefully kept my expression blank and closed my mind. On the off chance that he'd felt the push from my mind, I didn't want him to know it was from me. Or that I'd failed.

"My morals align more closely with the Light Guardians," I finally said, straightening up as Luke blew the whistle to end the drills. "I care about protecting Normals, not killing or controlling them like the Dark Guardians. But that doesn't mean that I'm willing to blindly follow the Light Guardians. Nor does it mean that I think they're right all the time. Every situation calls for analysis. And fighting for improvement within the group seems to me to be as important as fighting for improvement outside the group. Whether or not the Light Guardians see it that way."

Damian frowned but didn't respond.

"You're from a border town," I said as we waited for Matt to roll out the racks of practice weapons. Today we'd be using daggers. "You fight for the Light Guardians as well. Do you blindly follow *your* orders?" I raised an eyebrow shrewdly at him. It'd felt like he'd been judging me for my role on the Light Guardian side. But his situation was the same as mine.

Damian shrugged noncommittally. "I suppose I do. The price of where I was born. And to whom," he added, an edge of bitterness to his voice, his eyes the coldest I'd seen them. "We don't all have a choice."

I frowned. It sounded like his parents were border town enthusiasts like my mother. They were the ones who rejoiced in raising their children in the thick of war zones, forcing them to reckon with the front lines of war at impossibly young ages. They believed their children would be the next great generation of soldiers. That they'd be revered as heroes and would obtain high rank and notoriety. But the reality was that they'd probably just die super young. And if they didn't, they'd be pretty damn fucked up. But border town enthusiasts often forgot about that part. Or didn't truly care. They tended to care about rank and power more than their own children.

"I thought that too," I said quietly, as we raised our daggers and took

367

our starting stances, waiting for Luke to blow the whistle again. "That I didn't have a choice. I believed that until I came to the Academy."

Luke blew the whistle and Damian and I circled each other, daggers at the ready.

"My mother abandoned me in the worst border town in the country when I was a baby because she wanted to forge me into the best warrior possible—to be an obedient weapon more than a person." I grimaced.

Damian's brow furrowed slightly as he considered me. I lunged and struck out with my daggers, and we fought back and forth for a bit until we both pushed back and circled each other again.

"She mostly succeeded," I continued, "until I came here and started questioning all that. When I finally had some separation from my border town, I began taking more ownership over myself and my power, and I started truly appreciating that it's mine to choose what to do with and whom to fight for. It was also when I realized the Light Guardians have upheld cruel policies that've left people behind and without support. And . . . I finally realized I don't have to go back to Dagmar if I don't want to. They can't force me to go back—not now that I'm an adult. And if they try, they'll be supremely sorry," I added, my voice going hard.

Damian observed me neutrally for a moment before lashing out with his daggers, lightning fast. He gave no warning before the attack. Nothing about his manner or expression gave him away. But I managed to block him, and went through another round of intense, back-and-forth maneuvers, neither of us gaining more ground than the other. Damian was incredibly skilled and incredibly fast, but so was I. I used daggers most often when I fought Demons in my non-transformed state. I was good with them. And I'd almost completely recovered my old speed and strength.

We finally broke away from each other again, realizing that neither of us was going to win that round. But we had a newfound, if grudging, respect for each other's fighting abilities.

"For someone who doesn't share things with strangers," Damian said coolly, circling me again, "you sure spilled a lot of info about yourself."

I glared at him. He was baiting me, because deep down, I'd upset him with what I'd said. I wasn't sure which part had gained his ire, but I felt instinctively that a part of it had. But I'd also shared with a purpose, and I'd been careful about how much I'd revealed. His words had reminded me so much of my own thought processes—of feeling stuck, used, and alone— that I'd wanted to reveal there could be another way. That maybe he didn't have to go back to wherever he'd escaped from. And I'd seen him in my visions so often that I felt like I owed him some advice, since he'd be around a lot. But based on Damian's cool amusement, bordering on disgust, I'd wasted the information on him.

I calmly circled him. "I only revealed basic and well-known things about my life for *your* benefit. Take or leave them. It literally doesn't affect me at all. I don't give a shit about your world view and your life choices. But you started this conversation, so I finished it. Next time, you could spare us both and just not talk."

I lashed out with my daggers before he could respond, taking him slightly off guard. I moved with increasing speed as I launched attack after attack, moving continuously, striking, slashing, and dodging with smooth speed. Damian kept up with me, but only just. I was duly impressed, though. Basically anyone else would've been defeated immediately. But Damian moved with instinct and obvious, immense practice.

I finally saw an opening and took it. I twisted my dagger forcefully around his, causing it to fly from his hand, then I kicked his other dagger, so he lost his grip on it. It flew in an arc and landed on the mat several feet away. Then I launched myself at him and brought the points of both daggers down where his shoulders met his neck and violently twisted them around the circumference of his neck. If they'd been real, he'd have been dead. And decapitated. As it was, he'd probably have bruises.

Damian stared at me, his eyes wide, and I saw a flicker of fear there. I suspected it'd been a *long* time since anyone had bested him in a fight. He was scared, not so much of me, but of what his defeat just now might mean. I was familiar with this type of fear since my injury—the fear that you were slipping, that you weren't good enough. But he had nothing to worry about on that front. He was one of the most amazing fighters I'd ever encountered. But he'd made me mad. And angry me could be *very* hard to defeat. Anger made me sharper, faster, and more lethal. Anger removed my inhibitions.

I smiled sweetly at Damian, baiting *him* this time, but I knew my eyes were cold and hard. Like his, for once. I'd given him a chance, which was more than I usually did for strangers, and he'd decided to be shitty about it. I didn't plan on giving him any more chances. If he wanted anything from me, he'd have to do all the work. And I wouldn't make it easy for him. I might've opened up a little more over the last few months, but my openness had its limits, for everyone except Gabriel.

Damian eyed me warily. I could see he'd realized he'd fucked up when it came to dealing with me. And he seemed frustrated more than anything else. He closed his eyes for a second and took a deep, calming breath.

"You're right," he finally said, opening his eyes again and ignoring for a moment how he'd just lost. "I did start it. And I did push you to share. Talking about being trapped and being forced to follow orders . . . puts me on edge," he added quietly.

He looked deeply uncomfortable. Like both apologizing and sharing how he felt were uncommon and unwelcome things for him. He bent to retrieve his daggers, his shoulders and jaw stiff. He wouldn't meet my eyes. But I had the sneaking suspicion that he was telling the truth for once.

"Anyway," he said, straightening up and facing me again, "sorry for being an ass. It's my natural state, I guess." He shrugged, a ghost of a smile appearing on his face.

"Wow, an *intentional* joke from the stoic Damian?" I feigned shock, placing my hand against my chest. "I didn't think you knew what humor was."

Damian leveled a glare at me, but there was no real animosity in his eyes for once. Just a flicker of amusement.

"I have no idea how Gabriel stands you," he finally said, shaking his head slowly in mock confusion, the corner of his mouth twitching in an almost smile.

"True love," I deadpanned. "And a great ass." I sent an exaggerated wink at him.

Damian mimed throwing up. "I'm sorry I asked." But the coldness in his eyes had receded slightly.

Against my better judgment, I felt myself smiling.

17
TEAM-UP

As we reached the end of February, the frost covering campus slowly thawed, turning the sharp edges of ice and the frosted ground into pools of mud and water, revealing the grass that'd browned during winter. The air started to warm a bit, not hurting our faces quite as much when the wind whipped by us. The sun was also peeking through the clouds more, allowing occasional beams of warmth and light to pierce the depressing gray that covered campus like a shroud. And with the increase in sunshine and the warming of the weather—along with the lack of further Demon attacks—the general mood on campus started to lift.

After a particularly grueling day of training, power-usage-heavy classes, and transformation training, Gabriel and I blew off studying and headed to the lounge for some much-needed relaxation. It was only Thursday, but the increased workload had us beyond ready for the weekend. Unfortunately, it looked like the rest of the school had had the same idea.

I scowled as we pushed open the door to the lounge and saw just how crowded it was.

"I think I see a table in the back corner," Gabriel murmured.

He took my hand and started forward, using his body to push through the crowd, leading me behind him. People stared at us and whispered as we passed—they hadn't stopped doing this since the start of the semester—but we did our best to ignore them. We were getting used to it at this point. When we reached the empty table in the back corner, Gabriel pulled me against him and wrapped his long arms around me. I smiled, surprised at his public display of affection.

"Are you okay?" I murmured against his shoulder, wrapping my arms around his waist.

"Mhmm." I felt the press of his lips against the top of my head. "Just had a long day. And I'm feeling extra grateful that I have you in my life."

My smile broadened, and I pressed a kiss to his shoulder. He was usually only this open when we were alone. "And I'm grateful to have you in mine. Who else could make me laugh after an afternoon filled with almost setting myself on fire."

I pulled back in time to see Gabriel's exasperated laugh. I'd told him over dinner about the larger things I'd been practicing in transformation training. He'd been intrigued, but also frustrated that I'd put myself in harm's way.

"I'm glad I can offer that service," he teased, a rueful smile pulling at his lips.

I bit my lip as I looked at his smile, and warmth pooled in my stomach. I tried not to think about the texture of his lips, the heat of his mouth, how it felt against my skin. I swallowed. I was failing.

"Sorry," Gabriel murmured, his voice going hoarse. I met his eyes again and saw that they'd gone molten, matching the heat currently churning through my body. He'd noticed my gaze. And my want. "I think I've passed the point of not making out with you in public."

I barely had time to laugh before his lips captured mine. And then I no longer cared about anyone else around us. I no longer cared that we were surrounded by about a hundred students and various teachers. I didn't even care that some people were probably still watching. All I cared about was the feel of Gabriel's lips against mine. How they firmly pulled, softly nibbled, coaxed me to let him in deeper. To let him take the kiss soul deep. And I always did. Because it was what I wanted too.

Gabriel finally pulled back, his chest heaving. But I stepped forward, grabbed the front of his jacket, and leaned up to kiss him one more time, a slow, lingering kiss that promised much more. For later. I released him and sent him a mischievous smile as I slid into the empty chair next to me. Gabriel's smile was heated, his cheeks still flushed. He pulled off his jacket and placed it on the back of the other chair. The sleeves of his black shirt were pushed up to his elbows, so I could admire his tattooed forearms. I bit the inside of my cheek and tried to take a deep, calming breath to steady my pounding heart. But gods, he made me want to fan myself.

"I'll get the first round," Gabriel said, his voice a little gravely, his eyes still heated as they met mine.

He tilted my chin up to kiss me one more time as he passed my chair, almost as though he truly couldn't help it. I smiled and watched him as he walked over to the bar. He moved confidently and gracefully, cutting through the packed crowd like it was nothing.

But my smile faded as I saw Matt sitting alone at the far end of the bar. He was glaring daggers at Gabriel as he approached, and he had . . . a broken glass in his hand—like he'd squeezed it too hard until he'd crushed it. Beer dripped from the bar onto the ground in front of him, but he didn't seem to notice. My stomach sank as I realized our rather intense public kiss had probably been the reason for his reaction and the glass's demise. Guilt turned my stomach into a collection of knots. It wasn't actually my goal to make Matt suffer more than he already was. It wasn't like we'd seen him and done it on purpose. We'd been too wrapped up in each other and the strangers staring at us to notice him. Gabriel was ignoring Matt's pointed glare, so I swallowed hard and looked away from him as well.

But no sooner had I glanced away, than my gaze slammed into Caleb's. He was sitting at a table in the middle of the room with Damian and a group of Caleb's followers. Damian was lounging back in his chair, sipping his beer, looking bored as he generally ignored the rest of the group. He did glance between Caleb, Matt, and Gabriel once though, and I wondered how much his bored expression was a mask for what he was really thinking and feeling. He always seemed to know what was going on around him.

Caleb's gaze, though, surprised me. We'd been forced to train together a lot more these past few weeks, so we'd naturally had to interact more than either of us wanted to, but he'd been pretty consistent about ignoring me at all other times. Given this, the directness of his gaze was startling. But his expression was even more so. He looked . . . almost shaken. Like he'd just realized something he'd rather not have realized. But as I stared back, he seemed to remember himself. He snapped his mouth shut and turned purposefully away from me, his jaw clenching, and his shoulders stiffening. Damian glanced at him appraisingly before looking away again, his expression unreadable. I wondered, briefly, if Caleb was reacting to my kiss with Gabriel as well.

I looked away, focusing instead on the table in front of me. I traced my finger lightly over a deep scratch in the shiny lacquer covering the dark wood and tried not to blush. It really wasn't ideal that all of us, with our complicated histories with each other, were forced to live and train in such close proximity. It made everything more difficult. It made it harder to just be myself when I was constantly questioning how my actions would affect certain people around me. Whether or not I'd make people unhappy—people who certainly weren't too bothered by how their own actions affected me. I was mad that I even cared. But I couldn't seem to help caring, at least a little.

Gabriel returned with two beers and sat across from me. His own expression seemed dampened as well, and I wondered how much he'd also seen Matt and Caleb's reactions. Probably as much as I had. He *was* one of the most observant people I'd ever met. I wondered how much it affected him—the visible reminder that us being together and happy made other people unhappy. But he managed to lift the corner of his mouth in a small smile as he slid his glass forward across the table and clinked it against mine.

"Happy Thursday," he murmured before taking a large sip.

I smiled a little and took a sip as well. It was very good—a medium brown color this time, with dark fruit and spice notes, and a slightly boozy finish.

"Mmm." I closed my eyes and took another sip. "This is perfect."

Gabriel's smile was warmer when I opened my eyes. "Glad you like it. The bartender recommended it, so I thought it would be worth a try."

"Definitely worth a try."

We sat in silence for a little bit, taking hearty sips of our beers while trying to look tough and unbothered. Inwardly, though, I knew we were both trying to ignore the array of conflict-filled emotions that surrounded us on all sides. From Matt, from Caleb, from Damian, from every damn person who couldn't mind their own business and put their gazes somewhere else. But finally, Gabriel seemed to pull himself back together. He pulled his chair around the small table, so he was sitting more next to me than across from me, and the expanse of his back did wonders to block people's view of us and our conversation. And we finally relaxed enough to talk again.

Finally, after midnight came and went, and after the lounge had cleared out considerably, Gabriel and I decided to head back to the room we now shared. As we donned our jackets, I allowed myself to look around for the first time since I'd noticed Matt, Caleb, and Damian earlier. It looked like Matt had left at some point, but Caleb and Damian were still sitting and sipping beers where they'd been before, engaged in conversation, now that the rest of Caleb's followers had left. It was a little weird seeing them both talking so much to another person, but they'd become friends over the past few weeks—well, as much as either of them could ever be friends with another—and spent most of their time together. It helped that Damian was such an exceptional fighter, and that he seemed to secretly enjoy helping us improve when he trained with us, almost despite himself. Caleb had quickly recognized how much having Damian and his skills close might benefit him down the road, so he'd embraced him as a friend faster than usual.

Apart from them, there were only a few other students left in the lounge. Most had gone, probably grudgingly realizing they'd still have to get up early for training in the morning. I slid my hand into Gabriel's as we walked back through the lounge, trying to ignore Caleb and Damian's gazes, and out the doors into the clear, starry night.

The breeze whispered past us, stirring our hair, and bringing the smell of the newly spouted grass and damp earth past our noses. The air still had a chill to it, but there was also a hint of warmth—of jacketless summer nights to come. I took a deep, calming breath, as I let my eyes slide closed. Winter was too damn long, and I had a deep yearning for the warmth. To spend time in the sun again. To not have to wear so many damn layers.

Gabriel and I took a meandering path back toward the dorms, savoring the freshness of the night air.

"I wish all our nights could be like this." I tilted my head back to look at the stars twinkling above us. "Spending time together. Planning for the future. Not planning everything around the war."

The corner of Gabriel's mouth pulled up in a wistful smile. "That would be nice. Maybe someday that'll be our reality. A quiet, normal life together."

I looked up and met his gaze. His expression was surprisingly earnest, filled with hope and longing. A swell of bittersweet emotion rose within me, and my heart clenched. I wanted that too. A quiet, normal life with him. I bit the inside of my cheek and looked down at the damp grass beneath my feet. I'd never seriously considered what I wanted my future to look like. I'd never thought I'd survive that long. Or that I'd ever let anyone in again—that I'd let anyone close enough for another person to ever be a part of my dream. But now . . .

I sighed and pushed the thoughts away, even as longing for that future flooded me. I doubted it'd ever be possible. Not while we were embroiled in a violent, horrendous war that seemed to be getting worse by the day. We were soldiers, whether we liked it or not. These dreams weren't something I should think about or long for. There was no pint. It'd only hurt us. There was no point in wanting more than our war-torn existence would ever allow for.

I swallowed hard and pushed the thoughts as firmly as I could from my mind. Then I forced my mouth to curve into a halfhearted smile. It was the best I could do, given the circumstances. I looked up at Gabriel and forced my mouth to move.

"I hope so." It was all I could get out. I hoped it'd be enough. I hoped he wouldn't sense the depth of my despair—how much it hurt that these dreams weren't realistic for the life we led.

Gabriel's eyebrows furrowed as he watched me, and his steps slowed as he turned to face me. "Terah," he murmured, his voice filling with worry, "what's wr—"

A terrible shriek tore through the night air before he could finish his sentence. My eyes slid closed, even as my pulse surged into frenzied action. I honestly wasn't surprised anymore. It always felt like an inevitability now. Violence. War. And that it'd happened right after I'd dared to dream about a different kind of future was almost hilariously ironic. The universe certainly seemed keen on reminding me what my real priorities should be.

I bent and pulled my daggers from my boots, almost matter-of-factly, and turned to face the Demon that was already barreling toward us. It was pretty damn large, though nowhere near as large as the last Demon I'd faced. I took a deep, centering breath as I shifted into battle position. I was recovered enough now to face it confidently. The speed and strength I'd lost over my long recovery had been back for weeks. I could do this. And I knew Gabriel could too. But . . . I glanced over at him, watching as he swore and retrieved his own daggers from his boots. My heart squeezed with dread. Nothing was a sure thing. And I didn't want him to get hurt. I didn't want him to—

Gabriel's gaze slammed into mine as he straightened up, and I saw the same worry mirrored in his eyes. Seeing it there, knowing we were both feeling the same thing about each other, gave me strength somehow. I smiled a little at him, momentarily ignoring the pounding footsteps of the Demon as it approached.

"I love you. Be careful. If you die, I'll kill you."

The ghost of a smile appeared on Gabriel's lips. "I love you too. And likewise."

I shot him a grin before turning back to face the Demon. It was pretty much on us now. I took a deep breath and tried not to think about how alarming it was that, once again, the Demon had found us, specifically. We were also much closer to the dorms this time. We'd have to be vigilant and push the Demon away from the buildings. Once again, the defense of the school and the students was coming down on our shoulders. What the hell was the point of the warrior faction if they kept letting Demons through like it was nothing?

I took a deep breath, then ran at the Demon. It was around forty feet tall, with the same thick gunmetal gray skin and glowing red eyes that all Demons had. It only had two arms and two legs, but both were larger than the thickest tree trunks I'd ever seen and were heavily muscled. Both its hands and feet ended in giant, curled, sharp-looking claws. The Demon also had giant horns protruding from its forehead, curling back over its unruly, matted hair, and giant fangs that dripped with venom as they extended out of its mouth, down past its chin. I'd definitely want to avoid those.

The Demon released a scream that pierced my insides with cold dread and made my eardrums throb in protest. It ran at us, its sharp claws extended, preparing to strike. I forced my lungs to take in air, even as the Demon's continued screams made it difficult, and aimed carefully as I ran. Then I threw one of my long daggers as hard as I could at the Demon's neck. It lodged deep in the thick gray column, cutting off the Demon's scream mid-note. A horrible gurgling sound filled the air instead, but at least I could draw air freely again. I sent a wave of purple fire at the Demon, charring its neck, trying to deepen the wound the dagger had started, before wrapping my power around my dagger and pulling it through the air back to me.

The Demon's leg shot out at me, its taloned foot extended, but I threw myself out of the way in time, rolling across the damp grass. It bent and swiped its claws at me next, trying to slice deeply into me, but I created a shield around myself, and its claws glanced off it. I was getting better at this—at seamlessly integrating my power into my fighting without having to transform.

As I drew the Demon's attention, Gabriel repeatedly struck the Demon's leg with both his daggers, trying to remove its mobility. He managed to slice through about half of one leg, but its limbs were just so thick. The Demon, whose throat was quickly healing, let out a half gurgle, half roar. It turned from me and swiped its claws at Gabriel instead, the long, deadly talons gleaming in the moonlight. Gabriel threw himself out of the way just in time.

With a growl, I threw myself onto the back of the Demon's enormous leg, and started climbing it, stabbing my daggers deep into its skin and pulling myself up. I wanted to make it to its shoulders so I could behead it. I also wanted to distract it so it wouldn't attack Gabriel. The Demon screamed and spun, its arms flailing, trying to dislodge me from its back. I clung to my daggers' handles and winced as the Demon landed some pretty rough blows on my back, some involving its claws. But I could tell that none of the punctures were very deep. My jacket was thankfully providing a certain amount of protection.

Gabriel threw thick beams of electric blue fire at the Demon's leg, slowly burning through its skin and muscle, all the way down to the bone. Then he ran at what was left of its limb. With a yell, he brought down his daggers on the charred bone. This time, it cracked and gave way. The Demon screamed and jerked violently as it collapsed onto its knees, no longer able to sustain a full standing position. I clung to the Demon's shoulders as it jerked forward, and smiled. Gabriel had stopped the Demon from advancing on the dorms. Pride swelled in my chest. He was a damn good soldier.

I finally climbed over its shoulder and straddled it, then stabbed violently into the base of its neck, directly into its spinal cord. The Demon screamed and swatted at me, but I created another purple shield around myself, keeping its scrambling claws from making any contact with me. I removed the dagger and stabbed again, even deeper this time. The Demon twitched uncontrollably as the blade severed nerve connections. I was hoping to incapacitate it enough that I could behead it without it being able to injure me badly in the process. I left that dagger in its spinal cord to prevent it from healing, then, with a cry, swung my remaining dagger across the Demon's throat as hard as I could. The blade sliced deep, and a gush of acidic blood spilled from the gash. But it wasn't deep enough. The Demon had already healed most of the damage I'd inflicted on its neck with my dagger and power only a few minutes earlier.

With a growl of frustration, I prepared to slice at its neck again. But, out of nowhere, a knife flew past me and embedded deep in the Demon's forehead. I gasped. The knife had flown closer to me than I'd liked. I looked down, confused, and saw that Gabriel still had both of his weapons. He looked up, confused as well. Then, two dark shapes emerged from the shadows—one tall and broad, brandishing a long knife that matched the one in the Demon's skull, the other shorter and athletic with longer hair. Then, in a flash of light, the shorter figure transformed, white bursting from his skin as enormous wings sprouted from his back, and armor closed around his body. Caleb and Damian had joined the fight.

The Demon screamed and shook its head back and forth, trying to dislodge the knife embedded in it. Blood spattered over me, burning holes in my jacket and stinging my skin. The Demon was distracted. I took advantage of the opportunity and yanked my dagger out of its spinal cord, then stabbed both daggers deep into the side of its neck where I'd already created a gash. I jerked them out again, then repeated, putting my entire body behind it. The Demon's blood coated my hands and burned my skin, but I ignored the discomfort. I needed to make deep cuts that could facilitate full decapitation. Its neck was just so thick—too thick for easy removal with the weapons we had.

The Demon screamed again as Caleb launched into the air, flying quickly toward us as he unsheathed his sword with a flash of bright white light. Damian simultaneously ran at the Demon with his remaining knife. It didn't seem like he was going to bother transforming. That was interesting. Most Divines immediately did when faced with a battle situation, like Caleb had just done. Only Gabriel and I refrained from immediate transformation due to our transformations' appearances. Maybe Damian thought this Demon wasn't worth the power-suck that transformation would entail.

Gabriel renewed his attack, now that Caleb was distracting it, sending electric blue fire at its other leg to keep it immobile, slowly burning through the thick skin. The Demon let out another gurgling screech and swiped its giant hand at Caleb, lethal claws extended. Caleb flooded his wings with power as he swung up his glowing sword, managing to counter the Demon's momentum and stop the blow. Several enormous, clawed fingers dropped from the Demon's hand as Caleb's blade sliced through.

I stabbed ferociously into the Demon's neck again, this time hitting bone. Then I shot a beam of purple fire into the wounds, severing muscle, burning away skin until the entire side of its neck was gone. We were so close. I just needed to burn through to the other side.

"Terah!" Caleb shouted, as he charged the Demon again, his sword raised.

I looked up, but not in time. The Demon had already grabbed me off its shoulder with its uninjured hand, its claws slicing shallowly into my sides. And before I could even think or move, I was flying through the chilled night air with enormous speed. The Demon had flung me with all its strength away from it. *Shit.* I should've been paying more attention to the Demon's hands. It was a mistake I felt too old and experienced to have made, and I was, even in that split second, disappointed with myself. I whipped my head up and saw Caleb trying to follow, trying to grab me from the air to save me from a deadly impact with the ground. His expression was desperate as he reached his hand out toward me, almost beseechingly. But he wasn't fast enough.

I closed my eyes and looked inside myself to the deep purple well of power and grasped it. I needed to transform as quickly as I could if I wanted to avoid the agonizing impact that was sure to follow. Because, gods, I didn't want to die again. But before I could fling the power outward, something closed around me.

I gasped, my eyes flying open. Strong, shadowy arms grabbed me tightly and pulled me out of my chaotic flight and into an embrace midair. A shuddering breath of relief left me as Gabriel's body, dark and speckled with star-like lights, wrapped around mine and pulled me down toward the ground, as light and as slow as a leaf gently falling from the branch of a tree. Shock reverberated through me. I hadn't known that was something he could do—move that fast. Faster than a Guardian. Fast enough to catch up to me and catch me midair.

"Thank the gods," Gabriel gasped as we floated back to the ground, his arms tightening around me. "I didn't even know I could do that."

"Yeah, me neither," I panted. "But I'm glad you can. Otherwise, I would've been flattened from the impact."

We landed on the ground and Gabriel released me. "Be careful." I could feel the intensity of his eyes on mine even though I could no longer see their color.

"I will. Be safe," I added as Gabriel transformed back into his human form.

He grinned at me. "Always am."

We ran together back toward the Demon, which was now heavily engaged in battle with Damian and Caleb. Damian had climbed the Demon as I'd done earlier and was working to deepen the neck injuries that I'd made. He'd managed to saw about halfway through the Demon's neckbone. Meanwhile, Caleb was attempting to keep the Demon's hands occupied, trying to give Damian more time. He flew within the proximity of the Demon's grasp, taunting it, striking it with his sword and white fire, before flying quickly backward before the Demon could grab him.

I flung my dagger up at the Demon as we ran toward them, and it embedded deep into the neck bone with a loud crack, breaking it the rest of the way. Damian jumped, startled, and glanced down at me. I shot him a grin. He'd startled me earlier with his knife. Now we were even. The Demon's head teetered, then fell sideways, lolling onto its own shoulder. But the skin and muscle on the other side of its neck were still attached. Which meant it could still heal itself, and it was still able to fight. Such was the power of Demons.

"I'll get up there and help sever it the rest of the way," Gabriel panted as we ran.

I nodded and reached out to squeeze his hand briefly. "I'll try to keep it busy."

Gabriel nodded and started running faster, then pushed electric blue power outward to fill every inch of his skin, transforming in a flash of blue light.

With a violent swipe of its injured hand, the Demon managed to grab Caleb out of the air, its head swinging as it continued to dangle from only a foot or two of remaining skin and muscle. It was horrifying sight. The stuff of nightmares. Even with its injured hand, the Demon managed to squeeze Caleb hard enough to crumple and puncture his torso armor. I cringed as I watched the Demon's claws enter deep into Caleb's skin. Caleb let out a grunt of pain, then sent bright white flames out from every part of his body, burning the Demon's hand almost down to bone, and shoving out of its grasp. Blood dripped from his side, down his shining armor, as his wings beat powerfully to move him a safe distance away. At the same moment, the Demon grabbed Damian from its shoulder with its other hand and threw him powerfully at Caleb. Caleb's eyes widened, and he tried to catch Damian, but the throw was too forceful, and Damian crashed into him, sending them both careening to the ground.

I picked up my speed as I used my power to pull my dagger from where it'd fallen as its head swung off its neck, back through the air toward me. I saw Gabriel leap off the ground and propel himself quickly upward, as though he were weightless, toward the Demon's neck. At least transformed, I wouldn't have to worry about him getting injured. The Demon's claws would just go straight through him.

I finally reached the Demon just as it was leaning down, stumbling forward on two charred stubs—what was left of its legs—toward the tangle of limbs and wings and blood that was Damian and Caleb on the ground. Damian managed to extricate himself and turned over just as the Demon was about to sink its claws into his chest. He had blood running down his face from his nose, probably from the impact of hitting Caleb and his armor midair.

I ran toward them at full speed, clutching my daggers tightly in my hands. I saw, as if in slow motion, Damian's eyes widen in disbelief as the Demon lowered its claws toward his chest, prepared to end his life. He didn't even have his knives or a shield at the ready. It was almost like he hadn't truly thought a Demon could ever kill him. Perhaps his success in his border town and his superb fighting skills had made him believe he was invincible. But no one really was. No matter how powerful. No matter how well trained. But I didn't want Damian to learn that lesson like this. Not today. Not at the expense of his life. So, with a burst of adrenaline, I charged forward and brought my daggers down over the Demon's thick wrist as hard as I physically could. Metal parted flesh just before its claws pierced Damian's chest. The enormous hand fell onto him in a gush of black acidic blood, the claws just missing him, propelled further to the side from the force of my strike. But at least it hadn't killed him.

Just as the Demon's hand fell, Gabriel unleashed a powerful stream of electric blue fire at the remaining portion of the Demon's neck. The Demon jerked around, flinging its remaining claws at Gabriel, but they passed straight through him. In another moment, Gabriel had burned through the rest of the neck, and with a sizzle of charred skin and a horrible squelch, the Demon's head fell from its body into the grass, now soaked with the Demon's blood. As the decapitated body teetered and started falling backward, Gabriel launched himself off its shoulders and floated gently back to the ground in front of us.

With a flash, he transformed back into his human form, then pulled me into his arms. One arm pinned me to him around my waist, and the other cupped the back of my head, bringing my cheek to rest on his chest. I could hear his heartbeat pounding through him. He didn't seem to care that the Demon blood covering me was burning into his jacket. He must've been more worried about me than he'd been letting on. I slid my arms around his waist and held him to me, breathing out a sigh of relief. We'd done it. The Demon was dead. And we were safe. He was safe.

Behind me, I heard a grunt of effort and then a thud. I lifted my head off Gabriel's chest and turned to look. Damian had shoved the Demon's giant hand off him and pushed to his feet. He quickly shed his blood-soaked jacket and abandoned it on the ground before the acidic blood could fully burn through to his skin. Then he reached forward and pulled Caleb to his feet. With a flash of light, Caleb transformed back into his human form. I could see blood soaking through the left side of his jacket, and I remembered how deeply the Demon's claws had sliced into him. He needed to be healed. I took a step toward him, but his hard, cold eyes met mine, stopping me. His expression was firm. Easy to read for once. He didn't want me to heal him. I sighed reluctantly. *Fine.* He could try healing on his own, but he'd lose a lot more blood that way. It'd take a long time for his quick healing to deal with punctures that deep.

Instead, I turned back to Damian, who was regarding me seriously, an odd expression on his face.

"You . . . saved my life," he finally said.

It was a question and a statement. But I didn't understand where it was coming from. I hadn't done anything out of the ordinary—just my job as a soldier. Which, as a fellow soldier, he should know. I stared at him for several long moments, waiting for him to say more. He didn't.

"Of course I saved your life," I finally said, giving him a weird look in return. "The Demon was going to claw you open and I was in a position to stop it. So I did. Why wouldn't I?"

The odd look in Damian's eyes intensified as he continued to stare at me in disbelief. "But . . . why? What was there for you to gain from it? You don't even like me."

I couldn't keep the smile from spreading across my face. He was just . . . so serious. So confused. I'd never seen him so flabbergasted before. It was a little funny.

"Well, I don't *hate* you." I tried to tamp down my humor so I wouldn't laugh at him. "But even if I did, I wouldn't just let you die. Not when I could keep it from happening. That's the whole point of being a soldier—protecting people. Is that not what it's like in your border town?" My smile faded, a dawning sense of unease steeling over me. Had it just been every soldier for themself where he came from? Had they just let each other die? As hellish as Dagmar was, even we'd never been that harsh. We may not have cared for each other, but we'd recognized that we were all on the same side. We'd all had each other's backs in battle.

Damian finally got his expression under control and pulled a mask of indifference back over his face as he shrugged in response. But he couldn't quite hide the odd look in his eyes. Like he was unsettled.

"Well, thanks," he finally said, looking away from me. "I'm . . . not used to that," he added so quietly I almost didn't hear him.

The knot in my stomach tightened. I was beginning to feel . . . bad for him. Bad that he'd had to grow up in a hellhole where they didn't even look out for each other in violent, life-threatening situations. That was the bare minimum one should do to be a decent person, not to mention a decent soldier.

"Not a problem," I said lightly, exchanging a curious glance with Gabriel before pulling my phone from my pocket.

I opened my contacts and hit the call button before I could lose my nerve. Someone needed to report the attack. Though I was surprised more people hadn't heard it already. I glanced around. We'd moved pretty far from the buildings, and it was late on a weeknight. Perhaps that was why nobody had noticed. The phone rang for a long time before I finally heard the click of it being answered. I could practically feel the hesitancy oozing from the phone.

"Yeah?" Matt said, his voice resigned. Closed off.

He always sounded so sad now. I remembered the glimpse of his sadness that I'd seen the last time I'd connected our minds, and I thought about the broken glass in front of him on the bar. How he'd shattered it without even noticing, because Gabriel and I had kissed, and he'd watched. My stomach clenched as my heart throbbed painfully. It gutted me.

"Hey, Matt." My voice was quiet and somber. "I thought you should know there was another Demon attack."

Silence extended on the other line for a long moment. Then he let out a stream of swears.

"How in the fucking hell did it get in?" he finally shouted when he could form sentences again. "I've been working my *ass* off to keep this campus safe, and it's like it doesn't even matter." There was a desperation in his voice that I didn't think was completely attributable to this situation. I was concerned for him. It sounded like he was going through quite a lot. Alone.

"I don't know," I murmured, aware of everyone's gazes on me as I talked to him. "But we're in the central green of campus, east of the chapel and dorms. You should come here or send someone else here quickly."

I heard Matt starting to gather his things. "I'm assuming you defeated it." His voice was heavy. "Any injuries?"

"We're mostly okay, though Caleb has some decent puncture wounds."

Caleb glared daggers at me, but I wasn't wrong. He'd removed his jacket and was using it to stem the flow of blood from his side. He was also getting paler. I wondered if we'd have to tackle him and force him to let one of us heal him.

"You're . . . with Caleb?" Matt sounded confused. Almost hurt.

"Gabriel, Damian, and Caleb," I said quickly. "Caleb and Damian joined the fight a few minutes after Gabriel and I encountered the Demon."

"Oh." I couldn't quite figure out what he was thinking, but there was something in his voice. "Okay. I'll be there soon." Then he hung up.

I sighed and put my phone back in my pocket. "Matt's on his way. He was pretty unhappy to hear about the attack, especially after all the work he's put into the Academy's defenses."

"Hmm." Damian pursed his lips and studied me closely. "Seems like he's pretty unhappy all the time, with or without a Demon attack." He lifted his eyebrow slightly at me, his gaze knowing. Accusing.

Gabriel stiffened beside me, and my shoulders tensed at Damian's insinuation. He was watching the two of us closely, almost amused. But calculating. Always calculating. It was like we were wild animals he was poking just to see how we'd react.

Caleb shot Damian a disgruntled look from behind his back. As though he could feel it, Damian turned and glanced at him. He looked, if anything, even more amused. But that odd look that'd appeared in his eyes after I'd saved him hadn't left. And I caught it there as he continued to observe us. Like he was unsettled about something and wanted to get rid of the feeling. Like when we'd trained together for the first time. When I'd unknowingly touched a nerve as I'd encouraged him to leave his past behind, and he'd lashed out at me to cover his own discomfort. I wondered what nerve I'd touched this time.

"Just an observation." Damian shrugged casually, amusement thick in his deep voice. I decided to ignore it and move on.

"When did you notice the attack?" I asked, looking from him to Caleb. "No one's ever come to help us before."

This time Caleb took a step forward, his eyes meeting mine more directly than they usually did. "We left the lounge a little while after you did and were walking back to the dorms. We heard the noise of your fight and ran to check it out. I was hoping you weren't the one fighting it—that you'd managed to avoid it this time . . ." he trailed off suddenly, looking self-conscious. Like he hadn't meant to say that. "I just mean you're at every attack, and it seems like the rest of us should start pulling our weight," he added quickly. Matter-of-factly.

But he looked away from me suddenly, and I watched, slightly astonished, as he tried to pull his cold mask back on, his cheeks faintly filling with color. Damian watched Caleb curiously, and Gabriel tensed next to me again. Alarm bells went off inside my head. I hadn't seen Caleb act like this since . . . Dagmar. I swallowed, discomfort slithering through me at the thought.

I turned in relief as I heard footsteps thundering through the ground and saw Matt jogging toward us. He had his phone to his ear and was ordering the warrior faction guards to check and secure the perimeter. His eyes homed in on me first and swept over me, like he was trying to make sure I wasn't hurt. They narrowed slightly as he saw the tears and burns in my coat. No doubt, he realized that I was mildly injured underneath. But he didn't say anything. He knew as well as I did that my injuries were probably ninety percent healed by now anyway.

Then his eyes swept over the rest of the group, pausing on Damian's bloody nose, which seemed to be healing on its own, and stopping on Caleb and his now blood-soaked jacket that he still had pressed to his side. Matt said a few more words to the person on the phone before hanging up and heading for Caleb.

"You need to let me heal that," he said firmly. "Now. Your quick healing isn't dealing with it fast enough and you're bleeding out."

Caleb's jaw clenched, and he glanced at me briefly before looking away. "It's nothing." His voice was hard. "It'll heal soon."

I rolled my eyes, even though I knew I'd said the same thing hundreds of times before. I wondered if people had been able to see through me as easily as we could now see through Caleb.

"It's not a negotiation," Matt said sharply. "I'm your trainer. Take off your shirt. I'm healing you. *Now*."

Caleb released a frustrated sound but obeyed. Not because Matt was his trainer, but because Matt was a high-ranking member of the warrior faction now, and Caleb knew it. I bit the inside of my cheek as I looked at Caleb's torn up, blood-covered torso. The Demon had really done a number on him with those claws. Even Damian looked sympathetic.

Matt knelt next to Caleb and placed his hands over Caleb's wounds. Caleb's jaw clenched, but otherwise he didn't move or react. Blinding white light glowed around Matt's fingers, and I watched with relief as Caleb's wounds were pulled together, the bruising eliminated, and his blood replenished. He might not be my favorite person, but I didn't want him to bleed out, either.

We described the attack to Matt as warrior faction guards arrived to surround, examine, and dispose of the Demon's body. He asked us questions in between giving orders and receiving information from the perimeter guards. He was clearly growing into his role as a ranking member of the warrior faction well, directing the chaos around him with authority and confidence. Having known him all my life, it was intense to watch. It was like he'd become . . . a different person. One now inextricably entrenched in the will and power of the Light Guardian side. The Matt I remembered from my childhood seemed to be growing further and further away. My stomach clenched, but I forced myself to refocus on the situation around us. From what I could hear of the reports, it didn't seem like the Demon had breached the perimeter when it came in. In fact, there were no traces of breaches . . . anywhere. It was a mystery. It was almost like the Demon had just popped into existence. Or had been here all along. I shivered at the thought.

Matt finally dismissed us, and the four of us trudged back toward the dorms, this time truly exhausted.

"I wish we didn't have to get up for training," I grumbled as we squelched through the damp grass, my fingers entwined with Gabriel's. "It's only a few hours away at this point, and I'm fucking exhausted."

Damian shrugged. "Do you think they'd really care if we skip? I bet Matt will tell Luke that we were all involved in the Demon battle. I can't imagine they'd be mad about it."

"We can't skip," Caleb interjected, sounding stern. Stubborn. "We need to learn to train and fight no matter the conditions. Even if we're tired. Or injured. Demons don't stop attacking just because we don't feel our best."

I raised a sardonic eyebrow at him. Glenhaven had turned him into a real bundle of joy. Damian gave Caleb a partially disgusted, partially amused look. Gabriel didn't bother reacting. He wasn't pleased that we were having to spend time with Caleb at all.

I eyed Caleb's blood-soaked clothes. "You of all people should skip. You practically bled out."

To my surprise, Caleb's cheeks flushed with color. "I was fine," he said quietly, not looking at me. "And I'm healed now, so it doesn't matter. I'll be fine to train in a few hours."

I shrugged, deciding not to push it. If he wanted to expend large amounts of energy forcing his still-healing body to do difficult shit, that was totally up to him. He clearly couldn't handle the concept that one day of missed training wouldn't mean the end of the world or the end of his career.

"Do *you* want to skip?" I asked Gabriel, pulling his arm around my shoulders and leaning into him. I looked up into his face and smiled. His stubble was showing now, and it made him look roguish and handsome. I wanted to rub my cheek against it—wanted to feel the gentle scrape of it across my skin. His eyes, almost luminescent in the dark, heated as they read my expression.

"Mhmm." He pulled me closer. "We wanted today to be Friday anyway. Might as well go all in and decide tomorrow's Saturday." A playful smirk touched his lips, and I laughed.

Damian sighed. "With them out and you in, I guess that means I can't skip. If I do, you won't have anyone to train with." He elbowed Caleb in the side, his expression mildly annoyed.

Caleb looked at him, his eyebrows lifting. "So . . . you'll still train with me tomorrow?"

Damian shrugged. "Guess so."

"Thanks."

They both looked uncomfortable, and the odd look in Damian's eyes returned. I fought to keep from smiling as I watched them. The two most closed off men in the world were forming the most reluctant friendship in the world. Almost like they couldn't help it. It was funny and almost endearing to watch. It would be if I truly trusted them. *But they fought with you. Defended you. Put their lives on the line with you.* I definitely trusted them more than I had a month ago, but something held me back. Kept me tentative. For Caleb, I knew our past was the roadblock. For Damian, though, I wasn't sure. Perhaps it was his newness in our lives. Or his unclear role in my visions.

We finally reached the dorms, and Damian and Caleb left us to head to their building, while Gabriel and I headed back to ours. When we reached our room, I immediately stripped out of the Demon-blood-soaked clothes, tossed them into a corner where the stone floor was exposed, and headed to the shower, Gabriel behind me.

I turned on the water as Gabriel stripped and placed his clothes on the bathroom counter. And as we waited for the water to heat up, Gabriel pulled me closer and gently traced the faint marks, now mostly faded, where the Demon's claws had shallowly sliced into me, and the burns from where its blood had marked me. Even as he traced them with the tips of his warm fingers, they faded even more. I met his gaze and saw that it'd grown intense. Warm shivers flowed through me in waves.

As he took my hips in his hands, I gently ran my fingers over his hands and wrists, purple power spilling from them, erasing the welts from the Demon's blood that'd splashed him during the battle. They thankfully weren't too bad. His jacket had protected him, and his transformation had protected him the rest of the time. Gabriel's chest rose and fell more quickly as I touched him. It made me not want to stop.

When I was done healing him, Gabriel pulled me flush against him and kissed me with a fervor he'd tried to curb while we'd been in public. But we weren't in public now. His fingers tangled around strands of my hair as he anchored my face to his, tilting my head back, delving deep, his tongue sliding against mine. A groan tore from his chest, reverberating through my mouth, like he'd been waiting to let go with me like this forever. I clutched him tightly to me and kissed him back, pressing my chest to his, the breath coming in and out of my lungs in desperate gasps as my fingers dug into his upper arms.

When I could no longer breathe, I pulled my mouth from his, gasping for air and laughing, even as desire pumped through me, intoxicating me and filling me with fiery tingles. "We're supposed to be showering."

Gabriel was breathing hard but grinned at me. He slid his arms around my waist, his fingers splaying over my skin, his eyes dark and intense with desire. I swallowed, my muscles clenching sweetly. I knew that look well by now, and it sent scorching heat through me, making goosebumps erupt over my skin in anticipation. It was a look that made me want to press myself to him and never let go.

"We can do that too," he murmured, his voice deep and liquid, a mischievous gleam in his eyes. Then he lifted me without warning into the shower and followed me in.

He pulled me under the spray of the water, before pulling me tightly to him. And then we were kissing again, and the sensations were at once enlightening and overwhelming. The steam filling my lungs. My wet hair plastered to my back and shoulders. The stubble on his chin scraping over mine. The hot water. Our wet, warm skin. His soft lips and deep, searing kisses. His talented tongue. His hands gliding over me. The feel of his firm muscles under my fingertips. The heaving of his chest against mine. I was lost in it all. And in him. But I also knew there was nowhere else I'd rather be.

It was dark. Pitch black. I couldn't see anything, not even myself. I couldn't tell if we were in a small room or a large cavern. There were no windows. No light. Barely any air. And the air that surrounded us was musty and stale, as though it hadn't been stirred in centuries. Instinctively, I reached out and found Gabriel's hand with mine. I didn't want to lose him in this darkness. I didn't want to be lost.

A bright light suddenly flared into being in front of me, and I saw Matt holding it in his palm, turning slowly so he could get a look at the room we were in. Caleb followed suit, making a light appear in his own hand. The twin pools merged and expanded, and Gabriel, Damian, and I looked around us. We were in a moderately-sized room made of ancient looking stone blocks, enclosed around us in a semicircle. The open end of the room seemed to disappear into darkness. As we stepped slowly toward it, bringing the light with us, a narrow staircase that descended downward slowly emerged from the shadows, enclosed on either side with the same stones that lined this room. I heard a sigh behind me.

"Well," Damian said, "there's no turning back now. Let's go."

I took a deep, centering breath and nodded. This needed to be done. Damian started descending the stairs, Matt and Caleb behind him providing the light. I squeezed Gabriel's hand, and we exchanged a worried look before following the rest of the group.

The image faded, and a new one appeared.

I was running. Trying to get to Gabriel and Matt. I knew I was running out of time. I'd been so wrong about . . . everything. How could this have happened? How had I *let* this happen? I should've known better. I should've realized sooner. I ran harder, heedless of the tears streaking down my cheeks. Now wasn't the time for them. The damage was done, and we needed to set up some kind of defense.

An explosion rent the air, violently shaking the ground beneath my feet. I looked up in horror and saw black fire blooming around the far edges of the trees and moving quickly inward, setting the vegetation ablaze. Clouds swirled overhead, and thunder rumbled as the alarms began blaring. A paralyzing terror flooded me. We were out of time. They were here.

The image faded, and another appeared.

A young woman stood in front of me, her eyes like flames, practically blazing with determination and stubbornness. But underneath her determination, I saw a deep worry that was taking a toll on her. She looked pale and drawn. Her eyes were rimmed with red. Worry tightened my stomach and a sense of dread washed over me. Something had happened. I wondered why he wasn't here with her.

"They took him" she said, as if in answer to my unspoken question.

Fear blazed through me like a fire. Paralyzing me. *No. They couldn't have.* My brain refused to believe what she was saying. There had to be a mistake. A misunderstanding. He was the best fighter I knew. He'd never let them overtake him. He couldn't be . . . gone . . .

"I was there. And they—" her voice broke, and I saw a sheen of tears flooding her eyes. She swallowed and shook her head, clenching her fists and trying to shake the swell of emotion away. "They ambushed us. I tried to stop them, but in the end he . . . he put a shield around me so they couldn't attack me anymore."

My mind whirred, thoughts spinning rapidly over one another until it was completely flooded. Overwhelmed. My hands clenched into fists as they began to shake. They'd taken him. *They'd taken him.* She'd seen it happen, and now he was gone. There was a ringing in my ears. Blood pounded through me at a frantic pace. They'd kill him. After everything he'd done, I knew they would. Torture him for information, then kill him. We needed to do something. *I* needed to do something. We needed to save him. He was . . . family. But . . . what could we do?

"We have to help him," the young woman continued. "We have to bring him back. We're the only ones willing to try." She gestured at the small group standing behind her. "Will you help us?" Her eyes held mine with desperation and . . . something else. My eyes widened slightly as the truth washed over me. *She loves him.*

The image faded, and a battle scene rose around me.

The sky was swirling and dark as thunder rumbled ominously overhead, blasts of power and screams filled the air around me. Everything had been reduced to rubble, and blood flew through the air like rain, coating everything in sight. It was horrible. We probably wouldn't survive this. We were far too outnumbered. But I'd fought with all of myself anyway. With everything I had. Because we had to try. We had to save as many as we could. We couldn't give up. Not even now. But I was tired. So tired.

The world spun around me, and my vision blurred as exhaustion, pain, and blood loss finally overtook me. I gritted my teeth, blinking hard, and my vision cleared slightly, but the world tilted around me again. I swayed.

I heard a shout—a familiar voice cutting through the echoey static around me. It was a desperate, frantic cry. But it was too far away for me to understand the words. Then there was a thud. So close. Too close. Gasping, I spun around just in time to see Caleb turning toward me. He reached his blood-covered hands out to cup my face as I stared at him, frozen. His expression was desperate as his thumbs ran gently down my cheeks.

"Terah."

I bolted upright in bed with a gasp, covered in a sheen of cold sweat. My entire body shook. I looked around, disoriented, and saw the sun was just starting to peek through the windows of my dorm room, sending rays of warm, golden light across the floor. I took a deep, unsteady breath and tried to calm my racing heart. I felt Gabriel's hands sliding around me, and when I looked down at him, I saw his eyes were open. He blinked sleepily at me, but I could see his worry.

"Visions," I murmured, my voice hoarse as though I'd been screaming.

Understanding filled his eyes, and he pulled me back down next to him and wrapped his arms tightly around me, folding me into his chest. I took a deep breath and savored his comforting scent as he pressed his lips against my hair. I tried to unclench my muscles and soak in his warmth and calm.

"Do you want to talk about it?" His voice was gravelly from sleep.

"Maybe later." I sighed, draping my arm around his waist, and closed my eyes. I just wanted to sleep again. To forget, at least for a little while. I just wanted to escape.

I felt Gabriel nod. He wasn't going to make me talk about it if I didn't want to, for which I was grateful. I relaxed fully into him as his warmth surrounded me like a cocoon, and I let my mind wander. Before long, I felt myself slipping back into sleep. This time, too deep for dreams.

18

FUTURES

BEFORE WE ALL KNEW IT, THE LAST FEW WEEKS OF THE SEMESTER were upon us, and there hadn't been any more attacks or hints of anything worse to come. It was almost like the last attack had been a fluke. Teachers, who'd clearly assumed the Academy would be closed before the end of the semester, were suddenly scrambling to prepare exams for their classes, and all the remaining students were suddenly flooded with exam-related stress.

Matt and Luke handled the uncertainty surrounding the Academy's future by pushing us in training. I'd been scared enough by my most recent set of visions that I'd told Matt about them, and I'd urged him to evacuate as many students as possible. I didn't know for sure when or if an attack would happen on the grounds, but the vision had been bad enough that I didn't want to take that chance. To his credit, Matt tried. He made clear to the administration that a bad attack could be coming and advised them to close the school. But they refused. Absent anything in my vision specifying the exact time, place, and circumstances, the president didn't think there was enough proof for such decisive action. The most she'd do was make a general announcement that the Academy couldn't guarantee against future Demon attacks. It was the most half-assed announcement regarding potential death that I'd ever heard. And I was furious. But her decision was made. Not even Matt, a warrior faction commander now, could do anything to force her hand.

In response, Matt and Luke were clearly switching from training us to theoretically join the warrior faction someday, to training us for battle. Just in case. It meant that someone, at least, was taking my worry seriously. So I didn't complain when my arms screamed with tiredness as I pushed open the training room door, knowing we'd be in for even more ass-kicking today. It was the first time in years that I'd been this consistently sore from training, even with my quick-healing abilities.

I tried not to wince as Gabriel and I walked across the room to the locker rooms, my legs still aching from yesterday. After changing into our uniforms, we joined the rest of the group on the mats. Unfortunately, I'd be training with Caleb today. Since the last Demon attack, where we'd been forced to interact way more than either of us wanted to, he'd tried not to make eye contact with me or even acknowledge me when we weren't training together. He was working even harder to build up the walls around himself, especially between me and him. But he seemed to be failing. I caught him watching me a lot, despite these efforts, his expression often uncertain or deeply conflicted. And when we trained together, those expressions intensified. No matter how much he wanted to completely remove himself mentally and physically from my presence, our new training situation didn't let him.

I sighed and took my place across the mat from him, trying not to let his nervous energy seep into me, and waited calmly, listening to Luke's instructions as I watched Caleb fidget, trying not to meet my eyes. I knew when he'd left Dagmar, he'd quickly thrown himself into a new town with new people and new immense danger. He'd probably succeeded in pushing me from his mind pretty quickly. He'd probably successfully kept himself from really having to deal with what he'd done and how he felt about it—to really *feel* the consequences of his own actions. But I got the feeling that he was starting to feel all of that now, as he was forced to be in regular close contact with me. And he was forced to see how I'd grown and moved on. Without him. I almost felt bad for him, but I certainly wouldn't help him navigate his feelings. Not anymore.

I ignored the coldness mixed with uncertainty in his gaze as he ran at me, and we began to fight. I fought my hardest, pushing through all my soreness and exhaustion to kick his ass. He'd started hesitating more and more whenever we fought, unwilling to fully commit to his usual moves—moves that might hurt me. Moves that he used to execute without a second thought, even when we were dating. I took advantage of his hesitation and pushed him hard, forcing him to defend himself. To engage and fight back. To make him angry and push him back to a place where he wouldn't pull his punches. I truly didn't give a damn about his feelings for me anymore, complicated or otherwise. I just wanted us to both get the most out of training while we still could. And his inconsistency was starting to piss me off.

We ended yet another fight as he threw me over his shoulder and slammed me into the mat, throwing his body across mine to pin me to the ground. His chest heaved with exertion and his gaze was dark and intense as it met mine. But I just smiled as I caught my breath. Like I'd *actually* let him pin me down. I pushed suddenly and forcefully on the outside of his upper arm and shoulder with my hands, altering his center of gravity, while simultaneously twisting my body. I locked my arm as I continued to push him, unbalancing him with my hip, and shoved him off me. Then I turned so I was over him, twisted my limbs around his to keep them from getting leverage on the mat, and pressed my forearm across his neck, restricting his airway. Caleb struggled, but he had no leverage to push or shove me from. I had him.

"I yield," he gasped as I increased the pressure across his neck. I grinned and released my hold on him.

Caleb drew in a deep, shuddering breath as I detangled my legs from his and pressed my hands into his shoulders so I could push myself off him. He closed his eyes for a moment as I sat up, briefly straddling him. When his eyes slid open, they were darker. Molten. Warning bells blared through me, and I shoved off him as quickly as I could, taking a few steps away until it felt like we were a safe distance apart. *What the hell?*

I bit the inside of my cheek as I stared at him. Nervous energy pumped through me as I watched him push to his feet, trying to pull his cold mask back into place. It really wasn't a good idea for us to train together anymore. It was clearly too much for him. And I'd moved on. I didn't want to deal with the fact that maybe he hadn't.

Suddenly, the room blurred as a loud buzzing filled my ears. Intense pressure squeezed my head from all directions, and I clutched it, gasping for breath. What was happening? I wanted to cry out, but I couldn't find my breath or my voice. *What . . .*

My knees buckled as my vision went black.

I was on a giant field in the middle of nowhere. A battlefield. I glanced down at myself. I was wearing full body armor. I frowned. Something about this felt familiar, like I'd been here before, but I knew I hadn't. Everything was silent this time. Eerily still and quiet. I spun around and took in the landscape around me—barren and empty. Full battle was raging, but was frozen in time, like a three-dimensional image that was paused mid-action. There were Light and Dark Guardians, Demons, Blessed, maybe even some Normals. The gloomy sky was colored with strange lights that illuminated the grim scene below—flying dirt, broken earth, blasts of fire, water, ice, stones, endless sprays of blood, bodies. So many bodies.

Blood pounded through my veins as I spun, trying to take in what was happening. Trying to determine what was going on and who was winning. Who was even fighting whom? Nothing looked unified. Nothing was clear. But we all looked like we were losing. So many were already dead. So many were dying. Too many. Far too many. And so many were young. It looked like, in the end, everyone would probably die here.

Tears filled my eyes and spilled down my cheeks. Was this a warning? Or was I simply glimpsing the future? What would we even do? How could we possibly prevent this without context? Was this the end of the world itself? Intense rage and sadness burned through me, battling it out. I was overwhelmed and overcome.

"Then why?" I shouted at the sky, my voice breaking. "Why show me this if you won't show me how to prevent it?" Tears dripped from my cheeks to the blood-soaked ground. I didn't even know who I was shouting at. I didn't know if anyone was listening. "Why was I even given this power?" I raged, the words coming out as sobs. Was it just to torment me? To show me exactly how I and everyone I loved would eventually die? Were the gods really that cruel? Was the universe?

I heard a sound behind me and spun around, more tears spilling down my cheeks. I gasped as my gaze slammed into a too-familiar pair of eyes. Wet like mine. Dark like mine. I felt the blood drain from my face. How could he be here? He wasn't a part of the frozen image. He was looking at it and moving within it. Like me. My mouth opened, but I couldn't think of what to say. I was too stunned. He looked stunned too. And a little scared.

Before either of us could move or even speak, deep purple power flared to life and encircled us. It swirled around and between us, connecting us. Pulling us closer together. Making our skin glow. I stared at him across from me, confused. Then I stared at the power connecting us. What did this mean? Was this some kind of direction? Did it mean there was something we could do? And why was he here? *How* was he even here?

"Terah? Can you hear me?"

A familiar warm voice, laced with worry and a little desperation, broke through the image around me. My heart clenched in response to it. I didn't want him to worry. I never wanted him to worry.

"I don't know what happened. She just collapsed. We weren't even fighting." Another familiar voice. Cold, but edged with concern.

"She's not the only one. Look over there." A third voice. Familiar. Comforting. Tense.

My consciousness grew little by little, my body reawakening. I felt the breath filling my lungs and the dull ache pounding in my head. Felt my body pressed into the hard mat beneath me. The light pressing on my closed eyelids from above.

I forced my eyes to open and blinked up, squinting against the light, into three worried faces.

"Terah!" Relief washed over Gabriel's face. "Are you okay? Are you hurt?"

I smiled a little, wanting to comfort him. "I'm okay. Not injured or anything." I would've told him what'd happened, but Caleb was still here. And Caleb didn't need to know about my visions. I winced and pushed onto my elbows.

"Caleb," Matt said suddenly, "go over there and see if Luke needs help with Damian." Caleb looked reluctant to leave but nodded and shoved to his feet.

"What's wrong with Damian?" I asked, pushing all the way up so I was sitting.

"He collapsed too," Gabriel murmured, meeting my eyes with his worried ones. "At the exact same time that you did."

I swallowed and glanced over at him. He was also lying on the mat, Luke and now Caleb crouched next to him. Caleb was speaking to him, and I saw him gesture in my direction. Damian suddenly shoved into a sitting position and glanced over at me. Once again, his startled gaze met mine. He looked deeply unsettled. Shock trickled through me as well.

Had he really been in my vision? Had that part been real somehow? But . . . how? Why? I glanced at Gabriel and noticed he was watching

Damian too, trying to figure out what was going on. Well, if he figured it out, I hoped he'd tell me, because I had no fucking clue what was happening.

"Was it another vision?" Matt asked quietly, pulling my attention back to our group. He spoke too quietly for anyone not directly next to me to hear. But Damian's gaze snapped to Matt as he spoke, and the unsettled look in his eyes intensified. I felt disoriented and a little afraid. Nothing was making sense.

"Yeah," I finally murmured quietly, turning away from Damian. "But I don't think we should talk about it here. We've already drawn enough attention." I jerked my head at the rest of the room. The entire training group had stopped their drills and were staring at us, whispering and trying to figure out what was going on. *Great.* Like I needed more unwanted attention.

Matt looked disappointed but nodded. Then he and Gabriel each took one of my hands and pulled me to my feet. Gabriel wrapped his arm around my waist and pulled me gently into his side, offering support. Matt's jaw clenched, but he quickly looked away.

"Do you still feel up to training?" Matt asked, his voice a little harder than before. "I don't want to force you to sit out if you don't want to, but it's fine if you're not feeling well."

I shook my head slowly, taking stock of myself. "No, I want to stay. But I don't have it in me to train with Caleb again today. I need to train with Gabriel."

Matt stiffened even more, and his gaze hardened as he looked at me.

"Please, Matt," I said quietly. "You don't know what I saw, and you don't know what it's like. I need to train with Gabriel. It's either that or I leave."

Matt rubbed the back of his head agitatedly, but his gaze softened as he continued to watch me. He no doubt noticed how exhausted I looked. How confused. Maybe even how scared.

"Fine," he finally said, though his voice didn't carry the aggression he'd likely wanted it to convey. "If that's what you need, then do it."

I smiled a little at him. My one-time best friend. My family. Now barely even an acquaintance. I pushed down the sadness.

"Thanks, Matt," I murmured.

Matt's eyes turned sad as he watched me. I saw him swallow hard as he turned away.

"No problem," he said quietly, his voice devoid of emotion.

I told Gabriel about the vision over lunch as we secluded ourselves on a wrought-iron table outside, as far from the dining hall as we could. Gabriel was as shocked as I was about Damian's presence in the vision. We didn't know how it was possible or why it'd happened, and it unnerved us both. It'd never happened before with anyone else. But it seemed like his proximity to me might've been a factor. Proximity and . . . something else. But we weren't sure what that something else was. We just knew there had to be something, since no one else in the vicinity had ever been pulled into my visions before. I couldn't shake the feeling that there was some conclusion we were supposed to be drawing from the vision. Something someone wanted us to see. But I couldn't make sense of it.

After our mutual collapse, Damian had also chosen to remain for the rest of training. But I'd caught him staring at me with that unnerved expression. I'd half expected him to corner me after training and demand an explanation from me. Not that I'd be able to give one. But if I were him and I'd been pulled into some random, chaotic, gruesome vision with another person, I'd try to figure out as much about what was going on as possible. But Damian never approached me about it. Nor did he give Caleb any answers as he threw question after question about it at Damian.

I'd noticed throughout the rest of the day, though, that Damian's gaze was following me. Through the dining hall as Gabriel and I grabbed food for lunch, through the halls of the main building as we walked from class to class, and through the classes that we shared. The unnerved expression had started to fade, replaced by calculation as the day wore on. I wondered if he'd figured something out about the experience that we'd shared—something I hadn't figured out yet. Or if he'd theorized that, apart from just being present with him, *I'd* been the cause of that unnerving experience. I hoped not. I didn't want people to know about my visions unless absolutely necessary. But his gaze made me nervous. I half wanted to confront him and make him explain what he thought had happened. But the other half of me was afraid that, in doing so, I'd reveal much more about my abilities than he knew. Much more than I wanted him to know.

That night, I dreamed. But no. It was too clear to be a dream. Even my drowsy brain knew it had to be something more. Something different. It must be a vision, then. But it was even clearer than any vision I'd had

399

before. Everything was brighter. Crisper. Smoother. A twinge of confusion had me frowning, but it quickly passed as I watched the detailed image form around me, solidifying and settling, almost like a picture turned three-dimensional.

I found myself hovering above a brightly lit room made of pearly-white marble pillars connected by marble arches, forming the foundation for the impressively tall, domed ceiling above me. These arches surrounded an imposing, round marble table in the middle of the room that had matching curved marble benches. Around the table sat about a dozen important-looking officials, their uniforms similar to that of the warrior faction, but with the deep green crests of the political faction on their jackets.

My stomach clenched. This was the group of leaders who worked most closely with the High Light Guardian. This was the group that made all the decisions about the war—who we'd fight, who we'd help, who we'd work with, and who we'd decide didn't matter. This was the group responsible for deciding border towns like Elareth remained unsupported, both the Normals and Divines deserted.

My jaw clenched as I watched them, and floated closer, trying to hear what they were discussing. It was clear that this meeting had been going on for some time.

"We don't have a choice," one elderly man said, placing his palms on the table in front of him, leaning forward for effect. "The time has come for drastic action. The book must be obtained. We must be the ones to find it, and we must be the ones to use it. Before the Dark Guardians get their hands on it!"

There was murmuring around the table. Some sounds of assent, some seeming less sure. I frowned. What book? What the hell were they talking about?

"Once we obtain the book," the elderly man continued, "we can use it to dissolve the boundaries that were placed around the realm of the gods at the beginning of the Divines' creation. The boundaries that keep the gods separated from our plane. It is time to release the gods back into our world! Only then may we have a chance of defeating the Dark Guardians and securing lasting peace."

The table practically erupted as many of the leaders clapped, nodded, and yelled their agreement, while a small number of people were exclaiming with anger and concern. Cold fear traveled like icy water down my back, and my hands started shaking as their words slowly sank in. *Dissolve* the barrier between us and the gods? Let all the gods back into the human realm? They were talking about the unthinkable. The impossible. Something that *couldn't* be done. No one had the power to release the gods back into our world—not even Divines. And even if there was a way, it should *never* be used.

If our legends were true, the new gods were responsible for removing all gods from the mortal plane and sealing them away—the benevolent, the violent, and the neutral alike. They'd removed them all to protect humanity from the wars and direct manipulations of the gods. The Divines had been created by those same gods to keep the peace in their absence. To bring neutral order to the planet, and to keep the Normals safe. We'd been given some divine power to do that job, but we could *never* rival or overcome the power of an actual god. It just wasn't possible. Nor should we ever try. It'd be beyond foolhardy. It could mean death for us all. And that was exactly what this group of leaders was suggesting— that we somehow overcome the will and power of the gods for the sake of our own war. One we weren't even supposed to be waging.

"As you all know," the elderly man continued, once the other members had settled into silence, "Divine legend speaks of a book created by the alliance of gods who formed the barrier between the divine and mortal realms. This book was meant to guide the Divines and aid them in their mission to protect the earth and the humans who inhabit it. Yet this book was more than simply a guide and a statement of our mission. It also contained instructions detailing how the Divines could undo what the alliance of new gods had done, if we ever saw a need to do so. It was meant to be a solution for only the direst of emergencies, yet it was a solution they trusted *us* to decide upon. And today, we may."

My hands clenched into tight fists. This man looked far too pleased with himself about this situation. About a thing that, if it actually existed, could and probably would destroy the world.

"While this book has been lost for centuries," the man continued, "our informants have told us that the Dark Guardians have finally narrowed down its location and are actively seeking it for their own nefarious purposes."

Gasps and frantic whispers filled the room.

"Then where is it?" an older woman asked, her eyes gleaming with ravenous curiosity. And greed. Another chill shuddered down my spine.

"One of the only places such an artifact could remain securely hidden for centuries," the elderly man said, seemingly not put off by the woman's expression. He calmly folded his hands together on the table in front of him. "If the Dark Guardians are correct, it is hidden at the Divine Academy."

People around the room gasped, and my stomach seemed to plummet through my body to the floor far below. I clenched my hands even tighter, my fingernails digging deep into my palms. If this was true, if the book really existed and the people at this meeting were correct about its location, then this could explain the Demon attacks on the school. But if it was true, and this book was what the Dark Guardian side was after, then the stakes were so much higher than I'd thought. This was no longer about creating a new front in the war or bringing the school under Dark Guardian control—this was about finally winning the war, and maybe even ending the world. *By design.* And it meant that everyone on campus could die. Because if these were the stakes, they wouldn't stop trying—stop attacking the school—until they had what they wanted.

My mind whirled quickly, thoughts spinning around each other like a tornado, as I tried to piece everything together, trying to understand why such a solution could appeal to either side. Perhaps the Dark Guardians viewed this book as their ultimate solution to ending the Normals' way of life on earth, by wiping everything they'd created from it, and reintroducing ancient, authoritarian rule. In the end, it was what they'd always believed would protect the Normals—rigidly controlling them. And it was absolute bullshit. But the Dark Guardians were even more foolish if they truly believed the authoritarian rule they'd bring down on the Normals by unleashing the gods wouldn't affect them too. And the Light Guardians were fools to believe they could control the outcome of breaking the barrier between the realms to suit their own needs. It was the most ridiculous thing I'd ever heard. The most ignorant, entitled, and dangerous assumptions on both sides.

I floated there in shock, blankly staring at the political faction members below me. They had to be wrong about the book and its contents. Why would the gods ever create something like that? Why would they ever trust us with something so destructive? They had to know something like this would eventually happen if they did. Humans—even Divine humans—couldn't be trusted with that power.

"Legend tells us that the book was protected throughout the centuries by a neutral collection of Divines," the older man continued after the murmurs around the table died down. "They were tasked with moving, protecting, and hiding the book. However, eventually the conflict between factions grew to be too intense, and neutral groups of Divines became rare.

The last neutral group at the time—those responsible for founding the Academy—decided the book needed to be expertly hidden until a time when it would be truly useful again. They therefore created a secret, well-guarded place within the Academy for the book to be concealed, and they transported it there in secret. Since then, sightings of the book have ceased, and people have largely forgotten about its existence."

"Then why should we use it?" an elderly woman across the table asked. "Why do you believe now is the time to undo what the gods worked so hard to put into place?" Several other members murmured in agreement, though they were the minority in the room.

The older man sighed deeply, looking resigned. "First and foremost, if we don't retrieve it, the Dark Guardians will. They are already trying, as we all know."

Several people around the table nodded sadly. One man murmured to the person next to him about his granddaughter leaving the Academy because of the recent attacks. My fingers trembled. Could that've really been the reason for the Demon attacks? This book? This world-ending plan?

"Even if we chose not to use it, we would still need to retrieve it," the older man continued. "However, the High Light Guardian and I believe it is imperative that we *do* use it. We have reached a precipice in the war. It is the worst it has been since the beginning, and Light Guardians and Blessed are being wiped out in record numbers. We cannot continue like this. We are losing. The Dark Guardians have somehow obtained power that we don't understand and cannot contend with, and at this rate, we will destroy the entire planet with our escalating conflict unless something changes. We need a miracle—a turning of the tides in our favor."

He cleared his throat emphatically and continued.

"We, the Light Guardians, are upholding the will of the gods by protecting the Normals and their realm. The gods will side with us when released back into the mortal realm and help us finally push the Dark Guardians back into their rightful place. They will restore order and true neutrality to the world, and they will end this war for good."

Most of the people around the table looked awe-struck and reverent, but all I could do was gape at the old man. *Seriously?* That was our grand plan? Release the gods back into the Normal realm and assume they'd help us fight a battle that they didn't even want us fighting in the first place? This man was forgetting that at least half the gods would believe the Dark Guardians were right. Many gods had never had qualms about killing Normals indiscriminately and would see nothing wrong with the Dark Guardians' actions. It was horrifying that the Light Guardians didn't seem to realize that.

If what they said was possible, and if they really chose to do this, then this small group of people would be responsible for killing us all. The gods would do what they'd done before—they'd destroy everyone and everything, either because they wanted to, or because our insignificant selves got in the way of their own divine struggles for power and territory. Our horrible, gruesome war would suddenly look like nothing when compared with the chaos and violence that would rain down on us then.

We couldn't let this happen. We couldn't let anyone get the book, and we certainly couldn't let anyone use it. None of us had the authority to decide like that for the whole world, especially not a room full of ancient, privileged, elitist Light Guardians. Something needed to be done. Someone needed to stop them. But what could I possibly do? Who would I even tell? Who would believe me?

"Any other questions before we vote?" the old man asked the room.

The older woman sat forward again. "And the High Light Guardian truly believes this is the best path forward?" She stared intently at the older man, her eyes piercing and direct.

The older man met her gaze calmly and nodded. "Yes. She has considered this option for a long time and analyzed it from every angle. It is her true belief that this is needed to finally end the war and have lasting peace. And I, for one, have great faith in the High Light Guardian and her wisdom."

My jaw clenched and rage flooded me. So much that I could barely think or move. I was surprised I didn't burst into flames from the intensity of it. *What could she possibly be thinking?* As much as I hated her, she was smarter than this. At least, I'd thought so. But apparently not. Once again, the High Light Guardian was making a decision that would lead to tremendous violence and suffering for the innocent, dooming Normals and Divines alike to a hellish future. And this room still trusted her. Agreed with her. It made me sick.

But I wasn't really here. I couldn't shout at them or try convincing them that this was the worst possible strategy. I could only watch, horrified, as the room voted to move forward with this terrible, absurd plan. They were dooming us all. Dooming the entire world. And they somehow didn't realize it.

"One last thing," the older man said after the room had unanimously voted. "This is a top-secret mission that will be assigned to the highest-ranking warrior faction member to complete. Only that one person, the High Light Guardian, and you within this room will know of this plan. It is imperative that we keep it that way. If others find out, you can imagine the conflict or even panic that might ensue. Most importantly, it is imperative that no word of our plan reaches the Dark Guardians. With that in mind, the High Light Guardian has ordered the immediate execution of anyone who finds out about any aspect of this plan." Eyebrows rose and mouths opened around the room, including mine. *What?* "It does not matter whose side they are on. It does not matter if they are family, friends, high ranking, or well-connected. Her orders remain the same. If they are not explicitly given permission by her to know, they must be eliminated. While this may seem extreme, it is for the greater good. We must, as unfortunate as it is, be prepared to sacrifice the few for the sake of a brighter future for the many."

Everyone nodded somberly, accepting the unacceptable. I shook my head, stunned. Speechless. Angry.

"Understood," one member murmured.

My heart pounded wildly as the room faded. This was too much to process. This changed everything. This could *destroy* everything. I was paralyzed with panic and horror. Once again, the vision felt like a warning. Like I was being told to do something, but what could I possibly do? Telling anyone about it would be placing them under an execution order. They'd be marked for dead. I couldn't do that to anyone. It wouldn't be right or fair.

Suddenly, I was yanked backward from the fading image of the room and into darkness. I felt like I was being sucked through a long, dark tunnel. Finally, I landed, slightly winded, on lush grass bathed in sunlight. I was back on the Academy's grounds, and I watched as students passed by and through me like I was made of smoke. I spun, half expecting to see something horrible happening. A battle raging. Blood and death. That was usually what happened in my visions. But nothing seemed out of place. I walked forward, through crowds of people gathering for lunch, smiling and basking in the warm sunshine. I frowned. Why was I here? What was I meant to see?

The crowd parted, revealing a wrought-iron table about fifteen feet in front of me, filled with familiar faces. Gabriel, Matt, Caleb, and Damian were all seated there, eating food and leisurely talking. I'd never seen them so relaxed before, especially in each other's company. A warm breeze blew around me and encircled me like a hug as I stood there, gazing at their peaceful faces.

"You can't do this alone," a warm voice murmured in my ear, carried on the breeze. My heart squeezed. It was Gabriel's voice. Though the Gabriel in front of me hadn't said it. I knew it came from within me somehow. But how could I put people I loved in danger by involving them in this? I couldn't. I *wouldn't*. It'd be a death sentence, and I wasn't willing to lose anyone else.

Suddenly, Gabriel looked up at me from his seat at the table. Like he was the only one who could see me. The intense electric blue held me, his expression knowing. Understanding. Comforting. And I knew what the vision was insinuating. How would I feel if Gabriel had been given this information instead of me? Would I expect him to face it alone? Would I prefer he protect me instead of telling me and letting me help him? No. I knew the answer was no. I'd gladly be in danger if it meant that I could support him. Fight for what was right with him. And I knew he'd feel the same way. He'd be incredibly upset if I *didn't* tell him.

But . . . what about the rest of them? I looked back at the table. At the rest of the faces there. My relationship with them was different. How could I put them in that position as well? Suddenly, Matt's voice encircled me.

"You need us, Terah," he murmured. His voice was calm. Warm. Firm. "You know you do."

I swallowed hard. For once, he was probably right. I had no idea where to start. No real familiarity with the Academy, or lore, or history. I had no idea how I was supposed to find something that'd been expertly hidden for centuries. I needed help. And if I found this book, if it even existed, what would I do with it then? How would I hide it from all the Divines looking for it? I needed a plan. And support. This wasn't something I could do alone. Not successfully.

I bit the inside of my cheek as I considered the table again. For whatever reason, the vision seemed to be pinpointing this particular group. I could understand Gabriel and Matt, but I was confused and conflicted about Damian and Caleb. I didn't fully trust them, and involving them in something like this . . .

But the vision made them seem important. Maybe they had skills or expertise that were needed to successfully accomplish this. And I remembered some of my past visions—ones that'd involved everyone at this table. Perhaps it was unavoidable, then. But it still didn't sit right with me—

putting all of them in such extreme danger for something they'd never asked to be a part of. Uncertainty boiled in my stomach, unsettling it.

Maybe . . . there was a way. Maybe I could give them a choice. Warn them, vaguely, about the danger and let them choose whether they wanted to be involved. Then they wouldn't be put in danger unless they explicitly chose to be. It seemed important enough, a desperate enough situation, to try.

"Trust us," Gabriel's voice whispered through my mind as the image in front of me faded. "We won't let you down."

Blackness engulfed me, and I was dropped out of my vision into a deep, sudden sleep.

19
RELIC

I woke up the next day feeling groggy. Out of it. My head throbbed—a dull, persistent ache. I didn't usually hurt like this unless I'd been injured in battle. Which I hadn't been. Not recently. But having two intense visions in one day had physically drained me in a way sleep alone hadn't managed to fix.

Once awake, I wasted no time in telling Gabriel about my vision. It was serious enough, and the stakes high enough, that we needed to immediately work on a plan to retrieve and hide the book. I ended up connecting our minds and showing him all that'd happened, replaying it like a video. When I finally pulled my mind from his, Gabriel looked stricken.

"How could they do this?" he'd shouted. "How could they possibly think that a fucking ridiculous plan like that would work and not just kill us all?" He'd slammed the side of his fist against the stone wall of my room in desperate anger.

I understood his rage and the panic underneath it. I'd felt the same as I'd witnessed it. How could anyone be expected to process something so mind-numbingly horrible with anything but rage? It was either anger or paralyzing fear, and Gabriel and I both knew that we didn't have the time or luxury to be paralyzed. We needed to stop this. Now. Preferably without dying.

I decided to tell Matt next. He was the person I trusted second most out of the people in my vision, though given the people in question, that wasn't saying much. But telling Matt had the potential to be the most complicated. He was in the warrior faction now. He was bound by orders to be strictly, militantly loyal to them above all others. Meaning he'd have to report us if we told him what we knew.

On the other hand, if he told them that we knew about the book, they'd kill us all, including Matt. Because none of us were allowed to know. Who knew how he'd react to that information, and which loyalty would win out—the value he held for his own life and for mine, or his extreme, unconditional loyalty to the Light Guardians. Gabriel thought Matt would value my life and his own more, especially because of his feelings for me. Lately, though, I wasn't so sure. And I didn't know if that would be enough to sway him from his orders, especially given the scope of the matter I'd be revealing to him. Either way, it was a hell of a risk. But I knew it had to be done.

After training the next day, I gave Gabriel a significant look and told him I'd meet him in a little bit for lunch. He sighed heavily, but nodded and walked away, leaving me to my Matt-related quest.

I caught up to him just before he left the training room.

"Hey, Matt," I murmured, skidding to a halt at his side. He slowed and turned to look at me, his expression reserved, as though he was steeling himself against more pain. My stomach clenched. "I need to talk to you. In private. It's . . . vision related. Can we go to your room? It'll be safer there."

Matt shoved both hands into his front pockets and ducked his head for a moment, considering. Finally, he raised his gaze to mine, the hazel depths shifting from enigmatic to something sadder, deeper.

"Okay. Let's go." He turned and led me from the training room, his shoulders stiff.

I followed him across the sun-lit grass toward the staff residence buildings, and breathed in the earthy, damp smell of spring. It'd rained last night, leaving the grounds greener. Brighter. More fragrant. The warm breeze danced around us, lifting and suspending my hair, almost like I was transformed. It was lovely. A needed reprieve after such a long, frigid winter.

We made our way up the stairs of building four in silence, and I tried not to remember the last time I'd made this journey. Bleeding and barely alive. The night Gabriel had first kissed me. The night I'd thought he'd rejected me. The night I'd kissed Matt to try to forget. I'd smeared blood all over the doors and floors of this building. I wondered who'd had to clean it up.

Matt glanced at me, and something in his gaze made me wonder if he was remembering the same things. My cheeks flushed, and I looked away quickly. I didn't want to remember that night. I didn't want to remember how destroyed I'd been, inside and out. How I'd used Matt and hurt both of us in the process.

Matt closed and locked the door behind us, and I headed straight for his couch, my legs sore and slightly wobbly from the intense training session that morning. I'd trained with Damian, and he, as usual, had attempted to soundly kick my ass. I'd held out, but only just.

"So," Matt said quietly, turning toward me and meandering slowly to the opposite end of the couch, his eyes never leaving mine, "what's going on?"

I took a deep breath, not sure where to begin. "I had a vision," I said slowly. "A bad one. But . . . I'm not sure where to start."

Matt settled into his end of the couch and turned to look at me, one of his arms slung casually over the back cushions, extended toward me. "Okay . . ."

Despite his casual posture, he seemed stiff. Uncomfortable. Guarded. We hadn't really been friends for months now. Not since he'd forced a kiss on me in the medical wing and Gabriel and I had both threatened to physically harm him if he did it again. We weren't what we'd been. I wasn't sure we ever could be again.

"It's difficult to tell you about," I started again, "because . . . well, because of your orders. My vision directed me to trust you." Matt's eyes widened. "But I know from experience that your orders tend to come first and tend to conflict with my best interests."

Matt's mouth twisted, like he wanted to say something. Like he wanted to defend himself. But, in the end, he remained quiet.

"So I guess I'll present it like this. I had a vision of a plan. The endgame strategy of the war for both sides. A plan that only a dozen or so political faction members are allowed to know about. Anyone, and I mean *anyone*, no matter their rank, who wasn't in that room will be executed if they find out about the plan. That means me, Matt. Regardless of who my mother is. And if I tell you, it means you too. We'd both be marked for dead. Even if you report the vision, they'd kill us both. No exceptions. The problem is," I continued in a rush, ignoring Matt's frozen, shocked expression, "their plan is completely irrational. It'd never work in a million years. I'm not exaggerating here—if their plan succeeds, it'll probably destroy the entire world. I think my vision was a warning. It was telling me to stop both sides from succeeding at this. But I can't do it alone."

I stopped and finally looked up at him, sucking in a deep breath. Matt looked torn. And terrified. The terrified part I understood. The torn part just pissed me off.

"I'm telling you this so you can understand the stakes. If you ask me to tell you and you won't report it, and then you do, I want you to know that they'll kill us both immediately. I promise you that, Matt. It was very, *very* clear in the vision. And if you ask me to tell you so you can help me, you need to know that you'll be betraying your orders. And, I guess finally, I'm telling you like this so you can say no if you want. I don't have to tell you. You don't have to help or know. I'm only coming to you because the vision directed me to."

Matt flinched and looked down at his lap.

"And," I continued slowly, "because I trust you more than several of the other people the vision directed me to tell."

Matt swallowed and stared at his hands in silence. Gone was the higher-ranking warrior faction commander. Gone was the confident, always-right guy who never second guessed himself. The Matt suddenly in front of me was unsure. He'd gone pale. Looked more like the twenty-two-year-old that he was than he had in a while.

"You can have some time to think about it," I finally said when the silence had stretched on for too long. "Just . . . please let me know if you plan to tell them. I'd like to know if I'm about to die." I sighed and pushed to my feet, but Matt suddenly reached out and grabbed my hand.

"Wait." He sounded . . . different. There was a hint of defeat in his voice that I'd never heard before. "I . . . I want to know. I want to help you."

I watched him, my brow furrowing. I wasn't sure whether to trust him. Trusting him hadn't gone well this past year—he'd only ever betrayed me. But he pulled on my hand until I collapsed back onto the couch. He'd pulled me so I was much closer to him this time.

"Are you asking just so you can turn me in?" I met his gaze intently, trying to read his expression. "Or rather, turn me *and* you in?"

Matt's mouth twisted in thought as he regarded me. He hadn't let go of

411

my hand. Though, if he really wasn't going to turn us in, I'd let him hold it for a little longer. But only a little—boundaries and all.

Matt took a deep breath. "If you're risking telling me, knowing you might die just by revealing it, then it's clearly incredibly serious. World-ending serious. I know you, Terah." He smiled sadly at me. "At this point, you wouldn't come to me with anything if it wasn't cataclysmic somehow. Not anymore." His voice caught in his throat.

My stomach tightened briefly with pain. But he wasn't wrong. Our friendship was broken, and I came to him now, not as a trusting friend, but as a wary acquaintance with few to no other places to turn.

"So, no," he finally said, resigned. "I won't turn you in. I may not be able to do much besides listen, given my current position, but I won't . . . I won't send them after you. I won't be the reason you die," he added, so quietly I almost couldn't hear him.

I met his gaze again, trying to see what he was really thinking and feeling. If he was telling the truth. If I could trust him not to betray me this time. He had dark shadows under his eyes that I hadn't noticed before. And a few lines that hadn't been there several months ago. But his expression was earnest. He might not directly help, but he'd listen. And not send them to execute me. What low standards the two of us were working with now. How sad it was that even this felt like progress.

"Thank you," I finally murmured, sliding my hand slowly from his and bringing it back to my lap. I didn't feel comfortable letting him hold it for any longer, and I was determined to listen to my feelings about that. "If you're sure, I'll just connect our minds and show you the vision. It's probably safer that way anyway," I added, looking around the room, nervously.

Matt nodded. He looked like he was headed to his grave, albeit willingly. "Okay. Whatever works best."

I nodded curtly, then closed my eyes and connected our minds. I was careful to only open a channel one way, and to only share that specific vision. I had everything else on lockdown. I didn't want Matt to have access to my thoughts, nor did I want to see his feelings or his pain.

I showed Matt my vision, including the table at the end. I wanted him to see who the vision had directed me to tell. Both because I wanted him to believe me, and because I wanted to make him less likely to turn everyone in.

When my vision faded and I pulled out of his mind, Matt just sat there, pale and silent. He'd slumped forward so his elbows rested on his knees, and was staring, almost blankly at the rug. He didn't react the way

Gabriel and I had—with explosive anger and despair. He was turning inward. Keeping everything on lockdown inside. If it wasn't for the fact that his fingers slightly shook, I might've believed the vision hadn't affected him at all.

"So . . ." I tentatively broke the silence. "What do you think?"

Matt's head fell forward, and he shook it. His shoulders sagged. He looked . . . defeated. It made me want to reach out to him. To place a hand between his shoulder blades where his tension was pooling and offer comfort. But I held back. I was trying to practice keeping my boundaries in place with him—something I'd historically been very bad at. But things were clearer in my mind now, and I was committed to listening to and honoring those feelings moving forward. So I kept my hands to myself. I didn't invite more complication where there didn't need to be any.

"Gods, Terah," Matt finally murmured, his voice hoarse. "What the hell am I supposed to do with that? What are we—*any of us*—supposed to do with that?" He finally raised his head so he could look at me. Tears pooled in his eyes, and I could see the hopelessness swimming there. There was frustration in his voice, but I knew it wasn't directed at me. It was toward the situation. Perhaps even the vision itself.

I sighed. "I don't know. Try to stop it from happening, I guess. Likely die while trying, per usual." I gave him a sardonic smile. "Their plan is horrific," I added, my smile fading. "There's no way it can work the way they think it will. You see that, right?" I bit my lip as anxiety simmered in my stomach.

Matt's gaze shifted to my mouth, and he watched as I worried my bottom lip with my teeth. The hazel seemed to deepen slightly. My shoulders tensed, and I abruptly stopped, releasing my lip from my teeth. Matt swallowed hard, and I shifted uncomfortably as his gaze lifted back to mine.

"I see that," he said, after taking a deep breath and finally looking away from me. I don't understand how—" he paused, rubbing the space between his eyebrows with his fingertips, like he was trying to stave off a headache. "I don't understand how the High Light Guardian could possibly think a plan that they *share* with the Dark Guardians could be a good or rational one. It just . . . doesn't make sense. I wish . . . I don't know. I wish I could ask Serafina about this. See if this is really her plan. If she sanctioned it. How she could've ever agreed to it."

I opened my mouth to speak, but Matt cut me off.

413

"I know I can't, Terah," he said, resignedly. "I know it'd get both of us killed. I just wish I could."

"So . . . you think the vision is credible?" I watched him closely.

Matt sighed heavily and sank back into the cushions of the couch. He let his head fall back until he was staring at the ceiling. "I've never heard of any book like that," he finally said, "but . . . it seems credible. I recognized one of the people in that room." Matt turned his head to look at me as I inhaled sharply.

"Really?" I was almost breathless. This was the reassurance I'd needed that this vision was real. Accurate. Even possible.

"Really." Matt looked unhappy. "One of the older women was a part of the political faction group that visited Dagmar when I was . . . I don't know, maybe twelve? It was after one of the really bad attacks where some of the Demons got past us and killed nearby Normals. It was one of the times that your mother . . . visited. So it was hard to forget."

Shock washed over me. That must mean that I'd seen her before, too. But I'd been too caught up in the fact that my mother was around and that I'd fought in that horrible battle, to really take notice. To be fair, I'd only been eight.

"Wow," I breathed, still feeling the waves of shock washing over me. "It must be real then."

Matt nodded slowly, his gaze raking over my face. "Probably."

"So what do we do?" I sank back into the couch. "How can we stop this and preferably not die?"

Matt made a sound, part frustration, part helplessness. "I don't know." His hands balled into fists on top of his thighs. "Doesn't seem like we can do much since no one's heard of the book. And . . . I have no idea how we'd find information about it without getting killed." He blew out a breath and shook his head. "This is such a shitty situation."

I nodded slowly. "Yeah, but when have we ever *not* been in shitty situations? We've managed to pull through so far." I gave him a small smile and nudged him with my shoulder, trying to lighten the mood a little.

Matt turned to look at me again, his face closer to mine than it'd been in months. Pain shot across his face. And longing. My stomach clenched, and I fought the urge to scoot away from him. It'd only hurt him if I did. And I didn't think he'd actually try anything. Not anymore.

"I suppose we have," he finally murmured, his voice hoarse. He stared into my eyes for a long moment, then turned away, clearing his throat.

"I'll need to think about it," he finally said, his voice a little more business-like now. A little more like the in-control Matt I'd seen this past year. The version of him that I knew the least. "I need to think about how we can best move forward without getting killed. And how we might start trying to figure out where the book is. We need to come up with a comprehensive plan that we stick to, especially if we don't want to be discovered."

"And we need to figure out how to tell the others," I added.

Matt looked at me quizzically. "Don't expect me to believe you haven't already told Gabriel." There was a bitter note to his voice. "Be real, Terah. You'd never tell me anything first."

I raised an eyebrow at him and leaned back, crossing my arms over my chest. "I would if I thought you'd tell on us and get him killed," I lied drily. He didn't need to know Gabriel knew. I'd only let him believe that once Caleb and Damian also knew. Then I'd have more confidence that Matt wouldn't report us.

Matt looked supremely unhappy with me, but he seemed to believe me. *Good.*

"Fine. Whatever," he grumbled. "I trust you can figure out how to tell him without my help."

I nodded stiffly.

"As for the other two," he continued, frustration thick in his voice, "maybe I can ask them to meet with me after training tomorrow in Luke's office. He clears out of there pretty fast. You and Gabriel can just meet us in there a minute or so later, so we don't raise any suspicions. And . . . I'll think about it overnight. Hopefully by tomorrow I'll have figured out some decent way of telling them. Some way to convince them not to get us all killed." He ran his hands anxiously through his hair.

"But you definitely think we should tell them?"

"I mean, from what you showed me, it looks like you have to. Just like you had to tell me. Maybe all of us are needed to pull this off."

I sighed, deflated, but nodded. "Okay. I just hope they don't get us killed." I pushed slowly to my feet and started heading for the door, but Matt pushed off the couch and grabbed my hand.

"Terah, wait." His voice was quiet.

I stiffened. I knew, somehow, what he wanted to say didn't have anything to do with this new mission. And that made me want to leave. I thought longingly of Gabriel waiting for me, and the lunch I was currently missing to be here. My stomach felt hollow from hunger.

"What is it, Matt?" I asked, resigned.

"It's just . . ." he squeezed my fingers gently. "Thank you. For trusting me. I know . . . I know it can't be easy for you right now. And . . ." he took a step closer to me, so his front was practically touching my back. I could feel the heat radiating off him as his familiar scent surrounded me. "I'm glad you came to me with this. I'm glad . . . you're here. I miss you, Terah. So, so much."

Without warning, he wrapped his arms around my waist and hugged me to him, my back firmly pressed to his front. I could practically feel the loneliness radiating from him. He buried his face against my hair briefly, rubbing the strands with his nose, inhaling, then released me just as suddenly and stepped away. Like he was trying not to cross too many boundaries, which I supposed was restraint for him.

I turned to stare at him, anger and pity warring against each other in my chest. I supposed he hadn't tried kissing me this time, but it still wasn't great. I wanted to yell at him about keeping his hands to himself. About asking first. Respecting my boundaries. He knew we weren't on hugging terms anymore. I'd barely let him touch my hand.

The tears in his eyes stopped me, though. And the trembling of his hands. Because I was weak. And because too much of me still deeply cared for Matt.

I swore internally, turned on my heel, and walked away. Disappointed in myself.

I got to train with Gabriel the next day, which was good because I was so nervous about telling Caleb and Damian about my vision—letting them know I had visions at all—that I was incredibly distracted and easily defeated. Gabriel overcame me multiple times during our hand-to-hand combat exercises—far more than he should've been able to since I'd healed —and threw me to the mat over and over again. He was gentle, at least.

"Earth to Terah," he said in my ear after throwing me to the mat again. He was smiling.

"I know, I know," I grumbled as he rolled off me and I pushed into a sitting position. "I'm sorry. I'm just nervous."

"I figured." He reached down and pulled me to my feet. "It's okay. I just feel like I'm participating in a one-sided fight. Either that or I've suddenly become the best fighter in the world." He smirked, and I shot him a glare.

"Is that your way of challenging me to destroy you in this next fight?" I raised an eyebrow at him. "Because you know I will."

Gabriel laughed and slid his arms around my waist, pulling me gently against him and pressing a kiss to my forehead. "Maybe it's just my way of distracting you so you won't be as nervous," he murmured against my skin.

I raised onto my toes and brushed a kiss over his lips. "Challenge accepted. Can't back out of it now, lover boy. You're going down."

Gabriel grinned and released me, then we took our fighting stances across from each other again.

Not even a full minute later, I had Gabriel on his back on the mat, pinned so he couldn't get leverage.

"I yield," he gasped, winded. I eased the pressure on him and sat up, watching as a broad grin spread across his face. "Wow, that world's best fighter comment really got to you, huh?"

"Well, you *did* want me to be less distracted, sooo . . . this is kinda what that means."

Gabriel laughed as he pushed to his feet, then swept me into a quick hug. "Welcome back," he murmured, humor dancing in his eyes.

Matt approached Caleb and Damian after training ended, and I watched out of the corner of my eye as he spoke to them, apprehension boiling in my stomach. Both young men looked confused, and Caleb looked defensive, as though he thought he was in trouble for something. But they both nodded after a few moments and headed toward Luke's office. Matt turned and met my eyes briefly, and I gave him a small nod. Gabriel and I loitered in the training room as everyone headed for the locker rooms. We didn't want it to look like we were going to Luke's office as well. We didn't want anyone asking questions or noticing we were all meeting privately. The less that people suspected, the safer we'd be.

We walked over once the training room cleared, and I pushed open the office door. Matt was leaning on the edge of the large wooden desk, one ankle crossed over the other, his hands on either side of his hips, braced against the edge of the tabletop. Caleb and Damian were sitting in the two chairs in front of the desk, both still looking confused.

"Ah, here they are." Matt sounded both relieved and nervous.

Damian and Caleb turned as Gabriel closed the door, and their eyes widened. I noted, wryly, that this was probably the only time I'd ever seen Damian confused. He always seemed to know what was going on around him. But apparently not this time.

Gabriel and I went to stand against the wall to the side of the desk so we could see the other three easily.

"I brought you two here today," Matt began, looking at Caleb and Damian, "because a situation has arisen that requires your help." He paused, and I knew he was working to keep his nerves under wraps. He wanted to look calm. In control. Not afraid. He was mostly succeeding—I could only see his underlying tension because I knew him so well.

"However, I want to give you both a choice," Matt continued, looking at each of them in turn, his expression serious. "This mission requires you to know things that you're prohibited from knowing. Knowing these things will place you in danger, and if anyone from either side of the war knows you know, you'll be executed, regardless of who you are or what side you're on."

Caleb frowned and glanced at me, presumably to see if this information was new to me. It obviously wasn't, so he turned his head slowly back to face Matt, a look of alarm warring with indecision and confusion on his face. Damian's eyebrows furrowed in the smallest frown, but he didn't say anything or really move at all. He just continued watching Matt. Waiting.

"We have an ally affiliated with the Light Guardians," Matt continued, "who has visions of the future. Visions of things that might happen if not prevented, visions of things that will happen but haven't happened yet, and so on. I know and have access to this person because of my position in the warrior faction."

Emotion swelled in my chest, and I fought to keep my expression neutral. He wasn't telling them that it was me. He wasn't revealing I was the one who had visions. He was . . . protecting me. Not giving them ammunition to hurt or report on me in the future. I was . . . really grateful for that. Matt's eyes briefly flicked to mine, and I saw warmth in the hazel depths.

"This person," Matt continued, returning his gaze to the two men in front of him, "had a vision of a shared Dark Guardian and Light Guardian plot that will result in the end of the world regardless of who is successful. It's a plot that both sides are relying on to help them win the war, but it's not a plot that'll work in either side's favor. It'll only result in death and destruction for the entire world."

Caleb's confusion was now tinged with horror. Damian's expression remained largely blank, but his fingers tightened around the arms of his chair.

"This person also saw a way of preventing this catastrophe," Matt

418

continued. "They saw all of you," he gestured to each of us with one hand, "working together to stop it. This person came to me and trusted me with their life by telling me this plan. They only did so because of my rank, and because I'm one of the only people who knows all of you. They trusted in the fact that, because I know you, I wouldn't want to be the one reporting this and getting you all killed. Nor would I want to die myself. They were right about both of those things. So I'm giving you a choice. You can choose to know the contents of that vision and forfeit your life, but ultimately help save the world; you can choose not to know and walk away, your life safe for now, but knowing the plan may not be preventable without you; or, you can choose to hear the contents of that vision, report it to those higher up, and result in all of us, including yourself, being executed."

Caleb sank back in his chair looking stunned. Damian's expression remained stony, but he couldn't hide the tension in his body—a crack in his mask.

"Obviously none of those options are great," Matt added, "but it's the reality of the situation. I told Terah and Gabriel about this first, since I ran into them earlier, and they've agreed to be told. But I wanted to wait to share the details until I have answers from the two of you. I won't put their lives in danger if either of you are planning to report this."

I bit the inside of my cheek. Matt was protecting both me *and* Gabriel now, at the possible expense of his own life. I genuinely never though he'd do that. I wondered if he was starting to grow beyond himself and his own more self-centered wants and needs into a real leader. One who put the safety and well-being of others before himself. Who took the responsibility, even if it wasn't solely his to shoulder. Unselfishly. That'd be a new trait for Matt. A good one.

"You can have time to think about it if you need to," Matt finally said. "You don't have to make that decision today. I get that it's a large one."

Caleb nodded slowly, his eyes now trained on the floor. I knew this was hard for him. Potentially harder than it'd been for Matt. Caleb's greatest wish was to be the highest-ranking member of the warrior faction. Being involved in this mission—in thwarting the Light Guardian side—directly opposed that plan. If he agreed to help, he might never achieve his dream. He might not even survive to try. And what Caleb wanted, over all else, was his own survival and success.

Damian, on the other hand, just ended up shrugging. "Fine, whatever. I'll help. It doesn't seem like we have much of a choice anyway. If we don't help, the world will supposedly end, and we'll all die. If we do help, the world may not end, but we'll still maybe die. Looks like death is on the table either way. Might as well at least try to do something."

All of us looked at Damian in surprise. I'd assumed he'd be difficult to convince. That he'd want to stay as far away from this as possible. That was the vibe he exuded—that he looked out for himself and himself alone. Not unlike Caleb. And that mentality didn't lend itself to a potential suicide mission like this one. But Damian *was* still a border town soldier. I had to remind myself of that sometimes. And border town soldiers were raised to be martyrs. To always be given impossible situations that we were somehow expected to deal with and survive through. And, above all else, we were raised to always protect the innocent—to save the world or liter-ally die trying. And all of us in the vision were border town kids. That couldn't be a coincidence. Perhaps Damian felt the pull of that responsi-bility just as strongly as I did, only he hid it better.

Matt nodded slowly at Damian, watching him closely, trying to read how genuine he was being before trusting him with our lives. But Dami-an's face was expressionless. He had it on lockdown. Probably to keep us from seeing any nervousness or fear that he might be feeling. I knew him well enough now to know he didn't like showing anyone his vulnerability. Another common border town trait.

Matt finally gave up trying to decipher his expression and turned to Caleb. "Do you need more time to decide?"

Caleb glanced up at Matt. He looked unhappy. A little panicky. And he still looked undecided. Clearly, Damian agreeing to be told had thrown Caleb. He'd probably hoped Damian would say no. Then he wouldn't have felt so guilty about refusing too. And he would've been able to convince himself that refusing was the right thing to do. But he couldn't do that now, so he was flailing.

After a few more moments of silence, Caleb turned his head until his eyes met mine again. His gaze raked over my face desperately as he pushed his hand nervously through his hair. I didn't know what he was trying to find there. Permission for him to say no? Some hint that I, also, didn't want to be involved? Whatever it was, he wouldn't find it there. I just stared back at him, resigned yet resolute. I knew we had to do this. We had to at least try.

Caleb turned away from me, almost frustrated, and pinched the bridge of his nose between his thumb and forefinger as he closed his eyes and took a deep, steadying breath. Then he swore and opened his eyes.

"Fine," he growled. "You can tell me too. I'll do my best to help. Like Damian said, it doesn't seem like we have much of a choice."

Matt nodded slowly at him before his eyes flicked to mine to gauge my reaction.

"All four of you promise not to report any of this to anyone?" Matt asked. All four of us murmured that we wouldn't. "Okay," Matt said heavily. Then he launched into a detailed description of the contents of my vision.

Gabriel and I tried our best to pretend we were hearing it for the first time. When Matt finally finished describing it, Caleb looked pale and like he might throw up. He was gripping the arms of his chair tightly with fingers that were going ghostly white. Damian's expression was still largely unreadable, though his eyebrows had furrowed slightly, and his jaw was clenched. He seemed at least a little upset.

"How can we even stop that?" Caleb finally murmured, a slight tremor in his voice. I sympathized. The reality before us wasn't a pretty one. "And even if we somehow find the book before they do, what would we do with it? How would we keep them from immediately finding and killing us anyway, and just taking the book then?"

Damian looked at Matt curiously. So did Gabriel and I. After all, none of us really had a plan.

"With research and incredibly careful planning," Matt finally said. "We need to be strategic about each step of this process, and we need to have it planned out before we even start. The fewer variables we have, and the quicker we can complete the mission, the less likely we are to make mistakes or be discovered."

None of us seemed to feel particularly soothed.

"We should meet in a different location each time," Matt continued. "And since we're running on a tight timeline here, our first meeting should be tonight after dinner. Does that work for all of you?"

We nodded.

"Okay, let's meet in Terah's room tonight, since it's the biggest of your dorms. We can work on mapping out what needs to be done, and by whom. Is that alright?" Matt asked, turning toward me.

I stiffened slightly, knowing Matt would be upset when he saw the obvious signs that Gabriel was living there with me, but I nodded anyway. He'd just have to get over that like he had to get over everything else. And it really shouldn't surprise him. But I knew, instinctively, that it would. My stomach clenched, and I bit the inside of my cheek.

"Okay, let's meet there at 7:00 then," Matt said. Caleb and Damian nodded. Gabriel, sensing my tension, slid his hand into mine and squeezed it gently. "You're all free to leave. See you later."

Damian and Caleb shoved to their feet and booked it out of the room. They clearly wanted space, and time to think about everything that'd just happened. I didn't blame them. We'd thrown a lot at them all at once. Gabriel pushed off the wall and began following them out, but I pulled back on his hand so I could briefly turn to Matt.

"Thanks for doing that," I murmured, keeping my voice low in case anyone else was nearby. "And thanks for protecting us. That was . . . really decent of you."

Matt smiled a little, his expression tinged with sadness. Perhaps that's just how he smiled now. Sadly. I couldn't remember the last time I'd seen him truly happy.

"It's fine, Terah," he said quietly, taking a step closer to me. "It needed to be done, and it was the right thing to do." He glanced briefly at Gabriel before clenching his jaw and looking back at me. He took a step back. "I'll see you tonight."

I nodded, backing away from him, then turned and walked with Gabriel from the room.

Caleb and Damian arrived first that night, lightly knocking on my door before slipping quickly inside. Damian whistled as he looked around, noting the size of my room. And that it had a fireplace and bathroom.

"Nice," he murmured.

Caleb didn't say anything, but I saw him glance at the bed and then away quickly, his cheeks tinged with pink. I rolled my eyes and plopped down in one of the armchairs near the fireplace. We'd turned them so they faced the foot of the bed, allowing us to sit in a circle for our meeting.

I sighed heavily as I leaned back and crossed my arms over my chest, extending my heeled-combat-boot-clad feet out in front of me on the floor. This whole thing was going to be so damn uncomfortable. It was almost enough to have me missing cigarettes. Gabriel shot me a commiserating look before taking the armchair next to me.

I let Matt in a couple minutes later, and he joined Damian and Caleb on the edge of my bed. I tried really hard not to think about all of them being here. And how much I really didn't want these three men in particular in my personal space.

I took a slow breath, trying to calm my nerves. This was for something much bigger than me. Much bigger than all of us. I could put the bad and awkward shit aside to get this done.

"Okay," I said, my voice a practiced calm. "What should our first steps be?"

Matt looked contemplative, Damian stoic. Caleb looked unhappy, but no surprises there.

"We should probably start with research," Gabriel said, his voice equally calm and matter of fact. "But we shouldn't just center our research on the book. Obviously, we want to learn more about it, but we should also attempt to learn more about the construction of the Academy, since everyone thinks the book is hidden here. Because the book was so secret, we're probably not going to find information about it in our history books. But the building of the Academy wasn't a secretive process, so we'd probably have more luck getting hints about where the book might be from the construction records. We should try to find building plans and sketches, records, journals, and historical accounts of the construction. Hopefully something in those will point us to where we should look or what we should do next."

I smiled a little. As always, he was smart and practical, and had a knack for looking at things in unique ways. Even Matt and Damian looked impressed.

Matt nodded slowly, pulling on his lip as he thought. "That's not a bad idea. I may actually have a friend who can help with that. Not directly—I won't tell him about the vision or anything—but he's spent a lot of time researching the historical relationships between different factions of Divines, so he can probably point us to where the information is about the Divines who built the Academy, and where any construction records are. I'll ask him about that tomorrow."

"He's here?" Damian asked, speaking for the first time. "Is he a student?"

Matt shook his head. "No. He graduated, but he's stuck around so he can work on his research for the book he's writing. He mostly stays for the library." Matt shrugged. "It's the largest collection of Divine literature, history, and historical journals in the world. Larger even than the Grand Archive. He pretty much spends all his time in there."

Damian nodded, the neutral expression descending over his face again.

"So, how are we going to do all this research without someone noticing?" Caleb asked, raising his eyebrows challengingly at Matt. "If we don't want to die, we need to make sure no one notices what we're doing. But it'll be hard to do that if all of us are suddenly spending all our time in the library pouring over blueprints of the school."

I shrugged. "We can take turns doing research. That wouldn't look too out of place since we're all supposed to be studying for our upcoming exams anyway. And we don't share all our classes with the same people, so people won't know that what we're doing isn't for some other class."

"If, for argument's sake, I believe we could really pull that off without being noticed," Caleb continued, sending a cold glare in my direction, "and if we actually find the book, what the hell do we do with it then? We can't just hide it somewhere else. There's no way that would stay a secret for very long. And I don't think we can just destroy it either. So what are we supposed to do? How does this not just end with them finding us, taking the book, and killing us?"

Damian gave Caleb a sardonic look—like he thought Caleb was being melodramatic. But Caleb maintained his resolve, and looked at each of us, challenging us to meaningfully respond to his question. I didn't know what to say. Because I was afraid of all those same things. Matt looked stumped. Gabriel's expression was carefully neutral, but I could tell he was worried too.

"We could try to do what the Dark Guardians have done," Damian finally said, leaning forward so his elbows could rest on his knees. "And what the neutral group of Divines did when they created the school. We could try opening a rip in the plane, creating a really small unsanctioned plane, hiding the book there, then sealing it."

We all turned to look at him like he'd lost his mind.

"But that's not possible." Caleb's voice was full of disbelief. "It can't be done without an enormous number of Divines all combining their powers. We'd need hundreds of people. Maybe thousands. Without that, we can only fortify and manipulate planes that are already there. Besides, from everything I've heard, the creation of new planes is kind of lost knowledge. Even closing plane tears has basically been impossible for us for a few hundred years without enormous amounts of power at our disposal."

"Plus, even if we could," I interjected, "I don't think we'd be able to keep it a secret for long. The Light Guardians pretty much always know when a new tear in the Normal plane is created."

"They only know that because Demons start pouring through those tears, and because those tears aren't ever closed," Damian said, seeming unbothered by our incredulity. "Demons won't be coming out of this tear, and it will be small enough for us to close it, so there's no way the Light Guardians or Dark Guardians will know about it."

"But what about Caleb's point?" I pushed. "How would we amass enough power to do that without recruiting a bunch of people and giving ourselves away? And how would we even figure out how to create a new plane in such a short amount of time when no one has that information anymore?"

Damian looked at us, his brow furrowing slightly, like he wasn't sure how much to tell us. "We *may*," he said slowly, "have recovered information about that from some Dark Guardians and Demons that we captured and, er, *questioned* in our border town."

Matt fully turned to face him now, looking both stunned and angry. "What? But the Light Guardian leadership doesn't have that information. Did your town not report it?"

Damian shrugged, still looking unconcerned. "I'm just a lowly soldier," he said, a ghost of a smile on his face, and a hint of bitterness in his voice. "I don't get to make the decisions about who knows what and what is or is not reported to the higher ups. Who knows—it might've been reported but the Light Guardian leadership is keeping the info from being widely known. I have no idea. I just fight when I'm told to fight. I don't have a choice. But . . . I did hear enough that I may be able to help with this. Maybe that's why the vision wanted me included." He shrugged.

Matt still looked angry, but I could tell Damian's words were getting to him. Maybe that *was* why Damian had been included in the vision. It certainly was a unique way of solving the what-to-do-with-the-book problem. It might even allow us to survive.

Matt met my gaze, and I shrugged. I didn't know what I was doing any more than he did.

"So how do you do it?" Gabriel asked, his gaze sharp and challenging. He clearly wasn't as convinced by Damian's speech as the rest of us were.

Damian slid his cool, calculating gaze over to Gabriel, and they stared at each other in silence for a few moments. Finally, Damian rolled his eyes and broke eye contact with Gabriel.

"It's less about huge amounts of power, and more about concentrated intensity," he finally said. "People don't tend to think about divine power like that, so it never occurs to people to use it that way. We just throw large, sloppy amounts of power at each other all the time, or make dramatic things happen with fire or water or plants, and that's all we think we can do. But we can create things, too, in a more abstract manner. Like matter-shifting, but on a more minute level. Yes, we'd need to combine our powers to do it, but we might be able to pull it off, especially if we're creating a really small space. You'd only need immense amounts of power if you wanted to create a large kingdom or a large plane rip. But that's not what we're trying to do."

I felt a bit thunderstruck by this information, but I didn't have time to process it right now, so I shoved the shock to the side. Right now, we needed to strategize and act. I'd fall apart about it all later. If we survived.

"And you know enough about how it's done to guide us in creating and closing a new plane quickly?" I stared intently at Damian. I was pushing this because his competency, or lack thereof, could be the difference between us surviving or dying. We had to be sure. "You only claimed that you overheard it. We don't even know that you heard the whole thing."

Damian stared back at me, his dark eyes piercing coldly into my own. And for the first time in several weeks, I thought I felt a tugging in my mind. A gentle push, as though someone else's consciousness had bumped gently into mine. But the feeling was gone almost as quickly as it'd come. I clenched my jaw, not sure whether I'd felt anything at all.

Damian tilted his head as he regarded me, a ghost of a smile pulling at his mouth. "Yeah, I heard enough. I didn't want to put you all off by going too much into it," he continued, glancing around at the rest of the group, sarcasm thick in his voice, "but I was there for the entire . . . questioning. I heard everything the captives said. Before they couldn't speak anymore . . ."

We all stared at him in horror. It sounded like . . . they'd tortured their captives. Like they weren't just defending and protecting their territory—they were harming and forcefully interrogating outside of the battle situation. That wasn't something that border town soldiers were supposed to do, and it certainly wasn't sanctioned by the Light Guardians. But . . . there were a lot of border towns, and a lot of people died horribly in them because of Demons and Dark Guardians. It wasn't unheard of for people to get carried away with their grief and anger and engage in unsanctioned behavior. And who knew how the Light Guardian leadership dealt with that. It wouldn't surprise me if there were those in the Light Guardian leadership who unofficially sanctioned those actions to benefit from whatever information such behavior could get them. I scowled. And they truly thought they were *so much better* than the Dark Guardians . . .

"I didn't participate in the questioning," Damian continued, almost amused, as he watched our judgmental discomfort, "but I was one of the soldiers assigned to guard the doors to the room in case the questioners lost control of the prisoners, so I had to be there the entire time. It's not like I had a choice."

Well, I supposed that was something. At least he hadn't been one of the torturers. But being there and just letting it happen wasn't much better, regardless of his orders.

Damian sighed, straightening up. "My point is, I learned enough that I'm confident that we can recreate it on a small scale in a short amount of time. And it's the only option *I* can think of where we can hide the book so it can't be found."

I stared at Damian, stony faced, thinking. Then I glanced at Gabriel and saw he was doing the same thing. I wondered if he felt as undecided as I did. Matt looked angry but was clearly considering Damian's words, likely airing on the side of believing him. Caleb looked mildly disgusted, but overall unbothered by what Damian had revealed. As though he thought torture was going too far but didn't care enough to be truly upset by it. Well, I supposed there was a reason they were friends.

"Does that answer your question?" Damian asked, turning to look at me again. He raised his eyebrow at me, like he thought I was the one being dramatic. I glared at him. I was being practical and trying to keep all of us —including him—from being murdered. Sometimes I really wanted to punch him in the face.

But in the end, all we had was his word. We didn't have a choice about trusting him and relying on him to recreate something he'd never actually seen or done. To recreate something solely based on a description. There was no time for indecision or doubt. Every day that passed was a day the Dark or Light Guardians could find the book and cause the end of life as we knew it. We'd just have to rely on the fact that Damian wouldn't want to die either. Because if he failed in this, he'd die too.

I sat back in my chair, letting it go for now.

"Good." Damian smiled mildly and leaned back.

"So," Gabriel said, turning to look at Matt, his jaw clenching like it always did when he was forced to interact with him, "once you talk to your friend about potential sources, who should be responsible for what research? And what should our timeline look like?"

Matt's shoulders stiffened as he regarded Gabriel. "Once we have some guidance on where to start, I suggest we work in groups and trade off who researches what. Each day, one group will research the book, and the other will research the building of the Academy. We can meet at the end of each day and compare notes. It's a lot of work, but it's an urgent situation. Hopefully we'll be able to make enough headway in a week or so that we can start looking for the book on the grounds. Though we'll have to do that at night, so people don't see us."

"Great," Caleb said bitterly. "We're not going to get any sleep at all. How are we supposed to pass our classes so we can still protect the Academy moving forward if all our time is spent on this mission?"

"You can't protect the Academy," I said coolly, "if the world ends. There won't be an Academy left to protect. Or a warrior faction left to join." I gave him a hard, quizzical look.

Caleb shot another cold glare at me. *Good.* I could handle him when he was mad at me. It was the softer more conflicted Caleb that I didn't want anywhere near me—that put me on edge and made me uncomfortable.

"Can we call it a night?" Gabriel asked curtly, clearly reaching his limit on how long he could deal with this particular group of people in our space. I felt the same. The sooner it was just us again, the better.

Matt sighed, resignedly. "Yeah. Let's regroup after dinner tomorrow night. We can meet in my room next time. Staff residence building four, room eighteen."

He pushed to his feet, and Damian and Caleb followed suit. Matt's eyes flicked over to Gabriel, and I wondered if he expected him to get up and leave too. My shoulders stiffened as I felt the ambient tension building.

Caleb and Damian made their way to the door and pulled it open, and Matt turned and followed slowly behind them. Caleb went through first, clearly eager to leave, but Damian paused as he was passing through the door and looked back at Matt, almost amused.

"Come on, Matt. They clearly want us out of their space."

I turned my head slightly to look. Matt had frozen halfway between the armchairs and the door, staring at my open closet. I glanced at it too and saw what he was seeing: half of the closet was still filled with my stuff, but the other half housed all of Gabriel's clothes, jackets, and shoes. He clearly lived here with me.

Matt's hands balled into fists so tight that his fingers turned a ghostly white. His body was so stiff that he looked like he'd turned to stone. He finally glanced back at me, and I saw fresh despair in his eyes. *Damnit.* I knew it'd be a bad idea to have him in here. He was never going to handle this well. But I felt no remorse. I loved Gabriel. I wanted to share a space with him. I just didn't want to see Matt as he was forced to face that reality. It was awkward. Uncomfortable. Painful.

Matt's jaw tightened, and he turned and stormed from the room without saying anything. Damian rolled his eyes, then followed Matt out. I quickly pushed to my feet and shoved the door closed behind them, then sank back against it, releasing a deep breath, suddenly completely exhausted.

20

THE DEEP UNKNOWN

THREE WEEKS LATER, I WAS CERTAIN ABOUT TWO THINGS: I'D NEVER been this tired before in my entire life, and we were no closer to figuring out where the book was hidden than we'd been when we'd started.

Initially, the five of us had switched off when and what we researched, then met each night to report our findings. But it quickly became clear that we couldn't sustain that level of activity and fatigue for much longer. That's when the group research sessions started. For the past two weeks, we'd all headed to the library after classes, to the deepest, darkest, most hidden section—the one Matt's friend Zamir had pointed us to. We'd realized after the first week that no other students or staff ever got close to this part of the library, so there really wasn't a reason to hide our presence there.

Each night, one of us would grab food from the dining hall for the whole group. We'd fill a bag with as many portable food items as possible, then we'd pile a tray high with warm food to share. Then we'd walk everything to the library, quickly disappearing between the tall stacks of books before anyone could really notice. The trick to all this was walking with confidence, like you weren't doing anything wrong or weird. If you did that, the most people would do was give you a quick, weird look before turning away and promptly forgetting about you.

Tonight was Damian's turn, and I sighed with relief as he finally found us in the back corner of the library. Training and classes had been especially hard today, and I was starving. Damian slid an iced coffee across the table to me as he balanced the tray of food in his other hand, a ghost of a smile pulling at his lips. The coldness that I'd gotten used to seeing in his eyes had receded to the background. It'd been less and less present these past few weeks.

I smiled. "Thanks."

I grabbed the coffee and took a long sip, grateful for the caffeine. After Gabriel had made a point to grab iced coffee for me several nights in a row during our first week of group research, Damian had realized it was not only my favorite drink, but also that I got irritated much quicker without it. So now, out of kindness or purely out of a desire to keep me from biting all their heads off, he made sure to grab one for me each time it was his or Caleb's turn to bring us food. Matt had caught on and did that as well. It was kind of funny, but I appreciated it all the same.

Damian had grown on me over the past few weeks, and I found myself appreciating his insight, quick wit, and dry, sharp humor. I was seeing more and more of the nice person beneath the cold mask—a person that he didn't seem to want anyone to see. But spending so much time with us seemed to be wearing down the walls around him. Hopefully for the better.

"Find anything?" Damian asked as he carefully deposited the tray of food in the middle of the table. He unloaded some silverware and a few more items from his bag before sitting next to Caleb and grabbing a book.

"Not really," Caleb grumbled, grabbing a fork. "But we did finish going through another stack. So that's something, I guess."

Damian looked a little disappointed, though not surprised. He shrugged and grabbed a fork, then stabbed a piece of roasted carrot and opened the book he'd grabbed. It looked like an old budget booklet, probably kept by a past Academy president.

After our unsuccessful first week with a more expansive search radius, we'd focused on records from the Academy's history. This included journals from teachers, old assignments from students, and occasionally building records and sketches of the Academy's different stages of construction. The problem was that none of it was organized by time or type of record. It was all just thrown onto the shelves nonsensically.

Of the ten or so long and tall stacks that carried Academy records, we'd completely looked through about eight. That meant that we'd gone through every book, record, and piece of paper on eight entire rows of bookshelves. And we still hadn't found anything useful. While we'd found

431

some construction sketches of the dorms our first week, those had been a dead end. And just yesterday we'd found construction sketches of the main classroom building. We'd spent the rest of the night pouring over the intricate drawings, trying to determine whether any secret areas were implied in the design—anywhere that they might've hidden something as important as the book—but after hours of scouring, we'd concluded there weren't any areas that we hadn't seen or had access to as students. After spending so much time on it, we'd all taken the realization hard, but Damian had actually shoved to his feet and walked out of the library. According to Caleb, he'd probably gone to the lounge so he could drown his frustration with beer. We'd all sympathized with that need.

Today, we'd started going through the ninth stack, each tackling a different row of books within it. We'd all skimmed through a few by the time Damian had arrived with food, but none of us had found anything compelling. I'd stumbled across a stack of student journals, some work-books filled in with homework assignments, and some random, frayed text-books. I rolled my eyes and tossed yet another workbook onto the reviewed pile in front of me. This one had been particularly bad, and had ended with a student's essay on why, despite the importance of neutrality at the Academy, Divines shouldn't marry and reproduce outside of their factions. It was pure ignorance and prejudice, and it deserved to be burned. If we weren't in the library, I probably would've set it ablaze.

I grabbed a fork and speared a piece of chicken, then pulled another book toward me. This one looked like a student journal. It didn't look very old, maybe fifty years or so, so I didn't have high hopes of finding anything useful in it. But I flipped it open anyway and skimmed through while I took bites of chicken. The journal had belonged to a person named Eliza, who . . . seemed to have been a Dark Guardian. Her parents had lived in the Normal world, generally abstaining from the war, but that hadn't mattered at the Academy. Eliza, who'd been a timid, quiet person, had been ostracized by her classmates. People had bullied her, hurt her, pushed her out. I wondered if this had happened before the rule existed that prohibited students from asking each other about their Divine faction, or if the rule hadn't ultimately protected her. Either way, her ostracization had caused her to seek refuge in out-of-the-way places where she could be alone. And she drew those places in beautiful, intricate detail, in the pages of her journal.

I found myself mesmerized by her rendition of a wrought-iron bench in front of the border of trees surrounding campus. Each curl of wrought iron looked like it was made of hammered metal, not pencil on paper, and the feet of the bench sank into plush-looking grass. Each tree was formed with hundreds of individual leaves, and the texture of the bark was drawn in such detail that I expected to feel the coarseness of the wood beneath my finger. Somehow, she'd made them look like they were swaying in the wind. I could almost feel the breeze, smell the freshness of the grass on the air. It was all so real. Eliza . . . had been really talented. I wondered if she'd managed to escape the war after she left the Academy. I wondered if she'd grown old. Or if she'd died young like so many of our kind.

I turned the pages and saw equally detailed renditions of the dining hall, a dorm common room, a medical wing room, the carving of the bar in the student lounge during daylight, the exterior of the main building from a variety of angles, and many drawings of the chapel. All the drawings had one thing in common: each space was empty. She'd drawn them all in the safety of solitude, when no one was around to torment her. My stomach tightened. Was I feeling . . . bad for a Dark Guardian? I shook myself and refocused. Pages and pages were filled with the chapel's high ceiling made of pointed arches, the wooden pews that filled the room, the carved stone altar and podium, the stained-glass windows that lined the walls. From the volume of drawings, it seemed like the chapel was the place that was empty most often and was therefore her most frequent refuge.

I turned yet another page and froze, my mouth opening in surprise. I'd come face to face with a drawing of something I'd seen before. And I was kicking myself for not remembering it sooner. How had I forgotten? I'd stared at it for minutes over winter break. It was a drawing of a stained-glass window—the one depicting four Divines, one of each faction, kneeling around a large book, each extending a hand forward to touch the cover. At the time, I'd assumed it was symbolic of our shared mission as Divines. And maybe it was. But . . . maybe it meant something more, too.

"Gabriel," I murmured, setting my fork down as I continued to stare at the drawing, "look at this."

Gabriel leaned over, his arm coming to rest on the back of my chair. "Oh, shit," he murmured as he stared at it too. "That's from the chapel, isn't it?"

"Yeah. I looked at it when we were in there over break, but I totally forgot about it."

"Did you find something?" Damian asked, looking back and forth between us intently.

"Maybe." I spun the book and slid it to the middle of the table for him to look. "It's a window in the chapel. We've seen it in person as well."

Damian, Matt, and Caleb all leaned forward to get a better look at the drawing. Almost as one, their eyes widened, and their mouths opened. Like they'd never actually expected to find information about the book.

Matt shook his head. "I can't believe I didn't remember that." His surprise was turning to frustration. "I've been in the chapel countless times over the past five years. How did I not fucking remember?"

I shrugged. "None of us had ever heard of the book. If you didn't associate the image with an actual object instead of symbolism, you wouldn't remember it in this context."

Matt frowned, still looking upset with himself, but Caleb leaned forward and pulled the journal closer.

"Do you think the book is hidden in the chapel, then?" He frowned as he flipped through a few adjacent pages.

Gabriel leaned back in his chair. "Who knows. But it's the first lead we've gotten. Might be worth checking it out."

Damian leaned back as well. "We should definitely check it out." He sounded calm, but I could see the hint of urgency in his eyes. We were all feeling it—the pressure to find the book and get it out of reach of the Light and Dark Guardians before the semester ended. "It was clear from the construction sketches that there aren't hiding places built into the dorms or main building, so the next logical place to look would probably be the chapel anyway. It's either that, the lounge, or the administrative building."

I frowned and leaned back, crossing my arms over my chest as I thought. The chapel was mainly just one large, open room, perhaps with a few storage rooms in the back. If it was really hidden there, it was probably underground somewhere. An image flared to life in my mind—a dark room, steep stairs leading down, seemingly vanishing into a black abyss. My jaw clenched, tension radiating out like forks of lightning through my body. Had this been what those visions were about?

I reached out to Gabriel with my mind and showed him what I'd seen.

"Those marks on the floor," Gabriel murmured silently. "Remember? The symbols of the gods that are on some stones and not others. Maybe they have something to do with this. Maybe we have to use them to find the hidden passageway. Like a code or something."

I turned to him in surprise, my heart pounding. That sounded . . . plausible at the very least. It was the closest thing we'd gotten to finding a lead.

I glanced across the table and noticed Matt studying us, his jaw clenched. He could tell we were talking in our minds. I could see curiosity there under the upset—he knew me well enough to know there was more we hadn't yet shared. I glanced quickly at the others to see if they'd noticed too. Caleb was still staring at the drawing, and Damian's eyes were on Matt, his brow furrowed slightly. Both looked deep in thought.

I shifted my gaze back to Matt. "Are there any other anomalies in the chapel? Anything else that's different from the other buildings? Any details that stand out or aren't present anywhere else on campus?"

I wanted to see if he'd noticed the symbols on the stones before. If he knew why they were there or had any other insights about the building. Matt watched me for a long moment, squinting slightly. He knew he was being led toward something. He sighed and rubbed a hand over his eyes.

"I guess there are a couple things. Most notable are the symbols on the floor. Symbols of the gods," he clarified as Caleb and Damian looked at him questioningly. "They're carved into some of the stones on the floor. Sat through enough boring assemblies during my time here that I eventually noticed them. I haven't seen anything similar in any of the other buildings. And the second anomaly is related—the chapel generally holds most of the iconography of the gods and the four factions of Divines on campus. Iconography that's absent in the rest of the buildings, except for the carving on the bar in the lounge."

"Don't you think that's just because it's a chapel?" Caleb interjected, an eyebrow raised. "It's meant to be the one religious building on campus. Everything else is academic and wouldn't necessarily require that iconography."

Matt shrugged. "That's possible. But it's something that stands out. And the iconography plus the window with the image of the book feels significant."

Damian ran his hand over his chin thoughtfully. "It's worth checking out. It's the best lead we have, and we're not working with a lot of time."

"I agree," I murmured.

"When should we do it then?" Caleb asked, resigned. "We need to make sure no one knows what we're doing."

"Night would be best," Gabriel murmured, glancing at me, his arm still across the back of my chair. "If it's tonight, we need time to change and gather supplies in case we find something. If we don't want to go tonight, we probably shouldn't put it off past tomorrow. I don't want to give anyone the opportunity to find or take the book before we get there."

"I think we should do it tomorrow night," Damian said, leaning forward and resting his arms on the table in front of him. His expression was neutral again. Colder. Like he was trying to hide his nerves. "We don't want to leave anything to chance, but I think it's safe to say we're all exhausted. If we go tonight, we won't be as alert. We might be setting ourselves up to fail. Tomorrow's the weekend. We can sleep in, gather supplies, and meet at the chapel around nightfall. The sooner we can get the book and hide it, the better, but we want to make sure we do it right."

Matt nodded slowly. "Does everyone agree with that?" He glanced around the table.

All of us nodded. We were all exhausted, and we knew Damian was right.

"Okay. Tomorrow night, make sure you pack an assortment of weapons, wear battle-ready clothes, and pack a few provisions. We don't know how long it'll take, what we'll face, or if we'll even find anything. It may be another dead end. But be prepared. Just in case."

All of us nodded solemnly. This was an adventure that none of us were happy to be a part of. While we might be closer to finding the book and thwarting the Light and Dark Guardians' horrible plan. We were also closer to death than we'd been so far in this process. And the further we pursued the book, the more unsafe we'd be.

We ended up meeting at the chapel around midnight the next night. While we'd intended to be there closer to dusk, the other students on campus had forced us to change our plans. Even though it was the last weekend before exams started, almost everyone was piled into their respective common areas, blowing off some last-minute steam before the crushing pressure of finals began. There was copious drinking, loud music, games, and movies blaring. And there were people *everywhere*. Which meant that we couldn't walk through our dorms heavily armed and carrying various combat and survival gear without drawing a lot of attention.

Instead, we waited in our respective dorm rooms, texting each other updates for several hours. I was going stir crazy, pacing around our room with no outlet for my nervous energy. Gabriel was sitting in one of the armchairs by the fireplace checking and rechecking our gear and sharpening all our weapons. It was his way of working through his nerves—

making sure we were as prepared as possible. I preferred to jump into the action. Fight. *Do* something. I hated waiting.

Eventually, I couldn't take it anymore. With a frustrated growl, I stalked to the window, threw it open, and climbed out of it, bypassing the common area altogether. I'd chance running into a couple students in the dark in all my gear over waiting any longer in this damn room. Gabriel just shrugged and followed me out. He'd had enough waiting as well. We texted the others as we made our way across the dark grounds to the chapel, occasionally ducking into the shadows, trying to avoid any wandering students.

When we reached the chapel, we slowly pushed open the doors, trying to prevent the creaking of the wood from reverberating through the quiet night air. Given the heavy partying, I doubted any students would've noticed anyway, but we didn't want to chance it. We slipped silently inside and pushed the doors closed behind us, then stood there for a moment, letting our eyes adjust to the darkness within the cavernous room. The large, stained-glass windows let in a good amount of moonlight, so once our eyes adjusted, we could see things in decent detail. Which was good. People outside were more likely to notice us if we conjured additional light.

Damian and Caleb arrived about five minutes later, as Gabriel and I were following paths of stones with markings, looking for patterns or clues. They each wore a backpack with supplies, heavy clothing that would put up at least a little resistance to being punctured or slashed, and a plethora of weapons stashed all over their bodies. I smiled as I watched them walking toward us. They looked like walking armories. But I couldn't judge. Gabriel and I were dressed similarly.

"We ended up climbing out of our windows too," Caleb said as they reached us, his eyes flitting over me. A little uncertain. A little nervous. A little less cold than usual. I shifted, uncomfortable. "Wasn't a big deal for me since my room is on the first floor, but Damian ended up jumping out of his second-floor window." Caleb smiled and shook his head in amused disbelief, glancing at Damian.

Damian shrugged. "It worked, didn't it? At least we're finally here now. I hate waiting."

I smiled. We had this in common.

"So, have you found anything?" Damian asked as he looked around the room appraisingly. I could see the dark shadows under his eyes, even in the dark of the room. He must not have slept well last night.

437

"Not really," I said. "Just following paths of the symbols on the floor and seeing if there are any patterns or anomalies. So far nothing, though."

Damian nodded, looking unsurprised. "We'll help." He walked over to a pew as he removed his backpack, then dropped it onto the seat and stretched his shoulders. "Alright, where have you looked so far?"

Gabriel and I showed him the paths we'd taken through the chapel, then Damian and Caleb went off to explore parts we hadn't gotten to yet.

Matt arrived a few minutes later, slipping quietly through the doors and squinting around, trying to find us as his eyes adjusted.

"Sorry it took me a little extra time to get here," he said as he walked toward us. "Ran into an Academy administrator who wanted to check in about security." He shrugged, looking unconcerned, but the rest of us stopped in our tracks and looked at him, worry widening our eyes. The administrator's timing was . . . troubling.

"He just saw my gear and assumed I was heading for the barrier wall to check its integrity," Matt clarified, noticing our worried gazes. "Said he had a dream last night that there'd be an attack on the school soon and just wanted to ask if there was any way for me to strengthen the barrier walls further." Matt sighed and shook his head. "I told him I was doing my best to fortify everything as much as possible. Which everyone already knows."

Damian frowned and shifted from one foot to the other. I frowned too and met Gabriel's gaze, worried. It wasn't exactly a secret that we thought there'd be more Demon attacks, but thus far, the school hadn't taken the warning very seriously. So why was this person coming to Matt now? Did he guess what we were up to and just used his story as a cover? Or . . . could it be that someone else was having visions about attacks too? Maybe this administrator hadn't had a dream at all, but something more substantial.

Matt looked at me, guessing at the direction of my thoughts. "I think it was a product of his own anxiety, and nothing more. He didn't have any specific knowledge about impending attacks or anything. Nothing clearer than the general worry. Honestly, the tension on campus has been building for a while, and not just with the students. Even though the administration has largely chosen to disregard worries of a more serious attack, there are individual staff members who feel the tension and aren't sure that the Academy is making the right decision. That's where I think he's coming from. I told him if he really wanted to make sure nothing bad would happen, he'd help evacuate the students and close the school. He didn't have much to say to that. Just left, still looking worried, so I left to come here. Took a slightly roundabout way to make sure he wasn't following me, though. Just in case." He shrugged again. "Anyway, that's why it took me so long. Did you find anything before I got here?"

The rest of us glanced at each other. I wondered if the others felt the same sense of foreboding growing in their chests that I was feeling. Something felt . . . off. But I didn't know what it was. I couldn't put my finger on anything specific. It was just a feeling—a growing apprehension.

"Not really," Gabriel said, pulling himself together first. "We've mainly been looking for patterns or clues in the markings on the floors."

Matt nodded and rubbed his chin in thought. "Okay," he finally said, "I think some of you should keep doing that. Damian, Caleb, and Gabriel, that can be you three. Terah and I should split up and look around the rest of the building—at the walls, back rooms, anything else that might give us clues. Just check in as you go. If you find something, no matter how small, inform the rest of the group. We're running out of time, so we should take every possible clue seriously."

Everyone nodded, then Gabriel, Damian, and Caleb headed to different clusters of symbols that we hadn't examined yet.

"I'll start looking at the walls if you want to get the back rooms," Matt said quietly, turning to me. His gaze flitted over my face and his mouth opened, like he wanted to say something else—something that didn't have to do with the mission. I nodded and turned to go, choosing to ignore this. We didn't have time for complicated feelings, nor did I have the patience for it right now. We needed to stay focused. On mission. The sooner this was over, the better and safer we'd all be.

The back rooms of the chapel had no windows, so I didn't feel bad conjuring light in my hand. I had to, anyway—the second I'd pushed open the door, I was met with a wall of pitch black. I quickly stepped inside and closed the door, then conjured an orb of bright white light in my hand. Then I spun, taking in the room around me. It was circular and couldn't be more than ten feet in diameter. The ceiling in here was much lower than the rest of the chapel—maybe twelve feet at its highest point, with a slanting roof that attached the room's outer wall to the chapel's main room.

I circled the room slowly, taking in every detail. From the contents of the low shelves on one side of the room that housed dozens of candles and boxes of matches, to the wooden rack leaning against the wall by the door holding various mops and brooms. I carefully pulled the shelves away from the walls to look at the stone, but I saw no marks. No symbols or other clues. Finally, I circled the room again and looked carefully at the stone floors. But again, nothing.

With a sigh, I dematerialized the light in my hand and exited the room. I walked quickly across the back of the chapel to the other side of the building where the other small room was, then walked into the darkness and pushed the door shut behind me. I conjured the ball of light again and looked around. This room was about twice the size of the first and seemed more like an office than a storage closet. There was a large wooden desk in the middle of the room with stacks of paper and various writing utensils strewn across the surface, and about a dozen bookshelves were pushed against the walls holding hundreds of different religious texts. It was mustier in here than in the previous room. It smelled of leather, dust, and stagnant decay.

I circled the room and examined the walls and ceiling as I'd done in the first room, lifting the light in my palm so its beam slid over the stones above me. But they were all uniform, marked only slightly by the passage of time. Then I did my best to shine light behind all the bookshelves—which were too heavy to move forward—to see if there were any markings or clues. Again, there was nothing. With a sigh, I circled the room one last time, looking closely at the floors. Nothing.

I extinguished the light in my hand and exited the room, coughing from the dust. Then I walked back toward the group where they were now congregating at the front of the chapel near the altar and podium, talking quietly.

"Find anything?" Matt asked, turning toward me as I approached.

I shook my head and wiped my hands on my pants. "Other than a ton of ancient religious books and more dust than I ever want to breathe again, no."

Caleb groaned. Damian scrubbed his hand down his face, not fully concealing his grimace.

Gabriel walked over to stand next to me. "We didn't find anything either. We looked at all the symbols, but there's nothing to indicate how we're supposed to use them. Also, no signs of trap doors or hidden compartments."

"And I didn't see any other symbols or irregularities around the walls either." Matt sounded even more frustrated than Caleb and Damian looked. "I just don't understand. This was the best lead we had. I don't know where it could be if it's not here."

Caleb sighed and went to sit on a pew in the front row. He pulled off his backpack and dropped it next to him before leaning forward and resting his elbows on his knees.

"So, what do we do now?" He looked around at all of us. "Where are we supposed to go from here?"

Everyone frowned, uncertain. We were stumped. We'd tried everything. Researched as much as we could. There weren't any other clues. We didn't have anywhere else to look. We were running out of time. If we didn't figure this out now, we'd fail at our mission. We'd fail at saving everyone and stopping the horrible vision from coming true. If we didn't figure this out, and incredibly soon, everyone could die.

I released a slow breath, trying to calm my racing heart and feverish brain, and turned away from the group. I walked toward the altar. It was a large rectangular table made of solid, polished stone like the podium in front of it, and stood about four feet off the ground. It was mostly plain, but the lip was modestly carved to look like two strands of thick rope twisting around each other to form a border around the top edge of the table. I pushed myself up so I could perch on the edge of it, my legs hanging over the side, and looked at the frustrated faces in front of me.

"Let's stop and think for a few minutes." My voice was low and even— my own version of practiced calm. "Even though we haven't figure it out yet, it's not like we know nothing. We know where the book isn't, and we've found several clues indicating where it might be. We just need to . . . I don't know . . . look at things from a different angle. Slow down for a minute."

Gabriel nodded slowly and walked over to me. He leaned back against the altar next to me, his hands gripping the ledge on either side of him. Damian sighed and went to sit on the pew next to Caleb, and Matt leaned against the solid stone podium, his brow furrowed.

"For one thing," I continued, "we might be looking at the symbols on the floor in the wrong way. We keep looking for repeated symbols or patterns, or a path that they form, but maybe that's not the right way to look at it. Maybe the symbols mean something else or are meant to be used in a different way."

"What other way could they be used?" Caleb asked, cold frustration flooding his voice.

I worked hard not to glare and snap at him to use his own damn brain for once. "What we *should* be asking, is what the benefit is of using hundreds of distinct symbols with no patterns, no repeats, and no central-ized location in the room. What does that tell us?"

There was silence for a few moments as everyone thought.

"That it's not meant to be a path or map," Gabriel murmured as he rubbed his hand absently over his jaw. "It's not meant to lead us to a particular spot. Maybe it's not even meant to be a clue. Maybe we're supposed to use something else to make sense of it. And perhaps the number and lack of repetition is also meant to overwhelm the looker. An added deterrent."

Matt nodded slowly. "So, maybe it's a tool." He turned to look at the floor again. "Maybe it's part of a mechanism that we're supposed to use to open wherever the book is hidden."

Caleb released a humorless laugh. "But what else is there to help us make sense of it? We looked through almost all the records and didn't find a damn thing to help us."

I bit the inside of my cheek as I thought for a moment. "Maybe we should look at the window again. There could be more in it than we initially noticed." I slid off the altar and walked across the chapel.

The group followed me, then spread out in a line in front of the window, gazing up at it as the moon illuminated the many-colored panes of glass. Once again, I was struck by the beauty of it. The scale. The complex composition. But I forced myself to look past the grandeur and focus on the smaller details. Focus on the book. The book itself was made from a large, but innocuous, solid piece of light brown glass that was easy to overlook. It wasn't dynamic or multi-faceted like the rest of the window. There was no movement or complexity there. It was just . . . brown. There wasn't even a title on it. Nor were there any symbols. It was arranged more as a prop for the Divines to place their hands on than as a true focal point. It seemed intentionally designed so that your eyes would slide easily away from it and back to the colorful, larger-than-life depictions of the Divines. The observer would notice it enough to draw meaning from it, but the book itself was never the focus. The only embellishment the book had was a thin, twisting border around the top cover, made of the same brown glass as the rest of the book. Too thin to really notice when standing a normal distance from the window. But up close, you could just make it out.

"I don't see anything new," Caleb murmured, though he didn't sound mad this time. Just disappointed. "Nothing that can help make sense of the floor or anything else."

"Me neither," Damian murmured, reluctantly.

I didn't bother responding. They could give up if they wanted to, but I wasn't going to. The stakes were too high for that. I tilted my head as I continued to stare at the book, my eyes drawn to the twisting border. The only embellishment. It could be a coincidence, but . . .

I turned on my heel and walked quickly back to the altar. When I reached it, I abandoned caution and formed a ball of light in my hand as I crouched to examine the stone. It had the same border around the top as the book. A border that didn't exist anywhere else in the chapel. The altar was the same general shape as the book. It was adorned minimally, exactly like the book. Maybe it meant something, or maybe it didn't, but it was all I had, so I was determined to check.

I heard footsteps following me, but I ignored them as I ran my fingers around and under the carved lip of stone. I wasn't sure what I was looking for. Something. *Anything.* Anything that was different. I made my way around the outer edge of the front and side of the altar, carefully feeling every carved knot and line of the twisted border for irregularities, before making my way down the back edge that was completely bathed in darkness.

"What are you—" Caleb began, but Matt and Gabriel both held up their hands, silencing him. Damian just watched me silently, his arms crossed over his chest, his expression enigmatic.

I slid my fingers slowly over the undermost edge of the back of the altar as I'd done with the front and side, while illuminating it with my other hand. But the light only made the space under the lip fall into deeper shadow, so I was mainly relying on touch at this point. I slid my fingers over knot after knot of smooth stone, feeling all the way from where the border attached to the side of the table under the lip, to where it ended at the top of the altar. Over and over again. Slowly. Thoroughly. I felt around for looseness, holes, missing pieces of stone, but was met again and again with cold, uniform smoothness.

My hope was starting to plummet as I reached the outer end of the back border. Nothing. This had been my best guess. The only other clue I'd managed to find, and it was turning out to be as useless as the rest of the clues we'd found so far. I sighed and crawled around to the last side of the altar, running my fingers around the border as it curved from the back to the side. But I froze as my fingers met a small patch of roughness. My pulse leapt and I ran my fingers over it again just to be sure. Yep. There was definitely a rough patch, tucked into the undermost portion of the lip, right where the border curved and met the pointed back corner of the altar.

I leaned forward and lifted the orb of light, then pressed my cheek to the cold stone, craning my neck to see the part of the lip that'd felt irregular. Its placement made it almost impossible to get a good angle, but there was definitely something there. It wasn't roughness born from aging—these looked like . . . patterns. Writing, or maybe symbols.

"I think I found something," I breathed as I squinted up at the stone. "I think there's something carved under here."

All four men crouched next to me and tried to see what I was pointing at, each forming their own orbs of light in their hands.

I scooted out of the way, making room. "You may have to lay down to get a good angle."

One by one, each of them pressed against the side of the altar to get a look at the small carvings. While they did this, I quickly ran my fingers over the border on the last side of the table to see if there were any other irregularities, just in case. But my fingertips met the same smoothness they'd encountered on each of the other sides. There were no other carvings.

After he'd looked at the underside of the altar, Matt pulled off his backpack and unzipped a front pocket. Then he pulled out a small notepad and pencil.

"We should draw what we see on here," he held up the notepad, "so we can get a better look at it without trying to bend like that each time."

Matt scooted back over and laid under the edge of the altar again.

"Can someone bring some light over here? I can't draw it and light it at the same time."

Caleb sighed and scooted closer, a ball of light appearing in his hand.

"How did you know where to look?" Damian asked. He drew a knee up in front of him on the floor and eyed my suspiciously, his gaze like ice. "It's not like the window had any new information. But somehow you knew . . ."

I drew up both knees in front of me and leaned back against the side of the altar, raising an eyebrow at Damian. He seemed . . . testy. Stressful situations seemed to do that to him. Gabriel reached over and entwined his fingers with mine, his gaze hard as he watched Damian. But Damian's temper didn't bother me. I'd had to deal with volatile soldiers for most of my life.

"Actually, the window did have a clue," I said coolly, "if you looked close enough."

Damian frowned. I could tell he was itching to turn around and look at it again—to try figuring out what I'd seen that he hadn't. But he didn't. He just waited, his jaw clenched.

"The book was the clue. There was nothing on it. No symbols, no writing—just a solid piece of glass. But it did have one detail. The border around the top of the cover. If you looked closely, you could see it had a twisted rope pattern." I tapped the embellishment on the altar behind me, and Damian's eyes widened. "The altar is also made of a rectangular piece of uniform material, undecorated except for an identical border around the top. They're the only two things in the chapel that have that feature."

Caleb glanced at me, still holding the light for Matt, looking taken aback. Damian raised both eyebrows at me.

I tried not to laugh at their incredulous expressions. "I'm not saying it was obvious, just that it was enough to make me want to check. And it's good that I did." I nodded to where Matt was still lying, his brow furrowed as he drew in the small notepad.

Damian rolled his eyes, but his posture relaxed a bit. "That's a ridiculous clue," he grumbled. But he didn't seem suspicious of me anymore.

"Got it," Matt said suddenly, ending our conversation. He sat up and scooted toward us, then placed the notepad on the ground in front of him. We all leaned forward as one, looking at the four symbols he'd drawn.

"They're—" Damian started.

"Symbols of the gods," Gabriel finished, as he stared at the page. "Like the symbols on the floor. I saw this one earlier." He pointed to the last symbol. It was a circle, the interior of which was completely carved out. Two lines touched the circle's sides, and each extended downward. It almost looked like an upside-down trash can. "It's under a pew over there." He gestured toward the right side of the chapel.

A smile broke across Matt's face as he turned to look at me. "Terah, you might've actually figured it out."

I tried not to be offended that he sounded so surprised. I shrugged one shoulder. "We'll see. Does anyone remember seeing any of the other symbols?"

"I recognize most of them," Damian murmured, his voice dark and resigned, as he stared at the page. There was a flicker of something in his eyes. Hesitancy? Fear? "But I don't remember seeing them in here."

"I saw that one." Caleb pointed to the humanoid figure with a curved animal head holding a long pole in one hand.

That left two symbols we hadn't seen. A circle with elaborate symmetrical patterns traced within it, surrounding a grinning face at the very center, and a figure holding an arrow in their right hand and a bow in their left.

"We need to find them all." I shoved to my feet and held out my hand to help Gabriel up. "Gabriel, you should try to find the one you saw again. Same goes for you, Caleb."

They each nodded and headed toward opposite sides of the chapel.

"The rest of us should try finding the two remaining symbols."

Matt and Damian nodded, then we split up and headed in different directions, scouring the floor. I followed a trail of symbol-filled stones that began near the center of the room and swooped in a large curve toward the smaller storage room. Matt followed a cluster that curved and twisted under some pews near the front of the chapel, and Damian followed a grouping that ran along the outer edge of the room near the windows.

Damian halted suddenly. "Wait, I think I found one." He crouched over a stone at the very edge, pressed against the chapel wall. "The symbol is so close to the wall it's hard to tell, but I'm pretty sure . . ."

I saw a faint glow as he conjured a ball of light to double-check.

"Yeah, it is," he confirmed. "It's the first symbol. The patterned circle with the face."

"Okay, so we just have to find the figure with the bow and arrow," Matt murmured. He conjured a light in his hand as well and crouched so he could see beneath the pews.

I turned and continued following the line of stones I was on, carefully looking at each symbol. My pulse pounded through me. We were *so close*. So close to solving this mystery and preventing apocalyptic harm. But I soon reached the end of the cluster without spotting the last symbol. My jaw clenched, and I spun, looking across the floor for another cluster that didn't intersect with the ones already being covered. As I looked, Matt climbed over pew after pew, crouching between each one to quickly examine the stones beneath them, before climbing over the next and repeating the process.

"Wait," Matt said as he slid between another row of pews, "I think I've got it."

The breath whooshed out of my lungs.

"Really?" Caleb's voice was slightly higher and tinnier than usual. "You're sure?"

"Yep," Matt murmured, holding the light directly above the stone. He reached forward and traced the carved pattern with the tip of his finger. "It looks exactly like the symbol on the altar."

I quickly walked to the back corner of the altar where the symbols were and placed my fingers on the carvings again. "And you're all standing on the stones with the marks?"

All of them nodded.

I touched the symbols again, but nothing happened. There were no clues about how to proceed. I pushed the altar, but it didn't move. I frowned, considering the stone in front of me. Naturally, just standing on the stones wouldn't be enough to trigger a reaction. This building was meant to hold assemblies—people would be stepping on the symbols all the time. There had to be something else. A more specific step we were supposed to take. I walked around the circumference of the altar slowly, thinking.

"Four symbols for the four Divines," I whispered, glancing up at the window again. At each Divine reaching forward and touching the book. Well, we definitely didn't have all four factions of Divines present, but I hoped that wouldn't matter. Maybe it just mattered that there were at least four Divines present.

"Try pouring some of your power directly into the symbols," I said suddenly, looking around at them.

All four of them crouched again. I saw the faint glow of Matt's power emerging from beneath the pews, but I couldn't see the others. I assumed they were all doing it.

"Nothing's happening," Caleb's voice echoed from somewhere within the pews.

I rolled my eyes. Had he always been this impatient? "Keep doing it. Keep pouring power into it."

"The symbol is starting to glow," Gabriel said a few seconds later. "It's like it's filling up with power."

"Mine's doing that too," Matt murmured.

"Same," Damian said.

"Mine too," Caleb grumbled, quieter this time.

"Keep going." I hoped as hard as I could that something would happen. That something would come of this at all.

"The symbol's pulsing," Gabriel said just as I heard a creaking behind me.

I spun, my heart pounding. "Something's happening! Keep doing what you're doing."

The creaking turned into a groan, and my mouth fell open as I saw the altar tremble and begin to lower slowly into the chapel floor.

"No way," I whispered in awe as I watched it gradually sink into the ground, leaving a large hole in the floor behind it. Then there was a *thunk*, like stone hitting stone, followed by silence. The altar had stopped moving.

"Grab your stuff and come over here quick," I called. "A trapdoor opened, but I don't know how long it'll stay like this."

I heard sounds of surprise and hurried footsteps. Matt and Gabriel joined me first, their eyes widening as they saw the large hole that the altar had left behind. Caleb and Damian quickly grabbed their backpacks off the pews before sprinting over.

"Holy shit," Caleb murmured, stunned, as he knelt next to us. "I can't believe we found it."

"We should get in before it closes," Damian said quickly, conjuring a light and lowering it to the edge of the hole so we could see what lay beneath us.

I peered over the edge and saw the altar maybe twelve feet below, resting on what looked like a solid stone floor.

"I'll go first," Damian said, the light in his hand going out as he slid his feet through the opening and gripped the ledge opposite him. We watched with bated breath as he lowered himself slowly through it, then let himself drop the several feet to the top of the altar. Then he hopped to the ground, clearing the altar for the next person. I released a slow breath. He'd been lucky there weren't any traps in place for him. We needed to be more careful—letting our eagerness take over would only lead to our deaths.

I tightened my backpack's straps, then swung my feet over the ledge and lowered myself in next. Gabriel followed me, then Matt and Caleb lowered themselves in. As Caleb jumped off the altar, it groaned and began to rise. Panic flooded me. What if it was our only way out?

"Should we try to stop it?" Anxiety made my words breathy. I wasn't sure how we possibly could, but I hated the idea of being sealed underground.

"I don't think so," Matt said as we all watched the altar rise, supported by a thick column of stone under its center. The column glowed faintly with a muddle of shifting colors. "Either there's another way out, or there's a way to lower it again. It clearly isn't meant to stay open the entire time we're down here. That wouldn't be very secure."

His voice was calm. Confident. I hoped he was right, because if he wasn't, I'd murder him for getting me stuck down here. Being buried alive was *not* how I wanted to die.

We all watched silently as the altar finally slid back into place with a grating of stone on stone. And then it was silent. And dark. Pitch black. I couldn't see anything—not the rest of the group, or even myself. I couldn't tell if we were in a small room or a large cavern. There were no windows. No light. Barely any air. And the air that surrounded us was musty and stale, as though it hadn't been stirred in centuries. Instinctively, I reached out and found Gabriel's hand with mine. I didn't want to lose him in this darkness. I didn't want to be lost.

A bright light suddenly flared into being in front of me, and I saw Matt holding it in his palm, turning slowly so he could get a look at the room we were in. Caleb followed suit, making a light appear in his own hand. The twin pools merged and expanded, and Gabriel, Damian, and I looked around us. We were in a moderately-sized room made of ancient looking stone blocks, enclosed around us in a semicircle. The room was empty, except for the thick column that supported the altar, but the open end of the room seemed to disappear into darkness. As we stepped slowly toward it, bringing the light with us, a narrow staircase that descended downward slowly emerged from the shadows, enclosed on either side with the same stones that lined this room. It was the only way forward. The only way out, now that the altar had slid back into place.

My stomach clenched. I'd seen this before. I'd seen us here. In a vision. A cold shiver ran down my spine, and my fingers tightened around Gabriel's hand.

I heard a sigh behind me.

"Well," Damian said, "there's no turning back now. Let's go."

I took a deep, centering breath and nodded. This needed to be done. Damian walked around us and started descending the stairs. Matt and Caleb trailed behind him, providing the light. I squeezed Gabriel's hand, and we exchanged a worried look before following the rest of the group.

We traveled carefully down the steep, narrow set of stairs that seemed to go on forever, eerily disappearing below us into the darkness. I swallowed down the fear and adrenaline that were pumping through me, trying not to feel like the oppressive stone walls were closing in on us. That they would suffocate and crush us.

Damian turned and glanced back at us, his expression serious. Cold. "Be on your guard." His voice was deep and quiet. "There are bound to be traps in here to keep out trespassers. There's a reason the book has been hidden for so long. It isn't meant to be easy to find or take."

I nodded—that'd been my guess, too—then took a deep, calming breath as we continued our descent. I had a bad feeling about this. An unease that was rising in my chest, growing with every step we took. I reached down and loosened the knife at my waist. I wanted to make sure it'd come out easy. Fast. Just in case.

We traveled down the stairs in silence for what felt like forever. Only the sounds of our feet on the stone, our shifting clothes and gear, and our breathing could be heard. The silence around us was eerie. Deafening. I could practically feel it pressing in on our ears. How far did this staircase go? Where was it taking us? Would it ever end? How long would it take for all of us to lose our minds, descending forever into the empty blackness below us? Probably not too long. It already felt oppressive. Stifling.

I couldn't tell anymore if the lack of air was because we were going so far underground, or if it was from the panic gnawing at my chest. I'd never been enclosed underground before, and I was finding I wasn't adapting to it well. It made me antsy. I felt like I was slowly suffocating. I wanted to escape. To transform and fly out of here. But I knew we needed to do this. I'd need to overcome this and push forward. I pressed my eyes closed for a second, then opened them and concentrated on putting one foot in front of the other. On taking deep, steady breaths. I reminded myself that I could breathe. There was enough air, so far at least. The suffocation was more in my mind than reality.

"What if it's a trap?" Caleb eventually asked, his quiet voice feeling as loud as a scream in the intense silence. I could hear the tension in it. The anxiety. "What if there's never an end? What if it's not taking us anywhere? What if we're just meant to die down here?"

"I doubt it," Matt responded quietly, his voice even, calm. "They wouldn't have gone to all the trouble of building something like this just to have it lead to nowhere. It's more likely that it goes on like this to force people to give up. To make people give in to fear and turn back. It's a deterrent to keep people from getting the book."

Caleb still looked unsettled, but Matt's words had eased some of the more acute panic. Matt's level-headedness in stressful situations was an asset. Maybe that was why the vision had directed me to include him.

We pushed forward until the orbs of light stopped reflecting off the stone walls around us and instead seemed to melt into the darkness. Damian slowed, holding up his hand to stop us.

"The walls disappear ahead. Only the stairs continue, but with no railings. There's nothing to hold onto. Be on your guard, and keep your balance," he added as he started down the stairs again, "there's no room for error."

We shifted into a single-file line—Damian went first and Gabriel last—and kept to the middle of the stairs as the walls abruptly ended. I squinted around us as we descended, and faintly saw stone walls far to our sides. Too far to be of any use to us.

"Careful," Damian murmured, what seemed like an eternity later. "The stairs are starting to get rougher. They're old and there doesn't seem to be much structural support. There are chunks missing, and it looks like some are starting to crumble. Watch where you step."

Caleb cursed under his breath. He looked as antsy and tense as I felt.

"We must be at least a mile down," I murmured as we carefully picked our way down the crumbling stairs. "Maybe two. How did they possibly build something like this on the Academy's limited plane?"

"They must've designed the plane to extend far beneath the school just to hide the book," Damian replied. "The majority of the plane is probably below visible ground. It must've taken an enormous amount of power to make it this large. I doubt it's much smaller than the Dark Guardian realm," he grumbled. "It's a wonder they managed to keep it a secret."

I frowned. So much effort had gone into hiding this book. I was growing increasingly nervous about what might still lay ahead of us. What other protections—or traps—they might've put in place.

A crack ripped through the earsplitting quiet, echoing painfully off the walls around us, as a chunk of stone broke off the stairs several feet in front of me. Caleb stumbled as the step fell into the darkness below him, leaving one of his feet without purchase. He swore, flailing as he tipped sideways off the stairs. Without thinking, I lunged forward and grabbed his hand. My arm jerked straight as he fell beneath the line of the stairs, then my body was yanked forward as I suddenly supported Caleb's full weight. And then I was tilting sideways too, my feet starting to leave the stone. I was going to fall with him. *Shit*. I hadn't thought this through.

Gabriel swore and lunged for me, his arms wrapping tightly around my waist as he yanked me down with his bodyweight toward the stairs so that I was sitting in the circle of his legs. Then, lightning fast, he braced his legs against the stairs on either side of me and released me with one arm to grab the opposite side of the step, keeping us all anchored in place.

My arm burned with pain as I supported Caleb's full weight, and Caleb grunted beneath me, his face strained. His hand and wrist were probably killing him.

"Just let go, Terah." His voice was tense. "I'll transform. It's fine."

451

"No," Matt said hurriedly, sprinting back up the stairs with Damian. "Don't let him go, Terah. We'll pull him up."

I nodded, my body tense with pain. Gabriel's arm around me shook from the strain of anchoring all three of us to the steps, and I could feel Caleb's hand slowly starting to slip from mine. I gripped it tighter.

"Hurry," I bit out through clenched teeth.

Matt and Damian braced themselves by grabbing the edge of the steps behind them, then reached forward and grabbed the parts of Caleb they could reach. As they grabbed him, the ball of light in Matt's hand went out, plunging us into darkness.

"Lift now!" Matt called.

With grunts of effort, all three of us pulled him up with all the strength we could, until he could reach up with his other hand and help pull himself back onto the stairs. A strain-filled moment later, Caleb was safely back on solid stone, and all of us collapsed, panting from the effort.

"Why didn't you just let me transform?" Caleb demanded, panting as he turned toward Matt who'd conjured another ball of light. Caleb was rubbing the wrist of the hand I'd grabbed, but he looked more angry than in pain. "Why risk pulling other people over too?" He glanced at me, then away quickly.

"Because transforming and getting upward momentum in flight isn't instantaneous," Matt said calmly, pushing off his elbow and straightening up. "You would've fallen for an unknown amount of time while working to transform, and then it would've taken you at least a couple more seconds to build enough momentum with your wings to actually fly up."

Caleb opened his mouth to argue, but Matt cut him off.

"We don't know how far down these stairs go. You could've hit the bottom before accomplishing upward flight. Then you probably would've died. Additionally, the stairs are here for a reason. I bet most Divines who could transform and fly to the bottom would be tempted to do that. And I'm sure the designers of the book's hiding place knew that. There are probably traps or things rigged to injure or kill anyone who tries using the space around the stairs to bypass them. If you'd fallen, even just long enough to transform, you likely would've triggered those traps. Terah probably just saved you from being speared or something." Matt shrugged. "It was smarter not to take that risk."

Caleb still looked grumpy, but he didn't argue anymore. Matt pushed to his feet, careful not to look at me while I was still in Gabriel's arms. Damian followed suit, and they started down the stairs. Caleb glanced at me again, his gaze uncertain. He looked torn—like he wanted to say something but wasn't sure if he should. But Caleb's gaze drifted to Gabriel's arms around me, and his expression quickly closed off. He abruptly turned and began walking down the steps behind the other two, conjuring another ball of light in his hand, his other fisted at his side.

I sighed, flexing my sore hand, and leaned back into Gabriel's chest for a moment. I turned my head and tilted my chin up so I could see his face.

"I'm sorry," I said quietly, so the others wouldn't hear. "For taking that risk and making you worry."

Gabriel let out a slow breath. "I can't really be mad at you for trying to save someone's life. I know it's who you are." A small smile pulled at the corner of his mouth. "It's your instinct to protect everyone around you, even at the cost of yourself." His arms tightened around me again, and I saw him swallow. "It's an admirable quality. Even if it drives me fucking wild with worry." He was fully smiling now.

I smiled too, but I knew it was true. "I know," I whispered. "That's why I'm sorry."

He bent and pressed a kiss to my forehead, then stood, pulling me up with him.

"Just to be clear," he murmured as we followed the others down the stairs, "I'd never ask you to stop being who you are. That's not what I want. I hope you know that."

"I know. But you also don't want to see me die again. I get it."

I glanced back in time to see him wince.

"Yeah." His voice was deep as he looked down, his expression shuttered. "Once was . . . bad enough."

The muscles over my stomach tightened and my heart throbbed as I watched his expression. I reached out and took his fingers in mine, then turned and started down the stairs again.

"Thank the fucking gods," Damian's voice echoed up from the front of our procession. "I think I finally see the end of the stairs. There's a landing at the very least. Maybe a hundred feet down from here."

There was a collective sigh of relief. This had become hellish before we'd even done anything. We all wanted it to be over.

We reached the landing a couple minutes later, and I tried to hide how happy I was to be back on solid ground. My legs practically shook with relief, and I fought the urge to sink to the floor just so I could feel its comforting solidness against my back. I looked around as Matt and Caleb held out their conjured lights. This room looked a lot like the landing room beneath the altar, but where the staircase had been there, this room had a large, heavy metal door. And instead of smooth, unmarked stone walls, the four gods' symbols were repeatedly carved on either side of the door over a dozen times, spreading across the room. They were large this time. About as large as our hands.

We glanced at each other before moving slowly toward the door, wary. When we reached it unscathed, Matt pushed against the metal, but it didn't budge.

"Maybe it's like the altar in the chapel," I murmured. "Maybe we have to give it our power for it to move."

Matt nodded slowly and looked around the room again. "Perhaps that's what the symbols on the wall are for. Let's try it."

We spread out, and each of us put our hand over a symbol. Then we started feeding power into them. Slowly, the symbol beneath my fingers began to pulse, filling with my power. I glanced at the door, but it remained firmly shut. I frowned. This was more power than the men had given for the altar. This door couldn't need much more.

Caleb's light went out a minute later. Perhaps he no longer had enough power to sustain it and feed the wall.

"How much do we have to give?" he asked, his voice strained.

"As much as it takes for the door to start opening," Matt replied grimly.

Matt's light went out a minute or so later, plunging us into darkness. Now, all I could see was the faint glow of my power around my fingers as I poured it into the wall. I gritted my teeth as my knees shook. This was too much. It was requiring too much power. If the door didn't open soon, we'd be completely drained. Dread stirred in my stomach. That couldn't be what the room required, could it? That would be unreasonable.

There was a thud behind me, and I glanced over to see Matt had fallen to his knees.

"Shit," he rasped. "It's making us give all our power."

My legs shook violently as a deep exhaustion swept through me. But I fought it as I stared at Matt, astonished. We couldn't go into this completely drained. We'd be totally without protection.

But the door hadn't opened yet.

Gabriel and Caleb went down next, and Damian collapsed forward against the wall, his body covering his hand and the symbol as he barely remained upright. My legs gave out next. My knees burned from where they'd made sharp contact with the stone, but I kept my hand on the symbol above me, still feeding it power. We had to get the door open.

Whatever it took. Even if it drained us. Because we needed to get the book and hide it. Before it could be used to end the world.

Finally, I collapsed to my hands and knees, fully drained except for my life force. The symbol above me no longer glowed. The power I'd given it seemed to have been sucked into the wall. We waited in complete darkness, panting.

For a minute, nothing happened. Dread churned in my stomach. Had we done the wrong thing? But before I could spiral too far, the swirling muddle of our combined powers filled the door until it was glowing with blinding light. I squinted against the overpowering brightness but refused to close my eyes. I didn't want to miss anything or leave myself unprotected. Ironic, as I was kneeling weakly on the floor.

Then, with a loud creak and a deep groan of metal that reverberated around us like thunder, the door slowly swung open.

21

FAITH

The door in front of us now stood ominously ajar, like a silent, gaping mouth, waiting to swallow us into the darkness. The swirling colors of our combined powers continued to pulse in the metal, almost like a heartbeat, sending an eerie glow through the shadows around us. Dread rose in my chest. Would they use our powers against us somehow? Why else would they take them?

I gritted my teeth. I hated this. I'd never thought we'd have to do any of this without the protection of our powers. We were essentially Normals now. Well trained, sure, but weaker, drained, and without any other means of protecting or healing ourselves. We were far more vulnerable now than we were ever meant to be as Divines. And my vision had brought us here. If anything bad happened to us, it'd be my fault. *Damnit.*

The four of us slowly pushed off the cold, dusty floor and got shakily to our feet as Damian pushed off the wall, straightening up. Weaker than we ever wanted to be before heading into danger. I pulled my long daggers from their sheaths and gripped them tightly in my palms. The others followed my lead.

"Enter the room carefully," Damian murmured from my left as I moved toward the beckoning darkness. "Anything could be a trap."

"Let me go first," Matt said suddenly, grabbing my shoulder and holding me back before I could step through the doorway. "I have more experience, plus it's my job as a member of the warrior faction to put myself in danger before you."

I raised an eyebrow at him but stepped to the side and let him take the lead. It seemed important to him, and I wasn't in the mood to fight his instinct to control this situation. I shrugged a shoulder and followed him through the doorway, Gabriel on my heels. Damian and Caleb quickly followed. We stopped in a tightly packed group just beyond the opening, squinting into the blackness in front of us, trying to see what lay ahead. We didn't have powers to light the way, and the miniscule amount of light filtering in from the room behind us was from the pulsing of our powers in the door.

Suddenly the door groaned and began closing.

"Hell no," Caleb said, turning around to stop it from shutting us in. Matt and Damian grabbed his arms.

"We need to let it close," Damian said, his voice firm and calm. "It's like the altar rising back into place. The door needs to close before our way forward becomes apparent."

Caleb made a noise of frustration but didn't fight them on it. He just watched, brow furrowed, as our view of the landing room became smaller and smaller until the door slammed back into place with a final bang that shook the stones under our feet. And then we were in complete darkness once again. Gabriel's free hand found my lower back as we waited in silence for something to happen. Only the sounds of our anxious breaths surrounded us, too loud in the extreme quiet.

Finally, the stones beneath our feet began to glow, our powers pooling in the symbols carved there. But now the stones only had carvings of one symbol—the first symbol from the altar. Our powers followed paths of the repeating symbols across the floor, moving toward the walls before climbing to reach wrought-iron torches attached there. Fires burst into each torch as our powers touched them, bathing the room in a dim, warm glow. Then the power traveled to the opposite end of the room where a giant carving was cut deep into a large, stone square.

This carving was different from the symbol on the floor. There was still a face, but it was part of an entire body now, with arms bent at the elbows and clawed hands open, reaching above the figure's head. Around the head was carved short, curling hair and large ears adorned with earrings reaching down past the figure's shoulders. The mouth was stretched open in a menacing grin with a tongue protruding, forming a shallow basin that morphed into a river-like canal extending in a wavy line from the mouth to the ground. The figure was squatting, elbows resting on knees, each joint ornamented with carvings of human-looking skulls. And around the figure's waist was a skirt made of what looked like human bones with a star border.

Our powers flowed from the floor into the carving, filling it until it glowed with eerie light.

"What is it?" I asked, staring at the carving that was taller than I was.

"It's the god," Damian said, his voice a little hoarse. Like he was more anxious than he was trying to let on.

"An Aztec god," Gabriel said, stepping forward to get a closer look. He sounded more intrigued than worried. I followed him, and we walked cautiously to the other side of the room, the rest of the group trailing behind us. "I remember seeing variations of this figure and that first symbol, the sun stone, in some of my parents' books on world religions. Gimme a sec."

He closed his eyes as though he was summoning the image forward from the vault of his memory.

"Tlaltecuhtli. That's who I think this is."

We all stared at him, mildly astonished.

Gabriel shrugged. "Once I see things, especially writing and images, I can pull them forward and see them in my mind in almost the same detail as when I first saw them. I've always been able to."

I put this new information aside for the moment and turned back to the statue. "What are we supposed to do?"

Gabriel walked closer to it and examined the tongue that protruded from the wall to form the basin and river-like canal to the floor.

"The bestower and devourer of life," Gabriel murmured as he traced the indentation of the canal with his finger. "She was sustained through blood and sacrifice."

He looked up, meeting my eyes, his almost luminescent in the dim room.

"I think we have to offer a sacrifice in here." He tapped the tongue basin.

"What kind of sacrifice?" Matt asked, his brow furrowing. He stepped closer to the carving and examined the tongue-basin as well.

"Probably blood." Gabriel crossed his arms over his chest, his mouth twisting in thought. "I think that would be the most traditional for her in particular."

"But we don't have any power to heal ourselves right now," Caleb said, upset. "It will weaken us."

"That's what makes it a real sacrifice," Gabriel responded, raising an eyebrow at Caleb drily.

"I have some medical supplies in my bag," Matt said, glancing at Caleb, "so it should be fine. I'll try first. See if blood from one of us is enough or if we all have to give some."

Gabriel nodded and moved back over to me, out of Matt's way. I glanced at Damian. He was being uncharacteristically silent, his cold expression barely covering his deep unease. I got the feeling that he didn't like anything to do with the gods.

Matt pushed up his sleeve, raised his arm above the basin, and lifted his dagger to his forearm. In a swift movement, he sliced into his skin and let the blood drip onto the stone tongue.

"How much?" He glanced at Gabriel.

Gabriel shrugged. "Don't know. Probably enough so that it travels down the canal to the floor."

Matt nodded and bit the handle of his dagger so he could use his hand to squeeze his arm around the gash, encouraging more blood to come out. Finally, enough filled the tongue basin that it spilled over the side and flowed down the curved canal, leaving a trail of bright red. The swirling powers in the carving pulsed once, but nothing else happened.

"Damnit." Matt stepped away from the carving and sheathed his knife. "Looks like we're all going to have to make the sacrifice before it lets us move on."

He pulled off his backpack, blood still dripping down his arm, and unzipped it, then reached in and grabbed a bag of sanitizing wipes and a role of gauze. I bit back a smile. Matt's tendency to be over-prepared was actually proving helpful in this situation. I was surprisingly grateful that my vision had included him. Matt quickly wiped down his arm, then secured some gauze around his injury, tightening the knot with his teeth.

Gabriel stepped up to the carving next and made a similar slice in his arm. I winced as I watched the thick stream of his blood dripping down his skin. He and I had done much worse to ourselves to practice healing in class, but I couldn't change the part of me that hated seeing him hurt, no matter how minor—a part of me that seemed to be growing the longer we were together. It made me antsy, just standing there and watching him bleed. To ease my tension, I went over to Matt and grabbed a wipe and a length of gauze for Gabriel's arm.

Finally, his blood spilled over the rim of the basin and down the canal, leaving his own trail of red, and the carving pulsed with power again. I stepped forward and grabbed Gabriel's arm, pulling him away from the carving, and gruffly began patching him up. A small smile tugged at his lips as he watched me work.

"Worried about me?" he teased quietly as Damian stepped forward to slice his arm next. I shot Gabriel a glare as I tied the final knot in the gauze and pulled his sleeve back down. Then I flipped him off. Gabriel grinned and leaned forward to press a soft kiss against my lips. "Thanks," he murmured warmly against me.

After Damian's blood made the carving pulse again, and Caleb handed him a wipe and some gauze, I stepped forward, pushed up my sleeve, and pulled my dagger from my belt. I sliced quickly into my arm and held it over the small basin, now shiny with our combined blood. I glanced at Gabriel as I waited for enough of my blood to pool. His arms were crossed casually over his chest as he watched me, but I'd seen him wince as the knife bit into my arm. And, like me, he started fidgeting after watching me bleed for over a minute. He finally turned and went to retrieve the medical supplies from Matt, unable to stand still and play it cool any longer. It was my turn to smile. Gabriel wasn't doing any better than I'd done. And I liked him more for it.

The carving pulsed again as my blood reached the floor, and Gabriel tugged on my arm, pulling me back to him so he could patch me up. Caleb stepped up to the carving and sliced into his arm as Gabriel wiped the blood from my skin and tied the gauze tightly around me with deft fingers. Then he lifted my chin and pressed another kiss against my lips. But there was no teasing this time. He didn't like seeing me hurt. I smiled and entwined my fingers with his.

Damian handed Caleb a wipe and gauze for his arm as the carving pulsed again.

"Was that all we needed to do?" Caleb asked as he wrapped his wound.

All of us turned to look at the carving, waiting for something to happen. Hoping a door would open to let us move on. Suddenly, the glowing light of our combined powers was sucked inward, away from the outer edges of the carved figure and toward the path that our blood had taken. The power filled the tongue basin, flowed down the canal, and pooled with the blood at the figure's feet. And then the power turned red. It was beginning to morph into something new. Something thick and opaque. It was like the blood was being soaked up from the stone and disseminated into the swirl of colors. Like the power itself was turning into blood.

And then the glowing red substance oozed away from the carving—a writhing, shifting blob—and surrounded us, pushing us together in a circle. I quickly glanced at the carving. It still glowed with our powers, but a little less brightly now. I released Gabriel's hand and pulled my long daggers from their sheaths again. I didn't know what was happening, but I'd rather be prepared. The others followed my lead and quickly pulled weapons.

Once the red goo had completely encircled us, it shot upward, dramatically growing and forming into huge, hulking figures that seemed neither human nor animal. The metallic smell of blood filled my nostrils as the blobs grew. Then weapons formed in their hands. *Shit.* We'd given our blood and all our power, only to have both used against us.

We fanned out as much as we could in the small circle we'd been forced into and turned to face the large blood-creatures. I couldn't believe this was happening. It was like a nightmare, except I didn't think my brain could dream up something this bizarre. And then they were charging at us, weapons drawn. I had no idea how weapons made of blood could be solid, let alone deadly, but the creature's spear made hard contact with my long daggers and left no doubt in my mind that, if I were to be on the receiving end of its point, I'd be very much dead.

I swore as the huge blood creature spun its spear around with such force that it almost wrenched my daggers from my grasp, then aimed the sharp point at me again, thrusting with lightning speed. I dodged the blow, but there wasn't a lot of room to maneuver, as all five of us were forced to fight in such a confined space. I dropped to the floor and lashed out at the creature's legs with my daggers, severing them at the knees. The creature tipped backward and fell with a loud thud.

I pushed to my feet, breathing hard. I hadn't killed it, but it should at least be incapacitated. I spun and began helping Gabriel fight his blood creature, which was brandishing an axe that it was swinging in ferocious arcs, causing Gabriel to have to repeatedly duck or be hacked in half like a tree. The thought of the creature embedding that axe in any part of him had my blood boiling with rage. With a growl, I leapt forward just as the creature swung the axe again and sliced off its entire arm. It crashed to the ground before it made it to Gabriel. He lunged forward and stabbed it deeply through the chest for good measure.

A breath of relief whooshed from my lungs. But movement in my periphery quickly drew my attention. I spun and my mouth fell open in astonished horror. The creature I'd brought down first had regrown its severed legs, and the two severed legs had each grown to form two more full sized blood creatures. There were now three creatures pushing to their feet where there'd only been one.

Gabriel swore behind me, and I turned to see the arm from his creature that I'd severed was quickly expanding into a new, fully formed blood creature.

"Shit." I started fighting the three creatures in front of me, twisting and ducking like I was practicing a damn dance, just to avoid all their spears. "What the hell do we do now?"

I heard harsh swears behind me and knew that Matt, Caleb, and Damian had discovered the blood creatures' seeming invincibility too. Gabriel grunted as he fought the two creatures in front of him who were rapidly stabbing and slashing an axe and spear in his direction. He was holding them off, but only just.

"I'm not sure," he called back. "It doesn't seem like they can be defeated with weapons."

"And we don't have our powers," I added, lunging and plunging my daggers into the stomach of the creature closest to me, "so we can't get rid of them any other way."

I pulled the daggers out and saw the wound immediately close again. Like I'd never stabbed it. My stomach dropped. It couldn't even be injured. What the hell were we supposed to do then? A sudden thought rushed to the front of my mind, and I took a gamble. I jumped as high as I could and slashed the creature viciously across the neck. The creature's head fell sideways off its body and landed hard on the floor. I tried to keep an eye on it as I kept battling the two other creatures, desperately hoping they were like Demons and decapitation would get rid of them.

But luck truly wasn't on our side. The headless body immediately formed a new head, while the decapitated head on the ground rapidly grew a body to support itself. All my experiment had done was create yet another creature for us to deal with. I looked quickly behind me as I blocked another blow, and my stomach dropped. It looked like the three of them had been even more cavalier about slicing appendages off the creatures before they'd figured out that they regenerated and multiplied. There were now eight blood creatures towering over them and fanning out to surround us on all sides.

This was now officially bad. The first pangs of real fear twinged in my chest. I couldn't think of a way out. If I still had my power, I could try burning them until nothing remained, or I could at least put up a shield between them and us. But now . . . now I couldn't do anything but dodge, block, and stab, knowing my stabs wouldn't accomplish anything. And every time we were forced to cut off a piece of a creature to keep ourselves from dying, it just added to the number of creatures trying to kill us.

The five of us backed even closer together, trying to use our proximity to each other as an extra defense. But it was clear now that we were far outnumbered and outpowered.

"We can't win this," Matt called a few minutes later, his voice strained as he was forced to one knee under the onslaught of four blood creatures. "There must be a way out, but I can't think of anything." His arms shook, but he managed to shove to his feet with a yell, kicking the creature in front of him back so he could disconnect his weapons from theirs.

"Without our powers, I can't think of a way to win," Caleb gasped as he and Damian worked together to trip one of the creatures, causing it to crash into and knock over several others.

"I don't even see a way out of the room," Damian grunted as he brought his knives up to block an overhead attack from yet another creature.

I tried to run through our options as Gabriel and I fended off a seemingly endless number of creatures. I couldn't distinguish them from each other anymore. With the dim lighting and constant movement, they'd morphed into countless bodies, limbs, and weapons. Countless spears coming at me from every direction, trying to end me. I did my best against them, but eventually, the edge of a spear raked across my upper arm, slicing through my thick clothing, and cutting deep. For the second time this evening, I felt my blood, warm and sticky, dripping down my arm. Normally, such an injury wouldn't phase me. Because normally, it'd heal itself in a matter of minutes. But now, there was nothing to stop the bleeding. Nothing to make sure my body remained whole enough to keep fighting. *Damnit*.

With a frustrated growl, I threw myself back into fighting with renewed energy. I couldn't give up—I had to think of another way out of this. There had to be a way. Blood seeped through my shirt as I thought about the sacrifice again. The blood we'd given earlier. And I thought about what blood meant to the god—why it was necessary.

"What was it that you said about the god when we first entered this room?" I called to Gabriel over the din of fighting. "When you first saw the carving."

Gabriel ducked another swing of a spear and stabbed forward into the creature's chest, while sending a simultaneous kick at another.

"I said this god was the bestower and devourer of life," Gabriel panted. "She was sustained through human sacrifice."

Through human sacrifice. Hm. I thought about it as I blocked vicious strikes from two blood creatures. Our blood had been a tangible physical sacrifice—a giving up of life and wholeness to the control of the god. And it had taken our offered life and had created new life—these blood creatures. But perhaps we hadn't sacrificed enough yet. Perhaps the sacrifice the god required now wasn't simply physical.

I rammed my foot against the stomach of another creature as it ran at me and tried to look at our situation with fresh eyes. I tried to think as I narrowly ducked another swinging spear, then raised both daggers to trap another spear between my weapons. This battle was designed so that we couldn't win it. At least, not by force. The creatures couldn't be injured, killed, or incapacitated. They healed and multiplied rapidly. Thanks to their use of our powers, their multiplication didn't seem to weaken them, and we had no power left for ourselves. There was nothing we could do to get rid of them by force. But we were soldiers. In fact, most Divines had been throughout history. And soldiers fought until the end, no matter what. We never gave up. We'd only stop when made to by death or severe injury. But one truth kept repeating itself over and over in my mind. *This is a battle we can't win. This is a battle* designed *to keep us from winning.*

And it finally hit me. There was no way out through fighting. If we continued to fight, we'd all die. I suddenly knew what we were being asked to do—what the *real* sacrifice was meant to be. Something even harder for most of us than giving our lives to protect others. I just hoped I wasn't wrong. If I was, we'd all die anyway.

"We need to put down our weapons," I yelled, trying to make my voice carry over the sounds of battle. "We need to stop fighting. As long as we fight, they'll keep attacking and multiplying. We can't win through force. The real sacrifice that the room is asking for is . . . surrender. An act of faith and a relinquishing of control."

Gabriel glanced at me, surprised, before whipping his head forward again to block another blow. I heard a grunt of pain from behind me and turned to see a creature yanking the tip of its spear out of Caleb's shoulder.

Damian swore and swung his weapons at the creature, forcing it back a few steps.

"That's fucking ridiculous," Damian gritted out angrily as he shifted his position so he could cover Caleb's injured side. "We can't stop fighting. If we do, they'll immediately kill us."

"If we keep fighting, they'll kill us all eventually," I said, stabbing into a creature that'd been moving to attack Gabriel while he was occupied with two other creatures. "There's no way to win by force. You have to see that. We're barely holding them off. We don't have any powers right now, and we can't keep doing this forever."

"So you're suggesting that we just give up?" Damian shouted back. There was an undercurrent of desperation in his voice beneath the anger.

"No. I'm suggesting we all consciously surrender at the same time. It's an intentional ceding of control. It's not the same as giving up. Think about it logically, Damian. What else could we possibly do?"

He didn't respond. He just kept fighting.

"What do the rest of you think?" I asked, narrowly dodging the point of another spear.

A blood creature charged at Matt and managed to hit him across the chest with the blunt end of the spear. Matt stumbled back, crashing into Gabriel, who stumbled forward, causing his block to miss its mark. He hissed in pain as the point of a spear scraped across his chest. My heart froze, paralyzing me with fear as I watched blood begin to stain his shirt.

"No." I stumbled toward him, forgetting for a moment about all the creatures trying to kill me.

Gabriel looked quickly down at the injury and grimaced slightly, before stabbing into the creature that'd drawn his blood.

"Don't worry." He sent a small smile in my direction. "It's not very deep."

I swallowed hard and brought my daggers up just in time to block another blow aimed at me. This needed to end. If nothing changed, this would be how the battle would progress—the creatures injuring us more and more, taking chunks out of us until we couldn't fight anymore. Until only our lifeless bodies were left on the stone floor. Anger burned through me again—a defense mechanism against the fear. I couldn't let that happen to us. I wouldn't let these stubborn men be the reason for our deaths.

"Listen to me," I growled at the rest of the group. "We have to do something different. We're all going to die if we don't. If no one else has any better ideas, we're doing my plan. *Now.*"

As it was, blood from my spear injury had already soaked through the entire sleeve of my shirt and burned each time I moved it to block and thrust. If we wanted to get the book before dying, we needed to try something else.

"We should do Terah's plan," Gabriel panted, winded as blood seeped down the front of his shirt. My stomach twisted with pain at the sight. "It's better than being slowly hacked to pieces with no way to heal ourselves and no way to win."

"I agree," Matt said a few moments later, though he sounded resigned. "If we're going to die anyway, we might as well try it. It's just going to keep getting worse. And I can't think of a better way out of this." He dodged and lunged, trying desperately to fend off five creatures at once.

"I . . . agree with them," Caleb said, his voice tight as he kept fighting with his injured arm. "We won't last much longer like this, Damian. You know that."

Damian swore—desperate, angry. Surrender wasn't easy for any of us, but I suspected it was even harder for him. Finally, Damian made another noise of frustration, but it was tinged with defeat this time.

"Fine," he growled. "I'll do it since we're probably going to die anyway."

Relief flooded me, but so did anxiety. My theory about surrender was just that. A theory. I had no way of knowing if I was right. No way of knowing whether it'd bring an end to this unwinnable battle, or if I'd just end up being the cause of our deaths.

I blocked an aggressive swing of an axe. "Okay. Put down your weapons and kneel on the count of three. Hold your intent to surrender in your minds. We need them to know it's intentional. Ready?"

Fear reflected back in all their eyes, and Caleb looked like he might be sick. But they nodded. Firm. Resolved.

"Okay. One . . . two . . . three!"

I dropped to my knees and threw my weapons to the ground, bowing my head forward in clear surrender. I slammed my eyes shut, desperate for it to work—hoping I wouldn't feel the bite of an axe in my back in the next moment—and reached my hand out blindly toward Gabriel. If this was how it was going to end, I wanted to at least be connected to him one last time. A breathless second later, his fingers closed tightly around mine.

I heard the creatures charging at us. Heard the violent swish of their weapons swinging through the air toward us. My grip around Gabriel's hand tightened as I waited for the pain. My heart pounded wildly in my chest—the terrified, pumping adrenaline of knowing you weren't meant to survive a given situation. Time seemed to slow. And I hoped. With all my might, I hoped my theory was right. I hoped I wouldn't cause the deaths of the people I cared about.

Silence suddenly fell around us. Too suddenly. Like all sound had simply been muted. I was too scared to open my eyes, but my desperation to know what was happening—whether we'd stopped them—won out. I squinted up in the in the dim light and saw the blood creatures frozen above us, their weapons inches from the backs of our heads. My hands shook. They'd gotten so close. So close to ending us.

The creatures straightened with a jerk, then began to dissolve, the blood weapons melding back into the figures before the figures, too, began to liquify, pouring to the ground and sliding back—a thick, gelatinous entity—to the carving of the god. The blood and light climbed the statue and bathed the stone in thick red, pulsing rhythmically. Then the stone began to move.

We shoved quickly to our feet, looking at each other with a mixture of anxiety and relief. Damian nodded tightly at me—a resigned acknowledgment that my guess had been right. But we knew it wasn't over yet. There'd been four gods on the altar, and this chamber only represented one.

Gabriel reached out and pulled me against him with a shuddering sigh of relief as we watched the stone slide slowly to the side, exposing a large opening in the wall. I could feel the rapid beats of his heart against my chest as his arms tightened around me. He pressed his forehead to mine and just shook his head slowly from side to side, letting out a deep breath.

"We need to bandage your chest," I murmured as I held him tightly in return. I knew holding me so close must be hurting him.

Gabriel let out a small laugh. "Says the woman who's bled through the *entire* arm of her clothes," he grumbled in my ear. "Don't think I haven't noticed." There was an almost dangerous edge to his voice, like he thought I'd deny it and refuse help. In the past, I would've. But not anymore.

I smiled wryly and pressed a kiss to his shoulder. We were both stubborn and protective. "Fine. We *both* need to be bandaged, then."

Gabriel's lips pursed as he tried not to smile. But I saw the warmth growing in his eyes.

"Hey, Matt." I turned to face the rest of the group as the stone door finally groaned to a halt, leaving a dark chasm yawning ominously open in front of us. "Do you have any more gauze in there? We need to bandage our wounds if we don't want to bleed out before we reach the book."

Matt turned to look at me and winced as he saw how much I'd bled.

"Gabriel and Caleb too." I nodded at their injuries.

Matt glanced at each of them in turn, then nodded curtly at me, his gaze flicking to where Gabriel's hand was curled around my waist. He looked quickly away and pulled off his backpack, his jaw tight. He rummaged through it, then tossed rolls of gauze to each of us.

"Bind those after we go through the door," he murmured, his tone clipped. He swung his bag onto his back again and turned toward the dark opening. "We don't want the door to close before we're through."

22

FEARS

We passed through the door as a tightly packed group, then lingered just on the other side as we'd done in the first chamber. It was impossible to see more than a foot or two in front of us. Only the dim light from the previous room illuminated the space.

Gabriel quickly unrolled the gauze Matt had tossed him and started wrapping it tightly around the gash in my upper arm. "Before we completely run out of light," he murmured. Once he'd thoroughly bandaged me, he tore the gauze with his teeth and tied a tight knot over the wound.

"Your turn." I took the roll of gauze from him and pushed up his arms so I could wrap it tightly around the gash in his chest.

Damian took a cue from us and grabbed the gauze from Caleb so he could wrap the spear injury in his shoulder for him.

"Oh, thanks," Caleb said, surprised. Damian just shrugged, his face an expressionless mask. Like he didn't want us to see he cared.

The door started closing behind us with a slow, ominous scraping of stone against stone. I hurriedly used the entire roll of gauze to wrap Gabriel's broad chest and tied it to the remainder of my roll to make sure his wound was adequately covered. Then, in the fading light, I quickly tied a tight knot, firmly securing the bandaging.

The door finally scraped to a stop, and we were plunged into darkness once more. But this time I knew what to expect. Instead of panicking in the intense dark and quiet, I waited, watching for the swirling colors of our powers to seep into the chamber and move around us. It only took about thirty seconds this time. Our powers began to glow in the symbols below our feet, filling the space with faint, eerie light as they traveled toward the center of the room where a large stone statute stood, almost as tall as the room itself.

The statue was a three-dimensional rendering of the second symbol on the altar. It was of a creature with the body of a human and the head of an animal I couldn't name. It had long, narrow, rectangular ears pointing up and slightly back from its head, a long, curved snout, and a headdress of thick, straight hair that framed its shoulders. The only clothing was a thigh-length cloth tied around its hips. It was standing with one leg slightly in front of the other and held a long scepter in front if it that was curved on top and had a small, two-pronged base. Beneath it was a broad circle of stones, beginning at the statue's base and moving outward at least fifteen feet in every direction, containing large carvings of the god's symbol that filled the entirety of each stone. It was in these symbols that our powers finally pooled.

I squinted and looked around the rest of the room, trying to see if there was anything else in here with us. The light was so dim that I could hardly tell, but I didn't think so. All I saw was a vague outline of another solid-looking door on the opposite end of the room. Clearly, then, the key to our passage forward was the statue and the stones surrounding it.

Caleb started toward it, but Damian gripped his shoulder tightly, holding him back. "Wait. We need to strategize for a second, so we're not stuck in a shitty situation. Like last time," he added, his deep voice growing darker.

Matt nodded in agreement. "That's a good idea." He turned toward us, his face partially bathed in the eerie glow of our combined powers. "We should consider what we know about the god first, so we have a hint about what to expect."

I turned to look at Gabriel. He seemed like the most likely of us to be able to identify the god, except for perhaps Damian.

Gabriel rubbed his chin absently as he considered the statue. "I believe it's the god Set." He glanced at Damian to see if he agreed. Damian nodded slightly, his expression neutral. Cold. But with the slightest hint of disconcertion. Gabriel sighed and crossed his arms over his chest, turning to look at the statue again. "Unfortunately, that's not good news for us," he murmured, his eyebrows furrowing. "Set was generally thought of as the god of trickery, violence, chaos, and envy. I doubt that any test inspired by him would be straight-forward or easy to pass."

I bit back a curse and instead bit the inside of my cheek. Caleb swore and shook his head. Matt looked resigned. Worried. Damian just looked . . . closed off. Like he'd shut down.

"So, what should we expect?" I tried to sound calm.

Gabriel's eyes trained on my injured arm, and I realized I'd unconsciously touched the blood-soaked sleeve with my fingers. I quickly brought my hand back to my side. I'd shown my nervousness anyway. *Great.*

Gabriel's gaze turned intense for a moment as his eyes left my blood-stained fingertips to meet mine. I desperately wished I could still connect our minds. That we could communicate silently again. I could tell he wanted to say something. Just to me. Instead, he stepped closer and slid his hand into mine, squeezing gently.

"We should expect deception," he finally said, looking up and addressing the group. "For things not to be as they appear. It wouldn't surprise me if we'll have to fight again. Other than that, I'm not sure how to prepare. I guess just knowing what the god is known for might give us a leg-up in the moment, but we won't know until we face it. Just stay sharp and question everything."

I nodded along with the others, anxiety churning in my gut.

"Ready?" Matt asked, his gaze sweeping over the group.

We nodded again, then moved forward until we were spread out within the glowing circle at the statue's feet. I squeezed Gabriel's hand one more time before releasing him so we'd both have quick access to our weapons, just in case. For about a minute, nothing happened. But then, the symbols on the stones beneath us pulsed as they had in the previous room. And the statue's eyes glowed with the same light. A shiver of fear undulated through me at the sight. It was otherworldly. Unnerving, especially in the darkness of the room.

Suddenly, the powers shot upward from each symbol, bathing us all in light and warmth until it created a dome around the entire circle, its center point the top of the god's statue. Then the powers expanded within the dome, turning increasingly opaque, until the entire space was filled with their light and color. It was like a thick fog descending over and between us, its density growing until we couldn't see each other anymore. I tried to reach out for Gabriel again, but I couldn't seem to move my arms anymore. Or my feet.

I blinked rapidly and shook my head, trying to clear the fog that seemed to be creeping into my brain. But I couldn't clear it. And every breath I took felt like I was inhaling the dense power directly into my lungs. I could almost feel it spreading inside me. I blinked a few more times, trying to stay calm. Trying to remember what Gabriel had told us—to look beyond what we could immediately see. To remember that all might not be as it appeared.

I blinked again and the fog slowly cleared around me. *Finally*. I sighed with relief. But instead of seeing the darkness and the stone walls again, I saw that I was outside. I squinted around, confused, turning in place as the last remnants of fog cleared. I felt like I'd seen this place before. A breeze whipped past my face, and I smelled burning. The metallic odor of blood. Then I heard screams. Blasts of power. The din of battle. My heart lurched and sped up. I looked up and saw strange colors covering the sky like I wasn't even on the earth anymore. And it was all hauntingly familiar.

I heard metal scraping metal as I turned. I glanced down at myself, and my stomach plummeted. I was wearing full body armor, smeared with mud and blood. I was carrying a sword that was also covered in blood. My chest rose and fell rapidly as a scene of complete and utter carnage came into focus in front of me. Desperation and fear gripped my chest, vicelike, as they'd done the last time I'd been here. In my vision. With Damian. But this didn't feel like a vision. It filled all my senses. It was too real.

Unlike my vision, this image wasn't frozen. No, this time chaos reigned, and violent, incessant battle ravaged the spaces around me. And before I could fully decide what to do—or determine what was even happening—a figure barreled toward me, larger than life. I couldn't nail down its specific form. Just that it had one. Shifting. Powerful. Enormous. It hurt to look at. Like I wasn't meant to be seeing it with human eyes. The figure brandished a weapon as it charged me. There was no time left to think.

I raised my sword and blocked the powerful blow that aimed to decapitate me. And my arms, usually so strong and sure in battle, immediately shook from the force and power behind the strike. Inhuman in scope. Unlike anything I'd ever fought or faced before. My eyes widened, and I realized with a sinking stomach, the audacity I'd have to have to think I could win against this being. There was no chance. None at all.

The being disconnected its weapon from my sword and swung at me again. I leapt backward, narrowly avoiding the blow, but the creature was quick and immediately swung again. This time, its weapon connected with mine, and I felt the impact in every bone and joint of my body. Excruciatingly painful. I'd be lucky if none of my bones had shattered. The being disconnected and swung again. But I knew I couldn't take another hit like that. Against this creature, I was weak. Not even a real opponent for it. I'd never felt so helpless in a fight before—not even against the Demon that'd almost ended me. Fear flooded me with an icy numbness. This was worse than any nightmare I'd ever had. I'd trained too hard and fought too long to die like this. But I knew we'd never get to choose our manner of death—least of all those of us who were soldiers.

I swung my sword to block the blow, and gritted my teeth, steeling myself for the pain I knew was coming. But before our weapons clashed, a figure gently merged with the space between us and caught the blow meant for me with hands filled with golden light. The figure looked human, but clearly wasn't. They were larger than life. Not even a Divine. Tendrils of golden fire like that in her hands, emanated from the top of her head, almost like a halo of light. I was frozen for a moment, awestruck.

But I jolted back into reality and backed quickly away as the figure engaged my attacker in a battle so intense and otherworldly that I struggled to comprehend it. Gasping, and trying to shake off the lingering pain, I spun and looked around me, trying to find faces in the chaos that I recognized. Trying to find Gabriel. Matt. Panic filled my chest as I started running through the battlefield, dodging blasts of power, swings of weapons, explosions, sprays of blood. I didn't want to think about what those two could be facing. What might've happened to them. My fear grew and grew as I jumped over and wound through body after body on the ground clad in armor like mine, their young faces smeared with blood, if they had faces left at all. Their eyes all closed forever.

My stomach lurched as I kept pushing forward. As I kept seeing face after lifeless face. So many Divines dead. The only figures left standing were . . . inhuman. Otherworldly. I couldn't tell who or what they fought for, or what side they were on, if any. Tears pooled in my eyes, and my chest heaved against my will. I couldn't tell if it was sobs or if I was hyperventilating. Maybe both. Probably both.

"Gabriel!" I called, my voice breaking as I kept running. I tripped occasionally and fell onto the dead. Tears streamed down my cheeks as I kept pushing to my feet, my hands sliding over bloody armor and clothes, again and again. I tried my best to push forward—to keep moving. "Gabriel!" I spun around as I ran. But I couldn't see him anywhere.

I tripped again as another sob escaped from me, uncontrollable. The bodies were so tightly packed now, overlapping and strewn across the ground, it was a miracle that I could find a path to walk through at all. I landed hard across a body on the ground, slippery with blood. I gasped, winded, and pushed myself up again, before glancing down. I couldn't help it. As though I needed to see the face of the person I'd crashed into— yet another face devoid of life. Another casualty of this horrible war. But as my brain registered the face I was seeing, the blood froze in my veins.

"M-Matt," I mouthed, though no sound came out of me. I didn't have any breath left. My mouth could barely form the shape of the word.

I reached a shaking hand forward and ran my fingertips down his ashen cheek. Devoid of blood or life. His eyes stared blankly up at the sky, the hazel dim and unseeing. I just sat there in shock, tremors coursing through my body, tears streaming down my face as I stared at him. I couldn't comprehend it. Why wasn't he moving? Why wasn't he waking up? He was my friend. My family.

I reached forward and shook his shoulders. "Matt, wake up," I whispered. His body moved limply under my grasp. I shook again, harder this time. "Wake up. Please please. Please wake up. Matt, wake up!" But he didn't.

Another explosion shook the ground around me, sending a spray of debris over me, and shook me from my disbelieving trance. I'd die if I stayed here like this. And I needed, now more than ever, to find Gabriel. I bent forward and pressed my lips against Matt's cold forehead, my sobs still shaking my body, and slid his eyes closed with my fingertips. Then I pushed to my feet and began running again.

"Gabriel!" I screamed, unable to measure my emotions. I was falling apart. My heart was already broken in so many ways. But I needed to find him. I needed to help him. To be with him.

Another blast of power blew me off my feet, rough debris raining down on me. I tasted blood as I pushed to my feet again, but I didn't register any pain. I was beyond physical discomfort at this point. Someone could cut off my arm and I probably wouldn't feel it. I ran, screaming Gabriel's name, dodging inhuman beings and bodies alike, just trying to find him. I was so focused that everything else around me blurred. I only stopped once, lurching to a halt as another familiar face loomed out of the mud and blood at my feet, shaking me out of my stupor.

474

My mother. A staggered breath left me, and I felt like I was cracking around the edges. I wrapped my arms around my middle, trying to hold myself together as I stared down at the woman who'd given me life more than once, but who'd rarely cared for me. I was surprised at the bone-deep agony I felt at seeing her lying there, lifeless. Covered in mud and blood like everyone else. No longer the High Light Guardian. No longer my mother. I knelt next to her and extended a shaking hand, placing it gently over her heart. Like she'd done for me once. But I knew there was no possibility of bringing her back. I couldn't return that favor. She'd been gone too long for that.

I swallowed and pushed to my feet again, swaying. Dazed. In shock. My brain felt like it was on fire. And it was telling me that Gabriel couldn't possibly still be alive. But my heart wouldn't accept that. I knew he was alive. He had to be. The love I felt for him burned in my chest, too vibrant to be one-sided. Too alive for him not to be. So I pushed forward. Called for him with my voice and my mind and my heart. Searched the horizon and the ground. Looked everywhere for him. I couldn't stop—wouldn't stop—until I found him. Not if it took days, weeks, or years. Not even if I had to fight a thousand creatures and live through a thousand explosions of power. For him, I'd never give up. I repeated that to myself an untold number of times as I kept searching. Kept pushing forward.

Until I found him.

With a gasp, I ran toward a figure in the distance whose black, messy hair was sticking up familiarly ahead of me. It looked like he was sitting upright, leaning back against a rock. Probably to rest. A breath of relief whooshed out of me as I weaved quickly through the bodies on the ground to reach him.

"Gabriel," I gasped as I knelt next to him, grabbing his shoulder.

Up close, I could see his eyes were closed. That was okay. He was probably resting. After all, this was a battle to end all battles. The battle to determine the fate of the world. One would have to measure themself to weather such a fight, and resting was a part of that. I moved in front of him and grabbed his other shoulder as well.

"Gabriel, wake up." My voice sounded gravelly and broken to my own ears. His face still looked peaceful, but his head lolled forward. And he didn't wake up. "Gabriel," I said, louder, not caring if I startled him. I just needed to see the electric blue of his eyes. I needed to see the warmth in their depths as he looked at me. How they almost glittered as he smirked at me. I needed to hear the warmth in his voice as he said my name. As he told me he loved me.

"Wake the hell up!" I practically shouted, shaking his shoulders again, more firmly this time. His head lolled back against the stone, but otherwise, he didn't move or react.

My whole body shook as I stared at him for a long moment. I couldn't comprehend what was happening. I couldn't understand why he wasn't waking up. Maybe he just couldn't hear me over the tumult of raging battle—the explosions shaking the ground and air around us. I reached forward and slid my hand through his hair, pushing it back, away from his face as I'd done so many times before. As I wanted to do hundreds of times more. I ran my fingers down the cool skin of his cheek. He was as white as a sheet. But it was fine. Completely fine. He'd always been pale. Far paler than me.

"Gabriel," I said again, leaning forward so my face was close to his. There was no way he couldn't hear me now. Not with me this close. But he didn't respond. "Gabriel, I swear to the gods, if you don't wake up right fucking now, I'll never forgive you!" My voice shook violently. I gave his broad shoulders another shake for good measure. But he didn't move.

A cold numbness overtook me as I reached forward, fingers shaking, and ran my fingertips gently down his cheek again. Then, pressing my eyes tightly closed, I touched my fingers to the side of his neck. Where his pulse should've been. But there was nothing there. No hint of movement.

"No," I breathed, the air constricting in my lungs. "No no no no no."

I looked desperately inside myself for power to heal him. There had to be a way. There was always a way. There was always something to try. This couldn't be it. But there was no purple fire inside me anymore. No divine power left somehow. Not even my life force. It didn't make any sense. But it was all gone. There was nothing I could do. He was . . . gone.

I collapsed against the front of his body, holding him desperately as broken sobs spilled from my mouth. And I cried like I'd never cried in my life. I pleaded with him to come back. To not leave me. I'd never leave him. He hadn't given up on me, and I'd never give up on him. I'd lead him home somehow, like he'd led me home. I'd save him like he'd saved me. In that moment, I traded my soul a thousand million times to the darkness, the light, and everything in between if it would only bring him back. For him, I'd do anything. Trade anything. The world needed him in it. *I* needed him in it.

But no one was listening. No one seemed to care. The universe didn't care. Who were we, after all, to anyone else? What did our love matter to those who weren't us?

"Please please please please," I whispered through my sobs against his neck, my tears soaking his skin. "Please come back. I love you, Gabriel. Please. Please come back to me." I pressed my lips there to his cold skin. Desperately. Trying to remind him of our love. Maybe if he remembered, he'd come back. Maybe. I tried again and again. Until my lips were numb. But nothing worked. He was still . . . gone.

Eons later, I eventually ran out of tears. I ran out of things to bargain with. I ran out of words to bring him back. I ran out of hope. And he hadn't returned. I supposed I knew, now, that he couldn't. And I had nothing left. Nothing in the world. We'd lost this battle. The Divines had been annihilated. The earth couldn't be saved from whatever fate was in store for it. We had no control over any of it anymore. The Normals were doomed. There was no one left to shield them. I had no divine power and no strength left to fight. If I stayed here, I'd just die horribly. And everyone I loved was dead. Gabriel . . . was dead. There was nothing. Nothing left for me here. I was empty. A cold, desolate husk. And all I wanted, all my aching soul longed for, was to be at peace . . . with him. Wherever he was now.

I nodded a little to myself and wiped the remnants of tears from my cheeks with a shaking, bloody hand. Then I leaned back on Gabriel's lap and pulled one of his long daggers from his stiff fingers. I held it in my hands for a few moments, gazing at it as memories washed over me. Memories of him. Of us. Of Matt. Of my mother. Of the world before it'd ended. Then I raised the dagger and placed it point-first against my neck. I chose its placement carefully. That way, it'd be quick and certain. I reached out with my other hand and placed it against Gabriel's heart. Tears filled my eyes again as I looked at him. But I closed them quickly. Took a deep breath. Prepared myself.

But an intense throbbing erupted in my chest before I could push. And I gasped, dropping the dagger in surprise, my eyes flying open. I clutched at my chest, confused. It almost felt like heart palpitations, but the intense hammering was steady and strong, not erratic or uneven. It was . . . alive. *Too* alive. It was like my body was trying to communicate something that my mind wasn't registering.

I glanced at Gabriel and the throbbing in my chest intensified. And then it hit me again. *My heart was too alive for him to not be.* Somehow, even though it didn't make complete sense . . . somehow, I knew it was true. I closed my eyes and flashes of a dark stone room appeared behind my eyelids. And Gabriel's voice drifted through.

"We should expect deception . . . For things not to be as they appear." His voice was warm as it filled my mind. Alive. *". . . question everything."*

My eyes flew open as I gasped. The book. The secret mission. The test. This wasn't real. *This wasn't real.* It couldn't be. Which meant . . . he was alive. Gabriel was alive! He had to be. Matt too. And my mother. The world wasn't doomed yet. All wasn't lost. Hope wasn't gone. Warmth bloomed in my chest, and life seeped back into me little by little.

"This isn't real!" I shouted at the darkening sky above me. Smoke and ash from the battlefield blew across my face, stinging my eyes. "I know this is an illusion! This. Is. Not. Real. Let me out!"

For a moment, nothing changed. But then my surroundings dissolved around me, fading into a thick mist. I blinked as the light grew dimmer and saw that I was kneeling on the stone floor of the second underground chamber, one of my long daggers on the stone in front of me. Where it hadn't been before. I stared at the dagger as a chill stole through me. Had I . . . almost used that on myself outside of the illusion?

"Oh, thank the gods," a voice panted from behind me, "you're back."

I spun and saw Matt crouching just behind my shoulder.

"You almost used that on yourself." His voice shook as he nodded at the dagger. He looked haunted. "I'd only just shaken off my own illusion when I saw you raising that to your neck. I ran over and grabbed your wrist just in time. And you dropped it a moment later."

I stared at Matt, my hands shaking. He was alive. Actually alive. It really had been an illusion—all that death and violence. Not real. Not even a vision. It'd been a horrible, horrifying falsehood that'd almost caused me to take my own life.

I shivered and reached out to take his hand. Then I held onto it. Tightly.

Matt looked at me in surprise. We weren't really on affectionate terms anymore. But right now, I didn't care. I'd seen him lying there in mud and blood, all lifeless, and I never wanted to see him like that again.

"Thank you," I finally managed to say. "And . . . I'm glad you're okay."

Matt's cheeks colored slightly, and he squeezed my hand in return. Then he reached out with his other hand and gently wiped the tears from my cheeks.

"Thanks," he murmured. "I'm glad you're okay too. Your illusion must've been pretty horrific if . . . if you were going to . . ." he swallowed, unable to finish. I couldn't blame him. I didn't want to think about it. I didn't want to talk about it.

"Is everyone else okay?" I released his hand and pushed gingerly to my feet. Then I bent over, grabbed my dagger, and quickly sheathed it.

"We're the only ones who've broken out so far." Matt's brows drew together as he glanced around us.

Ice filled my veins. My illusion had been horrifying. I could only imagine the same would be true for the others. I needed to find Gabriel. I spun and rushed through the thick fog of our powers and nearly tripped over him. He was lying prone, his back pressed to the stone floor, his breaths heavy and erratic. But he was moving. Alive. *Thank the fucking gods.* A part sob, part sigh left my mouth as I collapsed next to him and pressed shaking hands to his warm chest. Tears filled my eyes.

"Matt, go monitor the other two and make sure they don't hurt themselves." I couldn't leave Gabriel's side. Not now. Maybe not ever. I forgot to listen for Matt's response.

"Gabriel," I whispered, running my hands down his arms. I noticed, with a sharp clench of my stomach, he had tears seeping from his closed eyelids. "Gabriel, it's okay. It's just an illusion. You're okay. Come back to me. Push the illusion away and come back."

I stroked his warm cheeks, wiping away his tears, and ran my fingers through his soft hair. I pressed kisses to his forehead. His nose. His cheeks.

"Terah," he groaned, his eyes still closed. He was still in the illusion.

I laid on the hard stone floor next to him and wrapped my arm tightly around his waist, resting my cheek against his chest. I pressed into his side, giving him my warmth. Hoping he could feel me here with him somehow.

"I'm here," I murmured. "I'm okay, and so are you. We're in the underground chamber trying to retrieve the book. You're in an illusion. What you're seeing isn't real. Follow my voice. Push the illusion away and come back. Come back to me."

"You're . . . alive?" His voice broke.

Tears spilled down my cheeks. He looked like he was in agony, even with his eyes closed.

"Yes, I'm alive."

"Promise?" he whispered.

A sob broke from my lips, and I leaned up and kissed him. "I promise," I breathed against him, my tears falling on his cheek.

Suddenly, his arms encircled me and pulled me tightly against his chest. I felt his heartbeat thundering against my own. So alive. I glanced up and saw his eyes open. He'd managed to break free of the illusion. A sigh of relief shuddered from my lungs, and I gave him a tremulous smile before dissolving into tears against his chest. I would've felt embarrassed if we hadn't just been through hell. Now, I didn't care if the whole world saw me cry as long as I could hold Gabriel and feel how very much alive he was.

"Terah," Gabriel breathed. He sounded exhausted and he looked haunted—as haunted as I felt. "You're alive. You're okay." He held me tightly, pressing his lips to my hair. My tears spilled onto the gauze still wrapping his chest. From the faint quake of his chest, I gathered his eyes weren't tear-free either.

"You are too," I whispered. "In my illusion, you . . . you weren't. I couldn't . . . I just couldn't . . ." I didn't know how to continue. I didn't have words to describe the devastation I'd felt. Even now, even knowing it hadn't been real, I felt a deep tear in the fabric of my being that would take time to heal. The illusion had been too real. And I'd felt it like it *was* real.

"I know," Gabriel murmured against my hair. "I know how you felt. I couldn't either. I couldn't . . . go on. Either time. It . . . destroys you. Tears you apart." I felt him swallow.

"I'm sorry," I whispered, pressing my forehead to his chest. "Sorry you had to experience that . . . again."

"I don't want you to be sorry." His arms tightened around me, his voice going deep—almost gruff. "The only thing I want you to be right now is alive and here with me."

I tilted up my chin so I could look into his eyes. Warm. Bright. "I can do that."

Gabriel reached up and gently wiped an escaped tear from my cheek. Then he drew my face slowly to his and kissed me softly, his warm hands cupping my cheeks. And for a few moments, the world around us faded away.

"Caleb's out." Matt's voice drifted to us from somewhere within the fog to our left.

Gabriel and I pulled slowly apart and sat up, still holding onto each other.

Caleb groaned. "That was the worst." His voice was hoarse.

"Welcome back," Matt said quietly. "When did you realize it was an illusion?"

Caleb sighed, sounding weary. I could almost see him pinching the bridge of his nose between his fingers.

"When there was nothing left but I still kept . . . existing somehow," he murmured. "That's when I felt like there was something I was forgetting. Something felt off. I tried to remember, and I got a few flashes of this place, which helped jog my memory. I was able to put things together from there and eventually pull myself out."

Matt made a small sound of assent. "It was kind of like that for me, too. Terah and Gabriel made it out as well. Go a few feet that way to join them. I'm going to check on Damian."

Caleb sighed again, more resigned than weary this time, and pushed to his feet. He appeared in front of us a moment later.

"Hey," he said quietly, nodding at us. He looked haunted, dark circles prominent beneath his eyes where they hadn't been before. His gaze slid quickly over us, assessing, no doubt noticing our red eyes and the traces of tears. He wisely decided not to say anything else. He just sank back to the floor again, this time closer to us. We all knew at this point that it was better for us to stick together.

"He's not doing so well," Matt called through the thick fog a few minutes later. "I may need your help."

The three of us looked at each other for a moment, worried, then pushed quickly to our feet. We followed Matt's grunts of effort until they appeared out of the fog in front of us. Matt was crouched next to Damian, who was writhing like he was being tortured, trying to steady Damian's body by holding his shoulders solidly to the ground. It wasn't doing much to impede the violent convulsing, though. We stared at them in shock.

"I'm afraid he's going to hurt himself," Matt grunted, his voice strained.

I walked quickly around them and crouched behind Damian's head, then reached forward and placed my hands palms-up beneath the back of his skull to prevent him from slamming it against the stones, as he must've done multiple times by now.

"What do we do?" I glanced over at Matt. "Do we just wait until he comes out of it on his own?"

"I'm not sure what else we could do." Matt looked regretful as he glanced at Damian's tormented face.

I looked too. I'd never seen such a strong emotion there before—he was usually so good at keeping a cold, neutral mask in place. The sight made my muscles clench and sent sharp pangs of alarm through me. He must be experiencing something unspeakably horrible. I was afraid of the damage that might be done if we didn't get him out—emotionally, physically, or both. And if he didn't break free of his illusion, I wasn't sure we'd be able to move forward from this room to retrieve the book. Because, without him conquering his illusion, the door might never open.

All four of us gasped as Damian suddenly grabbed his knives from the sheathes at his sides and swung them quickly up, the sharp points facing his body.

"Grab his arms!" I yelled, still trying to shield his writhing head. I wasn't sure whether he was trying to use them on himself or someone else in the illusion, but either way, it likely wouldn't end well.

Gabriel and Matt lunged forward, and each grabbed one of Damian's arms, then shoved them down against the stones, using their bodyweight to keep them pinned there.

"Caleb," Matt grunted, straining against Damian's attempts to free himself, "see if you can get the knives out of his hands." Damian was writhing even more violently now.

Caleb quickly crouched and tried to wrest the knives from him, but there wasn't much of the knife that he could grab that wouldn't slice him open. Damian's hands swallowed the entirety of each handle, so Caleb tried pulling one by the narrow blade instead. But his gripping area was too small, and Damian's grip was too strong.

Caleb swore and shook his head. "I don't think I can get them."

I winced as Damian thrashed, his head slamming into my palms. At least my hands were softer than the floor. It didn't seem like Damian could shake free of his illusion on his own. And it looked like whatever he was experiencing was getting worse. We needed a way to break through it somehow. We needed to give his brain space to remember where we were and what we were doing. To figure out that he was in an illusion.

"Damian," I murmured, as close to his ear as I could get with his movements, "what you're experiencing right now isn't real. You're in an illusion. Remember. You're with us in an underground chamber at the Academy, trying to get the book. You're okay. We're here with you. Push away the illusion so you can come back."

Damian's twitching lessened for a moment, almost like he could hear me, but then he groaned, and his writhing intensified.

"Shit," I whispered, straightening up. "I was really hoping that would work.

"Damian," Caleb said, moving to sit near me so Damian could hear him clearly. "It's Caleb. Snap out of it and come back." His voice was firm. No-nonsense. But I could tell he cared, which surprised me. "I know what you're experiencing is probably really shitty, but it's not real. You can push it away and you'll come back to reality. Come on, man, you can do it. Just shove it away, and you'll come back."

I hadn't seen Caleb like this before—actually caring about someone instead of just using them to further his end goal. Not since Dagmar. But he looked like he was being genuine. Like he cared about Damian as a real friend.

I hid my surprise and carefully watched Damian's face to see if he'd have a reaction. His erratic movements slowed again, this time for longer, and his brow furrowed.

"Say more stuff to him," I said quickly, glancing at Caleb.

His cheeks tinged with pink as his eyes met mine, our faces only a foot or so apart. He swallowed, his gaze lingering on mine for a long moment. Then he jerked his head forward and looked back down at Damian. He pressed his eyes closed for a moment, like he was recentering himself, then opened them again, his jaw setting with determination.

"Damian, all of us are here, waiting for you. Me, Terah, Matt, and Gabriel. Do you remember? We faced those blood monsters together, then we each had to face our own illusions. What you're facing right now is just an illusion. No matter how real it seems, it isn't. We're all safe, including you. We're in the god Set's chamber, and this is a test. Fight the illusion. Push it away and come back. *Win.*"

Gabriel and Matt expelled relieved breaths as Damian finally relaxed his arms.

"The . . . the god." Damian's deep voice was gravelly. "The book. I . . . remember."

Caleb sighed and sat back on his heels. "That's right. That's where we are. Trying to get the book. You can come back now."

Damian looked like he wanted to believe Caleb, but then his body convulsed with what looked like intense pain.

"No, don't!" he cried, tormented. Then he convulsed again, his muscles tensing. "I knew it," he groaned, despair heavy in his voice. "Never . . . should have . . . tried . . . to save . . ."

Tears formed below the thick curtains of his lashes, and his arms strained against Matt and Gabriel's grips.

"We have to do something." There was a frantic edge to my voice. Because I'd never seen Damian like this. If it was enough to make him break composure to this extent, it must be truly horrific. "He clearly can't get out on his own."

"I just . . . don't know what to do." Matt's eyes met mine, wide and anxious. Almost fearful. And haunted, like they were when I'd first seen him after my own illusion. "We don't have any power. There isn't any other way to reach him."

I looked down at Damian's tortured face as he writhed against the unforgiving floor. And something jolted within my chest. Not exactly an emotion—it was more like a physical pull. Like a string was attached there and was yanking me forward toward Damian like we were tethered some-how. Like it wanted me to do something. My memory briefly flashed to the vision I'd had that day in the training room—the day he'd been pulled into it too. My power had tethered us together on the battlefield at the end. Like it wanted to communicate something.

Save him, save him, save him, something whispered inside me. Insis-tent. Rattling, like a ball pinging around inside me. Save him? I obviously wanted to. But how? I didn't have any power right now. I didn't know what to do. The invisible string in my chest gave another tug forward, demanding action from me.

I slid one of my hands from under his head and placed it against his forehead, trying to steady him. I knew what I'd do if I still had my power. I'd try to see into his mind to see what he was experiencing, then I'd form a two-way connection so I could talk to him and help him confront the situa-tion. Show him that it wasn't real. I closed my eyes, trying to think of another way to accomplish something similar, as another tug in my chest pulled me forward. But I didn't have any other ideas.

My eyes flew open, and I gasped as another more violent tug yanked me forward, this time physically, so that I was leaning over Damian. My hand shot out and braced against his chest to keep me from falling face-first into his ribs. To my surprise, I felt a warm pulsing there that wasn't his heart. It was . . . familiar somehow. Like I knew it. It felt like returning home after being away. Like seeing an old friend again. I stared at his chest, confused. What was it? What was calling to me?

Save him, save him, save him.

I closed my eyes again, ignoring the questions from the men around me, and focused on that familiar pulsing beneath my fingers. I concen-trated on it, feeling its rhythm. When I blocked everything else out, I could feel that the pulsing matched the pull in my own chest. Like there was something buried in him that called to something in me. What was it? It felt just out of reach. I needed to see it. I needed to figure it out. I opened my mind to that pulsing, familiar thing, and simultaneously felt something in my chest open. Almost like it was unlocking.

"Terah, what are you doing?" Matt's alarmed voice cut through my thoughts.

My eyes flew open, and I saw something I couldn't comprehend. A line of deep purple power was flowing from the well in my chest into Damian's beneath me. But . . . I didn't have my power anymore. How was that possible?

"Stop giving him your life force!" Matt yelled, frantically. "You'll die again!"

Gabriel looked sharply at him before meeting my gaze, his own startled.

"I'm not trying to!" I gasped. "I'm not trying to do anything! It's . . . it's out of my control. It's just happening!"

All three of them gaped at me in astonishment.

"Try closing it off," Matt growled, his voice dangerous. "*Now.*"

"Maybe he needs this to escape his illusion," I panted. The throbbing in my chest intensified, like I was feeling his heartbeats along with mine, suddenly combining into one erratic, pumping beat.

"Not at your expense," Matt said harshly.

I glanced at Gabriel again, and I could tell he agreed with Matt.

"Maybe I can use it to see into his mind," I said, keeping my eyes on Gabriel this time. "To communicate with him. Maybe the room is allowing it to help us get him out."

"Why would the room do that?" Matt asked, desperate anger overtaking his fear. "It *wants* us to fail so the book stays protected. It would never help us."

"Must be . . . something else, then . . ." I gasped as I felt another tug in my chest, my power still flowing into Damian in a thin stream. My head started to fog, like it'd done right before I'd entered my illusion.

Gabriel watched me for a long moment, his face carefully blank. I could tell he was thinking hard. Trying to figure out what was going on. What to do.

"Try to make it quick," he finally murmured. Somehow, he seemed to understand, even if he didn't like it. I nodded and gave him a small smile. He just swallowed and looked down. "Be safe," he whispered.

I closed my eyes and gave myself over to the fog.

I immediately fell into Damian's illusion. As the fog slowly cleared, I found myself standing in the middle of a large, circular room with ancient-looking curved stone walls and dark wood plank floors. It almost looked like we were in a tower, but there were no windows—it was just dark and cold, like a stone prison. It evoked misery.

A large, utilitarian wood bed stood against one curved wall, and a small bookcase and dilapidated armchair sat together on the opposite wall. But otherwise, the room was empty and undecorated, like no one really lived here. There were no rugs, no art, no keepsakes—nothing to make the room feel warmer or more comfortable.

A groan of pain snapped me back into the present, and I refocused on what I was doing. I was here to help Damian get out. I spun in the direction of the noise and gasped, my hands coming up to cover my mouth at the horror in front of me. Damian was lying on the ground near the wall, daggers clutched in his hands, his body covered in his own blood. Deep gashes peppered his skin, seeping blood in a pool around him. My stomach twisted as I saw daggers had been stabbed through his arms into the wooden planks below, pinning him to the ground. But even more horrifying, were the bodies that surrounded him on the floor, all in various stages of dismemberment. All dead, of course. There had to be at least ten. Maybe more. And it was clear from the smell that many of them hadn't died recently. Horror and nausea churned like roiling snakes in my stomach, trying to fight their way up my throat. I pressed my hand to my stomach, trying to keep it from heaving.

A large figure crouched over Damian, brandishing a knife, the tip of which was dripping with blood. Likely Damian's blood.

"What right do you think you have to exist?" the stranger hissed, his deep, powerful voice sending shivers of fear through me, even though I knew the figure wasn't real. At least not here. "Do you think you're better than they were? That you deserve to live when they didn't?"

Damian tried to mask his pain, but the agony was bleeding through. "Of course they deserved to live," he rasped, his voice unsteady. "I was never the one . . . who wanted them . . . dead."

The stranger slashed Damian viciously across the chest with his knife. Fresh blood welled over the wounds and saturated the front of his shirt.

"Insolent, useless boy," the man growled, shoving to his feet and prowling around Damian. Then he kicked him hard in the ribs. I winced as I saw the breath leave him on an uncontrollable groan. "Their deaths are *your fault*." The stranger's booming voice filled the room and echoed off the walls. "*You* disobeyed orders. *You* stepped outside of the role given to you. *You* betrayed your leader. Their blood is on *your hands*."

He plunged his knife through Damian's upper arm. Damian slammed his eyes closed against the pain, his jaw clenched tightly.

"I know," he finally rasped as he got his reaction under control. He sounded . . . defeated. Truly and completely overcome. His head fell back against the ground. "I know it's my fault."

The figure chuckled, oozing dark amusement. "You always *were* useless." He paced around Damian. "Weak. Pathetic. Sentimental. You'd be *nothing* if it weren't for me. You should be grateful that I've kept you around for this long. But I've reached the end of what I'll tolerate with this latest betrayal."

He gestured at two of the dismembered figures on the floor. I noticed, with a horrified jolt, they were Caleb and me. Ice filled my veins as I eyed my dismembered form. That must've been how the illusion had dealt with the two of us trying to speak to him from the outside. It'd simply incorporated us into this nightmare. I swallowed down the bile rising in my throat.

"Hiding them in your room when I explicitly ordered you to kill them," the man tsked, sneering. "You should've known it would end this way. It always does."

He leaned over and yanked the knife out of Damian's upper arm, then stabbed it violently through the other. Damian groaned.

"Just kill me then," Damian murmured. Ragged. Tired. "Do what you've threatened to do my whole life. Just . . . end it. Let me die, for once."

Shock widened my eyes as a foreign pain twisted my stomach. He was . . . almost begging for that outcome. Like he really wanted death. Like it would offer relief. I felt the tug in my chest again—insistent. Urgent. *Save him.* This, finally, spurred me out of my horrified paralysis and into action.

"Damian," I called, starting toward him. I had to stop this. It was too horrible. No one deserved to experience this. No one deserved to believe this was real. "This is an illusion. You're not really here! We're trying to get the book from the underground chamber at the Academy. None of this is real! You have to push it away!"

Damian's eyes flew open, and he gaped up at me. The stranger whipped around to stare at me as well, dark eyes flashing with anger. He looked to be in his late forties. Tall. Strong. He'd be handsome if he didn't look so cruel. Terrifying and murderous. I swallowed down my fear, reminding myself once again that this wasn't real. And I trusted the men

487

waiting for us back in the chamber to make sure that nothing bad actually happened to my body.

"T-Terah?" Damian's voice cracked. "How are you here? You . . . you're dead." He glanced at the remains of my body to his right just to make sure.

"I'm not dead because this isn't real," I said firmly. "And neither is Caleb. We're all fine. You're in an illusion. You can only see me right now because I'm using my life force to enter your mind to help you get out. We're all waiting for you in the underground chamber. Remember the chamber? We're going through a series of tests, trying to get the book. Push the illusion away and come back with me."

The older man snarled and pushed to his feet, yanking his knife out of Damian's arm and turning to face me.

"Terah, get out of here!" Damian groaned, his eyes frantic even through his pain. He desperately tried to push off the ground as the man prowled toward me, but he collapsed back against the floor, too weak and in pain to yank his lower arms free of the daggers that tethered him.

"He's not real, Damian," I said, standing my ground as the man charged at me. I looked past him and made eye contact with Damian. "Trust me. You're in an illusion right now. All you have to do is believe it's not real, and you'll be free."

Damian stared at me in horror as the man reached me and swung his knife at me. "No!" he cried, wrestling desperately against the daggers embedded in his lower arms, like he wanted to come help me. But even if this had been real, I wouldn't have needed his help. It was only one man.

I reached forward and grabbed the man's wrist with both hands, stopping the knife's descent before it made contact with me. "Nice try," I said, raising an eyebrow at the cruel man in front of me. "But you're not real."

The man snarled at me, enraged. He practically vibrated with it. Damian's eye widened, stunned.

"Trust me," I called to him as the man pulled free from my grasp and tried to swing at me again. I ducked. "This is an illusion. I know it feels real. Too real. My illusion did too. But it's not. Believe me, Damian. Please. You're at the Academy right now. Not wherever this place is."

I lunged to the side as the man swung his knife at me again. Then I delivered two swift punches to his stomach.

Damian's face suddenly transformed. He looked . . . astounded. Almost awestruck. "I . . . I think I remember." He tried to sit up again.

"The Academy. I *am* there." His voice was firmer now. "You're right. I remember."

He glanced around at the room. He looked horrible—beaten up and haunted. But a grim stubbornness overtook his expression.

"This isn't real," he said, his deep voice strong for the first time since I'd entered his illusion. "I know this isn't real. I remember now. I'm at the Academy. This is an illusion."

The stranger snarled at both of us now. "I'll kill you both!" he roared, pulling another knife from his waistband.

I ran over to Damian's side and knelt next to him. "That's right." I reached out and pushed his hair back from his face—the only uninjured part of him. I felt the jolt in my chest again. The urgent call to save him. "You can do it. Say it again. *Believe* it."

Damian looked up at me for a moment, his expression almost impossible to read. It wavered between the cold, indifferent mask he usually wore for the world, and a deep vulnerability that I'd never seen there before.

The stranger rushed at us, and Damian flinched. His eyes slid closed, like he didn't want to see either of us die. I pressed my palm against his forehead, trying to comfort him. Steady and ground him.

"It's okay." My voice was calm. Firm. "It's not real. He's not real."

Damian swallowed hard. I could see him wrestling with himself. With his fear. Then his eyes flew open. Firm. Determined. Dark. Angry.

"He's not real." His voice was full of conviction this time. "None of this is real. It's an illusion."

I nodded, and the room seemed to tremble around us. Like it was on the verge of dematerializing.

"This isn't real!" Damian shouted as the stranger lowered his knives toward us.

The room, the figure, and all the dead finally dissolved around us, the details bleeding back into fog and darkness.

And then we were on the stone floor of the second chamber again, gasping. I opened my eyes in time to see the thin stream of deep purple flowing back from Damian's chest and into mine, returning what I'd given. And then my power faded from vision, and I felt the well inside of me lock back into place. It was the strangest thing I'd ever experienced. And I had no way of explaining it.

Damian groaned and his eyes flew open. I realized I was still leaning over him, but my hand wasn't on his chest anymore. Neither of my hands were holding me up. There was a gentle tug on my shoulders, and I realized someone must be supporting me. I'd probably started to collapse onto Damian when I'd entered his illusion, and someone had caught me, keeping me from injuring either of us. The hands pulled me, guiding me back into an upright sitting position. But my legs had gone completely numb from kneeling on the hard stone floor, and they couldn't support me now. Instead, I toppled backward and fell against something hard.

"Oof." A deep voice in my ear. Arms encircled me, steadying me against the hard surface. I felt a rise and fall. A faint heartbeat. I blinked, trying to get my bearings, shaking the remnants of fog from my brain, and looked at the faces around me. Gabriel and Matt were still kneeling on either side of Damian, helping him sit up. Gabriel was looking over at me, his eyebrows furrowed with worry. Which meant . . .

I immediately shoved into a sitting position, extricating myself from the arms that held me, and pushing away so I could support myself while my legs slowly regained feeling. I glanced over my shoulder at Caleb and saw his cheeks burning as his eyes met mine. Of course he was the one who'd held me. He'd been the only person in a position to catch me when I'd entered Damian's illusion, since the other two had been holding down his arms. I shouldn't have been surprised. But being this close to him made me uncomfortable. I didn't want to prolong it.

Caleb sat up and attempted to pull a cold, neutral expression back onto his face. But I saw his eyes sweep over me again. Too warm. I had a hard time keeping the scowl off my face.

Gabriel pushed to his feet and moved toward me, still looking worried. "How do you feel?" He sank to the ground next to me and wrapped his arm around me.

I leaned into him with a sigh, trying to push the memories of the dismembered bodies, the smell of blood and decay, and the terrifying face of that stranger from my mind. "Physically, I feel fine," I murmured, so only he could hear. "Not drained from the power use since it was returned to me. Just a little tired and sore. But . . . that illusion was fucking horrible."

I didn't elaborate. It wasn't the time. And I didn't want to reveal Damian's vulnerabilities in front of the whole group, especially without his permission. He'd been traumatized enough for one day. Gabriel nodded, searching my expression, then pulled me tighter against him.

Damian shoved to his feet and turned to look at me. His expression was a cold, closed-off mask again, but that odd look had returned. Darker this time. Almost tinged with fear. Like . . . he was afraid I'd seen too much.

"How did you do that?"

I grimaced and pushed to my feet, my legs feeling mostly normal again. Just tingly. Gabriel stood and offered me a steadying arm.

"I'm not really sure." I stretched my aching muscles. My injured arm was throbbing steadily, and I saw that I'd completely bled through the gauze. "My life force was what allowed me access. It . . . connected us, I guess. But I don't know why or how. It wasn't intentional."

Damian frowned, and the odd look in his eyes intensified. I wondered if he was also thinking back to the vision we'd shared in training that day. To the way it'd similarly, inexplicably pulled our minds together.

"I'm glad it happened though," I added quietly. "It didn't look like you were going to push out of your illusion on your own."

Damian's eyes hardened as he continued to watch me. "You don't know that."

I raised an eyebrow at him as I crossed my arms over my chest. "Yeah, because you were doing *so well* on your own when I got there."

Anger flashed in his eyes, but so did that hint of vulnerability.

Matt stepped up behind him and grabbed his shoulder before he could respond. "Enough. It doesn't matter anymore. It's done. Besides, you were beginning to injure yourself outside of your illusion. Something had to be done. Don't bite our heads off for it."

Damian glared at Matt briefly. Then he pressed his eyes closed and sucked in a deep breath. "Fine." He opened his eyes again, his expression now as cold as his voice. "At least we get to move on now." He nodded at the swirling powers that were now streaming toward the door at the other end of the room.

Caleb finally shoved to his feet, and all of us turned toward the heavy door, watching as the powers covered it and the door began to creak open. "I can't believe we have to face two more things." He sounded tired. Unnerved. How we all felt.

We watched the door open wider and wider, revealing yet another pitch-black chasm.

"We've survived so far," Matt said, exuding calm authority. "We just have to keep pushing forward and working together."

Caleb sighed. I could see his spear injury had also bled through the gauze. He was probably in a decent amount of pain. I glanced at the gauze covering Gabriel's chest. There was dried blood showing through in some places, but the bleeding seemed to have stopped. That was good, at least. It meant the cut hadn't been too serious.

I took Gabriel's hand again, and his fingers tightened around mine. I just wanted this to be over. I didn't think we'd all make it if the remaining two tests were as horrible as the first two. I released a slow breath, trying to steel myself for whatever was coming next. No matter what it was, I had to have faith that we could face it. That we'd succeed. If we gave into doubt now, I knew we wouldn't survive.

23
REVELATIONS

We walked through the door to the next chamber and waited just beyond the opening. It was a familiar pattern now, but no less anxiety-inducing. I tried to remember what the third symbol looked like as we waited, the door creaking slowly closed behind us. It'd been some kind of human-like figure, holding a bow in one hand and an arrow in the other. But I hadn't recognized the style or significance of the iconography. Would we have to fight again? My stomach sank at the thought. The combat we'd already engaged in on top of my injury and the draining of my power was catching up with me. I was beginning to feel like I'd been trampled by a Demon.

The door finally slammed shut behind us, plunging us once again into darkness. And then our powers ran through the symbols carved into the stone floor. I could vaguely see the walls around us as the powers traveled forward. This room was a much different shape than the others had been. It was long and thin, and seemed to narrow more the further the room went. I squinted as the powers traveled to the far end of the room and filled what looked like a stone platform that jutted up several feet from the ground at the room's narrowest point. The top of the platform was carved, but not with the original symbol. It looked like an etching of a flower, with wide petals that laid flat at its outermost edges, moving more upright as they traveled inward.

We cautiously moved forward as our powers pulsed in the platform. It was small and circular, and touched the walls on each side of it—only wide enough for one person to stand on at a time. And there was no way to bypass it. We'd each have to interact with the platform to reach the door in the distance on the other side. I noticed, as we got close, that our powers also pulsed in a large, circular stone a few feet in front of the platform. The stone had a large carving of the god on it and, like the platform, was just large enough to hold one person.

As we approached the platform, our powers began to pulse within it more quickly. Suddenly, fire burst from the top of the platform, covering its entire surface in tall flames that reached the ceiling. I stepped back, my eyes widening, as the flames blasted us with heat. So much for an easier way forward.

"Any idea what we're supposed to do this time?" I glanced at Gabriel.

His eyebrows furrowed as he knelt to look at one of the smaller carvings of the god on the floor. He traced his finger over it lightly, but his gaze was far away.

"I think . . . I remember a story," he murmured, almost to himself, "about Rama and a test of truth with fire. Maybe it has to do with that."

"The test of his wife's truth and virtue," Damian said, his voice a hard monotone. He was clearly still irritable from our previous test. "I've read about it too. The lotus on the pedestal gives it away."

Gabriel looked at him and nodded slowly. "That's right. She faced a test to prove she was truthful when she claimed to still be virtuous after her kidnapping. She survived the fire, proving her honesty." He pushed to his feet, and we all turned to stare at the flames.

"So, do we just . . . walk through the fire?" I eyed the flames dubiously. They seemed *extremely* real. "What are we supposed to be proving?"

"Maybe just our general virtue as people?" Matt suggested, though he sounded uncertain. Nervous. "Prove we're not evil or trying to use the book for evil?"

"But we're soldiers," I said quietly, my stomach clenching. "Do we even still have virtue like that? We kill people. All the time."

The group turned to look at me, varying expressions of guilt and worry on their faces.

"But we haven't really had a choice," Matt finally said. "We only do what's required to protect people. Would it be virtuous to let all those Normals die? Sometimes you have to make a choice between bad choices. The lesser of two evils. That doesn't inherently make us evil."

I shrugged. I wanted to believe him, but I honestly wasn't sure. It didn't necessarily make us virtuous, either.

"I think the test would be more specific than whether or not we're generally virtuous," Gabriel finally said after a long silence. "When Sita, his wife, stepped into the fire, it wasn't just a general test of whether she was a good person. It was a test of her honesty, loyalty, and virtue in relation to Rama. It was specifically about whether she'd told the truth when she asserted she'd been loyal to him during her kidnapping. She answered, and the honesty of her answer was tested with the flames. It was her honesty that ultimately saved her from the fire."

He walked over to the wall of fire, carefully avoiding the one pulsing stone in front of it, and reached his hand toward it, feeling the heat with his fingers.

"The fire is as thick as the platform itself," he said. "We won't be able to just plow through it. That plus this larger stone that's illuminated in front of it makes me think each of us will need to stand on it and probably face some kind of question, and the answer to that question will probably be tested with the fire, like it was for Sita."

"How are we supposed to know what to answer?" Caleb's eyebrows pulled together as he stared at the pulsing stone.

Gabriel shrugged. "One of us will have to stand on the stone and try it. That's all I can guess from what I see. Unless Damian has anything to add."

Damian shook his head, his expression as closed off and stony as the platform in front of us. Caleb sighed, frustrated.

"Okay," Matt said quickly, before they could argue, "if that's the best idea we've got, we need to try it. I'll go first."

We watched as he walked forward until he was standing near the fire —as close as he could get without the heat becoming unbearable. Then he stepped onto the glowing stone in front of it. The powers in it pulsed, then thin tendrils of the glowing mixture twined around Matt's legs and climbed up his body like vines. They were too thin to be a restraint. Instead, they headed to his chest and settled near his heart—where his power lived, and his life force was stored. The power sat there like a glowing window into his soul and stayed like that for a long moment. Then, an image formed in the thick wall of fire in front of him. The image had no sound, but it moved like a projected movie, obscured only slightly by the flickering flames beneath it.

As the image solidified, I saw Matt, a small child of no more than four,

495

sitting next to his mother in one of the training house kitchens in Dagmar. And Serafina was there, holding an infant in her arms. I swallowed hard, knowing it was me. Serafina thrust the bundle at Matt's mother, Abigail, speaking quickly. Abigail reached out and took me carefully into her arms, then brought me close to her chest, cradling me. A smile broke across her face as she looked at my round cheeks and tiny fingers. One small hand lifted into the air, reaching. Abigail held out one of her fingers, her eyes twinkling, and my hand wrapped tightly around it.

Abigail turned toward Matt and introduced us. Her lips moved as she explained that she'd be taking care of me from now on. That I'd be staying with them. Matt nodded, looking solemn and a little uncertain, but he also looked curious. Abigail beckoned him closer, then shifted me into Matt's lap. Matt looked so nervous, like he was afraid he'd do something wrong— even at age four, he was taking the responsibility given to him quite seriously. But when he saw my hand reaching up to him as it had to his mother, he extended his finger as Abigail had. And when my tiny hand closed around it, Matt's face broke into a surprised smile, the nervousness melting away. Serafina watched all of this dispassionately, then said a few more words. Abigail nodded, and then Serafina turned and left the room.

The image faded and another appeared. Matt and I were waiting in one of the reinforced interior rooms of the training house that sheltered all the children too young to fight during Demon attacks. Matt, now six, held two-year-old me tightly in his lap as we listened to the loud booms of power that shook the house, sending dust cascading down on us from the ceiling. I remembered having to sit in that room and wait while Matt had been off fighting a few years later. How the sounds of battle had still permeated those reinforced walls. How we'd always been able to hear the screams, the sounds of claws on metal and weapons on flesh. How scared we'd all been, even as we'd tried to hide it. We always had to wait in that room until one of the soldiers returned to give us the all-clear. We'd always been afraid that no one would return.

Matt slid the sword resting on the ground next to him closer to his side. As the oldest, it was his job to protect the rest of us in the room if the soldiers didn't make it back, or if a Demon broke away and attacked the house. His expression, even then, was serious and composed. He knew what was expected of him. But I fidgeted in his lap and started crying, over-whelmed by the sounds of battle. Too little to be able to contain my fear. Only then did Matt's expression break from the serious, responsible mask he was wearing. Flashes of fear, sadness, and understanding crossed his face as he looked down at me. Then he turned me in his arms, gathering me closer to him, and pressed kisses against my wet cheek as he bounced me soothingly in his arms, whispering comforting things in my ear. I grabbed his shirt and buried my wet face and runny nose against his shoulder.

The door burst open a few seconds later, and a soldier stood there. An adult. Injured, but not badly. Matt immediately stood, bringing me with him, his mask of responsibility back on. The soldier moved forward and knelt in front of Matt. I bit the inside of my cheek as I watched, knowing, even though I couldn't remember this, what was about to happen. The soldiers reached forward and placed her hands on Matt's shoulders, her expression solemn as she spoke. I knew she was telling him that his mother had just died in battle.

Pain gripped my stomach as Matt's face crumpled with sadness, and sobs of despair shook his body. The soldier in front of him wore a mild expression of sympathy, but she'd clearly locked down her own emotions a long time ago. Then she reached forward and tried to take me from Matt's arms, likely to dump my care onto someone else. Someone older. But Matt jerked away, holding me even tighter to him, his expression growing dark and fierce. He spoke to the soldier, firm, even as tears continued rolling down his cheeks. Then he bent, retrieved his sword, and carried me resolutely from the room.

The image faded and another appeared. It was maybe a year later, and Matt sat with me on my bed, a stack of old books in front of us, the covers faded, and the bindings frayed. These were the only young children's books in all the training houses in Dagmar. I remembered Matt had gone around, rounding them up so I'd have enough books to practice reading with. They'd taught us to read in school, but only the bare minimum, and mostly on chalkboards. But Matt had taken his role as my caretaker seriously. He'd wanted me to have more than the bare minimum, just as his mother had done for him.

Matt sat next to me, both of us leaning against the pillows, and he touched the page below each word as my mouth moved, sounding out the letters. We looked peaceful and enthusiastic—a rare quiet moment in our war-torn town. We worked diligently through the last couple pages of the book, reading the words and identifying things in the pictures. When we finally reached the end, Matt set the book back on the pile and grinned at me. Then he ruffled my hair and gave me a high-five. He was proud of me.

I'd thrown myself into his arms, giggling and happy, burying my face in his shirt.

The image faded and another appeared. This time Matt looked to be around fourteen, and I was around ten. We were in the training room together, both clutching practice weapons as we circled each other. Matt and I had often trained together after hours to ensure I'd be placed in the higher training group with him and his age group rather than my own. He'd never trusted I was being trained well enough when he couldn't see it happening and couldn't participate in it. And ensuring I received more than the minimum in training was important to him.

Matt spoke to me as we circled each other, likely talking me through the next round of moves and what he wanted to see from me. I nodded, and then we launched ourselves at each other, battling with a sword and dagger each. Matt pushed me as we fought, forcing me to move quickly and think strategically, especially since he was so much larger than me. He also pushed my strength, forcing my arms to hold and fend off attacks where he utilized his weight against me. Trying to ensure I got strong and could defend myself no matter the strength and size of my opponent.

I fought well against him, especially given our disparity in age and size, and I watched as we went back and forth on who was pushing back whom. Matt smiled occasionally as we fought. He was proud of my progress. Eventually, though, he managed to disarm me and fling me over his shoulder and onto the mat before pinning me down. I twisted underneath him, trying to break free, but I couldn't dislodge him. He had me.

Matt grinned down at me, his face close to mine as he spoke again. I remembered he'd been telling me how well I was doing. That I'd almost beaten him. My stomach clenched as I watched the image of me blush as I gazed into his eyes, clearly mesmerized by his closeness. But Matt hadn't noticed. He just pushed off me and reached down to help me up, still talking about the fight and what I should work on next time. I'd just swallowed and nodded, trying to push down my feelings and smooth my expression into a neutral mask.

The image faded and another appeared. Matt and I were standing outside the training house we'd lived in, with several packed bags at his feet. He was eighteen now, and this was the day that he'd left me in Dagmar so he could attend the Academy. Matt leaned down and took a firm hold of my shoulders. I'd been shorter and smaller then. I hadn't fully grown and settled into myself for another two years. Matt was clearly saying words of comfort as he squeezed my shoulders in his hands, trying to calm and reassure me. He was promising he'd write. That he'd visit as often as possible. That this wasn't really goodbye. But I'd clung to him anyway, burying my face in his chest while tears streamed down my cheeks. I'd clung to him like the world was ending, because for me in that moment, it was. I'd been heartbroken.

After a few moments, Matt pulled away from me and took several steps back, severing our connection, and forcing me to release him. Matt swung his bags over his shoulders, then looked back and gave me a small, tremulous smile. But he turned away quickly, clearly unable to look at the pain so clearly etched across my face. Or my endless stream of tears. He walked firmly away from me toward the edge of town. Not looking back.

The image faded and another appeared. Matt at the Academy, sitting around a table in the dining hall with a large group of friends, laughing, and more carefree than I'd ever seen him in Dagmar. They were a rambunctious group—laughing, joking around, drawing more and more people to crowd around the seats. People looked over at his table admirably, and many young women around the room eyed him with interest. Matt and his friend group seemed to be the center of attention, and he clearly knew it and liked it. A lot.

His friend Simon pushed through the crowd to take the saved seat to Matt's right. He was carrying a stack of letters and started tossing them at the recipients in their group, smiling. He'd clearly taken it upon himself to grab everyone's mail. Then he turned to Matt and handed him a letter, his smile fading slightly as he searched Matt's face. I wondered what he was looking for. Matt wasn't paying attention to him, though. His gaze was focused on the letter. I knew it was from me. Matt swallowed and took it from Simon, a brooding, guilty expression filling his face. He looked . . . almost resentful. Like he hated the reminder of me. My jaw tightened, and pain stung the inner cavity of my chest. It was like . . . he'd felt my existence was a burden on him. That I was ruining this new carefree life he was trying to lead. I knew he'd felt the pressure of so much responsibility put on him so young, but I'd never thought his resentment was toward me. I'd never felt like I was a burden on him, because I'd always thought we were in it together. We'd both been left alone. We loved and took care of each other. It was us against the world. But apparently, he'd never showed me how he really felt—that I was another burden on his shoulders. The sting of hurt grew, but now it was tinged with anger.

Matt turned and stuffed the letter quickly in his bag, shoving it between his books. Not bothering to read it. He turned back toward his group of friends and pulled his grin back on. He said something, and everyone laughed, enamored with his presence. My hands clenched into fists at my sides.

The image faded and another took its place. Matt was sitting in his dorm room reading a letter, at least a year later. His jaw looked a little more angular now, his expression a little more reserved. Even without looking too closely at the letter, I knew it was from me. I squinted to see it better and spotted smeared ink where I'd cried as I wrote. It was the letter I'd written after Caleb had left me. Matt dropped it on his desk and ran a hand down his face. He looked upset. Unsure. Deeply guilty. He swore. Then he grabbed the letter and crumpled it tightly in his fist, his fingers turning white from the force of his grasp. Without warning, he turned and threw it forcefully at the wall. Then he walked slowly to the edge of his bed and sank onto it, curling over so his elbows rested on his knees, his head hanging low. He looked defeated. Unhappy.

He stayed there like that for a while, like he wasn't sure what to do. But before he could decide, his head jerked up and turned toward the door. He must've heard a knock. He pushed to his feet and walked over to it before pulling it open. A very pretty young woman stood on the other side. She smiled coyly at Matt and said something, her head tilting slightly to the side. Matt glanced back at my letter, now crumpled on the floor, for a split second, before turning back to her and pulling on a charming smile as he responded. The young woman beamed and threw her arms around his neck, pressing close. Matt wrapped his arm around her waist and pulled her into his room before shoving his door closed. A split second later, they were frantically kissing. I scrunched my nose as I watched.

The image thankfully faded quickly, and another formed. Matt was walking down the street with his friend in the town he'd taken me to, clouds of steam puffing from their mouths as they spoke. It was snowing, and holiday lights were strung from every streetlight and storefront. It must've been over one of his winter breaks—the breaks he'd been too busy to visit me during.

They pushed open the door to a coffee shop, moving quickly inside to escape the cold, and were immediately confronted with a large display of flashy merchandise, mugs, ornaments, and cards. A large, glittering sign sat atop the mountain of merchandise and said, "This holiday season, show your family how much you care! See our gifts for every price range." As far as signs went, it seemed fairly standard. But Matt stared at it for too long, his face pinched with remorse. I wondered if he felt guilty about not being able to visit me in Dagmar. I frowned. As painful as it'd been for both of us, he'd had important work for the Academy that'd kept him away. It'd largely been out of our hands. And as sad and lonely as it'd made me, I'd known he'd never abandon me in a warzone for no reason. His absence wasn't his fault. So I'd pushed through and survived it, knowing it wouldn't be permanent. Knowing I'd see him again someday. If I survived.

His friend walked back over to him and spoke, gesturing at the pile of merchandise. Probably asking if Matt wanted to buy something. Matt jerked back into himself and looked quickly away from the sign. Then he pulled on a carefree smile and shook his head. Instead, he and his friend headed toward the order line.

The image faded as a new one formed. It was of Matt, looking close to the age he was now, setting another letter on top of a thick pile of them in a box in his room. It looked like he'd kept most, if not all, of the letters I'd sent him. He stared at the box and its contents for a long time, a now-familiar expression of guilt and regret filling his face. It'd been years since he'd seen me. Years since he'd left Dagmar—a reality conveyed succinctly by the inches-tall stack of letters in front of him. It was clear that his decision to leave had weighed on him the whole time.

A couple of Matt's friends walked into his room through his open door, laughing and joking around. Matt quickly covered the box and shoved it under some books on his desk, smoothing out his expression, hiding his guilt from them. Then he stood and pulled a grin onto his face as he turned to address them. As he did so, he surreptitiously pushed the box to the back of his desk, so it wasn't noticeable. Then he calmly walked away from it and left his room with the group.

The images in the flames disappeared, and the fire returned to normal again. I wondered what, specifically, Matt was supposed to answer for. What truth the room wanted him to speak. Was it clearer to Matt than it was to us?

Matt turned slowly, his gaze almost hesitant as it met mine, guilt and regret swimming thick in the depths. "It wants me to explain why I never returned to Dagmar," Matt said quietly. "Even though we were so important to each other. Even though I promised you I would."

He swallowed, tense. Nervous.

"I . . . I lied to you." His voice was barely audible. His fists clenched at his sides as he looked at the ground. I frowned, assessing his expression, trying to determine what he meant. "I lied when I said . . . when I told you I was too busy to return to Dagmar over breaks. I . . . wasn't too busy. I didn't work for the Academy yet. I stayed with my friends instead. I just . . . didn't want to return. I *couldn't* return."

The breath whooshed out of me as shock rushed in, icy and paralyzing. Along with a deep, burning pain. He'd . . . lied to me? He could've returned to Dagmar, but he'd chosen not to. He'd *chosen not to.* He'd intentionally left me in a hellish warzone, with no promise that I'd survive, when he could've returned for me. I was a child, someone he'd professed to love, his family, and he'd left me to die alone, because he just hadn't wanted to return. My fingers shook, and I clenched them into fists at my sides.

"I was selfish and afraid," he finally said, looking deeply uncomfortable.

He took a deep breath and looked up again, meeting my eyes. But he couldn't hold them for long. Instead, he turned to look at the others.

"Dagmar made me miserable. I never traveled, never left, never experienced anything other than death, destruction, and decay. More and more responsibility was always thrown onto my shoulders regardless of how little I had left in me to manage it all. I felt like I was trapped in hell—drowning and burning. That's why the Academy held such a draw for me. My parents had both broken tradition and attended before returning to Dagmar. It was a connection to them, and it was also a different, unknown way of life.

"I was so burned out from the constant death and constant fighting. I needed something different. A break from the front. So I decided to leave even though it'd mean leaving Terah behind. Even though I knew I was all she had." His voice faintly wavered. "But there was no way to bring her, and I couldn't pass up my chance to escape and experience a different way of life.

"People at the Academy were so different. They actually sought me out. They wanted my opinion for a change, and to hear my stories. They wanted me for me, not just as a soldier. I made friends for the first time in my life. A lot of them. Friends who were actually my age. And it was . . . surprisingly nice."

My fingernails dug into my palms as he spoke. Friends for the first time. Friends his own age. Of course he'd wanted that. He wasn't wrong to want that. But the truth stung. I'd always considered him to be my friend, regardless of age. My best and only friend. But it'd been different for him. He'd just seen me as the kid he needed to take care of. A kid he cared about, sure, but still just a kid. A responsibility. Not a friend. Not a real one.

"The more friends I made, and the longer I was away from the war zone, the harder it was to envision returning. I'd never lived like this before —free of constant fear, sadness, death, and injury. And once I had, I couldn't imagine giving it up. Not even for—" He stopped, his expression filling with guilt again.

Me. Not even for me. He didn't have to finish his sentence for the impact to land. I'd heard those words too many times in my life from too many people. And the sting went deeper this time, my heart turning colder toward Matt, hardening like ice in my chest. I refused to outwardly react, but the wound was there, deep and open. Gabriel's fingers touched my lower back, their warmth offering grounding. Comfort. I took in a slow breath and released it. I could see, in my periphery, that Gabriel's whole body was tense. I glanced at him—he was glaring at Matt, his expression as hard as stone.

"I was afraid to go back to Dagmar. Even to make sure you were okay. I knew that, if I actually saw you again, I wouldn't be able to leave you there like I had before. The first time was the hardest thing I'd ever done, and I knew I couldn't do it again. Besides, I knew your mother would never let you leave until you were eighteen. To stay with you, I would've had to drop out of the Academy. And . . . I didn't want that.

"I knew you wouldn't understand, so I told you I couldn't return because I was too busy doing work for the Academy. And I wrote to you a lot. I told myself it was a decent compromise—being in so much contact with you even though I didn't visit. I . . . know it wasn't, though," he admitted quietly, breaking eye contact with me. "It was just a lie I told myself to feel better about my decision. But I always felt guilty about it. And I know it hurt you. I'm . . . sorry Terah. I shouldn't have lied to you."

He shouldn't have lied to me? That apology was woefully insufficient. He shouldn't have left me behind as a child on the front lines so he could feel a bit freer. He shouldn't have abandoned someone he claimed to care about to death and destruction so he could run away and have fun. I clenched my jaw tightly, anger burning through me, as the fire behind Matt flared brighter for a second in tandem with the powers that'd settled over his chest. Then the powers streamed back down his body and into the stone at his feet, and the fire behind him returned to its regular flicker. I wondered if that was the signal that he'd adequately and truthfully answered the question that was asked of him. Or if it just sensed that he was done and was now allowing him to test the truthfulness of his response in the flames.

I didn't say anything as Matt looked at me. I didn't even alter my expression. I didn't think I could right now. I needed to keep everything on lockdown. Because I knew we all needed to work together to keep going. To survive this series of tests and get out of here with the book. Unleashing any of the emotions I was currently feeling wouldn't make that easy or perhaps even possible. So I just pressed my teeth into the side of my tongue and shoved everything down. I hadn't had to do this to myself—repress my emotions like this—for months. Not to this extent. I resented having to do it now. I resented Matt for forcing me back into this place of emotional survival.

Matt swallowed, his shoulders falling as he watched me. He knew me well enough to see, even through my practiced neutrality, that I was upset. But instead of trying to comfort me, he turned on his heel and stepped onto the platform into the flames. My stomach tightened again, tense and conflicted, as Matt disappeared into the fire. Even after all that he'd done to hurt me, I didn't want him to be hurt. I never wanted what I'd seen in my illusion to come true.

"I made it through to the other side," Matt said a moment later, his voice subdued. "I'm fine. It didn't hurt or anything. Just felt like warm air."

I turned to look at the rest of the group. "Who wants to go next?"

Caleb and Damian stared at me, like they were trying to figure out how I was feeling. What my reaction was to the obviously highly personal and painful things we'd just seen and heard. But my defensive walls were already up, and my expression was carefully neutral. I wouldn't let them see how I was feeling. I refused to let Matt's past actions hurt me any further right now. Not in the middle of this mission. Only Gabriel knew me and my history well enough to know how I was really feeling, and he was the only one I trusted enough to know.

"I'll go next," Damian finally said, his expression going curiously blank as he stepped forward. "Might as well get it over with."

I nodded and stepped back to stand next to Gabriel. We turned as a group to face the fire again as Damian stepped onto the glowing stone. Only then did I reach out to find the side of Gabriel's hand with my fingertips, seeking comfort. His hand quickly enveloped mine and held on tightly, steady and warm.

The powers pulsed then climbed Damian's limbs as they'd done with Matt, until they reached his chest. Then they formed a circular, glowing pool over his heart. But where Matt had looked nervous, Damian just looked bored and cold. I knew by now, though, that this was his own version of emotional lockdown. Of practiced control. A mask to hide whatever he was really thinking and feeling. The powers sat there on his chest for a long moment before an image appeared in the flames in front of us once again.

I had a hard time not stepping backward as the handsome-yet-cruel man from Damian's illusion appeared suddenly before us. And from the way Damian's hands clenched for a split second, he was having the same difficulty. But with beyond military self-control, Damian managed to unclench his hands and relax his shoulders until he looked unbothered again. Strong and unphased.

We watched as the man in the flames silently screamed at what looked like a very young Damian. He couldn't have been more than seven. The man shoved a large sword into his hand and pushed him back toward the center of the room where another young boy stood, similarly armed. The man pointed at the other young boy, screaming directions at Damian. And Damian looked . . . terrified. But he struggled to pull a tough mask onto his small face. Then he hoisted the sword with his little arms and charged the other young boy in what was clearly a fight to the death. These were no practice weapons.

I watched, partially in awe and partially in horror. Even at that young age, Damian had been an amazing fighter. And he overcame the other boy in only a couple minutes, pinning him to the ground with the point of his sword against the boy's throat. But he hesitated. Froze. His throat undulated as he swallowed hard. The cruel man launched himself at Damian, screaming again. But Damian's eyes hardened, his expression turning stubborn, and he withdrew his sword from the other boy's skin, shaking his head, his mouth pressed into a firm line. The man lunged forward, grabbing the sword still wrapped in Damian's hands, and forced him to plunge it tip-first into the other boy's throat.

I inhaled sharply, taking a startled step back. Gabriel's mouth fell open, and even Caleb let out a quiet curse. We all watched in horror as the man then yanked the sword from Damian's grip and slashed it viciously across Damian's chest, slicing deep into his skin. Damian tried valiantly not to react, but I saw the tears welling in his eyes as blood spilled rapidly down his front. Then the man laughed and turned, walking from the room, leaving Damian heavily bleeding and with the lifeless body of the other boy.

Damian only let the tears free once the man was gone, and he sank to the ground, clutching his own bleeding front. But he pulled himself together enough to crawl over to the boy and reached out a shaking hand to touch his throat. He scrunched his eyes closed in intense concentration, like he was trying to heal him, but nothing happened. He kept trying, though. Again and again, even as the puddle of blood from his own injury grew and mixed with the other boy's blood, spreading across the floor. But he wasn't able to do it. Damian finally gave up, crying harder now. He crawled to the corner of the room, pressing himself into the wall and burying his head against his knees, blood dripping freely from his wound to the ground. I gripped Gabriel's hand tighter as I watched, horror and remorse mixing in my gut.

The image vanished and another appeared. This time Damian looked to be about twelve. He was taller, stronger, colder. He stood in a circle of other children his age and older, all dressed in training clothes, and all brandishing weapons. In the center of the circle with him stood another boy who was a little taller and older than Damian. They circled each other calmly, almost stoically, before lashing out at each other with their daggers, lightning fast. They seemed pretty evenly matched, and very, *very* skilled, especially for their age. As the fight continued, the children around them began chanting and screaming wildly for whoever they wanted to win. Once again, there were no practice weapons in sight. These fights were meant to be deadly. I frowned. This wasn't what training usually looked like, even in border towns.

The older boy stabbed Damian viciously in the shoulder, but Damian barely reacted. Instead, he quickly disarmed the other boy before spinning and driving his daggers into the other boy's stomach. The boy gasped, his eyes widening, as blood bloomed from the impact point, spreading across his shirt. Damian had stabbed him deep. But . . . I knew Damian had stabbed him in one of the least lethal places possible. And the cold, unsurprised look on Damian's young face told me that he knew that too. It'd been intentional. He wasn't trying to kill the other boy, but he'd still established he'd won the fight.

Damian sheathed his weapons, then turned and strode from the room, his expression still neutral and cold. But the trainer followed him, pointing back to the center of the room. To his opponent who was injured but still alive. Damian just kept walking, his pace steady, almost leisurely, as he ignored the trainer. Until they ran into that cruel man again. Damian tried to keep his composure as he faced him, but his hands automatically clenched. The man spoke to the trainer, and the trainer gestured back toward the training room as he spoke. The cruel man looked livid. He dismissed the trainer with a wave of his hand, then turned on Damian and grabbed him by the throat, yelling unintelligibly. He slammed him hard against the stone wall. I could almost hear the crack of Damian's head against the rock. Then the man grabbed one of Damian's daggers from its sheath and ran him through with it, a cruel smile turning up his lips.

Gabriel glanced at me, horrified and almost disbelieving. But I believed it. After what I'd seen in Damian's illusion, it was hard not to. It was hard not to guess what his life must've been like. The only thing that surprised me was that this man had managed to get away with this kind of conduct for so long, even in a distant border town. Gabriel's eyebrows lifted as he studied my expression—my lack of surprise. And I saw the moment he realized what I must've seen in Damian's illusion. He swallowed and pulled me into his side, wrapping his arm around my waist. I almost wished we could give Damian the same comfort somehow—that he'd somehow let us. Because reliving all of this must be hell, especially in front of other people. But I knew he never would. I didn't know if he'd ever let anyone that close to him, and after seeing this, I wasn't sure I could blame him.

The image vanished and another appeared. Damian was solidly a teenager now. Maybe fifteen or sixteen. His eyes were the coldest and hollowest we'd seen yet. He moved with precision and fluidity as he fought a fully-grown man who looked to be in his late twenties. No emotion bled onto Damian's face. No signs of effort or fatigue. He moved and struck with graceful ease. Deadly. Exact. Easily keeping up with the man he fought, who was clearly an expert.

This time, they were fighting in a larger room than the previous two, filled with even more onlookers, many seeming to be trainees of all ages. I grimaced as I looked at the youngest trainees in the room—they couldn't be more than six—their faces already hardening into masks of cool aloofness. I'd thought Dagmar was bad, but wherever this town was, it was clearly completely out of control. A literal hell on earth. No wonder Damian had been so surprised when I'd saved his life earlier in the semester.

My focus shifted briefly from the young men fighting to the onlookers. Curiously, everyone seemed to be glaring at Damian, whispering to each other and shooting him disdainful looks. Like this was his fault somehow, or his idea. But based on what we'd seen of Damian's reluctance to kill his opponents, my guess was that the cruel man, not Damian, was the mastermind behind these horrible fights, and the kill or be killed mentality that seemed prevalent in the training here. From the little I'd seen, it didn't look like Damian had much control over his life in general.

The young man and Damian continued to spin around each other, engaged in fierce battle, their swords clashing hard enough to send sparks flying through the air. But I could see the other man was beginning to tire. To slow just a little. And from the sharpness of Damian's eyes, it was clear that he'd seen it too. But he was patient. He pushed the man even more, forcing him into elaborate passages of movement. Forcing him to use up his strength quickly. And Damian's patience paid off. He finally caused the man to stumble. It was an almost indistinguishable falter, but enough to give Damian a small opening. He swung his sword around the man's and sent it flying, then kicked him hard in the chest, causing him to stagger backward and trip. The man landed hard on the ground and Damian leapt on top of him, raising his sword to end the man's life.

But a small child ran forward at that moment, clearly screaming, tears streaming down her face. She was in a training uniform, but she couldn't have been more than five or six years old. Pain flashed across Damian's face as he glanced at her. It was his first real expression during any of this. And he hesitated, his sword hovering above the man in the air. The girl ran toward the man, but a trainer stepped forward and grabbed her roughly, pulling her back. It was clear that this man meant something to her. I glanced at him again, assessing his features. The color of his hair. All similar to hers. He . . . could've been her father.

Damian stared at the little girl, conflict brewing on his face, for a breathless moment. And then he lowered his sword and released the man. He pushed to his feet and said something to the rest of the room, his expression firm. Cold. Almost haughty. It looked like he was trying to end the fight without killing his opponent. But the cruel man from before stepped forward, emerging from the shadows almost like he was made of them. Damian paled but kept his expression of firm resolve. It was clear, though, that he hadn't known the man was present.

The cruel man strode toward him and grabbed the little girl by her hair, dragging her forward. A look of panic flashed across Damian's face, and he took a step toward them, almost as though he wanted to stop the man. But the man quickly pulled a knife and pressed it against the girl's throat. And he said something that caused her to start crying even harder, and for a look of deep helplessness to cross Damian's face. Damian looked at the girl, seemingly hesitating. Undecided. And a thin stream of blood trickled down her throat from where the cruel man held the knife to her.

Damian's resolve firmed. Without another glance he turned around and plunged his sword through the neck of the man still lying on the floor, killing him almost instantly. The little girl screamed, but Damian ignored her. His face was hard with anger as he turned back around and faced the cruel man. Then Damian yelled at him, gesturing at the little girl. And suddenly I knew that the man had threatened to kill her if Damian didn't finish the man he'd been fighting. So he had. To save her. And now he wanted to cruel man to release her. My stomach tightened, dread spiraling through me.

The cruel man just smiled. And before Damian could do anything else, the man sliced the little girl's throat and let her body fall to the ground. Damian lurched forward, his arm outstretched in horror as the little girl crumpled. And I saw tears fill his eyes. And then pure rage. With a yell, he started toward the man, brandishing his sword, clearly intent on killing him. But the man made a gesture, and all the trainers in the room moved swiftly forward to restrain Damian. It took a lot of them to keep him in his place, but they just barely managed to. The cruel man smiled evilly as he watched.

Then he spoke, gesturing at the dead man and girl on the floor. Based on what I'd seen in the illusion, he was probably blaming Damian for everything. Defeat filled Damian's expression, along with torment and despair. The more the man said, the less Damian fought the trainers who held him, and the emptier and colder his expression got. His eyes became so hollow that almost nothing human remained. It was frightening to see. The guards loosened their grip on him as he went limp. But Damian wasn't done yet. A moment later, he wrenched his arms free, then plunged his sword through his own stomach, all the way to the hilt.

I gasped as we watched Damian yank the sword from his body and fall to his knees, blood pouring quickly from the wound. But he looked up at the man, almost in triumph. The man looked furious. But as Damian sank to the ground in a pool of his own blood, the man shouted at the people around him. Shouted and pointed at Damian. And they all rushed forward, even as Damian was losing consciousness, and placed their hands on him. I knew, with a twisting of my stomach, that the man had ordered them to heal Damian. He truly couldn't escape the man. Not even through death.

Tears stung my eyes as the image faded until nothing remained but the dancing flames. No wonder Damian had been willing to leave that place to come to the Academy in a different country in the middle of the year. I bet he'd be willing to do almost anything to escape that man. He'd made Damian's life truly horrific.

Damian turned slowly on the spot to face us again, his shoulders tense, but his expression carefully blank. And cold. Gods, it must've been horrible to experience all of that again and to have us see it too. No one should have their deepest secrets revealed without their permission. Especially ones like this. I bit the inside of my cheek and pushed down the sorrow. Gabriel's fingers tightened around mine as he tried to get his own reaction under control. I glanced at Caleb and saw him wrestling with his emotions as well. He was clearly horrified and upset on Damian's behalf. We all were.

"It wants me to explain who that man is to me," Damian said, his voice emotionless, "and the situation I grew up in that led me here." His tone was matter of fact. Detached.

"I grew up in a place where one's fighting skill and one's capacity for violence were prized above everything else. We fought with real weapons and real stakes from the beginning, no matter how young you were. It was supposed to motivate us to improve quickly. Improve or die. That man was the leader there, and no one questioned his methods, no matter how horrible they were.

"That man . . . is my father." Damian looked past us to stare blankly at the dark space behind us. As though he wanted to pretend we weren't there. His eyes darkened, but I couldn't tell what emotion was dominant.

My stomach clenched. *His father.* I'd thought my mother was bad, but his father was on a different level.

"He forced me to participate in these yearly matches where the top two fighters at each training level fought to the death to establish the new highest-ranking fighter at that level. And . . . I was always expected to win. My father wanted me to be the best, so I could be his weapon." Damian glanced at me for a brief second before looking away. This was something he knew we had in common. "The fighter who won would get the best training, the best opportunities, and the best assignments, so people were motivated to work hard and win. Everyone participated, no matter their age or rank. We were forced to fight to the death, whether or not we wanted to. But most people there were so indoctrinated in my father's ways and methods that they relished the fight, the hierarchy, the violence. They *wanted* to participate. I tried to save as many people as I could. To skirt his rules if I could. But it never worked." His voice grew quieter now. Darker. And I glimpsed that empty, haunted look in his eyes again.

"He always found a way to make it worse—to turn what I'd tried to do against me. Eventually, I just tried to take myself out of the equation. He couldn't force me to keep hurting people if I wasn't . . . around for him to control. But he fixed that, too. He just had me healed, over and over again. I was trapped under his control with no hope of freedom. Following his orders whether I wanted to or not. And I still am. His orders just happened to lead me here this time. A small escape." His voice grew bitter. "But only a temporary one."

His gaze returned to us, assessing. Trying to read our expressions. I didn't know what he saw there, but he didn't give anything away.

The fire flared brightly behind Damian for a second, in tandem with the pool of powers over his chest, and then returned to normal as the powers flowed back down his body and into the stone beneath him. With one last calculating look at us, he turned and stepped through the fire.

"Made it," he said, a second later.

"What town is that?" Matt asked harshly from the other side of the flames. "No border town should operate like that. No Light Guardian leadership would ever allow it. If that's really a border town, it needs to be reported."

Damian sighed. "Look, I don't know what to tell you." His voice was a calm drawl. "My father has a lot of friends in high places. Friends he helps stay in power, who help him do the same. And the oversight on border towns in Europe isn't quite the same as it is here, since the High Light Guardian is stationed here. The leadership is stretched thinner and is less unified. They don't visit as often. As long as we do what we're supposed to when it comes to defeating Demons and protecting Normals, they don't care."

"But—" Matt started, still angry.

"Hey," Damian cut him off, his tone betraying only a little frustration, "as much as I'd love to help you overthrow my father, this is not the best time to discuss the finer details. We still have three more people to get through and one more test after this. Save the questions for a better time."

Matt made a frustrated sound but ultimately fell quiet, dropping the matter for now.

"Who's next?" Damian asked through the flames.

"I'll go." I glanced up at Gabriel, and he nodded before pressing a kiss to the side of my head. Then he released me. I gave him a small smile before turning and walking forward to stand on the glowing stone in front of the flames. Even here, the heat was almost unbearable. I took a calming breath and waited.

I felt a gentle tingling as the powers in the stone pulsed and began winding their way up my legs and torso toward my chest. It wasn't a bad feeling—it was mostly a combination of powers that I'd interacted with before. And some were my own. After all we'd faced thus far, it was almost comforting. The powers settled over my chest, and I felt tendrils sliding beneath my skin and congregating where my life force was stored. They pulsed there, searching through me for whatever the room wanted me to reveal. I just waited, staring at the flames until an image formed, little by little, in the fire.

I tensed, my hands clamping shut, as I saw my mother materializing in the image before me. But I forced my muscles to unclench as I took a calming breath. I'd dealt with the damage she'd inflicted on me my whole life. I could do it again here. I'd be fine.

I watched, jaw tight, as a toddler version of me saw my mother arrive at the training house in Dagmar. My face lit up as I slid off my chair, abandoning the book that Matt had been helping me read. I ran toward her, my arms raised for a hug that I never should've expected. Something she'd never offered freely. She was nothing like Matt's mother had been—what little I could remember of her. Serafina regarded me coolly for a moment before stepping around me and heading to the table where Matt was sitting. She sat down in my now-empty seat and began talking with him. Matt shot me an apologetic look, regret briefly filling his eyes, then turned to speak with her, his expression becoming animated. She'd probably asked him about training. That was usually what he'd gotten excited over. I just stood there watching them, my small face growing sad. Tears filled my eyes, and my hands clenched into little fists at my sides. Then I turned and ran from the room.

The image faded and another appeared. I was six this time and spattered with blood. I'd just come from my first battle. I was a little injured, definitely exhausted, but overall fine. Matt walked next to me as we made our way back to our training house to get cleaned up. I was smiling, and Matt was ruffling my hair affectionately. He was proud of me for how well I'd done. I'd trained hard in my short life thus far so that I could survive my first battles—a tough milestone that not everyone lived through. I remembered how proud I'd felt after that battle. Proud that I'd held my own against Demons that I'd viewed more as monsters than enemies at the

512

time. I'd barely been able to comprehend at that age that Demons, not transformed, were just like me.

As we reached the front door of the training house, it opened and my mother walked through, a group of the town's warrior faction leadership trailing closely behind her. And my face had lit up again, this time against my will. But I'd irrationally hoped she'd find it within herself to be proud of me. After all, I'd just fought in my first battle. *Survived* my first battle.

Serafina barely glanced at me as she walked past, still talking with the adults around her. But she briefly rested her hand on Matt's shoulder. And that was it. She didn't even acknowledge me. My jaw tightened further as I watched the hurt filling my eyes. I almost wished I could reach into the flames and comfort myself. Hug my younger self and tell her to move on. That she'd be fine without Serafina . . . eventually. Matt wrapped his arm around me and pulled me against his side as we kept walking toward the training house, speaking encouragingly to me. I vaguely remembered he'd tried to console me. He'd said my mother was just really busy right now, but that she'd be sure to come visit me later. She hadn't, though. And I remembered already knowing she wouldn't, even as he'd been reassuring me. We'd both known it was a lie.

The image dissolved and another formed. This time I was eight. It was the day after the huge battle where they'd thought the plane tear might've widened. The battle that'd destroyed a lot of the town, killed many of the soldiers, and had spilled over into some nearby Normal towns. It was the battle that'd brought to Dagmar that older political faction woman who'd appeared in my most recent vision. Those of us who'd survived and were physically recovered enough, were piled into one of the training buildings, running through drills and one-on-one fights. Thanks to Matt's continuous help, I was always in a training group far above my age group. I was always assigned to *his* age group. And usually to him as a training partner.

We watched as Matt and I engaged in a one-on-one fight, pretty evenly matched even though Matt had started growing more around that time. We went back and forth for a while as we fought, trading off on who was pushing the other back more in a given moment. Our faces were filled with enthusiasm—we'd always loved the challenge of a good fight.

It was during our battle that Serafina slipped into the building. I hadn't noticed her at first since I was concentrating so hard on fending off Matt. She meandered slowly toward the trainer, watching us, a shrewd, almost hungry expression on her face. I wondered which of us she was reacting to. When Serafina reached the trainer, she leaned in and exchanged quiet words with her, glancing occasionally at the two of us. It seemed like she was getting an update on our progress. Or maybe just Matt's, since I knew how this scene ended.

But my younger self had eventually noticed Serafina in the room. And that was what'd ruined things for me. The second I saw her—and her cold disinterest bordering on disdain—I faltered. Just long enough for Matt to eviscerate me in front of everyone. In front of her. After Matt released me from his hold against the mat, he spoke to me, looking confused. He asked what'd happened. How he'd defeated me with so little effort. It was uncharacteristic. But I just stared in Serafina's direction until he turned and saw for himself. As he turned back to me, his expression filled with regret and understanding. But Serafina was already on her way over.

She placed her arm around Matt's shoulders when she reached us, openly showing her preference for him over me as she praised him and our trainer. Then she turned on me, her expression becoming harsh and cold, her words biting as she told me how inadequate I was. How I could be so much better if I just tried harder—if I really *wanted it*, like Matt did. And she said how lucky I was that Matt stooped to training with me when he could clearly work with much better soldiers. How inconsiderate it was for me to be repaying his selflessness with such mediocrity. With such lack of motivation and ambition. I watched my younger self glower at her, my eyes filled with fire, fury, and hurt. My fists clenched so tightly at my sides that my fingers began to go white. I glared at her until I couldn't take her presence anymore. Then I turned and stormed from the training building.

The image faded and another appeared. I sighed, wondering how many there'd be. Surely, we didn't need to watch every interaction I'd ever had with my mother. I felt like we'd gotten the point already. But apparently the room didn't agree. Perhaps part of this test was simply to emotionally punish us. So I just waited as an image of me at sixteen formed in the flames. Well, at least we'd skipped a few. This was after Matt had left. After Caleb had left. After I'd closed myself off. Hardened. Grown up fast. This was the last time I'd seen her before the first Demon attack at the Academy. And she hadn't even spoken to me—not directly. But by that age, I hadn't wanted her to. All I'd wanted was for her to stay the hell away from me.

One of the commanders spoke with Serafina, gesturing at the small group I was standing with. Everyone around me looked proud of themselves. We were the ones who'd rallied and defeated the Demons in the most recent attack, ultimately saving Dagmar from complete destruction, and saving many Normals in the surrounding towns from dying horribly. We'd been vastly outnumbered, and we'd only managed because we'd been clever, persistent, and ultimately powerful enough. More powerful than the Demons. I'd even been forced to transform. All of that was why we were there. To explain how we'd done it, and to receive her praise. I hadn't wanted it. I hadn't wanted to be there at all. But no one said no to the High Light Guardian. So I just stood there, in my now-favorite ripped up black clothes, my arms crossed over my chest, and watched her coldly, my face a blank mask.

She glanced at me a few times but didn't say anything. And I didn't react to her at all. It'd thrown her off. That and the fact that Matt wasn't here for her to put all her focus on so that she didn't have to focus on me. But she pulled herself together and praised all the surviving soldiers, making eye contact with all of them except me. I watched as my jaw tightened a little at this, but I otherwise managed to maintain a bored expression. Then we were dismissed, and I immediately headed for the door. Not seeing her hesitation like I saw it now—like she'd wanted to say something to me. But it only lasted for a moment. Almost too short a time to really believe it'd happened. She turned toward the commander instead as I vanished through the door.

The image faded and another appeared. It was recent. Gabriel, Matt, and I were standing in the meeting room with Serafina after the first attack on the Academy last semester, where the administration had voted to let the warrior faction onto campus to protect the school. I watched as she revealed that Matt had told her about my new abilities. As she ordered me to train with him to further develop those abilities. As she told me how much my power would help the Light Guardians. As she lied and said she was proud of me.

It was hard not to get angry again, even watching the scene unfold without sound. Watching how manipulative and cruel Serafina was. Watching how Matt bent to her will without any hesitation. Watching how she clearly wanted me to do the same. But my gaze turned firm and hard as I told her no. I refused to be used by her or controlled by the Light Guardians. Serafina looked at me in stunned silence. Then her eyes slowly filled with rage. We exchanged a few more words, but it was clear she'd lost with me. She'd lost . . . me. I walked past her with sure strides and left her and her rage behind me in the room.

The image faded and the fire returned to its former state. I released a breath of relief. It was done. I turned to face Gabriel and Caleb. I knew, somehow, what I was supposed to tell them. I knew I'd have to reveal the nature of my relationship with Serafina before I'd be able to move on. It was a curious choice for the room—the only people who didn't know the history were Caleb and Damian. But perhaps that was enough to sow discord, as I suspected was the room's ultimate goal.

I met Gabriel's gaze first and saw understanding and sorrow on my behalf there. He already knew how much Serafina had hurt me. He'd seen how horrible she was to me—and had experienced first-hand how horrible she was in general—and now he'd seen a small example of what she'd been like when I was younger. I could see how much witnessing her conduct toward me upset him. Because she hadn't loved me. And she should've.

Caleb, on the other hand, looked confused. Because he knew her in her official capacity. He knew she was the High Light Guardian. He'd interacted with her. She was his idol—the person whose position he eventually wanted. The person he strived to be. But he had no idea what her relationship was to me, or why I had so many memories with her. I sighed. It wasn't something I wanted to talk about.

I sucked in a deep breath, steeling myself. "The High Light Guardian is my mother," I finally said, my voice firm. It was better to get it out of the way quickly than to prolong the discomfort.

Shock filled Caleb's face. Followed by anger. Because he now knew how hard I'd worked to keep that information from him, even when we were dating. Even after knowing what his aspirations within the warrior faction were. But I just stared coldly back at him. I didn't regret keeping it from him. He would've used me for it and hurt me even more.

"She left me in Dagmar when I was a baby to be trained. Formed into a weapon she could manipulate and wield. That's all that she wanted from me. I was raised for a bit by Matt's mother, then by Matt after she died. Serafina came to check on our progress sometimes, but mostly just on Matt's. She was never very impressed with me. That obviously sucked for me when I was younger and desperately wanted her attention and care, but I eventually learned to move past those wants. I learned to stop expecting anything other than negativity and coldness from her. To stop trying to seek her approval.

"Since that shift, our dynamic changed. She wants me to want her approval, even though she'll never give it, because she believes it will allow her to control me. But she's noticed that I've stopped wanting it. And that angers her. She wants me to feel emotionally obligated to follow her orders because of her relationship to me, but I don't. She's never been willing to put in any work to form or maintain an emotional connection with me. I don't even think she knows how.

"Since I've been at the Academy, she's sought to control me and my abilities, now that I've shown I might be worth something to her in the war, but I've refused to directly help her or be controlled by her. And I've made it clear that I no longer have any intention of joining the warrior faction, so her chance to control me from that arena is gone. And she dislikes that."

I shrugged.

"So . . . yeah . . . I think that's it." I felt the weight of the question somehow lift off me. The fire behind me flared for a moment as the powers over my chest did the same. And then they drifted back to the stone at my feet.

Caleb's expression had closed off as I'd spoken. The cold mask was back, and I had no idea what he was thinking. He was probably furious with me right now. But I didn't care. Any feelings of animosity he might have toward me over this were his own problem. As long as it didn't impede our path forward on this mission, I didn't care what he thought. I glanced at Gabriel one more time before turning to face the flames. He gave me a small smile and nod of encouragement. Then, with a deep breath, I stepped onto the platform and into the fire.

Matt was right. The fire felt like a warm breeze on my skin as I walked across the small platform. The oppressive heat I'd felt in front of it was gone. I jumped off the other side and joined Matt and Damian. Both men were looking at me—Matt regretful again, Damian assessing. I ignored them and squinted around instead. The room widened again on this side of the platform and was large enough for a decent sized group to fit between the fire and the heavy door that would hopefully lead us to our last test.

"I made it through," I called quickly as I turned back to face the flames so Gabriel wouldn't worry.

"I'll go next," Gabriel said quickly.

Caleb sighed. "Fine," he grumbled. He probably didn't want to be the last one left on that side.

There was silence as Gabriel walked to stand on the stone and waited for the powers to wrap around him. Under a minute later, an image formed within the fire. When I'd been on the other side of it, I'd thought the image had been on the surface of the fire like a projection. But I could see the image clearly from this side as well. It was like the image lived within the fire itself, filling it entirely. Like the room wanted everyone to see, whether or not they'd already completed the test. I frowned. It supported my theory that the room was trying to sow discontent between the people traversing it, threatening our unity and our ability to complete our mission.

We watched a group of small children playing together in the grass outdoors in the fading light of sunset. They couldn't have been more than four years old. A tiny Gabriel, distinguishable by his jet-black hair, pale skin, and vibrant blue eyes, laughed and ran with them. He looked care-free. The sight made me smile. Then one of the other children screwed up his face in concentration and transformed in a burst of green light. Vines twisted around his small limbs, his skin was tinged with green, and he made leaves erupt from his hand. The rest of the children laughed with delight and transformed as well. One shot little water spouts out of her hand. Another made some of the dirt at their feet fly into the air. Yet another made the wind dance around them, swirling everyone's hair up into the sky.

Gabriel transformed in a flash of electric blue, and the laughter abruptly stopped. The small children around him staggered backward, pointing at his dark, shadowy skin, pseudo transparent and speckled with little white lights. So different from their own transformations. They didn't see the beauty in it, only the darkness. The difference. And they were afraid. My jaw clenched as I watched their reactions to him. I knew too well how this felt. The pain it caused.

The group of children turned and ran from him, leaving him alone in the yard. Gabriel transformed back and sat on the grass, looking sad. A girl a few years older than him walked over and sat next to him, then wrapped an arm around him comfortingly. She also had jet-black hair, but had brown, not blue, eyes. This must be his sister. She said something to him. It looked like she was trying to cheer him up. But his lower lip trembled, and tears streamed down his cheeks. My heart clenched.

The image dissolved and another formed. Gabriel was older now—maybe eleven or twelve—and he was training alongside a young boy his age. They were working hard on some mixed-weapon drills as an older man walked around them, offering pointers and corrections. Then the man blew his whistle and collected the practice weapons from them. He clapped the boys on the shoulders encouragingly before dismissing them. The boys grinned, slightly sweaty, and walked from the training house, talking and laughing. They were clearly good friends.

But as they rounded the corner of the building, they saw a group of Demons smashing through the end of the town closest to them. I watched as their smiles faded and hardened expressions—a melding of fear, resignation, and determination—took their place. They looked older now. Less joyous. Less like children. It was a common transformation for border town kids, but it was hard to watch.

Both boys pulled weapons—real ones this time—from their waistbands and ran toward the Demons. They were joined by a few other Divines on their way. A handful of teens. An adult or two. A few people emerged from buildings and tried to produce shields to keep the Demons from getting further into town. Trying to protect the Normals and Divines within. But the Demons had successfully taken the town by surprise. And there weren't nearly enough Divines nearby to deal with them.

When the group reached the Demons, each person transformed. Except Gabriel. Stubborn expression firmly in place, Gabriel relied solely on his weapons and his training to protect him and those around him. He was trusting in his fighting skills alone to take on the Demons. And for a while, that was enough. He and his friend—a Light Guardian—worked together to take down and behead one of the largest Demons. It was impressive. But as one of the teens was torn apart by a Demon she'd been trying to behead, and one of the adults was viciously crushed by another, the tide of the battle turned against them, and things became truly desperate.

Gabriel looked around frantically, trying to see if there were any other people nearby to help. But no one came. His friend grabbed his arm and yelled something. But a flash of fear shot across Gabriel's face, and he shook his head. A refusal. Instead, he ran at the Demon again. He managed to cause it some significant damage, distracting it while his friend flew up and tried to behead it. But the Demon managed to get its claws around his friend and threw him brutally to the ground.

Gabriel stabbed the Demon again, then ran to help his friend. He pulled him to his feet, and his friend shook himself, trying to shake off the effects of the impact. And then he shouted at Gabriel again, gesturing at the Demons. Gabriel looked uncertain for a moment, but then he nodded. He and the boy turned and charged forward again.

In a flash of electric blue, Gabriel turned into a shadow. He ran at the Demon and leapt into the air, traveling far higher than he could ever jump in his human form, then sliced the Demon viciously across the throat. It wasn't quite enough to behead it, but he'd deeply injured it. He landed back on the ground and looked over at his friend. But his friend was frozen, staring at Gabriel's transformation, startled and perhaps even afraid. It was clear that Gabriel had managed to keep it from him until now—that he'd managed to fight without transforming for a long time.

The Demon lurched forward, blood from its injury spilling to the ground in droves as the boy continued to stare at Gabriel. Then it plunged its long claws through the boy's chest, deep and true. Gabriel fell out of his transformation, terror flooding his face as the Demon yanked its claws out of his friend. Then he ran toward him. He tried to catch him as the other boy's knees gave out, blood spilling rapidly down his punctured armor. But the Demon staggered forward again, intent on finishing them both. With a growl of rage, Gabriel transformed again and launched into the air, then hacked ferociously into the Demon's neck over and over. The Demon's mouth opened in a silent scream and swiped its claws at Gabriel. But they just went through him, not touching or harming him at all. And with another yell, Gabriel managed to behead it.

He floated back to the ground as the Demon fell, knocking over and pinning down another Demon that was behind it, allowing what was left of the fighting group to descend on it and quickly behead it as well. And then Gabriel transformed back and ran over to his friend. Tears streamed down his face as he gathered his friend into his arms. He summoned electric blue power to his fingertips and placed his hands over the deep wounds, then tried and tried to heal his friend as he bled out. But the boy was clearly too injured, and Gabriel too inexperienced with healing, to undo what the Demon had done. The life ebbed from his friend's eyes, and he went limp in Gabriel's arms. Self-hatred and despair flooded Gabriel's expression, and it was clear that he was blaming himself—his transformation—for everything that'd just happened. Tears stung my eyes, my heart hurting for that younger version of Gabriel.

The image vanished and another appeared. Gabriel was a teenager now. Maybe fifteen or sixteen. He'd adopted more of his current style by this point, and had quite a few of his tattoos, and he was training hard, running through drills in his human form while other trainees around him worked on their transformation-specific abilities. Then the trainer, the same older man as before, walked through the room and paired people off for one-on-one fights. Everyone was transformed except Gabriel.

The trainer blew the whistle and the fights began. Gabriel was amazing. Not only had he vastly improved as a fighter since the previous fight we'd seen, but he also had a good instinct for how to evade and address the other person's powers. He moved fluidly around them, almost catlike, dodging and biding his time until he saw an opening. And then he moved in swiftly and powerfully, overcoming his opponent, causing them to yield. It seemed like he'd decided he no longer wanted to engage with his transformation, at least in front of other people. Not when he didn't have to.

The image faded and another appeared. This time it was familiar. It was of the two of us sitting on the wrought-iron benches outside the main building last semester, smoking. I looked pale and exhausted, and my hand shook as I raised the cigarette to my mouth. This must've been after my first transformation training with Matt. Our mouths silently moved as we talked, his expression dark and concerned, mine sad and closed off. I was explaining why I was mad at Matt. How Matt had been scared of me. Repelled by me. Because of something I couldn't control or change about myself. How Matt believed my transformation was somehow more dangerous because it looked darker than his. Tears fell down my cheeks and a flash of surprise and pain crossed Gabriel's face. Then he lifted his hand and trailed the backs of his fingers slowly down my cheeks, gently wiping away the tears.

The image disappeared and another formed. It was of the two of us heavily engaged in battle with a Demon last semester—the first Demon we'd faced—and neither of us were transformed. We worked to bring it down strategically and methodically. Without powers.

My cheeks heated as a new image formed. The two of us sitting in one chair, me straddling him, our foreheads pressed together, our eyes closed. It was Christmas night. When we'd fully opened our minds to each other. Showed each other what we thought of each other's transformations. Showed how much we'd meant to each other all along. And then we were kissing urgently, grabbing at, and starting to pull off, each other's clothes. Caught up in the moment and each other.

Matt shifted tensely, his hands clenching into tight fists. I clenched my jaw and sighed. I wished these private moments could stay private. I resented our lives being put on display, especially to this group of people.

Thankfully, the image faded before too many of our clothes were off, and another appeared. It was of the Demon attack this semester where we'd fought alongside Damian and Caleb. We watched as the Demon suddenly grabbed me from its shoulder and flung me away from it with all its strength. Caleb tried and failed to catch me. A look of utter panic spread across Gabriel's face as he saw what was happening. And then he transformed without even thinking about it and sped after me. A streak of electric blue—almost too fast to see. He caught up with me and launched into the air, wrapping himself around me, saving me from the impact that'd been imminent. And then we floated gently back to the ground together, and I turned in his arms, pressing my cheek to his shadowy one, completely unphased by his transformation. He pulled me flush against him and murmured to me, his deep relief apparent even in this form. The image faded until only the fire remained.

I stared at the flickering wall of flames. What was the room trying to force him to tell us? Gabriel sighed from the other side of the fire. I could almost see him running his hand agitatedly through his hair, making it stand on end.

"It wants me to explain my relationship with my transformation and the evolution of my feelings about them. Especially how that evolution is tied to Terah and my feelings for her." His voice was low and even. Surprisingly, he didn't sound nervous.

My cheeks prickled with heat again as Matt glanced at me, his body taught with tension. The room was successfully enhancing the conflict within our group.

"As you saw, I was born with a transformation that looks different from most other Blessed," Gabriel said, resigned. "At least different from the ones who lived in Elareth. I was shunned for it when I was younger. People looked at it and saw power that wasn't as tied to the natural elements like it was for a lot of other Blessed, so they decided it must be darker or more dangerous. Maybe even tainted somehow. I looked frightening to them, especially to the kids. But even the adults who'd seen it didn't trust me. Not fully. It was like they thought I was closer to being a Demon or Dark Guardian, even though that's not how divine power works."

He sighed again, and I heard him shifting.

"I learned pretty quickly that, if I wanted to have any friends who were Divines beyond my older sister, I'd need to hide my transformation from other people as much as possible. I threw myself into learning how to rely more on pure fighting skills so I wouldn't need to transform during Demon attacks. People thought it was strange that I didn't transform, but they mainly assumed my power was especially weak, and that I just chose not to bother transforming because it wouldn't help me much in battle.

"As a result, I started making friends again, with people who'd never seen me transform, or who didn't remember. But I never stopped resenting my transformation, even after I'd successfully hidden it.

522

Everyone else was allowed to be proud of their power and their identities as Divines, and they got to enjoy the leg-up that that power gave them in battle. But I wasn't allowed those same things. I had to hide who I was. I had to hide something I couldn't control or change about myself.

"This resentment deepened after my best friend, Cainan, died in battle. I blamed myself for my friend's reaction, and then I blamed my power for not at least being able to save him. After that, I refused to transform at all in battle. I only worked on honing my transformation skills when I was alone at night, when no one could see me. But I rarely even did that. It wasn't until I was older that I realized the unfairness and hypocrisy of it all. The unfair prejudice. I eventually started blaming myself less for my difference and people's reactions to me and blaming other people more for their responses and their 'darker is bad' mentality. I started forgiving myself for the part of me I couldn't change.

"But having a better awareness of what was happening and why didn't make the situation feel any better, it just explained it. I still hid my transformation from people. I still sought acceptability by not showing all of who I was, and I still felt bitter about the reality I'd been given. And it hurt knowing no one would ever truly accept all of me—not even my family had fully managed to do that.

"It wasn't until I met Terah that I began thinking about my transformation differently. I'd never met another person who'd been shunned for their transformation like I had. Who wouldn't transform unless there was no other option, and who instead relied on pure fighting skills to survive like I did. But she had. She understood what it felt like."

Damian glanced at me, curious. Surprised. He was the only one here who'd never seen me transform.

"Seeing her pain and watching her struggle with the same things I'd struggled with allowed me to see my own situation from a different perspective. I knew without a doubt that Terah shouldn't feel bad for or ashamed of her transformation. I knew the people who'd reacted poorly to her transformation had failed *her*, and not the other way around."

Matt shifted uncomfortably next to me again.

"I knew, no matter what her transformation looked like, she was worthy of care and respect. She deserved to be loved for all of who she was, including her transformation. And . . . if that was true for her, I knew, deep down, it had to be true for me too." He sighed. "It was something I'd told myself before, but I never fully believed it until I met her."

I bit the inside of my cheek as I stared at the flames, warmth expanding in my chest. I wished I could see his face right now.

"But even then, I was still reluctant to transform. I believed, when faced with my actual transformation, no one would be able to accept that part of me without being repulsed, distrustful, or scared. They'd only see the darkness, and they'd fear it. And I didn't want to lose Terah because of it. I knew it was why she still didn't want to transform in front of me either. We were both afraid of that rejection.

"But the Demon attacks forced our hands. When we finally fully saw each other's transformations for the first time, I couldn't believe people had been so horrible to Terah her whole life for hers. I couldn't understand how anyone could ever reject her because of it. But the thing that surprised me most was her reaction to mine. I waited for her to flinch, back away, or look scared or repulsed, just like everyone else. But she never did. She just . . . smiled at me. Moved closer. Told me that my transformation was beautiful. And it floored me. She wanted me to accept and appreciate the part of me that I had the hardest time accepting. She did what no other person had ever done for me—what I thought was impossible. She accepted all of me, loved all of me, without condition. And I did the same for her.

"Her acceptance lifted a huge weight off my shoulders. I truly stopped caring about what other people thought of my transformation. I stopped trying to hide it, and I slowly started actively accepting and appreciating it. I decided to transform in battle again whenever it would be helpful. And all of that was tested when we fought the Demon this semester. My transformation not only allowed me to save Terah from severe injury, but also allowed me to end the battle and protect the people around me more quickly and without getting injured. I'd never been more grateful for my transformation and everything it allowed me to do. I knew I could never resent it or hide it again. Thanks to her."

My cheeks flushed as I watched the wall of fire separating us pulse once. A few moments later, Gabriel emerged from the flames and hopped off the platform. The corner of his mouth hitched up in a small smile as he saw my blush. Then he walked toward me, ignoring Matt's angry glare, and pulled me into his arms.

"Sorry that it showed so much personal stuff," he murmured into my ear as he held me against him. But I just shook my head. I couldn't be too upset about it. Not when it'd showed me in yet another way how much Gabriel cared about me, and how much we'd helped each other grow.

He pulled back slightly to look at my face and assess my reaction. I just smiled up at him, a little ruefully, my gaze warm as it met the darkening blue depths of his. Telling him, in my own way, that I loved him. His smiled broadened into his familiar smirk as he watched me, and he leaned down and brushed his lips over mine.

"Love you too," he breathed.

A few moments later, another image formed in the flames, and Gabriel and I turned to face it. It was Caleb's test.

A ravaged town appeared, smoke billowing around the remains of buildings, thick enough to dim the glow of the sun. It looked like a massacre had just taken place. Bodies of Demons and Divine soldiers were liberally strewn across the ground, blood staining the grass and dirt, pooling and trickling across the earth to form horrible rivers and lakes of carnage. A lone Light Guardian walked through the wreckage, still transformed, glowing sword dripping with black Demon blood still held at the ready. The figure was looking around, searching for something. He began shoving through debris with this free hand, moving broken chunks of stone and splintered wood until he uncovered what he sought. A small child, no more than two years old, with caramel-colored hair was screaming and crying, partially buried under the remains of a house. It was Caleb.

The man quickly sheathed his sword and knelt, swiftly pulling away the debris. When he'd unburied him, the man scooped Caleb into his arms and carefully wiped away a trickle of blood trailing down Caleb's round cheek from a small cut there. Caleb clutched the man's armor with one small, chubby hand, and pointed toward the devastation, tears still streaming down his face. It looked like he was saying something. Calling for someone. The man's face filled with regret, and he shook his head. He said something to Caleb, then placed his hand gently on top of Caleb's head—a gesture of comfort. Then, with one last look around the devastated town, the man extended his wings and leapt into the air, taking Caleb with him. Away from the carnage and destruction. Away from the scorched earth and blackened sky.

The image dissolved and another appeared. In many ways, this image was the opposite of the last. Instead of death and ruin, ash and darkness, this image was lush, green, and bright. Grass swayed in the wind outside a small, rural-looking cottage. Vibrant flowers surrounded the structure in little beds, neatly tended. The sun shone brightly, illuminating the cheerful faces of Caleb, now maybe five, and the man who'd rescued him. They'd crafted some makeshift wooden training weapons, and the man was leading Caleb through some sword drills, adjusting his stance occasionally. Caleb looked enthusiastic. Happy and carefree. He gazed up at the man with adoration as he watched him demonstrate drill after drill with incredible precision and power, clearly the result of many years serving as a soldier. And Caleb did his best to follow along. To be just as precise and powerful. He looked determined to learn, but he had none of the usual signs of desperation or anguish of someone raised in a border town. There was no deep bleakness or sadness clouding his eyes. No heavy soul. No motivation born from the pure need to survive. It looked like the man had managed to take Caleb away from it all, completely separating them from the war and violence.

The image faded and another appeared. Caleb looked to be around eight, now. He and the man were still training outside the small house, but this time both were transformed. The man and Caleb practiced forming shields of light, throwing fire, and finally pulled their swords and worked on transformed combat. It was clear that this man had been working incredibly hard to train Caleb as well as he possibly could, because Caleb showed impressive skill in his transformed state, especially for his age. At his current level, if he'd been living in a border town, they probably would've put him on the front lines. When the fight ended, Caleb and the man returned to the ground and transformed back. Both were smiling, and the man ruffled Caleb's hair, looking proud.

The image dissolved and another formed. Caleb and the man were moving around the small interior of their home, folding things and placing essential items into bags. The man looked cheerful. Caleb, who appeared to be about ten now, looked a little nervous. But the man spoke to him as they packed, animatedly moving his hands. Explaining. Caleb nodded as the man spoke, clearly trying to take the words to heart and push down his nerves. The man finally knelt in front of him and placed his hands on his shoulders bracingly. His expression was filled with earnestness and affection. Then he reached toward the table and grabbed a pair of daggers with beautifully carved handles that looked well-used, but also well-maintained. He held them out to Caleb. A gift. Caleb's eyes widened as he reached out and carefully, almost reverently, took the daggers from the man's hands.

The image vanished and another formed. Caleb looked to be around the same age, and he and the man were being shown around a crowded building filled with children and teenagers of all ages. My stomach tightened as I looked at the familiar set-up. The common area, the large eating area, the numbered rooms and shared bathrooms. This looked like a training house. A border town training house. The woman showing them around pointed to different areas of the building, her mouth moving in explanation. The man looked calm and nodded along politely as she spoke. Caleb, though, looked nervous. Out of his element. A little scared and maybe even homesick—all expressions I never thought I'd see on his face. This young boy was nothing like the Caleb I knew now, or the Caleb I'd known when I was younger. What . . . had happened?

The woman finally led them up some stairs and down a hall to another set of bedrooms. She pushed open one of the doors and pointed at one of the beds within. Caleb's new room. A couple other boys his age looked up from their respective beds, eyeing Caleb with hard eyes and clenched jaws, bleak and mistrusting beyond their young years. Caleb swallowed but walked forward, head high, and placed his things on his new bed. The man came over and rested his hand briefly on Caleb's shoulder, leaning down and murmuring something to him. Caleb nodded and managed a small smile before the man rejoined their guide and left the room. Then he looked over at the other two boys in the room, but they'd already turned away from him and were diligently ignoring his presence. He sighed and went to sit next to his bag on the bed. Lonely.

The image faded and another appeared. Caleb was in training gear now, taking part in one-on-one hand-to-hand combat fights under the watchful supervision of a stern looking trainer. Caleb, though still around the same age, looked less happy now. More reserved. More closed off. He didn't engage with the people around him. And while he still seemed to be taking training very seriously, the joy and enthusiasm for it that we'd seen in the previous images was gone. Border towns had a way of doing that to people. Taking away their happiness and hope. Slowly eating away at their souls.

Even in this new environment, Caleb was very good. He defeated partner after partner in record time. But where he'd previously gotten smiles and praise from the older man as they'd trained, here Caleb got nothing but disdainful looks from his fellow trainees. They probably resented him—were jealous of him because he was new and way more advanced than they were. Border town kids weren't known for being particularly nice or welcoming. How could they be when they'd been exposed to so much carnage and complete and utter destruction their whole lives? When all their focus every day was so heavily placed on their own survival to the exclusion of others?

Suddenly, all heads jerked around toward the training room door, and my stomach sank. Because this was familiar too. It was the unified reaction to the sound of the town's sirens. I could almost hear them now, signaling an attack. Calling for all available soldiers. Suddenly the image before us was one of frenzied action. People hurriedly re-racked practice weapons and transformed before running outside and pulling real weapons from their sheaths. Caleb followed, scared and uncertain, but transformed along with the rest of them, and launched into the darkening sky.

It became clear very quickly that Caleb was out of his depth. He was an amazing fighter, but he clearly had no real battle experience. He'd never fought an actual Demon before. He'd never had to push through the physical and psychological fear that the Demons produced with their appearance and powers. He'd never been faced with the carnage and destruction. And he looked completely overwhelmed.

Sorrow gripped my stomach as I watched Caleb trying to find his bearings as he engaged in the fight. He got in some blows, but they were half-hearted, and none were very strategic. He was pushed to the outskirts pretty quickly. I knew, as I watched Caleb continue to struggle, what the man who'd saved him as an infant had tried to do. He'd tried to keep Caleb safe and happy for as long as possible while trying to make sure he learned to fight well enough to actually survive. He'd tried to shield him for as long as he could from what it meant for so many of us to be Divines. And it had sort of worked. Caleb had been safe, happy, and well-trained for a lot of his childhood. But the man's plan hadn't taken into account that surviving and doing well in battle went beyond just knowing how to fight well. It was learning how to deal with . . . everything. Learning to push through so many emotions and so much fear so that you even *could* fight well. And watching Caleb now, I knew he hadn't been ready. He shouldn't be fighting like this yet. They'd thrown him in because of his skill, but it'd been too much for him to face all at once. He was still too young and inexperienced to know how to process it all on his own. And all of this made him sloppy. An easy target. I truly didn't know how he'd survived this.

Anxiety pulsed through me as I saw a Demon finally notice Caleb, small and uncertain, trying to hold the far end of the line. But Caleb hadn't noticed it. He hadn't seen the Demon's sinister grin as it singled him out. He hadn't seen the Demon starting to charge at him, claws as long and sharp as swords, brandished and ready. But the man who'd raised Caleb noticed. His mouth frantically formed the shape of Caleb's name, calling to him. Trying to warn him. But Caleb couldn't hear him. So the man shoved away from the fight and flew as fast as he could to Caleb's aid. At the last moment, Caleb spun around, just in time to see the enormous Demon raising its claws to kill him. Caleb's eyes widened, fear and astonishment flooding their depths. He raised his sword with a shaking hand to counter the blow, but I already knew it wouldn't be enough to deflect it or save him. So did the man.

With a yell, the man threw himself between Caleb and the Demon, shoving Caleb to safety. And he took the blow meant for him. The Demon's razor-sharp claws tore through the man's armor and slashed deeply into his body, almost tearing him in half. The man fell out of the sky and hit the ground on his back, blood spilling rapidly from his body. Caleb's mouth opened in horror and anguish flooded his features. He flew quickly to the ground as the Demon was swarmed by other Light Guardians. And as he sobbed, he placed his hands over the man's wounds. Frantically trying to hold the man together. To heal him. Caleb looked around and screamed for help. He needed more power. The man was quickly dying. But the other Light Guardians just looked down at Caleb and the man, faces hard, then turned away. Ignoring them. They were choosing not to expend their powers on healing rather than fighting.

The man raised a shaking hand and placed his fingers against Caleb's cheek, cupping the side of his face. His expression, even now, was peaceful and serene. There was no anger, fear, or pain there. Caleb clutched the front of the man's clothes, crying. Yelling. He looked desperate and angry. Emotionally torn apart. But the man just smiled and gently responded, his eyes filled with the same affection that was always there when he looked at Caleb. And then he went limp, his hand falling from Caleb's cheek to the ground, his eyes going vacant.

Caleb yelled and cried as though his heart was the one that'd been torn out, clutching the man to him with bloody, shaking hands. And then his expression changed. It filled with rage, almost feral. With another yell, Caleb threw himself into the air, drawing his sword in a flash of bright white light, and flew at the Demon that'd killed the man. The Demon was engaged in heavy battle with the group of Light Guardians that'd surrounded it, but Caleb shoved violently through them all, not caring that they were technically his allies as he kicked and punched them out of the way. Caleb's power burned even brighter now in his rage, and by the time he reached the Demon, he was almost blinding.

He flew directly at the Demon without hesitation, heedless of all danger, and hit it across the neck with his glowing sword with all his strength. Black blood burst from the gash as the Demon's eyes widened in surprise, but Caleb didn't stop. He kept hitting it there, over and over, blood flying, liberally coating him and burning the skin not protected by his armor, as tears streamed down his face. Until the Demon's head fell to the ground and its body followed closely after.

The rest of the Light Guardians watched, astonished, as Caleb landed, transformed back into his human form, and walked away from the battle, back toward the training house that contained his room. He didn't seem to care that the battle still raged around him. His expression was blank. Devoid of life and emotion.

He ran up the stairs and shoved open the door to his room. Then he grabbed his few possessions and shoved them into his bag. He grabbed the daggers the man had given him from his side table drawer and stared at them for a long moment, emotions traveling over his face as continuous and indistinguishable as drops of water in a river. Caleb finally secured the daggers around his waist, then grabbed his bag and walked back down the stairs. And then he just . . . walked away from the town. He glanced back once, on the very outskirts, his expression a mix of rage and desperate loneliness. Then he turned his head forward again and kept walking.

The image faded and another formed. Caleb looked a couple years older here. Maybe twelve or thirteen. And he was fighting in another training building. He must've relocated to another border town after he'd left the last one. Caleb's expression was much more closed off and cold now than it'd been before, and he fought with a ruthlessness that'd never been a part of his style when he'd been training with the man who'd raised him. This was a different Caleb. A Caleb who didn't pull his punches. A Caleb who didn't want to get emotionally close to anyone. This was a Caleb closer to the one I was most familiar with.

We watched as he defeated all the older, larger trainees, one right after another. His expression remained cold through the entire exercise. It didn't even change when the trainer nodded approvingly and seemed to be complimenting him. Caleb just looked around dispassionately, then turned and walked out of the building. He made his way back to another, larger trainee residence building, with more signs of damage and repair. That usually pointed to it being a larger border town—constantly rebuilding as they were constantly attacked.

Caleb paused to grab a few items of food, then made his way to his room. And he started packing again, his expression stony. I wondered if he'd run out of people to beat in this town. Perhaps it wasn't challenging for him anymore. And he seemed to be looking for a challenge. Perhaps he'd already decided he wanted to be the highest-ranking warrior faction member and no longer felt that this town would be able to help him achieve that goal. Or perhaps he just didn't like staying put for very long anymore. But whatever the reason, Caleb finished packing in a matter of minutes and left the residence house, and the town, before the rest of the trainees had even returned.

The image faded and another appeared. Caleb was maybe fourteen or fifteen this time, closer in appearance to how he'd looked when I'd first met him, and he appeared to be in yet another training building. This one looked even bleaker than the last. Larger and more disheveled, with mismatched wooden boards haphazardly patched over various holes in the walls and roof—signs of continuous repair. An even larger border town than the last, then. Caleb's expression was closed off and cold, but he seemed to be surrounded by admirers this time, rather than scornful looks. Fellow trainees looked at him in awe. Some were clearly very taken with him. But he didn't pay much attention to them. He just focused on what the trainer was saying. Focused on the next fight.

A tall, heavily muscled young man moved forward to stand in front of Caleb as the trainer blew the whistle, wooden sword in hand. He was at least two feet taller than Caleb, and much, much broader. But Caleb just looked at him with cold calm, waiting for the whistle to be blown again. When it was, Caleb attacked the young man in front of him lightning fast, disorienting and disabling him before he'd really had a chance to move. In under a minute, he had the man on the floor, pinned with his sword tip to the back of the man's neck. The man held up his hands in a yield as the trainer blew the whistle again.

The other trainees clapped, looking at Caleb with naked admiration, but Caleb just frowned. He looked dissatisfied. Restless. Then he left the training building yet again and made his way to the residence buildings. And yet again, he packed his bag and left the town behind. I frowned at the image, crossing my arms over my chest. Leaving things behind seemed to be a consistent pattern for him. I wished I'd known that when I'd met him.

The image faded and another appeared. Caleb threw his bag with all his things onto yet another training house bed, clearly having just arrived, then made his way down the stairs and outside. Matt and I both shifted as we watched him walk toward the training buildings. A familiar path with familiar structures. This was Dagmar. This was when I'd first met him.

Caleb walked through the large barn-like door of the main training building, looking around with mild interest. This was certainly the largest border town he'd been to thus far. Training was still in full swing, however, so Caleb stood to the side and leaned against the wall, watching a fight that was taking place in front of him. Sizing up the fighters around him and comparing his skills to theirs. My stomach tightened as I watched, and I felt myself closing off. I remembered this.

Caleb watched as a fourteen-year-old me fought off four seventeen-year-old young men in a round of hand-to-hand combat. It was a pretty rough fight. None of them were holding back—I remembered being covered in deep bruises after the match—but neither was I. Matt had left Dagmar not that long ago, and I had plenty of anger to spare. He watched as I roundly and viciously defeated the men around me, one after another, until they were lying on the ground, barely able to move. Caleb's eyebrows rose in surprise.

The men pushed to their feet as the trainer blew the whistle and ended morning training. They all glared at me—none of them found it flattering to be defeated by a small-statured, young teenage girl—but I just smirked at them, their anger clearly amusing me. The men muttered darkly, calling me some pretty uncomplimentary names, then quickly exited the building. I just extended my middle finger after them. Caleb's mouth curled into a small smile as he watched me—the first I'd seen in these images since the death of the man who'd raised him. And then he pushed off the wall and strode leisurely over to me.

I crossed my arms over my chest and raised an eyebrow coolly at him as he approached and spoke to me. I was distrusting of him, both as a new person to town, and as a person who wasn't Matt. Because no one besides Matt had ever stayed near me long. I didn't expect Caleb to either. As Caleb continued to speak, I looked up at him, my expression a little disbelieving. But I'd eventually nodded, shrugging. I remembered that Caleb had said he was new and had been impressed with the fight he'd just watched. He'd asked if he could have a fight with me, and I'd agreed.

We centered ourselves on the mat and Caleb counted us down since the trainer was no longer present to blow the whistle. And then we ran at each other. My jaw tightened as I watched the two of us move around each other with fluid skill. Striking, dodging, throwing, recovering, again and again. It almost looked like a dance and not an exercise in violence and domination. We looked evenly matched for a while, but Caleb eventually got the upper hand a few minutes in and threw me into the mat hard, pinning me with his weight so I couldn't move. Anger and frustration had filled my face—I was no longer used to being beaten at this point—but Caleb immediately released me and offered me a hand up. Then he smiled at me, slow and warm. It actually reached his eyes. And he complimented my fighting and offered to be my training partner. To teach me what he knew and to help me improve even more. I stared at him for a long moment in silence, expression unreadable, but I eventually nodded sharply in reluctant agreement.

The image faded and another appeared. Caleb and I were in the training room, maybe a month later, working on our one-on-one fights after hours. We'd become training partners during the day, training partners after hours, and friends in between. Since the moment he'd arrived in Dagmar, he'd shoved himself into every part of my life. And, out of loneliness and a growing infatuation, I'd let him. He'd helped me and had stuck by me this past month, making my time in Damar less solitary and hellish, so I'd allowed myself to open up to him just a little. It was hard not to when he was so warm and charming all the time. And constant like no one other than Matt had been up to that point. Caleb pushed me to fight better and to improve quickly. He didn't ignore or hate me. And these were all things I'd highly valued at the time. They were things no one else in Dagmar would ever give me.

No longer strangers, we joked around even as we moved through drills. Caleb displayed certain moves for me, then watched me repeat the moves quickly and precisely, a small smile on his lips. He looked . . . so different from the person he'd been even a month before. More open. Happier. And his enthusiasm for fighting seemed to have returned. It didn't make a lot of sense to me now. He'd been so closed off before. How could that've changed so quickly? At the time, I'd just thought he was always like that—charming and funny, if a little distrusting of others. I'd assumed that he must naturally draw people to him and make friends easily wherever he went. But now, seeing everything that'd come before, the drastic difference in his affect and behavior really stood out. It wasn't that he couldn't form connections with people—it's that he'd never tried to until now.

My teeth clenched as I watched Caleb walk over to reposition me as I stood preparing to run through the next drill with him. His hands slid slowly over me as he adjusted my stance, his body pressed closely behind mine. Both our cheeks turned a little pink as I turned my head and our eyes met for a long moment. I scowled. I hated how he'd so proficiently used training to get physically and emotionally close to me so quickly. I hated how easy I'd made it for him. And I wished I didn't have to see this again. Experiencing it once had been enough. Experiencing it again with an audience was basically a nightmare. But the Caleb in the image had just smiled at me warmly, pulling me closer for a brief moment, making me breathless, before releasing me and going to stand across from me again, mirroring my stance. And then, once I'd pulled my wits back around me, we'd launched into another fight. Even after only a month or so, I already looked like I'd improved. I was faster, stronger, more prepared for those compound attacks he favored, and I recovered more quickly.

This fight lasted significantly longer than the first, and I managed to land quite a few hard hits to Caleb's person. I'd even succeeded in pinning him down for a bit before he'd managed to shove his way out of the hold. But he'd eventually overcome me again, pinning me, chest heaving from exertion, to the mat. But he didn't let me up immediately this time, even after I yielded. His smile slipped from his face as a brief look of uncertainty flashed across it. And then warmth flooded in, replacing the uncertainty as his gaze skimmed over my face. My flushed cheeks. My lips. He seemed mesmerized. And he leaned slowly forward, his eyes sliding closed, and brushed his lips over mine. Just once. Then he pulled back to see my reaction.

My cheeks were burning, and my eyes were wide with confusion and astonishment. Caleb shifted his weight so he could free his hand, and he brought it up to cup my cheek, his thumb rubbing warmly over my skin. I swallowed hard at the contact—at his warmth and closeness. Caleb smiled at me again, that slow burning smile that'd always weakened my knees, and he watched me melt. Then his lips were on mine again, his arms slipping under me and winding around my back to pull me closely against him as he deepened the kiss, knowing now that I wouldn't stop him. Knowing he'd won this battle too.

The image dissolved and I bit back a curse as another image appeared, from almost a year later. Caleb and I in the tent in the woods on our day off, the day before he'd left Dagmar—and me—behind for good. Gabriel reached for me and laced his fingers through mine, squeezing them reassuringly as we stared at the image. He knew just how much this was sucking for me. Just how much I didn't want to relive this. I squeezed his fingers in return. It couldn't be easy for him to watch either.

I bit the inside of my cheek as it showed Caleb and I lying under some blankets together, my cheek pressed against his bare shoulder and chest as he held me tightly to him, still slightly out of breath from our previous activities. He pressed kisses to my forehead and hair as he told me over and over how much he loved me. How he'd never loved anyone like this before, but how he hadn't been able to help falling for me. And then he tilted my face up and kissed me, deep and slow.

But suddenly, we jerked apart, and both looked at the tent flap in alarm. The town's sirens had started blaring. Panic flooded Caleb's face as he looked back at me. He stroked his fingers slowly down my cheek, almost like he didn't know what else to do. And then he was pushing into a sitting position and grabbing a shirt, starting to beg me to stay in the tent. To stay away from the fight. I looked stubborn and uncertain, but I finally gave in, nodding and looking defeated, pulling the blankets more tightly around me. I hadn't been able to say no to him.

The image vanished and another appeared. Caleb and the surviving soldiers ran toward where I'd fallen from the sky onto the ground after the Demon battle. Where I lay with a wooden beam still run partially through my torso. I'd fallen out of my transformation moments before, totally burned out, after I'd finally managed to slay the last Demon. And I'd consequently fallen a great distance in my human form, slamming into the ground with nothing left to cushion the impact. I was quickly dying.

I squeezed Gabriel's hand as we watched my blood rapidly pooling around me. Caleb's expression was filled with terror, horror, and desperation as he reached me and collapsed onto the ground next to me. Tears pooled in his eyes and spilled quickly over, down his blood and dirt covered cheeks. He grabbed me and was frantically yelling, but I hadn't really been able to make out what he'd been saying at the time. I'd been on the cusp of unconsciousness—far too out of it. As he cried over me, two of the adult Light Guardians pulled the beam from my torso, and I passed out from pain and blood loss, my eyes sliding closed. And, as he'd done when the man who'd raised him was dying, Caleb lost control. He sobbed over my body, his own heaving, and clutched frantically at my torso, trying to hold me together with his shaking, bloody fingers. Desperate. Angry. Desolate.

One of the adults pushed on his shoulder, saying something. Caleb didn't seem able to comprehend his words, though, because the man shook his head, frustrated, and pushed Caleb out of the way more forcefully. Then he scooped me up, blood dripping quickly from my body onto the already-blood-soaked ground, turned, and jogged with me to the medical area. Caleb just stared after him, numb, his hands forming shaking fists in his lap.

And then his expression slowly changed. First there was intense despair—a deep chasm of pain and helplessness. Then rage took over, overwhelming and powerful. I could almost see it coming off him like waves of heat. He shoved to his feet, still looking after me, anger and regret mixing in a powerful, frenzied combination. Then the regret won out for a long moment, deep and bitter. And then the coldness descended over his expression like a barrel of ice water being dumped over his head. His jaw clenched as his eyes hardened and filled with ice. He tightly clutched the handles of the daggers at his sides—the ones the man who'd raised him had given him—until his fingers were as white as a sheet. And then, as he released the daggers again, the fire and ice left him, leaving only emptiness in their wake. He looked almost gaunt now. Completely unlike his usual self. Devoid of life or expression. And exactly how he'd looked when he'd come to tell me that he was leaving me behind.

Caleb turned on his heel and returned to his residence building. He walked slowly this time. No sense of purpose, urgency, or ambition leading him for once. He dragged himself up the stairs, his expression cold and vacant, and made his way to his room. Then he pushed through the door into the dim space beyond, grabbed his bag, and started packing, shoving his things in without any real thought or care, his hands shaking. When he finished, he sank onto the edge of his mattress in the dark and stared at the blank opposite wall. He just sat there for a while, still and silent. Then he grabbed his bag, like he was going to sling it on and walk out the door again. He held it like that for a long moment, before he dropped it back onto the bed and clamped his hands into tight, shaking fists.

Suddenly, he shoved to his feet and ran back down the hall, down the stairs, and out the front door, heading toward the medical area. He burst through the door and came to a skidding halt as he saw a large group of Light Guardians surrounding my unconscious form on one of the cots, the circle of them glowing with blinding white light as they worked together to heal me. He looked on in awe until the group stepped away from me, the glow dissipating, and the medic pulled a blanket over my body. Caleb caught one of the Light Guardian's eyes as she was leaving, and she offered Caleb a small nod and quick smile, placing a hand on his shoulder as she passed. Reassuring him that they'd been able to save me.

Caleb staggered forward until he reached the side of my bed, then he stood there and stared at my face, conflict brewing on his own again. He

536

reached forward slowly and trailed the backs of his fingers down my cheek. A look of intense pain overtook him as he touched me. As he confronted how injured I was. How close to death I'd come. Tears burned in his eyes again, and he clutched his chest with his other hand over the healing gash above his heart, like he was hurting, but internally. But he slowly worked to shove down the tears again. To conquer his emotions and imprison them behind steel doors inside. He finally took a step back from me, bringing his hands rigidly to his sides again. His whole body had tensed, and a look of hard stubbornness descended over his face like a black cloud, ice returning to his eyes. Then he turned on his heel and walked purposefully from the room.

The image faded and another formed. It was the next day. Caleb had waited all of one day to leave. He'd waited until almost the very moment I'd regained consciousness to tell me his decision. To spring his abandonment on me while I'd barely been able to handle being awake. Honestly, though, after seeing everything we'd seen, I was surprised he'd waited at all. I was surprised he hadn't just left me while I was unconscious. It would've been easier that way. For him.

This time, as Caleb stood next to my cot in the medical area, his face was a cold and empty void, so unlike any of the expressions I'd seen on it in the year he'd lived in Dagmar. And I remembered how it'd scared me. We watched in silence as he explained to me that it'd been a mistake to fall in love with me. That he regretted it. He regretted our love. That it weakened him, which was unacceptable. And he told me that he was leaving. Now. That he'd do his best to forget me and forget that I'd ever been in his life. How he hoped I'd do the same for him. My gut clenched and tears stung the corners of my eyes as I watched my younger face fill with shock, disbelief, and deep hurt as he spoke. But I could barely do anything to respond to his words. I was too weak to argue or fight for him to stay. I was still healing from almost dying the day before. And Caleb didn't leave any room for my words.

Once his speech was finished, he backed slowly away from me, gazing at my heartbroken face one last time, before turning and leaving the room. He grabbed his packed bag from the floor outside the door, slung it across his body, and walked toward the edge of town. When he reached it, he paused and looked back for a couple seconds. The briefest flash of uncertainty crossed his face as he stared at the medical building I was still lying in, but the cold, stubborn emptiness descended quickly again. And he determinedly faced forward, hiked up his bag, and firmly strode away. The image faded and the fire returned to shifting, imageless flames.

There was silence for a while. Without being able to see Caleb, I had no idea what emotions he was currently feeling. No idea what seeing all of this play out in front of him was doing to him. It'd been uncomfortable for me, but significantly less so now that I'd spent time processing what'd happened and had moved on in so many areas of my life. I had no idea how it'd hit him, though, since he'd worked his hardest to never have to deal with the fallout of his actions.

Finally, I heard a deep sigh from the other side of the fire. A resigned giving up and giving in. "It wants me to explain who that man was to me, and how what happened to him relates to . . . to my decision to leave Dagmar . . . and Terah . . . behind."

Matt and Damian both glanced at me—Matt worried, Damian assessing—both looking for my reaction. But once again, I refused to show any emotion. I just tightened my grip on Gabriel's hand. Nothing Caleb could reveal now would ever be worse than the actual experience of him leaving all those years ago, so at this point, I was just waiting for the explanation to be over. I got the impression that Caleb's reasons for leaving had been more complex than I'd known at the time, but that really didn't change anything for me. Because he'd still said those things to me, he'd still concluded that loving me was a mistake and a weakness, he'd still ambushed me with all this while I was gravely injured, and he'd still left me behind with no warning. No insight would erase or significantly alter any of that for me.

"I was born in a border town to two Light Guardian soldiers," Caleb said, sounding reluctant and closed off. "Both were only twenty-two. They'd grown up in that town and had fallen in love. They'd always wanted to be a part of the warrior faction but decided when they got married that they no longer wanted that. They didn't want to risk being separated due to orders or different assignments, and they wanted to have kids. In the end, they decided to just stay in their town indefinitely, with no rank or status beyond regular soldiers.

"Two years after I was born, the border town was hit with the largest Demon attack it had ever experienced. It completely obliterated the town and killed every single person there, except for me and . . . Mannan. Mannan was around forty at the time and was the best soldier in our town. He was the rare adult there who wasn't a member of the warrior faction. I don't know why he never joined—perhaps he just wasn't ambitious—but he was powerful enough and skilled enough to have had any warrior faction position he wanted. He could've risen through the ranks quicker than anyone. But he never wanted that." Caleb sounded bitter.

"Anyway, he'd known my parents well since they'd grown up with and were trained by him, and he thought it was some kind of sign from the gods that he and I had both survived. He thought his duty was being clearly shown to him. He took me away and found a secluded home for us, far away from any battles or even other Divine towns. The war never touched us there.

"When I was ten, Mannan finally decided we should move from where we'd been living to a small border town. He deeply believed in our obligation as Divines to protect those who couldn't protect themselves and to use our powers for good. He'd decided I was finally ready to start fulfilling that obligation myself, like my parents had done before me. He told me they'd be proud of who I was becoming, and that he was proud of me too. Even though we weren't related by blood, he considered me to be his son. And then he gave me those daggers—heirlooms passed down from his father to him, and now, from him to me.

"We packed up and moved to a small border town a few hours from where we'd been living. Almost a month into our stay, the town experienced a large Demon attack. Mannan had tried to prepare me for battle, but nothing we'd worked on could've really equipped me to deal with a real battle scenario. It was total chaos, destruction, carnage, and fear. I'd barely seen blood before that day. I was too overwhelmed, and it made me a liability. An easy target. And it resulted in Mannan sacrificing himself to save me."

Caleb let out a slow breath.

"He was the one person I knew, the one person I trusted, the only parent I remembered, and the only person I loved. But he was too torn apart for me to heal on my own, so I turned to the other soldiers for help. I needed more power. A better healer. I needed adults to take charge of the situation and help save his life. And I thought, surely, they'd help save him after how hard he'd worked since moving there and how hard he'd fought in battle thus far. He was always kind and caring to everyone. He would've helped any of them in a heartbeat. But they just looked at us with complete disinterest and didn't bother. They had no care or empathy. They just let him die. Just as they would've let me die. We were nothing to them, and we had no rank or other pull to *make* them care about us. We had nothing to make them acknowledge our humanity and worth.

"My heart broke for the first time as I watched Mannan dying, and I felt this overwhelming rage at him for taking us away from our perfect lives and bringing us to this town in the first place. And I was so angry that he'd saved me at the expense of himself and left me alone in the world. I lost control and demanded to know why he'd wasted his life just for mine. Why he'd been so irrational and hadn't found a different, better way other than using his body as a shield. But he just smiled at me and told me that he loved me. And then he died."

Caleb paused for an extended moment. I wondered if he was wrestling with his emotions—trying to subdue them again.

"After his death, I was furious at . . . everyone. At him, myself, my parents, every person in that horrible town. And in that moment, I realized things I'd never realized before: that love makes people act irrationally and not in their own best interests, that love is painful and the loss of someone you love can tear you apart far deeper than I'd thought possible, and that rank and importance had the power to save, if you were smart enough and skillful enough to go for it.

"I thought about my parents—how their love for each other had made them irrationally give up on their dreams and ambitions to stay, rank-less and unimportant, in a small town only to die young without accomplishing much. I thought about how Mannan had foregone his chance to obtain a high-ranking position in order to stay a lowly soldier in a small border town. How, even after the town was destroyed, he didn't try to better his position in life. Instead, he gave up all personal opportunities to raise me, because love had made him feel beholden to my dead parents and to me. And then his love for me had made him act irrationally, sacrificing himself instead of trying to find a way to intervene that we could've both survived. Love made them all foolish and weak. Love led them to waste their lives and die before they should have. And the devastation I felt when Mannan was dying told me that I'd succumbed to the same irrationality and weakness. Because I loved him.

"That's when I realized I didn't have to have an ending like theirs. I could change. I could break that cycle of meaningless death and *make* my life matter. I could ensure it meant something. That *I* meant something. I wouldn't have to die unknown and alone. I decided right then to leave and devote myself to training so I could do what none of them had—join the warrior faction and rise through the ranks until no one could ignore me. Until I knew my life would amount to something, and I'd have the benefits of notoriety and protection.

"I packed up and left the town behind. And I went on like that for years. I entered a new town, learned as much as I could, then left when there was nothing more I could gain there. I kept moving to larger and larger border towns, convinced that, if I could survive the most horrible places and become the best fighter there, I'd have a decent shot at getting a high-ranking warrior faction position when I came of age. And it was all going to plan until I got to Dagmar.

"Everyone knew it was the biggest and most attacked border town in the country, so I'd saved it until I was sure my fighting skills were indisputably at warrior faction levels. My plan was to work hard, make a name for myself there, and hopefully make some connection that would push me closer to my goal. But almost the second I got there I . . . saw Terah.

I sighed heavily, wishing this was over. Gabriel sent me a commiserating look.

"In front of me was this small, ferocious girl taking on a group of men twice her size and completely kicking their asses. She fought rough in a way that not a lot of other people fought in training, and she clearly didn't hold anything back. It was refreshing. It reminded me of me. And it was clear that she truly didn't give a shit that those guys were pissed at her for being better. She and her skills stood on their own. She was mesmerizing to watch. I was immediately struck by how skilled, powerful, and . . ." he cleared his throat, "beautiful she was. Despite everything I already knew about attachment and why I needed to avoid it, it was impossible for me at the time to resist engaging with her.

"She was the first person in a while to actually challenge me in a fight, even though I ultimately won. And I saw the same fierce determination and stubbornness in her that had guided me for years. Something in all that made me want to stay near her. Train with her. Spend time with her. To help her achieve her goals too. I had no idea where those feelings were coming from, but I didn't resist them too hard in the moment. I was . . . too drawn to her."

Caleb paused and cleared his throat again, clearly uncomfortable.

"From that moment on, we trained together, and I taught her techniques I'd learned in other border towns, while she challenged my strength, stamina, and persistence. She learned so fast, and it pushed me like I hadn't been pushed in any other border town. But I also found myself developing feelings for her pretty quickly, and, without thinking too much about it, I let myself act on those feelings. I vaguely rationalized it with myself by telling myself that our relationship didn't have to be deep or long-lasting. I convinced myself that I wouldn't be putting myself in the exact position I'd been trying for years to escape and avoid.

"But I . . . fell pretty hard for her." He spoke more quietly now, almost like he was hoping we couldn't hear him anymore. "And I opened up to her in a way that I hadn't been open since Mannan was alive. I pushed her to open up to me too. I pushed her to accept me and my feelings. I wanted to be with her so unbelievably badly, probably because I'd cut myself off from every other person for five years, and she was the first person I was letting myself connect with even a little in all that time. And I could see her slowly giving in and developing feelings for me, too, even though she'd been initially closed off as well. So, just over a month after I got there, we were officially together. And for that year I was a happy fool. But I was even more foolish for not confronting what it would mean to be in love. The universe eventually fixed that for me, though, and forced me to confront all that with an enormous Demon attack.

"It was the day that I finally fully told Terah how I felt, where I fully expressed how much I . . . loved her . . . that the sirens went off. I was paralyzed with fear at the thought of Terah getting hurt or dying in battle. I was terrified of losing the only other person that I'd ever loved besides Mannan. Obviously, we'd fought Demons together countless times, but something had shifted for me after openly acknowledging—to her and myself—how much I really loved her. I was already getting more irrational. I felt strongly that I wouldn't be able to fight if she was there and I was worried, so I begged her to stay in the tent and sit this fight out.

"I ran off to battle, but it became clear very quickly that we were outnumbered and outpowered. I knew we needed her there, but at that point, I would've rather died than have her be in harm's way—another irrational thought. But Terah showed up anyway and joined the fight. But I'd been right earlier—I was distracted with her there. All I could do was worry and think about all the ways that this could go badly for her. I was terrified, and it made me less focused. Sloppy in a way I hadn't been since my first Demon battle.

"Terah defeated the Demon, but got seriously injured in the process, and all my fears were suddenly realized. I was torn apart again as I saw her dying, and I felt my heart breaking like it had when Mannan had died. The fear and pain stripped away all rational thought, and I knew, if Terah hadn't already killed the Demon, I would've done something completely reckless in retaliation for injuring her. Something that would've probably led to my death.

"It was while she was being carried away to the medical area that it hit me. I'd just proven true everything I'd concluded about love almost six years earlier. My love for Terah had distracted me from my warrior faction goals and had also seriously distracted me in battle. It had made me an easier target. Less capable. I would've thrown everything away for her. I would've died a meaningless death for her, like my parents and Mannan had done for love before me. And seeing her suffer like that had completely ripped me apart. I didn't think I could survive feeling that way again. Love had once again weakened me, devastated me, and pushed me away from the path I was meant to take. The path I *wanted* to take. So . . . I finally came to my senses. I had to leave her, love, and Dagmar behind. I decided to leave and find a different border town. To start over again."

He paused, and I heard him shifting on the other side of the fire. Almost like he was pacing.

"I knew she loved me back," he continued quietly. "And I knew she'd fight me on this if I waited until she was healed to tell her. I wasn't sure I'd have it in me to refuse or resist her if that happened. But I also couldn't bring myself to leave without talking to her one last time—another weakness. I waited a day. Just long enough for her to wake up, but immediate enough that she was still too weak and injured to challenge my decision. Then I left Dagmar behind. It was the hardest thing I'd ever done, but I knew I had to do it to save myself. I needed to ensure that Mannan's sacrifice of his life for mine wasn't in vain. That all my hard work wasn't in vain. I realized in war, you have to make the hardest choices, and in the end, I had to choose myself over Terah."

Gabriel couldn't suppress an angry scoff, his expression dark and disgusted. I glanced up at his face, a small smile forming on my own. Having him here made watching and listening to this less painful. He glanced down at me, and I saw the distress on my behalf in his eyes. My smile broadened. I wished I could tell him that this wasn't hurting me the way it used to, even a few months ago. Instead of a fresh, open wound, reliving this felt like an irritating sting—like the throbbing aftershocks of hitting your knee on a table. Unpleasant, but not really painful. More jarring than anything else.

I pressed a kiss to Gabriel's shoulder and watched as his gaze flitted over my face, reading my expression. It warmed as he saw I was okay. He wrapped his arm around my shoulders and pulled me against his side, wordlessly telling me that he'd never hurt me like Caleb had. I smiled again, looking back at the flames. I already knew he wouldn't. Gabriel, unlike anyone before him, had my complete trust.

"I had to choose myself to ensure my own survival," Caleb continued, "because I knew no one else would save me." He sounded like he was trying to convince someone. Himself? Me? "It was a lesson burned into me when I was ten, but I've carried it with me since then. I made a new life for myself in Glenhaven, where I lived until I came here. I never thought I'd see Terah again, and I never thought I'd have to face all the consequences of leaving her behind. Obviously, the universe had other plans," he concluded, his voice trailing off in a bitter murmur.

He sighed deeply and the fire pulsed. He'd finally finished revealing all that the room wanted him to reveal.

A moment later, Caleb emerged from the fire and stepped off the platform. His body was tense, and he wouldn't look at me. He just went and stood near Damian, his expression blank and cold as he stared at the heavy door blocking our way. I hadn't really expected him to learn anything from this test, or to apologize. That wasn't his style. But a spark of irritation lit inside my chest anyway.

I looked at the faces around me as the fire behind us dimmed little by little. Matt, who'd chosen to leave me behind, lie to me, and never visit, even while knowing I had no one else and was in constant danger. Caleb, who'd forcefully shoved himself into my life because of how badly he'd needed connection, only to abandon me when he'd finally succeeded in making himself invaluable to me. Damian, whose life had been a fucking horror show, and who carried the fallout of that around him like a dark, mysterious, untrustworthy shroud. The others were similarly looking around. Eyeing each other. We'd seen a lot about each other in this room, and I could see that there'd be consequences from that. Trust was shaken. Feelings were hurt. Guilt was stirred. Pain and trauma were forcefully pulled forward then divulged without our consent. And it would only make it harder for us to work together moving forward.

"For a god who's supposed to focus on truth and virtue," I murmured to Gabriel, "this room seems to have created a shit ton of conflict between all of us now. How is that representative of this god?"

Gabriel frowned in thought. "Well . . . I think we need to remember who made this room."

I tilted my head, frowning.

"This wasn't a room designed by the god," he whispered. "It was designed by Divines. It's what that specific group of Divines' conceptions were of these gods, further influenced and warped by the fact that they were using those conceptions toward a particular end: as a trap and a protective measure for the book."

"That's true." I worried my lower lip with my teeth. "I hope it doesn't make it impossible for us to get through the last test, though." I looked pointedly around at the others—at their wary, distrustful, and distressed expressions. Gabriel sighed and nodded, silently agreeing.

The fire behind us finally extinguished and plunged us into darkness again. Our remaining powers streamed out of the platform and through the symbols on the floor under our feet until they reached the door. They were much dimmer now than they'd been when we'd entered the first room. Only a small amount remained for the last test. I desperately hoped that meant it wouldn't be as long and extreme.

With a screech of stone on stone, the door lurched as our powers filled the final symbol carved into its surface. It groaned—a deep, ominous howl —as the large stone slab dragged slowly across the floor, revealing yet another dark opening. Hopefully to the final room. The final test.

24

SYNERGY

THE DOOR FINALLY GROUND TO A HALT, AND WE WALKED SLOWLY toward the opening as a group. But it wasn't a normal doorway like the others had been. This looked like a tunnel. Carved to be the same height and width as the door, the tunnel extended out in front of us as far as we could see, melting into complete darkness. Ominous. Claustrophobic. Like a tomb.

"Shit." Caleb's whisper was more to himself than anyone else. He looked more antsy than he had so far during this entire ordeal, which was saying something.

"We should go through it quickly." Matt's voice betrayed some of his own anxiety as he paused in front of the opening. "Before we completely run out of light."

He glanced at me before moving forward, his gaze searching. Vulnerable. Almost like he wanted my approval. Or my absolution. I broke eye contact with him, my jaw clenching, and stared into the darkness pooling on the other side of the door. I didn't want to interact with him right now. I was too emotionally and physically exhausted, not to mention injured.

Matt sighed and turned back around. "Let's go." His voice was darker now. Edged with anger.

I knew he was upset that there was a chasm between us once again. I wished he could see he was the one whose decisions kept putting it there. He was the one who'd been willing to sacrifice our relationship so he could go off on his own and experience something different. He'd only remembered what we'd meant to each other again, treated me like family and acted on his love for me again, when I'd conveniently reappeared where he'd already decided to be. That never would've happened if I hadn't decided to attend the Academy. Even now, we'd still be apart, separated by the great physical and emotional distance *he'd* put there. And I was angrier about it all now than I'd ever been, because I could finally fully see the extent to which it'd all been his choice.

Matt roughly pulled a dagger from his waistband and walked purposefully through the doorway, his shoulders stiff. The rest of us pulled our weapons as well and followed quickly behind him, pushing into the eerie darkness until it swallowed us up. The light from the previous room barely reached ten feet past the door, and we quickly found ourselves walking through the inky darkness, hands braced against the wall to help guide us forward. I vaguely heard the heavy stone door sliding back into place far behind us, but I tried to push that from my mind. I didn't want to think about being trapped in here, especially now that it felt like the walls were closing in around us, burying us alive.

I eventually saw the faint glow of our powers racing through the stones at our feet, then rushing into the darkness ahead of us. We sped up, trying to follow them before the light was gone. It vanished suddenly, not too far ahead. That had to mean the tunnel was coming to an end. Or that it curved or dropped off.

The group slowed, and we crept along the rest of the tunnel, fingers sliding tentatively over the roughly hewn stone walls, trying to keep our footing. Trying to sense any changes to our surroundings.

"The wall just ended," Matt murmured, only a few steps ahead of us. "Let me check it out before you all come in."

The group slowed and waited, listening as Matt's footsteps suddenly echoed in a way they hadn't in the tunnel.

"It's a large, circular room." Matt's shoes scraped against stone as he turned and looked around. "The powers are glowing faintly around the walls. It's difficult to see what else is in here, but it looks safe for you all to come in."

The rest of us stepped carefully into the room and fanned out, squinting, trying to see what lay around us. There was barely any light at all—I could see the others now, but not in any detail. They looked more like shadows than people. Our remaining powers were glowing in what looked like the fourth and final symbol from the altar, carved hundreds of times into the stone walls around the circumference of the large, circular room. But there wasn't enough light for us to make out what was above or around us. Everything just melted into darkness.

It took a minute for anything to happen. But the powers finally moved, half traveling toward the floor while the other half merged into a large carving of the symbol in the wall before traveling quickly upward through a line of identical carvings, eventually disappearing into the darkness far above. My fingers tightened around my daggers. This room must not have a ceiling like the others. At least not one that was anywhere near us. That was . . . troubling.

The powers that'd traveled to the floor vanished, but a moment later, fire burst from the ground and spread around the circumference of the room, circling us, and bathing us with intense heat. I squinted against the sudden brightness and stepped back. The flames shot at least fifteen feet into the air and continued to sustain that height. We were completely walled in by it.

I turned and quickly looked around the room again. It was large—maybe forty feet in diameter—and at the very center sat a sizable bronze anvil standing over four feet high and six feet long with thick, lengthy chains attached to it, one longer than the rest. I looked up and saw the walls surrounding us continued upward for at least two hundred feet. Maybe more. It was hard to see that far in the dark, even with the fire, but it almost seemed like . . . we were in a pit.

I turned and walked toward the anvil slowly. It wasn't glowing like the objects in the other rooms had, but it was the only thing in here. Surely, we needed to interact with it somehow in order to get out. I glanced up at the walls again, dread churning in my stomach. There wasn't any other door forward like in the other rooms. No other carvings or giant slabs of stone. I wondered if we'd have to somehow get to the top of the walls in order to move on, but I had no idea how we'd do that with the fire creating such a tall barrier.

I reached forward tentatively and touched the anvil with the tips of my fingers as the men watched. But nothing happened.

I turned to look at Gabriel, frowning. "What is this? What're we supposed to do?"

Gabriel's expression was uneasy as he looked at the walls towering into blackness above us, his body tense. I glanced at Damian and saw he was staring at the large anvil in the center of the room, his expression similar to Gabriel's. I had a feeling they knew or at least suspected what was going on, but neither wanted to break it to the rest of us.

Finally, though, Gabriel let out a deep sigh and turned back to me. "I wasn't initially sure, just from the symbol, but it looks like this room is supposed to represent Tartarus—the ancient Greek god of the deep abyss, also represented as a giant pit where other gods were imprisoned."

I glanced at Damian. His expression had turned enigmatic, but he didn't bother contradicting Gabriel, so I assumed he agreed. I stared between them in silence for a long moment.

"A prison." I looked up at the walls again. "Does that mean we have to somehow climb out of here?"

"How can we?" Caleb burst out, angrily, his nerves ratcheting up again. "The fire goes up too high, we have nothing to climb with, and the walls are too smooth. There has to be another way out."

I sheathed my daggers and walked back to the anvil, then crouched to examine it like I'd examined the altar in the chapel. I looked and felt for any abnormalities. Any symbols. Anything to give us a clue about how to move forward. I ran my fingers over the cool metal feeling for any ridges or carvings. Nothing. I stood again and shoved the anvil with all my strength, trying to see if I could move it. It didn't budge. Not even a little. Matt and Gabriel came over and we pushed against it together, but it still didn't move.

"Maybe we should check the chains too? Just in case?"

Matt and Gabriel nodded, and we each crouched at a different chain to check. Caleb came over and knelt too, grabbing one of the shorter chains and looking it over. Damian didn't help—he just stood there, arms crossed over his chest, looking at the trail of symbols that climbed the wall. He seemed lost in thought.

It only took a couple minutes to ascertain there was nothing significant to be found on the chains, so we all turned toward the walls again. It seemed like our only way out. I wasn't sure how, though. Caleb had been right when he'd scoffed at the idea. It didn't seem possible, even if we figured out how to bypass the fire.

I walked as close as I could to the wall without burning myself, and squinted at the line of ascending symbols, trying to see how deep they cut into the stone. If they could maybe serve as a climbing surface.

"They're too shallow to offer good enough foot or fingerholds," Damian murmured, coming to stand next to me. "We'd fall if we tried going that way. Even if we took off our shoes."

549

I frowned. He was right about the carvings, but I knew there had to be a way. I shifted my focus from the symbols to the stones themselves. They were smooth, but they weren't perfectly flush with each other. There were thin gaps between all the stones in my sightline, almost like the mortar holding them together hadn't been spread all the way to the front of each stone. It'd be a gamble—I didn't know if the spaces would exist or be consistent all the way up—but it might be our only shot.

"Look at the spaces between the stones," I murmured back.

"The cracks are even smaller than the symbols," Damian's tone bordered on condescending. "How would that help us at all?"

I pulled out my daggers, smiling ruefully at him. "Think these would fit?"

Damian's eyes widened as he finally saw what I was suggesting. "Possibly. Though I'm not sure how deep we'd be able to get those in the cracks. If it's only an inch or so, I doubt the weapons would hold our weight."

I shrugged. "Only one way to find out. Unless you have a better idea."

Damian pressed his mouth into a straight line. It was clear that he didn't.

"It's high, though," he finally said, looking back at the wall appraisingly. "Think your strength would hold for that long? It would be all in your arms, and you're injured. As is Caleb."

I shrugged again, trying to keep my expression dispassionate. But I was concerned about that too.

"Only one way to find out," I said again. "I could die falling or I could die trapped in here. I'd rather die at least trying to escape."

Damian observed me shrewdly for a moment before turning to the rest of the group who'd slowly walked over to join us.

"Terah thinks we might be able to climb out of here using our weapons as climbing implements between the stones. What do you all think of that?"

Gabriel, Matt, and Caleb all pulled their weapons and examined them, then squinted at the stone wall, trying to determine whether the metal was thin enough.

"It's . . . possible," Matt finally murmured, "though I don't know how we'd all get over the fire."

I bit the inside of my cheek. That *was* a problem. There was nothing in the room that could help us bypass the wall of flames. Even if we could've moved the anvil, it wasn't tall enough to help us.

"We could lift someone up," Gabriel suggested, considering the flames. "It would take maybe two of us standing on each other to bypass the flames to get a third person past them, but it might be possible."

I turned to look at him. "But not everyone would be able to climb up, then. Two people would have to stay down here, which isn't acceptable." I didn't like where this was going. I sure as hell wouldn't leave him behind.

Gabriel met my gaze for a moment, before looking down, his shoulders tense. I knew he wanted to make sure I got out of here, but he should know better than to think I'd just leave if he couldn't come too.

Matt turned and walked back to the anvil, scrutinizing it. "When we first entered the room, half of the remaining powers traveled to the top of the wall, which means that there's probably another step to this challenge. Something more to face. Perhaps the next step will make it more possible for the rest of us to get out."

He bent and lifted the one long chain on the anvil. It had to be at least forty feet long fully stretched out.

"Maybe something up there will explain how the rest of us can use this." He dropped the chain and shoved to his feet. "It seems like our best way forward."

"Do we just send up one person and have them report back on what they find?" Caleb asked, shoving his long hair back over his head.

"That's probably best," Matt replied. "At least then, if we discover it wasn't what we were supposed to do, we've avoided having more people needlessly expend that amount of energy."

"How do we decide who gets to go up, then?" Caleb asked.

"Terah should go," Damian said.

The group turned to look at him. I almost wondered if he was joking—he hadn't seemed impressed with my earlier assertion that I could make it. But Damian didn't look like he was joking. He looked calmly back at us, his cool and disinterested mask back on.

"It's the most practical option," he said evenly. "She's the smallest and lightest, so we'll be able to lift her over the fire the easiest, and she won't have to pull as much weight up the wall with her, which means she won't get tired as quickly, and her daggers will probably hold her weight, whereas ours might bend or break."

"But she's injured," Matt said, glancing at my blood encrusted arm and the wet bandages around the wound—signs that the bleeding had slowed but not stopped.

Damian shrugged. "So are Caleb and Gabriel, and they're much larger than her. Besides, she's already told me she thinks she can make it."

They all turned to look at me, and I just shrugged.

"I probably can. It'd help if we could rewrap my arm, though." I glanced down at the bandage. I needed something clean and more tightly wrapped. I also needed to take off some of my blood-soaked layers—they weren't helping me anymore and would only weigh me down.

"Do you have any more gauze?" I asked, glancing at Matt.

He shook his head, his expression stormy with worry. "No, we went through all of it, and I don't have anything else that would work like it."

"Here." Gabriel pulled off his backpack, cut the now-dry gauze off his chest, and began stripping off his outer layers. "We can use my shirt. It has less blood on it than any of yours," he added, his gaze sweeping over my saturated clothes.

I pulled off my backpack and dropped it on the floor before grabbing my dagger and slicing through the wet gauze on my arm. Then I stripped down to my bottom layer—a black tank top that was thankfully free from blood.

Gabriel used his dagger to slice his shirt, then tore it into one long strip. He walked over and took my upper arm in his hand, examining the wound. I glanced down at it—it was swollen and angry looking, only partially crusted over with the beginnings of a scab, and it was still slowly oozing blood from one side. Gabriel swallowed as he tried to keep his expression calm and neutral.

"It's deeper than I thought it was," he murmured, finally meeting my gaze. The worry there was intense, but I could see he was trying not to dump it all on me. "Are you sure you can climb with it like that?"

"Yes." I said it calmly, firmly. I needed to believe that I could do it, otherwise I really wouldn't stand a chance. And I needed him to believe it, too, or the worry would torture him. Would it be painful? Definitely. But I could handle pain. And to get us out? To keep him safe? I could do it. He searched my expression silently for a few moments, before finally nodding.

He didn't say anything more. He just focused on wrapping my arm tightly with the scraps of his shirt.

Matt stared at the wall appraisingly. "The fire looks like it's at least fifteen feet high. But, if we can stand two of us on top of each other like Gabriel said, with the other two bracing the person on the bottom, we can boost Terah up and hopefully she can reach far enough past the flames to start climbing without getting burned."

"It's risky," Caleb murmured, almost to himself, looking at how high the flames reached up the wall. He glanced at me, worry flickering in the depths of his eyes, but he looked away quickly. He still didn't want to interact with me. Especially after what I'd seen in the last room.

"Damian and Gabriel should be the ones to lift me up, since they're the tallest," I said as Gabriel finished the binding on my arm with a tight knot. I turned to look at the rest of the group as he started pulling his layers back on. Matt looked slightly annoyed, but it hadn't been a slight on him—he simply wasn't as tall. "Which one of you should be on the bottom?"

Gabriel and Damian turned to look at each other, assessing.

"Damian is stronger," Gabriel finally said. "He'd be better able to handle the weight of two other people."

Damian pursed his lips slightly but nodded. "I can certainly try."

"Okay." I turned to look at Matt and Caleb. "That means Matt should boost me up, since he's the third tallest. Once boosted, Gabriel can help me get on his shoulders. Then Matt can join Caleb in steadying Damian."

Matt and Caleb nodded, each looking reluctant for different reasons.

"And I guess my job is to not die by fire," I murmured. I chewed on my lip as I turned to look at the wall of flames again. It looked so tall. So imposing. One wrong move, one moment of imbalance, and I'd fall into it. And there'd be no recovering from that. "Or by falling."

I shook myself and faced the group again. They were all watching me, worry on their faces.

I took a deep, fortifying sigh. "Okay. I'm ready."

Each of them nodded. Everyone was reserved now—grim and serious.

Damian positioned himself in a sturdy stance three feet from the flames, his feet hip-width apart. Matt stood in front of him in a slightly lunged position, gripping Damian's sides with his hands, steadying him.

"Ready," Damian said.

Caleb and I turned to look at Gabriel. It was time for us to lift him. But Gabriel had a fierce look on his face. He ignored Caleb and reached for me, pulling me into him. His arms wrapped tightly around me, squeezing almost all the air from my lungs.

"Promise me that you'll make it," he said gruffly into my hair, no longer caring that everyone could hear him. I buried my face against the front of his shirt and breathed deeply, inhaling his scent. Telling myself firmly that this wouldn't be the last time I'd smell it. That this wouldn't be the last time he held me.

"I promise."

He cradled me against him for a long moment before I felt him nod. He pulled back slightly and leaned down, brushing his lips slowly over mine. I wanted to melt into him. To forget everything and everyone around us and give into the exhaustion that I felt down to my bones. Instead, I swallowed hard, firming my resolve, and released him.

"Be careful," I murmured, staring up into his vibrant eyes. "And keep your balance."

He swallowed and nodded. "I will. Promise."

He turned and positioned himself between Caleb and me, directly behind Damian, then braced a hand on each of our shoulders. Caleb and I bent and cupped our hands so he could step into them. He stepped up into Caleb's hand, then brought his second foot into mine.

"Lift on the count of three," I said to Caleb. "One, two, three!"

We lifted with all our strength and managed to get Gabriel high enough that he could step onto Damian's shoulders. Damian raised his arms and grabbed Gabriel's legs just in time, steadying him so he wouldn't tip forward, and Matt kept Damian from swaying toward the flames with the momentum of all this movement. In a few breathless moments, Gabriel was standing, relatively stable, on Damian.

I released a relieved breath and moved out of the way so Caleb could start bracing Damian from behind.

"Okay, Terah," Matt said, meeting my eyes. "You're up."

I nodded and walked toward him, steely resolve filling me. There was no room for me to be nervous now. I had a job and I needed to do it.

"Caleb," Matt called, "make sure you're bracing Damian well. I'm about to let go."

"Got it."

Matt released Damian, and I stepped quickly between them, facing Matt. There was a lot in his expression as he looked at me, but for once, he put his feelings to the side.

"You can do this," he said quietly. Firmly. He was in leadership mode now. "It's just another mission. Just another challenge. You're good at those. Remember your strength and pull through no matter what, like always. Okay?"

I nodded. He regarded me for a moment longer before kneeling and cupping his hands to boost me.

"Brace yourself on my shoulders."

I grabbed them firmly and placed my foot in his hands.

"Everyone ready?" he asked.

"Yes," they all replied.

"Okay. One . . . two . . . three."

I stepped up, putting all my weight onto Matt as he lifted, boosting me up past Damian and toward Gabriel. But all I could see was the wall of fire looming in front of me, way closer than it'd seemed on the ground. It was violently flickering—hot and severe.

"You're still a few feet off, so I'm going to lift you the rest of the way onto my shoulders," Gabriel said from close behind me.

"Okay," I breathed. I hated not being able to see how far he was or what he was doing. I wanted to help—to have even a little control over this dangerous situation.

Gabriel's hands closed around my waist. "Brace yourself." I nodded, then Gabriel hoisted me out of Matt's hands and into the air above him. I scrambled for his shoulders with my feet, trying not to unbalance him, then slowly, holding my breath, holding all my muscles taught, I straightened up, my arms extended outward for balance. Gabriel immediately wrapped his hands around my knees, stabilizing me.

My legs shook as I stared at the top few feet of flames in front of me, catching my breath. I tried not to think about how high up I was. *Just don't look down.*

"I'm bracing Damian again," Matt said from below us, "so you can lift her to the wall whenever you're ready."

"I need to grab my daggers first," I said, trying to sound calm. "One second."

I carefully lowered my arms back to my sides, moving slowly, trying to preserve my balance. Then I pulled my daggers from their sheaths. I took a few deep breaths and pulled forward every last ounce of focus and strength I had left. This next part would be hard. Painful. But I knew I could do it. I *had* to do it.

"Okay. I'm ready."

Gabriel's hands slid slowly, carefully, from my knees to my ankles.

"On the count of three again," he said quietly. He counted, then hoisted me by the ankles with a grunt of effort.

My heart dropped through my stomach as I tilted toward the wall, but I shoved down the fear and concentrated on finding the nearest cracks between the stones above me. I reached up, dug my daggers as deeply as I could into the cracks, then pushed free of Gabriel's hands.

"Are you okay?" I called. I needed to make sure I hadn't unbalanced them.

"We're fine," Gabriel said quickly. He sounded winded. "You?"

"I'm fine." I braced my feet against the stones, the fire only half a foot beneath me. The heat was starting to burn my soles. I needed to move. Now.

With a grunt of effort, I pulled myself up purely with the strength of my arms. When my chest was level with the daggers, I braced my feet against the wall again, pulled one dagger free, then plunged it into another crack higher up. Then I pulled my lower dagger free, pulled myself up to the higher dagger, then plunged the free dagger even higher. I repeated this movement over and over, slowly beginning to ascend the wall.

I had to block out all other thought as I climbed. I had to ignore all the sounds of the men below me extricating themselves from the precarious position they'd been in. The climb was so difficult, and I was already so tired. If I thought about them now, or worried about their safety, I'd fall. I had to trust in their capabilities and believe they'd be fine.

I tried to put aside thoughts of time, distance, and height as I climbed, instead focusing all my concentration on each movement. Brace, stab, lift, pull. Brace, stab, lift, pull. My hands shook from gripping my daggers so tightly, and my upper arms burned with pain. I'd never had to do this many pull-ups in a row before. Especially after multiple battles and with no sleep or divine power to fortify me. But I shoved aside the pain and ignored the shaking. If I wanted to stop, I'd have to keep climbing. I thought instead about the relief I'd feel when I made it to the top. This was the last test. I could do this.

Brace, stab, lift, pull. Brace, stab, lift, pull. Concentrate. Push through. Breathe. Again. Keep going.

Several minutes later, searing pain, different from my screaming muscles, shot through my upper arm as I dragged myself toward my higher dagger once again. A sharp ripping, followed by a warm rush.

"Shit."

I didn't need to look to know what'd happened. Despite the new bandage, I'd finally managed to rip open the flimsy scab over my injury, and fresh blood was now pouring out, spurred on by the heavy use of my arm muscles. I could feel the blood quickly saturating the strips of Gabriel's shirt and pouring in rivulets down my skin. *Damnit.* It was another thing I'd have to think about now. I'd have to keep that arm positioned above my shoulder at all times, or the blood would drip down to the hand clutching my dagger. And the last thing I needed was a slippery handle. I'd definitely fall.

With renewed urgency, I started climbing again, as quickly as I possibly could without being reckless. Blood dripped freely from my arm to the fire and ground below me and was quickly saturating the chest and shoulder of my tank top. My whole upper arm felt wet. I hazarded a quick glance up for the first time since I'd started climbing, trying to see how much further I had to go. I'd known that I was making decent progress just based on how much dimmer it was getting around me—how much further I was from the fire. I was starting to have to squint now to see the minute cracks between the stones above me.

"Thank the fucking gods," I whispered as I looked back at the wall and kept climbing. I was only about fifteen feet from the top. I could do that. That was manageable.

Brace, stab, lift, pull. My arms were shaking violently now, and my breath was coming in gasps. *Come on, you're so close.* Brace, stab, lift, pull. Brace, stab, lift . . . I dropped my dagger on the ledge and grabbed the top of the wall. *Finally.* I pulled my other dagger free and dropped it on the ledge as well, then grasped the top of the wall with that hand. Then I took a deep breath and lifted one last time, propelling myself over the top.

I collapsed onto solid stone with a dry sob I was grateful no one else could hear. The pain in my body was unbelievable. I just laid there, legs still dangling over the edge of the wall, trying to catch my breath and slow the manic pounding of my heart. My hands were numb, and I could feel my pulse throbbing in the injury in my arm. I just hoped I wasn't actually bleeding out this time. Not yet. I still had work to do. I still had to figure out how to get the others out.

It was Gabriel's voice that finally cut through the thick haze of pain and exhaustion and jolted me into action again. It was the tone of it— worried with a hint of frantic.

I finally pushed myself into a sitting position and pulled my legs onto solid ground. I glanced briefly around me before leaning over the edge of the pit.

"I'm okay," I called down to them. "Just drained. Sorry, I needed a few minutes to recover."

I saw Gabriel heave a sigh of relief as he scrubbed his hand down his face, shaking his head slightly. He was stressed. Matt sagged against the anvil in relief. Caleb was pacing, pinching the bridge of his nose between his fingers.

"What do you see up there?" Damian asked. He seemed to be the only one who'd kept his calm.

I looked around again, squinting. I was sitting on a large expanse of smooth stone that bordered this side of the pit. It extended several feet past the pit's forty-foot diameter and the landing was about twenty feet from the ledge to the wall. While a flat ledge encircled the entire deep cavity, this was the only side that had substantial ground to stand on. Thank the gods we'd chosen to climb up this side.

I noticed another anvil on the landing with me, a little smaller than the one below, sitting pressed against the wall furthest from the pit. The anvil had one long chain attached to it, and unlike the anvil below, it was glowing with the remainder of our powers. Along the same wall, about ten feet to the right, was a door. Our way out.

I pushed to my feet, groaning slightly, and walked over to the glowing anvil. The chain attached to it was thick and heavy looking, like the ones below. This chain, however, was much longer than even the longest chain in the pit. It sat in a large coil, reaching almost to my shoulders. Squinting at the chain in the dim glow of the pulsing powers, I noticed that the very end of it concluded in a large hook. Hope bloomed in my chest for the first time since starting this journey.

I walked quickly back to the edge and looked down at the group several hundred feet beneath me. "I think I've found a way for you all to get out."

They tilted their heads to look up at me again, squinting, trying to see me through the dim light near the top of the cavern.

"There's another anvil up here, close to the wall, and it has a giant chain attached to it with a hook on the end. It must attach to the longer chain down there. If the connection is taut, it should let you pass over the fire and climb out without getting burnt."

"So, it's not long enough to reach the ground?" Matt asked, looking worried. I knew why.

"No. Definitely not long enough for that. It means someone else will have to climb part of the wall while carrying the longer chain and connect it to the end of this chain once I let it down."

Matt swore while the rest of the group groaned. They'd have to repeat the process of getting me over the fire and onto the wall with someone else, and this time, they'd have one less person to ensure their stability. They turned and started talking to each other, but too low for me to hear this time. I waited, the *drip, drip* of blood trickling from my arm onto the smooth stone at my feet—the only sound marring the silence up here.

Finally, Matt glanced up again. "You work on letting down the chain and we'll work out who's going to go and how we're going to do it. It might take us a few minutes."

"Okay," I called back before heading toward the anvil again.

I grabbed the heavy hook at the end of the chain with my blood-free hand and dragged it to the edge of the pit, slowly unraveling it from its large coil. As I moved further from the wall, I felt a pulse travel through the metal pressed to my palm—an ominous vibration—and glanced back at the anvil. The glowing powers contained within it had begun to pulse. *Shit.* If the other rooms had been any indication, that pulsing meant that something else was coming.

I moved more quickly, reaching the edge of the pit and released the end of the chain over the side. It fell a few feet but didn't pull the rest of the chain down with it like I'd hoped. Scrambling, I pulled the heavy chain as quickly as I could, feeding the hook deeper and deeper into the pit. From my periphery, I saw a hulking form materializing on top of the pulsing anvil, made from the glowing remnants of our powers, but hardening into something infinitely more solid.

"I'm about to have company," I called into the pit. "I got the chain over, so you can start climbing now, but I won't be able to help much."

"What kind of company?" Gabriel called, worry thick in his voice.

"The kind that requires weapons," I yelled, unsheathing my daggers. I heard a screech from behind me and spun around.

My mouth opened in horror as I saw the creature before me, towering above me by at least ten feet. I'd thought, after all my encounters with Demons and their endless, terrifying forms, I'd be immune to the fear that a monstrous being could inspire. Apparently not. The creature in front of me looked almost humanoid—like a woman from its head to its chest—but that's where the similarity ended. From the chest down, the creature was covered in dark, iridescent scales that wrapped around its powerful, almost dragon-like legs that ended in large, clawed feet. From the back of its body sprouted a huge scorpion tail that curved up and over the figure's head, and large black wings, almost like a bat's, erupted from its shoulders. Snakes slithered and hissed around its ankles, coiling tightly around the sinewy muscles.

But most horrifying were the heads. Heads of a variety of animals—snakes, bears, wolves, lions—*bubbled* around the creature's waist, dozens of heads aggressively rearing before melting into the head of a different creature. It looked . . . wrong. Unnatural. It made my stomach lurch. If I'd still had my power, I would've transformed immediately. But, as that wasn't an option right now, I just gritted my teeth and tightened my grip on my daggers. I wished I hadn't bled so much. That I wasn't so tired. That my body didn't hurt so much.

The creature thundered toward me, a scythe appearing in its hands. I widened my stance, making it look like I was going to stand my ground and face the creature head-on. I wanted all its energy and momentum moving forward. As it reached me, I dove to the side, rolling out of its way, and lashed out with my daggers, slicing viciously across its scaly legs. But the scales functioned like heavy armor, and my daggers glanced off them without cutting through or even scratching them. *Damn.* I wouldn't be able to incapacitate it this way.

I rolled to my feet as the creature screeched and spun to face me again, its beautiful face vanishing and transforming into a grotesque mask of demonic rage—more animal than human, now. It came at me again, its thundering footfalls shaking the stones at my feet. It'd expect me to dodge to the side as I had last time, so instead, I threw myself through the creature's legs, summersaulting and swinging my daggers sharply up as I stood, severing the scorpion's tail in a rush of dark goo that sizzled and steamed as it hit the stone.

The creature screamed, and the snakes that'd coiled around its ankles suddenly thudded to the ground and slithered rapidly toward me. I lunged to the side, trying to escape them, and sent my dagger out in an arc that managed to slice off one of the snake's heads. But the other managed to reach me and wrapped itself tightly around my leg before biting into the flesh of my thigh. I swore and quickly sliced it in half with my other dagger. The snake's body fell to the ground. I gritted my teeth as I looked down at the deep puncture marks in my thigh, just starting to seep blood. I hoped the snake hadn't been venomous, but with how this day was going, I knew I couldn't count on that. I quickly bit the handle of my dagger and pulled a clean knife from my belt. In a swift movement, I slashed my thigh in a deep "X" over the snake bite, causing a rush of blood to quickly darken my jeans. It was all I had time to do. I just hoped the quick flow of blood in the opposite direction would be enough to at least slow the spread of any venom until my power returned.

I spun back toward the monster and threw my small knife at its throat. It embedded at the base of its neck, between the clavicle bones. It wouldn't cause the most damage, but I considered every injury I inflicted, every step toward weakening it, a success. The creature released a frustrated, strangled cry and pulled the small knife from its skin, then tossed it to the ground.

Then it ran at me again and swung the scythe in a violent arc toward me. I raised both daggers and blocked the powerful strike, sliding back a few inches from the force of the attack. A shock of pain ran through my injured arm at the impact, and I gritted my teeth to keep my reaction concealed. I couldn't show this creature how weak I currently felt.

I broke away from the scythe and the creature immediately swung at me again. I sidestepped the blow but couldn't completely dodge it, so I raised my daggers again, blocking the strike so the blade wouldn't sink into my shoulder. The weapons collided with bone-jarring force and a screech of metal on metal. My arms shook. I wasn't sure how much longer I'd be able to keep blocking blows like that after everything else I'd had to do with my arms over the last few hours. I broke away before my arms gave out and retreated toward the wall, trying to regather myself.

I studied the creature again as it let out another aggressive cry, blood oozing from the dagger hole in its neck and streaming down its chest and over its scales. I needed to find a weakness. A real one. With my failing strength, it'd become increasingly imperative that I figure out a way to finish this battle as quickly as possible. I'd usually go for beheading, as I did with Demons, but those roiling, snarling animal heads at the creature's waist made getting that close, or trying to climb it to reach its neck, virtually impossible.

With another scream, the creature ran at me before I'd determined what to do next. I managed to duck at the last minute and the scythe narrowly missed me. As the blade traveled barely an inch over my face, I got a good look at the creature's arms. Its *human* arms. Sure, its hands were clawed with sharp talons to match the ones on its feet, but its arms looked as human as mine, and were, at the very least, not covered in armor-like scales. The length of the scythe would keep its arms far enough away from me to prevent major damage, though, so I'd need to deal with that first.

With as much speed and strength as I could muster, I swung my daggers up as the weapon arced past me and brought the blades down on the wooden handle of the scythe. With a crack, the wood splintered beneath my blades, the weapon cleaved in two. The scythe's blade dropped to the ground with a heavy clang, and I kicked it away from us, almost to the edge of the pit. There wasn't enough wooden handle still attached for the creature to use it again. I didn't wait to see the creature's reaction to the destruction of its weapon—I turned and ran to the anvil ten feet behind me and jumped onto it. I needed the added height to reach the creature's arms.

The creature screamed and swept up my small knife from the ground before rushing me again. Even on the anvil, I was decently shorter than it, but without its scythe, it'd have to get much closer to me now. The creature bent as it reached me and swung the blade at my throat. I blocked it with one dagger and quickly swung my other at its thrusting arm, severing its flesh just above its elbow. Its arm and my small knife fell to the ground in a rush of dark blood. The creature screeched and I lunged at its other arm, wanting to take it out too before the creature recovered. But it knew what I wanted, and lifted its arm out of the way, straightening up and crowding me with its horrifying body.

The growling, bubbling heads were level with me, now, and reached out toward me, snapping eagerly. I leaned back as far as I could on the anvil, but I was against the wall, cornered. I tried to use my daggers to fend off all the snapping teeth, but the second my dagger managed to slice off one of the heads, the creature grabbed me around the neck and slammed me into the stone wall behind me, squeezing so tightly that I couldn't draw breath.

A sharp pain tore through my side, and I knew, even though I couldn't see, one of the animal heads had managed to sink its teeth into me. Even though I couldn't breathe or break free, my arms were still free, so I swung my dagger at the space between me and the creature. Uncontrollable tears flooded my eyes as a sharp tug from the teeth pulled at the mangled flesh of my side, but then the bite loosened, and the head fell mercifully to the ground. I'd managed to sever it.

My vision went dark around the edges as the creature continued starving me of oxygen, slamming me back into the wall again in retaliation for my dagger's successful hit. But determination filled me again. The creature was close, and I was still armed. I could do this. I sagged against the stone, closing my eyes briefly, making it look like I was giving up. Losing consciousness. I forced my muscles to go slack for a brief second. Then, lightning fast, I swung one of my daggers at the creature's other arm and severed it before opening my eyes and lunging forward, plunging my other dagger hilt-deep into the creature's heart.

On a startled cry, the creature jerked away from me, taking my dagger with it. I collapsed back against the wall, sucking air desperately into my lungs as the creature's severed arm released me and fell to the ground. My vision cleared, but I was beginning to feel dizzy and unsteady on my feet. I didn't know if it was from exhaustion, all the blood loss and pain, or whether the snake had actually been venomous, but I wasn't going to remain conscious for too much longer. Fortunately, the dagger directly to the heart along with all its other injuries seemed to be affecting the creature more than I'd expected it to. More than the same would ever affect a Demon.

I sank to my knees on top of the anvil and watched as the creature collapsed onto the ground, writing and screeching in pain, my dagger still deep in its heart. Blood from its many injuries was pooling around it now, and it seemed like it'd probably die in another minute or so. *Thank the fucking gods.* I slid off the anvil and pushed shakily to my feet, blood dripping freely from my wounds as I stumbled toward the creature again, knowing I still needed to finish it. I didn't think it could heal like a Demon, but I wasn't going to take any chances.

At that moment, hands appeared over the edge of the pit where the chain was hanging, and with a grunt of effort, Caleb propelled himself over the ledge and onto the landing. He must've been the one they'd sent to connect the chains. As the second smallest and lightest of the group, it made sense. He was breathing hard, and the injury in his shoulder was heavily bleeding again, but he pushed quickly to his feet, his expression wary as he looked quickly around him. He'd known he was climbing toward a battle.

His gaze slid quickly over me and widened as he took in all my injuries. I was pretty much completely covered in my own blood, now. But hey, I thought it was pretty impressive that I was standing at all given everything I'd faced this evening. Caleb's jaw clenched and his expression turned murderous as he spun toward the creature still writhing on the ground.

Without a word, Caleb marched over to where the creature lay dying on the stone and pulled his daggers from their sheaths. With a grunt of effort, he swung them forcefully down and cut the creature's head from its body. The creature twitched a couple times, then fell still. Dead.

Caleb sheathed his daggers, then grabbed mine from the creature's chest before jogging back over to me as I swayed on my feet. Without hesitation, he wrapped his arm around me and supported my weight, then started walking me back to the anvil.

"The others are coming," he murmured. "They weren't too far behind me, so they should be here in a second." I nodded mutely, wincing in pain as we walked.

Caleb sheathed my daggers for me before lowering me onto the anvil. He pulled off his backpack and started stripping out of his layers. I clutched the edge of the anvil as the world swayed around me and watched as Caleb unzipped his backpack and pulled out a bottle of water. Then he pulled a smaller dagger from his waistband and came over to stand in front of my knees.

"I'm going to patch you up a little," he said quickly, no traces of coldness in his voice for once. "Hopefully enough to get you by until you get your power back."

"Okay," I murmured, swaying again. My eyes were on the chain where it dropped over the edge of the pit. I needed to see the moment that Gabriel and Matt emerged unscathed.

Caleb cut away the now-soaked bandage around my upper arm and proceeded to pour water over the wound, cleaning enough of the wet and dried blood from my skin so he could see what he was doing. With a quick slice of his dagger and a deft yank, he tore his long-sleeved shirt into a long strip and began tightly binding my arm again. When that was secured, he knelt in front of me and pushed my torn and bloody tank top up my torso, revealing the deep, oozing bite in my side from the animal head. Caleb let out a stream of swears, his voice gruff, as he examined the wound. Then he pulled me gently to my feet, poured water over the wound, and began wrapping the rest of his shirt tightly around my torso.

I shuddered with pain as he pressed and jostled the deep bite while wrapping it, tears seeping from the corners of my eyes. I dashed them away as quickly as I could, though—I didn't want him, of all people, to see me cry. Caleb bound the wound as well as he could and tied a tight knot over the injury, but it was a bad one, and no amount of binding would keep it contained for long. It would need to be quickly healed once we got out of here.

Finally, Caleb sat me back down and poured the rest of the water over the gashes and snake bite on my thigh. He quickly pulled his T-shirt over his head and ripped it into more bandages. Then he knelt and wrapped the new strips tightly around me, securing the end in a tight knot. I swayed again, half on fire with pain and half completely numb. Caleb straightened up and reached forward to steady me by the shoulders.

"Are you okay?" Worry was thick in his voice. He wasn't being as guarded as usual. I wondered if it was because of worry, exhaustion, or because no one else was around right now.

"Not really." I tried keeping my voice strong and steady. Matter of fact. But my whole body was shaking. "I need to be healed and I'm fucking exhausted."

Caleb nodded, his brow furrowing as he watched me. I wasn't sure what he was thinking. Or feeling. He squeezed my shoulders, trying to be comforting.

"Hopefully that was all of this test," he said quietly, his gaze boring into mine. "We should be able to move forward now. We can grab the book and hopefully get out quickly. And once we get our powers back, we can heal you."

His gaze shifted to my neck as I nodded, and I saw a flash of distress cross his face. He reached a hesitant hand forward and slid his fingertips gently down my skin. Where the creature had strangled me.

"You have horrible bruises," he murmured.

I heard a grunt of effort near the edge of the pit, and quickly turned my head, leaning around Caleb so I could see. Gabriel was holding onto the chain in one hand and was pulling himself over the ledge with the other. He looked exhausted, but otherwise unharmed. A breath of relief whooshed from my lungs.

Caleb stepped back as Gabriel, panting heavily, pushed to his feet and stumbled toward me.

"Terah," he gasped, his gaze sliding over me before quickly glancing at Caleb's shirtless form. His expression grew more worried as he looked back at me, his eyes finding all my bound injuries before flicking to the dead creature behind him. "Gods, I'm so sorry you had to deal with that on your own."

He knelt in front of me and took my hands in his, his gaze searching mine, trying to determine how I was feeling. How hurt I was. I could feel he was trembling from exhaustion. I wanted to throw my arms around him and hug him to me, but I was too injured to do that.

"It's fine," I murmured, squeezing his fingers. "I'm glad you made it up okay." I swayed as the world lurched around me again. *Damnit.* "It'd be cool if we could move forward soon, though." I managed a wry smile. "I could use a healing."

"How bad is it?" Gabriel's voice shook a little as he glanced at my bound torso. Caleb had done a thorough enough job that he couldn't see the wound beneath. I bit the inside of my cheek, not sure what to tell him.

"It's bad," Caleb said matter-of-factly from behind Gabriel. "She's got a huge bite mark in her side, some bad gashes on her thigh, her arm injury was ripped deeper, and she was strangled. Plus, she's lost enough blood to have passed out a while ago. It's a miracle that she hasn't yet."

I tensed, shooting a glare in Caleb's direction, but I knew I had no right to be mad at him. He'd only spoken the truth. And bandaged me. But I didn't like him speaking for me or making me feel any weaker than I already felt.

"Shit." Worry swamped Gabriel's expression. "We need to get you out of here. *Now.*"

We heard a grunt and turned to see Damian pushing over the top of the pit onto the landing. He looked around quickly to make sure there was no imminent danger, then collapsed back on the stone for a few moments, trying to catch his breath.

Gabriel turned back to face me, leaned forward, and pressed his lips to my forehead. Then he pushed to his feet and placed his hands on my shoulders to steady me as I swayed again. "Matt, hurry up. We need to go," he called urgently toward the pit.

Damian sat up and then shoved to his feet. He walked quickly over to us, his gaze assessing.

"I'm . . . coming," Matt finally panted, just below the lip. In another second, I saw his hands emerging, grasping the chain with one hand and grabbing the stone ledge with the other. With a mighty shove, Matt propelled himself over the top and collapsed onto the stone landing, panting. "Shit, that was hard," he breathed heavily.

I heard a sharp rip and glanced behind Gabriel to see Damian tearing into his own long-sleeved shirt, making a bandage for Caleb's shoulder since Caleb had used all his shirts on me.

"I hope the room hurries up," Gabriel muttered darkly. "We have too many injuries to linger here much longer."

Matt shoved to his feet and walked over to us, glancing at Caleb's injury before coming over to me.

He quickly looked me over "How—"

"It's bad," Gabriel gruffly cut him off before he could finish speaking. "We need to move as quickly as we can once the door opens."

Matt looked mildly annoyed at being cut off, but his worry overtook his annoyance as he knelt next to me. Gabriel still held my shoulders steady.

"We'll do that." He carefully assessed my expression. He'd gotten good over the years at telling how much pain I was in and how injured I was, especially as I'd often been reluctant to let people heal me. We'd been so conditioned not to show vulnerability or weakness. But Matt, as my care-taker, had learned to see through that so he could determine when I really needed to be healed, and when I'd probably be fine without external help.

"You look dizzy," he murmured, his hazel eyes holding mine. "Obviously a lot of blood loss and exhaustion."

He squinted a little, and I schooled my expression into as neutral a mask as I could muster. I didn't like him trying to read me like this. He already knew I was injured. Now it just felt like he was trying to prove a point. Like he wanted to prove he still knew me. Like that would fix things between us.

"In pain." His voice softened. He lifted his arm and pressed his wrist against my forehead. "And a fever." His brow furrowed. He glanced at the slain creature on the ground behind him, looking for something, but it was starting to disintegrate—the power that'd created it finally fading into nothingness. Perhaps the snake had been venomous after all.

Suddenly, we were plunged into darkness. The flames at the bottom of the pit had extinguished. I heard Matt push to his feet, and I looked to where I knew the edge of the pit was. Since the powers up here had faded, I assumed the powers that'd sustained the flames would now, hopefully, open the door so we could move forward.

A few moments later, I saw the dim glow of our powers rushing over the side of the pit, following the trail of the god's symbol in the stone. Instead of diverting toward the anvil again, the powers moved straight ahead to the heavy stone door separating us from the book. They filled the carved symbol on its surface and pulsed quickly.

I gritted my teeth and pushed to my feet, trying to ignore all the points of throbbing pain in my body. Gabriel shifted his hold on me, his arm sliding around my back to steady me against him. I felt his muscles tense.

"I know you want to pick me up, but it'd hurt my side less if I walk," I murmured. The thought of the mangled bite in my side getting scrunched up like that made my stomach turn over.

Gabriel sighed, but he shifted his hold a little higher, stabilizing me and taking some of my weight. "Okay. Just let me know if it becomes too much.

I wrapped my uninjured arm around his waist and briefly rested my head against his chest. "I will."

The door slowly opened, the stone heavily scraping across the floor, and the group of us moved toward the dark opening, me limping slightly. It creaked to a halt once the opening was fully revealed, and we moved gingerly to stand just on the other side of the door as we'd done in each prior room. It was impossible to see more than a foot in front of us, so we stood there, clumped together, waiting for the door to slide closed again so that maybe the miniscule remnants of our powers could provide us with some light.

The door took its time closing, but once it did, we were plunged into darkness. This made it even harder to tell up from down in my dizzy state. I tightened my grip around Gabriel's waist, trying to steady myself. Finally, the dimmest flow of powers ebbed from the door and streamed across the wall. In a flash, a single torch burst into flames, providing some dim lighting. I glanced quickly around and saw we were in a small, rectangular stone room. Maybe thirty feet by fifteen feet.

And the room was completely empty.

There were no carvings beyond the line to the torch, no statues, no irregularities. *No book*. Nothing.

We just stood there for a few moments in stunned silence. None of us were sure what to do or say. I wasn't even sure what to think. Confusion swam through my brain, cutting through the pain and exhaustion. Had the book been removed? Had someone in the past few hundred years discovered its hiding place and succeeded in taking it? Had we done all of this for nothing? But . . . that wouldn't make sense. My vision had told me it was here.

I frowned. That wasn't entirely true. My vision had shown me that everyone *else* thought the book was here. It'd shown me that this was where each side planned to send its agents to retrieve it. But it'd never shown me definitive proof that the book was still here.

I sighed heavily, deflating. My knees shook with exhaustion, and I tried to shove down the tears threatening to fall. Had I brought everyone here for nothing? Risked our lives for nothing? Gabriel's arm tightened around me. I glanced up and saw his firm, knowing look. He shook his head, telling me it wasn't my fault. But it was hard to agree when my vision had been responsible for sending us here.

"It doesn't make sense," Matt said, glancing around before glancing at me. "The vision indicated the book was still here. Plus, there were no signs that anyone else has ever made this journey before us. There's not even a place for a book to sit in here. No pedestal or box. Nothing."

I pressed my lips together, guilt filling me. I wasn't sure what to say. I looked around at Damian and Caleb. Damian's fists were clenched tightly at his sides and his jaw looked like it'd fused closed. But he looked deep in thought, not paying attention to us. Caleb looked half furious, half despairing. He took a deep, slow breath.

"How are we even supposed to get out?" he asked quietly, more calmly than I'd expected him to sound.

My eyebrows rose, and I looked around again. He had a point. There should be a way out. There was no way to get back through all the rooms we'd just been through, especially since the rooms had expended almost all the available power. And nothing in here suggested we needed the book to access an exit. There was nothing for the book to interact with—no doors, symbols, or other keys.

"He's right." I limped forward a few steps, trying to get a better look at the walls. "There has to be a way out. There's something about this room we need to figure out. A dead end here doesn't make sense."

I met Caleb's gaze, and he smiled a little, his expression warming in a very un-Caleb-like way. I didn't have it in me to smile back, so I turned quickly and examined the walls again. I gently extricated myself from Gabriel and braced myself against the nearest stone wall. Then I slowly made my way around the room, touching the walls as I moved, carefully examining them for even the slightest anomalies. In a couple minutes, I'd made a full circle and hadn't seen anything that stood out.

I sighed, leaning back against the door that'd led us here, and watched as the others did their own explorations of the room. I worried my bottom lip with my teeth. There had to be a way, just like every step in this process so far. I trailed my gaze over the dimly lit walls, trying to pay close attention to even my most basic observations about the space. That was how I'd found the clue in the chapel.

I noticed the door into the room had deposited us in the middle of one of the long ends of the rectangle. This meant that the opposite wall was the other long end, and the shorter walls were to our right and left. This was dramatically different from the layout of every other room. Maybe there was some significance to that, maybe there wasn't. I also noted the small torch was in the left corner of the wall I was leaning against. I frowned at it. Maybe there was something near it that I hadn't seen?"

I limped over to it, looking more closely at and around it for any clues. I slid my finger down the thin trail of four symbols that'd led our powers to the torch, but it really didn't seem like they were meant to do anything other than light it. I doubted they'd have anything to do with our way out. There were no other symbols or carvings, so I reached up and carefully touched the torch itself. It was made of sturdy wrought iron, smooth, and firmly attached to the wall. It didn't budge at all when I tried to move it. It wasn't a part of some lever or other mechanism that'd open the door. *Damn.*

I turned my back to the wall and leaned my weight against it, thinking again. The world tilted around me, but I shook my head impatiently, trying to settle it. Trying to focus. The room was a rectangle. Like the book. Like the altar.

Like the altar.

I turned my head and looked at the corner of the room across from me. The back left corner from the door into the room. The same corner on which I'd found the carved symbols on the altar far above us. I squinted at it, tilting my head. I knew there were no carvings there, but maybe that wasn't what we were meant to look for this time. Perhaps there was something else we were supposed to notice. I moved my head a little, still examining that corner. There was something about it . . .

I limped forward, still staring at it. There was almost . . . a shimmer to it. A slight distortion, almost too minor to notice in the dim firelight, like looking at something through an especially thick piece of glass. I frowned as I moved closer. It was hard to trust my own perception right now—I was completely drained and fairly dizzy—but I needed to check it out anyway, even if it was nothing.

I finally reached the corner and squinted at it again. Up close, with my body blocking most of the light, I didn't see anything out of the ordinary. It looked just as it had when I'd first walked past it. I stepped to the side, allowing the light to hit the back corner again, and turned my head to examine it. This time, I caught the slight distortion again—something that wasn't quite right.

"Hm."

I stepped in front of it again, and tentatively reached forward to the place where the two walls met—where the distortion seemed to center. It was a place I hadn't bothered touching on my first examination of the room. Instead of feeling cool, hard stone, my fingertips seemed to snag on jelly-like air. But . . . there was nothing there. Nothing to cause such resistance.

On a sharp intake of breath, I snatched my hand back to look at it. But nothing seemed out of the ordinary. There was no substance or any kind of mark on my skin. Frowning, I reached toward the corner again, this time intent on reaching the stone. My fingers sank into the jelly-like air again. This time, I pushed them forward. But instead of making contact with stone, my fingers simply disappeared.

"Holy shit!" I whispered, stepping back and snatching my hand away. My fingers reappeared. I stared at my hand, flabbergasted. "What the hell?"

I stared at the corner, frowning. It was definitely weird but . . . I'd experienced something similar before. Three times, to be exact. Each time I'd crossed through a portal into and out of the Academy's plane. The portals that'd been created by the same Divines who'd created this elaborate hiding place for the book. But the portals I'd seen had looked different from this. More like opaque holes in the middle of reality, not like transparent, largely undetectable sheens. But maybe that was just because this one was much smaller. Or perhaps it was because it didn't connect different planes of reality like the ones around the Academy did.

I reached forward again, just to make sure. My fingers vanished into the mildly rippling air, followed by my wrist and forearm as I pushed forward. A grin spread across my face. This had to be our way out! I was in up to my bicep before I turned my head toward the others, who were still engrossed in their own explorations.

"Hey, I think I found our way out." They all spun to look at me, surprised. "Back left corner, just like the symbols on the altar." I wobbled a little, dizzy, and disappeared up to my shoulder as the men looked around the room, noticing for the first time its shape and significance.

"Oh!" I exclaimed in surprise as I was yanked forward uncontrollably. Half my body was just . . . gone. I felt it pulling, now, almost like the sucking of water down a drain. I probably wasn't meant to linger half-in and half-out of a portal like this. It was trying to transport me all the way through. The suction intensified, and I glanced up quickly, wanting to explain before I vanished. Gabriel jogged toward me, his confusion turning into horror as he realized half my body was gone.

"It's okay," I said quickly. "It's a portal."

I gasped as a wave of nausea hit me, the suction intensifying. I stopped fighting it, and with a sound almost like a slurp, it pulled me from the dimly lit rectangular chamber and deposited me onto another stone floor. I groaned as the violent throbbing of my various injuries intensified.

"Damnit," I whispered. I tried pushing myself up without aggravating the wounds too much, but that seemed like a losing battle. The bite in my side was on fire with pain and my consciousness flickered.

Winded and incredibly dizzy, I managed to push through the agony and shove shakily to my feet. Unfortunately, I was in yet another pitch-black space. I took a few shaky steps, stretching out my hands blindly in the dark. Finally, my fingers brushed against a stone wall, and I sank against it in relief, trying to make room for the others.

A few seconds later, I heard the sliding of shoes over the stone floor, almost like someone had come through at a run.

"Gods," Gabriel gasped, skidding to a halt. "Terah?"

"I'm here. Against the wall."

I heard him move toward me, and I reached out my hand, trying to find him. My fingers brushed his jacket, and I closed my hand around the fabric, pulling him toward me.

"Hey," he murmured as he bumped gently into my front with his.

He wrapped his arms around me, carefully avoiding as many of my injuries as he could. I sighed and pressed my forehead against his chest. I was tired. So tired. So dizzy. My body wanted to sink to the floor and surrender to sleep. I wouldn't be able to sustain consciousness much longer.

Damian came through next, followed by Caleb, then Matt.

"Nice job, Terah," Matt said from somewhere to my left. "I don't think I would've ever noticed such a small portal. We could've been stuck in there forever."

I shrugged but realized too late that no one could see it. "I'm just glad we got out. What are the chances that our remaining powers will travel to this room so we can see where the hell we are?"

"They'd better," Gabriel grumbled, "or we'll be stuck in here forever. With how dark it is, we could be standing right next to the book for all eternity and never know it."

"Just give it a minute," Matt murmured in his practiced calm. But I could hear the exhaustion finally cracking his façade of control.

We waited, the quiet darkness pressing in around us, musty smelling air filling our lungs. Minutes passed in silence, and I felt the last dregs of my endurance leave me. I could hear my heartbeat too loud and fast in my ears, like an incessant drum in my head, and my legs finally gave out. I didn't have much control over it anymore. I leaned weakly back against the wall and slowly slid to the floor. I hardly registered the pain anymore, even as my injuries were tugged and jostled by the motion. I finally reached the ground, more a collapsed heap than a seated person. But there was some relief in not having to hold myself up anymore. My head fell back against the wall as I heard a familiar rushing in my ears, almost like a waterfall. *Shit.* I was going to pass out here.

The ground began to glow around us with very faint light, emanating from hundreds of small carvings of the four symbols that'd led us here. So little of our powers were left that, were there any other light in here at all, we never would've noticed the dim glow. But instead of conjuring another trap or even fire to provide us light, this time the powers split up and pooled around each of us, gathering in the stones beneath our feet. I could just faintly see that the power beneath me was purple. My power had returned to me. Warmth filled me, little by little. It was like feeling the sun's rays on my skin after a cold, dark night—a subtle comfort. A distant heat. My breath entered and exited my lungs a little easier as the gentle warmth centered in my chest, and my dizziness lessened slightly. I felt fuller.

I pressed my eyes closed and looked quickly inside myself, searching for the well of power that'd been empty, save for my life force, ever since we'd reached the landing room. A small glow of dark purple met my gaze—not anywhere near the amount of power I usually had, but more than nothing. This was what remained after the rooms had used our powers for all the tests. *Finally.* Maybe now I'd be able to heal enough to keep from passing out until we were back in our rooms.

"Our powers are back." Matt quickly conjured a ball of white light in his hand.

I squinted, looking quickly around us, and saw we were in a moderately-sized circular room with a solid stone altar, matching the one in the chapel, set in the center of the room. I sighed, relieved, as I saw the wall behind the altar, where a large circle of dark, distorted air rippled gently. Another portal. Here, finally, was our way out.

"It's here," Caleb murmured, staring at the altar in wonder.

I looked quickly back at it and strained to see the surface from the floor. On it was a large, thin book sitting in a stone stand. My heart jumped. This had to be the book we'd come for. *At last.* I wasn't sure if I was relieved or terrified. Perhaps a bit of both. Fear knotted my stomach as I stared at it. After all, the book was supposedly created directly by the gods. It seemed like something no mortal should fuck with. Part of me wished I could push to my feet and walk over to examine it, and the other part of me wanted to get as far away from it as possible. Being near it felt like playing with fire. Tempting fate. But I stayed put—even with a bit of my power returned, I wasn't healing fast or well enough to follow either instinct.

Everyone turned toward the book except Gabriel. He glanced at it only briefly before kneeling in front of me. "Am I right in assuming you don't have enough power left to heal your wounds?"

I nodded. "It's helping, but there's not enough to meaningfully fix anything. But it's keeping me from passing out as soon, so that's something."

Gabriel's expression darkened with worry as his gaze swept over my face. "Which wound needs to be stabilized the most?"

"Probably the bite in my side," I murmured.

"Okay." Gabriel looked determined. "Lay down on your uninjured side."

I looked up at him in surprise. Was he planning to try healing it? This was a much larger and more complex injury than he'd ever dealt with. And it'd probably require more power than he currently had.

"Don't push yourself too much." I lowered myself onto my side, wincing. "A partial heal is good enough for now."

Gabriel nodded tightly, but something in his expression told me he was going to try anyway. With a quick slice of his knife, he cut the blood-soaked binding away from the wound and hastily pulled my shirt up my torso.

"Holy shit," he whispered as he finally saw the mangled skin. Agony flashed across his face. "Gods, that's horrible. I'm so sorry, Terah."

I managed a half-hearted shrug as I pressed my eyes shut against the pain. It was overwhelming. Like each individual nerve on that side of my torso had been set on fire.

Gabriel quicky placed his hand over the angry wound, and I hissed in pain, gritting my teeth against it.

"I'm so sorry," he whispered. But we both knew it was necessary.

After taking a deep breath, Gabriel pulled power to his hands, electric blue shimmering around his fingers, making my skin tingle with warmth.

"*Heal,*" I heard him think in my head. I started a little in surprise, then a small smile formed on my lips. I'd missed this—connecting with his mind. Gabriel closed his eyes, concentrating fiercely as he sent his power burrowing into my skin. "*Heal.*"

I felt the soothing rush of electric blue delve into my lacerated, tender flesh, slowly starting to repair the torn and punctured muscles, the broken veins, the nicked organs, the shredded skin. I had no idea how he was doing it—how he was managing to so completely pull me back together with such a small amount of power remaining.

"*Pure determination and incredibly careful rationing of power,*" he responded in my mind, surprising me. "*Almost there.*" His hands shook against my skin, but the pain was easing now. The wound was almost completely gone.

Gabriel gasped and sat back a few moments later, electric blue fading from around his fingers. He must've used all his remaining power.

"I did it," he panted, a tired smile spreading across his face. "I healed it."

I glanced down at my side and saw all traces of the wound were gone. Smooth skin now stretched over my side like I'd never been injured there.

"That's amazing," I breathed. "I can't believe you did that. You've improved so much."

Gabriel's cheeks flushed, but he just shook his head and smiled. "Had a good reason to practice." He helped me up then wrapped his arm around my waist and supported me as I limped over to the altar to join the rest of the group.

"How are you doing?" Matt asked, turning toward us as we reached them, his gaze sliding over my side. Caleb glanced at it too, the smallest expression of concern furrowing his brow.

"A bit better." I turned to look at the book in front of us—the much more pressing matter. "Gabriel healed my side, so that's helping. What've you discovered?"

Everyone faced the book again.

"Not much," Matt said. "We were waiting for you two before doing anything, just in case, but it doesn't seem like there are any traps rigged around it or anything. None that are observable without touching it."

I nodded, my gaze sliding over the deep beige cover of the book. It looked like it was covered in some kind of animal skin stamped with an elaborate, intertwining pattern set in a large, indented rectangle in the center of the cover. It was beautiful in an ancient relic kind of way, but somehow also innocuous. It wasn't covered in gold or jewels or made of stone or metals. It wasn't overly flashy or ornate. It reminded me of the pictures of early biblical codices I'd seen in our History of the Divines textbook.

"Should we . . . open it?" I limped a step closer to the altar. "Just to make sure it's what we came here for and not a decoy of some kind? Or is that asking for too much trouble?"

"We should definitely make sure," Damian said from Matt's other side.

He sounded tired but firm. "We came all this way—it would be bad form not to double check, especially given all the deception we've encountered in these rooms already."

I nodded slowly. He had a point.

Matt took a deep, steadying breath, then reached slowly toward the book. "I'll do it." He hesitated as his fingers neared the bottom corner of the cover, clearly afraid of what might happen if he touched it. It was a text made by the gods thousands of years ago for Divines who were never really supposed to use it. It felt like we'd all be cursed for this somehow.

In a smooth, swift motion, Matt carefully gripped the cover of the book and opened it to the first page before stepping back again. We all held our breath. I wasn't sure what we were waiting for—a ghostly scream, the room to start collapsing, a crack of thunder from above—but even after a few breathless moments, nothing happened. I exhaled slowly, then leaned a little closer to see the first page. It looked like it was made from the same material as the cover, but thinner, and contained line after line of neat writing in a language I couldn't identify.

"How are we supposed to know for sure that it's the right book if we can't read it?" I reached out and lightly traced the text. But as I pulled my hand back, I saw the text morph smoothly into English in front of my eyes. "Holy shit. Look at that."

"It changes into the language of the user," Gabriel breathed, leaning over next to me. "That's amazing."

"It must be the right book, then." I looked at the others. Matt, Caleb, and Damian all looked astonished.

"Probably," Damian finally said, "but we should double check the contents just in case."

I frowned. "I don't know if that's a good idea. What it contains . . . that's not information we should have. It's not information *anyone* should have. It's dangerous on a variety of levels."

Damian opened his mouth to argue, but Matt held up his hand to silence us.

"As the only member of the warrior faction here, I'll be the only one interacting with it." Matt's voice was firm. "I'll flip through it quickly just to make sure it's the book we want. I won't read full sentences—I'll just look for relevant context clues. Then we can get out of here."

Damian's brows pulled together, and he opened his mouth to argue, but Matt gave him a hard look.

"Knowing the contents will put you in more danger, and it also makes you more dangerous to all of us. I'm not letting you read it. I'll make sure without reading too much, and then we'll figure out how to hide it so no one can be tempted to use it again. Understood?"

Damian's jaw clenched tightly—so tightly I was surprised I couldn't hear his bones grinding together—but he eventually gave a curt nod. The rest of us took a few steps back as Matt moved to stand directly in front of it, blocking the pages from us with his body.

"Okay," he murmured, reaching forward and beginning to carefully turn the pages. We waited with bated breath as Matt flipped through the book, silent, but for the slight dry crackle of the pages as they turned. Suddenly, Matt slammed the book shut, his head bowed. His entire body tensed. "This is it." His voice was quiet. Hoarse. "We shouldn't open it again. Not for anything or anyone." He turned his head to look at us, his face pale and drawn. "I'm going to wrap it to make sure it stays closed and is disguised, and then we should get out of here."

Fear tightened my stomach, and I glanced at the others as Matt pulled off his backpack and stripped out of his jacket. Gabriel looked tense and very, *very* serious. Caleb looked like he wanted to run. Damian looked both intensely curious and deeply troubled. Perhaps the magnitude of what the book was had finally hit him.

Matt carefully draped his jacket over the book and scooped it off the altar, then wrapped it within the jacket as tightly as he could.

"I don't think it'll fit in any of our bags, so I'll just have to carry it back like this. Once we get out and figure out what time of day it is, we can plan our next steps."

We nodded, then made our way to the exit portal. I leaned heavily on Gabriel as I limped, the gashes in my thigh starting to ooze blood down my leg again. The binding Caleb had put on had soaked all the way through.

"I should go first since I have the book." Matt moved to the front. "Make sure you all follow as quickly as you can. I'm not sure what'll be on the other side of the portal." He glanced back briefly, his expression unreadable, then he stepped through the opaque air, vanishing quickly.

We were plunged into darkness, Matt's conjured light having vanished with him. I quickly conjured another ball of light and held it aloft in my free hand. It was dim, given that my power was so low, but it was at least enough for us to see again.

Damian stepped through the portal next, followed closely by Caleb. I limped toward it and Gabriel took a step away from me.

"You should go first," he said. "I don't want you to be the last person in here, especially in your injured state."

I frowned. It wasn't like I wanted him to be the last one in here either, but I knew he was right. I was hovering too close to unconsciousness to chance it.

"Fine," I sighed, "but follow quickly. Oh, and it'll get dark once I go through," I reminded him. He didn't have any power left to conjure light. Gabriel nodded.

I took a deep breath and stepped forward into the dark, distorted air. The jelly-like atmosphere closed around me and swallowed me up, whisking me away from the dark stone room in a rush. And then I was falling, falling.

"Oof." Two sets of arms caught me. I gasped, winded from the fall and impact, and blinked rapidly, trying to figure out what'd happened.

"Put her down quickly," another voice said, urgently. "Gabriel will be coming through soon."

The arms lowered me to the ground, and I stood on shaky legs, backing away as Caleb and Damian prepared to catch Gabriel. Disoriented, I looked around the dimly lit room and saw that we were once again in the circular room just beneath the chapel where the stairs began. But where had I fallen from?

The dim light approached me, and I turned to see Matt stepping up to me.

"It's alright," he murmured, quickly assessing my expression. "I know it's disorienting. The portal spit us back into this first room, but from the ceiling. Found that out the hard way after a twelve-foot drop onto stone." He grimaced and rubbed the back of his head. I glanced at him and saw he had the book tucked under the arm holding the light. A shiver traveled through me, and I looked quickly away from it, fighting the urge to put more physical space between me and it.

"I managed to mostly catch Damian," Matt continued, "but Caleb basically fell on top of both of us."

I nodded and watched as Gabriel appeared through the ceiling and fell toward the ground. To their credit, Damian and Caleb mostly succeeded in catching him, even though he was the tallest of the group, and quite broad.

Gabriel shoved to his feet, quickly thanked them, and looked around for me. I limped toward him and slid my arm around his waist.

"We're in the room just below the altar again," I said as Matt, Caleb, and Damian came to stand around us.

Gabriel nodded and draped his arm over my shoulders. "How do we get out?" He frowned. "Last time, four of us needed to give some of our power so that the altar could lower into the room. Is there a way to do that from in here?"

Matt approached the thick pillar in the middle of the room that supported the altar above, lifting the dim light in his hand to examine it.

"Hm." He circled it, slowly lowering the light as he went. "The same symbols are carved into the stone here," he finally said. "Each one is in a different place, so it'll likely require four of us again, one on each symbol."

"I don't have any power left," Gabriel said, worry bleeding into his voice. "Do you think you'll have enough?" He looked down and met my gaze.

"Maybe just barely. But only if we do it now. My body is using what I have left to heal me and keep me conscious, so I'm losing more and more power by the second."

"Okay, let's do it now, then," Matt said, briskly. "Terah, you get the lowest symbol. Over here." He gestured. I nodded and limped over to where the fourth symbol—Tartarus—was near the base of the pillar.

"Caleb, Damian, you take these two." Matt gestured at two other points on the pillar. "I'll take this top one, but it'll make the light go out, so just be prepared for that. On the count of three."

Matt counted down and all four of us poured what little power we had into the symbols. We had so little left that the carvings barely glowed with light. I could hardly even see the color of my own power in front of me. I just hoped it'd be enough. I felt my power completely empty once again, and a wave of exhaustion washed over me. My hand shook against the cold stone. Fortunately, I felt the pillar start to rumble and heard the creak of stone on stone as the altar lowered into the room again. *Thank the gods.*

I released a shaky sigh as we backed away to make room. I could see faint light coming through the opening above us as the altar continued to descend. Daylight. We'd been down here all night. My knees shook, the effects of my blood loss and exhaustion no longer stymied by my power, and I grabbed Gabriel's arm to keep from collapsing as the world spun again. He quickly wrapped his arm around my waist and held me up against him.

"Hang in there," he murmured. "I'll get you out and back to the dorms as soon as I can." I nodded and leaned my head against his chest, trying to slow the spinning.

The altar hit the stone floor in front of us with a muffled thud, then stilled.

"Quickly." Matt hopped onto the altar. "It didn't stay down here long last time."

Gabriel bent and swung me up in his arms, taking me by surprise. He walked quickly toward the altar and set me on top of it.

"Her first," he said, firmly. "She's not going to be conscious for much longer. We need to get her out." Matt's gaze swept over my face and saw how pale and dizzy I was. He nodded, worry filling his expression, then bent and carefully set down the book at his feet.

"I'll boost you up." He turned to me and grabbed my shoulders as I swayed. "Once I lift you, grab the ledge and try to pull yourself up. I'll help you as much as I can from here."

I nodded, then Matt grabbed me around the waist and hoisted me up. I was glad Gabriel had healed the bite wound in my side, because otherwise this would've been excruciating. I managed to grab the ledge of the opening above me and lifted myself as much as I could, my poor arm muscles screaming. Matt grabbed my legs and boosted me the rest of the way through, and I rolled onto the sun-lit stones of the chapel floor with a sigh of relief.

"Terah, grab the book," Matt called urgently from below.

I sat up, wincing, trying to force the world to settle around me and stop tilting, then leaned back over the opening in the floor. I reached down and managed to grab the wrapped book by its corner and brought it swiftly out of the hole and into my lap. I tried to ignore how my heart hammered once I'd grabbed it. I didn't want the book near me. The sooner we hid it forever, the better.

Matt quickly jumped up and grabbed the ledge, then pulled himself up and through. He glanced around, making sure no one else was in the chapel, then took the book from me and helped me move a few feet away from the hole to give the others more room. Gabriel quickly followed him out, trailed directly by Damian. The altar creaked and began rising, but Damian reached back through the opening and grabbed Caleb's hand, helping him out before it had risen too much.

We all sat back on the stones, breathing hard as we watched the altar shift back into place with the soft grumble of settling rock.

"What now?" Caleb asked a moment later. "We don't have enough power left to hide the book like we'd planned."

Damian frowned slightly in troubled thought. I felt a stir of discomfort as well. It wasn't safe for us to just have the book in our possession, either. We'd removed it from all its intense protections—it'd never been easier to take than it was right now.

"We need to rest and let our powers regenerate for a few hours," Damian said slowly, "but we shouldn't leave the book with any one of us. That wouldn't provide much protection for it if someone decides to come after it. We should stay together until we've actually managed to hide it."

Matt nodded and rubbed his hand down his face. "Let's take it back to my room." He reached into his pocket and pulled out his phone, then checked the screen. "It's 6:00 a.m. on a Sunday. I don't think any other staff members will be up yet. If we hurry, we can all make it to my room without running into anyone else. Then we can rest and regroup there before we try to hide it."

The rest of us nodded and began pushing to our feet. I tried to stand, but my legs wouldn't hold me anymore. The world lurched again, and everything blurred around me. I could barely see. I couldn't even tell which way was up anymore. *Shit.* I sagged back against the stone. My breaths were coming in shallow now, and my heart beat too quickly. Darkness flickered around the edges of my vision.

I vaguely felt arms slide under me and lift.

"Don't worry, I've got you," Gabriel's warm voice murmured in my ear. I felt his lips pressing against my forehead. "Hang in there."

I distantly registered that we were moving, but I was too out of it to take in any of the details or to register what was being said around me. An indeterminate amount of time later, I felt myself being lowered onto a soft surface.

"I have a little power left," I heard Matt's voice echo somewhere above me. "I can at least replenish some of her blood." I felt hands on my shoulders, then a faint white heat slowly sliding through me. A few moments passed and I began feeling slightly more lucid, but my heart still beat too quickly, and my breaths were only slightly less shallow.

"Shit," Matt panted, flickering in and out of focus above me. "I didn't have as much left as I thought."

"I can help," Caleb said from somewhere to the side of me. "My shoulder isn't as bad anymore, and I have a little power left."

Matt stepped to the side, and suddenly Caleb's face loomed over me, his cold, distant expression betrayed by the blatant worry in his eyes. He grasped my shoulders, and then white-hot power was burning through me again, healing my veins and replenishing my blood. He'd obviously had more power left than Matt. Caleb didn't touch my surface wounds—not enough power for that—but he managed to heal enough interior damage and replenish enough blood to stabilize me.

I sucked in a deep breath of air as he lifted his hands away from me, now completely drained, and I blinked, my vision slowly clearing. I saw I was lying on the couch in Matt's room, the four of them all standing around me, worry in their eyes.

"Thanks," I murmured, glancing at Matt and Caleb as I pushed gingerly into a sitting position. I was still injured and shaky, but at least I didn't feel like I'd pass out. I looked around. "Where's the book?" Gabriel sank onto the couch next to me and handed me a protein bar from his bag.

"It's in my bedroom closet right now," Matt responded. "I'll keep it closer moving forward, but I wanted it out of the way while we healed you and figured out food and sleeping arrangements."

I nodded and bit into the protein bar. I hadn't thought about food or hunger all night, but the second the food touched my tongue, I realized I was starving.

"I have enough sandwich ingredients in the fridge for all of us," he continued, "and I should have enough blankets for everyone to sleep out here."

Gabriel and Caleb made sandwiches for the group while Damian and Matt located and brought out all of Matt's spare blankets and pillows. Once we'd all scarfed down our food, we traded off taking showers and rebinding what was left of our wounds. Matt lent Gabriel and Caleb a couple of his shirts to wear since theirs were torn and bloody, or in Caleb's case, non-existent, and also provided me with some of his clothes so I could sleep in something other than ripped, blood-encrusted garments.

In under an hour, we were all settled in the living room under blankets, with the exception of Matt who'd taken to his bedroom with the book. The group had insisted I take the couch, given that I was currently the most injured and unwell among us, and I'd decided not to fight them on it. I was too exhausted, and the thought of getting to sleep on soft cushions instead of the hard floor was too tempting.

Damian and Caleb had moved the coffee table so the rest of them could settle on the rug. It offered a little cushion, at least. Gabriel had set up on the floor next to the couch, and we all sank back against our pillows, finally allowing our bodies and minds to relax after so many harrowing hours. So much physical and mental exhaustion. So much pain. I didn't know if I'd ever felt this tired before.

Gabriel reached up from the floor and took my hand. I was already fading, sucked into sleep like it was a vortex, but I managed to squeeze his fingers in response. I saw the side of his mouth pull up in a gentle smile before closing my eyes, finally, to sleep.

25

DARKNESS RISING

I woke up slowly, like I was being pulled sluggishly from the depths of a mud pit. I felt groggy, disoriented. Almost nauseous. Like I wasn't supposed to be awake yet. Like something was trying to pull me back under. My head throbbed dully behind my temples. It reminded me of how I'd felt the morning after my vision about the book. Perhaps, like then, it was just a product of sheer exhaustion. But a sense of unease tingled around the edges of my being as I tried to open my eyes. It felt like something inside me was prodding at me like I'd forgotten something. An internal, mental itch. Perhaps that was what'd woken me up—this feeling of . . . restlessness. Of wrongness.

I managed to peel my eyes open with difficulty and stared up at the ceiling of Matt's living room. The room was bathed in dim light from the windows, but I had no idea whether it was sunrise or sunset. I had no idea how much time had passed. With a groan, I pushed into a sitting position, my blanket falling into my lap. My arm and leg didn't burn with pain anymore, meaning that my power must've regenerated enough to heal them while I'd been asleep. Which meant . . . I'd been asleep for a really long time. I looked down and saw that Gabriel was still lying on the ground next to me. Just past him lay Caleb. Damian was . . . gone.

I pushed shakily to my feet and looked around. Maybe he'd woken up already and was in the bathroom. I stretched a little and made my way down the hall that led to Matt's bedroom and the bathroom. Matt's bedroom door was closed, but the bathroom was open. He wasn't there. Worry and something akin to fear began pumping through me. Where was he? Had something happened to him? Had someone taken him? Had he just left? No . . . that wouldn't make sense. He was the one who'd stressed how important it was for us to stay together until we'd hidden the book. For the book's protection.

Frowning, I cracked open the door to Matt's room and peered inside. Matt was lying on his side, still asleep. No Damian here, either. I pulled his door shut again and hurried back to the living room, picking up my phone from the side table along the way. The screen informed me that it was 7:00 a.m. On Monday. The day our exams were meant to start. A chill stole through me. We'd been asleep for almost twenty-four hours straight. We'd missed all of Sunday. The feelings of unease and fear grew until my chest felt like it was filled with lead. Why hadn't anyone else woken up yet? And why the hell was Damian gone?

I knelt next to Gabriel and gently shook his shoulder. I needed to wake them. We needed to hide the book and figure out what was going on. Too much time had passed, both since we'd gone to sleep and since we'd retrieved the book. At this rate, we'd miss training and our exams. Not that I thought they were super important compared to the book, but it'd bring unwanted attention to us if we all missed both. Especially if Matt—a trainer—missed training.

"Gabriel, wake up," I murmured in his ear, giving him another little shake. But his breaths stayed deep and even, and he didn't move. I shook his shoulder a little harder. "Gabriel, wake up." Nothing. Panic stole through me like ice water filling my veins, and tears gathered along the lower rim of my eyes as I clutched his shoulders, but I tried to shove down both. At least he was breathing. He was okay. He was alive. This wasn't like the illusion in the god's chamber. I took a deep, steadying breath, trying to calm myself and slow my racing heart. Then I turned and crawled over to Caleb.

"Wake up," I said, shaking his shoulder. I needed to see if it was just Gabriel or if all of them were like this. Caleb shifted a little, his head turning slightly, but he didn't wake. I shook him again. Tapped his face gently with my fingers. "Caleb, you need to wake up." He didn't.

"Shit," I whispered, shoving to my feet. Not trying to be quiet this time, I ran down the hall to Matt's room and shoved open the door. "Matt, wake up!" I jogged over to his bed, then grabbed his shoulder and shook him as well, pushing him until he was lying on his back. "Wake up! Something's happening and I need your help!" Matt didn't move. He just let out a small snore.

"Damnit!"

I pulled my phone from my pocket, opened the contacts, and hit Damian's number. The phone went straight to voicemail. I didn't know if it was because something had happened to him, or if it was because he was the source of this somehow.

I shoved my phone back into my pocket and looked around frantically for the book. I had no idea where Matt had put it, but he did mention wanting to keep it close until it was hidden. I grabbed the blankets on his bed and pulled them back, trying to see if he'd tucked the book around him. But it wasn't there. I pulled the blankets back up, then checked under his pillow, under the bed, in his nightstands, in the drawers of his dresser. Finally, I checked his closet. But it was gone. The book was gone. And so was Damian.

An icy chill descended over me as I clenched my hands into tight fists at my sides. Pieces of past visions were gnawing at me, flooding my brain, but I couldn't figure out how it all fit together. I couldn't make sense of it. But standing here in shock wouldn't fix anything. I needed to find Damian. I needed to figure out what was happening. I needed to get the book back. And I needed to wake Gabriel, Matt, and Caleb somehow.

I ran back to the living room and quickly stripped out of Matt's boxers and shirt to don my blood-encrusted clothes from yesterday. At least they fit me. I hurriedly pulled on my boots and grabbed my weapons. Just in case. Then I dashed out of Matt's room and out of the staff residence building.

The morning was cool and misty, and dew still clung to the grass in opalescent beads. I shivered a little and looked around. Nothing looked out of the ordinary. A few people were walking to and from the main classroom building for breakfast, but most people were still in their dorms. How was I going to find him? I couldn't just run around campus, covered in dried blood, ripped clothes, and heavily armed, and not expect to be stopped and questioned. And I didn't have time to go back to my dorm and change. I needed to find him another way.

I ran around the back of the building where fewer people would be able to see me, and leaned against the cool stone wall, closing my eyes and concentrating hard. I'd been given these amazing extra abilities. I might as well try using them. I took a deep breath and opened my mind as broadly as I could. More broadly than I'd ever opened it before. I cast a wide net, expanding my consciousness to take in the entire surface area of campus. Every single person. Every single thought.

What felt like a million thoughts and feelings suddenly flooded my mind, tumbling over each other like water in a turbulent river, giving me impressions of the people behind them. Like echoes of faces. Silhouettes of beings. It was loud. So loud. So chaotic. I clutched the wall behind me and braced myself, feeling suddenly nauseous. But I forced myself to take a deep, slow breath. To hold onto the connection. Try not to panic. Focus. Slowly, I began sifting through everything—all the voices, all the feelings, all the people—searching. It felt extremely vulnerable and incredibly overwhelming, opening my mind like this, but I set aside the discomfort for now. Everything was on the line. I needed this to work. I needed to find him.

As my focus sharpened and my panic decreased, I felt a tugging in my mind. Like the tugging I'd felt in Set's chamber when Damian needed to be saved. When my power had pulled me toward him like a pull on a line connecting the two of us. I didn't understand it. But right now, I'd listen to it. I gritted my teeth and opened myself to the tugging. Followed it in my mind. It created a faint purple path that cut through all the thoughts and shadows, buildings and trees. I sped down it in my mind, weaving through the tumult. Pushing down the extraneous sounds and images until they were a faint whisper instead of a roar. I focused all my energy on the line connecting us. Finally, I reached him.

I couldn't see him. Not like I could see all the other people in my mind. But I could see a sort of bubble of energy, and I could feel, somehow, that he was inside it. I wasn't sure if he was shielding himself, or if someone else was shielding him from me, but it clearly wasn't enough to completely throw off my power or sever whatever connection we seemed to have. I knew, now, he was in the forest on the north side of campus. I didn't know what state he was in—kidnapped, injured, unconscious—but I knew where he was and that he was alive.

I broke the connection and opened my eyes as I shoved off the side of the building. Without further thought, I ran as fast as I could, cutting across the large, grassy expanse of the grounds. I needed to reach him before he moved or was moved. I needed to figure out what was going on. And why.

I reached the edge of the trees a couple minutes later, gasping for breath, and slowed. I needed to take this next part more slowly. I tread carefully and silently through the dense trees, a soft spring breeze gently tugging on my hair and rustling the leaves above me. I knew Damian was decently far in, though not far enough to be anywhere near the perimeter guards.

Anxiety pulled at my stomach as I pushed forward, and a feverish frenzy of things I hadn't deeply thought about before—things that were gnawing at me that I'd pushed to the back corners of my mind—tumbled to the forefront. My vision about the book had made it seem like the Demon attacks on the Academy were connected with the Dark Guardians' plot to retrieve it. But . . . the more I thought about it, the less sense that made. Sending transformed Demons was the most conspicuous way possible to enter the grounds. It'd inherently draw attention and put the Academy on high alert—the opposite of what they should've wanted for such a covert mission. It didn't make sense strategically. If they wanted the book, they should've sent someone undercover as a student or teacher to get it covertly. So . . . why *had* the Demons been sent? If they'd just wanted to attack the Academy and bring it into the war, why send just one at a time? Why not start with the largest one? And why had they all appeared when I was there? Fear slid through me. Had my murder been their purpose?

Goosebumps raced down my arms. Why me, though? I didn't stand in the way of them getting the book or conquering the Academy more than any other person in the administration or warrior faction. I wasn't the only person on campus who could fight well. And the first attack had taken place before anyone beyond Matt, Gabriel, and my mother even knew I had visions. They wouldn't have known I even had the ability to see their plans in the future, so it couldn't have been about that.

I frowned and stepped carefully over and around the twigs scattered liberally across the forest floor. I tried to look at the situation from every angle. Could the Demon attacks have been an attempt to kill me as a method of revenge on my mother given her position as the High Light Guardian? Maybe. But why now? And why go to such lengths to do so at the Academy? Creating portals or rips in a heavily fortified plane and transporting Demons here without anyone noticing was *way* harder and required way more power than just murdering me in Dagmar, where they'd had much easier access to me.

And most troubling of all, if the Demon attacks weren't actually book-related, why had my vision asserted they were?

All the thoughts and possibilities spun over and over in my head in a feverish swirl as I neared where I knew Damian had been. None of this made sense. Nothing seemed to completely fit. I had to be missing something. Some key that'd connect all these pieces.

I heard a faint rustling to my left and stilled, then crouched behind the thick trunk of a knobby tree. I waited a few seconds before carefully peering around the trunk in the direction of the sound. And my stomach dropped at what I saw.

Damian was crouched on the forest floor, the book open on the ground in front of him. There was no one else around. No kidnapper, no one there to injure him or force him to do anything. My heart sank, but I was mainly confused. What was he doing? Why had he taken the book? To what end? As bad as this looked, there had to be more to it than I could glean just from watching him. While he was rough around the edges and had a past darker than anyone I'd ever met, I'd also seen into his fears and cares in his illusion and in the fire. I'd seen genuine kindness peeking through his gruff and neutral facades over the past few months. I knew, deep down, he cared about people. He cared about . . . us. When he'd thought his father was about to kill me in the illusion, he'd tried to warn me. He'd tried to stop it. And I'd seen in the fire that he cared about doing the least harm possible in a given situation, even if he was painfully punished for it. Even if he ultimately failed. He always tried. None of that lined up with a betrayal. There had to be something I was missing.

Damian slammed the book shut and swore gruffly as he straightened up. Without warning, he spun and slammed his fist into the tree nearest him, letting out a frustrated, almost anguished sound. Then he sank back against the trunk and slid his hands into his hair, grasping the strands tightly as he breathed hard. He looked . . . scared. Haunted.

I straightened up slowly, trying not to make any sound. But Damian's head spun in my direction, and I ducked behind the trunk again. I hadn't made any sound, but I had a feeling he'd heard me in a different way. I felt a warmth pushing at my head—a foreign presence. I shoved the walls up around my mind, but I knew it was too late.

"Who's there?" Damian barked, his voice harsh and gruff. I heard him draw a weapon.

I bit the inside of my cheek. I didn't have a choice now. I needed to talk to him anyway. So, with a fortifying breath, I stepped out from behind the tree and took a few steps toward him.

"Terah." The blood drained from his face, and his leg moved a little, almost like he wanted to take a step away from me, but he tensed his muscles, controlling the impulse. Standing firm. And he didn't lower his weapon.

"What are you doing?" I sounded much calmer than I felt. But with him, I knew this was a battle of wills and control. Of calm coolness. A test to see who could retain a grasp on their self-control for the longest. Who could stay the sharpest. We were similar in that way, when we felt cornered or challenged. Far more similar than he'd probably ever acknowledge.

Damian was quiet for a moment, sizing me up. Like he was trying to determine what he wanted to say. How much he wanted to say. What I might already know.

"Following my orders," he finally said. His face and voice were both devoid of expression or emotion, but I knew by now that he usually only looked like that when he was thinking and feeling the most.

"And whose orders are those?" I narrowed my eyes, wishing I could see into his mind. That I could shove past the dense walls he'd erected around his thoughts, impenetrable even by me.

Damian's jaw tightened, and I saw the muscle there flex sharply. He was quiet for another long moment. Thinking. Weighing.

"My father's."

My blood turned to ice. So, he wasn't even secretly working for the High Light Guardian. That was what I'd suspected first, given where he was from and the timing of his arrival. But no. He'd been sent by his father —the tyrannical border town leader who thirsted for complete control over everything and everyone around him. The leader who killed his own people and tortured his son like it was nothing. Like it was *fun*. The book in his hands would be . . . world ending. I couldn't even fathom what he'd do with it or why he wanted it. It'd be as bad as if we placed it straight into the hands of the Dark or Light Guardian leaders.

"What does he want you to do?" Maybe there was something we could do to stop this. Some way to thwart his father without getting Damian killed.

"What did your vision tell you?" He raised an eyebrow at me mockingly.

My jaw clenched as ice filled my veins again. So, he'd figured it out. That it was my vision. That I'd been the one responsible for sending us on the mission to retrieve the book. I kept my expression carefully blank.

"You know very well what it told me. What *both* visions told me." He had, after all, been inexplicably sucked into one of them. That was probably why he'd figured it out.

Damian's eyes hardened as he watched me, but he didn't respond.

"You were there with me in that vision. You saw that horrible battle. What if that's what happens if someone gets their hands on the book? It could be the end of the world. The end of all of us. I *know* you were affected by it like I was. Please. Don't do anything that'll ensure that end. We can find another way. We can report your father and have him removed. Then you won't have to follow his orders anymore. You'll be safe. I know it's hard to trust people, and I know your father made your life a living hell, but we can help you escape from it. He's not invincible. I *know* you don't want all of us to die. I know that, Damian."

Damian's stare remained cold and hard. He looked unmoved. Unconcerned. Unemotional.

"You understand very little about what you're speaking of," he finally said, drawing the words out slowly. He began spinning his knife around in his hand, almost leisurely. Then he gave me a cold, smug smile. "And very little about what you're up against." He almost looked like he was taking pleasure in this—in upsetting me. But his eyes held no mirth. Not even scorn. They just looked . . . empty.

"Then *make* me understand," I said quietly, returning his hard stare.

Damian spun his knife around one more time before pointing it at me again. I itched to draw my weapon as well, but I knew it'd only escalate the situation. And he wouldn't tell me anything more if I did.

"There's no one who my father can be reported to. No one who can hold him accountable for anything. There are no personal consequences he can ever feel. There is no point in trying to go against his will. For better or worse, *you will not win.*" A grimness settled over his expression for a moment before it returned to a blank, cold mask.

"The High Light Guardian could do something," I finally said, even though I hated saying it. Even though I hated relying on her for anything. "I know he's powerful, but he can't have every person in his pocket and on his side. I know for a fact that she can't be bought like that. She's too selfish, and she'd *never* let anyone besides herself amass that much power under her leadership."

Damian tilted his head slightly as he watched me, and his eyebrows rose in an almost pitying expression. "You really haven't figured it out, have you?" I clenched my jaw but didn't respond. I didn't know what he was talking about. "My father isn't beholden to the High Light Guardian. He isn't beholden to *any* Light Guardian."

I frowned, confused. It didn't make sense . . . unless . . .

My hand did go to my dagger this time, and I whipped it from my sheath as the cold truth washed over me. Icy fear and boiling rage warred within me as reality dropped on me like weighted armor, making my body feel heavy and stiff. Making me feel like I was sinking into the dirt beneath my feet.

"I see you now appreciate the situation." Damian's eyes carefully followed my hand, his gaze sharp. But I didn't throw my dagger at him. Not yet. I needed to know what he'd done. I needed to understand. The keen sting of betrayal spread from the middle of my chest outward.

"You're . . . a Dark Guardian." There was a small tremor in my voice. Not entirely from fear, but from an overwhelming rush of emotions.

No wonder I'd never seen him transform. No wonder he'd been so careful not to use his power in a visible way in front of us. Suddenly, everything I'd ever thought or assumed about him went up in smoke. Every warm feeling of friendship I'd ever had toward him—and I'd had more and more of them this past month—turned into stabbing pains in my chest. I hadn't expected his betrayal to hurt this much. Even when I'd been suspicious of him, I'd never thought he was so categorically on the opposite side. Him being wholly evil just hadn't made sense with my other visions—visions of the future that hadn't happened yet. Instead, I'd considered him to be on par with Caleb—not to be fully trusted, but ultimately not too harmful. I'd thought there was some goodness inside him. That maybe he was stuck in a horrible situation and just needed permission to leave. But this . . . this was different. This changed everything. He was a Dark Guardian spy, and he'd made us trust him. We'd let him in.

Damian watched me carefully, his eyes traveling over my face.

"Your father is—"

"The king of the Dark Guardian realm," he interjected, his voice dark. Deep. A final confirmation. "That's where I'm from."

Boiling anger coursed through me, triggering a burst of adrenaline, sharpening my thoughts, tightening my muscles. I needed to be vigilant. Now that I knew who he really was, I was in more danger. We all were. This was now a situation I'd need to survive. And I had a feeling Damian wasn't supposed to let me. My grip on my dagger tightened.

"So, you were sent here to retrieve the book." Ice laced my voice, hardening it like steel. But I still needed information from him. I needed to understand the extent of his treachery. As many details of the Dark Guardians' plan as possible. Maybe then I could stop it.

"Among other things." The icy smile was back on his face.

"And we just made it incredibly easy for you, didn't we?" Bitterness crept through my calm exterior. "Including you in that mission. Getting the book and essentially delivering it into your hands."

Damian ran his free hand through his hair agitatedly, still pointing his knife at me. "It was anything but easy." His voice was dark. "I'd been searching for that damn book for months. The only reason I involved you all was because I was running out of time. I had to find it before the end of the semester. I needed help."

Wait . . . he'd involved us?

"What do you mean?" I bit out sharply. "My vision was what brought you into that mission."

Damian shifted his weight slowly from one foot to the other and raised an eyebrow at me. "Was it your vision?" he taunted. "Really?"

I glared at him, even as confusion filled me. What was he insinuating?

Damian laughed, though the sound was humorless. "You're out of your depth, Terah." His tone was condescending and dark. My eyes hardened as I stared at him, but he wasn't going to get a rise out of me that way. I was used to handling abrasiveness. He should know that by now.

"Then explain it to me," I said coolly, almost surprised at how calm I sounded.

Damian stared at me for a long moment, assessing. Calculating.

"It won't help you to know," he finally said, his tone indifferent.

I just shrugged, waiting. I wouldn't let him out of this until I understood what was going on. What he'd done.

Damian sighed, shaking his head. "Fine. I guess it can't hurt now." He sounded resigned. Tired. "My father had two objectives: get the book, and . . . kill or acquire you."

My stomach clenched with cold dread, but I was careful not to visibly react. "Why me? What could he possibly want with me?"

Damian stared at me again in silence, almost like he was warring with himself. "I'm not sure," he finally said. His gaze traveled over me again, curiosity filling his eyes like it had when we'd first met. "My father doesn't always reveal why he wants something done. He just orders me to do it, and I . . . must."

His eyes darkened slightly.

"He found out about you a little less than a year ago. Right before you came to the Academy. He was furious. He said you were too much of a threat to have on the Light Guardian side. He either wanted you dead or wanted you under his control. That's why he sent the Demons to the Academy. If they ended up killing you, then that took care of the problem, and meant you weren't too much of a threat anyway. But if you defeated them all, as you did," he inclined his head at me, "then he would know how powerful you really were—that you were worth his while—and he could send me in to convince you to join us, or to take you out should you refuse."

Shock and confusion filled me in equal measures. His father had heard about me before I'd even come to the Academy. Before I or anyone else knew about my extra abilities. My sense of dread, of wrongness, grew. Now I *really* didn't understand what he could want with me.

"So, you don't even know why you're here to kill me, but you'd do it anyway." I shook my head in disgust.

"I don't *have* to kill you." His voice was smooth, nonchalant. Like he didn't care one way or the other. "I was originally planning to kidnap you while you were still asleep, but that plan's obviously shot. You could make my job easier and agree to come back with me to the Dark Guardian plane. It would be best for everyone if you did. I'd fulfill my orders, and you'd survive."

I narrowed my eyes at him, my unease increasing by the moment. I needed to figure out how deep this went. What his father's final intentions were. This could be our only opportunity to get the answers we needed.

"How did he have enough power to break through the Academy plane border and transport Demons here at will? That would take huge amounts of power. More power than the Dark Guardians should have access to. More than they ever have."

Damian's mouth pressed into a thin line, and I could see he wasn't going to answer that particular question. *Damn.*

"Fine then. How did they always manage to find me? How did they know where I was on campus?"

Damian shrugged. "We have someone working for us here. An administrator. The same one who tried to 'warn' Matt about fortifying the barrier the other night." He shook his head, dispassionately. "If my father finds out about that, he'll kill him. Though he'll probably kill him anyway." He shrugged again, his eyes cold. But he hadn't said *he'd* tell his father.

I bit the inside of my cheek as I thought. So, this administrator wasn't inherently loyal to the Dark Guardians. They'd wanted to prevent further attacks even while helping them happen.

"Why would anyone on this campus help the Dark Guardians? This is pretty much a Light Guardian stronghold, especially within the school's leadership."

Damian's eyes clouded with an emotion I couldn't identify for a split second, before returning to the blank cold. "He was compelled to help us," he said, coolly. "In exchange for the safety of his family, who are currently being held captive in the Dark Guardian realm."

My fingers went white from how tightly I was holding the dagger now, and bile rose in my throat.

"Your father would never keep them alive." I'd seen enough of him in Damian's fire sequences to know that.

"It's more likely that he will if his orders are followed." Damian's voice had gone quieter. Hollower. "If he's not obeyed, they'll definitely be killed."

Anger seethed through me at the cruelty of it all. At the cruelty of the Dark Guardians. At Damian for helping them. For being one of them.

"And this administrator followed me around and somehow communicated my position to the Dark Guardians?"

"Essentially. He had easy access to the Academy's technology to communicate off-plane. There were preferred days, times, and circumstances on our end, but he alerted us to your position within those. And we had the . . . capacity to send Demons to your reported locations very quickly."

My jaw tightened. Another display of power the Dark Guardians shouldn't have. How the hell had they done it?

"And what about the Demon this semester? The one we fought together."

"It was to gain your trust and establish which side of the battle I was on." His eyes emptied of emotion again. "He traveled with me onto campus in his human form disguised as another student—one who didn't return—and waited for the planned day and time in here." He gestured at the trees around us.

"You brought him here just to die?" Horror seeped into my voice. "Why would he agree to that?"

Damian was silent for a few moments.

"You don't understand what it's like in the Dark Guardian realm." He sounded detached. Emotionless. Like none of this was a big deal. But something bleak flickered briefly in his eyes. "You don't know the brutal hierarchy. The forced sacrifice. The levels and degrees of servitude. He probably did it because he was promised an elevation in life for his family. Perhaps heightened safety and better opportunities for them. That tends to be why."

That tends to be why. A chill of disquiet stole through me. He made it sound like Demons didn't always have a choice in fighting. Not much of one, anyway. That was . . . troubling. That could change things. I blinked quickly, trying to recenter myself, and tucked the disquiet away for a later time. I couldn't afford to focus on it right now.

"But he tried to kill you," I reminded Damian. Taunting him. Pushing him to give me more information. "He almost took you down with him."

"Yes." Damian's lips pursed slightly. "His idea of revenge. Imprudent of him. If my father had found out, or if he'd succeeded in killing me, his whole family would have been killed. His sacrifice would have been for nothing."

Another thing Damian hadn't told and wasn't going to tell his father. It seemed like he was keeping a lot from him, for a loyal spy and all. But discomfort continued to swirl within me as I stared at him. I'd stopped that Demon from killing him. I'd saved Damian's life that day. Conflict squirmed in my stomach. Had I caused all this by letting him live?

No . . . I couldn't accept that. The king of the Dark Guardians would've found another way to get what he wanted, even if Damian hadn't survived. I was sure of that. He always did. He was a lot like my mother that way.

"So you got close to us in an attempt to make me switch sides, and to kill me if I didn't?"

Damian frowned and looked past me in thought. "You were harder to get close to than I thought you'd be. I mean, I expected border town soldiers to be a certain degree of tough, but you and Gabriel essentially fortressed yourselves away from most other people. And I couldn't . . . *read* either of you. Not without fully revealing myself, which I couldn't do then. It was so frustrating—a roadblock I hadn't expected."

I remembered the pushes into our minds when we'd first met him. The foreign warmth. His look of surprised frustration. That made it seem like . . .

"You *can* read minds?" My mask of calmness slipped. I'd thought I was the only Divine who could do that. I'd never heard of anyone else having that ability. Ever.

"Yes." He carefully observed my reaction. "Usually. Though there are some people who are harder to read. People who feel me there and try to block me out. I can still get through, but not without alerting them to my presence."

My hand shook, making the dagger bob a little in the air in front of me. How could he, a Dark Guardian, share that ability with me? It wasn't one that *any* Guardian usually had. No other Divine did.

"You and Gabriel had too many blocks up, so I knew I needed to get close to someone who was around you a lot. Someone who couldn't feel my presence in their mind who I could get information from."

"Caleb," I murmured, darkly.

"He was the easiest." His mouth pulled into a taunting, rueful smile. "Always looking at you. Thinking about you. He had a history with you. He unknowingly gave me a lot of information. As did Matt. Matt was too distracted by you and Gabriel to really notice me in his mind. He was particularly useful in letting me hear your conversations since I couldn't hear them through you. But it was more difficult to find reasons to be around him since he's a staff member. That's why I mainly stuck with Caleb."

"What did you do to them?" I demanded, taking a predatory step toward him. "Why won't they wake up?" If he'd hurt them in any way, I'd make him wish he'd never been born.

"The same thing I did to you. The same thing I did to make all of this happen. I used my mind. Specifically, I used my mind to invade theirs and keep them asleep—to keep their brains stuck in dream-mode."

Rage warred with curiosity in my head. How had he done that? Could *I* do that?

"You broke free from it, though." He tilted his head as he regarded me. "I guess that makes sense, since you have the same ability. To see into minds," he clarified. The curiosity grew in his eyes again. "I've never met anyone else who could do that. I thought I was the only one."

Dread cut through my curiosity. He knew about that ability of mine, too. I supposed it made sense, since he'd had access to Matt's mind. But it was dangerous. The Dark Guardians knowing the extent of my abilities was dangerous. They'd wanted me dead *before* they'd known about them. They'd try even harder to eliminate me now.

"I found that out rather late," Damian said, almost absently. "In the library when you found that clue in the journal. Matt noticed you and Gabriel speaking mind-to-mind and was jealous about it." He rolled his eyes. "That was the first time he'd thought about you having that ability while I was in his mind. That's when I found out why you seemed so skilled at keeping me out. And it made sense that Gabriel was too, since he spent so much time speaking with you in that way. He was attuned to the feeling. Caleb doesn't seem to know about it, though."

I neither confirmed nor denied this. I just waited for him to continue.

"We knew from our . . . source . . . that the book was hidden at the Academy, but it was taking me too long to find it. I couldn't find any clear information in the library on where it could be hidden, and I knew I wouldn't be able to get through every book before the semester was done. I was getting desperate. I knew my father would make things worse for everyone if I failed. More people would die if I didn't succeed in the given timeframe. That's why I eventually brought you all into my mission.

"It was the day we shared a vision." His voice grew distant again, as though he was remembering it. "When we came out of it, I listened to your conversation through Matt's mind and heard him ask if you'd had a vision. *Another* vision. Meaning you must've had them before. I was shocked. I didn't understand how you, of all people, could have that power. It just didn't make sense. But I realized I was focusing on the wrong thing. I could *use* the fact that you had visions. All I needed to do was wait for you to fall asleep that night, leaving your mind less guarded. That's how I got in."

Terror gripped me as I realized what he must've done. What I was responsible for because of it. My muscles tensed down the entire length of my body.

"I guided your mind into deeper sleep, then projected a story from my mind into yours. I created a false vision and filled it with a few details I'd managed to gather from Matt's mind to make you believe it. Real people you'd seen before in positions of power. Dynamics and behaviors that you hated about the Light Guardians. I knew they were there, based on how you'd talked about their leadership when we trained together. All I had to do was suggest an apocalyptic plan approved by the High Light Guardian, and I knew you'd immediately believe it and want to stop it. Your hatred for her would make you believe pretty much anything bad or unreasonable about her. To your detriment."

I glared at him, the nails of my free hand digging deeply into my palm as I clenched my fist.

"I inserted the secrecy requirement into the vision for obvious reasons, so you couldn't talk with any leadership about the book or any plans they might have with it. They don't have any, by the way," he added, almost smug. "They don't even know about the book. And then I showed you a table of people I wanted you to trust the plan with. I knew the group of you together would probably be motivated enough and martyr-like enough to agree to the mission and find the book in the given time, but you'd be too distracted with each other and all your interpersonal angst to pay much attention to me or any other details that didn't fully add up. And I was right.

"Then I used your distrust of me to make you believe I'd been included in the vision because I had a secret way to hide the book that I'd heard from captives. You were so caught up with the thought that I'd participated in torture that you accepted that story without a lot of push-back. You decided it *must* be true because I wouldn't make up something that made me look bad." He smiled a little, but it didn't reach his eyes. "Negative perception and bias are dangerous things and can be easily manipulated to get what you want if you pay attention. Just like lack of trust. You can use lack of trust to make people trust you in smaller or different ways. If you're creative."

I scowled at him, not appreciating the spy lesson. But he was right. We'd believed him because, ultimately, we hadn't trusted him to be a person who *wouldn't* just stand by and watch torture happen. He'd preyed on our preconceived notions of him to get exactly what he wanted, and we'd let him with remarkable ease. Just as I'd believed his story that my mother would sanction the use of the book to win the war. I'd let my distrust and hatred of her cloud my judgment. And I'd brought everyone down with me. *Shit.*

"I should thank you, though," he continued, a carefully amused expression touching his features. "Both for keeping everyone else in the group too distracted to pay attention to me, and for figuring out the clues to finding the book so quickly. You've single-handedly allowed me to fulfill my orders, and right on time." He sent a cold grin my way. He was needling me, now.

I dug my heels into the ground to prevent myself from charging at him and punching him in the face. "Right on time for what?" I asked through gritted teeth.

"For my backup to arrive." He bent quickly and grabbed the book. My eyes widened. *Backup?*

"Drop it!" I stepped toward him aggressively. "Or I'll kill you right now!"

Damian straightened up with the book, the ghost of a smile on his face. It almost reached his eyes. "I have no doubt you'd try, but I'll give you two compelling reasons not to. First, you really should agree to return with me to the Dark Guardian realm like my father wants. By doing so, you'll save all your friends, and all the students here. You'll save Gabriel and Matt. Because, if you don't agree, my father will kill them all. And you. Today. After what you've seen of him, you know it's true. And you can't return with me if you kill me." He shrugged.

I opened my mouth to speak, shock washing over me, but he cut me off.

"Second, even if you decide not to come with me, you won't want to waste time trying to fight me now. Your chance for that passed. You know by now that killing me won't be easy. The fight would take time. My backup would arrive before you succeed in taking the book, and then you'll have wasted your chance to warn everyone about the army that's coming," he glanced at his watch, "right about now."

My mouth fell open. *An army?* Not just another Demon attack? Fear and panic flooded me in overwhelming waves of hot and cold, making it hard to breathe. There weren't enough well-trained people at the Academy to defend it against an army, even a smaller one. We'd be unbelievably outnumbered. Decimated. And all the students who couldn't defend themselves? My fingers shook. I didn't want to think about what'd happen to them.

I took a step back. I'd unknowingly wasted too much time. Anger with myself rushed through me, and I backed up another step, away from him, not sure what to do. He'd successfully distracted me for too long. I needed to warn the school and prepare for the imminent attack. But I couldn't just leave Damian with the book—he'd hand it over to the king of the Dark Guardians, who'd use it and destroy the world. Indecision churned in my gut like snakes twisting over each other.

"You know I can't go with you." I tried to keep my voice steady as panic continued pumping through me. "Your father would do to me what he's done to you—hurt me, control me, use my skills and power to kill others. I'd rather die than be used that way. And I know, even if you don't, that agreeing to go with you won't make him call off the attack."

Damian's eyes filled with sharp denial, but I saw hesitation there as well. "That was our deal," he said firmly, pushing the hesitation away. His expression became resolved and cold again. "The book and you in exchange for the safety of the school and the students."

"Are you really naïve enough to believe that?" I laughed with disbelief. He of all people should know that his father would never abide by a deal like that. Not when he could take down the Academy and ruin a Light Guardian stronghold.

Damian's jaw tightened like a vice.

"Do you really think he'd call back an army after bothering to send it here? No, he'll destroy everything regardless of what either of us does, even if I come with you. You have to know that."

Damian just stared at me in silence, his face stony. Immovable.

"Please don't give him the book." I backed up another step. I had to warn the Academy. Surviving the army was now the most urgent problem. We'd worry about the book if we lived. But I had to try one last time. "You know what'll happen if he has it. He'll bring the gods down on us. He'll destroy the world, and you won't be protected from it. *You* put that in my vision yourself. You have to know. Everyone will die."

Damian's expression closed off and his body stiffened. "I don't have a choice. Nothing else can be done. He'll find and take the book, regardless of what I do. The earth is already doomed, Terah. Following his orders just buys everyone a little more time. A little more life."

"Please don't do this. We can find another way. We'll help you find another way."

"There is no other way!" He was losing some of his carefully crafted control. "We're out of time. Either you come with me, or you'll all die!"

I shook my head, tears pooling along my lower lashes, and reached out for Gabriel in my mind. I needed to wake him. He needed to warn the school. But he was still deep in artificially enforced sleep. I tried desperately to fight Damian's hold on him, to pull him past the block, but I couldn't. It was like trying to grip a wet bar of soap—slippery and impossible to firmly hold onto. Damian clearly had much more experience invading and manipulating people's minds. It was still so new for me. He'd probably been using that power his entire life, instead of ignoring and suppressing his power like I had.

Damian frowned at me. "You won't get them out that way." He'd pulled his control back around him. "My hold on them is too strong."

"Then release them." My voice broke. "Give them at least a fighting chance. You've already won! We're going to be so outnumbered. At least let them defend themselves!"

Damian's gaze hardened. He wasn't going to let them go.

I backed away, the tears threatening to overflow from my eyes as I stared at his cold, stony face. Could he really do this to us? Could he really just sit back and watch all of us die? After all the time we'd spent together and all the things we'd done for and with each other?

"*None of it was real,*" his cold voice slithered through my mind. I gasped. I must've let my guard down somehow. Enough to let him in. "*I was never really your friend, Terah. You were just blinded by emotion. You only saw what you wanted to see.*" His laugh echoed through my mind. "*You grew soft,*" he whispered, taunting me with my own fears. He was dangerous out of my mind, but he was even more dangerous within it.

My jaw clenched tightly in response, my teeth grinding together, and I shoved him out of my mind, trying to ignore the unexpected spear of pain in my chest. I wished his betrayal hurt less. I wished I could take back how much I'd come to like him over the past few months. But I could see, now, he wasn't the person I'd thought he was. He never had been. And he was going to let all of us die.

I took another step away. And another. Would he try stopping me? Would he try killing me right now?

"You could still stop this," Damian said, aloud this time. He took a step toward me. His gaze was intense on mine, and there was an undercurrent in his voice. Urgency, maybe? "You could agree to the offer. Join our side. Save everybody here, at least for a little longer."

I shook my head, backing further away. "It won't make a difference. And you know I can't do that. I'd rather die than have my power used for so much evil."

"Then you will die." Damian's voice had grown hard again. Almost angry. "Everyone here will. And it will be *your fault*. Is that what you want?"

"It's not my fault," I said quietly. "And I think you know that."

It was his father's fault. The endless war's fault. The Dark Guardians' fault. His fault. Damian's eyes filled with pain for a split second before going blank again. But he didn't respond.

I spun and sprinted back toward the open expanse of campus as fast as I could. Surprisingly, he didn't stop me. Perhaps because he knew I'd die anyway. I wove through the trees as fast as I could, sprinting like the world was going to end. Because it was. An *army* was coming. Everything had led to this moment. All the attacks. All that violence. It all came down to this. His choice, and mine. But it hadn't really been a choice for me. I knew it wouldn't have made a difference—saying yes—and I could never turn my back on everything and everyone I loved. And now I'd probably die. We all would.

I'd been so wrong about . . . everything. How could this have happened? How had I *let* this happen? I should've known better. I should've realized sooner. All those visions, and I still hadn't managed to prevent this. What use were they? What use was I?

I ran harder, heedless of the tears streaking down my cheeks. Now wasn't the time for them. It was too late, anyway. The damage was done. I needed to reach Gabriel and Matt in time. I needed to save them from the artificial sleep and warn the school. We needed to set up some kind of defense.

I exited the trees and sprinted across the grass toward Matt's dorm. I looked around, wanting to shout a warning to whoever I saw, but no one was in sight. Everyone was either in training or preparing for exams.

An explosion rent the air around the perimeter of campus, violently shaking the ground beneath my feet. I stumbled but managed to catch myself. Then I looked up in horror as black fire bloomed around the far edges of campus and moved quickly inward, surrounding us on all sides, setting the vegetation ablaze with Dark Guardian fire. Clearing away the trees for the army that was likely pouring through the barrier like it wasn't even there. Perhaps it wasn't anymore. Dark clouds swiftly gathered overhead, swirling dangerously. Thunder rumbled through the air as the alarms around campus, never before used, began blaring. A paralyzing terror flooded me. We were out of time. They were here.

"Terah!"

I spun and saw Gabriel, Matt, and Caleb sprinting toward me, varying looks of horror and confusion on their faces as they saw the black fire surrounding us. How had they gotten free? Had Damian released them? Or had he just become too distracted with the imminent battle to monitor them anymore?

"Gabriel!" I ran into his arms at full speed, thudding into his chest and holding on for a moment. "It was Damian," I gasped, pulling back to look at all of them. "He has the book. He's been working for the Dark Guardians this whole time. He was responsible for the vision about the book—it wasn't a real vision. He used his power to project it into my head while I was sleeping. His father is the *king of the Dark Guardians*. He tried to keep us all asleep while he took the book, but I broke free. I wasn't able to stop him in time, and now their army is here to destroy the Academy. We have to protect the students!"

All three of them gaped at me, horrified. Caleb had gone particularly pale, stumbling back a few steps. I knew the betrayal hit him the hardest. He'd let Damian in the most. He'd spent the most time with him. Considered him a real friend—something he'd almost never allowed himself. And Damian had betrayed him.

Matt pulled out his phone, his face contorting with grim rage as thunder rumbled around us, louder now. The black fire was spreading toward us, rapidly burning the trees. It'd reach the inner edge in a few minutes. Matt raised the phone to his ear, but a moment later, he hung up, swearing. Whoever he'd called hadn't answered. He hit another number. This time the call went through.

"The Dark Guardians are attacking the Academy," he yelled into the phone. "Order all students back to the dorms and instruct them to enable the armored walls in their rooms. Immediately!" He hung up and hit another number. "Luke, the Academy is under attack. Grab as many trainers, professors, and well-trained students as you can and meet me outside. We have to put up some kind of defense. Send everyone else back to their dorms and tell them to enable the armored walls in their rooms."

Then he pulled out a second phone and hit another number. This one rang for a while. "Serafina, the Academy is under attack. The Dark Guardians have sent an entire army and they've already broken down the plane barrier. I don't think any warrior faction perimeter guards survived the destruction. We're going to be outnumbered, and we need backup as soon as possible. Please help us." He was silent for a moment, then hung up.

"I had to leave a message." He turned back to me, despair in his eyes. "I don't know if she'll come. Even if she does, it might be too late."

We all stared at each other for a breathless moment, hopelessness and fear pooling between and around us. We all felt responsible for bringing this down on everyone. We'd found the book. We'd made it possible for Damian to take it. And so few on campus could fight well. There were so few of us here to protect it. We should've thought things through more. Found a way to shut down the school before things escalated this much.

Students poured out of the main building as we stood there. People were screaming. Crying. Professors were shouting. Directing students back to their dorms as the sirens continued blaring around us, thunder cracking sharply through the air.

"Armor your dorm rooms as soon as you're in!" a professor shouted as students screamed. Shoved each other. Trampled over each other. All trying to get back to their buildings first.

The swirling clouds had completely blocked out the sun, now, covering the grounds in a dark, green-gray glow. It was almost as dark as night. Wind whipped around us as lightning shot with jagged electricity across the sky.

"We're all going to die!" a younger student sobbed, falling to her knees in despair as she stared at the black fire approaching us.

"No," her friend said firmly, hauling her back to her feet and dragging her forward toward the buildings. "I'll protect you. I will. I promise."

Tears spilled down my cheeks. I looked at Gabriel, Matt, and Caleb. They looked as stricken as I felt. What could we possibly do? How could we save them? The armored barricades wouldn't hold for long—not against an entire army. They weren't meant for that. Eventually, they'd break through.

"We have to try," Matt said, correctly guessing at my thoughts. "We'll try our best to protect them. Just like we've always done. It's . . . all we can do." His voice shook a little, but his expression was firm. Determined.

Gabriel and Caleb nodded their agreement, their expressions grim.

Gabriel wrapped his arm around me and pulled me into his side. "Whatever happens, we'll face it together." I nodded, wiping my tears with my arm.

Footsteps thundered through the grass toward us, and I saw Luke approaching with a large group of trainers, professors, and intermediate to advanced trainees. I saw Simon and Omer—Matt's friends who were assistant trainers—among them. The president was also there, pale and shocked, but determined. There were maybe one hundred people total, including the professors directing students to their dorms, prepared to defend the Academy. Not nothing, but not anywhere near enough. My stomach sank.

"This is everyone I could find," Luke said, stopping next to Matt. His gaze was on the flames that'd just engulfed the last layer of trees around campus. The army would be here soon. "We'll have to do our best with this."

Matt met and held Luke's gaze for a moment, and some kind of understanding passed between them. Luke reached forward and grasped Matt's shoulder briefly, resignation on his face.

"I'll start preparing them," Luke murmured before walking back to the group of trainers and trainees.

"*Terah*," a voice whispered through my mind. Cold as ice.

I bit back a curse. It seemed like I wasn't successfully keeping my mind closed right now. Too much was happening. I was feeling too many things. I spun around and saw him standing there, maybe fifty feet away from us, his back to the blazing trees. He still had the book.

"Damian," I growled. What could he possibly want now? Why would he confront us like this? I didn't see how it'd benefit him. Not after he'd already won.

I yanked my daggers free and jogged toward him, Gabriel, Matt, and Caleb on my heels, each pulling weapons as well.

Damian regarded us silently as we approached him, his eyes lingering on Caleb, whose expression had gone as cold and dark as I'd ever seen it. He was livid. Hurt. We all were.

"There's still time." Damian looked back at me as we skidded to a halt maybe ten feet from him.

I wanted to just attack him. Kill him for his betrayal and for bringing all this down on us. But something in me made me hesitate. A feeling. A pull. *Damn the pull!* I gritted my teeth and brandished my daggers.

Regret flashed briefly in his eyes before his expression went blank again. "There's still time to stop this. To save everyone. It's in your hands."

"No, it's not!" I growled. "It won't change anything! And I won't follow your father's orders!"

"You've made the wrong choice." His words were firm, but his gaze flitted over the people around me. The people who'd become his friends. Uncertainty wavered briefly in their depths. "If you don't choose differently, you'll die. All of you."

Anger speared through me. "Look around you, Damian! The army won't stop now! Me agreeing to help the Dark Guardians won't change that. Your father would never waste this opportunity, no matter what he promised you. *He always intended to destroy the Academy.* Open your eyes! You know it's true!"

Daman's eyes flickered for a moment, before he turned to look behind him at the army shoving through the burned remnants of the trees, smoke swirling around them. Hordes of Dark Guardians and huge, misshapen Demons. His fists clenched and unclenched at his sides.

"It's too late," he murmured, his voice hollow as he turned back to us. "There's nothing I can do."

"You can help us! You can keep the book from them! You can keep it from your father! Please, Damian. You know what'll happen if he gets his hands on it. Please."

Damian swallowed, his gaze sweeping over us again. Me, Gabriel, Matt, Caleb. The group of students and teachers behind us, shakily preparing to fight. The terrified students sprinting to their dorms. His head dropped forward for a moment.

"I . . . tried to destroy it," he finally said, looking up again, his deep voice going hoarse. "Right before you found me in the trees. I tried destroying the part that's about demolishing the barrier between realms. I planned to give my father an incomplete text and claim it must've been tampered with at some point in history. But the pages won't tear or burn. None of the book will. It's indestructible. I don't . . . know what else to do."

My lips parted in surprise. He'd . . . tried to disobey his orders? That was more than I'd thought he'd do. I hadn't thought he'd felt bad about what he'd done and was going to do. Or was he just lying? My head spun. What was real with him and what wasn't? Did he truly want to prevent further harm, or was he just stalling? Was he just manipulating us again?

I shook my head slowly, not sure how to react. What to believe. Images —memories—swam through my frenzied mind as I tried piecing it all together, trying to figure out who he really was. What he really wanted. I remembered Damian and I joking with each other during training, the amusement reaching his eyes as we'd teased each other. The enthusiasm he'd shown as he'd taught each of us to fight better, even against his better judgment. How much he'd talked and engaged with Caleb each day. His astonishment when I'd saved his life. Offering to train with Caleb rather than skipping training like he'd wanted to, so Caleb wouldn't be on his own. The tears that'd filled his eyes as he'd experienced that horrible apocalyptic vision with me. His eyes becoming less and less cold over the past few months. How he'd brought me iced coffees during our research sessions, his expression full of warm amusement. How he'd shielded and aided Caleb in battle after Caleb had been injured in the first god's chamber. How he'd bound Caleb's wounds for him. How Caleb's voice had almost succeeded in pulling him out of his illusion when he'd been stuck. How horrified he'd looked when he'd thought his father was about to kill me in his illusion. He'd tried to warn me. He'd tried to stop it. How he'd tried so hard throughout his life to save people. To defy his father. To do the least amount of harm. How much he'd suffered because of it.

Damian stared at the ground, pain streaking across his face. His grip on the book was so tight his fingers looked bloodless, and I detected the slightest tremble. The memories faded from my mind. Perhaps all of that had been contrived too. Maybe I'd only seen what I'd wanted to see. What he'd *meant* for me to see. Perhaps everything really had been cold and calculated. Perhaps we really didn't know him at all.

Damian lifted his gaze and met mine again. There was a flash of vulnerability before he smoothed the cold neutrality back into place.

"Your mind opens more when you're emotional," he murmured. There was no vitriol in his voice this time. No accusation. No taunting or judgment. I wasn't sure why he'd said it. To tell me that he'd seen my memories too? To what end? It didn't change anything. He'd proven himself not to be that person.

A roar sounded from behind Damian, deep and painful and loud. It sucked the breath from my lungs and made my knees tremble. I peered around him, and my stomach clenched. An army—bigger than I'd expected—was stepping beyond the burning trees. We were out of time.

Flashes of light illuminated the dark sky as everyone behind us started transforming.

"Matt!" I spun to look at him. "We need to try putting a barrier around the dorms. We need to keep them away from the buildings for as long as possible. Until we have a better plan."

Matt nodded, then turned and ran back toward Luke. Caleb shot Damian one last furious look before turning and following Matt. They fanned everyone out in a wide circle around the dorms, instructing them on how to conjure, expand, and connect their shields to others. It'd be a big energy drain. We wouldn't be able to hold them forever.

Gabriel transformed and took my hand, tugging a little. "We need to join the others. The army will reach us in a minute."

I nodded and turned to look at Damian one last time. *Try again. Try again.* The same voice that'd told me to save him. The same pull that'd led me to him in the forest. I sighed and warily considered Damian for a moment in silence.

"Join us," I finally said, even as I knew he wouldn't. "It's not too late. Fight with us. Fight for these students. Fight for your friends."

Damian's gaze slammed into mine, startled. *Friends.* I knew, now, that he'd never had any. But he did now. Or he had, before he'd betrayed us.

"There's still time to do the right thing."

Damian swallowed hard, despair seeming to fill every inch of his being. Surprisingly, he didn't try to mask it this time. He clenched his free fist, his body going rigid.

"He'd kill me. Or continuously torture me and never let me die." His voice was quiet and hollow.

"He's already killing and torturing you. Every day. Can't you see that?"

Damian flinched, but didn't respond. I sighed. We didn't have time for this anymore. With a frustrated sound, I spun away from him and jogged with Gabriel back to the rest of the group. I closed my eyes as we ran and found the well of purple power in my chest, thankfully full again. I grabbed it and threw it outward, filling my skin with my power. With a burst of light, I transformed. Huge purple wings sprouted from my back, my hair lifted around me, armor closed over my limbs, and a sword of fire and lightning formed at my side. Several students and professors gasped and backed away from me, but I didn't have time for their ridiculous fear. More Demon screams had begun to crack and bleed through the air as the army closed in around us, sowing fear and pain through our too-small group of fighters.

"Shields up now!" I yelled, drawing my sword, lightning crackling up and down the blade. Light flashed all around me as the students, professors, and trainers conjured different colored shields, expanding them out and up as far as they could. I turned back toward the tree line in front of us and quickly conjured one as well, carefully connecting it to Gabriel's and Caleb's on either side of me, and extending it high into the air, over the top of the closest dorm, until it touched the edge of yet another shield.

I looked through the deep purple barrier in front of me and saw that Damian was still standing where we'd left him, but he was staring at me, his mouth open in naked astonishment as he gawked at my transformation. I supposed he'd never seen it. His gaze swept over me, taking in all the details, even as the army closed in behind him. He knew, now, I wasn't a Light Guardian, or any other recognizable Divine. I was something strange and different. His hand shook as he brought it up to his mouth, covering it. Grabbing at his own jaw. He shook his head and took a step closer. Then another. And another. Until he was jogging toward me.

"How is that possible?" Astonishment and confusion filled his voice as he skidded to a halt in front of me.

I didn't respond. It wasn't like I knew. No one knew what I was. Or *why* I was. And it was far from the most important thing right now.

"I thought . . ." he stepped up to me and ran the tips of his fingers over

609

my shield. "I thought I was alone." His eyes continued to devour my transformation, even as he withdrew his hand.

Alone?

"My father told me there was no one else. That it was just me—the lone abomination, destined to be reviled wherever I went. No use to anyone but him—he, who'd overlook my difference to gain a weapon. But . . . he was wrong." Damian took a step back from me, amazement widening his eyes, his chest rapidly rising and falling. "I'm not the only one."

He met my gaze squarely for a moment. Reading my confusion.

"And neither are you."

In a brilliant flash of deep purple, Damian transformed in front of me. Purple wings sprang from his back, purple armor closed around his body, a sword of fire and lightning formed at his side, purple light shone from his skin and eyes, and his hair lifted, as though it was caught in the wind.

I gasped and stepped back, my sword falling from my fingers, my shield flickering and fading. He was . . . like me. *Exactly* like me. I wasn't the only one.

"What the hell," I murmured weakly, staring at him. "How is that even possible?"

Damian stepped toward me again and extended his hand, palm up. I looked up and met his gaze, purple like mine. Amazed like mine. I hesitated for a moment, then placed my palm to his. A jolt shot through my body. Not of electricity or awareness or anything, but of wholeness. Like completing a circuit. Uniting something that'd been broken. Purple swirled around our connected hands almost like a halo. Like it wanted to bind us together.

"What does it mean?"

"I don't know." His brow furrowed as he stared at our connected hands. "But it . . . wants us to stay together."

That broke whatever trance of amazement I was in. I yanked back my hand and bent to pick up my sword.

"You chose the wrong side, Damian," I reminded him, voice hard. "You're the enemy now."

Damian sighed deep and long, like it was being pulled from his soul. He was silent for a long moment.

"I chose the only course of action I thought I had." His expression was surprisingly earnest as he stepped forward to stand between me and Caleb. "I was never on their side ideologically. I was just on the side I was born into, like so many of us. It was the side that had control over me. But . . . if I'm going to die anyway . . ." he paused, looking down at the book in his hand, then up at the army that was closing in around us, ". . . I might as well choose to do what's right." His voice had grown gravelly and raw, but he sounded sincere.

He drew his sword quickly, tucked the book under his arm, and conjured a shield with his other hand, bolstering the protections around the dorms.

I blinked at him, not sure how to feel. I didn't know whether I could believe him. Or forgive him. I didn't know if I could ever trust him again.

"You can yell at me more later," Damian said, glancing at me, the ghost of a smile on his lips. "Let's focus on them for now." He nodded at the soldiers and Demons surrounding us.

I regarded him for a long moment before nodding tightly and facing forward, conjuring my shield again. I wouldn't turn down such a good soldier offering to fight on our side. Not when we were so outnumbered. But uncertainty still churned in my gut. I hoped trusting him in this moment wouldn't backfire as it had before.

"My father must have known," Damian murmured, his gaze on the army surrounding our giant shield. "He must have known you were like me." He glanced at me briefly, his eyes flitting over my transformation again. "That must be why he wanted you on our side or eliminated."

I bit the inside of my cheek, considering. "Maybe."

It'd certainly explain why he'd wanted me eliminated before I'd known about my additional abilities. If he was familiar with Damian's, he must've known what the outcome of mine would be or had assumed I'd connected with those abilities already. I wondered what else he knew about us that we didn't.

On a shouted command, the Dark Guardians surrounding us on all sides began blasting the shield with black fire, drawing my attention back to the battle. The fire engulfed the entire dome we'd managed to create over the dorms. Several students stumbled backward, under the onslaught of power, struggling to hold on.

"Steady!" Luke called. "Concentrate on feeding a continual stream of power to your shield. Don't over or underdo it. Just keep it constant."

The shield rippled and bent.

"Brace yourselves!" Matt yelled down the line to my left. "Get yourself into a sturdy stance and concentrate!"

"How many soldiers are there?" I asked quietly, so only Damian, Gabriel, and Caleb could hear.

Damian stared at the wall of black fire in front of us, his expression grim. "About two thousand."

My heart sank as Caleb and Gabriel both swore. Around a hundred of us against *two thousand* soldiers? Even if the few hundred barricaded students were helping us, we'd still be devastatingly outnumbered. Our chances of getting out of this alive were essentially nonexistent. I nodded and pushed down the waves of fear and grief threatening to pull me under. We weren't powerless yet. Not completely. Backup could be on its way. And we could still prevent the world from ending, if we could keep the book from his father.

"Okay. We need to get rid of the book. We need to make sure they can't give it to your father if they . . . win."

Strained sounds of effort echoed around the dome, and the shield bent and warped again as more Dark Guardians joined the bombardment. The amount of power hitting us now was seriously straining the integrity of the shield. I widened my stance, bracing myself to better handle the pressure of the onslaught. But keeping it up would be a huge power drain for our side—more than it'd be for theirs. The Demons weren't being affected by this at all. They, unlike other factions of Divines, couldn't use their power for things outside of their transformation and specialized quick healing when transformed. They were just biding their time, filling the air with their terror-inducing screams while the Dark Guardians, and those of us defending the Academy, expended power.

"Damian, that method of hiding the book you mentioned a few weeks ago . . . was it complete bullshit, or was there some truth behind it?" I glanced at him and saw him frown.

"It was based in truth, but it isn't as doable as I made it sound. It may not be possible with so few of us."

Caleb's expressed turned even more stormy, his mouth pressed into a grim line as he shook his head in disgust. He clearly wasn't in a place to put aside Damian's betrayal, even for the moment. Regret flickered in Damian's eyes as he glanced at Caleb. He could hear what Caleb was thinking—he seemed to use that power much more than I did—and I could only imagine those thoughts were pretty brutal toward him right now.

"Unless you have a better idea about how to keep the book away from your father, we should still try it," I said, trying to refocus everyone.

612

"We can try. Just don't count on it working. We'll need someone to cover this portion of the shield, though. We'll need at least the four of us."

I nodded and looked at our shields, assessing. It'd be quite a gap to fill, but I knew one person who was powerful enough to do it.

"Matt! We need you over here for a few minutes!" I couldn't see where he was, but I knew he was within earshot.

"Give me a second," he called back from a moderate distance. "I need to make sure my shield area is covered first."

"We'll need to work quickly," I said quietly, turning back to Damian. "The shield isn't going to last for long. We need to make sure the book is hidden and we're ready to fight by the time that happens."

Damian nodded shortly at me, his expression firm and neutral. Rigidly under control. Which was how I knew he was actually worried.

"Understood."

I turned as footsteps thundered through the grass toward us. Matt skidded to a halt as he caught sight of Damian and his transformation.

"W-what?" He looked back and forth between us in astonishment. "How is that possible?" He took a step closer to us, slowly, flabbergasted. His gaze swept over Damian, taking in the details of his transformation from top to bottom, before sweeping over me. Comparing. Ascertaining if we really were the same somehow. His hand shook as he ran it through his hair. "How . . . how is he . . . *like you?*

Horror filled Matt's eyes, eclipsing the shock, and my chest felt heavy, like it was turning to stone. He'd had a hard enough time dealing with just my transformation. Two of us like this was clearly more than he could wrap his mind around. It was more than he could accept.

"We don't know," I murmured. I took a centering breath, refusing to let the old hurt touch me now. His lack of acceptance couldn't be my problem anymore. "We only just discovered it."

Matt shook his head, speechless, as he stared back and forth between the two of us. Finally, he shook himself out of his daze and looked at Damian, his eyes turning to steel as his jaw clenched with rage.

"What the hell is he even doing here?" He shot me an accusing look. "He betrayed us! He's responsible for almost leading us to our deaths under false pretenses and unleashing this hell on us and all the students. How could you let him be here?"

Damian's jaw clenched, and his cold mask descended again, but he didn't say anything.

I sighed. "I know, Matt." He had every right to be furious at Damian, but now wasn't the time for angry confrontations. We needed to prioritize survival first. "But we still have a chance to hide the book and keep it out of the Dark Guardians' hands, and Damian is willing to help us do that. I need you to put aside your anger for a moment and help us. Please, Matt."

Matt's gaze slid over my face, seeing my desperation. Seeing how much I needed him on our side. His anger softened just a little.

"Fine," he gritted out. "But don't think this is over," he growled at Damian. Damian nodded at him slowly, his expression unreadable. "What do you need from me?" Matt turned back to me.

"We need you to create a shield big enough to cover the area we're about to vacate. Hiding the book will take all four of us, and you're strong enough to make and hold a shield that large."

He sighed and scrubbed a hand down his face but finally nodded. "I can do that." He moved to stand between me and Damian. "Let me conjure one behind yours first so there's no gap when yours come down."

We nodded and the four of us took a couple steps back, making more room for him. Matt extended his hand in front of him and shot bright white power into the air, forming a shield that quickly climbed outward and up, expanding to cover a huge section of fortifications in front of this particular dorm. He was seriously powerful.

"Okay," he said a moment later, "you can let go of your shields now. Just hurry. I don't want to drain my power too quickly."

"We'll do our best." I gave him a small smile before dropping my hand and following the others.

We jogged to the dorm wall behind us and knelt in a circle around the book.

"Alright," Damian said, rubbing his jaw, "what we're about to try is advanced power theory—like what the Academy founders did with their powers to protect the book. Most of us have never learned about, or even seen, power use like that. We've been focused on war and survival for so long that we've lost our deeper connection to ourselves as Divines. We've forgotten what we're capable of. We have a whole group of scholar-soldiers back home who spend their entire lives studying and practicing these techniques so they can open new plane rips. As a child, I was curious about what they did, so I stole and read many of the books containing their notes—that's how I know the general theory. It's also how I know how difficult this will be. Maybe impossible."

He rubbed a hand over his eyes and released a breath.

"Alright. First thing we need to do is make a cut in this plane. Think about it like gliding the tip of a knife lightly down your skin with just enough pressure to open it but not damage anything beyond. In this case, the knife is your power. You aren't trying to cut an object or even air—you're trying to cut *space*. You're not isolating matter like you would for normal matter-shifting, you're isolating matter so you can exclude it and solely focus on the space *around* the matter."

"How the hell are we supposed to do that?" Caleb asked, incensed. "That doesn't make any sense!"

"It takes massive concentration," Damian responded calmly. "You have to clear your mind and *feel* the matter around you, like you would with any other matter-shifting. Concentrate on feeling the particles of earth and water in the air. You need to look beyond and between those substances to feel the presence of the space that all of that is in. Remember, the plane itself is a thing—space is both an absence and an entity—and as an entity, you can impact it with your power. Once you can feel that space, you can direct your power to treat it like a solid object, and you'll be able to cut it."

"This is complete bullshit!" Caleb burst out angrily. "Do you believe this?" He turned to look at me incredulously. "I've never heard of anyone using their power like this. He's probably lying! Stalling so some other horrible shit can happen to us!"

I glanced at Damian in time to see hurt flash across his face before he smoothed out his expression again. But he didn't say anything to defend himself. He probably knew it wouldn't help. Caleb was furious with him and would undoubtedly stay that way.

"I don't think it's bullshit." I held Caleb's gaze. "Our proof lies in the Dark Guardians' own actions—they've managed to slice open the Normal plane and attach it to theirs throughout the war, even in recent memory, and that's all we're trying to do here. Besides," I added, glancing at the black fire engulfing the shield, "we're fucked anyway. We lose nothing by trying."

Caleb's expression turned grim as he looked around us as well, before returning his gaze to mine. "Fine," he grumbled, refusing to look at Damian.

"We need to aim our power at the same point and move together." Damian extended his hand into the space between us and pointed at where he wanted us to start. "We don't have enough power individually to do any of it."

I nodded and reached forward, mirroring him. Gabriel and Caleb followed suit.

"Close your eyes and focus on the matter around you. When you're finally able to feel and isolate the space from the matter in front of our hands, tell the rest of us. We all need to be at that same mental place before we try making the cut. Ready?"

The three of us nodded before closing our eyes. I concentrated with every bit of energy I had, trying to *feel* the matter that made up the air and all the particles within it, and beyond to the space that those entities existed within. I let a little power drift out from each of my fingers like tiny vines to touch the air there, gently feeling. This was such an abstract concept of substance and being. I'd never tried using my power on something as wholly existent and nonexistent as space—something so tangible yet illusory. But I tried looking beyond my own senses to see through my power.

Slowly, so slowly, I began to sense what I hadn't been able to detect with my eyes—the solidness of the matter in front of us. The fleeting tangibility of the spaces between. It was like parting hundreds of translucent curtains to reach the window behind it all—invisible yet palpable. On a deep, slow breath, I directed my power into the spaces between and touched that almost imperceptible entity. *Space.*

"I'm ready." My voice came out slow and quiet through my concentration.

"So am I," Damian murmured.

There was silence as we waited for Gabriel and Caleb. I had no idea how long we sat there—my mind was entirely occupied with feeling and holding onto the space in front of us.

"I'm ready," Gabriel finally said, his voice deep and quiet, almost like he was in a trance.

"Ready," Caleb said a long moment later.

"Now we need to move our hands across the space, focusing our power on slicing the plane. Remember, your power is the knife, and you're slicing the space, not the matter." He took a deep breath and let it out slowly. "Now."

I kept my eyes closed, needing to only see with my power, but I could feel the others' powers spilling from their fingers and combining with mine to make a blinding beam. I could feel their concentration. Their connection to the space around us. I could almost feel their thoughts, even without connecting my mind to theirs. Slowly, as a unit, we created a thin slice in the space between us, moving our hands millimeter by millimeter, not daring to go any faster for fear we'd mess up or lose our grasp on our concentration. Goosebumps erupted over my skin in waves as we went. This felt . . . wrong, somehow. Tearing reality and leaving an open gash in it felt abnormal. Vulnerable. Like it needed to be healed. I reminded myself that we *would* heal it, once the book was safe inside the new plane.

"Good," Damian finally murmured. "That should be enough."

I opened my eyes to look at the slice we'd made. It didn't look like I'd expected it to. It wasn't a violent, jagged tear in the fabric of reality. Instead, reality just kind of rippled above and below the cut, like lightly bunched cloth. And within the thin slice—nothing. Just perfect darkness. Perfect absence. *Weird.*

"The next part is the hardest." Damian's expression was grim. "We may not be able to do it. Be prepared for that. We might just have to seal up the tear we made and walk away from this plan. There's a reason it takes whole lives of study to do things like this."

The rest of us looked at each other uneasily.

"We need to channel raw power across the slice and concentrate on creation. Focus on turning your power into space as a three-dimensional entity. The space you're creating isn't matter, but if you need to think about it in terms of matter-shifting, think about shifting your raw power into tiny, three-dimensional, invisible and fillable cubes beyond the tear. You're essentially creating potential—a place where things can and will go, but that aren't there yet. Picture what you want to create and push your power through that image. Are you ready to try?"

I glanced at the shield again—at the consuming black fire and the students and professors faltering under its weight. The stakes were high, but I tried to let that fuel me. We *would* do this. We had to.

"I'm ready."

Damian nodded, then looked at Gabriel and Caleb. They nodded as well, their expressions more resigned than determined.

"Alright. Close your eyes and begin."

I took a deep breath and raised my hand again as I closed my eyes. I felt, rather than saw, our fingertips hovering over the gap in reality. I filled it with my power along with the others in a flood of multi-colored light. It was weird, because . . . nothing existed in the gap, yet we could still interact with it somehow. It was somehow fillable like a dry riverbed searching for water. Yet it was the absence of everything. I could *feel* the nothingness. A fathomless, terrifying absence. But somehow our powers could float on that nothingness. Could touch it somehow. There was no way to explain it other than that our powers were . . . truly divine. Something more than the laws guiding reality. An exception to the rules of the universe.

I concentrated on the power we'd collectively pooled in that area of nothingness. Then I pictured what I wanted to create. I filled every part of me with that image. I focused every fiber of my being, every thought and feeling, on the need for its creation. Then I flooded the image, the concept, the need, with my power. My hand shook with the strain of it. I could feel a sheen of sweat forming on my forehead. I could feel all of us straining. Pushing ourselves beyond what we thought was possible. I felt our powers writhing and shifting, trying to do what we were asking of them. But . . . it just wasn't happening.

"We're just . . . not . . . strong enough," Caleb panted.

"Don't give up," Gabriel huffed. "Think of what's at stake. We have to . . . keep . . . trying."

But I could feel what Caleb was saying. It felt like there was a block. Something keeping us from taking that final step of creation. But it didn't feel like an internal block from any of us. It just felt like . . . we didn't have enough power to do what we were asking our powers to do. The strength for that final push just wasn't there.

My stomach dropped as despair flooded me. "We . . . we have to do it," I gasped. "There has to be a way."

But there wasn't. No matter how hard we tried, we weren't able to cross that threshold. Even with four powerful Divines, we didn't have enough power to create space from nothing. *Shit*. My head drooped forward. Our success or failure here would be the difference between preserving the world, and its complete destruction at the Dark Guardian king's hands. We *had* to find a way to do this. No matter the cost.

Through my despair, I suddenly felt a tugging in the vicinity of my chest, almost like a throb. The same tugging from the illusion chamber. The same tugging that'd allowed me to find and follow Damian. It was that invisible, insistent tether that inexplicably reached from my chest into his, somehow always there. Now it was pulling me toward him like it had a mind of its own.

Without consciously trying, my mind reached out and connected to Damian's with a snap. I wasn't sure if instinct was driving me or if this was somehow out of my control. I was sucked into a trance-like state. The world seemed to slow around me, the sounds of impending battle fading into a muffled jumble at the back of my mind. I could hear my breath filling and exiting my lungs. My heart pounding loudly in my ears. My blood rushing through my veins. And I could *feel* Damian. The pulsing of his power matching mine—familiar, like a piece of me. And I could see, like we were there again, the battlefield from our shared vision. The deep purple power swirling between us as the world fell apart around us. It'd been trying to tell us something. To show us something. There was something it needed us to do. The power connected us. Linked us to each other. Pulled us closer. Together, we created . . . *something more.*

I gasped as Damian suddenly grabbed my hand and closed his fingers tightly around it. I felt him opening himself to the connection, whatever it was. He felt the pull too. The call toward unity. Our power hummed back and forth between us quickly. Intensifying. Yet something about it felt stabilizing. Whole. Instead of the steady drain of power I usually felt while transformed, it suddenly seemed to slow almost to a stop. No more bleeding of power like a newly opened gash. Now, it was more like the power was flowing back and forth between us in a circle. Like it was on standby. Like we'd only lose power if we used it for something. I wondered, fleetingly, if this was what it felt like for all other Divines to be transformed. I'd always drained so much faster than them, and we'd never known why.

"*More*," I murmured silently to Damian. I knew, somehow, we needed to give ourselves completely to this unity. We needed to become vulnerable to it so we could become stronger. So we could become something more.

"*More*," Damian echoed—a confirmation, an agreement—his voice in my mind almost otherworldly. It whispered through me as our power vibrated, barely contained by our skin.

We both opened to the pull—the unity—even more. Letting go. Giving in. Losing ourselves. We knew it was the only way. I could feel the breath in his chest. It had become my breath. His heartbeat had become my heartbeat. His power and mine could no longer be distinguished or disentangled. We were somehow . . . one. One being. One entity. One power. *More.*

"What's happening?" Caleb gasped as he and Gabriel sat back, pulling their hands from the space in front of us. I could feel his voice drifting toward us from far, far away.

A pulse shuddered through us, and we felt the cages around our life forces—the things separating and protecting our most sacred power—opening. And we were flooded. With everything we had and everything we were. All of our divine. It pooled inside us, mixing with our normal power, becoming a light so blinding and a power so fierce and raw that it nearly burned us from the inside. We felt like a living ember. An unearthly being boiling with power. Neither mortal nor immortal. Not really human anymore. My grip tightened around Damian's hand. I didn't want to lose control of this, whatever it was. If we did, I knew it'd rip us apart. No mortal was meant to withstand this much power. No mortal could without dying. But somehow, together, we could survive it. *Use* it.

We opened our eyes and felt them burning with raw, otherworldly force. Glowing more brightly than they ever had before. The power radiated off us in waves, stirring the air around us. We glowed like beacons as our hair danced in slow motion through the air. Caleb and Gabriel gaped at us, astonished. Speechless. We weren't just transformed anymore. We were . . . something else. Something new.

Damian and I stretched our joined hands toward the rip in reality, the air around us shimmering with power. We knew we could do this now. Just the two of us. We knew whatever we were was strong enough. We pressed our glowing fingertips to the nothingness within the plane tear and concentrated.

"*Create space*," we murmured simultaneously in our minds.

We shared all thought now. Pictured the same thing we wanted to create. Pushed our power into and through that image. Willing it to come into being. We were unified. We moved as one, almost like a dance. We wondered if this was why we could read minds. For when we came together like this. It allowed us to be as one. To work and act as one. To think as one. Our thoughts were untouchable to others. Our communication was silent and instantaneous. Merged. Ours.

Power bloomed from our fingers, impossibly bright, and spilled through the tear in reality, expanding beyond the opening little by little—the mixture of our combined life forces and our normal power finally strong enough to breach the threshold and allow for creation. Our life forces were the strongest parts of us. The most purely divine. And usually off-limits to those who didn't want to die. But connected like this, morphed into whatever we'd become through our shared, unusual power, we could use that previously untouchable force to do the unimaginable.

Together, we pushed forward, the space growing larger and larger beyond our fingertips until it was large enough to encompass the book. It was time to create the air.

Damian reached down and grabbed a handful of grass next to his leg, then raised the delicate blades to the newly created space.

"*Shift into air*," we thought in tandem, picturing what we wanted them to become.

In mere moments, we filled the new plane, giving it atmosphere and usability. It was much easier than creating space. Then we reached down together and grabbed the book. It pulsed beneath our fingers, sending tiny vibrations like static electricity through our hands. It felt like it was . . . seeing us somehow. Watching us as we watched it. Like it was conscious. Sentient.

Damian's chest grew heavy as he looked at it. I could still feel his every emotion and thought like they were my own, and I was suddenly flooded by his guilt, pain, and regret—for all that he'd done, for all that he wished he could do, for what he wished he could change, for what he knew he was about to lose. For all that could never be. For all that he'd never deserve.

He usually concealed everything so well, but he couldn't hide how vast and deep his pain was when we were connected like this. It felt like an internal wound, catastrophically hemorrhaging, but invisible. But it was a pain he knew well—a constant companion his whole life. And I had no idea how he didn't drown in it all.

Damian's glowing eyes met mine for a brief moment, and I felt his answer. He *did* drown in it. It was his own personal torture. But it was, perhaps, the only method of penance truly open to him. The only way he could even slightly atone for all he'd done and would still be forced to do. So he bore it, silently and alone. Always.

I frowned. "*But you're not alone. Not anymore.*" My grip tightened around his hand. Comforting. Connecting. "*And you deserve more than your father and more than that pain.*" I knew what he'd done. I knew what he was. But I also knew who he *could* be. He just needed to see it too.

Damian's mouth curled into the smallest smile as he looked at me. He was surprised. Warmth crept back into him despite himself.

We turned back to the new plane and lifted the book, then placed it within the dark space we'd created. It'd be safe there, hidden forever, as it should be. Then we touched our joined fingers to the tear in the plane and slowly fused the cut, knitting reality back together like reforming skin over a gash. Fusing what'd been torn. Reunifying what'd been broken. Until there was no sign of the new plane in front of us. Just a slight feeling in the air when you touched it. Almost like a scar, but an invisible one. You'd only notice it if you were looking for it. But it was done. *Finally.*

I looked at Damian, and he nodded. It was time for us to let go of this . . . unity. Before we used too much of our life force. I wasn't sure if there'd be consequences for using a power that Divines were never supposed to use. We closed our eyes again and concentrated on pulling our life forces back inside their confines in our chests. Then we divided our remaining power, sending half back into me and half back into him. I was surprised to see that, even after being transformed for so long and unleashing whatever we'd just unleashed in ourselves, we were only drained about halfway. Well, half our normal power, and part of our life force. Finally, we unclasped hands.

With a jolt, Damian and I fell out of our transformations, no longer connected. I gasped, swaying slightly. Gabriel wrapped his arm around me, steadying me. I felt drained, tired, but mostly fine.

"Are you okay?" Gabriel's gaze flitted over my face, worried. At least he didn't look afraid of me.

I glanced at Damian and trepidation slid through me. We'd become capable of the unimaginable. It'd felt like . . . we were no longer human. No longer myself. But what had we become? And how? What did it mean? We'd once again done something no Divine should be able to do.

I shivered a little as Damian gazed back, his expression unreadable. I wondered if he felt as disconcerted as I did. I leaned into Gabriel and tried pushing the fear and questions away. The unity—whatever it was—had helped us.

"Yeah." I pulled on a tremulous smile. "I'm a little drained, but overall, not too bad."

Gabriel nodded, his hand coming up to cup my cheek. He still looked worried. "How's your power level? You look pale."

I shrugged. "About half drained." The worry in his gaze intensified. He knew I drained just by transforming, and we still had a battle ahead of us.

"I'll just wait to transform until the last possible moment. It'll be fine, I promise."

"What the hell *was* that?" Caleb cut in, before Gabriel could respond. He was looking back and forth between me and Damian.

Damian and I glanced at each other before turning to Caleb and shrugging.

"We're not sure," I said. "But it must be some kind of benefit of sharing the same weird power. Whatever it was, it was helpful, at least."

Caleb's eyes slid over our faces, taking in how pale we'd become.

Worry grew in their depths. "What did it do to you?" His voice was quieter now. "You both look, I don't know, weakened somehow. Can you still fight?"

"We'll be fine," Damian said firmly, not looking at Caleb. "And now's not a great time for us to figure any of this out." He jerked his chin toward the shield surrounding the dorms.

I turned and saw that significant cracks were starting to form in the multi-colored barrier. Spaces that hadn't been there before were gaping open, letting black fire through. It looked like it could fall apart at any moment.

"Shit," I whispered, pushing quickly to my feet and pulling Gabriel up with me. We'd taken too long. "We need to help them. Now."

26

DARKNESS VISIBLE

WE QUICKLY JOGGED BACK OVER TO MATT, WHO'D SHIFTED INTO A more braced position.

"Thank the gods," he panted as he saw us return. Sweat was pouring down his face from the effort of holding up so much of the shield on his own. "Did it work?"

"Yes," I said quickly. "The book is sealed away and undetectable."

Matt released a relieved breath. "Well, at least one thing has gone right. I need you all to take over this area again so I can try to patch up the cracks in the rest of the shield."

We nodded and got into position behind him, then quickly conjured our shields and carefully connected them to the ones around us.

"We need a better plan." I turned to look at Matt once he'd let go of his shield. "We can't hold them out forever, and we don't know whether any backup will come. There are two thousand Dark Guardian and Demon soldiers," I added quietly. "If we don't have a better plan when the shield falls, everyone here will die."

Despair spread across Matt's face for a moment as my words sank in. He hadn't guessed there were so many. He'd known we were hopelessly outnumbered, but he hadn't known by how much.

"I don't know what else we can do," he finally responded, quiet enough that only I could hear him. He scrubbed his hand down his face. "All we can do is put our most experienced fighters in front and hold out for as long as we can. Try to keep the army away from the dorms for as long as we can and hope for backup. I don't think there's anything else we can do, Terah. This is just . . . a battle we can't win." His voice had become gravelly, dejection spilling from his eyes. "We were probably never going to make it out of this, even with backup. The odds were always against us."

I clenched my jaw and tried to fight my own frustration and despair. I didn't like that he was giving up. Our entire lives had been filled with odds that weren't good, but we'd always pushed forward. Always tried to outsmart the situations designed to end us. We'd survived so much that way. Where had that determination gone? Where was that ceaseless drive for survival? Perhaps this was another way he'd changed when he'd taken on his warrior faction position. He'd become less recklessly hopeful and more resigned and pragmatic. That wasn't wholly a bad thing, but if there was ever a moment where we needed reckless hope, it was now.

I knew he wasn't going to give up completely—he still meant to fight with everything he had and lead everyone here until he no longer could—but I could see, now, that he was also preparing to die. Preparing to watch all of us die. Resigning himself to it. He had been since the army had first arrived. I swallowed down my frustration and was surprised to feel tears prickling the corners of my eyes. I didn't have a better plan either. I'd just hoped that someone would. Because I wasn't ready to give up yet. I wasn't ready to resign myself to death again.

Matt stepped closer to me, his eyes searching mine. Then he reached out and gently ran the tips of his glowing fingers down my cheek—something he hadn't dared to do for months. His fingers shook a little as his eyes overflowed with emotion. With unspoken words. My heart clenched as I watched him, my chest feeling constricted. With a jolt, I realized he was . . . saying goodbye.

"Matt," I whispered, not sure what to say. There was so much hurt and negativity between us. So much complicated history. But he'd always been my friend and my family. I still cared deeply for him, and I didn't want to lose him. I didn't want to see him die like I had in my illusion.

"Be strong, Terah. Like you always are. I . . . I love you."

My mouth opened a little, but I felt frozen. Overwhelmed. Unsure how to express everything I was feeling. Matt just gave me a small, sad smile and backed away.

I blinked away the stinging remnants of tears as I watched him go, maybe for the last time. It felt like he was taking a piece of me with him. Like he'd torn out a small part of my chest, leaving a hollow chasm in its wake. *No.* I shook myself and faced resolutely forward again. We'd see each other again. I refused to believe this was the end.

I gritted my teeth, concentrating on keeping my shield steady and strong. I felt the Dark Guardians' powers pushing against it like it was a door they were trying to shove open that I was just barely holding closed. It took a lot of strength to keep them out. No wonder all the students were starting to seriously falter. A few minutes of this would be draining and painful for anyone. And we'd still have to fight after it fell. I didn't know if the students would be able to do it. Not for very long. I bit back a curse and shook my head. We *needed* a better plan.

The Demons continued to roar horrifically outside the shield's bubble. I shivered, the sound seeping into my bones. *Damn Demons and their fear-based powers.* I gritted my teeth for a moment, collecting myself.

"Should we transform into that . . . that *thing* again?" I glanced at Damian.

He shook his head. "That form uses our life force, and we've already expended some, on top of draining half our powers. We don't have enough left to make a significant dent in two thousand soldiers before completely burning out and dying. Maybe, if we were at full power, but as of right now, we'd be more useful as normal soldiers. It's better to save that form for when there's nothing more we can do. Because it will probably be the last thing we do."

I nodded grimly. He was right. We'd be deadly for a moment in one area, then gone forever. And then they'd have two less highly trained soldiers protecting the Academy.

I chewed on my lower lip, dread pinging around in my chest, as I tried to think of a plan. We couldn't let all the students behind us be murdered in cold blood. They weren't battle-hardened soldiers. They hadn't grown up in border towns and had their lives shaped by loss, unfairness, and trauma. They'd barely stepped into adulthood. And they didn't deserve this. None of us did.

I glanced around, trying to look at our assets in a new way. The other side had Demons on their side, but we had an advantage in the form of Blessed. Their powers were almost never completely identical, were much more diverse than any other faction's powers, and were often much harder to predict. There were no Blessed soldiers in Dagmar, so I'd never considered how strategically important they could be in battle until now. Perhaps the Dark Guardian army hadn't considered them as a unique threat either. Perhaps the Blessed students, professors, and trainers could use their powers in unpredictable ways to gain us an advantage or at least buy us more time. But that alone wouldn't help us hold off two thousand soldiers forever. We'd still need significant additional help. But how could we alert people outside the Academy's plane about the massacre that was about to happen here? And who could possibly get here in time?

"Damian," I turned to glance at his profile, "is the protective barrier around the Academy completely gone? Can people enter and exit the portals freely now?"

Damian's brows furrowed slightly. "I believe the barrier is completely gone, so I'd assume that would make the portals available for use. We didn't use or mess with them. Why? You know we can't evacuate everyone that way—we'd never make it through the army to the barrier with all the students. And even if some of us managed to survive, the army would just follow us out and take this battle to the Normal plane."

"I know. That's not what I was thinking about."

"Then what?" He glanced at me.

"I'm not sure yet." I rubbed my hand over my forehead. "Still working on it."

He nodded and faced forward again. "Work on it fast. In a minute or two we won't have any more time for brainstorming." He nodded at the cracks spanning over the top of the domed shield around us and the dorms. They were widening. Splintering out like cracks in shattered glass, new fractures appearing every moment.

I faced forward again and tried to catalogue all the transformations I'd seen around me. How many Blessed there were surrounding the dorms. What their powers were. How we could use their abilities to shield the dorms and keep the army away from us for longer. There were maybe twenty Blessed on this side of the dorms, so maybe thirty to forty total, and most had earth and water-based transformations, though there were a few with wind and fire. But could any of their powers allow them to bypass the army to escape through one of the portals to get help off-plane?

Before I could come to any conclusions, screams erupted around me as several students in my line of sight fell to their knees. I whipped my head around, my heart pounding frantically, and saw that the shield had failed in multiple places, leaving large portions of area around the dorms completely unprotected. Black fire shot through and hit the sides of the dorm, blackening the stone in wide swaths. A few students lay motionless on the ground—the fire must've hit them as they'd lost hold of their

627

sections of the shield. I had no way of telling whether they were dead, injured, or just knocked unconscious.

"Shit." I summoned more power to my hands, then threw it outward, expanding my shield to cover a much larger area. Damian, Caleb, and Gabriel followed suit, all of us spreading out to cover more ground.

It barely helped. Student after student lost hold of their shield, collapsing under the pressure of the power they were trying to hold out. As soon as I saw someone starting to fall, I expanded my shield as quickly as I could into their area, trying to protect them from the blasts of black fire. But that was only a temporary solution—none of us had enough power to keep a shield up over all the dorms with only a few of us powering it.

"Spread out!" Luke yelled from somewhere behind us. "All those who still have shields up, spread out and cover as much area as you can. Everyone else, spread out behind them and prepare yourself to fight when the shields fall."

People helped each other to their feet and lined up behind us. Some professors and trainers were healing students who'd been burned as their shields had fallen. Not everyone got up, though. There were still a handful of students in our area alone who were lying motionless in the grass. My stomach clenched painfully, but I tried to push the grief away. I needed to focus on pushing forward. Save as many as I could. Survive, if possible. I'd grieve later if I was alive to do so.

Gabriel and I glanced at each other as we moved further and further away from one another, each trying to hold up larger and larger portions of the shield. I knew we felt the same—we didn't want to lose sight of each other. Not now. Not when the battle would . . . end the way we guessed it would.

"Matt, take Simon and Omer to the farthest dorms on the other side," Luke shouted. "We need you three to hold up the shields over there. We're losing them fast. I'll cover your shields here."

"On it," I heard Matt say before running footsteps retreated.

I sent a silent prayer to the universe that he'd be okay. He'd be too far away from us to know for sure for a while. Dread churned in my stomach, making me glad I hadn't eaten anything today. I tried to remind myself that he was one of the best fighters I knew, and one of the most powerful Divines I'd ever met. He was in a better position to survive than most. All I could do was have faith in his abilities.

I faced forward again, panting. Sweat gathered on my forehead and dripped down my cheeks. I was holding up so much of the shield now, and the weight of the Dark Guardians' powers against it made it feel like I was holding up a giant Demon. My arms shook as another student fell on the other side of the building, and I expanded my shield again. I had most of an entire dorm covered on my own now. And Gabriel was over a hundred feet away. I didn't know how long I could hold it like this. I wasn't sure how much more I could expand my shield. At some point, I'd hit my limit —we all would—and we'd be screwed.

I glanced around, trying to see how many of us were still supporting it. It looked like only a little over twenty of us still held it up. Less than a quarter of what we'd started with. And cracks were forming again. We were spread too thin.

The shield shuddered and buckled as a large crack formed in Caleb's shield, spreading hair-like fractures rapidly through it. He'd reached his limit, and it'd shatter at any moment. With a grunt of effort, Damian extended his shield to cover all of Caleb's, filling in the cracks and protecting him just before it fell. His hands were shaking too. None of us would be able to hold out for much longer.

Another shudder in the shield corresponded with a grunt of effort from my other side. *Gabriel.* I spun my head to look at him and my stomach dropped. His shield was rapidly cracking just as Caleb's had. He braced himself, straining as he tried to hold it together, even as he dematerialized more, growing more transparent. Preparing for when his shield would fail and the black fire would engulf him and the dorm behind him.

"No," I gritted out, even as my arms violently shook from the weight of the barrier I already carried. I wouldn't let that whole side of the dorm be unprotected.

On a cry, I expanded my shield and covered all of his. Just as his fell. I gasped, widening my stance as the new weight of my expanded shield and even more Dark Guardians' powers pressed down on me. It felt like I was holding up a building now.

"Terah, no!" Gabriel cried as he saw what I'd done. "You can't hold that much of the shield! Let me make another one and cover this area again."

"No," I called back, my voice strained and shaking almost as much as my arms. "It's too late now. If I let go of that part, I'll let go of all of it. I don't have that much control over it anymore."

Gabriel gaped at me helplessly and ran his hands desperately through his hair. "What can I do? What do we do?" He jogged over to me, his gaze sweeping over my shaking limbs. "Can I give you my power? Would that help?"

"No. Keep your power. You'll need it."

Another shudder rocked the shield and the professor on Gabriel's other side lost her hold on her section. It rapidly splintered, and black fire shot through, burning her arms. A student ran up to her and tried to conjure a shield behind hers, but the student couldn't hold back the amount of fire the professor had been blocking. Few could. Their shield just sputtered out. Another ran up and tried to help, but to no avail. Instead, they conjured shields around the three of them to protect themselves from the fire. On a last cry of strained effort, the professor's shield fell.

A huge beam of black fire erupted through and engulfed them and the whole side of the dorm they'd been covering. The vegetation was set ablaze and the stone quickly blackened under the onslaught. I faintly saw Luke through the fire trying to expand his shield to cover the breach, but he was already stretched thin. He only managed to cover a fourth of it. But someone had to. If we didn't close it fast, the army would get through.

With a deep, shuddering breath, I pulled more power forward. I tried not to think about how much less was there than I wanted to be at this point in the battle. With another breath, I threw the power into my shield. With a cry of effort, I forced it to expand inch by agonizing inch, slowly closing the gap left by the professor. My whole body shook with the effort, and I felt lightheaded, but I managed to seal the gap.

Tears streamed down my face as I fell to one knee under the pressure. It was excruciatingly painful. It felt like I was holding up the planet now. A planet that would, at any moment, simply crush me.

"Terah," Gabriel gasped, kneeling in front of me and taking my face in his hands. "Let me help you."

I felt him pouring some of his power into me—warm and electric blue —but it didn't really help. It wasn't an injury he could heal. It was more about the amount of power I was holding out. How much power I was countering with my own. How heavy it was and how much concentration and will-power it took.

"Don't waste your power," I panted. "It doesn't help with the shield. Save it. Save it for later."

The stream of power trailed off, but he shook his head a little, his expression desperate and pained as he watched me. He ran his fingertips down my cheeks, wiping away the tears. He wanted to help me, but he didn't know what to do. And it was hurting him. I wanted to reach out and touch his cheek, comfort him, but I was holding the shield with both hands now. But I kept my eyes on him, trying to derive comfort from his presence. Trying to distract myself from the pain. His skin looked like a velvety midnight sky glittering with thousands of tiny stars. I knew he'd spent much of his life hating and resenting his difference, but I was so grateful for it. His transformation could protect him, even in an unwinnable situation such as this. He could make himself untouchable. Gabriel, out of all of us, actually had a chance of surviving, if he wanted to. If he'd only take it.

My lips parted on a gasp as it finally hit me. Gabriel could make himself untouchable. Gabriel could be extremely fast—faster than a Guardian. Gabriel could . . . make it through the army to the portals unscathed. *Gabriel could get help.*

"What is it? What's wrong?" he asked anxiously, cupping my face between his hands.

"I just thought of something," I panted. "A plan."

His eyebrows rose in the first expression of hope I'd seen since the army arrived. "What's your idea?"

"We need backup," I gasped, trying to force words out as my body shook with strain. "We need others who are willing to fight for the students here. The warrior faction may not come—we can't rely on them. But what about Divines from the towns closest to the portals? There are enough portals to enough places across the country, and all of them have Divine settlements nearby. If someone could get to all of them quickly and unscathed and gather as many people willing to fight as possible, we might have some sort of chance."

I raised my face to look into his eyes again, my expression already pleading. I knew he wouldn't want to. And I knew why.

"It has to be you. You're the only one who can make yourself untouchable, and you're the only one who can outrun their army. You're as fast as the wind—faster than Demons and Guardians. You could make it to all those towns and raise the alarms there in less time than anyone else."

Gabriel fell abruptly out of his transformation and shoved to his feet, startled. Hurt. Scared. Defiant.

"You . . . want me to *leave* you?" he demanded, running his hands through his hair, his voice tinged with anger.

At that moment, another shudder went through the shield, and I turned my head to see Luke's cracking, about a dorm's-length away, black fire beginning to seep through. My heart sank. No one was moving to cover his shield—everyone was stretched too thin, and they all knew it. No one had the strength to hold up the amount he was holding up, even working together. We were officially out of time.

Another cry tore from my lips as I expanded my shield as far as it could go to cover Luke's area. My body felt like it would crack apart at any moment, now, just like the shield. Nausea spiraled through me as the pain intensified.

"No." My voice was ragged as tears streamed down my face again. I looked desperately into Gabriel's beautiful, vibrant eyes. "I want you to *save us*."

His expression shifted from desperate anger to resolve in a split second. He knelt before me again and tenderly took my face between his hands, wiping my tears with the pads of his thumbs.

"I can do that." His gaze traveled over every inch of my face like he was trying to memorize it. "For you."

I nodded, more tears forging salty trails down my skin. Even if he was able to bring help, I might not survive that long. This could be the last time I'd see him. And my heart broke.

"You have to promise me, though," Gabriel continued, his expression growing firm and fierce as he watched me carefully, "that you'll be here, alive, when I return. Promise me that, Terah."

I didn't know what to say. I couldn't promise that. Not truthfully. Not when we were this outnumbered. Tears filled his eyes, and my heart went from broken to shattered.

"I can't leave you if you don't promise me that." His voice broke.

Tears were threatening to blind me now, but I pulled a tremulous smile onto my face. If he could do this for me, I could do that for him. I could make that promise. I could mean it. For him.

"I promise."

Gabriel leaned forward, slowly, deliberately, and pressed his lips warmly to mine. It was a simple kiss—one meant not to distract or make me lose my hold on the shield—but it seared through me anyway, warming me, patching up the cracks inside of me that were threatening to break me.

Gabriel pulled back and pressed soft kisses to my forehead, my cheeks, the tip of my nose.

"I'll be back as fast as I can, and I'll bring as many people as I can.

You're an amazing fighter, Terah, and you have an amazing transformation. Believe in yourself. Believe you can survive. And I'll be back by your side before you know it."

I nodded, and he leaned forward and kissed me one last time.

"I love you," he said simply, the truth of his statement radiating from his eyes.

Even through the strain, I couldn't keep a smile from forming. "I love you too."

Gabriel smiled gently before shoving to his feet. In a flash of electric blue, he transformed again, then became more transparent as he dematerialized as much as possible. He faced the shield in front of us and shook out his limbs, preparing. Then, with one last look at me, he shot forward, straight through the shield and out of sight. So fast I couldn't even see him running. He just disappeared in an electric blue streak. I released a shuddering sigh and hoped like I'd never hoped before that he'd be safe and that I'd see him again.

"Where did he go?" Damian yelled from my other side. He'd also fallen to one knee at some point as he'd expanded his shield by necessity as well. It looked like there were only about ten of us holding up the whole thing.

"To get help," I yelled back. "From towns near each portal. When he dematerializes, nothing can touch him. And he's fast. He's the only one who could make it there and back unscathed."

Damian's features lit with surprise. "That's . . . a good idea." His voice shook with strain.

Caleb moved to stand between us, and pulled power to his hands, preparing to jump in to help if either of our shields cracked. That was nice of him, but the shield was coming down, one way or another. Caleb wasn't powerful enough to hold up both sides if ours fell.

"Everybody, listen up!" Luke yelled from my other side, his voice shaking with effort. He'd reformed his shield and was trying to reinforce as much of the upper dome as he could. But even through the shaking, there was a firmness and strength to his tone that I had to admire. He was a true leader. No wonder Matt looked up to him so much.

"The shield is about to fall, and we must prepare to fight." The dome of the shield projected his words through the expansive space beneath it. "Many of you have never fought in battle before, and those of you who have, have fought Demons. *This will be different*. You will no longer only be fighting creatures whose appearance makes it easy to dehumanize them

—to forget they are like us. Now you will also be fighting Dark Guardians. You will look into their faces that look like yours. You will hear their screams that sound like yours. You will watch them bleed and suffer like you bleed and suffer. That will be incredibly difficult to push past. It will be horrific, because war, itself, is horrific. It's not fair that you're in this position. It's not fair that you'll be made to fight for your lives today. But you *will* push past it, and you *will* fight with bravery, conviction, and strength. Why? Because your life matters and means something! Because the lives of all the students in the dorms unable to defend themselves matter and mean something! Because this is your home, and these are your friends! Because senseless violence like this has no place in the world! You will fight with everything you have and everything you are. You will fight for your future and for theirs. Win, lose, or draw, we will show the world today that goodness, bravery, and honor still exist. I am proud to stand here and fight beside each and every one of you. Now, prepare yourselves!"

The students around us nodded. Many looked terrified. Others looked resigned. Some had tears streaming down their cheeks. But all of them moved into position, standing shoulder to shoulder with their trainers, professors, and peers, pulling weapons and readying their powers. My respect for every one of them grew—these few brave souls willing to die for their friends. Willing to fight a terrifying, unwinnable battle.

I took a deep, shuddering breath, and let it out slowly. Then another. And another. My body was still quaking under the pressure of the shield, and I felt my hold on it slipping. I glanced toward Damian and Caleb. Damian's whole body shook under the weight of his shield, and I could see his muscles straining. Our eyes met and he nodded shakily at me. I glanced quickly at Caleb, and he nodded at me as well, his eyes filling with regret and some deeper emotion as his gaze swept over my face. I took another shuddering breath and nodded slowly back. We knew what was about to happen, and we were promising to have each other's backs.

The shield shuddered as a crack ripped through the barrier at the other end of the dorm buildings—a huge rip in a bright white shield. *Matt.* My heart clenched desperately. I hoped he was okay. I cried out and Damian grunted in pain as the weight on our shields increased, the structure rippling and swaying over all the buildings. We were losing it. I desperately tried holding on, to buy us more time, but there wasn't anything more I could do. In the same horrible moment, my shield and Damian's both cracked. Black fire burst through as Caleb made a wide shield around the three of us, only leaving our hands free so it wouldn't impede our shields.

"Luke!" I called as loud as my shaking voice would let me. I needed to tell him what Gabriel was doing. We needed a plan to buy him more time. "I sent Gabriel off-plane to get help from the closest Divine towns. But we need to buy him time."

"You believe he was able to make it through?" He wasn't familiar with Gabriel's transformation.

"Yes," I said as firmly as I could. "He made it through. We should try using the Blessed's powers strategically to keep the army away from the dorms as long as possible. The Dark Guardians aren't used to fighting them and won't be able to easily predict or counter their powers. We need to use that against them."

I cried out again as my shield rapidly cracked above and around me. It was too much. I couldn't hold it anymore. Caleb stepped closer and shored up his shield around me.

"That's a good strategy," Luke called. "Blessed! To the front! Our mission now is to buy time. Use your powers to create barriers, blockades, ditches, anything else that might keep the army away from us and the dorms. Be creative. Don't focus on individual soldiers, focus on keeping the swarm of them back. The rest of the group can focus on defending you and taking out any soldiers who manage to get through. Spread out and prepare! Work together!"

The Blessed students, trainers, and professors started running, spreading out around the dorm buildings, preparing to act as a blockade.

"Everyone still holding the shield," Luke called, "let go on the count of three. Everyone else, make sure your individual shields are up." He looked around to make sure everyone was in position. "One . . . two . . . three!"

With a gasp, I finally released my hold on the last thing protecting us. The weight immediately lifted from me, and I watched, trying to catch my breath, as the dome of protection dissipated around us, letting the black fire engulf the buildings.

"Blessed! Now!" Luke shouted.

Through their smaller, many-colored shields, I saw the Blessed around us raise their hands, calling forward their different, more elemental powers. Then, in a burst of movement and color, they sent their many-formed powers toward the now-advancing army.

I shoved to my feet, panting, gaping in awe at the spectacle now taking shape in front of us. I'd never seen anything like it. Several Blessed directed their powers deep into the grass and soil, and with a groaning of the earth beneath our feet, the ground cracked open and shifted, forming a deep, wide chasm separating the dorms on this side of the line from the smaller Demons who didn't have the size to traverse it. Simultaneously, other Blessed created walls of thick, twisting branches in an enormous circle around the dorms, climbing up and over the buildings like our shield had done before, blocking out the sight of the Dark Guardians and larger Demons who'd managed to traverse the deep chasm in the ground. Others shot thick vines from their hands, binding and reinforcing the cage of branches surrounding and protecting us like a giant basket.

Thirty feet to my left, another Blessed shot water from his hand, spraying the branches in front of him in thick jets as he ran while a Blessed next to him raised her hand, sending out aqua-colored power, freezing the water into a thick barrier of ice, further fortifying the wall and filling the cracks between the branches. The two of them moved quickly around the dorms, trying to strengthen as much of this new barrier with ice as they could. Those with air powers blasted the army back with hurricane-force winds, or restrained them with thick, twisting ropes of air. Those with fire powers struck the army with wide beams of flame, shoving them back while the other Blessed worked on closing up any holes in this new, physical barrier around the dorms.

Another Blessed ran around the perimeter, raising earth from the ground and turning it into large stones, at least a foot deep, lining the branch barrier up to fifteen feet in the air. Another Blessed shot molten lava at the rocks, filling the cracks and transforming everything into glowing, sweltering magma. A Blessed with ice power followed close behind, quickly cooling the magma so it instantaneously settled into a thick slab of dark rock. Building a stone wall around us. Caleb lowered his shield as we watched this new barrier being reinforced.

"Good! Very good!" Luke called. His hands were raised above his head, sending thick branches surrounded by his own deep green power to the top of the dome, reinforcing where the cooled magma couldn't go. "Maintain the barriers you've created. Keep them out as long as possible. Fix and reform the structures as much as you can. Remember, we're trying to buy time."

The ground shook as hundreds of enormous Demons—the ones large enough to traverse the large gashes in the earth—approached the shield of branches, ice, and stone. Their horrifying screams, simultaneously the highest, lowest, and sharpest sounds I'd ever heard, thickened the air with agonizing noise. Students and professors alike clutched their heads as the volume grew with proximity, trying to block out the piercing, terror-inducing shrieks. My hair stood on end as nausea clutched my stomach and pain burned my ears. I saw a few students retching, casting up their breakfast as the physical effects of the Demon screams overwhelmed them. Others fell to their knees, intense shaking overtaking their bodies and weakening their limbs.

"Keep your minds and wills strong!" Luke called. "It's a part of a Demon's power to sow terror and hopelessness in their enemies. But *you* control your bodies, minds, and emotions. Remember you're strong! Remember what you're fighting for! Push away the fear and focus on protecting yourselves and your friends!"

Damian, Caleb, and I, along with a handful of less-affected trainers, started toward those who'd fallen, pulling them to their feet and steadying them. Those affected most were those who'd never encountered Demons before. It wasn't that Demon screams lessened in impact over time, but rather that one learned to compartmentalize the fear and separate it from movement and functionality. But it took years of being a soldier to really master that. None of the inexperienced people here would have enough time to adjust. They were being coached to push through, but I had no doubt that people here would die because they wouldn't be able to over-come their fear in time. It was why Demons were built that way in the first place—to incapacitate through pure terror, leaving their enemies power-less and broken.

The sounds of metal against wood filled the air. Black fire and glowing black swords punctured through the unfilled spaces and thinner ice, as the Dark Guardians tried creating wide enough cavities to reach us through. The cage around us shook as Demons hit the outside with astonishing force. Huge branches the size of tree trunks snapped and fell all around us, and everyone started conjuring shields above their heads to keep from getting struck by them. The cage was a protection, but it could also crush us alive.

"Keep filling in whatever holes they make!" Luke shouted, hitting a Dark Guardian in the face with a blast of green fire, before closing the hole they'd created with thick layers of branches.

All around us, Blessed ran past, patching up holes and blasting Dark Guardians and Demons with power to keep them from crossing through. Some Light Guardians—those whose favored weapons included a bow—shot glowing arrows through all the distant gaps and cracks forming under the Demons' vicious onslaught, injuring and repelling the attacking forces to buy time until more Blessed could patch the holes. This worked well for a while. We were actually managing to hold off the enormous army, which was more than I'd thought we could do even for a few minutes. But we were too outnumbered for it to last long.

A loud crack tore through the air on our side of the barricade as the branches and hardened lava split under the assault of what must've been a huge Demon. The barrier shook as the spot was hit again and again, sending an ominous ringing boom around the buildings. The branches splintered and gave way, the ice shattered, and the magma started to crumble, sending chunks of rock tumbling to the ground. Multiple Blessed ran toward the area, trying to shore it up again, but nothing they created was able to withstand the sheer force behind the relentless attack for long.

I glanced at Damian as more Blessed ran toward the area. Damian nodded at me, understanding and agreement in his eyes. We might be partially drained, but it was time for us to transform again and help, though individually this time. We were needed. But once we transformed, we'd start steadily bleeding power again. There was a finite amount of time that we'd be powerful and protected through our transformations before we'd burn out. After that, we'd just have our human forms and whatever remained of our life forces. We'd have to use our limited time wisely.

In identical flashes of purple light, Damian and I transformed and pulled our swords from their sheaths. With Caleb at our side, we jogged toward the breach point which was quickly growing wider and wider. Some Light Guardian students and professors joined us, and the Blessed near the breach nodded at us gratefully, not even wary of our transformations anymore.

I glanced at the group, assessing, as we spread out to cover the breach. There were no trainers here, nor were there any of our fellow advanced trainees. There was no one to strategize or unify the group. No one with battle experience besides me, Damian, and Caleb. I glanced at them, but neither moved to step into the leadership role. They were used to fighting with people who knew what they were doing. They hadn't considered this group didn't. I gritted my teeth. If they didn't step in, I'd have to.

"Work together to shove as many Demons and Dark Guardians back as you can," I called to the group of Blessed. "Focus on that instead of repairing the barricade. With them constantly hitting it, no repairs will last for long. You'll just waste power. The rest of us will protect you and deal with anyone who gets past you."

The Blessed students and professors nodded and formed a semicircle in front of us, facing the breach that was gaping open now. The rest of us fanned out behind them and to their sides.

"Shields up," I said firmly, as another large piece of the barrier in front of us cracked and fell to the ground. The Dark Guardians could get in now, and the Demons were sure to follow.

White and multicolored shields went up all around me and everyone lifted their power-filled hands or brandished weapons, ready. The barrier shook and the hole widened as a five-foot chunk of the stone wall shattered and tumbled to the ground, the branches behind it reduced to smoking and splintered shards of wood. And then the Dark Guardian soldiers burst through.

"Attack now!" I shouted, planting my feet and firmly holding my shield in front of me.

I caught a brief look at the Dark Guardians, transformed and covered in their black armor, as dark and matte as a midnight sky, before they hit us with a powerful blast of black fire, entirely engulfing us. But the Blessed shot powerful streams of air at the attacking group, forcing their fire back onto them, and shoving them back toward the opening in the barrier. Others shot fire, covering the entire breach with thick, scorching flames. The Dark Guardian soldiers quickly conjured shields around themselves to keep the flames—their own and those of the Blessed—away from them. But their shields couldn't keep the force of the streams of air from pushing them backward.

The wind bowled over a handful of their soldiers, but others fought against the pressure, using their wings to counter the force, allowing them to move forward again, though more slowly. In response, several Blessed liquefied the ground like quicksand at the soldiers' feet, causing them to sink up to their thighs, before solidifying the ground again, trapping them. A couple others formed heavy boulders around the soldiers' feet whose shields didn't reach the ground, fusing them to the earth so they couldn't move forward.

But the Demon attacks on the dome around us didn't cease. Horrifying screams and guttural roars surrounded us as the pounding on the dome shook the structure and the ground at our feet. Branches fell in a steady rain from the top, some still burning with black fire. Cracks split through the stones as the Demons assailed the structure, and more and more chunks of cooled magma broke away and tumbled to the ground. Wider holes were starting to form around the whole barrier, and Dark Guardians began pushing through.

"Spread out!" I pointed my sword at the points nearest us where soldiers were starting to enter. "Cover as many of the breach points as you can. Keep them out!"

I turned to look at Damian and Caleb next to me.

"You both should go cover the other breaches with them. I'll stay at this one. We can't afford to have all three of us in one spot anymore. There aren't enough well-trained soldiers here for that."

Damian and Caleb both turned to look at me grimly. Neither moved.

"It's time," I murmured. "We have to protect and help them for as long as we can." I nodded at the inexperienced students in front of me. "That's our job now. We can't afford to stick together anymore."

Damian's jaw was clenched tightly, his shoulders tense, but he finally nodded. Worry overtook his expression as he looked at me and then Caleb. Caleb didn't move or speak, but his expression was oddly intense as he stared at me. Almost fierce. I sheathed my sword and reached out, grasping each of them by the shoulders.

"Good luck," I murmured, my heart squeezing.

I wasn't sure what expression was on my face. Worry, resignation, sadness, fear. Perhaps a combination. But for once, I didn't try to feign neutrality. I couldn't. Not now. Despite everything, I'd grown to care about them. Despite our complex history and their betrayals, despite all the harm they'd caused, I knew each had a core of goodness. When everything else was stripped away, they were two people willing to die, to give up everything, to protect those who couldn't protect themselves. And I knew, despite it all, that my heart would hurt if I lost either of them.

They looked surprised for a brief moment before each of them reached up and clasped their hands over my shoulders in return, hints of warmth entering both of their expressions.

"Good luck," Damian replied, giving my shoulder a squeeze. "Both of you," he added, glancing at Caleb.

Caleb was still pissed with him, but I could see his anger was tempered with worry. Damian had become his friend—he didn't want him to die.

Caleb managed a slow nod at Damian. "Likewise," he said, a little stiffly. Then he turned to look at me again. There was a long moment where it looked like he was struggling to find the right words. "Fight like I know you can," he eventually said, his expression turning tight. Almost pained.

I nodded at him, my throat oddly constricting. I had to swallow before I could speak. "You too."

Caleb nodded. His mouth opened again, almost like he was going to say something more, but after a moment, he just closed it, turned, and walked firmly toward one of the other breach points, taking a few of the Light Guardians with him. Damian's mouth twisted a little as he watched Caleb go, no doubt knowing what Caleb had almost said. How he felt. Damian sighed then looked back at me. He gave my shoulder one last squeeze, then turned, motioned to a few other Light Guardians in our group to follow him, then jogged to another breach point to my left.

I took a deep breath, trying to refocus on the battle, and unsheathed my sword, then turned to face the widening hole in the barrier in front of me. There were only five Blessed and four Light Guardians with me now, and they were barely holding off the Dark Guardian soldiers attempting to enter. I shook out my arms and adjusted my grip on my sword. I was ready. I could do this. After all, battle was what I knew best.

With a roar that left a sharp ringing in my ears, a huge Demon smashed the cage of branches in front of us, ripping open a massive hole. And before anyone could react or build another blockade, Dark Guardians began pouring through.

"Shit," I ground out through my teeth before throwing my shield around myself again.

Then, with a growl, I ran at the wave of incoming soldiers, several Blessed and Light Guardians at my back. As we ran, several Blessed wrapped parts of their chests and limbs in thick branches, stone, and ice, forming makeshift armor. At the last moment, I spread my wings and launched into the air.

The Blessed bathed the oncoming soldiers in waves of fire and weighed them down with deadly twining branches and unwieldy stones, then the Light Guardians cut down the trapped soldiers from the sides. I attacked from above, bringing my sword down in powerful, violent arcs, killing soldiers while they were distracted and ensnared. And I knew in an instant that Luke had been right. It *was* different fighting Dark Guardians instead of Demons. The heads I cut off didn't look monstrous. Those I killed weren't horrifying creatures of nightmares. They looked human. And despite their hardened expressions, their faces weren't different from ours or from the Light Guardian soldiers I'd grown up with. They ranged from young to middle aged, like us. And I couldn't distance myself from what I was doing like I could with Demons, no matter how bloody things had gotten. I was killing *people*. And while that'd always been true, it hit me differently when they *looked* like people.

But I didn't have a choice. They were here to systematically kill us all. They were here to slaughter hundreds of young, untrained students without mercy. I couldn't afford to hold back, for any of our sakes. But I felt a little piece of myself withering inside me, knowing this was what all of us had been reduced to, their side and ours: slaughtering each other when we didn't have to. Continuing a centuries-long war that left bloodshed and devastation on both sides. None of us were innocent. And I knew, deep down, it didn't have to be like this. It *shouldn't* be like this. But I also knew none of us had the power to stop it right now. All we could do was pick a side and fight or die.

The Blessed hit the incoming Dark Guardians with blinding jets of fire as more soldiers poured through the large break in the barricade, shoving past their dead and trapped comrades. I swung around to different sides of the incoming horde, diving and attacking as they were blinded, taking them by surprise before withdrawing and diving from a different angle. But it almost didn't matter. More and more soldiers pushed through, quickly replacing those who'd been slain, and sending more bursts of fire, black arrows, and weapons flying our way. There were so many more of them than us, and more and more holes were opening around us as the cage of branches and stone burned and broke apart on all sides.

The heat was intense, now, below me and around me, and I shook sweat from my eyes as I continued attacking the Dark Guardians and swooping in to protect the Blessed and lesser-trained Light Guardians. But the Dark Guardian forces grew under the burning dome, and I saw groups of them heading our way. They were going to surround us on all sides, and the Blessed wouldn't be able to escape as easily. They couldn't fly.

"Fuck," I growled, landing and running toward the small group who'd been fighting with me.

I threw a shield around all of us, feeling the power draining from the well in my chest.

"Run toward the closest dorm!" I yelled over the din of fighting and screams of Demons. "We need the dorm at our backs so they can't surround us!"

The students, already looking exhausted and terrified, nodded and ran frantically through the falling, burning branches and blasts of power. I ran to the front of the group and led them through the chaos, cutting Dark Guardian soldiers out of our way, clearing our path as much as I could. We finally reached the wall as the dome cracked fully open, revealing the dark, swirling sky again, and giving Dark Guardians and Demons complete access to us and the dorms. The last traces of the barrier would be gone in a matter of minutes.

"Gods," one of the students cried behind me, his voice shaking, "we've lost. We've already lost."

I whipped my head around and sent him a fierce glare. "It's not over until all of us are dead." I was unable to keep the harshness from my voice. "We fight until we no longer can. Until there's no one left to protect. Pull yourselves together. This is *not* over. Everyone in the dorms needs you. Don't let them down."

The small group nodded, grim and scared, pressing their backs into the stone wall of the dorm.

"We can't keep them away from us anymore." I faced forward again. "Now we have to focus on keeping them from destroying the dorms. That means taking down Demons. The Dark Guardians can burn up the sides of the buildings, but only Demons can break through the stone and armored walls. So we focus on them. If you've never fought Demons before, attack them from as far away as possible so you lessen your chances of injury. And make sure to keep the dorm wall at your backs. Don't let their army surround you. I'll try to go in and behead as many as I can while you all attack from here. Got it?" They murmured their assent.

I watched carefully as Dark Guardians swarmed the area around the dorms, this time accompanied by an endless number of Demons that shook the ground with each step. There were countless misshapen, hulking bodies, monstrous faces, numerous arms, clawed hands and feet. Some oozed acid, some shot it from their mouths as they roared. All were gunmetal gray with thick skin and glowing red eyes. More horrifying than the worst nightmares. More Demons than I'd ever seen in one place at one time.

"Don't focus on the forms they take. That only heightens the fear." My eyes narrowed in on the Demon fast approaching our section of the dorm. This one was a little over twenty feet tall, with thick limbs, a misshapen body, four glowing eyes that all blinked at different times, and a long, forked tongue that dripped acid. "Focus on where we need to hit them to kill them. That's all. It doesn't matter how horrifying they look if we can quickly behead them."

The Demon roared—an earsplitting shriek that felt like shards of ice cutting through my chest—as it saw the group of us pressed to the dorm wall.

"Light Guardians, attack with me from the air. Stay behind me and don't let that dripping acid touch you. Blessed, attack and protect us from here. Try to take away its ability to move. Now!"

I jumped into the air, my wings beating until I was eye-level with the charging Demon. The four Light Guardians rose in the air with me. The Demon screamed and lumbered toward us, lifting its thick arm and sharp claws to swipe at us. Its tongue slithered out of its mouth wildly like a snake's as it roared, spraying the air around it with acid.

"Those claws can pierce armor if it strikes hard enough," I called at the Light Guardians behind me. "Be careful."

I dove around the Demon's extended arm, bringing myself closer to its face. If I could keep its attention on me, it'd give the others a chance to attack and incapacitate it with less chance of injury. I quickly slashed the tip of my sword across the Demon's neck, taking off a chunk of its lolling tongue in the same movement. Then I spun away, dodging the claws it flung at me. My strike hadn't beheaded it—I hadn't been able to get close enough with all the acid it'd been spewing—but it was enough to send a gush of black blood down its body and draw all its attention to me. *Good.*

As I flew around to its side, making room for the Light Guardians to injure it with white fire, I saw one of the Blessed had formed heavy stone around the Demon's feet and lower legs, keeping it stationary and limiting its ability to attack. I swung around as the Demon struggled against the rock and brought my sword down on the arm closest to me, hacking into it several times until it severed just below the elbow.

The Demon roared with rage and twisted its body, sending black acidic blood flying in its frenzy, attempting to slash me with its remaining claws. I dodged as another Blessed shot thick branches at the Demon's remaining arm, twining tightly around it before coiling the branches force-fully around the Demon's body, cinching it to its side. The Demon roared and struggled, its muscles swelling with exertion. I doubted the branches would last long against it. I dove quickly, dodging as much of the spraying blood and acid as I could, and hit the Demon across the neck with my sword again. This time the blade sank deep, severing muscle and bone. With a grim squelch, the Demon's head fell to the ground, followed by its body.

644

"Nice work," I called to my group. "Take some deep breaths and prepare for the next round."

But even as I spoke, I saw several Demons break away from another nearby group and turn toward us, roaring in outrage as they saw their dead comrade in front of us. My jaw clenched. We'd taken on one Demon successfully, but three at once might be too much for this inexperienced group to handle. I wasn't sure if I could protect them all.

I quickly assessed the Demons, trying to think of a strategy. Two of them were only about fifteen to twenty feet tall, but their forms were still dangerous and horrible. One was a lumpy, misshapen monster with six arms that ended in claws as long and sharp as short swords. The other looked like a huge, furless cat who'd had all its bones broken then healed incorrectly. Its fangs were long and pointed, and it spewed acid from its mouth in a wide arc each time it roared. At the end of each foot were taloned claws that looked like they could easily tear through a Guardian's armor.

The third Demon was large. A four-legged creature at least thirty feet tall, covered in short metal spikes almost like scales, with horns that extended forward away from its face, sharp metal claws, and at least ten independently moving tails, each ending in heavy-looking spiked metal balls almost like maces. Its roar cut through the air, a vibrating, high-pitched wail like a boiling kettle mixed with a thousand agonized screams. It took all the self-control I had not to clap my hands over my ears to protect myself from the sound like I had when I was a child. I took a deep breath. I had to fight this one. It was the deadliest of the three.

"Okay," I called to the group, trying to sound calm and firm, to be like the leader I'd never wanted to be. "We'll split into three groups for this one. Who's in the highest training group here?"

One Blessed and Light Guardian raised their hands.

"We're both in the intermediate training level," the Light Guardian said. My stomach clenched. Only in intermediate, and they were the best trained in the group. I wasn't sure they could do this. Not successfully.

"Okay," I said, hiding my reaction, "you two will fight with me. We'll be taking on the big one. What groups are the rest of you in?"

"We're all in beginner-intermediate," one of the other Light Guardians said quickly, "though me and those two," she added, pointing at two of the Blessed, "are going to be moved to intermediate next semester."

I nodded quickly. "Then you three can work together to take on the cat-like Demon. And you four," I pointed to the two remaining Blessed and the two remaining Light Guardians, "can work together to take down the Demon with six arms. Call for me if you need my help. Split up now and stay near the group and the dorm wall—we don't want to be separated or surrounded. Go!"

I flew higher into the air with the intermediate Light Guardian at my back as the Demons reached us, so we'd be at our Demon's eye level. The Blessed in our group backed up so he was against the dorm wall, then fire spiraled down his arms and collected in his hands, ready. The Demon let out another shriek that made my eardrums feel like they were going to explode, then charged at us, its mouth wide, sharp teeth already glistening with red blood.

"Watch out for those tails," I called to the Light Guardian behind me.

"Will do," he said grimly, pulling his sword from its sheath in a flash of bright white.

I sheathed my sword and summoned my bow and arrows instead. It'd be better to injure this one from afar for as long as possible. I flew higher as I poured power into the arrow, then pulled it back on the bow and carefully aimed at the Demon's neck. I released the string, and the arrow shot through the air with a crackle of lightning but bounced off one of the Demon's metal spikes. I swore and notched another arrow. The spikes shielded so much of its skin that I wasn't sure where to hit it.

The Demon roared again and went up on its hind legs, swiping its claws at us. I flew higher as I charged my arrow and aimed at the only vulnerable part of the Demon I could see—its open mouth. I released the arrow, and it flew straight, embedding deep in its throat, and exploded with lightning and a loud boom of thunder. Chunks of the Demon's face and throat tore off as the lightning shot through its body, burning it alive with electric heat and power, and it fell back to all fours again, blood streaming thickly and steadily from its head.

"Yes!" the Light Guardian exclaimed from behind me. He flew around me and dove toward the Demon, intent on beheading it.

"Wait!" I yelled. "It's still dangerous!" But it was too late. The Demon, seeing the young Light Guardian about to attack, spun its body violently so its mace-ended tails whipped through the air toward him.

I swore and dove, my hand extending in front of me as I pulled power down my arm to conjure a shield around him. But he'd flown too quickly and too far. Before the power could leave my fingers, three of the mace-ended tails tore across his chest and propelled him forcefully back into the wall of the dorm with a sickening smack. The Light Guardian crumpled to the ground.

"*Damnit!*" I was furious at him for being so reckless, and at myself for not saving him in time. "Protect him!" I shouted to the Blessed on my team, who'd run over to where the Light Guardian had landed. "I'll deal with the Demon."

I turned back to it as a rolling gurgle left its destroyed throat, like laughter. My insides burned with murderous rage. I'd make it pay for what it'd done to that inexperienced student. I dematerialized my bow and arrows and lifted my arms instead, pulling power to my hands. Then I dove to the Demon's height and unleashed a torrent of swirling fire and lightning at its head, fully engulfing its upper shoulders in a tornado-like structure of burning power. The Demon screamed and whipped around again, trying to break the connection and hit me with its tails, but I flew up in time, keeping the stream of fire and lightning steady and continuous. I wouldn't be able to do this for long—it used far too much power—but its metal scales would protect its neck from beheading in any other way. This was our best shot.

With another grunt of effort, I unleashed a final wave of power at the Demon, swirling the fire and lightning so tightly around its head and shoulders it couldn't escape or even breathe. And within a few seconds, its entire head burned down to bone, then disintegrated, leaving the Demon's lifeless body to collapse heavily onto the blood-soaked ground.

I quickly glanced at the other two groups as I flew swiftly to the ground. One Blessed from the first group was suffocating their Demon by sucking the air from its lungs and using air to strangle it, while the other Blessed burned off its many arms. The Light Guardians were working together to behead it. In the second group, one Blessed had formed stone around the Demon's face so it couldn't spew acid from its mouth, while the other had tied its front and back legs together with a tangle of large branches. The Light Guardian was working to behead it around the stone. Feeling confident that they'd be okay without me, I landed and ran toward the fallen Light Guardian from my group.

"I . . . I think he's gone," the Blessed said, looking at me with tears in his eyes.

I bit the inside of my cheek and knelt next to him, reaching forward and feeling for a pulse. I didn't feel one. *Shit.* Carefully, I lifted the Light Guardian's head to inspect the damage, and my stomach lurched. Apart from the deep gashes in his front from the maces, his head had cracked open when he'd hit the dorm wall. I lowered his head gently back to the ground. The Blessed was right—he was gone.

I clenched my fists tightly, my eyes sliding closed for a second. *Damnit. Damnit!* But nothing could be done now. I couldn't bring him back to life. I couldn't undo what'd happened. Tears stung my eyes, but I quickly blinked them away.

"You're right," I finally murmured, looking at the Blessed. "He fought bravely, but he's gone. We need to push forward so we can help the others. Okay?"

He swallowed hard and blinked quickly, trying to clear his own tears. Then he nodded. "Okay."

I helped him to his feet, and we ran over to join the others who'd finally managed to kill their respective Demons.

"Good work." I nodded at the group of heavily panting students in front of me. "Unfortunately, we lost a group member." My stomach tightened as I watched their triumph turn to stricken devastation. "Please don't act recklessly when you're fighting," I continued, my voice low and serious. "Demons are still incredibly dangerous, even when gravely injured. *Especially* when they're injured. Don't get close to them unless you're absolutely sure they can't hurt you anymore. There are too few of us here defending the Academy to take any chances with our lives. Understood?"

The group nodded, some wiping away tears.

I turned and quickly scanned the area around us again. The Demons we'd slain were acting as a kind of barrier, shielding us from view, but I doubted that'd last long.

"Let's—"

The dorm wall exploded above us, sending chunks of heavy stone and debris raining down on us. I covered my head with my arms and conjured a shield over as much of the group as I could. But I heard cries of pain and knew it hadn't been enough.

I blinked rapidly, trying to see through the dust slowly settling around us, and caught some movement from above.

"Put up your shields!"

Another explosion sent more chunks of the dorm tumbling over us. Heavy stone after heavy stone hit my weakening shield before tumbling to the ground, and I felt my power draining even more. I just hoped the others had gotten their shields up in time.

"Whoever isn't injured, keep your shields up around yourself and anyone near you who's injured. I'm going to find out what's happening. Stay here."

I pushed into the air, keeping my shield around me, and flew to the top of the dorm. Standing on the roof was a huge Demon built like a boulder. It was taller than the dorm and extremely wide—a hulking figure of solid muscle and misshapen proportions, with a small, rock-like head, and giant limbs, fists, and feet. It was crushing the roof and sides of the dorm just by stomping it. And if it could break through the stone like it was nothing, it could probably break into or crush the armored rooms protecting the students once it uncovered them. We needed to get it off the dorm and eliminate it before it did that.

I flew back down as the Demon stomped on the edge of the roof again, uncovering the edge of an armored room and sending more debris tumbling over the group.

"There's a Demon on the roof strong enough to break through the stone and armored rooms. We need to get it off the dorm and eliminate it. Who's still able to fight?"

Many of them were covered in scrapes and blood from the falling debris. Six out of eight raised their hands.

"I'm sorry," gasped one of the Blessed, still on the ground with tears running down her face. "A few larger stones landed on us before we could put up a shield. I think my arm and collarbone are broken, and his leg and knee are broken." She nodded at the Blessed next to her who was white with pain.

"It's okay—it's not your fault," I said quickly, trying not to think about how hard it'd be to keep them alive now. No one had the excess power to heal them. "Just stay where you are and keep your shields up. There will be more debris, and likely more Demons."

She nodded and widened her shield to cover the injured Blessed next to her who seemed to be in too much pain to keep his own steady. I turned to look at the rest of the group, who'd come to stand around me, their shields still up. There were three Light Guardians and three Blessed left.

I gestured at the Blessed. "You three, stay down here and try pulling the Demon from the roof with your powers. It'll keep you a little further from harm. And you three," I turned to the Light Guardians, "follow me up there. We'll get behind the Demon and help force it off the roof. Then we'll all work together to behead it. Blessed, make sure you're out of range when the Demon starts to fall—I don't want any of you getting crushed. Let's go."

I pushed into the air with the Light Guardians at my back, and we flew over and behind the Demon who was repeatedly stomping on the corner of the exposed armored room, slowly crushing the metal. I could only imagine how terrified the student inside must be.

I pulled power from the well in my chest to my palms. "Now!" I raised my hands and blasted the middle of the Demon's back with purple fire. The Light Guardians raised their hands and shot fire at the back of its neck and each of its legs. The Demon bellowed—a deep sound of surprise and pain—and momentarily stopped stomping on the armored room.

"Blessed, now!" I yelled.

A split second later, thick branches wrapped around the Demon's arms and began pulling it toward the ledge. But the Demon stumbled backward, yanking violently on the branches, snapping many of them in the process.

"Intensify the fire," I said to the Light Guardians around me as the Blessed sent more branches, yanking and binding the Demon's wrists together before tightly wrapping its arms to its torso.

The two other Blessed raised their hands then. One sent a beam of light brown power at the branches around the Demon's middle, and I watched in awe as they were encased in stone. The other Blessed sent a beam of fire at the Demon's head and shoulders as he'd seen me do with the large Demon earlier. The Demon bellowed and flailed, trying to wrench its arms free, stumbling closer to the edge of the dorm.

The Light Guardians and I flew closer to its back, blasting it with another wave of fire, forcing it a few more steps forward as the Blessed started wrapping its legs together with branches. But the Demon repeatedly yanked its legs apart, snapping the branches and sending the Blessed sprawling forward onto the ground. Then it stomped a section of the roof near where they were standing, sending a new wave of rubble tumbling over them. Fortunately, the two other Blessed managed to raise shields in time.

Then a terrifying roar shook the air around us as a large Demon appeared behind the Blessed on the ground, climbing over the pile of Demon bodies that'd been shielding us. This Demon took the form of a giant, mutilated dog with multiple heads, its many mouths gnashing, overflowing with jagged teeth. The Blessed released their hold on the Demon in front of me and turned to face the new Demon. But they didn't stand a chance against it without armor or the ability to fly. Not without better training.

I spun in the air to face the Light Guardians with me. "Go help them. I'll deal with this Demon."

They nodded and quickly swooped away, then dropped in between the charging Demon and the Blessed on the ground, pulling their swords and sending beams of white fire at the roaring heads to slow it down.

I quickly materialized my bow and arrows and charged an arrow with my dwindling power. Then I took aim and released the shot at the Demon's charred neck. The arrow struck true, shooting bolts of lightning outward from the impact point as thunder shook the air. Some of the Demon's thick skin blew off and burned with the blast, but it was so solidly built that the hit hadn't come close to beheading it, and it was already healing quickly from the damage the Blessed's fire had caused.

Before it could recover, I pulled my sword again and flew at the Demon, then struck it across the back of its neck, cutting deep before it jerked forward away from me. It spun to face me, snarling, rage burning from its red eyes. I flew at it again as one of the Blessed on the ground shot branches at its middle, still trying to pull it off the roof, even as they were trapped between two Demons. The Demon jerked to the side, causing my strike to hit its chest instead of its neck, but a thick wave of blood still spilled down its front.

The Demon roared as another Blessed started reforming the stone around its legs, weighing it down and unbalancing it. I flew at the Demon and stabbed it through the chest, shoving it backward with all my strength as the other Blessed wrapped more branches around its middle and pulled again. And this time, with its legs fused together and immobile, the Demon tilted. *Yes!*

"Keep pulling!" I yelled as I hit the Demon's neck with another shot of purple fire.

With a scream, the Demon fell off the side of the roof, crashing to the ground with enough force to shake the building and send more broken stones cascading from the roof.

"Pin it down!" I shouted as I flew down to join the Blessed.

The two Blessed quickly built up a thick structure of branches and stone around the Demon's middle, pinning it to the ground while the third threw fire at its neck. But before I could bring my sword down to behead it, a roar and a cry of pain from behind us diverted our attention. I whipped my head around and my stomach turned over at the horrifying sight. One of the dog heads had managed to grab a Light Guardian out of the air, and its teeth were clamped through her middle. Blood, red and human, poured from its mouth as the Light Guardian screamed in pain.

"Go help them," I yelled at the Blessed. "I'll be there in a second."

I swallowed down the desperation and hopelessness that were starting to rise in my throat like bile, and turned back to the enormous Demon, partially pinned to the ground. I charged at it with a cry, my sword glowing brighter with my anger. Then I hit it across its thick tree trunk neck over and over until my arms shook. It screamed, then gurgled and thrashed as I cut deeper and deeper. Acidic blood spilled to the ground, burning the soles of my boots, and spattered across my armor, but I ignored it. I kept hacking until my sword sank into the ground beneath the Demon's neck, and its head rolled away from its body.

Then I threw myself back into the air and flew as fast as I could at the dog-like Demon, now engaged in heavy battle with the rest of my group. I dodged shots of burning red and white fire aimed at the Demon as I flew straight toward the head that still held the Light Guardian, now silent, in its teeth. I landed on its back, and with a yell, swung my sword at its neck with all the strength I had. The sword passed clean through, severing muscle and bone, sending the head tumbling along with the Light Guardian, to the ground with a rush of acidic blood.

The Demon reared onto its hind legs, its remaining heads roaring, teeth gnashing, as it tried to bite me out of the air as it'd done to the Light Guardian.

"Remove its mobility!" I yelled down at the Blessed.

They ran forward and shot branches and stone at the Demon's back legs, weighing it down and fusing its limbs together. The Demon fell back onto all fours, twisting, trying to reach the Blessed. But I flew quickly down and struck another neck, severing it and redrawing its attention. There were only two heads left now. The two uninjured Light Guardians flew over to join me and burned the Demon's remaining necks with white fire from above. The Demon roared and tried to jump up and bite the Light Guardians, but its fused limbs caused it to lose balance instead, and with a keening scream, it fell onto its side.

"Combine your fire to burn off one head," I called to the Light Guardians. "I'll cut off the other."

The three of us flew to the ground, and the Light Guardians along with the Blessed with fire powers threw beams of fire at one of the Demon's remaining necks. I quickly ran to the other, and with a swift, powerful strike, I beheaded it. The head tumbled to the ground on a wave of black blood. I sheathed my sword as the Demon's other head was burned off its body, collapsing into a pile of ash on the grass. It was defeated.

Without sparing it another glance, I ran over to the Light Guardian who'd tumbled from the Demon's jaws as the beheaded skull had hit the ground. She was on her side and wasn't moving. I could see the teeth marks that'd pierced her armor had also pierced straight through her body. My jaw clenched and I rolled her carefully onto her back, even knowing from the amount of blood on the ground that she couldn't still be alive. But, wisely or not, I had a small amount of hope that she'd hung on somehow—that she hadn't died horribly and alone.

The rest of the group crowded around me as I brushed her hair from her face and off her neck so I could feel for a pulse. I tried a few times, desperately looking for any signs of life, first on her neck and then her wrist, and then with my power. But there wasn't even the slightest remnant of a pulse. No hint of life in her body. I doubted there was any blood left in her to pump through her veins. She was gone.

My shoulders fell as an aching pain grew in my chest. I swallowed hard and leaned back again, looking up at the others. I could see in their faces that they knew.

"I'm sorry. She's gone."

Tears filled the eyes around me. Crumpled expressions of sadness, hopelessness, and fear that they'd be next. I didn't know what to say. I didn't know how to provide comfort in such an unwinnable situation. I didn't think it was possible anymore.

"We should move her to the dorm wall," I finally said. "So her body's protected."

I crouched behind her head and grabbed her from under her arms as the rest of the group slid their hands under her. We lifted as one and walked her body to the closest part of the wall that was free from rubble.

As we straightened, an explosion rent the air to our left. We fell back against the wall as stone, wrought iron, and metal erupted through the air, raining down a wide radius of debris. I stood there, stunned for a second, my ears still ringing from the sound as I watched the air slowly clear. I pushed quickly away from the wall and saw the Demons had demolished two-thirds of the dorm next to ours. It was just . . . rubble. A pile of broken stones and torn open or crushed metal boxes that no longer resembled a structure at all. Demons and Dark Guardians quickly descended on the wreckage with triumphant yells and roars.

And then the screams began. A sound I could never forget. The purest sounds of agony and fear from the students who'd survived the demolition and were now injured and exposed.

"We have to help them!" one of the Light Guardians yelled at me, clutching my shoulder, her eyes wild with fear. "We have to save them!"

I wanted to agree with her. I wanted that with all my heart. I wished more than anything that we could save every student here. But I looked at the number of Dark Guardians and Demons that'd descended on that dorm, and then I looked at us. Six of us, and only one trained enough to be a soldier. We wouldn't even make it to those students before our entire group was cut down. Then I looked at the dorm behind us. This dorm was still mostly intact and was probably sheltering over sixty students. If we stopped protecting it, this dorm would quickly be reduced to rubble as well. Then there'd be even more dead students. And if we split up, neither group would be strong enough to hold off any Demons.

"We can't," I murmured, my voice hoarse as my hands shook at my sides. I clenched them into tight fists. "We need to stay here and prevent that from happening to this dorm."

She opened her mouth, disbelieving and furious. "But—"

"We can't be everywhere at once," I said firmly, cutting her off as I turned to face her. "There are only six of us who can still fight. We're already spread too thin, and we're far too outnumbered to save everyone. We wouldn't even make it to those students before they'd kill us all. The best we can do is try to keep that from happening to more students. We need to protect this dorm."

I looked around us and saw, even as I spoke, swarms of Demons descending on each of the remaining dorms. They'd gained confidence in their ability to decimate the buildings now—to fulfill their mission of killing every single person at the Academy. And we were next.

"They're coming."

An ever-growing swarm of Demons gathered around the building, blocking our view of the demolished dorm and the inexperienced, injured students fighting desperately to stay alive. I wondered, briefly, where Damian, Caleb, and Matt were. If they were even alive. The ache in my chest grew. I hoped so. And I hoped they could help the students that I couldn't. Even now, I knew I didn't have enough power left to put a shield over even one side of the dorm, let alone the entire building. All I could do was fight and cling desperately to my transformation for as long as possible.

654

A loud boom sounded from the other side of the dorm. Demons must've reached it and were trying to breach the walls.

"Shields up. And expect more debris."

Shields—two white, one light brown, one orange, and one light green—went up on either side of me as I formed my own deep purple barrier around myself. Another boom sounded from the other side of the dorm as the Demon shrieks grew to an unbearable volume. Shivers cascaded over my skin in response to the sound as I drew my sword and scanned the group of approaching Demons.

There was a snake-like creature slithering toward us, at least fifteen feet tall with sharp teeth as long as swords, dripping acid, and metal spikes covering its back from the crown of its head to the end of its tail. There was a Demon with a muscled body of a four-legged animal, with curling sharp claws and a disturbingly human face. But when it opened its mouth to roar, its jaw unhinged, opening far too wide, exposing row after row of jagged, sharp teeth. There was a giant featherless bird with sharp spikes where wings would be, whose beak was elongated, sharp metal. There was a Demon whose body was dragon-like, but instead of wings, it had multiple hulking arms, each ending in sharp pincers. There was a Demon whose body and head were like a panther but had at least eight legs ending in vicious claws. There was a large blob-like creature that oozed thick acid all over its body, whose face was entirely smooth and blank except for two burning red eyes. It had multiple tentacle arms sprouting from its shoulders, each one ending in a gaping mouth filled with razor-sharp teeth.

All I could see was Demon after Demon. Too many to count. Too many to fight. I wasn't even sure which was the biggest threat to focus on. I felt paralyzed. How could I even create a battle strategy when there were only six of us against an uncountable number of Demons?

But at the last moment, the Demons stopped advancing and hovered around the perimeter of the building, like they were waiting for something. An eerie dread built in my chest. Whatever it was, it couldn't be good.

Suddenly, at least fifty Dark Guardians descended on the dorm, and the air above us turned black as they encased the walls and roof in their fire. What were they doing? Their fire wasn't hot enough to break through stone. At least, I didn't think it was. Our small group stumbled forward as the heat grew intense behind us. And then I heard a sound that sent icy dread trickling through my body—the cracking and popping of stone. The Demons roared with triumph, the sound shaking the ground beneath us. And I realized the Dark Guardians' fire didn't have to melt stone—it just had to damage its integrity enough for the Demons to hit the sides of the dorm. That pressure on top of the heat damage would shatter the structure into a pile of rubble like the other dorm.

I spun and quickly explained this to my group. "We need to stop the Dark Guardians before that can happen. They don't have their shields up right now. We need to hit them from below with powerful fire and take them by surprise."

The group nodded grimly.

"We'll need to temporarily split up and spread out around the dorm so we can hit them all simultaneously. Keep your shields up as much as possible, keep out of sight of the Demons if you can, and get back here as quickly as you can. You two," I pointed at the two remaining Blessed, "each of you should go with a Light Guardian, so they can fly you out if they need to. And you," I pointed at the remaining Blessed who had fire abilities, "can stay on this side of the dorm with me, and I'll watch your back. Okay? Let's go."

We ran, hunched over so we wouldn't be spotted, and spread out around the dorm as much as we could. I looked over at the Blessed thirty feet to my left and nodded at him. It was time. Flames burst from both our hands, shooting straight up, and completely encasing the Dark Guardians above us. We quickly widened the flames until the entire side of the dorm was covered. Shouts of surprise and pain filled the air above us as I drew even more power from the well in my chest and funneled it down my arms and out my hands, blasting them with more heat. Dark Guardians fell from the sky—burned, injured, some dead—and I directed one hand of flames down at them, making sure they couldn't get up again. I kept my other hand pointed upward, sending a thick beam of purple fire at the few Dark Guardians who'd managed to shield themselves after being hit by the first wave of flames.

"Try to overwhelm their shields!" I called to the Blessed.

He nodded, fire spiraling down his arms, then flames practically erupted from his palms, encasing the small remaining group above him in a giant fireball. I raised both hands, the Dark Guardians on the ground now subdued, and pulled more power to my palms. A wave of tiredness swept through me as I drained even further. But I gritted my teeth and sent a giant beam of fire at the remaining Dark Guardians above me, encasing their shields in a swirling ball of flame so tight they couldn't escape. I tightened it further and further, pressing in on them, suffocating them with heat. Finally, one after one, their shields failed under the pressure, and they were encased in flames. Then they fell from the sky, burned and defeated.

Before I could feel relief, a scream ripped through the air to our right—a chilling, terrified sound. A human sound. And then the Demons moved in, snarling and furious.

"Shit." I ran to the Blessed on my side of the dorm, wrapped my arms around his chest, then kicked off the ground, my wings carrying us up and over the top of the dorm. I deposited him on the roof, then pushed into the air again. "Stay here. I'm going to get the rest of our group."

He nodded, then turned and shot a wide beam of flames at the encroaching Demons as I flew to the other side of the dorm where the scream had come from. I didn't hear screams anymore, but I did hear the pounding of fists and the screeching scrape of claws against rock. A stony dread filled me before I even reached the edge. I could see the Demons covering the entire wall unimpeded, cracking the now-vulnerable stone, and sending heavy pieces tumbling to the ground. Where were the members of my group?

With a growl, I pulled power down my arms and shot a wave of fire and lightning at the Demons, electrocuting and burning them. Forcing them away from the wall. Then I flew out past the ledge, trying to get a look at the ground where the Blessed and Light Guardian should've been. I squinted through the dust and debris beneath me. There was so much rubble. Too much. More than the stones from the dorm. My heart sank as I flew closer to the ground. It looked like the Blessed had tried to build a wall of thick rock along this side, to shield the damaged walls from the advancing Demons. But there'd been too many Demons, and it looked like they'd crushed the still-forming wall, pushing and hitting it until it collapsed backward onto the Blessed and Light Guardian.

I looked around desperately, trying to see them through the wreckage. Trying to tell if they were trapped but maybe still alive. But the debris was too thick, piled too high, and the Demons had crushed it even more when they'd moved forward, scaling the collapsed wall to continue their incursion on the charred dorm. If the Blessed and Light Guardian had been alive after the wall collapsed on them, I didn't know how they could be now.

My hands shook and the fire and lightning trailed off. Regret burned through me. Half of me wished I hadn't sent them off on their own—that I hadn't divided the group at all. But the other half of me knew it'd been our best strategy to save the integrity of the dorm and protect the students inside. This was the result of being so incredibly outnumbered. But that didn't make it hurt any less to lose people. People I was supposed to protect.

I clenched my fists and turned in the air, flying quickly back to the Blessed on the roof. He'd been joined by the last remaining Light Guardian and Blessed.

"We lost the other two," I panted as I landed next to them. "The Demons buried them under stones and crushed them. It's just us now."

The group stared back at me, horror in their eyes. The fear had overtaken the sadness now. They knew as well as I did how this was going to continue. And I could see on their faces that none of them were ready to die. Well, neither was I, and I'd work my ass off to keep us alive for as long as I could. But I knew we couldn't fight like this forever. I glanced at the horizon, at the forest of burned trees that led to the edge of the plane and the portals, hoping with every fiber of my being to see backup on its way. To see Gabriel and a better-trained army of Divines who could help us. Even the warrior faction. To not be abandoned and left to die by my mother yet again.

My throat burned as I swallowed the smoke and dust filled air, and I pressed my eyes closed for a second. There was no backup in sight. Just an endless sea of Demons descending on this and every other standing dorm, of which there were only a few.

"I'm almost out of power," the Light Guardian murmured to me, his voice shaking, as the four of us moved to stand in the middle of the dorm roof, back-to-back so we could each see one side of the building.

"Me too," the Blessed with fire abilities murmured. "I used up a lot taking out the Dark Guardians around the dorm."

"I have a little left," murmured the other Blessed, who could conjure branches, "but not much."

I pulled my sword from its sheath. It glowed only dimly now. But I didn't want to tell them I was almost out of power too. I didn't want them to feel any more afraid or helpless.

"Just do the best you can for as long as you can," I finally said. "Do you have any weapons on you?"

All three of them shook their heads. Of course they didn't. They weren't from border towns, where they'd hammered into us from an early age that we should always be armed. They weren't soldiers.

"Here," I said quickly, reaching under my glowing armor to grab a couple small daggers from my waistband. I handed one to each Blessed.

Then I bent and grabbed a knife hidden in my boot and handed it to the Light Guardian. "Use those to defend yourselves if you run out of power."

"What about you?" the Light Guardian asked. "You're running out of power too," he added quietly as he glanced at my fading sword. He shared too much of my transformation not to see the signs.

"I have a couple daggers left. I'll be fine," I murmured, watching as multiple Demons made it over the edge of the roof and lumbered toward us. "Now brace yourselves and stay with me."

There were maybe twenty small to medium sized Demons pouring onto the roof now. Most of the larger ones had stayed on the ground so they could use their size and power to crush the outer walls of the dorm. With so few of us left, all we could hope for was that we'd stopped the Dark Guardians before they'd done enough damage to the walls to make destroying them as easy for the Demons as it'd been for the dorm next to us.

I quickly sheathed my sword and materialized my bow instead. My legs shook with exhaustion as I drained further, but I needed a quick way to injure multiple Demons at a distance. I grabbed an arrow and aimed at a fast-approaching Demon, then let it loose. Its scream cut off as my arrow embedded deep in the column of its throat and shot burning lightning from the impact point. I turned and shot another Demon in the same way, this time burning through its thin neck. The Demon collapsed, pinning another down with it. The Light Guardian next to me quickly materialized his bow and joined me.

"Aim for their necks," I panted as I aimed then let loose another shot. "If they're small enough, it might behead them, and if not, it'll slow them down."

The Light Guardian and I shot arrow after arrow—his full of bright white light, and mine full of crackling purple lightning—turning as a group so he and I could face whatever Demon was getting closest to us. We managed to behead a handful of smaller Demons this way, and injured many others, but the Demons still managed to close in around us.

"Get your sword," I said to the Light Guardian, dematerializing my bow and pulling my dim sword from its sheath. The Demons were too close now. "Blessed, try to restrain or injure as many Demons as you can, and we'll move to behead them. Prioritize the closest Demons."

The Light Guardian and I kicked off the ground as the Blessed moved together, back-to-back. Then they began hitting any Demon that got within fifteen feet of us with power. The Blessed with fire abilities surrounded Demons' heads and necks with fire, burning through their flesh and beheading some and injuring others, while the other Blessed shot thick branches, binding their limbs and strangling them. Both distracted them enough so the Light Guardian and I could swoop in and behead them with our swords.

We scrambled to keep up as line after line of Demons ran at us from all directions. The Blessed hit them as quickly as they could while the Light Guardian and I swung our swords again and again, hacking through thick skin, sinew, and bone until our arms shook, dodging Demon strikes, bites, and acid sprays as best we could. But both of us were liberally spattered with acid and the Demons' burning black blood. There was no avoiding it from the amount of beheading we were doing, and I was starting to feel the sharp sting as the acid made its way between the pieces of my armor, burning through my torn-up clothes to the skin beneath. And my sword dimmed further as what little power I had left tried to heal my skin. I wished I could stop it. Right now, I'd trade healing for having power for a little longer.

A yell pierced the air behind me, and I spun to see a Demon with its teeth clamped around the Light Guardian's arm, its head and neck charred from the Blessed's power. I flew quickly over and swung my sword at the Demon's neck, slicing quickly through the little remaining flesh. The Demon's jaws released the Light Guardian's arm as its head tumbled to the ground.

"Shit. It's using the rest of my power to heal me," he gasped as blood dripped quickly from his arm.

His transformation dimmed and flickered as the bleeding slowed. He paled, and his arms shook. Cursing, I grabbed him out of the air just as he fell out of his transformation. He'd officially burned out. I lowered him quickly to the roof before flying at another Demon and beheading it right before it lunged at the Blessed. There were only a few Demons left—the group had done an incredible job of holding them off.

I beheaded another Demon and kicked off its falling body, propelling myself toward another whose head was now wrapped in the Blessed's fire. I propelled my sword straight through its neck, cutting off its wail before removing my sword and cleaving off its head in one strike.

"Over here!" the other Blessed yelled as she threw quick branches around the legs of a charging Demon.

It fell, legs bound, and skidded across the surface toward the group, its jaws open and ready. I charged at it and beheaded it mid-slide. There was only one Demon left now. I spun and flew at it as the other Blessed shot fire at it. But the stream petered out, and with a grunt, the Blessed fell out of his transformation. *Shit.*

I swooped down and put myself between the group and the charging Demon. At the last moment, the other Blessed managed to twine branches around the Demon's front legs, tripping it. I flew over its head as it fell, landed on its shoulders, and drove my sword through the base of its neck before pulling it free and beheading the Demon.

With a breath of relief, I pushed off its body and landed next to the group with a thud. I braced the tip of my sword against the roof and leaned on it, breathing hard and trying to force my legs to hold steady. Trying desperately to hang onto my transformation. The booming sounds of the Demons' continued attacks on the dorm walls filled the air around us, partially drowning out the horrific sounds of their screams and roars.

"What do we do now?" the Light Guardian asked, his face pale and drawn with exhaustion and fear.

I stared at him, slightly at a loss. I didn't know. I didn't know what we could do, especially without bringing down a ton of Demons on us. And we wouldn't be able to hold them off again. Not without the Blessed and Light Guardian's powers. What I *did* know was that we needed to get off the roof before I fell out of my transformation. We didn't want to be trapped up here. But before I could say this, a horrible bellowing shriek ripped through the air from the opposite end of the roof.

I spun and shoved into the air so I could see over the pile of Demon bodies surrounding us like a wall. Every drop of blood in my body turned to ice as I saw the huge Demon slithering over the side of the roof. It was in the form of a centipede, at least twenty feet tall and twelve feet wide. I had no idea how long it was. Its body just kept going as leg after sharply pointed leg made its way over the side and onto the roof. It let out another bellowing shriek as it saw me, and glided quickly toward us, its many legs moving in way that caused shivers to cascade through my body in repulsion. It was too big. Too deadly. Without power and training, the students with me wouldn't stand a chance.

"Run!" I yelled down to the group. "Get to the edge of the roof over there and I'll try to get us down!"

They quickly scrambled over the expansive pile of Demon bodies, hissing as the blood and acid burned through their clothes and skin. I spun back around, gripping my sword tightly. The Demon was advancing too quickly. I needed to buy them time. I took a deep breath, then flew at the

Demon and swung my sword in a wide arc, slamming the blade into its spike-covered antennae, severing the long feelers from its body. Then I spun away from its fang-filled mouth and brought my sword down over one of its front legs, severing it. The Demon twisted and lunged at me, then lifted the front of its body off the ground as I flew higher, trying to reach me. Several of its sharp metal legs scraped across my armor before my wings pulled me out of reach.

I glanced behind me and saw the others had made it as close to the opposite side of the dorm as they could without engaging any of the Demons attacking the walls from below. I needed to incapacitate this Demon so I could get them off the roof. I swooped down again and brought my sword down over its neck. But the Demon lurched back as I swung, and my blade slashed through its head instead, slicing open its skull from its crown through its jaw, causing its head to fall open in the front like a partially cracked egg. The Demon bellowed, twitching uncontrollably as blood rained from its face, obscuring its vision. But it had enough control to shield its face and neck with its numerous front legs, creating almost a spiky crown around itself that would take a while to get through.

Making a quick decision, I turned and flew toward the rest of the group. Whatever we did, we'd have to hurry. The Demon's ultra-fast healing would have it repaired enough to attack us again in only a couple minutes.

"There's no place to go even if we get off the roof," the Light Guardian said, turning to face me as I touched down next to them. "Look. They're everywhere." His voice was filled with grim despair.

I looked out over the expanse of campus, once so beautiful and green, now scorched beyond recognition and covered in rubble, bodies, and blood. He was right. The Dark Guardian army was still so large that there was nowhere I could take them where they wouldn't be surrounded. And I couldn't fly them all to the burned forest in time. We'd probably be intercepted by hundreds of Dark Guardians anyway. I spun to look at the Demon again, whose head was quickly fusing back together. I didn't know what to do.

"We have a better chance up here with only one Demon than down there with hundreds," said the Blessed who controlled branches.

I glanced at the other Blessed and the Light Guardian. They both looked terrified. But they nodded in agreement.

"I don't know if I can protect you against it." I tried to tamp down the panic clawing its way up my throat. "It's too big. Too fast. It has too many sharp legs. It can and will quickly overwhelm you, especially without your powers."

"It wouldn't be any better down there," the Light Guardian said, jerking his head at the hundreds of deadly Demons on the ground. "We're in a bad position no matter what."

The Demon bellowed again behind us, and I knew we were out of time. I looked out over the chaos on the ground again, sweeping the area for any place the group could land or take cover. I'd grab them all and drag them there if I had to. They didn't know what they were committing to by staying up here. They didn't have the experience to know. They thought they had some chance, but with this Demon, I didn't agree. They'd be overwhelmed in a matter of seconds, and I didn't have enough power left to keep them safe.

"Damnit," I whispered, as I was once again met with an endless sea of Dark Guardian forces. If there were allies alive and fighting somewhere, I couldn't see them. There was no place to run. No place that was safer than here. "Shield yourself and them," I growled at the Blessed who still had a little power left. "And don't take the shield down for anything, understand?"

She nodded. "But what about you?"

"I'm a soldier," I said firmly. "I've trained for this. You three haven't. So put up your shield. *Now*." I didn't want to be an ass to them, but I'd do what I had to, to make them understand the stakes and to keep them safe. They weren't trained enough for this battle, and they needed to stay out of it.

The Blessed's lips pressed together in a frustrated line, but she put a light green shield around the three of them as the Demon charged us again, its bellows making my ears burn with pain. The shield didn't look very strong. My stomach clenched. She must be running even lower on power than I'd thought.

I spun, gripping my sword tightly, and ran forward to meet the Demon. If I'd known we wouldn't have the chance to escape the roof, I never would've let it this close to my team. It was too late now, though. I could only hope they had enough survival instincts to stay away from this fight.

I threw myself into the air at the last moment, shooting straight up and surprising the Demon. Then I tucked my wings and plummeted rapidly, then plunged my sword clean through its back. I shoved off it quickly, scraping my sword down its body as I flew to its rear, deeply cutting into the skin there. But its body was so thick that I doubted it felt the injury more than a paper cut. When I reached its rear, I brought my sword down over several of its back legs, severing them. It had so many legs that I doubted losing some would affect it, but I wanted it to turn around. To follow we away from my group.

The Demon swung around on a scream, bending its body almost in half so it could attack me with the deadly points of its front legs. My wings beat frantically, carrying me out of range just in time. Then I spun and flew quickly forward, leading the Demon toward the center of the roof again. But as it swung the rest of its body around to follow me, its back legs hit the Blessed's shield. I turned my head and watched in horror as they tumbled across the surface of the roof, still enclosed in the green bubble, skidding toward the edge. They stopped rolling just before the edge, but it'd been close. At least the Blessed's shield had held up under the impact.

The Demon charged at me with a bellow that made the dorm vibrate. I flew up, hovering high above it at the other end of the roof. From here, I could see the entire length of its horrifying body. All fifty feet of it. I couldn't help the icy shudder that vibrated through me. I'd seen a lot of horrifying Demons in my lifetime, but never anything quite like this.

I dove again as the Demon launched the front of its body off the ground, stabilizing itself with its back legs, and punching all its front legs at me repeatedly in the hopes of impaling me. I pulled in my wings and spun through the maze of limbs, getting only slightly nicked, before swinging my sword up and cutting off the bottom of the Demon's face. I swung again and managed to cut part way through its neck. *Finally!* If I could manage one more powerful strike, I might be able to behead it. I quickly raised my sword, determined to end this, but the Demon swung to the side, blood flying from its face, and hit me in the side with multiple legs.

The blow sent me careening to the roof, and I only just managed to keep ahold of my sword as I tumbled across the surface. I skidded to a halt on my back just as the Demon slammed its legs down over me. I quickly raised my sword, deflecting as many legs as I could with a wide, powerful swing, hitting the points away from me before they could make contact. But a sharp tug and fiery burn in my leg told me I hadn't gotten all of them.

I cried out as the Demon yanked the metal point out of my thigh. I felt the warm rush of blood and knew it was bad. I cursed, scrambling backward, trying to get out from under its legs. But it was too big. Too long. There were too many legs. I was trapped.

The Demon brought its legs down over me again, but I rolled away, toward the center of its body. As I rolled, I faintly heard footsteps running toward me. More than one set of footsteps. Fear sliced through me. I turned, trying to see past the erratically moving legs, and saw my group members running over from the other side of the dorm, weapons in hand and no shield in sight. They wanted to help.

"No!" I tried pushing to my feet as blood dripped from my leg. "Stay in your shield! Stay back!"

The Demon swung around again and knocked me over before I could find my way out from under it. I rolled, desperately trying to avoid getting stabbed again as leg after leg pummeled me, trying to get purchase. The Demon's legs screeched across my armor as I rolled, denting and scraping it with its weight, but it couldn't get a good enough angle on me to punch through again. I finally managed to extricate myself from its legs and make it to the middle of its body underneath it again. I shoved quickly to my feet and stabbed up through its stomach with all my strength, driving in my sword up to the hilt. Then I ran with my sword still in it, dragging the blade forcefully down its body, cutting deep and unleashing a torrent of burning black blood.

The Demon screamed and jerked around, throwing me out from under it and sending me tumbling across the roof. I winced as the stab wound in my leg was knocked around, but I managed to halt my flailing progress and shove to my feet just in time to see the Demon charging at me again. I jumped into the air, but it lunged after me and hit me in the torso with what was left of its face, throwing me back with astonishing force. I caught myself with my wings before I fell out of the air, then tried to fly out of its reach. But the Demon raised itself on its back legs again and hit me across the side with multiple legs. This time I did fall out of the air, and went tumbling across the roof again, barely able to hang onto my sword. I was winded. Exhausted. Almost out of power.

My transformation shuddered around me as I finally came to a halt on my back.

"Stay with me," I whispered desperately to it. "Please. Stay with me."

The Demon loomed over me before I could shove to my feet, and with a roar of triumph, brought its legs down violently over me. I dropped my sword and threw both hands into the air, shoving a shield in front of me. It flickered as the sharp legs pounded into it, and my arms shook wildly. I didn't know how many more hits it could survive. I cried out as the Demon brought down its legs over my shield again. I felt the force of the blow through my whole body, even as my shield deflected the lethal metal.

But suddenly the Demon jerked away from me and disappeared from my field of vision. *What?* Gasping, I shoved into a sitting position, my shield fading, and I saw the last thing I wanted to see—the Blessed dragging the Demon backward, thick branches wrapped around the back of its body, and the other Blessed and Light Guardian attacking its back legs with their small weapons.

"No!" I picked up my sword and ran at the Demon. "Get back in your shield! Now!"

But the Demon swung the front of its body around with an enraged bellow, bending in half, and jerked the back of its body violently away from them, sending the Blessed flying. Away from the other two.

I swore and ran as hard as I could, ignoring the pain in my leg, and reached the back of the Demon just as it charged the two young men. I launched into the air then stabbed down into its back, trying to distract it, as the Blessed and Light Guardian tried to throw themselves out of its path. The Demon screamed as I shoved my sword deep and ran with it up its body toward its head, leaving a trail of blood—my own and the Demon's —behind me. But it didn't turn around or even throw me off. It'd homed in on the two young men. And on their current lack of divine power.

With a triumphant bellow, the Demon skittered forward, bowling over the Blessed with a violent head-butt to the chest, smearing his front with black blood, then turned and struck the Light Guardian across the torso with its sharp legs, cutting deep. Blood seeped through the front of his shirt as he stumbled back, and he looked down at the gashes, stunned. He raised his free hand shakily to the wounds, almost like he was trying to cover them. To stop the flow of blood with his palm. But it'd already soaked the entire front of his shirt.

Panicking, I threw myself into the air and sped toward the front of the Demon, my legs not carrying me fast enough over its elongated body.

"Run!" I shouted as I sped toward them. "Run away from it!"

The Light Guardian stumbled back a few more steps, looking at me, but I wasn't sure if he'd comprehended what I'd said. He looked frozen. Like shock was taking over his body. The Demon was barreling down on him, and he wasn't moving away fast enough. Desperate, I threw my sword forward and down as hard as I could, aiming for the Demon's neck. I had to stop it. Distract it. Refocus its attention on me. The sword tore through the Demon's neck and lodged there, hilt-deep, cutting off the Demon's bellow. But the Demon didn't stop or divert its course. It just launched forward again, aiming the sharp points of its legs at the Light Guardian's chest. Ready to end him.

With a cry, the Blessed who'd been thrown to the ground, flung himself forward, ramming into the Light Guardian's side, knocking him out of the way and to the ground. I dove and grabbed my sword from the Demon's neck as they tumbled across the roof, the Light Guardian leaving a pool of blood behind him. With a yell, I brought down my sword over the Demon's neck, severing it halfway. *Shit.* Its neck was almost as thick as the rest of its body. I jerked my sword free and raised it again to deliver another blow. But the Demon bucked wildly, throwing me off my feet, then off its back.

I beat my wings desperately and managed to right myself enough to land hard on my knees, bolts of pain radiating up my thighs. I shoved shakily to my feet, using my sword as a brace, and felt blood gushing from the puncture in my leg. But I just threw myself back into the air and flew forward, trying to reach its neck again. The Demon was still moving toward the Blessed who was trying to drag the Light Guardian back with him, its head dangling forward at an odd angle, blood pouring down its face from its neck, obscuring its vision.

With a squelching hiss, the Demon lunged clumsily forward, wildly stabbing its legs out in front of it, trying to pierce through them even though it could no longer see them. The Blessed fell to the ground, trying to dodge the blows, the Light Guardian collapsing on top of him. A deluge of black blood spilled from the Demon's neck over the two young men as it lunged forward again, and the Light Guardian cried out in pain as the acidic blood sank into the deep gashes in his front. With a garbled hiss of triumph, the Demon homed in on their location from the sound, and brought its legs swiftly down over them, running them both through.

"No!" I yelled frantically, finally reaching its head. I swung my sword again.

But the Demon was jerked suddenly backward, and my sword glanced off the front of its rapidly healing head. I spun to see the remaining Blessed had wrapped branches around the back of the Demon's body and was dragging it backward, away from the young men with all her strength. The Demon let out a guttural scream of rage, and bent its body in half again, quickly scuttling away from me with uncanny speed. With a roar, it brought its remaining front legs down over the branches restraining it, severing them with a loud crack.

I glanced down at the Blessed and Light Guardian quickly, trying to see if there was anything I could do to help them. Both were unconscious and rapidly bleeding out. I could see, now, that they'd been stabbed too many times and in too many important places to survive for long. And I had no power left to heal them. There was nothing I could do. I swallowed down the burning sting in my throat as fury and despair battled for supremacy inside me.

With a growl of rage, I flew at the Demon again as it scuttled toward the remaining Blessed. She threw branches from her hands, wrapping them tightly around many of the Demon's front legs and cinching them together, causing the front of its body to thud to the roof and skid forward. Then she ran backwards, trying to distance herself from it. But the Demon recovered quickly and pulled itself up, so it was standing on its unbound back legs. I reached the back of its body as it roared and wrenched its front legs apart, snapping the branches and raining splinters of wood over the roof.

I quickly brought down my sword over the Demon's back, slicing viciously into it again and again. Unwilling to let it ignore me as it had when it'd attacked the two young men. With one last cry of effort, I managed to completely cut through the entire back ten feet of its body. Finally unbalanced, the Demon screamed and jerked forward, the front of its body thudding to the roof's surface. It bent in half, spinning to focus on me, and I pushed into the air, preparing to avoid the thrusting metal legs I knew were coming. The Demon lifted its front into the air, punching its legs up at me. But without the back ten feet of its body, it wasn't stable, and it fell heavily back to the roof. I dove, wanting to take advantage of this new instability, and swung my sword over its neck again. But the Demon thrust into the air at the last moment, narrowly avoiding my blade, and head-butted my stomach with enough force to knock all the air from my body. And to knock me out of the air.

I fell with a clatter of metal as my sword bounced off my armor. I'd barely avoided cutting myself. And with another scream of triumph, the Demon brought its legs down over me. With a burst of adrenaline, I rolled toward the middle of its body, but the Demon moved with me, remarkably nimble even now. With another scream, it brought its legs down over me again. I swung my sword in an arc in front of me and managed to knock away most of the sharp points. But another leg came quickly down and slammed through my upper left arm. I gasped as the Demon wrenched its leg free on another bellow of triumph, and blood spilled from the wound. Satisfied, the Demon spun away from me, then lurched forward, scuttling quickly to the other end of the roof, its sights set on the remaining Blessed.

"Fuck."

I shoved to my feet, ignoring the screaming pain in my limbs and the soreness that went bone deep, scooped my sword from the roof, and pushed into the air, flying as fast as I could to reach them. The Blessed threw a shield around herself as the Demon reached her and swung its front legs at her. The metal points bounced off the shield, but the hit was forceful enough to throw the Blessed back several feet. Her shield sputtered out as she hit the roof.

I pulled power down my arms as fast as I could as the Demon charged her. Then I unleashed a torrent of purple flames at it.

"Come on!" I growled as I burned through leg after leg as I flew up its body as fast as I could. "Pay attention to *me!*"

The Demon bellowed but didn't alter its course. The Blessed was scrambling quickly backward, unable to get back on her feet. But she was running out of roof. I poured more fire out of my hands, draining almost completely, trying to stop the Demon. Burn through its body. Burn off enough of its legs. Anything, so it'd stop advancing on her.

The Blessed screamed as the Demon finally reached her. She threw her hands up in panic, creating a cage of thick branches around her, trying to shield herself. On a roar of triumph, the Demon lunged forward and crawled over the cage of branches, before violently stabbing its many legs into the wooden structure.

The Blessed screamed—a sound of pure terror.

"No!"

I finally reached the Demon's head and blasted its neck with fire. But it dimmed mere seconds later, and the flames sputtered out as my transformation shuddered around me again.

"No," I gasped, "not now!"

I tried to summon more flames to my hands, but none came. So I yanked my sword from its sheath and dove. With as much strength as I could muster, I brought my sword down in an arc over the Demon's neck.

The Demon's head swung forward, attached by only a foot or two of tissue on the other side of its neck bone. But the Blessed's screams had ceased. Terrified, I pulled my sword free and swung at the Demon's neck again. It cleaved through the remaining tissue, severing the Demon's head from its body. It writhed and jerked as its head rolled away, and then its body thudded to the roof, hard enough to shake the building, and its legs curled into its back. It was dead.

I landed hard on the roof, my wings barely able to maintain flight anymore, and ran to the cage of branches around the Blessed. I lifted the structure with all my strength, shoving the thick enclosure off her. My stomach pitched as I saw what remained. It was . . . horrible. I turned around and fell to my knees, a dry heave forcing itself from my body as tears spilled down my cheeks. I clutched my stomach, gasping for air. I'd failed her. I'd failed them all.

I pushed shakily to my feet as a new wave of Dark Guardians surrounded the dorm and blasted the exterior with black fire, as though all our efforts to protect it had meant nothing. I stumbled away from the edge, heading toward the middle of the roof as the intense heat surrounded me. Stone after stone cracked under the onslaught, and a few even shattered, showering the area with burning rubble. I needed to get off the roof, but I wasn't sure my wings would hold me.

Before I could decide what to do, a wall of bright red flames shot from the ground on one side of the dorm, blasting the line of Dark Guardians. I stared at the flames for a moment, dumbstruck, as I watched at least forty Dark Guardians burn alive. Who could possibly still have that much power left at this point in the battle? But I had my answer in the next moment when a wall of wind rose from the same spot, sending the intense flames around the entire exterior of the dorm, engulfing every Dark Guardian who'd been attacking the structure. The Blessed. This attack was coming from the two injured Blessed who'd stayed on the ground. They must've decided to stop shielding themselves and jump into battle. But they'd die. They'd die the second the Demons got close to them, because they couldn't run or move or fight.

I ran desperately toward their edge of the roof, unwilling to lose any more group members, but the Blessed's flames kept me from flying down to them. I was trapped in four walls of violently swirling fire that went up at least thirty feet above me and was quickly sucking all oxygen from the roof. I fell to me knees, gasping for breath as the Dark Guardians fell like flies around me, burned to death and thrown violently from flight. I wondered vaguely, as my vision began to flicker and darken, whether I'd burn too or die of suffocation first.

But just as suddenly, the flames dissipated, and the wind died down. I desperately sucked in a breath of air, clutching my burning chest as my vision slowly cleared, then pushed quickly to my feet, wobbling on unsteady legs. I jumped back into the air before I'd fully recovered and flew back toward the side of the roof. My wings were carrying me only a little above the roof now. *Come on, transformation. Stay with me. Stay for just a little longer.*

I pulled my sword from my sheath and dove, intent on putting myself between them and the Demons. Desperate to save these two. Desperate to get to them before the Demons could. But a blast of wind knocked me out of controlled flight and propelled me back along with the attacking Demons. I slammed into the ground forty feet away, the breath punched from my lungs at the force of impact. A ringing filled my ears as stars burst in front of my eyes. But I quickly rolled over, gasping, and shoved to my feet, before jumping back into the air.

I tried to fly back toward the Blessed. It looked like the young man with fire abilities had already fallen out of his transformation, burned out after creating such a giant fire. The Blessed next to him was trying desperately to shield them both with powerful bursts of wind, but I could feel them getting weaker as I shoved against them, trying to maintain flight. Trying to reach them. But I realized in the next moment that if I reached them, so would the Demons. So I turned and cut down as many Demons as I could while they struggled with the wind. I didn't know what else I could do.

I hacked through Demon after Demon, trying to clear the area in front of the Blessed, but there were just too many. It didn't seem to matter how many I injured, incapacitated, or killed. There were always more stepping forward to replace them.

With a last cry of effort, and a last feeble wave of wind, the Blessed fell out of her transformation. I turned and flew desperately toward them, trying to beat the wave of Demons doing the same, but there were so many of them, and many were huge—large enough to reach them in only a few steps. I extended my hand frantically and threw power at the Blessed, trying to form a shield between them and the Demons. But my power shimmered only briefly before vanishing. My transformation flickered. I clenched my teeth and tried to draw more power down my arms anyway. Anything to make another shield. A lasting one. But nothing came out. There was no power left.

"No," I gasped, my outstretched hand shaking wildly as I saw the first Demons reach them.

And in a matter of seconds, they'd crushed them.

"No." It came out as a shaky whisper this time. I'd failed. Again. I'd failed to protect them.

I slowed in the air, shock and devastation drowning me in overwhelming waves. Then I watched, numb and helpless, as the Demons swarmed all sides of the dorm, the largest at the front. And as one, they hit the charred and weakened stones as they had with the other dorms. And the walls exploded under the onslaught. I flew backward as stone debris burst from the building in a wide arc. My skin burned as chunks of rock sprayed over me, dragging across the exposed parts of me.

I managed to get about fifty feet away before it finally happened. With a shudder, I fell roughly out of my transformation, twenty feet to the ground. I'd officially burned out.

27
SOMETHING MORE

I hit the ground and tried to roll, dispersing the impact across my body. But even then, it hurt, and bolts of pain shot through my legs like an electric shock. I rolled to my feet, groaning, and pulled my two long daggers from their sheaths at my hips—my last remaining weapons. I'd have to be more careful now. I no longer had armor or quick healing to protect me. No wings to pull me out of dangerous positions. But students still needed my help and protection, regardless of the state of my power. I needed to evacuate any students who'd survived the dorm's destruction. If any had.

I crouched, making myself as small and unnoticeable as possible, and ran to the large body of a fallen Demon a few feet to my right. Then I sprinted down the length of it back toward the dorm, using its corpse to shield me from sight. When I reached the end of its body, I crouched and ran a few feet to the left where there was another. I dodged pools of acidic blood and Demon goo spilling from it as I ran down its length, then crouched again, scouting another. With a quick look around, I ran to the left and slid into the thin space between two dead Demons. Unable to avoid the acidic blood now, I ran down the gap between the two, hoping my boots would hold up against it. But I remained unseen by the Dark Guardian forces, which was the most important thing right now. I'd deal with burned boots and feet if it kept me alive for longer.

When I reached the end of the gap, I peered from the crack and realized I'd managed to make it to the corner of the dorm. Or what'd been the corner when the dorm had still been standing. Now, it was a mess of broken, charred stones, pieces of mangled wrought iron, and smashed up remains of armored rooms. My heart ached at the sight. Not many people could've survived. Especially since the Demons had immediately swarmed over the ruins the second the dust had cleared, crushing and tearing through anything that hadn't been completely demolished. But there were some armored boxes along the edges that looked mostly intact, where the Demons were thinnest. Maybe I could find some survivors.

I quickly made sure no one was looking in my direction, then crouched and ran toward the back of the dorm where I saw the most intact armored rooms, partially hidden under the rubble from the rest of the building. They all looked dented and torn, but not crushed at least. Not yet. Breathing hard, I plastered myself against one of the armored rooms as a group of Dark Guardians flew overhead, willing them not to notice me. A breathless moment later, they passed.

I blew out a breath of relief, then turned to examine this back row of rooms. There were six on the first floor and four on the second that were mostly intact, though each was ripped open at least a little. But maybe that was a good thing. At this point, the students weren't any safer in their armored rooms than they'd be out of them. The rooms, so good at offering protection under lighter attacks, were now becoming metal tombs, trapping and crushing the students inside them. The sooner they escaped their confines, the better. And the cracks in the metal might give them a way out.

I crouched near the bottom of the room I'd pressed against and examined the tear in the structure. It was maybe three feet tall and a foot and a half wide at its widest point. Potentially enough room for someone to get out. I could barely see into the room, though. Beyond the first couple feet, the space melted into darkness.

"Hey," I called quietly into the tear, "this is Terah, another student. Are you okay? Are you injured?"

There was silence for a moment before I heard shuffling from the other side.

"T-Terah?" The voice was thin and shaky.

I squinted as the person crouched in front of the mangled metal. As the light hit her face, I recognized her as another first year from class.

"It's Ivy, right?" I asked, trying to sound calm. Comforting. Not exhausted and injured. "Are you hurt? Do you think you can slide through this tear? The Demons are smashing the rest of this dorm—it's no longer safe for you to stay in here."

"I'm a little injured, but mostly alright," Ivy murmured back. "I have a couple friends in here with me. I think we can all get out, but . . . is it safe?"

I bit the inside of my cheek for a moment, thinking. "No," I finally said, deciding on the truth. "It's not safe. But it's potentially safer than staying in here. There are a ton of huge Demons smashing all the intact armored rooms they find. They can and will crush this room. If you have power left, it's better for you to leave the room and work together to shield yourselves out here than to stay and hope they don't crush you. But it's up to you all. I can't force you to come out."

"No, I, I'll come out." Her voice trembled even more. "Will you come with me?" she asked, turning to her friends in the room, still shrouded in darkness.

"Yeah. I think that would be best."

"I will too."

"Good," I said quickly, peering around to make sure no one had spotted me. "It's clear right now. Come out as fast as you can and immediately put up your shields. Be careful exiting. Don't cut yourself on the jagged metal."

I moved to the side and Ivy climbed through the tear headfirst. I helped her quickly to her feet. She looked a little banged up, but not too bad.

"Shield up," I reminded her, "and stay as close to the wall as you can."

Ivy nodded and materialized a bright white shield around herself as one of her friends began sliding through the tear sideways. I stepped forward and grabbed her under the armpits, supporting her weight so she could keep pushing out without cutting herself.

"Sorry about the blood," I mumbled as a liberal amount from my injured arm smeared across her shirt.

"It's fine," she whispered as she finally pushed to her feet and conjured a white shield around herself. Katara—another first year from class.

"You're injured!" Ivy whispered, her eyes widening as she looked at my blood encrusted left arm and the leg of my pants, shredded and soaked through with blood.

"Yeah," I grunted as I helped her other friend—Mary—through the tear. "That can happen when you fight a shit ton of Demons."

She ignored my snark. "Do you want me to heal you?"

I looked up at her, surprised. She was . . . offering to help me? To use her power on me in the middle of a battle? To my surprise as much as hers, I felt myself smiling. A genuine one.

"No, it's okay. Save your power to protect yourself. You'll need it."

I helped Mary to her feet, then she put a shield around herself.

Ivy nodded but continued to scrutinize me. "Are you out of power?"

I sighed, straightening up. "Yeah. All but some of my life force." I didn't know why I was telling her this. It wouldn't make them feel better to know I could barely protect them anymore.

Ivy nodded, determination filling her face. "Then we'll have to work together to protect you too."

I stared at her, stunned, my throat feeling suddenly tight. She'd surprised me again. I swallowed and sent her a tight smile as we moved as a group to the next armored room.

"That's nice of you." I tried to keep my voice matter of fact. "But don't worry about me. I'm well-trained. It's more important that you all look after each other until backup arrives. I'll be fine." I tried to sound like I believed my own words. But I was exhausted. In pain. Rapidly weakening.

Her response was cut off by another group of Dark Guardians flying overhead. I pulled them all down beneath a part of the structure that was jutting out from the rest. It offered a tiny bit of coverage.

"Stay under here. I'm going to see if there are any other survivors."

I ran to the next room over, which was partially smashed. The tear in the armoring was at the corner and had also torn into the room next to it.

"Hey," I called, as loudly as I could without being overheard by the army around us, "are there any survivors here? This is Terah, another student. I'm trying to help survivors out of the building before the Demons crush the rest of it."

I heard a sob from the partially crushed room, but also shuffling, like someone was crawling over.

"I-I'm alive," a soft voice murmured, sounding frayed around the edges, perhaps from screaming. "But my friend, he . . . he was crushed with the other half of my room." I heard another sob.

My stomach clenched. "I'm so sorry." That must've been horrible to witness. "Do you think you'll be able to climb out?" The tear in this room and the next started about six feet off the ground. It'd be harder for them to get out than it'd been for Ivy, Katara, and Mary.

"Yeah," she sniffled. She took a deep breath. "Let me pull my desk over."

676

"I can get out too," a deeper voice said from the room next to hers. "And I can help you get the others out. My room was torn open on the other side too, so some others have climbed through from the rooms behind mine."

My heart lifted a little at this news. There were more survivors than I thought.

"That's good to hear. Come out as quickly as you can. We don't have a lot of time."

I heard furniture moving in his room as the young woman from the room in front of me climbed out of the tear, legs first. She had a nasty gash on one shin, but otherwise looked alright. I moved forward and grabbed her around the knees, helping her lower herself out without scraping her torso on the jagged metal.

"Go join the others over there, and put up your shield," I said once she was on the ground.

She limped over to join them under the overhang and quickly put up a blue shield. I turned and watched as a tall young man lowered himself out of the tear in his room.

"Okay," he called quietly through the tear once his feet touched the ground, "we're ready for the next person. We'll help you from this side."

I nodded at him gratefully as he and I positioned ourselves in front of, and in my case below, the tear. Working together, we lowered four more people out of his room and sent them to huddle with the rest of the group. There were a few injuries and bruises, a couple smaller broken bones, but nothing life-threatening yet. A few other students from the first floor began climbing from their rooms as they heard us extricating the others, and a few from the second floor peered out of their rooms down at us.

"I'm a Light Guardian. I can transform and get them out," the young man murmured once we'd cleared all survivors out of the first floor.

A Demon roared right as he spoke—closer than any had been thus far. We plastered ourselves against the side of the dorm again, waiting with bated breath. They must be moving to this side now.

"Hurry," I whispered, once it was clear that a Demon wasn't going to immediately crush us. "And don't let the Demons see you, or they'll attack."

He nodded, equal parts worried and determined, then transformed in a flash of bright white. Then he flew to the second floor, keeping his wings as low as he could, and peered into each intact room. One by one, he pulled students out and carried them to the ground as I kept watch. While only four rooms remained standing on the second floor, they'd sheltered seven students. There were twenty survivors in total—more than I could've hoped for given the state of the dorm. But the group had grown too large to remain hidden under the alcove. We'd be noticed any second, especially with the variety of bright shields all the students had around themselves. We needed to get away from the dorm, and fast.

I looked around, appraisingly. We were pretty close to the main classroom building. It was too crushed to hide in it, but we might be able to use it for cover. No one was swarming it—the army was currently focused on the dorms.

"The main building is damaged, but we can use what's left of it to hide behind and then block you so you can get into the woods. The portals around the perimeter of the plane are open now. Head for them and try to get off plane. But stay together once you're in the trees. If you're attacked, working together to shield yourselves is your best chance of surviving. I'm going to send you a few at a time from here. Run as fast as you can and stop behind the main building. I'll protect each of you as you go." I tightened my grip on my daggers. "If they notice us, I'll try holding them off. If you see that happening, the rest of you should run behind the main building and then into the trees. Don't wait for me. Just get out if you can. Got it?"

I looked around at the terrified faces surrounding me. But they all nodded.

"Don't have your shield up while you're running to the main building unless you're attacked. The bright colors and lights will attract notice. You can put them up once you're out of sight behind the building."

I stood and looked around us quickly, making sure no Dark Guardians or Demons were too close. They were nearing us, roaring and smashing, but they weren't at the edge yet. It was the best we could hope for at this point.

"Okay," I turned back to the group, "you two go first." I pointed my dagger at a couple injured students near me. I wanted to make sure that those least able to fight had the most cover.

The two students looked at each other, then nodded, dropping their shields.

"Go now. As fast as you can."

The students took off, running through the pain of their injuries. My heart hammered wildly as I looked around, watching to see if the army noticed. But within a few seconds, the students disappeared behind the large building. I took a deep breath and pointed at two more injured students.

"You next."

I sent the last two pairs of injured students as the Demon roars reached deafening levels. They'd be on us at any moment. And I'd only cleared eight students so far.

I cursed under my breath as a Demon near us kicked a large piece of stone façade over the edge of the building, narrowly missing us as it crashed to the ground. And then the horrible sound of screeching metal met our ears as the Demons started smashing the armored dorm rooms on the second floor that we'd just evacuated.

"Go!" I whispered to the next two students as crushed stone rained over us. "You two next." I turned and pointed to two more students who were clutching each other, their faces stiff with fear. "And tell the rest of the group to run into the trees toward the portals. Don't wait any longer. Just try to get off plane."

They nodded, their limbs shaking wildly as they pushed to their feet. On a deep breath, they ran, breaking away from the dorm and streaking toward the back of the main building. I held my breath, hoping the Demons were too distracted to notice them. In another moment, the students disappeared behind the building. I hoped the group was now running toward the portals. I hoped they'd manage to get out.

I turned to look at the rest of the group—eight students in all—who were still waiting to go. Most were staring at the top of the dorm, now, which was closer to us than it'd been several minutes ago.

"Okay, you two go," I whispered urgently pointing at Ivy and Katara. "Be ready to shield yourselves. Run behind the main building for cover but keep running until you get through a portal. That goes for all of you." I looked at the remaining students. Everyone nodded as Ivy and Katara straightened up. Ivy counted to three, her voice shaking, then they took off.

A Demon roared directly above us, making the group jump, and my heart sputtered into overdrive. I looked up and saw a Demon staring after them as they ran, its long talons curling over the edge of the closest destroyed dorm room. We'd finally been spotted—we were out of time. Cursing, I gestured at the rest of the group to stand. They'd have to make a run for it. All of them.

The Demon stepped off the dorm, its heavy footfalls shaking the ground, and it started after Ivy and Katara with another roar.

"Go now!" I called to the group as I ran after the Demon. "I'll try to hold it off!"

The remaining students made a break for it, running in a wide arc around the Demon as I jumped and plunged both daggers into its lower back, pulling them down with my bodyweight, slicing deep. The Demon screeched and spun around, jerking free of my blades. It roared again as it saw me and trundled forward, its long claws extended, ready to strike. I ran at it again, dodging the swipe of its claws, and brought my daggers down over its thick, trunk-like forearm, slicing clean through it. At least this wasn't one of the bigger Demons.

Blood sprayed from the wound as the Demon jerked away from me and swiped its other set of claws at me. I dove forward, through its legs, then shoved quickly to my feet. With a growl of effort, I swung my daggers at its thick leg, cutting most of the way through. The Demon screamed and spun again, gnashing its sharp teeth and swinging its claws wildly through the air, but it stumbled, its balance thrown as its partially severed leg wobbled underneath it. I ducked and spun around to its side, then brought my daggers down over its leg again, this time severing it completely.

I glanced quickly over my shoulder as the Demon teetered on its one remaining leg, and a wave of relief washed over me. The last group of students had disappeared behind the main building. Using myself as a distraction had worked. With any luck, all of them would be running for the portals now. I sent a silent prayer to the universe, hoping they'd make it. Hoping they, at least, would survive this.

I faced the Demon again and dove forward, shoving my daggers into its stomach up to their hilts, trying to unbalance it. The Demon screamed, swaying as it lashed out at me again, but it didn't fall. I ducked under it, lunging through its legs, hissing as the blood from its severed limb spattered across my injured arm, burning the skin over and around my stab wound. But the payoff would be worth it. I shoved to my feet, then swung my daggers as fast and hard as I could across the back of the Demon's remaining knee.

Its leg buckled from the force of my strike. With a keening screech and wildly flailing arms, the Demon lost its balance and fell forward onto the ground. I ran around its body before it could move and brought my daggers down on its neck. The Demon's yell of rage cut off in a horrible gurgle as its head rolled forward, away from its body.

I straightened up, panting, only to see a group of Dark Guardians swarming over from the destroyed dorm. My fight with the Demon must've been loud enough to attract attention. At least they were swarming me and not the trees behind me where the students had run. I gripped my daggers tightly and planted my feet, wishing I had something substantial at my back. But it was too late to move now—the Dark Guardians surrounded me in a circle, hovering in the air above me.

I gritted my teeth against the panic that wanted to escape my chest and overflow into the rest of my body. I didn't have power anymore. I couldn't shield myself from their attacks. If they chose to aim their black fire at me, I'd burn alive in a matter of seconds.

My hands shook as I stared defiantly up at the soldiers surrounding me. Their armor and swords were caked in red blood. My stomach knotted. I wondered how many students they'd killed. How many students we'd failed to save. I'd never felt this helpless in battle before. Perhaps I'd never felt this helpless ever. Not even in Dagmar. Everything was out of my control. It didn't matter how many Demons or Dark Guardians I'd defeated. There were more. Always more.

I glanced at the rest of campus—at the other fallen dorms. It didn't even look like we'd made a dent in their army's numbers. My heart sank, and the last dregs of hope I'd clung to died. The Academy was gone. The students were dead. And I'd fall like everyone else. I'd be brutally torn apart or burned beyond recognition. I'd die alone and without saving the school. I'd fail.

"You have to promise me, though," Gabriel's voice whispered through my mind, *"that you'll be here, alive, when I return. Promise me that, Terah . . . I can't leave you if you don't promise me that."* Tears burned in my eyes as I remembered his fierce expression. His breaking voice. His tears.

"I promise," I whispered. I tightened my shaking grip on my daggers. I couldn't give up. I couldn't give in to death or hopelessness. Not now. I'd promised. I still had to try.

I watched as the Dark Guardians pulled spirals of black power down their arms toward their hands, preparing to end me.

"Fuck this," I growled, and started sprinting as fast as I could toward the heart of campus. Toward the rest of the dorms. My leg burned with pain, and I felt more blood leaking from the wound, but I pushed forward.

The Dark Guardians, taken by surprise, turned and flew after me, shooting beams of black fire at me. I dodged as I ran, causing the blasts to hit the ground, spraying dirt and charred grass around me like explosions. But I wouldn't be able to outrun them for long. I veered closer to the dorms, then dove into the fray that was countless hulking Demons charging the buildings to take part in crushing whatever remained. This slowed down the Dark Guardians. Their shots of fire ceased as I weaved through and under Demon after Demon, shielding myself from sight and a clean shot.

As I ran, I looked around for survivors—anyone who was still alive and fighting. Any familiar faces. But it was so hard to see past the constantly moving throng of giant creatures. There could be whole groups of survivors and I wouldn't be able to see them from this vantage point. I cursed as I rolled through the legs of another Demon and made my way between two dorms on the far north side of campus. Maybe I could lose the Dark Guardians under some rubble. Already, many had broken away, unable to determine which direction I'd gone. It was as hard for them to spot me through the throng as it was for me to find others.

I dodged swiping claws and a spray of acid as I rounded another dorm and finally saw what was left of my own. It was as crushed as all the others —completely demolished, no hint left of the building it'd once been. I dodged another blast of black fire as I ran around the perimeter, looking for an overhang or some kind of cover. Something to help even the odds. As I rounded the last corner, I finally saw an option. An armored room on the second floor had been torn open and crushed, but one of the walls had been pulled down so it jutted over the side of the building, offering a small amount of cover. It'd have to do. I veered toward the wall and skidded to a halt underneath the outcropping just as a Demon lumbered by.

I panted, waiting. Hoping it'd been enough to lose the rest of the Dark Guardians. But before I could check, a scream pierced the din—blood-chilling, and sharp enough to cut through the Demon screams that weighed down the air. The scream had been distinctly human. If it was a Dark Guardian, it meant there were survivors nearby putting up a fight, and if it was someone from the Academy, it meant there were survivors who needed help. Either way, I needed to find them.

I took a deep breath, then sheathed my left dagger and bent to grab a sheet of torn metal from the ground. It was big enough to be a shield. I'd need it if any other Dark Guardians wanted to throw fire at me. Then I pushed back into the fray. I shoved under and around Demons, disappearing into the throng before they could fully register my presence, and running as fast as I could in the direction of the scream. It hadn't sounded far. Finally, I reached the side of one of the middle dorms.

I ducked behind a large chunk of the façade, now on the ground, and peered around, looking for any hint of the survivors. It was hard to see far, given the demolished state of the dorm, but after a few moments, I saw a blast of white fire about forty feet to my right, shooting forward to engulf a group of Dark Guardians. Hope loosened the knot in my chest, and I shoved to my feet, then ran toward the fire, my makeshift shield still clutched tightly in my left hand.

The white fire died away as I approached a large outcropping of rubble, and I saw Dark Guardians stepping over their burned and dying fellow soldiers to move forward and attack whoever was putting up the fight. I ran as quickly as I could around the rubble and launched myself at the charging Dark Guardians, taking them by surprise. I slammed my shield into one soldier's face, smashing his nose and blinding him, as I plunged my dagger through the neck of another. Then I ducked and used his body to shield myself from the shots of black fire that were aimed my way as he clutched his neck, trying to breath. Then, with my shield, I shoved that soldier's body into the soldier next to him, causing them both to collapse in a bloody pile of dark armor and wings.

I glanced quickly behind me as I backed up and saw that at least ten students were taking shelter in the crevice of the outcropping made from debris. One of them was the Light Guardian whose beam of flames I'd spotted. From the terror on her face and the shaking of her hands, I assumed she wasn't one of the better-trained students. It was a good hiding place—invisible to those above, and only visible to those below if they looked in at the right angle. But with all the Demons and Dark Guardians surrounding every dorm, they'd eventually been spotted. There were a couple fallen bodies where the crevice widened and melded into the crumbled outer wall of the dorm. Fallen students who'd tried to fight once they'd been discovered. They'd been cut down mercilessly.

Anger churned in my gut as I turned to face the new wave of Dark Guardians moving in. I gripped my dagger tightly, scoping out their weaknesses—the gaps in their armor, parts of themselves that they left vulnerable as they moved—preparing my strategy. One good thing about this outcropping was that it limited how many Dark Guardians could get close to the students at a time. It made this position slightly more defensible. At the very least, I couldn't be surrounded here like I'd been before.

I lunged at the Dark Guardian on the far right, stabbing between her plates of leg armor and hitting the femoral artery with my long blade. She fell, blood pouring from her body as I deflected shots of fire and the swing of a sword with the shield angled slightly upward in my left hand. The fire rebounded at two of the Dark Guardians, burning their heads and necks, causing them to collapse. I spun and blocked the middle Dark Guardian's sword with my dagger before swinging my shield around to smash him in the side of the head. Before he could recover, I cut his throat.

I barely had time to recover before another group of Dark Guardians stormed the opening of the crevice. I shook sweat out of my eyes and tried to slow my gasping breaths. I'd never fought for this long and this hard. I wasn't sure how much longer I'd be able to adequately defend anyone.

"Put a shield up around all of you," I yelled to the group of students cowering behind me. "Don't lower it for anything. Work together to make it stronger."

The Light Guardian nodded shakily, moving back to sit with the rest of the students. Then they formed a bright shield around their group, securing themselves in a bubble of protection. Hopefully it'd hold.

I stepped over the pile of bodies in front of me, and moved forward, out of the crevice to its very mouth. It was too full of bodies to move precisely and accurately anymore without letting the Dark Guardians get too close to the sheltering students. I had no choice but to take on more opponents in exchange for the students' safety. I stepped into the open space beyond the crevice and immediately had to duck behind my shield as several Dark Guardians shot beams of black fire at me. I angled the shield as much as I could and directed the flames back at the approaching soldiers. I managed to hit a few, and they screamed as the intensified fire blasted through their armor. But there were too many of them and my shield was too small to adequately protect me for long.

I cried out in pain as a beam of fire hit me in the shin. I could feel my pants burning from my boot line to my knee. I brought my knee quickly to the ground and snuffed out the flames in the dirt. But my skin was badly burned, and I felt the boiling, mind-numbing pain spreading up my leg like continuous, searing electricity.

"*Damnit.*" I shoved to my feet. I'd have to change my strategy. The shield couldn't protect me against this many opponents.

I took a deep breath, then propelled myself forward into the line of Dark Guardians. I hit a few head on, and we tumbled to the ground, rolling over each other. The Dark Guardians stopped throwing flames, unable to hit me without hitting some of their own soldiers. With a grunt of effort, I dragged my dagger across one Dark Guardian's neck, then slammed the sharp edge of my shield across the head of another. Suddenly, shouts sounded from around and above us, and different colored powers blasted the Dark Guardians. I vaguely thought I saw something plant-like and shards of something shower over the army, but I could barely see in my current position.

I shoved from underneath the Dark Guardians' bodies, shaking my hair from my eyes, and saw two students from my advanced training group along with two younger trainers from the lower-level training groups jumping from the dorm's rubble at my back.

"We heard the scream and came as fast as we could," David, one of my fellow trainees said, panting as he sent a spray of sharp ice shards from his hands, aimed at the heads and necks of the approaching Dark Guardians.

"I heard it too," I panted, limping over to them. "Only got here a couple minutes ago. There's a whole group of students hiding in this crevice." I jerked my head toward the space under the rubble. "A few were killed before I got here."

David nodded, glancing at the shield they'd erected, his blood-smeared face grim and tired. "We'll help you. I still have a little power left, at least."

"Lucky you," I grumbled as I planted my feet, gritting my teeth against the pain in my burned leg, preparing for the Dark Guardians who were charging us again. David sent an amused-but-exhausted smile my way before pulling more icy blue power down his arms to his ice-encrusted hands.

David, his Light Guardian friend Elliott, and the two Blessed trainers fought hard alongside me. David pierced through the exposed skin of Dark Guardian after Dark Guardian, while the Blessed trainers incapacitated them with vines and shoved them back or drowned them with water. Elliott and I dealt with any Dark Guardians who got through their onslaught, cutting them down with our blades and occasional blasts of Elliott's white fire. But soon, more Dark Guardians descended on us, some from the air, and some over the ruins of the dorm behind us. We were surrounded on all sides now.

"I'll take the ones in the air if you get the ones on the dorm," Elliott called to me. The Blessed were too busy dealing with all the Dark Guardians in front of them to help with these new ones.

"Sounds good," I called as I beheaded the Dark Guardian I'd been grappling with.

Elliott jogged over and grabbed me around the waist before extending his wings and pushing off the ground. He flew up and deposited me on top of the outcropping where the students were hiding, then flew up to engage the circling Dark Guardians above us. We'd done it fast enough that we'd taken them by surprise. Not wanting to waste the moment, I dove headfirst into the group of Dark Guardians on the ridge, quickly stabbing into all the weak spaces between their armor again and again as I blocked sword strike after sword strike with my shield. In this one small way, it was helpful that my transformation was so like theirs—all those weak spaces between armor plates that I usually worried about for myself, I could now take advantage of to defeat them. And we were all too close for them to safely use fire on me.

I kept up this frantic pace as I slashed Dark Guardian after Dark Guardian around me. One started bleeding into another as enemy after enemy crowded close, trying to end me. Endless weapons aimed at me that I had to dodge, block, thwart. Countless people I had to kill to stay alive. I was so exhausted and in so much pain that I could barely think anymore. Every movement felt automatic—based more on instinct than intention—but I was surviving at least, and I was keeping this group too preoccupied to surround and attack the students and fellow fighters below. Finally, after a harrowing struggle with the last two surviving Dark Guardians, they crumpled to the ground, their blood spilling into the substantial pool already at my feet that dripped over the side of the outcropping.

I gasped, trying to catch my breath as the world spun and jerked around me. Exhaustion, pain, and blood loss were finally overtaking me. I blinked repeatedly, trying to clear my vision. But the rubble and bodies around me blurred as the sounds of fighting turned weirdly hollow, like I was hearing them through a long tube. I stumbled as my pulse hammered in my ears. Fear sliced through me, and I knew I had to shake this off if I wanted to survive, especially here, where I was so exposed. I gritted my teeth, blinking hard, and shook my head. My vision cleared slightly, but the world tilted again, and my makeshift shield slipped from my hand and clattered against the rubble at my feet as I swayed.

I heard a shout—a familiar voice cut through the echoey static around me, and I turned my head in the direction of the sound. Vaguely, in the distance, I saw a glowing white figure shifting in and out of focus, too far for me to make out. But there was something off about it. Like it was filled with some kind of emotion. What was it? Pain burned through my shoulder before I could figure it out, and I cried out, snapping out of my dazed reverie, and stumbling forward a few steps. Black fire burned through the back of my tank top and blistered the skin around the stab wound in my arm. I gasped as the pain paralyzed me. It felt like all my nerves were on fire, each one tortured with its own individual flame. Each one melting into oblivion.

Before I could recover, before I could even move, I heard the voice shout again, slightly closer this time. It was a desperate, frantic cry. *Fear.* That's what it was. It was fear that was distorting the voice. But it was still too far for me to understand the words.

I heard footsteps pounding through the rubble behind me, then a sharp thud and a groan of pain. So close. Too close. Gasping, I spun around in time to see an untransformed Caleb standing right behind me, violently beheading the Dark Guardian who'd been attacking me. As the Dark Guardian's body fell onto the rubble, Caleb turned slowly toward me and shock washed over me, dragging the air from my lungs. The Dark Guardian's sword was embedded deep in Caleb's chest. A sword that'd clearly been meant for me. Caleb stumbled forward as the sword began to evaporate, and blood quickly bloomed across his chest.

"No," I whispered as I stared at him, frozen with shock and horror.

"Terah," he rasped, reaching his blood-covered hands out to cup my face. His expression was desperate as he ran his thumbs gently down my cheeks. With a jolt, I realized they were wet, already covered with my own tears.

Caleb's knees buckled as blood dripped from his already-soaked shirt, and I threw my arms out, trying to catch him. But I was too injured and weak. In the end, we both tumbled to the ground.

I grunted with effort as I pulled Caleb's upper body into my lap. "I-It's okay," I gasped, placing my wildly shaking hands over the wound in his chest. "I'll heal it. I, I'll just heal it."

Caleb smiled at me slowly. A familiar smile. A devastating smile. A smile that, for a period of time, had made my life more livable. A smile that'd given me a tiny bit of hope when I hadn't had any in so long.

"You don't have any power left, Terah." Each word sounded like it took a lot of effort to say.

"I don't care!" I shouted, my voice shaking as much as my hands. "I'll use my life force!" I couldn't explain it or rationalize it, but there was just something in me that couldn't watch him die. That couldn't lose him, too. An unreasonable, desperate part of me that couldn't handle this reality. That couldn't watch someone I'd loved die like this.

"No." Caleb reached up and pulled my hands from his chest into his own instead. "You wouldn't survive the rest of the battle if you did that. And you wouldn't be able to help anyone else. I don't want you to do that. I won't . . . let you do that." He sucked in a breath. It sounded like it was hard for him to do.

A sob burst from my mouth as my tears dripped onto him. "I'm sorry," I cried as I clutched his fingers with mine. "The sword was meant for me. It should've been me. I'm s-sorry."

"No," Caleb said again, his fingers tightening around mine even as he grew paler. "I would never . . . have let it be you. Not when I could stop it. I . . . I get it now," he murmured, his voice growing weaker. "I never thought I would. I never thought I'd . . . agree. But . . . I get it now. What Mannan did for me. What he meant . . . how he felt . . . when he saved me."

I stared at him through my tears, confusion mingling with deep sadness.

"Love," Caleb said, his voice fading more. "Loving someone so completely that you'd . . . give up everything you are and everything you could be . . . just to keep them safe. I . . . I get that now."

He raised a pale, shaking hand and stroked my cheek again.

"I was s-such a fool before," he rasped, his hand falling to rest on mine again. "Th-thinking that loving you could be a w-weakness. How could . . . keeping you alive . . . keeping you in the world . . . make me weak? No . . . n-no . . . loving you made me strong. S-strong enough to do the right thing. Strong enough t-to see . . . what's really important f-for once in . . . my life. I'm . . . s-sorry, Terah," he gasped. "For . . . everything."

I shook my head as another sob spilled from my mouth. I brought our entwined hands up to my chest, clutching them over my heart.

"It's okay," I whispered. "I forgive you. It doesn't matter anymore. I forgive you."

Caleb smiled again, even as his hands fell slack in mine.

"Take . . . my daggers . . . from Mannan," he whispered shakily, his voice fading as he stared up at the dark sky above us. "That way . . . a piece of me . . . w-will always be there . . . t-to . . . p-protect . . . you . . . Terah . . ."

A rattling breath left his chest as his face went slack, his eyes reflecting the swirling, dark sky above us even as they hollowed. The world around me blurred, the blasts of power, the spray of rubble, the rain of blood coating everything, all faded away as I hunched over his body and sobbed.

"Terah," I vaguely heard that same familiar voice from before say, this time close to me, "I'm putting up a shield around us, but I won't be able to hold them out for long. We need to go help the others."

I looked up, tears still streaming from my eyes, and saw Matt standing over me, his hands extended above him, holding up a bright white shield. He was still transformed. Still had some power left.

"Matt," I sobbed. I felt broken inside. Hollowed out. "He's gone. He saved me, but n-now he's gone."

Matt's expression softened as he looked down at me. "I know," he murmured. "I saw. I tried to come help, but Simon, Omer, and I got waylaid by another group of Dark Guardians. I'm so sorry, Terah."

A fresh wave of tears spilled down my cheeks as I turned to look at Caleb again. I reached a shaking hand forward and gently closed his eyes. He deserved to be at peace. I hoped with all my heart that he'd found it, now. That, wherever he was, he was finally able to be happy.

"H-he wanted me to keep his daggers." My shaking fingers fumbled with the sheaths at his waist. "I should . . . I should do what he wanted."

I finally slid the strap with the two sheaths from his waist and clutched them to my chest, my eyes sliding closed. Then I placed them on the ground next to me and carefully shifted Caleb's body from my lap to the blood-covered rubble beneath us. I tried not to look at how much of his blood covered me.

"Damian's coming," Matt murmured as I pushed to my feet. I shakily secured Caleb's daggers around my hips.

"Let him in." I wiped my tears with the cleanest part of my arm I could find. "Caleb was his friend."

Matt didn't move or lower the shield for a moment, but he finally sighed. "Fine."

He dropped the shield as Damian reached us, then quickly put it up again as Damian stepped closer, his eyes glued on Caleb.

I watched him closely as he walked to Caleb's side, then dropped onto one knee next to his body. Shock and grief rippled across his face in a way I hadn't seen emotion do since the illusion chamber when his father had been torturing him. He reached a shaking hand forward and placed it over Caleb's blood-covered chest.

"He saved me," I murmured, my heart aching. "At the expense of his life."

Damian's head dropped forward so I couldn't see his expression anymore, his hand still gripping Caleb's body. He didn't move for at least a minute, but finally he nodded his head and raised it again.

"That makes sense." His voice was hoarse. I was surprised to see he actually had tears running down his face. I half expected him to be angry with me, but he wasn't. Just sad. Deeply sad. "He did love you, even if he fought the feeling until the end."

Another tear trailed down my cheek.

"He was . . . my first real friend." Damian's voice was so quiet it was barely more than a whisper. He moved his hand to grip Caleb's shoulder. "Even when he was pissed at me for betraying him, he still worried about me. Didn't want me to die." He squeezed his shoulder before leaning back again. "No one's ever cared about me like that before."

I stepped forward and gripped Damian's shoulder gently, trying to impart some comfort. "Caleb needed a real friend. As did you."

Damian glanced up at me and smiled a little. He didn't contradict me. They'd let each other in, despite themselves, and something that'd started as a convenience for both of them had ended up being something much deeper.

"And I care about you too, for what it's worth."

Damian sniffed and wiped his sleeve across his face. "Thanks." He pushed to his feet, then, in a very uncharacteristic move, wrapped his arm around me and pulled me into his side for a brief hug. "What do we do now?" he asked, releasing me and glancing at Matt before looking at the battle still raging all around us. "I'm out of power, and we're still overrun."

A look of helplessness settled over Matt's face as he, too, looked at the campus around us. But a cool calmness settled over me as I followed their gazes. I knew what needed to be done. There were no more feasible options.

"It's time," I said, looking at Damian. "Assuming you still have some of your life force left."

Damian's gaze snapped to mine, and he searched my expression. "I do. Are you sure you're ready? What about Gabriel?"

My heart burned, like it was being ripped violently apart, and tears flooded my eyes. "It's the only way to ensure anyone is still alive by the time he comes back with backup. We don't have any other options left."

Damian nodded slowly, his eyes still flitting over my expression. "I agree," he said quietly. "As long as you're prepared for what it might mean."

I nodded again, unable to speak. If I opened my mouth now, only sobs would emerge.

"Wait a minute." Matt took a step toward me, his shield flickering as worry overtook his expression. "What are you talking about? What are you planning to do?"

I stepped toward him and placed my burned and bloody hand over the armor covering his chest.

"Don't worry about us." I looked up at his face. Memorizing it. Saying goodbye to it. "We'll be fine. Just make sure the surviving students are safe." I lifted onto the balls of my feet and pressed a kiss to his cheek.

Matt's shield flickered and fell as I stepped away from him, toward Damian. Damian held out his hand, palm up, and I clasped mine over his.

"Ready?"

"Ready."

"Wait!" Panic widened Matt's eyes as he stepped toward us. He knew me too well to believe me. He knew I was saying goodbye. "Don't—"

But it was too late. Damian and I closed our eyes and reached inside our chests, unleashing our life forces—the only power we had left. Deep purple spilled outward, filling our skin with warmth. Flooding us with the divine. The power overflowed, seeping out of us, covering us with shining armor again, forming wings of bright purple light on our backs, lifting our hair to float around us, and filling our eyes with fire. I felt all my injuries starting to heal, the burning pain turning to a small sting before vanishing altogether in record time.

"*It's time,*" Damian murmured, his voice whispering through my mind. His grip on my hand tightened. "*It's time to become—*"

"*Something more.*"

"*Something more.*"

Both of us opened to the power, to the pull that was always there, making ourselves vulnerable to the connection. To unity. I let go of myself, reaching out to Damian with everything I had. It was easy this time. Almost too easy. My power entangled with his. Our heartbeats merged, our thoughts combined, and our breaths united. Our souls became inseparable. Our powers became one. We were one being now. One otherworldly, ethereal entity. *Something more.*

We opened our eyes as one, feeling the raw, unearthly power boiling through us. Contained only through our unity. The power radiated off us, stirring and distorting the air as we glowed with blinding light. Matt stumbled away from us, astonishment and fear mixing on his face. We didn't blame him this time. We were no longer quite human. No longer quite mortal. We looked untouchable. Unapproachable. Purely divine.

As one, we extended our wings and glided upward, far above the ruins we'd been standing on. Far above the tallest building on campus. We could see everything from here. Every Demon. Every Dark Guardian. Every person from the Academy who was fighting for their lives. All the bodies of those who'd fallen. How much of the army remained. There hadn't been enough of us fighting back to truly make a dent in their numbers.

We gathered our power around us, then directed some down our free hands until we were holding crackling balls of electric light. We slowly raised our hands, extending them out and down. We could feel where every being was. *Who* every being was.

"*Lightning*," we thought as one, visualizing what we wanted. Transforming the power in our hands into the form we wanted.

We chose our targets, seeing them more in our minds than with our eyes, and let go of the power. Huge beams of lightning erupted from our palms, traveling out in a wide circle around all the dorms, striking down hundreds of Demons and Dark Guardians. Burning them alive instantly. Screams of terror filled the air as chaos ensued. All eyes turned to us, fear and awe filling the air like electricity. We felt the army below us panic. We heard their thoughts. Felt their fear and rage. They'd expected an easy battle with little push-back. They'd expected to win. To arrive, slaughter, and leave. It was the outcome they'd been promised.

We pulled more power down our arms. "*Lightning*."

We released another deluge of electric bolts, aiming for the remaining Demons and Dark Guardians on or around the dorms. Trying to ensure the safety of any surviving students and staff around, in, and under the buildings. Screams and roars echoed through the grounds as the Demons and Dark Guardians retreated, moving away from the buildings and the piles of ash where their comrades had stood only moments before.

We watched calmly as hundreds of Dark Guardians took to the skies, flying at us from every direction. Intent on ending us. Stopping us from burning their army alive.

"*Fire*." We gathered more power and sent it down our arms.

Flames erupted, swirling around us—a giant sphere of roiling purple heat. Then it shot outward, engulfing all the approaching Dark Guardians and blasting through their armor. Disintegrating their flesh and bones. Ash rained from the sky as more Dark Guardians pushed into the air, but they kept more of a distance this time. Their rage thickened the ether like a stormy cloud. We felt them gathering their power down their arms before we even saw it. Then black fire shot at us from all sides, growing in intensity as more and more Dark Guardians pushed into the air, joining the attack.

A shield materialized from our bodies and encircled us in a bright, transparent orb, blocking the intense, dark heat before it could touch us. Black fire filled the air around us, blocking our sight of the grounds, of the Dark Guardians, of our friends, of everything besides the flames. But we could still feel everything. Hear everything. And everyone. We felt more Dark Guardians taking flight, adding their flames to the air around us, trying to overwhelm our shield. We looked inside ourselves, taking stock of what power we had left. What we could do and for how long.

I took over the shield as Damian gathered more of our power into his free hand.

"*Lightning,*" we thought as he lifted his hand above our heads.

We opened the top of the shield, then, with an eruption of crackling heat, more lightning than we'd conjured before burst from his palm and shot out in all directions at the forces attacking us. Thunder crashed around us in response, a deep, bone-shaking baritone that shook the entire plane. Hundreds of Dark Guardians fell from the sky, even as more swarmed closer, the heat of their fire unceasing. I kept up the shield, steadily feeding it power, keeping us safe. But we'd used a lot of power on top of the portion of our life force we'd expended earlier. We wouldn't be able to sustain this for much longer.

"*We'll take down as many as we can,*" I murmured silently to Damian.

"*As many as we can for as long as we can,*" he agreed.

He gathered more of our power into his free hand, his grip tightening around mine as he concentrated, and I felt power flowing from my arm into his. Feeding him as he raised his free hand above us again. Power burst from his fingers and swirled, forming a huge tornado of fire and lightning around our shield, deflecting the fire. I dropped the shield and raised my hand, sharing the weight of the power with him. Sharing the control. We worked better as one.

The fire and lightning swirled around us, gaining speed. Growing far above and below us, but not low enough to hurt anyone on the ground. Then we expanded it, widening it, sucking the Dark Guardians surrounding us into the vortex. Causing them to tumble through the burning mass until there was nothing left of their bodies. The tornado grew and grew as thunder cracked through the air. We were determined to make this count. To make the fight more winnable for the students below. To make sure that some, at least, survived until backup arrived to help them.

We could feel our power drain as we grew the tornado more and more, until it extended at least a hundred feet from us on all sides. Drawing in and obliterating more and more Dark Guardians. We could feel our limits even as this otherworldly being. And we were starting to reach them. When we ran out of power, our ability to be this being would cease, as would we. Our hands shook as we lowered them back to our sides, allowing the remaining fire and lightning to dissipate around us. Ash filled the air, fluttering toward the ground like black snow. We'd managed to take out at least a few hundred Dark Guardians. But there were more. So many more. And more Demons as well.

We conjured another shield around us as more Dark Guardians filled the sky by the hundreds. Perhaps they guessed we were running out of power. Or perhaps they were angry and scared enough not to care what happened to them. Whatever their reasoning, they climbed toward us, surrounded us, and blasted us with intense heat. We could feel the pressure on us from every side, pushing inward with unimaginable force. And it was quickly draining what little power we had left.

Frustration grew in our chests. We wanted to do more. We wanted to have more of an impact before we burned out. We didn't want to waste time and power on a shield. That wasn't why we'd become this being. It wasn't why we'd given up our individual selves, our humanity, our lives. This wasn't enough. We hadn't done enough to save everyone.

Our eyes slid closed as our hands shook under the onslaught. We knew we only had moments left. Regret burned through us as I thought of Gabriel. Of the promise I'd made and had hoped to keep for him. Of how much I loved him—more than anything.

"You made sure he survived," Damian's voice whispered through my mind. "And you made sure his battle is more winnable."

I felt his own regret burn through us as he thought of Caleb. How he wished he'd been able to do the same for him, somehow.

"You did more for him than you realize," I murmured, seeing what he was seeing. Feeling what he was feeling. "You opened him up. You cared about him and helped him grow."

Damian swallowed but managed to nod. "I know. I did for him what he did for me."

We gripped each other's hands tightly as our shield dimmed, the last of our power fading away. We hoped it'd be quick, at least. Not too painful. We hoped we'd made a big enough dent in the army to give our friends and all the survivors a chance.

A pulse throbbed in our chests as our shield dimmed further, and we gasped at the force of it. It felt like . . . the pull. But stronger. Bigger. Confused, we looked inward at where the dregs of power were quickly fading. Where the tug was centralized. With another violent tug, it sucked us in, grabbing our minds. Pulling us from the present.

694

Images flashed before our eyes like visions, but not of the future this time. We saw Damian as a young boy, practicing with his transformation in an empty training room. We watched as he bounced blasts of fire and lightning off the repellant walls and caught the power in his hands instead of being burned by it. Soaking the power he'd caught back into his body. I'd never seen a Divine do that before. If you were hit with the products of your own power, it'd hurt you like it'd hurt anyone else. You weren't immune to it just because it came from you. I'd proven that when I'd almost burned myself to death with my own rebounding power first semester. So . . . how had he done it?

The image shifted to another of Damian, this time as a young teenager. One of his first solo missions. A group of Light Guardians were bombarding his shield with a continuous blast of powerful white flames as they chased him. I could see Damian cringing with the effort of holding them out. But then something shifted. Instead of repelling the flames, his shield grew brighter and brighter, holding the Light Guardian fire. Finally, on a yell, Damian released his shield, sending all their power back at them. The Light Guardians were bowled over, overwhelmed by the rebounding of their own power.

Shock gripped my insides as the image morphed into another. What he'd done shouldn't be possible. I could feel Damian's surprise too. He didn't remember either of these instances well. It hadn't been intentional on his part. Whatever had happened, had occurred through pure instinct and desperation, unexplainable by him even now.

An image of me alone in an Academy training room formed around us. I was transformed and was using the metal-encased walls to throw blasts of my power and have it rebound at me. We watched as I deflected shot after shot with my shield, the power dispersing and fading after impact like it always did if one's shield was sufficiently strong. Then, with a look of intense concentration, I sent another shot of power at the wall, and this time when it rebounded, I caught the power with my shield, reabsorbing it instead of deflecting it. My shield glowed brighter in response, strengthened by the addition of power. The image faded as our hearts pounded through our chests, waves of shock crashing through us. I'd forgotten I'd done that. I hadn't thought too deeply about it at the time. I'd assumed it'd only worked because it was my own power. That it was out of the norm, but not too noteworthy. I hadn't thought I could apply it to other people's powers.

The pull in our chests released us as our power faded to nothing, and our minds snapped back to the present. Where we were about to die. I turned my head to look at Damian, determination filling me, and he nodded, silently agreeing. We knew what we had to do. If it didn't work, we'd die. But if it did . . .

We turned to face our almost nonexistent shield and raised our free hands in front of us. Then we closed our eyes and concentrated harder than we had thus far. We saw, as if in slow motion, every particle of power being shot at us. Every atom composing the flames. Every spark of energy creating the heat, the light. And we welcomed them. Beckoned them forward with our outstretched hands. We invited them to touch our shield. To sink into its surface. To meld with it. We were no longer trying to deflect, but to absorb. To unify.

Even without seeing it, we could feel the power in our shield growing and growing. Purple and black power pooling together. Mingling. But we were still drained. The Dark Guardians' power was fortifying the shield, but there was nothing left within us to support our own transformations. And without it, we couldn't use this power we were harvesting. We groaned as we felt our bodies weakening. Draining. Dying. We needed . . .

My consciousness began slipping. We needed . . .

"*More power,*" Damian whispered as the world darkened around us.

Yes. More power. Inside of us, not around us.

My grip tightened around Damian's hand, and I reached out with my last shreds of consciousness toward the shield surrounding us. On pure instinct, I pulled desperately with my mind. Pulled the blazing power around us inward, toward my hand. Telling it to merge with me. Not to hurt me, but to *become* me. I pulled it in through my palm, and it flowed up my arm and into the empty well in my chest. Then I sent some through my body and into Damian. It was *our* power now. It could no longer hurt us.

Damian lifted his hand and joined me, our thoughts and actions melded again. Fused as they only could when we truly became one being—when we let go of our individual selves and gave ourselves over to this ethereal entity. This unearthly oneness. The power flowed into us quickly now, like we were some giant force of suction. Black fire filled our chests as we pulled in every foreign ounce of power that'd collected in our shield until only faint purple remained. But it wasn't enough. The wells in our chests were barely filled. Just enough to keep us alive.

"*More,*" we thought, extending our hands forward again, out toward the Dark Guardians who surrounded us, now gaping at us in disbelief, abject fear filling their faces. *"We need more."*

Closing our eyes, we began to pull again, this time not from power that was aimed at us but pulling power directly from each Dark Guardian surrounding us. Raw, unformed power. Pure divine. Hundreds of beams of black, fluid power seeped from their bodies, pulled from their chests like venom from a wound toward us. We caught the power with our palms, soaking it into us. Pulling more and more. We were empty. *Hungry.* Starving for it.

We could feel it now, as the power filled our skin. As it poured into the wells in our chests. We could feel what it meant to be a Dark Guardian. Their essence. The shape of their souls. Everything their power could do. Every form it could take. We could feel it all.

"No," we thought as the power moved through us. It was more than that. It wasn't just that we could feel it. There was something . . . else. We opened our eyes again, but they were filled with black fire now, swirling with a foreign darkness. Our skin tingled with a thousand pinpricks of unfamiliar power as it danced through us, as though in anticipation.

"*That's it,*" we thought through our otherworldly, trance-like haze. "*That's what it is.*"

It wasn't just that we could feel the power. It wasn't just that it was keeping us alive. It was . . . at our disposal. It had become our own. As though we were the Dark Guardians it'd originated from.

A commotion snapped us out of our trance as dozens of Dark Guardians broke away from behind those we were draining, and flew at us, teeth bared, swords drawn. We could hear their thoughts. They were intent on ending us—purging the world of the abominations they saw before them. The terrifying beings with unnatural power that they didn't understand and refused to let exist. The beings that should never have been allowed to live from the start.

We blinked, lowering our hands, no longer pulling in power. Instead, we drew the dark, smoldering power from the moderately filled wells in our chests, down our arms and into our hands. Then, as one, we raised our hands and shot black fire outward, swirling it around us, creating an enormous vortex of blazing heat and scorching, shadowy flames. We engulfed Dark Guardian after Dark Guardian in their own power as it churned forcefully around us. Burning them alive. We could feel their numbers dwindling as we expanded the structure, pouring power into it. Filling the sky with black fire.

This was what we'd wanted. This was the impact we'd hoped for before our own power had run out. The ability to give all the students below us a fighting chance. The ability to save our friends.

The well in our chests steadily drained again as we determinedly expanded the flames, growing the sweltering, churning structure into something larger than either of us had ever made before. Reaching line after line of Dark Guardians, now flying away from us as fast as they could. But we wouldn't let them escape. With a cry, we threw most of our remaining power from our fingertips, expanding the vortex of flame until it filled the entire upper dome of the plane. Our hands shook, but we sustained it for as long as we could, finally burning the last of the Dark Guardians from the sky with inescapable heat.

Gasping, we lowered our hands to our sides, the world starting to blur again as the black flames dissipated. We should've filled ourselves with more power. But screams from below snapped us back into focus even as the power faded from our skin. A handful of Dark Guardians, frantic with terror, had found and grabbed most of the surviving students while all eyes had been on the sky. They were holding swords across their throats with shaking hands, holding them hostage. Using the students to shield themselves. Perhaps they thought it was their only way out of here alive. Dread made our stomachs jump as we saw blood starting to trickle down the necks of many students. The Dark Guardians were too agitated to measure their force. They'd end up killing them on accident.

We looked around desperately, trying to see where the more trained students and staff were. Where Matt, Simon, Omer, David, and Elliott were. But our spirits sank as we spotted them. They were at least fifty feet from the hostages, and they'd all fallen out of their transformations. They were also completely surrounded by Demons. They were in no position to help.

We thought frantically, trying to consider our options. We needed more power if we were going to do anything. We needed—

A student on the ground cried out as the sword pierced deeper into her throat.

"*No time,*" we thought, pulling power to our hands again. It wasn't truly a conscious decision. We knew if we moved, if we tried to take more power from them, the Dark Guardians on the ground would kill the students they'd grabbed. We had no choice. All we could do was use what we had left. All of it.

As one, we pulled the last of our power down our arms, into our palms.

Then we concentrated, finding and isolating every Dark Guardian anywhere near the students. We closed our eyes, took a deep breath, then released the last of our power. Beams of lightning shot from our fingertips and simultaneously hit every Dark Guardian we'd isolated, cutting them down precisely and instantaneously. Burning them alive. What was left of their bodies crumpled to the ground, smoking. The students were free.

We exhaled our relief even as our vision blurred and darkened. At least we'd been able to do one last thing. Save a few more people. Our bodies shuddered as the last of our power faded from our beings, ebbing quietly from our skin. There was nothing left now. No foreign power. No life force. Not enough left within us to try taking more power. The divine was leaving us. And once it did, we'd die.

Color bloomed over the horizon in front of us as our vision grew foggier. It mixed with bright light, intertwining, cracking open the dark clouds filling the plane. We gazed at it in awe, even as the armor disintegrated from our skin, and our wings evaporated into nothingness. The color and light grew brighter and brighter as we faded. It was . . . beautiful. So beautiful. Like the first flower to bloom in spring. Like the first kiss of the sun against your skin after a long winter. It made us want to cry. It filled us with peace.

"*Is this . . . what death is?*" Damian thought, his voice slowly fading from my mind as our hair stopped floating and the fire faded from our eyes. He sounded surprised. Almost hopeful.

"*I . . . don't know,*" I whispered, not sure if he could hear me anymore.

Last time, death had been darkness, not light. An endless ocean of nothingness. But I hadn't really died then. Maybe that wasn't what death was after all. Maybe . . . there was something more . . .

Darkness enveloped us, and we fell, our hands unclasping as we tumbled through the air, separate once again, just in time for our deaths. One last moment to be me. One last breath as Terah.

I faded as I fell, no longer able to see or feel. No longer able to sense the terrifying plummet. Perhaps my soul had detached from my body, already departing this plane of existence. I was weightless. Bodyless. Floating. Suspended in the ether somewhere beyond the realm of life but not quite to death. Everything I knew, everything I was, dimmed, fading to nothing. Dispersing like a wisp of smoke in the air.

"Stay with me," a voice growled, the sound echoing through me. Whispering around what was left of me. "You promised. Stay with me!"

The last of me instinctively reached for the voice. Almost like this wasn't the first time. Like I'd done this before, somehow. I reached with all that was left of my soul, desperately scrambling for a hold. Desperately straining to return to the voice's familiar warmth.

But the fading remnants of my being met with only air. There was nothing close enough for me to grab. No surface for me to hold onto, no matter how hard I tried.

"Stay with me! Stay . . ."

The voice was fading, the sound dissolving into blank nothingness, leaving only the abysmal static of complete silence. And what was left of my being splintered into endless pieces, flaking gently away from itself. My soul quietly dispersed, disintegrating into millions of miniscule particles in the darkness. Floating away. Undoing everything that I was.

The last whisp of my existence faded.

It was . . . too late now.

. . . he was . . . too far . . . to reach . . .

. . . too far to . . .

. . . too far . . .

. . . too . . .

28

A NEW BEGINNING

"... HANG ON ... STAY WITH ME ... JUST A LITTLE LONGER ..."

"... it's a miracle ... it shouldn't be poss ..."

"... who are they? How did ..."

"... I don't know. I'm not sure if they'll ..."

"No! They'll be f ..."

"... still unresponsive. We should ..."

"I'm not sure how they're still alive. No other Divine ..."

"I'm staying, no matter how ..."

"She's received fifteen donations since arriving. He's received twelve ..."

"They're at comparable levels of stability. I wouldn't worry about the exact ..."

"I'm here, Terah. I ..."

"... how is she today?"

"... the High Light Guardian wants regular updates ..."

"There weren't any injuries on their bodies when they got here, however ..."

"With their life forces gone, it's unclear if ..."

"They've been out for a while. At what point ..."

"It's not her first time coming back from this. She just needs time ..."

"I've never seen anything like it before ..."

"I was there. It was ... scary. What even are they?"

"It was like they *became* Dark Guardians . . ."

". . . they saved your life. All your lives. You should be grateful, not judgmental . . ."

"We've been checking their vitals every few hours. They're stable, but no sign of . . ."

"Just give them time . . ."

"Five more donations to her, and three to him. We'll have to see if . . ."

"I love you, Terah. I'm not giving up on you . . ."

". . . she wants a report. I'm not sure what to . . ."

"Make sure you're resting too. I know you're . . ."

"It's okay, Terah. I'm here with you. I'm not going to leave. I love you . . ."

"I sent Mom and Dad a message. They're wor . . ."

". . . I love you, Terah. I . . ."

The first thing I felt was my soul. It was heavy. Different. It wasn't *us* . . . I mean . . . *me*. It was foreign and unknown. A substitute—enough, but not filling. The shape of it didn't quite fit the shape of me. Like it was scratchy instead of smooth. Sharp instead of rounded. But it weighed me down like it was a rock over the thin paper of my existence. It pinned me where I was and didn't let go. Even as the edges of me wavered, delicate and breakable, it didn't release the heart of me. It clung and waited for the gale to die down. For my being to settle.

Then there were the voices, wavering in and out of focus. Jumping through time and place. I could barely hear them. Only sometimes turn the shape of the words into meaning. Only sometimes feel the pangs of recognition. The warmth behind the sounds. But the words often faded before I could put faces to the voices.

Yet . . . it wasn't quite the same darkness as last time. It didn't consume me the way it had before. I wasn't surrounded—wasn't continuously drowning—in it. Beams of light pierced through, creating brighter spots and wavering rays of warmth in the void. I didn't feel as lost as I had last time. I still knew who I was even if I didn't know what'd happened. Even if some memories were foggy, and I couldn't quite escape this internal wasteland.

Last time I'd hovered on the edge of death, body and soul both broken. Both on the brink. I'd been torn apart in every way imaginable. But this time, only my soul felt harmed. Drained and stripped of the divine. It was enough to kill any other Divine. It *would* kill any other Divine. No one could come back from completely draining their life force, no matter how many people tried to give them power to save them. It was something you couldn't heal. A piece of you that other power couldn't replace. But . . . I'd managed to come back from that before. It was inexplicable, but so were many things about my power. So this time, I knew I wasn't fully gone. I hadn't fully died. But I was still . . . *absent* somehow. Suspended in limbo. Attached, but distant. I wasn't sure if I could return. I didn't know how I had last time. I'd just reached. Hard. Desperate. I'd followed a path back, clinging with all my strength to the one who'd been reaching for me.

But this time there were too many voices. Too much sound, swirling in and out. Overwhelming. But I heard it—the voice—mixed in. Reaching for me. Staying for me. And I tried to grab it, aiming between the words I didn't recognize. The voices that brought no warmth. But each time I thought I'd reached it, the sound would fade, drowned out by the other voices and the distance between us. And so it went, again and again, and I remained in the partial darkness. Frozen, without concept of time or place.

"I love you, Terah. I'm here."

The voice was clearer this time. Closer. I could understand it. *Feel* it. Warmth blossomed within me as the meaning soaked in, sending ripples of heat from my center to the furthest edges of my being. Filling me with light. Connecting me with more pieces of myself.

"*Gabriel.*" I reached out, the sound traveling through the pillars of darkness and light, bouncing off the emptiness around me. Searching. Needing a response. Needing more of his voice.

"*Terah.*" His voice rushed through the void, cutting paths of light through the patches of gaping darkness. Cutting through the extraneous voices and sounds. "*It's alright. You're safe. Come back to me.*"

The warmth of his voice and his words wrapped around me, sheathing my being in a protective cloak. Shielding me from the dark and the cold. Pulling me somehow. Perhaps that's what I needed. A guide. A true guardian of the light to lead me back from the darkness. To connect me with myself again.

"*Stay with me . . . please stay.*"

"*I'm not going anywhere. I'll be with you . . . always.*"

"*Please help me . . . help me come back.*"

"*I will.*"

I could feel him, now. No longer just a voice. A presence, reaching for me. Straining from his plane of existence into mine. I could almost see his fingers stretching toward me, searching for my hand. He felt so close. *So close.* Yearning throbbed through me. I wanted to see him again. I wanted to be with him again.

"*I can feel you. Just beyond my grip. Reach for me, Terah. Fight. Come back to me.*"

I reached forward, straining, trying to move closer to him. To move further from this strange realm of piercing darkness and shadowy light. The timeless in-between. I tried to move through the hazy veil that seemed to separate us.

"*I'm trying,*" I gasped as I stretched as far as I could. Pushing against the veil with all my strength. I wanted to reach him. I wanted to return. I wanted to be whole again.

"*You're so close.*" He strained forward. "*I can feel how close you are. Keep reaching. Don't give up. Just don't give up.*"

I shoved forward with all my strength, pressing against the veil. Pushing through its gauzy layers. Reaching for the tangible. The solid. The warmth.

"*Gabriel,*" I panted, straining. I wasn't sure how much further I could push. It felt like the darkness wasn't letting go. But neither was the light. I was being pulled in both directions, stretching past the limits of my being.

"*I know,*" he panted, straining toward me as hard as he could. "*Just a little more. Come on, love. Just a little more.*"

The warmth of his words washed over me, lifting me further from the rigid clutches of darkness. Pulling me closer to the light. Pulling me through the veil. I could feel his determination. He'd stay here, reaching, for as long as he had to. Until he found me again. Until we were reunited.

Love for him swept through me, filling me with light until I was glowing. Burning away the last traces of the darkness in and around me. Freeing my mind and soul. With a cry, I shoved forward with all my strength, through the last layers of the veil, reaching desperately for his hand.

Finally, warmth surrounded my fingers, and I felt him smile. "*I've got you.*" He pulled me forward, wrapping me in his warmth. "*Welcome home.*"

With a gasp, I opened my eyes.

The first things I saw were round, florescent lights hanging from an unfamiliar ceiling high above me. I blinked a few times, trying to clear my blurry vision. To make the world settle more firmly around me. Then I turned my head and saw Gabriel looking down at me, anxiety swimming in his eyes. His fingers tightened around mine, like he was afraid to let go. Like he thought I'd fall back into the darkness again if he did.

"Gabriel," I whispered, squeezing his fingers. Then I pushed gingerly into a sitting position, wincing slightly. I wasn't injured, exactly, but I was sore. My body had been through a lot recently. My throat tightened and my eyes stung with tears as I stared up into his face. He looked so tired. So worried.

"Terah," he whispered, his own eyes filling as he cupped my cheek.

What little control I had snapped. I threw my arms around him and collapsed against him, tears overflowing down my cheeks in a torrent. It was something I never would've allowed myself to do last year. Something I never would've let myself show another person until recently. But I trusted Gabriel. I knew he wouldn't think less of me. He'd helped show me that my emotions were a valid part of me, not a weakness. Not something to ignore or push away. That I needed to know them, acknowledge them, and face them to truly live.

Gabriel held me tightly as I sobbed. I wasn't sure what'd come over me, but once the tears started, I couldn't make them stop. Everything poured out of me like water released from a dam. Every feeling I'd suppressed as we were put through test after harrowing test to get the book. Every emotion I'd shoved down for survival's sake in the battle that'd followed. Every stab of fear, moment of panic, of hopelessness, horror, terror, and terrible sadness. Every experience of pain, betrayal, despair. Of loss. It was too much to stay shoved down forever. And here, now, safe and with him, it demanded to be released.

I cried against him until no more tears could fall. Until my heaving breaths mellowed again, and the shoulder of his shirt was soaked through.

"Sorry," I finally murmured, resting my head against his shoulder and gently rubbing the tip of my nose against his neck, before brushing my lips across the skin there. "I guess I had a lot of emotional build-up to release."

Gabriel pressed his lips against the top of my head as his hand continued to stroke gently down my hair, comforting me. "It's okay. I understand. It's been hell." He shook his head, his expression growing bleak as he wiped the tears from my cheeks. "I only saw the aftermath. I can't imagine what you experienced. What you saw."

I swallowed hard, my throat tightening again as I pressed my forehead into his shoulder. "Too much." It was all I could get out right now. All I could say to describe the hollow pain that felt like a black hole rooted in my chest. Someday, I'd tell him the details—what I'd done, what I'd seen, who I'd saved, who I'd lost. But I couldn't make my mouth form the words now. My soul felt tired. Far too tired.

"I'm sorry." Gabriel's voice grew hoarse.

I lifted my head to look at him, and he took my face between his hands. Tears were swimming in his eyes again.

"I wish I hadn't left." Pain sliced through his gaze. "I wish I'd been with you for every moment of that battle. For every hardship and every painful thing that you saw and experienced. I never wanted you to go through that alone."

I raised my hands and covered his. I could see the guilt burning through him. Eating at him. Guilt that he hadn't been there. That he hadn't suffered enough or done enough. But . . . he had. He'd lost everything that I'd lost. He'd felt the same fear. He'd pushed forward, trying to get as many reinforcements as he could, all the while not knowing if anyone would be alive by the time he returned. Not knowing if he'd lost me. And he'd seen the horrible aftermath—the death that covered every inch of the once-green grounds of our home. His fight might've been different, but it hadn't been less difficult or painful.

"You did what you had to do to save us. There wouldn't have been any survivors if you hadn't arrived with backup. I would've died. We all would've. What you did was so important." I leaned forward and brushed my lips lightly over his, lending him my warmth and comfort now. "Please don't feel guilty. We needed you to do what you did. We needed you to get help."

Gabriel swallowed hard and leaned his forehead against mine, his eyes sliding closed. But finally, he nodded.

I leaned forward, sliding my nose along his until our lips met again. And this time, he responded. His arms snaked around me, and he held me close as he kissed me thoroughly. Warmth swept through my veins, filling my skin with tingles. Grounding me. Banishing the dark and the cold from where they wanted to take root in me. I could feel the desperation in it as we clung to each other. I could feel our pain, our love, our relief that we'd somehow survived. That we were together again.

We finally pulled apart, our chests heaving, and I reached up to wipe a tear from Gabriel's cheek, my heart squeezing painfully at the sight.

"I could've lost you," he whispered, his eyes roving over my face, taking in every feature and detail. "I was terrified every moment I was gone. Afraid I'd come back and you wouldn't be there."

I slid my fingers through his, intertwining them. "I know." I rubbed the back of his hand with my thumb. "But you didn't lose me. You saved all of us who were still alive."

Gabriel smiled a little, but I could tell it was hard for him.

"You barely survived," he murmured, pain filling his eyes again. "I saw you, right when I crossed back through the portal with reinforcements. I saw you and Damian high above the school. I saw the light around you both fading, and I just started running as fast as I could without even thinking. And then the light vanished, and you fell. I've never been that scared in my entire life. I ran like hell and jumped as high as my transformation would let me. I managed to grab you both out of the air and slow your descent to the ground, but it was close. Too close."

I nodded, trying to remember those last moments. I remembered draining. Falling. Fading. And his voice. Desperate as he'd begged me to stay with him. I swallowed hard and looked down at our intertwined fingers. I wished he hadn't had to go through that. Again.

"I wondered how we'd survived the fall," I said, quietly. "I should've known it was you. You're the only one who could've reached us in time. Thank you for doing that."

His fingers tightened around mine.

"I had to wait until we reached the ground to give you both any power." His voice grew hoarse again, torment tightening his features. "If I didn't, I'd have fallen out of my transformation, and we'd all have fallen out of the sky. But you were fading so fast. When I finally reached the ground and began pouring power into you both, I didn't know if it would work, or if it was too late. I gave you everything I had, hoping it would be enough to keep you alive.

"That's when the survivors ran over to us. The reinforcements were starting to engage the remainder of the Dark Guardian army, and Matt and the others wanted to get everyone in one place and out of the way. None of the fighters had any power left when they reached us, but some of the surviving students did—the ones who weren't too injured. They took turns pouring power into you both while Matt and the others surrounded the group and protected everyone until the battle was over. It was enough to keep you going, but only just. I stood watch over you and protected you until the Dark Guardian army was gone. Fortunately, it didn't take long."

He ran his other hand absently through his hair.

"There were about five hundred surviving Dark Guardians and Demons when we got there, and I'd managed to get a little over that number from the fifteen towns near the portals. Plus, the High Light Guardian sent a company of warrior faction soldiers to help, which was another two hundred and fifty highly trained people. They arrived at one of the portals just as we were starting to send people through. Those numbers on top of how burned out most of the Dark Guardian soldiers were by that point made victory quick. And bloody. A lot of people from those towns had kids at the Academy. The rage over their loss was definitely taken out on those remaining soldiers and Demons. I can't even describe it."

He shook his head, his gaze far away, like he was seeing it again.

"The second the last soldier died, I picked you up and ran to the portal that had the largest town near it. Iverly. That's where the reinforcements had all agreed to meet once the battle was over. That's where we are, by the way." He nodded at the large room around us. "They set up a medical area in the school gym. One of the trainers grabbed Damian, and Matt and the others helped the surviving students follow us. When we got here, we immediately brough you, Damian, and all the surviving students in here for treatment and observation. You each received a lot more donations from townspeople, some of the reinforcements, and some students who said you'd managed to evacuate them off-plane during the battle. It was enough to stabilize you both and keep you alive, but not enough to bring back your consciousness. You've been out for a week," he added, pain creeping back into his voice.

A week. I squeezed his fingers again, guilt churning through me. "I'm sorry," I whispered, looking down. I knew how much he must've suffered during that time. How much it must've taken out of him.

"No," he said quickly, "I don't want you to apologize. You didn't do anything wrong. You did what you had to do to save as many people as you could, and it was the right thing to do. I'm proud of you." He ran his thumb down my chin, and I looked up at him again, meeting the vibrant blue of his eyes. They never failed to draw me in. "But I can still worry about you," he murmured, running his thumb down my chin again. "I'll always worry about you. It's a part of love."

Warmth bloomed in my chest and my cheeks prickled with heat. "I just wish you didn't have to worry so much."

Gabriel smiled, the warmth of it filling his eyes. Then he leaned forward and brushed his lips gently over mine. "We'll just have to find a way to end the war for good, then." He kissed my nose, my forehead, my cheeks, then my lips again. "Then we won't always be fighting. We'll be free."

Free. And our future would be ours to do what we wanted with. We could do anything. Go anywhere. Have the life together we'd dreamed of.

"That would be amazing." My heart simultaneously ached for and shut out the possibility of that ever happening. After a lifetime of fighting, loss, and pain, after generations of battle and trauma, and slaughtering people for my own and others' survival, I wanted that—peace, freedom—more than anything. I wanted the war to end for good. But I knew better than most that the war was only escalating. We were further from resolution and peace than we'd maybe ever been.

I sighed. "I wish it was possible."

"We never truly know what is and isn't possible," Gabriel said, taking my hands again with both of his. "But if we don't preserve hope, if we don't dream and fight for that dream, it really won't be possible. We owe it to ourselves and the world to try, don't we?"

A smile pulled at my lips. His capacity for hope would never fail to amaze me. Even after everything he'd been through, it was like he had this inexhaustible well of it inside of him. It . . . inspired me. Lifted me from the darkest places in my mind and being. It made me want to be better. To fight for a better world. To find a better way forward.

"Yes," I finally murmured. "I guess we do."

"You're awake!" An unfamiliar voice exclaimed from the doorway across the gym.

I turned to see a woman walking toward us, clad in the warrior faction uniform. She looked a little older than us—more around Matt's age. I tilted my head a little. There was something familiar about her . . .

"We were getting really worried," she added, smiling at me, her eyes warm. "Especially that one." She nodded at Gabriel.

I glanced at him and saw that he was smiling and shaking his head a little. He was relaxed, like he knew this person well.

"Terah, this is my sister, Rebekah Edom. She's a lieutenant for one of the platoons in the company of warrior faction reinforcements. They were the closest company to one of the portals, so they volunteered to come to our aid. And, as you know," he said, turning to his sister, "this is Terah Alexander. Badass warrior, awesome human, and also my girlfriend."

My cheeks burned at his introduction, and I shot a teasing glare in his direction. He just smirked back.

"Nice to meet you," I said, turning to look at Rebekah. Even though I'd seen her in his memories in the fire, she'd been much younger at the time. I hadn't recognized her. Now, though, I could see the family resemblance. She had the same pale skin, jet-black hair, eye and nose shape, and a similar face shape, though hers was softer and less angular than his. The main difference was in their eyes—where his were electric blue, hers were a rich brown.

"Nice to meet you as well," she said warmly, as she came to a halt next to my cot. "I've heard a lot about you this past year. I've never seen Gabriel so head-over-heels." She shot a smirk at him.

I smiled as Gabriel rolled his eyes at her. Apparently, teasing ran in the family.

"In all seriousness," she continued, grabbing a folding chair and setting it next to my cot before sitting, "I'm relieved you're awake. You gave us all quite a scare. How do you feel?"

I pulled my legs in so I could sit cross-legged on the cot. I was still wearing the clothes I'd worn in battle. "A little sore and tired, but nothing too bad."

She nodded, watching me closely. Assessing. I wondered how much she knew about my power. I was sure the surviving students had probably told people what Damian and I had done near the end of the battle. What we'd become. I wondered how she felt about it.

"That's good to hear. You didn't have any physical injuries when you got here, but with all your power and your life force gone, we weren't sure you could come back. Gabriel insisted you could, though, so we've kept feeding you both power and hoping it would sustain you for long enough that your own power could start to return. I'm glad he was right," she added, placing a hand on Gabriel's shoulder and squeezing gently. I could see worry for him in her eyes. It must've been hard for her to see him so upset this past week.

"Is Damian awake too?" I turned to look at the gym around me for the first time. There were a bunch of cots strewn throughout the space, most of them empty, but some of them on the far side of the room still had people in them. Medics walked around the cots, tending to people and speaking to family members.

"He's not," Rebekah said, sounding hesitant, like she didn't want to upset me.

I turned to look at Gabriel, worry drawing my brows together.

Gabriel squeezed my hand. "He's on the other side of the room." He nodded to where the medics were. "He's had a similar amount of power donations as you, but he hasn't woken up."

Fear mixed with the worry in my chest, making it feel heavy—almost leaded. "Maybe he can't return without help. Like me."

Gabriel's brow furrowed slightly as he nodded. "You might be right. But I'm not sure how to help him. My connection with you is what made that possible. You were reaching for me, and I was reaching for you. We were searching for each other and managed to connect. He doesn't have that with anyone anymore."

My stomach tightened. He was right. Caleb was gone. But . . . Damian and I had a connection. Whether it was through our shared unique power or something else, something pulled us together. Something allowed us to become one being—one power. And that something had allowed me to enter his mind and save him before. Maybe it could again.

"I'm going to try." I swung my feet over the side of the cot and stood. My muscles twinged as I straightened up, but after the battle we'd had and the injuries I'd sustained, a little twinge wasn't so bad. "Maybe I can help him like I did in the illusion chamber."

Gabriel stood and nodded, but I could see his hesitation. He was worried he'd lose me to the darkness again.

"It'll be fine," I murmured, taking his hand as we started walking across the room, Rebekah behind us. "And I have you to bring me back if I get lost."

Gabriel took a deep breath in and released it slowly. Like he was trying to calm himself. But he nodded again, squeezing my hand.

"Just be careful."

"I will. I promise."

We gathered around Damian's cot and looked down at him. He was still wearing his clothes from battle, and streaks of dried blood and dirt covered him from head to toe. And there was a paleness beneath the light brown of his skin that tightened the knot in my stomach. He looked barely alive.

I felt the familiar tug in my chest, even though not all of my own power had regenerated. The pull to save him. To bring him back from the brink. I closed my eyes and placed my hand over his chest, opening my mind to him. Seeking connection.

"*Damian*," I called in my mind. "*Are you there?*"

There was no response. No flicker of his mind in mine. No feeling of his presence. *Damnit.* I took a deep breath and opened my mind more, letting myself feel how much I wanted to find him. How much I wanted to save him.

"*Damian,*" I called again, "*can you hear me? Are you there?*"

The tug in my chest intensified as the silence elongated. Something was wrong. I should be able to reach him this way. He should be able to reach back. But he wasn't. Something wasn't letting him. I wouldn't be able to bring him back this way. I'd have to try something else. Go deeper.

"Don't let go of me, Gabriel. Whatever you do, don't let go."

He wrapped his arms tightly around me, pressing his torso into my back. "I won't. I'll be here with you. As long as it takes."

I nodded and reached both hands forward this time, placing them against Damian's chest. Then I looked inside my chest, to where my power usually lived. It was a mixture of colors now, of all the different powers that'd sustained me this past week. But I could see where my own was growing again—a core of deep purple that was starting to take over. I reached for it, knowing somehow that I needed only it this time. I pulled a strand of deep purple down my arm and directed it into Damian's chest as I opened my mind to him again, giving in to the pull.

I was quickly sucked away from the world of light and was plunged back into darkness.

"*Damian, can you hear me? Where are you?*"

I pushed forward through the thick emptiness around me—the darkness that now felt more like a malicious entity than a void. It felt different from when I'd been here earlier on my own. There had been more light then. More balance. It hadn't been this oppressive. I shoved in deeper, through the wavering, ominous shadows. The air felt thick like blood-soaked mud and seemed to get thicker the deeper I went.

"*Damian!*" I called again, louder this time as I shoved forward.

I could barely see anything around me. It was like black fog filled the space, making it impossible to tell where I was going. I stilled and closed my eyes again. He wasn't responding. I needed to find him another way.

On a deep breath, I cleared my mind, ignoring the thick, dark air that seemed to press in on me from all sides, its presence suffocating. Then I opened my mind to everything around me. To the darkness, the hints of light, the density, to any traces of Damian in this place. It felt exposing—vulnerable—to let myself sink so deeply and reach so hard toward something I'd only minutes before been trying with all my strength to escape. But I knew from last time that it was the only way to access this part of my power. It was my only shot at finding Damian when we weren't both intentionally connecting with each other. So, instead of panicking, I breathed deeply, concentrating hard, and started sifting. Feeling every detail of everything around me, then letting everything that wasn't Damian fade into the background.

Slowly, so slowly, I started feeling hints of him. Corresponding pulls. A weak, vague glow of purple in my mind. It wasn't like before—I wasn't able to pinpoint Damian's specific geographical location—but, if I kept my eyes closed and concentrated, I could feel a vague glowing vibration in the darkness. A being who didn't belong here. And a tug pulled me toward him. I followed, keeping my eyes closed as I began walking again, pressing through the thick air. As I walked, the glow became more tangible. I could see the purple in my mind, the shadow of Damian that still barely permeated the darkness. Something was wrong. He should be able to feel me here. To hear me. Reach out to me. But he either didn't want to or couldn't.

"Damian." I was getting close. I could feel him somewhere nearby. "Can you hear me? Can you say something? Please, Damian. Say something."

I felt more than heard the shuddering breath coming from ahead of me, where the glow was brightest. He hadn't said anything, but he'd reacted. He must've heard me. I hurried forward, shoving through the last few feet of darkness before reaching the heart of his purple glow. I quickly opened my eyes, no longer needing the internal guide, and drew in a quick, startled breath. Damian was lying on the ground, pale and cold, inky black tendrils of darkness twined over and around every part of him, pinning him to the ground, just out of reach of the shadowy light.

"Damian," I breathed, kneeling next to him. "What happened to you?"

This wasn't what it'd been like for me. It'd been difficult to push free of the darkness on my own, but I hadn't been restrained like this, literally imprisoned in the shadows, unable to move or reach for the light.

Damian turned his head slowly to look at me. His eyes looked empty. Devoid of emotion or expression. It was frightening—he almost didn't look human anymore.

"Can you hear me? Do you recognize me?"

He blinked slowly but didn't respond.

"It's me. Terah. The one who shares a power with you. I'm here to bring you back with me. Back to the light."

I reached forward and gently touched his face. He was as cold as stone. Maybe he just needed warmth. Needed to remember what that was.

I reached my other hand forward and held both sides of his face between my palms, letting him soak in the heat.

"*It's okay. You're okay. You're alive and safe now. You can come back to the light. Come back with me.*"

Damian swallowed and blinked again, some recognition filling his eyes now. I wondered if he was having trouble remembering. Remembering who he was. What'd happened. What he'd done. Perhaps it was his mind's way of protecting him.

"*T-Terah,*" he whispered back, his voice sounding faint in my mind. "*I . . . I remember you.*"

I released a relieved breath. "*Good. I'm here to bring you home.*"

"*Home,*" Damian repeated, his voice going hollow. "*I . . . don't have a home.*"

I frowned, moving my hands to his shoulders. "*Yes, you do. Your home is in the world of the living, with your friends. It's not here. Don't let that thought keep you here. You belong in the light.*"

"*I don't . . . deserve the light.*" His chest rose and fell more quickly now. He looked upset. In pain. But more like himself. "*It's coming back to me. Everything is coming back. Seeing you . . . I . . . I remember now. Everything I did. Everything I didn't do. Everyone I hurt or killed. Caleb.*" His voice shook as his body tensed. Several more strands of ropey blackness rose from the ground beneath him and wrapped around his limbs, securing him more tightly to the darkness. "*The Academy. All those students. I remember it all. I don't deserve to come back.*" He looked at me again, pain bleeding from his eyes. "*There's nothing there for me now. This is . . . for the best. Just leave me here, Terah. Leave me. Death is . . . all I wanted anyway. I don't deserve to exist out there anymore. Not after everything I've done.*"

A desperate panic gripped me as I watched more ropes of darkness spiraling around him, covering him so thickly now that I could barely see him beneath. This wasn't right. Leaving him here, letting him succumb to the darkness, it didn't feel right. The tug pulled at my chest again, urging me to do something. To save him.

"*This wasn't only your fault, Damian.*" I reached forward and brushed his hair back from his forehead. Warmth. I needed to remind him of the warmth. Of connection. Of the light. "*We both know that your father would've found a way to do all those things without you. If anyone deserves to be here, it's him, not you.*"

Damian's gaze jerked to mine, startled.

"He abused and tortured you your whole life. He showed you again and again that there was no way out for you. That the only respite you and anyone around you could ever hope for could only come from following his orders. He made that true. I watched you in your memories try again and again to find ways around his orders. To disobey him. To save people. To escape, even through death. He never let you. That's not your fault."

Pain filled Damian's eyes again. I could tell he didn't believe me. He wanted to, he was desperate to, but he didn't. He thought everything did and should land on his shoulders. That the evil was his own, and he'd never overcome it. That he didn't *deserve* to overcome it.

"The things he made you do isn't who you are or who you have to be." I reached forward and laid my hand on his shoulder again. "I'm not saying there are no consequences for the things you did, or that you won't have to face those consequences when you return, but you can. I know you can. What you've experienced at his hands—all that pain and despair, all you were forced to do—none of that speaks to who you are or can be as a person. It doesn't make you less worthy or good. And it doesn't have to define your actions moving forward. You can make amends, discover and redefine yourself. You can actually live. You deserve a chance at life away from him."

Damian's eyes slid closed, despair crumpling his face. He didn't think any of that applied to him. He didn't think he deserved another chance.

"I hope someday you'll realize and believe it." I squeezed his shoulder. "But it's okay if you can't today. Today, I can believe it for you."

I pushed to my feet. I knew what to do now. He couldn't pull himself out of the darkness on his own. Too much of it still lived within him, drowning him. Imprisoning him in shadow. But that was okay. I knew better than most that deep healing couldn't happen overnight. Believing in oneself and one's own worth was a process. It took time and space. And sometimes you needed other people to lean on to help you move through and beyond the darkness. To see the light again. And I was here. He didn't have to do it alone. He could lean on me.

I pulled a strand of purple power down my arm, concentrated on what I wanted it to form, and fed the power into the image. This wasn't exactly how our power worked outside our minds, but I knew, somehow, it'd work here. With a flash, a purple sword materialized in my hand. Without wasting another moment, I swung it down in a forceful arc, severing the dark restraints binding Damian to the floor. Then I walked around him and did the same on his other side. I dematerialized the sword and knelt again, tearing away the rest of his shackles with my hands, banishing them back to the darkness. Then I grabbed his hand and pulled him to his feet.

He sagged forward against me, unable to carry his full weight in the thick void.

"*Oof.*" I readjusted him so his arm was over my shoulders instead. I could better handle his weight this way. "*Okay. I've got you. Let's go home.*"

We stumbled forward and pushed slowly through the darkness together, but it was so hard to see. So hard to tell which way the light was.

I opened my mind and reached out as we pushed forward. "*Gabriel. Can you hear me? Are you there?*"

"*I'm here,*" his warm voice echoed through the darkness. "*I've got you. Follow my voice.*"

Relief whooshed from my lungs. I could feel him again, like a path of warmth had opened in the cold darkness around us. I'd keep us in this warmth. On this path. We'd make it back to him.

"*Good. You're getting closer. I can almost see you. Keep pushing.*"

My grip around Damian's waist tightened as the air around us seemed to thicken more and more with every step. It was like the darkness didn't want to let us go. Like it was grabbing and restraining us with hundreds of invisible hands. I wasn't sure how much of it came from Damian's mind, and how much of it was some force beyond the two of us, but I knew I couldn't let it win. I wouldn't let it take us down now. Not after everything we'd already been through and survived.

"*Come on, Damian,*" I gasped as I pulled him forward, step after agonizing step. "*Push. You deserve better than this ending! Push!*"

To my surprise, Damian shifted, and with a grunt of effort, he stood more on his own feet, taking more of his weight. And then he pushed, shoving with me through the inky blackness and wavering light. Shoving back through the veil that'd had its talons sunk so deeply into him. The pressure eased step by step as we built momentum. As Damian seemed to gain some strength on his own again.

"*Good.*" I felt the warmth increasing. "*Keep going. Keep pushing. You can do it. We can do it.*"

"*I can almost reach you,*" Gabriel's voice whispered around us. "*Just a little further.*"

I felt him reaching forward, ready to grab me again. To steer us the rest of the way home. And I reached back with everything I had, clutching

716

Damian tightly, making sure we wouldn't lose him. That he wouldn't be left behind.

"*Just a little more,*" I gasped, stretching, pushing against the darkness with everything I had.

Damian's arm tightened around my shoulders, and he pushed with me. He wanted to leave. He actually wanted to leave the darkness. Elation filled me, and I smiled. The veil parted in front of us, and I felt Gabriel's arms curling around me again.

"*You're home.*"

With a gasp, I opened my eyes.

I quickly looked down and saw Damian blinking up at the bright gym lights above us, looking dazed. We'd done it. We'd managed to bring him back. I sank back against Gabriel's chest with a sigh of relief.

"What . . . just happened?" Rebekah asked, her voice quiet. She sounded confused. Maybe a little afraid.

My stomach clenched. How could I explain things in a way that wouldn't scare her? I didn't want her to think badly of me. Not when she meant so much to Gabriel. I rested the back of my head against Gabriel's chest and tilted my chin up to meet his gaze. I wasn't sure what to do. Gabriel's arms tightened around me, and he brushed a kiss over my forehead before looking at his sister.

"Terah and Damian share the same unique power and transformation," he said calmly, taking the responsibility of explaining off my shoulders. "It's a power that seems to be unique from other Divines. Because of this, they can connect through their shared power and accomplish things together that no other Divine can do. It's what allowed them to save so many students at the Academy before we got there. Terah accessed Damian's mind through their shared power and helped guide him home. And I helped guide her home through her mind."

Rebekah gaped at him. Like she was having a hard time wrapping her head around it all.

"Some people just have different powers, Bekah," he murmured. "Like me. It doesn't make them bad or frightening."

Rebekah's mouth snapped closed, and she took a step toward us, guilt filling her eyes. "I know." She reached out and placed a hand on Gabriel's shoulder. "That's not what I meant." She looked at me, earnestness filling her eyes. "I'm sorry. I didn't mean to imply that you're . . . bad or dangerous. I've just never heard of powers that can do any of that. It was a little overwhelming to process."

"Well, join the club," a dry voice said.

We turned to see Damian pushing into a sitting position.

"We don't understand it either. But I'm not going to complain about it after everything it's let us do thus far."

He shot Rebekah a cold, arrogant look, before turning to look at me for a long moment, his expression becoming unreadable. His familiar mask had returned.

"Thanks," he finally said, quieter now. Serious. "That's two times you've saved me. Guess I owe you," he added, a ghost of a smile on his face.

"Don't worry about it. *It's what friends do*," I added in my mind. His eyes flickered, and I knew he'd heard me. It was getting easier to connect with him.

"Anyway," I added, turning to look at Gabriel and Rebekah, "is there anywhere we can clean up and change? I don't think these clothes can be salvaged." I looked down at my heavily torn, burned, and blood-and-grime-encrusted clothes. "I could also use a haircut," I grumbled, running my hand down the strands. I'd noticed a whole chunk of it had been burned off when that Dark Guardian had hit me in the back with fire. There was a reason why I'd kept it short when I was younger.

"Yes," Rebekah said, her voice cheery now. She was less guarded than Gabriel. It seemed like she wanted to make up for her earlier shock. "The gym has locker rooms with showers. I can find you both some new clothes and then I'll come help you with your hair. I'll give Gabriel your clothes and he can bring them into the locker room for you," she added, turning to look at Damian again. He was eyeing her warrior faction uniform with distrust. His eyes flicked to hers, and he nodded slowly, his expression unreadable again.

Rebekah grabbed some towels and showed us where the locker rooms were before leaving so she could find us clothes. I quickly peeled off the horrible torn and bloody remnants of my outfit, then jogged over to one of the shower stalls.

I sighed as the hot water finally hit my skin. Steam billowed around me, and I slowly felt the deep ache in my muscles starting to ease. I released the tension I'd been storing in my muscles and closed my eyes under the stream. I needed this. This moment of stillness after everything that'd happened. Everything had been one overwhelming whirlwind after another, and then I'd been lost, closer to death than I'd ever wanted to be again. I hadn't had a moment to just . . . be. To breathe and collect myself.

So I let myself be still for a few minutes. Just concentrating on the feel of the water on my skin, on the rhythm and sound of my breaths, the feel of my heart beating beneath my chest, on the warmth of the steam, the sound of the water hitting the shower floor and streaming down the drain. Grounding myself again.

I took my time showering, making sure I lathered every part of my skin with soap. Working shampoo through every strand of my hair. I didn't want any remnants of the battle on me. When I finally emerged from the stall, towel wrapped tightly around me, I saw Rebekah had returned with a pair of scissors, a brush, and some clothes.

"Feel a little better?" She looked up from the bench, her expression soft and her smile kind.

I wondered how someone who was a soldier for a living could still smile like that. How she could retain so much light and joy with the devastation she must regularly see. It reminded me of Gabriel's unyielding hopefulness. His ability to keep part of himself open to the good and joyful in the world despite the horrors and loss he'd experienced. It was something I still struggled with—not shutting down. Not succumbing to the devastation and giving up. I wondered if it came naturally for them—if it was just built into them somehow—or if it was something they had to practice.

I smiled back a little. "Yeah. Definitely feeling better. Did you find clothes for me?" I eyed the pile of folded fabric.

"Yes!" She grabbed it from the bench and held it out to me. "A lot of people in town have donated clothes to the survivors. I picked this out for you, though I had to guess at the sizing, but you can go grab a few more outfits from the donation room later, since I'm guessing most of your belongings were lost with the Academy."

I nodded, reaching out to take the clothes, my throat tight. It wasn't like I'd had very many belongings to begin with, but everything I did have had been in that room. It was just another way I'd have to start over.

"Gabriel said you like black," she called as I disappeared into the shower stall again. "I tried to find some clothes that might suit you."

I couldn't help smiling as I looked down at the items she'd picked. She'd managed to find a pair of black jeans around the right size, a black cotton tank top, and a black knit cardigan. She'd also included a sports bra, socks, and a pair of underwear still wrapped in its packaging. It was sweet. The pair of them were pretty thoughtful.

"Thanks," I called as I quickly dressed. "They're great."

I donned the cardigan last and pushed up the sleeves to my elbows before grabbing the socks and emerging. I didn't want to put them on until I'd fixed my shoes—they'd only get wet.

Rebekah smiled as she looked at me. "You two really do share a style, don't you? All black all the time. Lots of tattoos. He really did find his counterpart."

I laughed a little as I sat beside her on the bench. "It was definitely one of the first things we noticed about each other," I admitted. "Though obviously it wasn't the only qualification."

"I'm glad he found you." She leaned forward and squeezed my arm. "Despite the circumstances, I've never seen him so relaxed and happy with another person. I've never seen him so comfortable being himself. You two must be good for each other."

I shifted a little, uncomfortable, heat prickling beneath my cheeks. I wasn't used to talking like this with people. Especially people I didn't know well. I wasn't used to letting someone new in so quickly. But something about it was . . . nice. I tried not to push away the feeling.

"I think we are," I managed to say. "I'm just grateful he decided he wanted to be my friend and wasn't put off by how difficult I initially made that for him. I wasn't . . . the most open person when we met."

"Hm." She leaned back and looked at me appraisingly. "Well, he's always been good at seeing through and into people. Plus, he grew up in a border town and is familiar with how that can shut people down. He's not put off by a bit of roughness. Especially if you intrigued him," she added, elbowing me playfully in the ribs. "Anyway, I'll reign in my older sister instincts to torment the young, and I'll stop embarrassing you." She grinned. "Shall we cut your hair now?"

I laughed and shook my head a little. I could see how she and Gabriel had caused so much mischief together when they were younger.

"Sure. I'm not sure what we'll be able to salvage, though, since a pretty big chunk was burned off."

Rebekah turned me on the bench, so my back was to her, and ran her fingers through my wet hair. "It looks like it burned up to your shoulder on one side." She picked up the brush and pulled it gently through my hair. "I can cut a little above it all the way around, and it should be fine. Your hair will just be a little above your shoulders. Are you okay with that?"

"Yeah," I murmured, resigned. "That's how I used to wear it when I was younger, for exactly this reason."

Rebekah laughed. "I understand the struggle." She put down the brush and picked up the scissors. "Had mine mangled one too many times in battle and decided to just wear it braided tightly around my head while on duty. If it gets hit now, well, that will be the least of my problems since I probably won't have a head."

I smiled a little, but I felt the heaviness beneath her light tone. It was my first glimpse of it in her—she was experienced enough to hide it well. But she, too, carried the uncertainty that every soldier bore. Of the death that followed all of us like a shadow, biding its time. Never knowing when it'd catch up to each of us. When the shadow would finally consume us.

"Alright," she said, once she'd arranged the towel over my shoulders to keep hair off my clothes, "I'm going to start cutting now. Don't worry, it should be fairly even. Most people at my base cut each other's hair on the reg, so I'm pretty good at it now."

I nodded and let her get to work. Fortunately, it didn't take long. In under ten minutes, she put down the scissors and collected the towel from around my shoulders so she could throw away all the fallen hair.

"It looks nice!" she exclaimed when I turned to face her. "It frames your face and draws attention to your features. You should go show my brother," she added, a mischievous smile stealing across her face.

I rolled my eyes at her, silently amused, but grabbed my socks and walked out of the locker room anyway. Gabriel was waiting in a chair next to my cot, talking to Damian. Based on their serious expressions, Gabriel was probably filling him in on what'd happened after we'd passed out.

"Hey," I murmured, as I reached them. "Sorry that took so long."

Gabriel glanced up at me mid-sentence and froze. His eyes roved over my newly cut hair, then over my face, and finally landed on my mouth. His cheeks warmed.

"That bad, huh?" I smirked at him.

"No," he murmured, reaching out and grabbing my fingers, then drawing me closer to him. He reached up and ran his fingers through the short strands. "No," he murmured again, pulling me gently down so I landed on his lap. He cupped my cheek and rubbed his thumb slowly over my bottom lip. "It's . . . you're . . . beautiful."

I smiled, my cheeks burning. It was sweet, but I wished we didn't have an audience. Gabriel had either forgotten or didn't care anymore. But after his lips met mine, I didn't care anymore either.

"Gods," Damian said a few moments later, "can you two at least wait until you're alone?"

Gabriel and I broke apart. Damian was looking at us, eyebrows slightly raised, but he didn't really seem upset. More amused.

Rebekah laughed as she walked over from the locker rooms. "See?" She sent me a mischievous wink. "Told you he'd like it."

"I do," Gabriel murmured, brushing his lips against my neck before releasing me so I could stand again.

"By the way," Rebekah continued, coming to stand between me and Damian, "we cleaned and kept the weapons you had on you when you got here. They're under each of your cots along with your shoes. We had those cleaned and repaired so you could wear them again, since there weren't a ton of shoe donations."

"Thanks."

I knelt and pulled out the items from under my cot. It looked like they'd only salvaged one of my long daggers and the two daggers with sheaths that Caleb had given me. My throat tightened as I straightened up, staring down at the daggers in my hand. They really were beautiful. Intricately carved wood handles partially wrapped in leather for grip. Leather sheaths with matching patterns carved across the surface, softened from use over time. Passed down from generation to generation, and now in my care.

"That way . . . a piece of me . . . w-will always be there . . . t-to . . . p-protect . . . you . . . Terah . . ."

Tears clouded my eyes as I stared down at them, my fingers closing more tightly around them. The dark, hollow feeling of loss gaped open in my chest again. *Caleb.* He'd done the exact thing he'd tried to avoid his whole life—sacrificing his own future for someone else. Dying without rank or recognition. Just so he could keep me alive. Guilt swamped through me, paralyzing and cold. Making it hard to breathe.

I felt an arm slide around my waist and a hand grip my shoulder. I looked up, startled, and saw Gabriel standing on my left and Damian on my right. Both were looking at Caleb's daggers in my hands.

"Matt told me what happened," Gabriel said, his eyes sad as they met mine. He'd never liked Caleb, but I knew he hadn't wanted him to die, either. Neither had I. "I'm so sorry. That must've been hard to see."

I nodded, a tear escaping down my cheek. All I could think about was how that sword had been meant for me. It was never supposed to be him. His death was my fault.

"It wasn't your fault," Damian said firmly, his hand tightening on my shoulder. I wasn't sure if he'd heard or just guessed at my thoughts. "He made that choice, just as Mannan did for him. He knew what he was doing, he knew what the outcome would be, and he chose to do it anyway. He wasn't a victim of your actions, Terah. He was a brave person who finally stopped lying to himself and made the only choice he felt was right. Don't take that away from him by putting the results of that choice on your own shoulders. He wouldn't want that."

I nodded, looking down and quickly wiping another tear from my cheek.

"I heard you were awake," a familiar voice said from the doorway of the gym. *Matt.*

I spun to look at him, but my words died in my throat as I saw what he was wearing. The official warrior faction uniform. Crisp, formal. His rank was even attached to the front. My stomach clenched at the sight.

Matt smiled at me as he walked forward, across the room toward us. He looked older—more serious and put together like this. It made me feel even further away from him. Like the person I'd known was even more out of reach. The dark, empty feeling of loss hollowed out my chest again.

"Thank you for letting me know, Lieutenant." He nodded at Rebekah.

She nodded in return. "Of course, Commander."

Commander. So, he'd retained the rank my mother had given him at the Academy. But it was more official now. Its significance much greater, the impact broader. He'd lead troops now. Whole companies. He'd be forever entrenched in the war, under Light Guardian orders until he died. My hand clenched into a fist at my side.

"I'm glad you're okay." Matt stopped in front of me. Looking only at me. "I was worried about you."

My shoulders tensed as I looked up into his face. I could see he wanted to step closer. To pull me into his arms and not let me go. But he was refraining. I realized, as his eyes flicked from Rebekah back to me, that he wasn't refraining because of my boundaries. But because she was here—someone beneath him in rank. He wanted to live up to his new title. To seem unemotional. In control. My insides grew colder.

"I'm going to grab my weapons and shoes," Damian said, breaking the silence.

Matt glanced at him, his eyes hardening as he watched Damian walk back over to his cot to retrieve his things. He clearly wasn't happy that Damian was still here. He clearly didn't like or trust him.

"The High Light Guardian has actually asked to speak privately with the two of you," Matt said, his voice growing serious. Firm. "That's why I'm here."

Somehow, that didn't surprise me. Matt was always at her beck and call.

"Once you get your things together, I'll take you to her. Unfortunately, *you* won't be able to join them," Matt added, his gaze enigmatic as he looked at Gabriel.

Gabriel's shoulders tensed, but he nodded curtly. Rebekah looked back and forth between them, her expression serious. Worried.

I squeezed Gabriel's hand, then sank into the chair he'd been sitting in, pulling my boots toward me. The sooner we got this over with, the better.

As soon as Damian returned and I'd strapped Caleb's daggers around my hips, we followed Matt out of the gym and down a series of halls, passing classroom after classroom, many of them rearranged to accommodate the surviving students, their parents, and the large number of warrior faction soldiers who seemed to be here now. We finally made it to the far side of the building, and Matt pushed open yet another classroom door. Sitting at the desk at the front of the room was the High Light Guardian.

She glanced at us. "Ah, yes." Her expression grew haughty. Cold. "Come in you two. Have a seat." She gestured at the students' desks in front of her.

Damian and I walked over, but we remained standing, our arms crossed over our chests.

"I will send for you later, Matthew," she added, glancing at him.

He nodded solemnly at her before briefly meeting my eyes. He looked curious. He must not know what she was going to say to us. He turned slowly and closed the door, then disappeared down the hall.

"Well." Serafina stood and walked to the front of the desk to face us. "This is certainly unexpected. I never thought I'd see you two in the same place." Her eyes swept over both our faces before she turned quickly and walked to the window.

I glanced at Damian, confused. He was staring at Serafina, his brows furrowed in frustration. It was a look I'd seen before. I wondered if he was having a hard time reading her thoughts. It wouldn't surprise me—Serafina valued control over all else. The moment she'd learned I could read minds, I bet she'd worked hard to figure out how to close her mind to others. She'd never willingly allow anyone in like that, especially me. Or perhaps her mind had always been closed.

"I hear," Serafina began again, turning her back to the window, but remaining distanced from us, "the two of you did some spectacular things with your power as well as the Dark Guardians' power during the battle. Please explain what happened from your perspective." Her expression was carefully curious, but I could see the dark hint of greed in her eyes. She wanted to use us. My insides turned to ice.

Damian glanced at me, quickly reading my expression. It was clear I didn't want to talk with her. I didn't want to be here at all.

"We are connected through the same power," Damian said carefully, turning to face her again. "We simply used that connection to combine our power and life forces, which allowed us to do much larger things than we could do apart."

"I see." Greed was taking over her expression now. "And what about your manipulation of the Dark Guardians' powers?"

I glanced at Damian and saw his expression had turned wary as well. He noticed her greed too and knew how she'd treated me and my power my whole life. We needed to tread carefully.

"In desperate moments," he said slowly, "when we're almost out of power, it seems like we can siphon power from other Divines and use it as our own. It's not something we fully understand or know how to control. That was the first time we've ever done it."

"I see." Serafina turned to look out the window. "That is an extraordinary power. It holds potential to help our side greatly, but an equal potential to hurt us. Tell me, Damian, what made you decide to help our side of the war? I am aware that you grew up in the Dark Guardian realm under Gedeon Eliel's care, and I have it on good authority from Matthew that you were a spy for him up until the battle."

Her eyes pierced him as she turned to face us again.

"I was." Damian crossed his arms over his chest as he stared straight back at her. "I've been a spy my whole life. I've been his pawn since I was old enough to do anything. I've stolen for him, killed for him, used my power and unique abilities to help him take power, infiltrate spaces, destabilize governments, and widen his influence."

My fists clenched at my sides as I watched Serafina's expression. I was worried for him. Worried about what she'd do to him.

"But," Damian said slowly, uncrossing his arms and leaning against the desk behind him, "I was never free. He forced me to do horrible things that I never wanted to do. He tortured me for not complying every time I tried to get around his orders and do less harm, and every time I failed to accomplish what he wanted. He killed people I cared about or people I was trying to save just to show me how futile it was to disobey him. And every time I tried to escape him through death, he just healed me. There was no way out."

Serafina's expression crumpled for a second. Almost as though she felt . . . pained. Or perhaps guilty. But she smoothed out her expression before I could decipher more.

"I went to the Academy on a mission," Damian continued, "to obtain an item for my father and convert or eliminate Terah. I was resigned to follow his orders by that point—he'd broken me down enough that I no longer saw another way. But when I got to the Academy, I got to experience a different way of living. A place that wasn't dark with fear, evil, and death. I got to see people genuinely caring about each other and genuinely experiencing happiness. It was so foreign to me."

He rubbed the back of his head absently as he glanced out the window, watching the breeze move the branches of the tree next to the building.

"People I'd connected with just to complete my mission became real friends." His voice was quieter now. "It reminded me of all those feelings I'd had when I was younger—that there had to be a better way. A way to do less harm and get around his orders. But even as I thought that, even as I opened up and connected with people more, I knew my father would never let me go, and if I didn't follow his orders, he'd kill all the people I'd come to care about. That's why I stuck to my mission.

"Before I left for the Academy, I'd come to an agreement with my father—if I could convert Terah and bring her back to the Dark Guardian realm along with the object he sought, he wouldn't attack the school. He'd spare everyone else. It wasn't until the army was already on its way that I really saw what Terah was trying to make me see—that my father had never intended to keep that promise. He'd always intended to attack the Academy regardless of what I did. And I couldn't just stand by this time and watch everyone die. I couldn't watch all the innocent students be slaughtered. So, I figured, if I was going to die no matter what I did, I might as well fight for what I really wanted to fight for. That's why I switched sides."

"Hm." Serafina continued to study Damian. "And what was it that Gedeon wanted you to obtain? Matthew was not as forthcoming about this as I'd expected him to be." Her brow furrowed deeper. She wasn't used to Matt not completely falling in line with her wishes and orders, especially now that he was in the warrior faction.

Damian glanced at me, a question in his eyes. He wanted to know whether we should tell her about the book.

"It was a book hidden beneath the Academy grounds that would help Divines undo the barrier between the mortal realm and the realm of the gods," I said quickly, deciding on an abridged truth. Serafina's eyes widened with shock. "But Damian and I used our combined power to hide it so no one from either side of the conflict can get their hands on it. It's gone—as out of your hands as it is Gedeon's." My voice was firm. Hard.

"And how can you be so sure of that?" Her eyes were icy as they met mine.

I met her gaze unflinchingly. "Because it's sealed on a plane that no one else can find or access."

Surprise lifted her brows as a hint of anger shot across her face.

"Additionally," I continued, "Damian proved his loyalty to our side by keeping the book out of his father's hands, by fighting against the side he grew up with even though the odds were so against us, and by willingly giving his life to save as many students as he could with me. He's proven himself enough."

Serafina glared at me in silence for a long moment before turning away from me. She didn't bother responding. She didn't like engaging with me.

"Explain the Demons that gained access to the Academy last semester." Her voice was a little impatient now, her frustration seeping through her calm, haughty façade.

"They were meant to test or eliminate Terah. I was only sent after she'd proven she was powerful enough to defeat some of our most formidable Demons. My father wouldn't have wanted to use her otherwise. But they were also a display of power and an opportunity to damage the Academy—one of the last Light Guardian refuges. He wanted the Light Guardian side to know he had the power to attack them anywhere and everywhere, no matter how protected."

"And how did he have such power?" Serafina prompted, her hands twitching at her sides. "It is not a feat he should be able to accomplish."

Damian was silent for a moment, his gaze on the window again. "I wasn't supposed to know," he finally said, his voice quiet. "But he raised me as a spy. I couldn't help noticing something had changed. He could suddenly do things he'd never been able to do before. Things that shouldn't be possible. So . . . I waited until he was deep in sleep one night and crept into his mind. It was something he'd forbidden me from ever doing, and I'd never disobeyed him about that before. The punishment

727

would've been unbelievably severe. His mind was always carefully closed anyway. But in sleep, his guard slipped a little."

Damian traced his fingers absently over the edges of the desk behind him.

"My father has always been fascinated by the gods. I think it's their limitless power that enthralls him the most. Especially their ability to have endless access to power without burnout, and to command unquestioning, unwavering worship from their followers. It's always what he's emulated. It's why he's been so set on controlling me and using my unique abilities for his own gain. His intense interest in the gods covers the entire castle. It's full of books and scrolls about every god imaginable. His own personal quarters are filled with relics from every religion he can get his hands on. He devotes all his free time to studying them and ascertaining whether any contain or can direct power. He even goes on missions to the Normal plane to acquire or search for relics. He's obsessed.

"When I pushed into his mind that night, I saw he'd acquired a new relic several months earlier. Something old, stolen from a collection of protected artifacts guarded by Normals. It's a small stone statute—a depiction of a god. I got a look at it in his mind, though I've never seen it in person. But the statute speaks to him somehow. When I first saw that in his mind, I thought he'd lost it. But then I dug deeper and saw him interacting with it. Somehow, it's preserved a connection with the god it depicts, even though the god is in a separate realm. And it can do more than communicate. It can feed him power."

Silence filled the room as shock settled over us.

"That . . . is not possible." Serafina's voice wavered. "It is well known that the alliance of new gods completely separated themselves and the old gods from the mortal world. In order to protect humanity, they are only able to interact with their worshipers in the most distant of ways. Gedeon cannot be communicating directly with a god. He cannot receive power from it."

Damian shrugged, crossing his arms over his chest again as he observed Serafina. "I don't know what to tell you. I saw what I saw. Maybe the gods aren't as distant as we've always thought. Or maybe the barrier between our planes is weakening. Whatever the reason, somehow this artifact has kept or reformed a connection with the god, and my father has not only discovered that, but has somehow managed to use it. It was on the god's orders that he tried to retrieve the book. He wouldn't have known about it or where it was hidden without the god's information. And it was with the god's help that he was able to easily push through the protections around the Academy's plane whenever and however he wanted to send Demons and the army there. And in exchange for doing the god's bidding, my father was promised the god-like power he's always wanted. Enough power to finally win the war. What he *hasn't* paid much attention to is the god's end goal. He's been far too eager to take the power given to him to ask enough questions. But it seems like, at the very least, the god wants to dissolve the barrier between our world and theirs, which would be catastrophic. My father thinks he'd have the god's allegiance and protection in the conflict that would follow, but I highly doubt that."

Serafina just gaped at him, her expression wavering from disbelief and distrust to panic.

"The god must not have a very strong connection to this plane, though," Damian continued, ignoring her expression. "If it did, it would just do all of this itself instead of using my father and his resources as pawns. It would also have more specific knowledge. It knew where the book was generally located, but not its exact position or how to get to it. And even though the god can give power, it's like that power has to be directed through someone—the god can't seem to act much on its own. Not yet at least. Which probably means there are limits to the amount of power the god can give and the chosen mortal can withstand receiving."

"If . . . what you're saying is true," Serafina murmured, starting to pace in front of the window, "this relic must be removed from Gedeon's possession immediately. Do you know where it is being kept?"

"I do not. Somewhere in the Dark Guardian realm, likely with him most of the time, and hidden and guarded the rest of the time. But I imagine he moves it around a lot. He's always been paranoid."

"And you can't access his mind to find out?" she pressed, returning her piercing gaze to his.

"Not from this distance," Damian responded. "I'd not only have to return to the Dark Guardian plane, but I'd have to be relatively close to him to hear him. And based on how I've betrayed them this past week, they'd overpower and kill me long before I could make it anywhere near him."

Serafina pursed her lips, her gaze going distant. She was probably trying to think of ways around this. Ways she could still use Damian to retrieve the relic.

"Do you know what god this artifact is connected to?"

"No." Damian's brow furrowed slightly. "It wasn't in any of his surface thoughts. I've looked for information about a god depicted like the statue since then, but I haven't found anything resembling it in the Academy library."

Serafina nodded, disappointed, but unsurprised. "I will have to think on that," she finally said, refocusing on us as she walked back over to stand in front of the desk, facing us again. "As for the other part of your mission," she said, her voice cool and calm again, "did Gedeon tell you why he wanted you to convert or eliminate Terah?" Her gaze was sharp again as she considered Damian.

"No." He met her gaze steadily. He was good at interrogations. Good at not getting flustered. Being a spy probably helped. "He usually only gave me enough information to complete my missions, not the reasoning behind them, though I often guessed correctly. He never trusted me or anyone else enough to give a full picture of what he wanted and why. It was easier to keep us all beneath him that way. But my guess is that it has something to do with the fact that she has the same power as me."

Serafina nodded slowly, looking back and forth between us. Like she was deliberating.

"And is it your intention to remain on our side and fight against those you grew up around? Against those who raised you?" She raised her eyebrows quizzically at him.

Damian took a deep breath and let it out slowly, running his hand agitatedly through his hair. "Yes," he finally said, quiet again, his eyes trained on the ground. "I can never go back there now. Not after directly disobeying his orders. Not to mention hiding the book and fighting against his army. And even if I could, I wouldn't want to return. I'd rather work with people I care about doing something I actually believe in for once. If you'll let me," he added, raising his gaze to hers again.

He knew as well as I that Serafina held the key to his future. She could punish him for his role in the Academy's attack and his work as a spy, or she could forgive him and potentially gain access to his power and allegiance. She'd face criticism no matter what choice she made. I wondered what'd win out.

"I am willing to pardon you for all your past misdeeds against us, Damian, on one condition," she said smoothly. "You swear allegiance to the Light Guardian cause—to *me*—and fight exclusively for our side in this war. If you do that, and continue to prove your loyalty through your actions, then I would be happy to have you on our side."

I stiffened as I watched her. While it was probably the best outcome we could've hoped for, I knew she was only offering this because of the potential she saw in having the two of us together. She wanted access to the extra power and otherworldly abilities we seemed to gain as a unit. She wasn't benevolent. She was coolly transactional, willing to trade with him for the promise of power and control.

Damian nodded slowly, scrutinizing her carefully. "I swear allegiance to the Light Guardian side of this war," he finally said, "and promise to protect Normals as well as the general welfare of the world, as is your mission." He hadn't said exactly what she'd asked him to. I wondered if she'd notice or care.

Serafina watched him for a long moment in return before stepping forward and holding out her hand. "Then it is done," she said as he shook it. "You are now formally sworn to the Light Guardian side. In return, I pardon you of all treasonous activity taken against us up to this point. Do not disappoint me, Damian," she added, stepping back. "Do not prove wrong my willingness to pardon you."

Damian nodded slowly, calm, but serious.

"Now, I suppose, it is my turn to shed some light on this situation," she continued, her tone matter of fact again as she looked between the two of us.

I leaned against the desk behind me as I watched her, waiting. Her hands clenched and unclenched at her sides. She looked . . . almost nervous. I'd never seen her like this before.

"You two seem to have discovered your connection to each other through your shared powers on your own," she began, "but there is more to it than that. Much more."

I quickly glanced at Damian. His expression was carefully blank, but I saw his fingers turning white as he gripped the edge of the desk. It was his only tell.

"There was a prophecy made in the early days of our existence as Divines. Made by a Divine who had a dream so real and recurring so often that it had to be something more than a dream. The Divines of the time acknowledged it for what it was and recorded it. However, the written prophecy was lost through the passage of time and has largely been forgotten. Yet some Divines correctly guessed its importance and preserved it by passing the knowledge down to their children.

"I heard it first from my grandmother," she continued, staring over our heads to the wall at the back of the room, "though my mother made sure to recite it to me as well. The prophecy predicted a great and lasting war, one in which the Divines would participate and pay heavily for doing so. It spoke of a great tide-turner. A being who would finally have the power to end this great, devastating conflict forever. A being who would, finally, save all our souls. This being would be a child, a Divine, born from the most powerful dark and the most powerful light, but who would be neither. They would have mastery over land and sky, this world and the other. They would have the power to determine all our fates. They would be the god-chosen one."

My own fingers began to numb as I tightly gripped the edge of the desk. She couldn't mean . . . she couldn't be saying what I thought she was saying. I glanced at Damian again and saw that all the blood had left his face.

"I am the most powerful Light Guardian who has ever existed," Serafina continued, haughtiness inundating her voice again. "It was clear to me even from my childhood that I was destined to be the High Light Guardian. There were and are none who possess more power than I. I knew the moment I first heard the prophecy that I was to be the one destined to birth this miracle—this great weapon for our side. My conviction grew when I attended the Academy and saw Gedeon, your father." Her eyes strayed to Damian, who'd stiffened, his entire body going rigid. Waves of cold rippled through my body. It couldn't be. It couldn't be true. It would mean . . .

"He was a third year when I started," she continued, ignoring our shock. "He was the son of powerful, high-ranking Dark Guardian spies embedded in the Normal government, who resided in the Normal realm. He was already famed for being the most powerful Dark Guardian anyone had seen in known history. It was assumed from a young age that he would take over the Dark Guardian throne either by appointment or by force once he graduated. I knew the moment I saw him that he was the one who must make this weapon with me. The most powerful dark and the most powerful light."

I shoved off the desk and turned fully around, facing the back wall, and sucked in deep breaths through my nose, one hand covering my mouth. It meant . . . she meant . . .

My pulse pounded frantically through my veins as I turned my head slowly again. Damian's shocked eyes met mine. And I looked at him—really looked at him—for the first time. His face had always seemed familiar, but I'd never figured out why. But now . . .

My eyes swept over his features as his swept over mine. Noticing.

Cataloguing. His eyes were dark brown and almond shaped with thick lashes. Like mine. His skin was a warm light brown. Like mine. His hair color matched mine perfectly. His nose, his mouth, all were familiar. Similar. How had I not seen it before? How had I not connected those dots?

"Yes," Serafina said after a long pause, "I see you have put it together now."

I turned slowly to face her again, my heart still pounding feverishly. It was so much to wrap my head around. Too much.

"You are brother and sister," she said carefully. Quietly. Like the knowledge wouldn't hurt as much that way. "More than that, you are twins."

Waves of shock washed over me, a new one crashing in before I could recover from the one before. How? How could I have a brother and not know it? How could I have a *twin* and not know it? How could she not have told me? Why hadn't we grown up together? Why had we both been so . . . alone?

I sank back against the desk, shock paralyzing me. My hands shook as I tried to steady myself. If what she said was true, it meant that Gedeon, that horrible, torturing, abusive asshole was . . . my father. The *king of the Dark Guardians* was my father. Something in me broke at that realization. Perhaps it was a last strand of hope, long held onto. A hope that my father would one day come for me. That he'd take me away from the horrible, violent, and neglectful circumstances I'd grown up in. That he'd eventually find me and actually love me. But that was laughable now. A foolish, naïve dream. My real father was willing to send Demons after me. He was willing to kill me. Torture me. Use me.

Tears stung my eyes, but I tried to blink them away. I refused to let Serafina see me cry. Ever. I glanced at Damian again and saw that he was eyeing Serafina. Realizing what I'd just realized. She was his mother too. Damian tore his gaze from her and glanced at me. His expression held a vulnerability I'd rarely seen there. I wanted to reach out and take his hand, but I wasn't sure if I should. I didn't know where we stood now. Was he happy he had a sister? Did he hate that it was me?

"Anyway," Serafina continued, as though she hadn't just exploded our worlds, "I knew I needed to wait until I graduated and secured a high-level position in the warrior faction before having a child. I couldn't have it affecting my career trajectory. A few years after graduation, once I had secured a high-ranking position, I embarked on a journey to find Gedeon. I knew he had returned to the Dark Guardian realm and risen to their highest rank, and our intelligence told us that he was strategically placing himself in a position to take over the throne. I found out through several warrior faction spies that he was planning to leave the Dark Guardian plane and travel to Europe for a mission. Something about attempting to rig an election to destabilize the government there—more ill-conceived plans trying to weaken the Normals to make them easier to conquer and manipulate."

She paced a small path back and forth in front of the desk.

"I planned to cross paths with him while he was on his mission, in disguise of course. I did so after his mission was complete to ensure he was in a good mood. I used that to aid me. It took almost no convincing to seduce him at that point."

Damian and I both cringed.

She ignored our disgust. "I knew the prophecy was on my side, that it was referring to the child I would bear from my union with Gedeon, when I became pregnant from that one encounter. I returned to the Light Guardians, victorious, without anyone knowing the wiser."

I felt almost nauseous as I stared at her in horror. What a horrible way to make a decision. What a horrible way to bring a child . . . children . . . into the world. All for a story she'd been told in childhood. All to gain power. Damian and I had been emotionlessly created for our utility. We hadn't been wanted as children or even as living beings—we'd been wanted for our powers. As weapons. I'd always suspected that—had always assumed my mother had never really cared about me—but having it so categorically confirmed . . . hurt.

"Nine months later, I was in my grandmother's home for my delivery." She walked over to the window again and stared out through the glass, her gaze distant. "She was a great healer, and my mother was already dead, so she was my only remaining family. I trusted no one else to deliver this chosen child. Or children, rather. We knew by then that it would be two. My grandmother . . . she was so excited for you, even though she knew I never wanted to be a mother. Even though she knew this birth wasn't about that."

I stared daggers into the side of her face. I wanted to punch her. To hurt her as much as she was hurting me right now. But more than anything, I hated that she still could. That she could inflict more suffering on me. That I somehow still let her.

I jumped slightly as I felt fingers closing around mine. Squeezing gently before letting go. I glanced up in surprise, meeting Damian's eyes. It wasn't like him to offer comfort. But I saw a lot in his expression. Understanding, anger, hurt, confusion. Hearing this was a lot for him, too. Hearing what our lives did and didn't mean to her. *Our mother.*

"My grandmother insisted on naming you both," Serafina continued, drawing our gazes back to her. She was refusing to look at us—the living results of her grand plan. "I didn't have time to think about it with my warrior faction duties, nor was it something I cared greatly about, so I let her choose. She chose Terah and Damian. Only the gods know why—they aren't good Light Guardian names. Though, I suppose neither of you are Light Guardians," she added quietly.

"Anyway, I went into labor, and you were the first to be born." She glanced at Damian. "He arrived right after your umbilical cord was cut." Her voice darkened. "Gedeon. It turned out that he had known exactly who I was in Europe. His family, it seemed, was another line that had kept the prophecy alive through the generations. He had identified me as I had him, as soon as I started at the Academy. He had simply been biding his time, waiting for the right moment to put his plan into action. But in the end, I'd brought myself directly to him. He, however, wanted the child—the weapon—for himself and his own uses in the war. He had never intended to let me keep you."

She took a deep, shuddering breath before continuing.

"He came to steal you away from me—from the Light Guardian side—at the moment of your birth. He stormed into the house with a handful of followers, and they killed everyone inside. When he reached the room I was in, my grandmother stood in front of me, holding Damian and trying to shield us from Gedeon. He . . . killed her and took you." She glanced at Damian again, whose whole body had gone tense, then looked quickly away. "He didn't know there were two of you or else he would have taken Terah as well. We had kept that secret well, at least.

"I shouted your name as he took you away," she murmured, a slight waver in her voice. The first sign of real emotion I'd ever really seen from her. My hands clenched at my sides. "I suppose that's how he knew it. Apparently, he never saw fit to change it. I couldn't move to go after him. I was too weak, and Terah started coming out as he was leaving. Just ten minutes after your brother was born." She turned to look at me. "I delivered you by myself in a house full of the dead."

Serafina inhaled deeply as she stared at me, pressing a hand against her stomach, almost like she was reliving it. I was frozen. Not sure what to feel anymore. How to react. It was . . . horrifying.

She spun back around to look out the window again. "It took a little while after Terah was born for me to regain enough strength to do anything. When I could move again, I called for help. A team of warrior faction soldiers was sent to extract us, including Matthew's mother, my old friend. She was living in Dagmar with her young son at the time, and it was then that I decided Terah would live there as well. You would be looked after, trained well, and kept out of sight enough that Gedeon might not discover your existence for a long time. We would have a chance to raise you the right way. On the right side. Then, at least, one of you might fulfill the prophecy. In any case, I did not have time to raise you myself with all my warrior faction responsibilities."

My jaw was so tightly clenched that I could feel the tension radiating up into my skull. I hated this. I hated her.

Serafina turned to face us again, her expression guilt-free. "We brought you to Dagmar, and I left you in her care. And I am pleased to say that my plan worked. Gedeon only recently discovered your existence. How, I do not know. Damian could probably answer that better than I. Gedeon must have decided that he either needed both of you or needed Terah eliminated since she was raised on the Light Guardian side. You both have borne witness to his actions and the results of said actions since then, so I do not need to explain the rest to you." Her tone was almost clipped now. Like she was expecting retaliation from us.

I didn't know what to do or say. I felt numb and overwhelmed at the same time. I couldn't fully process all the information I'd received. I was flooded with droves of tangled emotions, feverish and frenzied. But one thought floated to the surface.

"Why didn't you try to get Damian back? Why did you let Gedeon keep him?"

Both Damian and Serafina looked at me. I couldn't read the expressions on either of their faces. But it mattered to me. The answer mattered. Damian was her son. My . . . brother. He'd been powerless and vulnerable. Violently stolen just as he'd entered the world. He'd deserved to be saved.

"Because it would have been folly to attempt to infiltrate the Dark Guardian realm to steal back the most well-protected child in existence," Serafina scoffed, as though my question was the most ignorant thing she'd ever heard. "We would not have succeeded, and countless numbers of our warrior faction soldiers would have died. We had no idea what Gedeon had already done to taint and control him. It was not worth the risk."

I stared at her, open mouthed. Didn't she hear what she was saying?

She'd just said that Damian, her own child, hadn't been worth the risk. Rage flared through me, hot and untamed, as the cruelty and unfairness of the situation sank in. I stepped forward, my fists clenching. I was practically vibrating with anger. I wasn't even sure what I was planning to do to her. Probably punch her. Repeatedly. Until she had some inkling of what she'd done to us. Of how cruel and horrible she really was. But Damian reached out and grabbed my arm, holding me back. I wanted to yank free of him so I could run at Serafina and pummel her—make her feel as low as she really was—but I couldn't bring myself to pull away from his grasp. Not now. Not after what she'd said about him. Not after she'd willingly left him behind. So I just gritted my teeth until my jaw burned with tension and stayed where I was.

Serafina huffed and moved to sit behind the desk again, putting the large slab of polished wood between herself and us. She didn't believe I had a right to be angry with her. That was clear from her haughty expression. She thought she'd made the right decision. The only decision. But she hadn't. She'd made the easiest decision. I'd never noticed how similar Matt was to my mother. How his attitude and actions mirrored hers. But now that I was looking at her, watching how she handled this situation, I couldn't unsee it. I wondered for the first time if this was where he'd learned it. From her. The only pseudo-maternal figure he'd had after his mother had died. After all, Serafina had communicated with him over the years much more than she'd communicated with me. She'd guided him. Given him advice. Groomed him for leadership. I clenched my fists again. Here was another thing she'd fucked up. Another person she'd damaged. Another way she'd negatively influenced those around her. And I hated her even more for it.

As I stood there fuming, I felt Damian reach out to me, trying to connect his mind to mine. And for once, I let him in.

"I guess both of our parents are horrible, huh?" He asked it drily, but I could feel the pain behind the question. The sting that lurked around the edges of the words. It was the same pain I felt. The realization that both our parents were . . .

"Evil," he supplied.

"Yes. Though in slightly different ways."

"Mhmm. I always hoped my mother would be . . . different. Better than him. Nicer than him. That she would care about me. But she—"

"Never can and never will," I finished for him. *"For either of us. They're never going to be who we want them to be."* I felt both our chests

737

tighten. It hurt. But we both knew it was true. *"They're never going to act like family or love us like family. They never wanted us. Not really. They've only ever wanted to use our power. That's all they care about. Our power and this supposed prophecy."*

I fell silent as Serafina looked back and forth between us. I wondered if she knew we were talking—communicating in a place she couldn't access.

"Maybe we should just be satisfied with each other," Damian said quietly, ignoring her stare. *"We don't need them. I think we've proven that much, at least."*

I turned to look at him, surprised. It was the last thing I'd expected him to say. Connection was never something he'd strived for. Not intentionally. Damian smiled a little, the coldness that still lived in his eyes receding to the back corners. The pain was still there, raw and sharp, but at least it wasn't remoteness or emptiness for once.

"You're right," I murmured. *"At least we have—"*

"Each other. Which is honestly more than I ever knew to hope for. I never thought I'd meet or even have any other family, let alone a sibling. A twin. I never thought there'd be anyone who'd understand what being like this is like. But . . . I was wrong. There are two of us. We're—"

"Not alone."

"Not alone."

Damian pushed gently from my mind before crossing his arms over his chest, eyeing Serafina again. "I think it's interesting that there are two of us—something not referenced by the prophecy at all—yet you somehow still think we fit the description. You still think you've created these 'chosen weapons.' Why? Just because you're so . . . powerful?" His voice was shrewd, sardonic, as he raked his gaze over her, raising a challenging eyebrow. He had a talent for this. He could take her haughtiness and raise it by a hundred if he wanted to. He'd never let her win on that front.

Serafina's eyes turned hard as she looked at him. As she looked at us together. She was the one on her own now.

"The prophecy has been passed down by word of mouth for centuries." Her voice was as cold and hard as stone. "No one knows the exact wording. It is highly probable that the prophecy originally allowed for such an inevitability. Besides, everything else fits perfectly. I have every belief that you are what the prophecy predicted."

"I think it's interesting," I said, crossing my arms over my chest this time, "that you thought you only needed one of us for the prophecy to come true." Challenge filled my voice. And anger. "Obviously there was a reason that two of us were born instead of one. You looked at us like there was a spare, when it makes far more sense that we're *both* needed for the intended effect. By not going after Damian, you jeopardized the prophecy, didn't you?"

I raised an eyebrow at her coolly as a ghost of a smile formed on Damian's face. Serafina's cheeks tinged pink, and she looked, for once, mildly flustered. She didn't like being called out, especially by us. Well, she shouldn't have had children, then.

"I stand behind my choices and beliefs," she said stiffly, standing once more. "And it hardly matters anymore. You are together now. The past is behind us. We must now focus on the future. Tell me, Damian," she trained her eyes on him again, "what insight can you give me about the Dark Guardians' plans moving forward?"

Damian stared at her, wordlessly, for a long moment. I knew he was angry at her as well, though he didn't show it as much as I did. Helping her was harder now that he knew who she was to him. What she hadn't done to protect him.

He blew out a breath and leaned back against the desk. "The Academy was just the beginning. It was a small display of my father's strength and power, and his willingness to kill everyone who inhabits Light Guardian controlled spaces. His real plans are much more far reaching and extreme. With the god's help, my father is now able to escalate the war. He has the ability and the resources to expand his attacks on a global scale beyond the border towns that have always been the front lines. He's no longer just tied to those plane rips for realm-crossing and battle. He can now create infinite plane rips and transport Demons, his army, and his spies anywhere at any time. And he will. He wants to . . . exterminate all Divines who do not follow him and his ideals. Every Divine town across the world will be susceptible, and he will strike them all. And once he exterminates the Divines who oppose him, he'll quickly topple the Normals' control over their own world and will institute his own. He's been planning this escalation for years, but he's now in a position to act on those plans."

Serafina stared at Damian in silence, her face pale and drawn. She was shocked, but also proud. Too proud to let us see just how much this news bothered her.

"My father has been assessing the warrior faction's numbers, locations, strategies, and weaknesses for years. He's made sure that his soldiers far outnumber yours, and that his plans of attack will put your forces at a disadvantage. You will be spread too thin to adequately counter him."

Her expression morphed from shock to rigid anger.

"And now that the Academy has fallen," Damian continued, ignoring her glare, "he will start initiating those widespread attacks before the warrior faction has time to prepare for them. To adequately counter his attacks, you'd have to expand your global fighting forces by at least double if not more in the next few months. Only then will you have enough soldiers in enough places to defend your people."

"That is impossible." Serafina's voice was low. Dangerous. But there was also a current of fear there. "Onboarding people into the warrior faction takes time. Every individual approved to join must pass rigorous physical, strategic, and power level tests. The standards are very high—only the elite are accepted and inducted in. We cannot simply eliminate that process and let in anyone."

"Then you'll lose," Damian said calmly. "Either adapt to the situation at hand or fall victim to it." They glared at each other in silence, neither backing down.

"You can expand forces without them all being warrior faction soldiers," I finally cut in. "There are a lot of people who can adequately fight who either have no interest in joining the warrior faction, or who wouldn't meet the warrior faction standards for other reasons. Think about what just happened at the Academy," I added, staring her down. I knew she didn't like the idea of soldiers being out of her control, but Damian was right. If she didn't adapt, we'd lose. "The majority of our reinforcements were civilians who could fight well enough to take out the rest of the Dark Guardian army, and none of them were members of the warrior faction. Only a fraction of our reinforcements were official soldiers."

"Terah's right. They don't necessarily have to have full military training and qualifications to be useful. You could recruit people who can already fight or who are interested in fighting, to respond to the attacks in areas that the warrior faction can't occupy or get to in time. You can provide some combat and strategy training to those recruits to better prepare them, but it won't have to be as in-depth or time-consuming as warrior faction training. That will allow you to quickly and efficiently expand your military presence globally."

Serafina stared back and forth between us for a while in silence. "It is something to consider," she finally said, her voice clipped. "And what role do you see yourselves having in all this? As you know, your importance in the resolution of this conflict cannot be overlooked. Whether or not you accept this reality, the two of you were prophesized. You cannot turn your backs on this war—you must help us end it. It is your purpose."

Damian and I glanced at each other, anger fresh in both our eyes. We both had our doubts about the legitimacy of this supposed prophecy, and we both hated how she was using it to try controlling us. But . . . we couldn't exactly explain our unique power and abilities either. Nor did we want to totally remove ourselves from the war. We wanted to protect people, but on our own terms.

I looked at Serafina again. "I've already told you that I'll never join the warrior faction. That hasn't changed, and it won't change no matter what you tell us. However," I added, cutting off her response—she was practically fuming, "I'm willing to be a part of these new non-warrior-faction forces as a trainer and fighter on four conditions."

Serafina raised her eyebrows at me, waiting, her eyes like ice. She wasn't a fan of negotiation or compromise. But I had bargaining power here. I held something she wanted and would have to pay for, metaphorically speaking.

"My conditions are that Gabriel can have the same position as I do if he wants it, that he'll never be assigned to a position that's in a different location than mine unless he wants to be, that Damian can stay with us for a few months at least, if he agrees, so he and I can practice using our joint power, and that Damian can also be a trainer for these new forces if he wants to."

Serafina considered me silently for a long moment. Then she turned to Damian. "Is that what you want as well?"

Damian frowned. He looked unsure.

"You'd make a good trainer," I murmured, our minds snapping together. *"You proved that by how you helped each of us improve in training this semester. It's natural for you. Plus, this would keep you out of the warrior faction and away from her direct orders."*

I could feel his grudging agreement, but also his hesitation. This was a complete unknown for him, and he didn't know how to move forward. He'd never formed a real life for himself outside the Dark Guardian realm and outside his father's control. He wasn't sure where he fit. He wasn't sure he deserved a chance to find out. He wasn't sure he'd live up to it.

"You will," I responded firmly. *"And you won't have to do it alone. Gabriel and I will be with you. Also . . . you've been using your power and unique abilities your whole life. You have a much better grasp on them than*

I do. You never shut yourself away from your power for years like I did. I need your help learning how to better connect with and use mine. Please."

Damian closed his eyes for a second, deliberating. But I could feel him giving in. He didn't want to say no to me. Not now. Nor did he want to take these next steps into a different life alone. My plan provided structure and opportunity, as well as protection against the Dark Guardians should his father come looking for him. Fear bubbled in my stomach as he thought this. Was that a possibility? Would his father really try to take him back by force after his betrayal?

"*He doesn't like losing,*" Damian murmured. "*Especially losing power. And I've been his weapon, an extension of his own power, my entire life. Let's just hope that, with his new powerful relic, he won't feel like he needs me anymore.*"

But I could feel the doubt in his mind. He didn't believe his father would ever willingly let him go free. He wasn't sure how long this new freedom would last.

"*We won't let him get to you,*" I said, firmly. "*I'd kill him before he gets close.*" I practically itched to punish Gedeon for what he'd done to Damian. To ruin him for what he'd done to the Academy. To Caleb. To all those innocent students. I'd make Gedeon pay. I'd make him afraid of *me*.

A ghost of a smile pulled at Damian's lips, and his eyes warmed slightly. "*While I'd pay good money to see that fight, it would probably be best if you stay clear of him. If we both do,*" he added, the smile fading.

"*Does that mean you'll say yes?*"

Damian shot me a small smile before turning to look at Serafina again. "Yes. That's what I want as well."

Serafina stared at us wordlessly for a long moment. At our unified front. Our partnership that she wasn't a part of. Her expression was unreadable, but there was something there, deep in her eyes. Some emotion I wasn't used to seeing there.

"So be it," she finally said, turning away before I could pinpoint it. "It will take a few months for these new training encampments to be acquired and modified, and for enough trainers to be found and appointed. You can use that time to train together as you need to, in the location of your choice, as long as I am informed of where you are. You must, however, be ready to relocate when the camps are ready. Is that clear?"

"Yes."

"Then you are free to go." She gestured vaguely at the door. She was done talking to us.

Damian and I pushed away from the desks and walked to the classroom door. I pulled it open and started down the hall, not looking back. I wanted to be away from Serafina and her cold, stifling presence.

"Do you think it's bullshit?" I asked Damian as we turned down another long hall, heading back toward the gym. "The prophecy?"

"I don't know," he murmured as we passed a group of warrior faction soldiers walking in the other direction. "I want to say yes, but . . . there are a lot of unexplainable things about us. I'm just not sure." He rubbed the back of his head.

"Me neither. And I can't see how our abilities could do anything to turn the tide of the war. Not long-term, at least. But you're right," I added as we walked around another group of warrior faction soldiers. "Some things about us aren't explainable."

He shrugged. "I guess we'll just have to wait and see. There's nothing else we can really do."

I nodded slowly, biting the inside of my cheek.

"Terah!"

I paused and slowly turned, my shoulders already filling with tension.

Matt jogged down the hall until he reached us. "Can I talk to you for a few minutes?" He refused to look at Damian.

Damian rolled his eyes. *"I'll go catch Gabriel up on what's happened."*

I glanced up at him. *"Thanks. Hopefully this won't take long."*

Damian raised an eyebrow as he pushed away from my mind and turned to leave. But I knew what he was thinking anyway. Things with Matt were never quick and simple. I sighed. He was right.

Matt watched Damian walk away, dislike thick in his eyes. "Let's go outside." His voice was less cheerful now.

He led me to the side door, then pushed outside and began walking toward a large field of grass behind the school. The warm air, heavily scented with the earthy fragrance of cut grass and damp soil, moved gently around us, making my hair dance around my shoulders and the leaves on the trees rustle.

"So, you're talking to him in your mind now too?" Matt finally asked as we started walking around the large field. He was smiling a little, but it didn't reach his eyes.

"Damian?" I clarified. Matt nodded. "Yeah, I guess I am. He's not so bad, especially now that he's ditched the Dark Guardian side."

"So he says," Matt grumbled darkly. "He can't be trusted, Terah. You should know that by now."

743

I sighed, deep and long. I didn't know how to make Matt see Damian's complexities. The bind he'd been in his entire life. His potential for so much good.

"I've had access to his mind, Matt. I know more than anyone that he *can* be trusted. You saw what it was like for him in his memories. He never really had a choice. He did some horrible things—he doesn't dispute that—but he finally has the opportunity to be free from his father and to act on his own beliefs and values. And he's choosing to help our side of the war. That's a good thing."

Matt shook his head, his expression darkening. "How can you forgive him so easily? Do you know how many people died at the Academy?"

I shook my head, my heart sinking. I knew it was a lot. We'd done our best with a small group of fighters, but we hadn't been able to save everyone.

"Of those barricaded in the dorms, only forty-three students and ten staff survived," his voice was low. Dangerous. My stomach dropped. So few. So few had survived. "Of the more than a hundred of us fighting outside the dorms, only seven trainers including me and six students including you, Gabriel, and Damian survived. Over fifty civilians from the reinforcements died. That's almost four hundred dead, most of them students. We spent the whole week you both were unconscious sifting through the remains of the Academy, trying to find survivors. Counting the dead."

Tears filled Matt's eyes as he looked out over the grassy field.

"So many of my friends are gone." His voice broke. "Only Simon and Omer survived. Luke . . . is gone." My heart sank and pain gripped my stomach. Luke had been a good trainer and a kind person. Matt had really looked up to him.

"I'm sorry." I wanted to reach out to him. Offer comfort. But something about how Matt was holding himself kept me away. He didn't want to be touched. He didn't want anyone getting close to him right now.

"The president is dead," he continued, "and almost all of our training group—all my students—are gone." He wiped the sleeve of his uniform over his eyes. "Everyone I commanded in the warrior faction died the moment the Dark Guardian army blew away the plane barrier. Hundreds of people. And you just want to *forgive him?*" Matt's hands shook as anger radiated off him, and he stopped walking to stare down at me.

"Damian wasn't solely responsible for the attack or its outcome," I said quietly. "His father would've attacked the Academy with or without him in the picture. The Academy also had multiple warning about a potential attack from my visions, but they chose to remain open. All I'm saying is that it's not a simple situation. The blame doesn't belong on one person, except for the Dark Guardian king. And when Damian was faced with what his father had done, he chose to fight with us and keep the book from his father. He chose to *die* with us, Matt. He abandoned the side he was raised on because he wanted to fight for the Academy and the students. All he wanted was to escape his father and find a way to do better with his life, and now he can. So yes, I'm willing to forgive him and give him a chance to do better."

Matt shook his head angrily. "I thought you were smarter than that." His voice was icy and low. It dripped with disdain. "He's clearly just setting himself up as a double-agent. He's a spy—it's what he does! Everything he's done, including fighting with us, was calculated. He knew he'd survive, and once he did, he knew he could trick our side into thinking he was an ally."

I stepped away from him, anger fizzling through me. "You don't know what you're talking about. Damian and I almost died. It was purely luck that Gabriel caught us in time and that we were given enough power in time to survive. And Damian didn't wake up on his own. I had to go into his mind and bring him back like I did in the illusion chamber. Part of him didn't *want* to survive. So don't speak about what he does and doesn't want. You don't know anything about him."

Matt stared down at me in disbelief. "You're speaking like you . . . care about him. How could you? Especially after what he did and how he betrayed you? How could you let in someone like him?"

I crossed my arms over my chest and stared back, my expression growing hard. "I do care about him. He's shown his ability to grow and to care about other people. He's proven himself to me and to the Light Guardian side. I've seen into his mind. I know his thoughts and feelings, his hopes and fears, as he knows mine. He's a good person, Matt. Let him have the opportunity to act on that."

Matt let out a humorless laugh. "Wow, he really got to you, didn't he?" He sneered down at me—an expression he'd never aimed at me before. "Well, it doesn't matter. The High Light Guardian will never let him go free after what he did. We won't have to worry about him for much longer."

"You're wrong," I said quietly. Anger and sadness swirled together and burned in my chest. Matt and I were the furthest from each other we'd ever been, and it hurt, regardless of the conflict between us. "Serafina pardoned him in exchange for his pledge of allegiance. He and I are going to train together to practice using our shared power before we become trainers in some new non-warrior-faction military camps that she'll be setting up in response to the Dark Guardian side's escalation."

Shock overtook his expression. "That can't be possible. She wouldn't . . . she can't . . ."

"I think she's more concerned about having access to our shared power than she is about his history as a spy. She offered to pardon him pretty quickly."

"I just . . . don't understand," he said, almost to himself. "He's clearly dangerous. Dark. I mean, look at who his father is! The *king* of the Dark Guardians! How could she just—"

"There's something else you should know," I cut him off, bracing for the reaction I knew was coming. "Damian . . . is my brother. My twin. It's why we have the same power. It means the High Light Guardian is also his mother, and the king of the Dark Guardians is also my father."

Matt gaped at me as all the blood drained from his face. He looked frozen. Overwhelmed.

"I . . . don't . . . believe you." The words sounded like they were being dragged from his lungs.

"Serafina told us everything. Why and how we were conceived, how Gedeon stole Damian and took him to the Dark Guardian realm right when he was born, why we share this unique power. Ask her. She'll probably tell you. He's my *family*, Matt. I have to give him a real chance."

This snapped Matt out of his frozen horror. He glared down at me, something fierce growing in his eyes.

"*I'm* your family," he said furiously. "Not him. That's always how it's been, since you were a baby. I've always been there for you. I *raised* you. I taught you how to read and fight. I've loved you and cared for you since the moment I met you. I've always been by your side. I've always fought for your happiness. *He's* only been here for a few months, and in that time, all he's done is hurt and betray you. You don't even know him. I don't care what your connection is to him. He's *not* your family. Not like me."

I bit the inside of my cheek. Matt wasn't completely wrong, but he wasn't completely right either. Matt *hadn't* always been at my side. He hadn't always been there for me. He'd left me when I was fourteen and never returned. He'd pushed me away when I'd really needed him. He'd stayed away by choice, even though he knew I was suffering without him.

He'd forced us to grow apart. And ever since I'd come to the Academy, he'd hurt me and betrayed my trust again and again. Yes, Matt was my family, but he wasn't the shining beacon of care, love, and comfort he was trying to reframe himself as. And his history with me didn't erase that Damian was my family too.

"Don't train with him, Terah," Matt murmured, his voice becoming gentler as he stepped forward and took my shoulders in his hands. "Don't trust him. Don't let him in. He'll only hurt you and betray you again." His hands slid up to cup either side of my neck. "I don't want anything bad to happen to you. I just want you to be safe. Happy." His fingers slid up into my hair. "Stay with me," he whispered, his eyes turning molten as his face neared mine. "Join my company in the warrior faction, and we'll never have to be separated again. We can stay together. Make up for lost time. We can be a family again." He trailed his thumbs down my cheeks as he leaned in, bringing his mouth close to mine.

"*Let me love you*," his thoughts whispered through my mind as his eyes closed. "*Please. Let me love you. Don't leave me.*"

I reached forward and placed my hands on his chest, stopping him before his lips could make contact with mine. I stepped back, pulling out of his grasp, and looked up at him, seeing him as though for the first time. Matt was . . . *scared*. Scared of being left behind. Of being alone. Of feeling what I'd felt when he'd left me in Dagmar. He was scared that Damian would replace him. That Serafina and I wouldn't need him anymore. That the only people he'd let himself love would abandon him.

"You'll always be my family, Matt. Damian's presence doesn't take away from that. It doesn't change our history or my care for you. But . . . I can't stay with you either. I'm not ever going to join the warrior faction. Not even for you. I need to forge my own path under my own rules. And I'm not going to ignore my connection with Damian just to make you happy. He deserves a chance. He deserves to have someone believe in him and care for him. To not abandon him. And he and I both deserve to better understand our power. Also . . . I won't leave Gabriel. I love him, Matt. More than anything. More than you love me."

Tears filled Matt's eyes as he clenched his fists at his sides. His whole body was rigid.

"I never had a chance, did I?" he asked darkly, his voice shaking as much as his hands. He was sad. Angry. Lonely. "It was never going to be me. You were never going to pick me first in anything, were you? Not as your family, not as your friend, not even as your lover."

747

I opened my mouth, but I wasn't sure what to say. He wasn't wrong. He and I had grown apart, and just as he'd picked his happiness and freedom over me all those years ago, I now had to pick my own path to fulfillment regardless of his feelings and wants. It was my turn to choose who I wanted to be and what I wanted to do with my life.

"I'm sorry, Matt." My voice was steady. Strong. I believed in what I was doing now. I believed in my choices and judgment. In myself. I knew what I wanted and how I felt. And Matt wouldn't be able to sway me. Not this time. "I'll always love and care about you. I'll always consider you as my family. You'll always have a place in my heart. But we each have our own paths to tread, and they're not together. I'm sorry that it hurts you. I hope . . . I hope you can find your own happiness."

Tears trailed down his cheeks as he looked at me, his expression shattered. The muscles in my legs tightened as I stopped myself from moving forward and hugging him. It wouldn't help. Not now. Tears filled my eyes and my chest ached fiercely. But I knew I wasn't the one who could ease his pain. He needed to find real love, trust, and companionship on his own. Without me. He needed to figure out what really made him happy. Only then would his pain truly ease.

Matt turned on his heel and strode away, his shoulders stiff with anger and despair. I didn't move to follow him. I just watched him until he disappeared around the side of the building.

I wiped a tear from my cheek as I faced forward again and kept walking until I'd reached the far end of the large field. Then I sank onto the grass with a sigh, stretching my legs out down the small hill that led to a road then a line of trees. It was nice here. Quiet. Green. Not a town usually accustomed to warfare.

I sighed again and laid back in the grass, staring up at the deepening blue sky above me. The sun would start setting soon, but I wasn't in a hurry to move. I just wanted to stay here for a little longer. To be free of expectation. Free of violence and sadness. Just for a moment. One peaceful moment.

I watched the sky change colors as the minutes passed and the sun moved closer to the tree line. Felt the light breeze dance over me, rustling the grass. I closed my eyes and smiled.

"Hey," a warm voice drifted over me a few minutes later. "Mind if I join you?"

I opened my eyes to see Gabriel standing over me, a warm smile on his lips.

I smiled and sat up. "I don't mind." He was the only person whose presence could add to the calmness and tranquility.

Gabriel stretched out on the grass next to me and was silent for a few moments as he looked out over the trees. "It's nice here," he murmured as the breeze whispered past us. "Even with all the warrior faction soldiers around, there's still something so calm about this place."

"Mhmm." I leaned over and rested my head against his shoulder. "I was thinking that too."

We sat there together for a while, breathing in the fresh air and watching the branches sway on the trees below us.

"How did your conversation with Matt go?"

I sighed. "About as well as it ever could." I still felt the remnants of the ache in my chest from cutting Matt free. "I told him we each needed to follow our own paths, and that those paths aren't together. I . . . broke his heart again. But I think, in the long run, it's what's best for both of us. He needs to move on. To grow beyond who he is with me. He may never talk to me again, though," I added, my heart heavy.

Gabriel nodded and took my hand in his. "I'm sorry," he murmured, leaning over to rest his head on mine. "I know how much that hurts you. I'm sorry it had to be that way."

I slid my thumb over the back of his hand, back and forth, feeling the warmth and smoothness of his skin. I smiled a little.

"It sucks. I'll miss him. But I don't regret it. I just hope he'll find his own way. His own happiness. And that, maybe, we can be friends again someday."

"I hope so too." Gabriel pressed his lips to the top of my head. "Damian told me what happened with your mother."

I straightened up and turned to look at him.

"That must've been a lot to process." His brows were furrowed with worry. "Suddenly having a brother, finding out who your father is, the potential prophecy. Plus, it sounds like your mother was shitty as usual." He leaned forward and tucked some hair that was blowing in front of my face behind my ear. "Are you doing okay?"

"I'm still processing everything," I admitted, picking at the blades of grass with my fingers. "All the losses at the Academy, all this new information about myself and my family. I don't think it's fully sunk in yet. I think it'll take time. But . . . I'm actually okay. Right now, at least," I added, smiling up at him.

He smiled, his eyes warm. "I'm glad. And you know I'm here for you if you're not okay at any point. You can take as much time as you need. We don't have to move forward until you're ready."

I nodded and laced my fingers through his again. "Thanks."

"Damian also told me that you both agreed to be civilian trainers moving forward." He glanced out over the trees again. "And that you'll train together for a few months first to better understand your shared power."

I nodded again, looking closely at his profile. I wondered if he wanted to do something else. If he didn't want to be involved in the war anymore. I wouldn't blame him if he didn't. And I wouldn't hold him back if he wanted to leave. But . . . it'd hurt. Losing him. It'd hurt so much.

"There's also a trainer position for you . . . if you want it," I said quietly.

Gabriel nodded, his brows furrowing in thought. "Damian told me."

My stomach clenched, and I tried to push down the panic. The only way I'd know what he was thinking was if I asked him.

"Will you . . . come with me? For the training with Damian and then to the training camps after that? Will you . . . stay with me?"

I knew I was asking a lot of him—to stay so engaged in the war, especially when he'd gone to the Academy to get away from it. To not be forced to fight.

Gabriel turned to look at me, and his eyes flitted quickly over my nervous expression. His eyebrows rose slightly in disbelief. "You already know the answer." His breath fanned gently over my lips, and I swallowed in spite of myself. His face was so close to mine.

Gabriel's eyes transformed from warm to smoldering as he watched my reaction, and a slow smirk curved up the corner of his mouth. He knew too well what he did to me.

"You know, there's a point after which you don't need to ask that anymore," he murmured, reaching forward and tracing his fingers up my neck until he was cupping the side of my face. "A point where you should just assume that if you're there, I will be too."

My cheeks heated as his thumb rubbed slowly over the skin there.

"And . . . are we at that point?" I was already breathless.

Gabriel grinned, then leaned forward, closing the small distance between us. His kiss was sweet and soft. Slow and lingering and deep. And everything in me melted and came alive at the same time. I gave myself over to it, breathing him in, filling my lungs with his warmth and his scent.

Electricity hummed through my body as his lips moved over mine. I could feel the warmth flooding his skin as my tongue slid over his. The frenzied beats of his heart as his hand stole around my waist, pulling me closer until I was pressed to him, the heaving of our chests now moving as one. And I could feel the infinite depth of his love. How much he wanted to be with me. How much he wanted to stay with me.

"*Always*," His voice whispered through my mind.

I sighed, wrapping my arms around him. My soul felt like it was soaring. Flying high above my body. Happy. Free.

"*Always*."

A while later, we sank back into the grass, lying side by side, our fingers intertwined as we watched the sun set. We heard the chirp of crickets growing in the distance. The last calls of the birds—mournful but sweet. The gentle rustle of the leaves in the trees. The earthy smell of sunlight and grass shifting to something cooler. Deeper. We soaked in the quiet beauty, bearing witness to the bittersweet end of day and the magical beginning of night. A natural, quiet changing of the guards.

I sighed, holding Gabriel's hand tightly in mine. I knew the war was far from over. That there'd be many trials we'd still have to face. Mysteries we'd still have to solve. Pain we'd still have to experience. Hardships we'd still have to overcome. But right now, all I could feel was happy. Happy to be alive. Happy to be in love. Happy to be with Gabriel. To have some hope restored in my life. To have a path forward of my own choosing.

We lay quietly, our sense of time fading as we watched the sky turn from red, orange, and purple to a deep blue. Watching as the stars emerged, filling the sky with bright points of twinkling light. The world lay before us, beautiful, quiet, and calm. Here, in this moment, there was peace.

ACKNOWLEDGMENTS

It truly takes a village to write and publish a book. First, I want to thank my spouse for being my alpha reader, research assistant, tech wrangler, sounding board, fantastic pep-talk giver, and my biggest and most constant cheerleader. You believed in me when I had trouble believing in myself, and you picked me up off the ground and set me back on my feet too many times to count. I love you, and thank you for being such an amazing partner.

A huge thank you to my beta readers Vee Haacke, C. Spence, and F. Shepard who took a chance on an unknown author and gave me their time, hard work, and generosity. Your feedback helped me improve the book, and your enthusiasm and kind words kept me going as I dragged myself through the 100th round of edits. A special thanks to Vee Haacke, who went above and beyond, and read through the manuscript multiple times to help me with the final editing process. You are a superhero!

I'd like to thank my friends and family for their support through this process, and as I transitioned from the legal field to the creative writing world. You valued my happiness above all else, and you stood by me as I changed my life for the better. Thank you for being in my life, and lots of love to you all.

Thank you to the online writing communities of both indie and trad authors. You all kept me company as I wrote and edited, hyped me up when I was having a hard time, wrote with me in the early hours of the morning, supported my marketing efforts, and answered publishing questions generously. I will keep striving to be as supportive and kind in return as you all have been to me.

Next, I'd like to thank my therapist, Avery. Your role may not be as visible as others, but you were just as integral in getting me through the writing and publishing process. Thank you so much for your insight, practical help, and overall support. I appreciate you!

Finally, I'd like to thank every reader who gave my book a chance. This series means so much to me, and I truly can't put into words how much I appreciate you giving your time to this world and these characters I've created. Thank you from the bottom of my heart.

ABOUT THE AUTHOR

Eden Sandoval is an Indigenous & Latine indie author who was born in Chile and grew up in Chicago. After subjecting themself to a law degree, they left the legal field to pursue their one true love: telling stories and creating worlds. Now, they craft narratives with complex protagonists navigating messy worlds, weaving in themes of growth through and beyond trauma, liberation & equity, and neurodivergence & disability. When not writing, they enjoy photography, archery, attending fandom conventions, making cosplays, and staring at the lake. Eden lives in Chicago with their spouse and rescue pup.

EDENSANDOVAL.COM

Up Next:
The Divine War Trilogy, Book 2
Divine Warriors